FLASH POINT

FLASH POINT

A NOVEL

JAMES W. HUSTON

WILLIAM MORROW | *AN IMPRINT OF* HARPERCOLLINS*PUBLISHERS*

HarperCollins books may be purchased for educational, business,
or sales promotional use. For information please write:
Special Markets Department, HarperCollins Publishers Inc.,
10 East 53rd Street, New York, NY 10022.

Library of Congress Cataloging-in-Publication Data

Huston, James W.
    Flash point : a novel / by James W. Huston. — 1st ed.
        p. cm.
    ISBN 0-688-17201-6
    1. Fighter pilots—Fiction.   2. Terrorists—Fiction.   3. Middle
East—Fiction.   I. Title.
PS3558.U8122 F57 2000
813'.54—dc21

                                                    00-026256

                                FIRST EDITION

                        Printed on acid-free paper

        DESIGNED BY MICHAEL MENDELSOHN AT MM DESIGN 2000, INC.

        00 01 02 03 04 RRD 10 9 8 7 6 5 4 3 2 1

In memory of my mother,
Florence Webb Huston,
who was afraid to fly
but encouraged me to follow my dreams

United States Constitution. Article I, Section 8: The Congress shall have Power . . . To declare War, Grant Letters of Marque and Reprisal, and make Rules concerning Captures on Land and Water.

FLASH
POINT

1

The dirty white van sputtered and stalled as it approached the Gaza checkpoint. The driver looked harried. He leaned forward and tried to start the van quickly. The engine caught, turned over, and stalled again. He glanced in his mirror and ahead of him at the other traffic.

One of the Palestinian guards watched the driver out of the corner of his eye as he waved two more cars through the border checkpoint. The van was about to block the morning's commuter traffic—the thousands of Palestinians who crossed into Israel every day to work the menial jobs the Israelis didn't want.

The Israeli soldiers on the other side of the border were much more serious about the traffic crossing into Israel. Exhausted from unending vigilance coupled with interminable boredom, they imagined a bomb in every car. They carried their loaded M-16s in their hands and sweated under their bulletproof vests. To them Gaza was just a large Trojan Horse.

The van had created a gap; only a lonely Fiat stood between it and the checkpoint. The Palestinian guard glanced toward the checkpoint and walked to the van. The van lurched, then started to move, inching along. It sat with its engine chugging reluctantly, waiting for the Fiat, now thirty feet in front of it, to pass through.

The rusty Fiat was waved on and the van was next. The van shuddered and the engine quit. The driver turned the key and the starter noisily cranked the engine. It wouldn't catch. Again and again he tried, without success. The Palestinian guard approached the window angrily. "What is the problem?" he asked gruffly in Arabic.

1

"I've had some engine trouble—" the driver replied, also in Arabic.

"Move it or we'll push it into the ditch! You're blocking the way!" The road into Israel was crowded. The bright morning sun was low in the eastern horizon, shining into the eyes of the Palestinian guards.

"Yes, yes. I'm trying . . ." The driver leaned forward as if lending his own energy to the van. He turned the key with his right hand, and reached subtly under the dash with his left and flipped a switch. The van chugged to life with half its cylinders working. The driver smiled at the guard apologetically and the vehicle began moving slowly toward the checkpoint. It was clear it would take the van a long time to make it.

"Get this thing off this road!" the guard finally yelled, exasperated with the slowness of the stupid white van that was now blocking the entire checkpoint. The Israelis watched and waited with concern. Anything out of the ordinary received humorless, intense scrutiny; any problem, any angry outburst, anything. It could be someone about to do something dramatic, or a diversion for someone else.

The driver nodded, surrendering, and began a Y-turn to go back the way he had come. The Palestinian guard, his rifle in one hand, watched in disgust. The van turned around, now headed toward Gaza City, the driver apparently abandoning any hope of getting to Tel Aviv. He reached under the dash again, and the van's engine coughed and died once more. The guard, barking obscenities, angrily advanced toward the window on the right side of the van. The driver suddenly raised an enormous handgun and fired, the bullet penetrating the man's bulletproof vest, throwing him back onto the side of the road, where he lay silently, his legs jerking involuntarily.

The rear doors of the van flew open and eight men with large machine guns rushed out and opened fire. The bullets made a distinctive, unusual sound as they flew toward the Israeli and Palestinian guards who fell quickly as the bullets tore through their protective vests. The eight fanned out and fired with precision, aiming at the targets each had been briefed to hit. The Israeli guardhouse on the other side of the border was splintered, the guards inside shredded. On both sides of the border, the cry went out for Palestinian and Israeli reinforcements. Six Palestinian guards lay dead on the Gaza side.

The shooters stood staring at the dead guards on both sides, as if waiting for something. An Israeli Armored Personnel Carrier raced for the border from its safe point a half mile away. There was a loud metallic sound and a TOW missile flew out the van's open doors from a tube bolted to the deck inside. The thin wire that carried the guidance information to the missile trailed behind it as the TOW raced toward the Israeli APC, slamming into the belly of the armored vehicle, instantly killing the Israeli soldiers inside.

The Palestinian and Israeli soldiers at the checkpoint were dead, but dozens of others were rushing to the border from their safe positions a mile away. The eight shooters, unharmed, ran back to the van, diving through the closing rear doors. The driver threw both of the switches under the dash and the finely tuned eight-cylinder engine roared to life. The van sped off in the direction of Gaza City.

Several soldiers standing in the back of an Israeli truck approaching the checkpoint began firing at the van. The M-16 bullets, small but fast, slammed into the back of the vehicle but fell harmlessly, bouncing off the van's inner lining of Kevlar. Small chips of rubber flew off the solid tires as the bullets hit, but nothing slowed the van.

It sped down the highway, back the way it had come. A Palestinian security truck raced toward the border near the retreating van. Too late, the truck driver realized that the target he was pursuing was the van about to pass them. The truck slowed but the van had already raced by, untouched. It reached the outskirts of the city and made a sharp turn into an alley. Another van pulled in front of the entrance to the alley, blocking it completely.

The white van stopped deep in the alley and the eight men and the driver quickly walked away, blending in with passers-by who were completely unaware of what had happened. Each of the shooters wore clothes different from those he had worn during the attack, and each left his weapon lying on the floor of the van next to the TOW launcher. They split up, each taking a different direction, then climbed into the unremarkable sedans that were waiting for them and disappeared.

⟋⟍

"Hey, Wink," Lieutenant Sean Woods, "Trey," as he was known, said into his oxygen mask.

"What?"

"This our last intercept of the night?"

Wink looked at the clock on the instrument panel in the backseat of the F-14. "Probably."

"Let's have some fun," Woods said.

"Always."

Woods glanced at his fuel indicator. They were fat. "You ready?"

"I'm ready," Wink replied, then immediately transmitted, *"Victory 207's ready."*

"Roger. Victory 207, your bogey is 284 for 42, angels unknown," Tiger replied. The bad guy—their wingman—bore 284 degrees from them, forty-two miles away, and the controller didn't know their altitude.

Wink slaved his radar toward the left side of the Tomcat's nose as Woods pulled around hard to the west in a three G turn. Wink picked out their wingman while still in the turn: *"207, contact 284 for 40. Judy,"* Wink transmitted, taking control of the intercept. Lieutenant Vialli and Sedge, his Radar Intercept Officer, RIO, in their F-14, were forty miles away and turning in at the same speed.

"Roger, out."

The radio went silent. Woods changed the mode on his HSD, his Horizontal Situation Display, to show the radar picture Wink was seeing in the backseat. He immediately knew what kind of intercept Wink would run. He checked his fuel ladder, a group of boxes he had drawn on his knee board to keep track of how much fuel he would need at what time to get back aboard the carrier with plenty of fuel left to go around if they couldn't trap the first time. They had fuel to burn.

"What's his altitude?"

Wink hooked the target on the PTID—the Programmable Tactical Information Display, which showed him the radar information. "Twenty-three." Twenty-three thousand feet above the ocean.

Woods pushed the throttles forward to the stops—as hard as the engines could work without afterburner—and pulled the nose of the Tomcat up ten degrees above the horizon.

The green glow of the screens reflected on their clear visors. The night was as dark as any night could be and still be illuminated by stars. Moonrise wasn't for another hour. The overcast cloud layer below blocked any light from the sea, not that there was much in the middle of the Mediterranean.

"Want to take him down the throat?" Wink asked.

"May as well since we're coming in high, but we'll need a little angle."

The F-14 climbed hungrily into the cool night sky. "Think they've got us?"

"Sure," Wink replied.

"Then they'll know what we're up to?"

"If they're paying attention. But it's the last one, they're the bogey.

May not notice our altitude. Starboard to 300 to build up some aspect angle." Wink wanted to come in from the side so they could roll out behind their target.

Woods turned the F-14 gently as he continued to climb. He steadied on a heading of 300.

"Okay, come port to 278."

Woods complied as they passed through thirty-four thousand feet, still climbing. He instinctively looked behind him to see if they were leaving contrails, but quickly realized he couldn't have seen them in the darkness even if they were there. They continued to climb straight ahead without speaking until they were at forty thousand feet.

"Ten miles," Wink said. "We'll start our normal intercept turn to kick him out about seven miles or so, then back in around five."

"Roger," Woods said, leaning forward to see down, but unable to pick out his wingman far below. "What are their angels now?"

Wink looked again. "Ten." Five miles below them.

"That asshole," Woods said, smiling under his mask. "They're sitting on the overcast."

"We'll just have to start down earlier, and watch our speed."

"Piece of cake," Woods said, grinning at the thought of screaming down thirty thousand feet in the dark upside down.

"Starboard hard," Wink called.

Woods turned the F-14 steeply but carefully in the thin air. After passing through whatever heading Wink was watching for, he called for a hard port turn.

Woods pushed the stick hard left until the Tomcat was on its back. He leaned back on the stick and let gravity pull them down toward the earth. Looking through the canopy toward the darkness below, he saw Vialli's red anticollision light. "Tallyho," Woods said.

"Got him," Wink responded, glancing up. "We're nearly on his line. Pull straight."

"Roger." Woods leveled the wings upside down and pulled back on the stick harder until they were pulling four Gs. Their speed increased through six hundred knots as the nose of the Tomcat pointed straight at the ocean. Woods eased the throttles back, no longer needing the full thrust of the engines; gravity could do most of the work. "Think he's got us?"

"They may be wondering what the hell we're doing up here."

"I doubt it," Woods said, grunting against the G forces. "How far behind them we going to be?"

"About a mile if you hold this."

"Perfect."

"Watch the speed," Wink said as they passed through 625 knots. Woods brought the throttles back more and pulled a little harder on the stick.

"Passing through twenty," Wink called calmly.

"You got him locked up?" Woods asked.

"Yep. Pull up at fifteen thousand feet, then we can descend to their altitude."

"Okay," Woods answered, taking a quick look at the engine instruments. They were still ahead of their fuel ladder. He pulled back harder on the stick and held five Gs to increase their altitude on pull-out.

Woods watched the nose of their Tomcat come through the horizon and back up toward the east. The artificial horizon told him he was approaching level flight again. He relaxed the back pressure on the stick and felt the bladders of his G-suit deflate against his abdomen and thighs.

"Dead ahead, one mile, two hundred fifty knots closure," Wink said to Woods, then on the radio: "*Fox two.*" The last transmission let everyone know they had completed the intercept and simulated the launch of an AIM-9 Sidewinder heat-seeking missile.

"Want to thump him?" Woods asked excitedly.

"Could get in trouble for that," Wink said warily.

"Rules were meant to be broken. So you want to?"

"Just don't hit him. That could *really* get us in trouble, and *wet*—I don't want to go swimming tonight. I'm not wearing my dry suit."

"Roger that." Woods pushed the throttles forward.

Tiger, the Air Intercept Controller on the carrier, transmitted: "*Victory 207, head outbound at 270—204, continue inbound 090 to set up another one.*"

"*That's it for us,*" Wink transmitted in reply. "*207's heading for marshall.*"

"*Roger that, 207. Good work. See you on deck.*"

"*Thanks, Tiger. Good work.*"

"Three hundred knots closure," Wink told Woods. He leaned to his left and studied the approaching lights of their wingman.

Woods also watched his wingman ahead. "He's skimming along the cloud layer. It's totally flat—he's completely in the clouds except his canopy and the two tails." He pondered their plan for a moment. "We'll have to go into the clouds to get below him."

"That's pretty marginal. Another time." Wink knew Woods was willing to lean on the boundaries.

"Nah, we'll be huge. You got a good lock?"

"Yeah."

"Tell me when we pass under him," Woods said, lowering the nose of the Tomcat and moving into the darkness of the cloud. The approaching lights of their wingman faded, then disappeared.

"One tenth of a mile—three hundred closure," Wink called, his eyes on the computerized radar image and the raw radarscope simultaneously. They were coming up to their wingman from dead behind with three hundred knots more speed. Wink saw the angle of the radar increase rapidly toward the top of the nose of the Tomcat, then felt the thud as the radar broke lock at a 65-degree up angle and the disappointed antenna returned to its neutral position. "Directly overhead," Wink said.

"Roger," Woods replied anxiously. "Think we're clear?"

"Should be," Wink replied.

"I'll give it a few," Woods said, counted to three in his mind, then pulled back hard on the stick. They came screaming up out of the cloud. The sky cleared and the stars were vivid again. "You got him?" Woods yelled.

Wink grabbed the handle on top of the radar console and used it to turn around and look between the two tails of the Tomcat. "Got him." Wink watched as their F-14 went straight up at five hundred fifty knots directly in front of their wingman, like a rocket.

Lieutenant Junior Grade Tony Vialli saw a flash of darkness outlined by anticollision lights and the green blur of the formation lights on the sides of the Tomcat directly in front of him. Realizing there was something in front of him, he tried to dump the nose of his Tomcat toward earth to avoid what he thought was an imminent collision. "Holy shit!" he yelled into his oxygen mask so loud that Sedge could hear it in the backseat even though Vialli's microphone was off. Coming out of their seats as the negative G forces from their evasive action pushed them up, they flew through Woods's jet wash and entered the clouds at the same time. Vialli, fighting to recover his bearings, forced himself to watch his artificial horizon to avoid vertigo, a loss of reference that could be fatal. He quickly checked his engine instruments to make sure the jet wash hadn't caused a flame-out.

In the other F-14 Woods and Wink were enjoying the rocket ride into the Mediterranean darkness. "That ought to do it," Woods said. "Think they saw us?"

The radio jumped to life. *"If that was you, you're dead."* Vialli didn't even have to say who he was talking to. He was using the radio in the front cockpit, reserved for squadron use, set to the squadron's private frequency. Woods was the only other squadron airplane airborne on this, the night's last flight. It was 0145.

Woods could hear the anger in Vialli's voice and realized he might have miscalculated. He keyed the radio with the switch on the throttle. *"Yeah, we overshot. Let's knock it off. See you at marshall."*

"You thumped *us,"* Vialli said furiously as he climbed the F-14 out of the clouds and leveled off.

"See you on deck," Woods replied.

Sedge answered, *"We're switching. See you guys in marshall."*

"I think they're pissed," Wink said as they flew straight up away from the earth.

"They'll get over it. Got to be ready for anything."

Wink switched the frequency on the digital display of his radio. *"Victory 207 checking in. We're on the 268 at 40, state 7.3."* They were forty miles from the carrier and had 7,300 pounds of jet fuel.

"Roger, 207," said the controller, the same one who was there every night, the one who mispronounced the same words every night, saying "Roger" with a long "o" and available with an extra "i," "availiable." His consistent mistakes had come to be highly regarded by the aircrew as signposts of the ship and a comforting familiarity.

"Contact, Victory 207. Stand by for your marshall instructions."

"Victory 207," Wink replied. Unlike Woods, he enjoyed marshall. It was where all the carrier's planes went before landing aboard the carrier at night, a finely choreographed holding pattern where they circled twenty or more miles from the carrier until their time came and they began their descent to the dreaded night landing.

"Want to go up on the roof?" Woods asked Wink.

"Sure. We've got time," Wink replied as he searched for a card on his knee board. "As long as we've got the gas."

"We've got it," Woods replied.

"Victory 207, Marshall at the 240 radial at 22 miles, angels 7. Your push time is . . . stand by."

"Passing thirty," Wink said to Woods as they passed through thirty thousand feet.

"Push time is 04."

"*Victory 207—240 at 22, angels 7, push at 04, roger,*" Wink replied. "Passing forty."

Woods started the nose of the Tomcat back toward the horizon. "How high do you want to go?"

"If we go above fifty we're supposed to wear a pressure suit. Wouldn't want our blood to boil."

"Forty-nine, aye," Woods said. He leveled off at forty-nine thousand feet and set the plane straight and level, heading in the direction of their assigned marshall location where they would begin their descent to the carrier for their landing. Their push time, when they were to begin their descent to the ship from a very specific spot, was four minutes after the hour—twenty-four minutes away. "Ready to darken ship?" Woods asked.

"Affirm," Wink replied. They both moved their hands around the cockpit expertly adjusting the lights, consoles, and switches that gave off any light at all, leaving faint indications of critical information, and turning off or dimming everything else. They lowered the radio receiver volume so they couldn't hear the other pilots checking in to marshall. Wink switched off his radarscope and PTID screen even though the radar stayed on. There were no reflections off the clear Plexiglas canopy which reached over their heads and down below their shoulders.

Woods adjusted the trim of the Tomcat so it would fly straight and level with his hands and feet off the controls and turned on the autopilot to hold their altitude and heading. As a last step he switched off the flashing red anticollision lights, which could be seen for miles and warned other planes of their presence. Tonight, there was no one else up that high and no risk of colliding with another airplane. The Tomcat blended in with the night, invisible to everyone but God.

Woods put his arms on the railings of the canopy and looked up at the stars. As beautiful as they were from the ship in the middle of the sea on a clear night, nothing compared to sitting on the roof, on top of the world, in a darkened airplane. Woods studied the patterns of galaxies and stars, the vast number and density of them. He loved to fly as high as he could go over the water, or anywhere else, for that matter. Even on top of the highest mountain, the view couldn't compare to the clear sky over the sea from fifty thousand feet—above the highest mountains, the highest clouds, the highest storms, and the highest airplane traffic. There was no sensation of movement at all. It was like sitting in a planetarium. But even the view in the best planetarium would pale in comparison to this. The planets had actual size. The stars were closer, clearer, and brighter. The ones he could see pointed to the ones behind them, dimmer but clear, and the ones behind them, dimmer still. They were gathered in groups, or clusters, so numerous he couldn't even count them in one section of the sky. God's living room.

Woods thought of the other Navy pilots flying their racetrack patterns aimlessly in marshall, waiting for their time to descend and land on the carrier, to go below and watch a movie, or eat ice cream, or do the never-ending Navy paperwork, all without ever looking up.

He leaned back and closed his eyes to moisten them. The oxygen leaking out of the top of his oxygen mask had dried them out. He opened his eyes again and looked toward the eastern horizon where the moon would be coming up in forty-five minutes. He could see the faint glow of white as the moon gathered its energy to rise and illuminate the night.

Wink broke the silence. "Two more months and we head back to Norfolk, Sean."

"Yep. But some good port calls before then. Like Israel."

"Never happen. Too much going on. They'll never let us go."

"I'll take that bet. I was on board last cruise when we stopped at Haifa. Same kind of deal."

"They'll probably blow somebody up and we won't get to go. We'll end up in Naples again."

"Roger that."

Woods sat for another minute breathing the pure oxygen. Real air was stale and warm compared to the Tomcat's pure oxygen, which seemed to rejuvenate him whenever he put on his mask. He didn't want to go to marshall and just drill around, waiting. They were supposed to get there early enough to set up their speed and arrive at their push time within ten seconds. He liked to get there as late as he could and still make it. Somehow they always made it. Maybe it was just his way of putting off the inevitable—landing aboard the carrier.

The mere thought of landing aboard the ship at night with no moon and an overcast caused his palms to sweat. He had never gotten used to it. He was good at it; one of the best in the squadron—but it was still an unnatural act. Woods turned up the instrument lights and switched on the anticollision lights. He rolled the F-14 over on its back and headed for marshall. "Let's do it."

2

Sami Haddad slowed as he turned into CIA Headquarters in Langley, Virginia. He had worked there for only three years but it was already becoming old hat. He had the apartment, the badge, the cool job, and the respect that came from lowering his voice when he told people where he worked. This was the New CIA. The one with a website. The one that acknowledged its existence and allowed people to say that was where they worked. At least the analysts. It was only the spooks who went odd places and did unspeakable things who couldn't tell people what they did.

He parked his ugly Nissan and slammed the door as hard as he could without being obvious about winding up. He listened for the telltale protest of the door with its trademark ping, the sound of a cheap, thin door. He wished his car would just die so he could have an excuse to buy another one. Until it broke he couldn't justify a new car. His father would never approve. Only replace things when they need replacing, especially transportation. You don't buy a car to make a statement or look good. That's what his father said. Mr. Pragmatic, who drove an S class Mercedes. So Sami didn't wash his car, or change its oil, or do any scheduled maintenance. He just waited for it to die, which it refused to do.

He walked to the building and held his key card in front of the red light on the other side of the window near the door. It recognized his card and let him in. The guard looked at him as he entered and nodded toward the X-ray machine and metal detector. All employees had to be checked every day. No exceptions. Too many people had too much against the Central Intelligence Agency to be sloppy about security.

"Morning," Sami said, putting his briefcase onto the conveyor belt. He wondered, as he did every morning, whether the X rays affected his sandwich. Probably not. If anything, they probably killed some bacteria. He knew the rays didn't affect the rest of the contents, the Arab newspapers, the Arabic dictionary, and the book he had taken home, *The History of the Crusades.*

Sami rode the elevator to the third floor and headed for his cubicle, where, like any good Dilbert, he put down his briefcase, took out his lunch to put in the refrigerator in the coffee room, turned on his computer, and sat down to work for the day. His mind immediately brought him back to where he had been the previous night at 9 P.M., the last time he had been at his desk. The very thoughts that had caused him to go to the Library of Congress and take advantage of the after-hours access that few ever used. He had checked out an obscure book on medieval Middle Eastern history and another on the Crusades.

He picked up the report that he had left on his desk. It was from the NSA. They had intercepted some communications they had found curious and sent them his way as they did many others in a given week. This was the only one he had kept.

It was from a very common transmitter, using ordinary voice codes that unsophisticated people used to allow themselves to think no one could figure out what they meant. But there had been a name that had been spoken in the signals. The name had created confusion at NSA, and caused them to make sure Sami was aware of it—he got all the unusual Arabic references.

Sami had a Ph.D. in Arabic studies from Georgetown, and was the son of a former Syrian diplomat. His father was a man who had found himself on the opposite side of Syrian President Hafez al-Assad, and had left the service of Syria to stay in the United States with his American wife. Sami had been born in the United States and had only a passing knowledge of Syria, based mostly on visits he had made to his cousins. But he knew Arabic, and he knew how Arabs thought. That made him invaluable to the Agency and in particular, the Middle Eastern Section, in the subdirectory of Emerging Terrorist Organizations.

"You still looking at that NSA report? It's not that long," Terry Cunningham said. Cunningham was a fellow analyst with a Ph.D. in political science. His strength was having knowledge of everything that had happened in the Middle East in the twentieth century. He knew all the political groups, angles, and implications. Although he wasn't perfect, his ability to predict what would happen next was uncanny. He also spoke passable Arabic.

"I'm worried," Sami said.

"Why?"

"I'm not sure."

"Talk to me."

"A new organization. That goes way back."

"Where?"

"I can't really talk about it and make sense yet."

"What do you have?"

"I need to think about this some more."

"The boss is going to want to hear about it."

"Not yet."

"I want in."

"When I've got something to say."

"Sounds to me like you do."

"Soon."

"Don't wait too long," Cunningham said, heading out of Sami's cubicle for his own.

"Don't worry."

⚓

"What the hell were you *thinking*?" Tony Vialli asked Woods as they stood facing each other in the paraloft, where all the pilots kept their flight gear and hung their G-suits and dry suits. Vialli knew he was a hothead, but he also knew when he was right. He pulled the zipper on the leg of his G-suit all the way to the top, freeing the zipper, which he angrily pulled apart. "Well?" he asked, waiting for Woods to reply.

Woods was taking his flight gear off slowly, methodically. Sedge, Vialli's RIO, and Wink were removing their flight gear and staying out of the discussion. Wink knew he was next. He and Woods were of virtually identical seniority in the squadron.

Woods finally replied, "What?"

"That stunt," Vialli answered instantly, knowing Woods was stalling.

"Cool your jets, Boomer. No harm done."

Vialli glared at him and continued, "Scared the shit out of me, man. That's harm to me."

"Keeps you on your toes."

"When I'm already skimming an overcast?"

"See? You weren't even complying with Visual Flight Rules. Violating cloud clearance requirements," Woods said as he hung his torso harness—the webbed harness they wore around their legs and chest and attached them to their ejection seats—on the hook with his name on it.

"I'm serious. You went IFR and then thumped me. That's reckless, Sean. Someone could have gotten hurt."

"All right. It won't happen again. Let's forget about it."

Vialli didn't say anything.

"Let's go to the wardroom. I need a slider. Wink's coming."

"Aren't we going to debrief the hop?"

"What's to debrief? We did twenty intercepts and didn't see anyone trying to attack the ship. Skip it. Wink's already done the intel debrief at CVIC."

Vialli hung the rest of his gear on his hook. He pulled his green flight suit and the T-shirt he wore under it away from his chest to break the seal his sweat caused and rolled up the cuffs twice, exposing his forearms slightly. He was still peeved, but not sure what to do about it. He didn't want to turn in his roommate, section leader, senior officer, and best friend for a flight violation. That would be a breach of the unwritten rules. "I'm going to hit the rack. Too damn late for a greaseburger." He walked toward the door of the ready room.

"You still want to go to Pompeii when we pull into Naples?" Woods called after him.

Vialli didn't even slow down as he let the door close behind him.

⚓

Sami stared at the pictures of the Gaza attack. "I don't know. How could I tell just by looking at pictures of dead people?" he asked, annoyed.

"Is there anything in your research to point to them?" Cunningham asked.

"I don't *have* any research. I have a bunch of history which may be interesting one day or may just make me look stupid."

"Talk to me, Sami. Bounce it off me."

Sami didn't want to talk about it yet. It was too easy to say too much. But he needed someone else's input. "The oldest secret society in the world. But they disappeared a long time ago."

Cunningham thought about it for a moment. "You're thinking maybe not?"

"Maybe."

"Because of one transmission?" Cunningham asked.

"That's what started me thinking. Now I'm seeing other things I hadn't noticed before."

"You haven't told anybody?"

"No reason to yet. I may be out of my mind."

Cunningham sat on the corner of Sami's desk. "Maybe it's time."

Sami wasn't sure what to do. He didn't want to overstate it.

"Want me to set up a brief with the section head?"

"I think I'll bring it up at our meeting this afternoon." He glanced at the pictures again. "What did the Palestinians say about the weapons?"

"American-made M-60 machine guns, American TOW missile launcher."

"Anybody trace them?"

"Actually, yes. Funny you should ask. The guns still had the serial numbers on them."

Sami frowned. "Why would they do that? And they left them in the van? They didn't care if anyone found them?"

"Nope. Like they wanted them to be found."

"Could they trace them?"

"Yeah. Easy. United States Marine Corps. In Lebanon. After the barracks were blown up they were never found. There has always been a suspicion a bunch of weapons ended up with the Druze in Beirut."

"Druze?"

"Yeah."

"You sure Druze?"

"Yeah. Why?"

Haddad didn't reply. He glanced at the NSA report. "The signals were from Lebanon, and the Druze . . . I don't want to jump to conclusions."

"Better bring it up at our meeting."

✒

Woods stood by the track in the Naples train station where he was supposed to meet Vialli, his reluctant co-tourist for the day. He had convinced his roommate to go with him to Pompeii. He glanced up again, scanning the crowd for Vialli, as he tried to open the triangular box of Toblerone chocolate he had just bought with Italian money, a piece of paper that had so many zeros on it it looked like monopoly money.

Woods checked the time. The big clock at the end of the track, past the engine, was five minutes behind his watch. Typical Italian efficiency. Can't even keep their clocks right. He had been in the Naples train station dozens of times. This was his fourth cruise to the Mediterranean, two with his first F-14 squadron, and one other with this squadron, VF-103, the Jolly Rogers, the ones carrying on the decades-old tradition and name of the most famous fighter squadron in the Navy. Woods loved their whole image, the tails with skull and crossbones, the traditional pirate flag. He was proud to be a Jolly Roger. And with this squadron and the one before, he knew Med cruises meant going to Naples, one of the finest ports in the Med, and the home of the Sixth Fleet.

He had been through this train station leaving on a ten-day skiing vacation in Switzerland, and for trips to Rome, to Venice, and to Paris. He was comfortable traveling in Europe even though he didn't speak any foreign languages. He had always taken advantage of the leave he accumulated to see Europe while in the Med. Few other officers did, so he often traveled alone.

Woods took his wallet from his jacket pocket, pulled out a small, two-inch square sticker, and peeled off the back. He looked around to see if he was being watched. He reached behind him and stuck the zapper—a sticker with the Jolly Rogers logo on it—on the light pole against which he was leaning. He smiled to himself.

Suddenly, he saw Vialli jogging toward him through the train station.

Vialli reached him breathless. "Hey! Sorry I'm late. I didn't think I'd make it at all. The boat I was on flamed-out. We had to do a mid-ocean transfer to another boat. What a flail." He glanced at the train. "Did you get the tickets?"

"Yeah. We've got to get on," Woods said, stuffing the Toblerone box into his back pocket like a set of drumsticks and moving quickly to the train.

They climbed up the stairs of a passenger car and walked down the hallway next to the compartments. Woods finally found an empty one, slid the door open, and they stepped in. Vialli closed the door behind him.

They sat down next to the window across from each other. Each had two empty seats beside him. Vialli leaned his head against the top of the vinyl seat and closed his eyes. Woods stared out the window. Vialli could sleep anywhere. Nothing troubled him. He was unflappable. Woods was pulling the bent chocolate box out of his pocket when something caught his eye by the door. A face. Someone had looked into the compartment and then moved away. There it was again. Woods watched the door, and suddenly it opened quickly. A woman stepped in and closed the door behind her.

She glanced at Vialli, who appeared to be sleeping, and sat down in the corner, on Vialli's side, placing her knit bag on the seat between them.

Woods, his mouth slightly open, tried not to stare—she was shockingly pretty—and nodded an acknowledgment. She smiled at him but didn't speak. Woods kicked Vialli's shoe, rousing him. Vialli sat up, baffled, looking at his squadron mate. Woods glanced casually at the woman, and Vialli followed the direction of his friend's eyes.

"Hi," Vialli said to her, no longer baffled and wasting no time. He brushed his hair back with his hand.

She looked past him out the window at the gray Naples morning. The train had picked up speed and was rocking softly sideways. She sat quietly with her hands on the armrests at her side. She wore a dark blue, loose-fitting flowery cotton dress, and had long, brown curly hair. Her dazzling light brown eyes had streaks of green and yellow in them. An even tan accentuated her outdoor, fit look. Vialli thought she was the most beautiful woman he'd ever seen.

"Are you Italian?" Vialli asked.

She glanced at him momentarily, then turned her eyes back to the window. The door suddenly flew open and the conductor came into their compartment. The train rocked, and the conductor leaned against the door to steady himself and free both hands. Addressing the woman in Italian, he stuck out his hand for her ticket. She smiled, handing the conductor her ticket with her left hand and speaking to him so rapidly that Vialli couldn't recognize any of the ten Italian words he knew.

She had a lovely smile, and her eyes sparkled as she joked with the conductor. He took the rest of the tickets and left the compartment.

Vialli shifted his gaze from the door to the woman, feeling his stomach tighten as he watched her. Woods studied Vialli and could tell his friend was about to do something rash. He tried to get his attention to discourage him. No luck.

"Do you speak English?" Vialli asked her.

Again, she didn't respond, not even to acknowledge that he had spoken. "*Sprechen-sie Deutsch?*" he asked.

Woods wondered what Vialli planned to do if she answered him, since Vialli didn't speak German. He leaned forward and gave Vialli a raised-eyebrow look.

Vialli gave him a look back, a "What?" look.

The woman transferred her gaze from the tranquil Mediterranean to her fellow traveler. "*Nein,*" she replied coolly, finally.

"I don't speak Italian," he said, happy to have gotten some response.

She gave him a cool smile and crossed her legs. She reached into her bag, pulled out a paperback book, and began to read. Vialli sighed audibly and looked out the window at the scenery he had seen so many times from the other side, on the sea. Suddenly he turned his head back toward her and looked again at the book she was reading. Hemingway. In English.

"You do speak English!" he said with a smile.

"A little," she replied without looking up as she found her place in the book.

"Why didn't you tell me?" he said sitting up, energized.

"Because you would have started talking to me and I wouldn't have been able to read my book, which I have been looking forward to for a long time." She returned to her book.

"How did you know I'd start talking to you?"

"Because you're an American, and Americans always talk to strangers."

"How'd you know I was an American?" he wondered.

She shook her head slowly, amazed. "Your haircut, your jacket, your shoes, your cord . . . what do you call them—corduroy pants. Your questions, and you've been staring at me since I came into this compartment."

Vialli grimaced. "Sorry . . ."

She started reading again.

"I didn't mean to offend you," Vialli said. He checked his watch. The trip was only thirty minutes, and they had left Naples fifteen minutes before. He tried to concentrate on the countryside as the rails clacked rhythmically beneath him. He could see Mt. Vesuvius in the distance, the now-dormant volcano that had buried Pompeii centuries ago. You could see it from Naples for that matter, or from thirty miles out at sea, or from a hundred miles if the weather was clear and you were flying high enough. He couldn't stand it. "Where are you from?"

She placed a bookmark in her book and laid it on her lap. "The American conversation," she said. "Where are you from, what do you do, where did you go to school. Right?"

He looked at her directly, and she noticed his intense brown eyes under his dark brown hair. "Doesn't hurt to be friendly," he said.

She relaxed slightly. "No, it won't hurt. I'm sorry." She took a deep breath and shrugged her shoulders. "I live in a town in northern Italy called Trento. It's just south of Austria."

"Must be nice."

"It is very pretty, and very old. A wonderful town."

"What do you do?"

"See?"

"Come on," he said.

"I am a schoolteacher, at least by training. I don't teach right now. I'm waiting for an opening."

He nodded and looked out the window again, trying not to show that he was really focusing on her reflection in the glass.

"What do you do?" she asked suddenly.

He looked at her with surprise. "I'm in the Navy."

"The American Navy?"

"Yeah."

"Are you on a ship?"

He nodded. "More or less. I'm a pilot—I fly off a carrier."

"Of course," she said. "You're on that big carrier in the bay."

He smiled and nodded. "That's me. The *George Washington*. Largest class of warship ever built. *Nimitz* class."

"Is it really?"

"Nothing else is even close. Some of the battleships were almost as heavy, but nothing nearly as big in every dimension."

"What do you fly?"

"Do you know airplanes?"

"Not really."

"Fighters. F-14s. Tomcats. You know, two tails, wings that move back and forth . . ."

"I think I've seen them. I think we have them too."

Vialli shook his head. "No, only the U.S. and, unfortunately, Iran."

"What do we have that looks like that?"

"We who? Italy?"

She looked puzzled, then understood. "Yes. Italy."

"Nothing really. Just Fiats and those sorts of things. Gnats. Bug-smashers. Noisemakers. Nothing serious."

"Well, you shouldn't belittle it . . ."

"I didn't mean to. I'm sure Italy's Air Force is *truly* formidable," he said. He tried to get her to look at him, which she was reluctant to do. "Do you mind if I ask you your name?"

She hesitated before she answered. "Irit."

"What?" he said, leaning forward, as if he hadn't heard her.

"Irit."

"That's an odd name. Is it Italian?"

"What's your name?"

"Tony Vialli."

"That's an odd name. Is it American?"

"Very funny. No such thing as an American name," he said, "except maybe Sitting Bull," he added. "No, my name is Italian, and my family, some time ago, I think my grandparents' parents, came over to the States. I've heard they were from Genoa, but I'm not really sure."

"Well, it's nice to meet you, Mr. Vialli."

"Thanks," he said. "Where are you going?"

She looked amused. "This train only goes to Pompeii."

He nodded, trying to imply he knew that. "But are you going to see the tourist trap, where all the dead people are, or what?"

"Yes, I'm going to see where the dead people are. What else would I be doing there?"

He shrugged. "Don't know. I figured there may be a town there too."

"Not really."

"So you're playing tourist today?"

"Yes I am."

"You want to come with us? With Sean and me? We can go to Pompeii together and see the dead people," he said. He suddenly realized he hadn't even asked Woods. "If that's okay with you?" he said to Sean. "We'll all go together."

Woods stared at him, amazed.

She studied Vialli carefully. "I don't really know you." She leaned back against the seat as the train rounded a curve. She considered. "Why not."

3

s of right now each of you is a member of a special task force to track the attack on the Gaza border, and identify the group responsible. This one has the Director's attention." Joe Kinkaid, Director of Counter-Terrorism at the CIA, had them hanging on every word. This was the kind of assignment they all longed for. It could launch a career. Kinkaid's unit had two hundred members. It was their job to identify and track all terrorist threats worldwide that might threaten American interests. He was overworked but he loved his job. He was one of the few people in Greater Washington who went home every night knowing he was making the world better for his children. In his mid-fifties, he was out of shape and didn't care. What he cared about was that his mind was working at full speed, which it always was.

Kinkaid pressed the space bar on the laptop computer sitting on the lectern and the screen in the front of the room lit up with the first slide of his presentation. The screen was blue with decorative red in the lower-right corner. In large white letters the slide said: GAZA TASK FORCE.

"This task force is classified Top Secret. I expect it will go code word in the not too distant future. No one outside this room has a need to know about us or what we're doing unless I say so. You know the drill." He touched the space bar again, and the next slide came up. It was in outline form and provided him with the bullet points he wanted to be sure to make. "The Gaza attack occurred after dawn, about eight in the morning, local time. Stranded truck, turned around, doors burst open. Big firefight."

The next slide showed a photograph of the checkpoint. There were several bodies on the road near one side, and a burning APC across the fence on the Israeli side. The high-quality color photo had words on the bottom: SECRET, NOFORN, WNINTEL. Classified secret, not to be released to foreign intelligence or military, and a warning notice, that intelligence sources or methods were involved in the acquisition of the photo that made it more sensitive than the usual secret photo.

"Note what we all know, and what we've all heard on CNN, that both Palestinian guards and Israeli guards were killed. This is different. I can't think of any time someone has taken on the Israelis *and* the Palestinians at the same time."

He touched his space bar. Another photo came up with the same inscription on the bottom. "Here is the van, and the weapons that were captured." The photo was a close-up of the van as it sat in the alley. It was dark, but the weapons could be seen.

A dark man in the back that Sami had never seen spoke. "They wanted them to be found."

Kinkaid looked at him quickly, agreeing. "That's how I see it. These weapons are all lined up. Like they're on display at a gun show." He went to the next slide, which was a well-lit close-up of one of the weapons. "Here, you can even see the serial number on the M-60." The members of the task force studied the photo. Kinkaid went on. "Not only are the guns neatly arranged, they were left in order—by serial number, lowest to highest."

The task force members were puzzled.

The dark man spoke again. "They're showing their escape went as planned. No hurry at all."

"What's the point of that?" Sami asked, unable to remain quiet.

"What indeed," Kinkaid asked. "Any ideas?"

"It's a message," the dark man said.

Kinkaid replied, "Clearly." Then to the others. "This is Mr. Ricketts. He is from the DO." Directorate of Operations. Spies. The ones who do the covert operations. "Like a few others of you, he is not a regular member of my counterterrorism section. He had some time and I asked him if he would join us, at least until he had to go about other things. He graciously accepted. He brings a different perspective—the perspective of someone who has actually fired weapons and knows what to do with them, instead of the rest of us, who study them in cubicles." He nodded to Ricketts. "So what's the message?"

"This op was easy," he said, speaking with just the slightest hint of an accent, but not one that was identifiable. He rubbed his unshaved chin. He could pass for an Arab, an Egyptian, an Armenian, an Israeli, or even a Serbian. His dark, pockmarked face was chameleon-like, and changed when he wasn't even trying. Sami was fascinated by him.

Ricketts went on. "They were willing to tidy up, sip a spot of tea, and watch a movie before heading off. They are very good, and very well trained. They just wanted to be sure we knew that."

"Who are they?" Cunningham asked.

"That's the big question, isn't it?" Kinkaid continued. He went to the next slide. It was a gruesome photograph of one of the Palestinian guards up close. A hand was holding open the dead man's bulletproof vest, sticking a finger through the hole in the vest and showing the entry wound on the dead man's chest at the same time. "Since we were talking about equipment, I thought we should note this. They had bullets for their M-60 machine guns that were designed to penetrate Kevlar vests. Steel-jacketed with a lead core. Experimental until very recently. The kicker is, these bullets had a Teflon coating outside the steel. Even our special forces don't have them. These guys are way ahead of the curve."

"Where'd they get them?" one of the women on the task force asked.

"We don't know. That's one of the things we'll be checking out." He brought up the next slide in his PowerPoint presentation. "Take a look at this van. No serial numbers at all, and the inside of the van— the sides actually—are lined with Kevlar. No bullets went through. And," he clicked, "solid rubber tires. In case someone tried to shoot them out. They meant business."

"Well planned," Ricketts commented.

Kinkaid continued, "So. Who are they, as Mr. Cunningham so aptly put it? We have no idea, and that's what we're going to find out. That's why we asked the Israelis for all the inside information they had, and we even got some from the Palestinians, although the idea of cooperating with us to track down Islamic terrorists—if that's what they are— is sort of new to them. They will definitely not give us their best information. I can guarantee that." He thought for a moment. "Nor will Israel, for that matter. But we may get some usable information from those sources, and we'll take a look at whatever we get." He got out of PowerPoint and closed the screen on his laptop. "You've all seen the photos of the shooting. These guys are a different breed." Kinkaid was clearly puzzled. "I've never seen this kind of operation. Anybody?"

No one wanted to sound stupid.

"They disappeared into Gaza City, which may mean two things. One, they had help. Two, they can probably pass as Palestinians. Which means either they are Palestinian, or close, or they're well hidden. Could be disguised too, I guess—"

"What about those weapons?"

"It's a little puzzling. Bottom line? The machine guns were probably on the arms market. Taken from the Marines in Beirut twenty years ago. Either kept by someone in Lebanon—which might mean the shooters are Lebanese—or someone just bought them, which then, of course, means nothing. We're trying to track that down."

"Anybody claiming responsibility?" Cunningham asked. He had already run through the list of the most likely suspects in his mind, the ones who would stand to gain the most. It wasn't a very long list because there weren't that many groups that had it in for the Israelis *and* the Palestinians.

"A few have called papers in the Middle East, but no one who had any inside information. Nothing we can use. And remember, they only attacked soldiers. No civilian casualties at all."

"Sounds like Hamas to me. Or Hezbollah," Terry Cunningham said, thinking out loud. "They've killed Palestinians before, when they were pissed at Arafat for dealing with Israel, and changing their charter."

"They both said they had nothing to do with it. Who else is out there that's unhappy at both? And goes so far out of their way to show both of them at the same time?"

Cunningham considered. "There are a few others, but none who could pull off this kind of thing."

"We may be dealing with something new. That's why I asked Sami to be part of this. He's an analyst with the Middle East Section. You should have all read his memo before now." He looked around the table. They nodded.

Sami watched Kinkaid for hints of what he thought of his memo. He had been forced to prepare it before it was ready. Kinkaid was in too much of a hurry to find the answer. Shortcuts are fine if they get you to the answer quicker. But sometimes shortcuts lead to trouble. Sami thought Kinkaid looked worn out. In fact he looked just plain dumpy. His mind was legendary, but he had heard other things about Kinkaid that troubled him. Sami figured Kinkaid was entitled to the benefit of the doubt for now.

Kinkaid continued. "You may be wondering why we're jumping

on this so early. No Americans injured, no American interests directly affected. The Israelis can look out for themselves, right? The way I see it, every terrorist event threatens American interests one way or another. It's just a matter of time. Sometimes it's way later than when we first hear about something. We've been taking a more pro-active approach for the last couple of years. We want to know everything about every terrorist we can. You can't have too much knowledge about people who are intent on destroying things. Maybe we'll save some lives. Hard to say. All I know is that it has paid off in the past, and I expect it to pay off now. And if Sami's memo is even close, we are in for a rude awakening. I will also be in touch with a friend from Israel who has helped me in the past. I'll find out what they know."

"She's the most beautiful woman I think I've ever seen," Vialli said as he sat back in his chair in the wardroom and scooped ice cream out of a drinking glass with a spoon.

"You were all over her as soon as you saw her. You didn't waste a second—"

"Dude, you *kicked* me! Made sure I saw her, and now you bust my chops for noticing her? What's up with that?" Vialli smiled. He scraped the bottom of the glass with his spoon and got up to get more from the automatic dispenser in the back of the wardroom, the Auto Dog as it was known. They were the only officers in the forward-most section of the aviators' wardroom, the dirty-shirt wardroom. It was on the 03 level, the same level as all the ready rooms and most of the aviators' staterooms. All they had to do to eat was walk forward. The other wardroom, on the second deck, was where most of the ship's company's officers ate.

Vialli pulled the lever and moved his glass back and forth to get all the chocolate ice cream the glass would hold. He filled a porcelain cup full of steaming coffee and sat down again. "You underestimate me. You think I'm—"

"I just watch."

"Well, she's different. I'm telling you. She's a class act. When you went off on your own into that cave we got to talk."

Woods frowned. "You didn't try to make out with her, did you?"

"I just put my arm around her for a second. She loved it. She snuggled right up to me—it was awesome."

"You're dreaming. She lives in northern Italy. You'll never see her again."

"We'll be in Venice in ten days, dude. Her city's only a couple of hours away by train and she had already planned to be there that weekend for a trip to a museum."

Woods suddenly had a bad feeling. "You've already *talked* to her about Venice?"

"Sure. Why not?"

"You hardly know her."

"I spent the whole day with her. After you went back to the ship we went for a walk in Naples—"

"Beautiful Naples—"

"We found a really cool farmer's market kind of place. Fresh vegetables, all kinds of stuff. It was great to walk around—"

"Wait, wait, don't tell me, you held hands—"

"Hey, bite me. Anyway, I like her a lot. And you'd better get used to it. I want to get to know her. What's wrong with that?"

"Nothing I guess." He actually couldn't think of anything that was wrong with it. It just struck him as odd that she just happened to have plans to be in Venice when the carrier pulls in. "Nice coincidence."

"Oh, what? She's scheming to get close to me or something? Why? So she can get my fortune from my parents' vegetable stand in New York? Give me a break."

"It's just an interesting coincidence." Woods stretched his arms out in his leather flight jacket and breathed deeply. He looked at his watch. "Aw, *man.*"

"What?"

"I've got Boat O in fifteen minutes. I just want to hit the rack."

"You're on at midnight?"

"Yep."

"Which boat?"

"E-boat."

"Damn, man. You get all the luck. Slamming through the waves for three or four hours with sailors throwing up and shit all over the boat?" He leaned back and looked envious. "Wish I could go."

Woods nodded. "Eat your heart out. If I'm really lucky it'll be raining and thirty-eight degrees and the visibility will be half a mile, and we'll get hit by some merchant ship and all be killed."

"That *would* be cool. Just like Barcelona."

Woods looked at his watch again. "I've got to head down. You gonna hit the rack?"

"Yeah. I've got to get up early. Evals due tomorrow. I haven't even started. I don't even know the names of the sailors in ops yet. But I'm supposed to rate them and say what great sailors they are."

Woods stood up. "You should know them by now," he scolded. He thought for a second. "What kind of name is Irit? Doesn't sound Italian. Doesn't end in a vowel, like Sophia, or . . . I don't know . . . Manuela or something."

"Manuela is Spanish, dude."

"No, it isn't. You're thinking of Consuela, or something. I met an Italian woman named Manuela."

"Whatever. Anyway, Irit is Italian. She's from northern Italy, near Austria. You heard her. Torentino, I think. Maybe it's part German."

"Yeah. Could be, except Torentino is in the southern part of Italy."

"Whatever. I probably got the city wrong. What time do you get off—0300?"

"Yeah. Maybe 0400."

"You're going to be tired tomorrow."

"I'm gonna to sleep in."

"No you're not. Quarters is at 0800 on the flight deck."

Woods groaned and hung his head. "I forgot."

"Hey, it's important. Sailor of the hour, or something."

"Think they'd notice if I didn't show?"

"XO would have your ass."

"The life of a Naval officer is one long battle for sleep." He zipped up his flight jacket. "There must be studies. People do hard things better when they're sleep-deprived."

"They're doing the studies now, dude. With *us*."

"I'll wake you up when I get in."

"If you do, I'll drop my alarm clock on your head." Vialli slept on the top bunk.

They walked aft from the wardroom together, stepping over the curved bulkhead openings that were nine inches off the deck—the knee knockers. The O3 level was just below the flight deck; their stateroom was exactly where the angled deck met the rest of the flight deck, forming a shoulder. Vialli stopped, unlocked the door, and closed it behind him. Woods turned outboard and descended the three ladders to the main deck, the hangar deck, where he would find the ladder to the enlisted boat he would be commanding for the next three or four hours. His seagoing command.

He walked along the nonskid hard steel of the hangar deck, detouring around the airplanes there for maintenance, making his way to the fantail. He passed the snaking line of enlisted men waiting to go ashore on liberty. Woods shuddered at the thought of these eighteen-year-olds going ashore at midnight in a city that had whatever they were looking for.

At the fantail, open to the sea air, the Masters at Arms were in place. A Warrant Officer was in charge.

Woods's Garrison cap—called a piss-cutter by those who wore it—was pulled down near his eyebrows and the simulated fur collar on his leather flight jacket was turned up to stop the biting breeze. The Warrant Officer saluted when he caught sight of Woods. The three enlisted men on duty saluted as well. "Good evening, sir," the Warrant said.

Woods returned the salutes and looked at the Warrant closely. He didn't recognize him. Woods nodded. "Any problems with the E-boats?"

The Warrant shook his head as he put his hands back into the olive green foul-weather jacket he wore over his dirty khakis. "No, sir. Nothing."

"How's the water?"

"Pretty calm. Three-, maybe four-foot swells."

Woods glanced past the fantail over the black water toward Naples. One of the ship's boats was plying its way back to the *Washington*, working against a rising tide. He could clearly see the city lights on the hills three miles away. "How's the visibility been?"

"Real good, sir. We've only lost the lights on the hills a couple of times. Mostly the vis seems to be unlimited."

"Much traffic?"

"Usual merchant traffic and smugglers."

"Here comes your boat, sir," the Warrant said as the coxswain gunned the loud diesel motor in reverse to line the boat up with the platform suspended behind the enormous aircraft carrier.

Woods watched the sailors disembark from the boat, most staggering, as a sailor played the line in and out to match the boat's rise and fall with the waves. The coxswain kept the engine in gear, pushing against the current to keep the boat in place. Finally the boat was empty except for the crew and they were ready to load another group.

Woods hurried down the ladder and jumped onto the boat. The center of the boat where the coxswain stood was elevated three feet above the passenger areas in the bow and stern. Fully loaded, it could hold about seventy-five sailors. The seating areas were open to the night sky. If the weather was bad they could rig canvas covers for all the seating area, but it made the ride very stuffy, especially when any of the sailors got sick.

Lieutenant Junior Grade Phil Cobb of Woods's squadron was the Boat Officer he was to relieve. Woods looked at the boat and then at Cobb. "Hey, Phil. How's it been?"

"Usual drunks."

Woods noticed the lights from the *Washington* reflecting off Cobb's green nylon flight jacket. "How'd you get so wet?" he asked unenthusiastically.

"Swells are getting worse. The whole way out you're going right into the waves. A couple made it all the way back to us."

"Great," Woods said.

"You'll have a blast. I'll bet it isn't below forty degrees."

Woods noticed Cobb was wearing gloves. "Mind if I borrow your gloves?" he asked.

Cobb shrugged. "I'll pick 'em up tomorrow."

"I appreciate it."

"You got your long johns on, Trey?"

"You bet," Woods said, as a chill caused him to shiver suddenly. "Wish I'd worn my green flight jacket."

"Use mine."

"Thanks." Cobb was taller and bigger than Woods, who was thin. People thought he was skinny, which he hated. He worked out all the time to get bigger, but only seemed to get stronger without adding any mass to his frame.

The sailors started down the ladder and filled in the seating areas quickly, anxious to go ashore.

"That's it for me," Cobb said cheerfully. "She's all yours, Trey."

Woods saluted Cobb and said, half jokingly, "I relieve you, sir."

Cobb smiled, returned the salute, and said, "I am relieved." He turned and dashed up the ladder to the well-lit hangar bay.

Woods watched as the sailors in their civilian clothes eagerly filled the boat, sitting close to each other so that there was no unused space. Liberty expired at 0400, except for those who had a special chit authorizing an all-night stay ashore. Woods knew most of the sailors would wander off the quay, past the Hey-Joes who would try to sell them something they didn't want, past the prostitutes who would try to sell them something they did want, past small restaurants they didn't like, only to end up at the USO club a few blocks from the waterfront listening to the same music they listened to all the time aboard the ship, and talking to the same people they talked to every day. But they could drink. They would consume more alcohol than any straight-thinking person would consume, stagger back to the quay, and get back aboard his boat just in time to throw up on someone, preferably some-one they knew, or a fistfight would ensue and they would get written up for being drunk and disorderly and have to explain their conduct to the ship's captain. Woods pulled his collar up more tightly around his neck. The night was getting colder by the minute, that Naples-on-the-water-bone-chilling-coldness that seemed to settle in when it was overcast and windy.

"Ready to go, sir?" the coxswain asked.

Woods nodded his head as he looked around for other shipping traffic that could be a factor on the trip in to the harbor. A twenty-minute ride, then a ten-minute wait on the quay. Then a twenty-minute ride back. The first of many. "Let's go."

The coxswain threw the throbbing diesel into reverse and backed away quickly from the *Washington,* turned into the waves, and started for shore. As he stood in the boat and strained his eyes ahead in the night, Woods felt like Washington crossing the Delaware. Except he had a motor. And Washington had a mission.

4

inkaid panted slightly as he counted the rings at the other end of the line. He was using the STU-III phone in his office, the encrypted phone that was cleared for conversations up to Top Secret if the person on the other end of the line had his STU-III properly encrypted, which was certainly the case this morning. Kinkaid checked his watch. Pick up, he ordered. Kinkaid had waited until midnight to catch the person he was calling at seven o'clock in the morning, when he was fresh.

The man on the other end answered. "Shalom," he said.

"Shalom," Kinkaid responded. "How have you been, Efraim? It is great to talk to you again." He already felt awkward.

"It has been a while."

"Yes, it has, I . . . It's a busy time."

"Which is, no doubt, why you called." His deep voice was soothing and threatening at the same time. It depended on what you were expecting.

"I am looking into the Gaza strip incident."

"Of course."

"We wondered if you knew who was involved."

"We are just beginning our investigation."

"Who do you think it was?"

"Why are you so interested?"

"It's my job to care. You know that."

"Yes. But this seems to be our problem."

"What are you going to do about it?"

31

"We're just trying to find out who did it first. Our response would depend on that, wouldn't it?"

"Do you have anything?"

Efraim paused. "There is so much we don't know."

"I've got to put together what we know over here. If you hear anything, or come up with anything, let me know. Anything, Efraim."

"Yes, obviously I will think about it. Right now I must go."

"Get back to me."

"I'll see what I can do."

"You have no idea? Really?"

"A few."

"Who?"

"It's too soon."

"Don't wait too long," Kinkaid warned. "If we're going to help, we need to know who we're dealing with."

"I'll see what I can do," he said again.

⚓

Woods walked into the ready room fifteen minutes before the scheduled brief. The Commanding Officer of VF-103, Fighter Squadron 103, Commander Mark Barnett, also known as Bark, was sitting in the first row reading through the message board in the front of the room. He glanced down at his watch. Woods knew what every other aviator in VF-103 knew—you were late to a brief only once in this squadron. Then you got to be Squadron Duty Officer for a week. No flying, just watching.

"Morning, Skipper," Woods said casually.

"Trey," Barnett replied, looking closely at Woods. "You ready to go?"

"I was born ready," Woods said.

"Right. I forgot," Bark said. "What kind of hop you on?"

"Strafing the spar."

"Don't hit it."

"Don't worry, Skipper."

"Did you see we got our new Intel Officer?"

"You're kidding me. Where is he?"

"It's a she. She's in the back, in the briefing area. Watching a brief from the receiving end first."

"What's her name?"

"Charlene Pritchard."

"She got any experience?"

"Yeah. She graduated from intel school at Dam Neck. *And* she has a gold bar on her collar." An Ensign, the lowest officer rank in the Navy.

"Damn good thing they send these Ensigns to tell us what's going on. Too bad Bruno had to go. He was just getting productive."

"Come on, Trey. You know you can't stick around here once you know what the hell is going on. That's what triggers getting *replaced.*"

Sean smiled as he looked toward the back. "She got a call sign yet?"

"Nope."

"I'll give it some thought," he said. He was one of the few officers in the squadron who could give someone a call sign and make it stick. He looked at the television. "Is she good-looking?"

"Trey," Bark said without looking up.

"Just making conversation. I'd better go brief. See you later, Skipper."

Commander Barnett didn't even acknowledge his departure, having already buried himself back in the message traffic on the metal board. He flipped one after another, initialing each message in the red ink only he used.

Woods wandered to the back of the ready room to the briefing area. It had charts of the Mediterranean on sliding boards next to the greenie board—where the landing grades of all pilots were kept in full view. There was an additional television for the closed circuit briefs from the carrier's intelligence center. Wink and Vialli were already there, as was the RIO with whom Vialli flew, Lieutenant Jack Sedgwick, known simply as Sedge. Wink's eyes began their characteristic exaggerated blinking, which had given him his name. No one in the squadron even noticed anymore. No one ever called him by his name, Kyle Martin. As a senior lieutenant, on his second squadron tour like Woods, he commanded a lot of respect, especially because he was regarded as the best RIO in the squadron. As the mission commander, Wink had arrived at the brief early and was prepared. The spare crew was there too in case Woods's or Vialli's plane broke and there was time to launch a replacement. They didn't want a scheduled sortie to go unfilled. Bark would rather die.

The television jumped to life at exactly 0815. The *Washington* had gotten underway at first light and was now well out of sight of Italy. The Ensign on the screen, the Intelligence Officer from VFA-81, one of the F/A-18 squadrons, showed the ship's position on the chart.

Woods resisted sitting down to listen to the brief. He saw the new Ensign standing behind the briefing area looking lost. Woods walked past the enormous steel and leather chairs to the large coffee urn. Removing his cup from the pegboard, he filled it with coffee. On the television the brief continued uninterrupted. Woods watched out of the corner of his eye.

"You're the new guy," he said.

"Yes, sir. Ensign Charlene Pritchard," she answered, extending her hand to Woods, checking him out. She had already heard about him and saw that his looks matched what she had heard. He was about six one, and had very dark brown hair, short but still unruly somehow. She was sure he wanted it to look that way. His eyes were an intense, dark gray and she noticed a faded hole in his ear from where it had been pierced.

"You don't have to call me sir, really," Woods said, shaking her hand. "I know you're supposed to, but we tend to ignore a lot of that kind of stuff around here."

"Thank you, sir."

He continued, not noticing. "Your name's Charlene?" She was of average height and thin, and had the curse of looking five years younger than she was. Her brown hair was in a French braid and her face had a clean, freshly scrubbed look to it. She carried herself with a confidence that Woods didn't expect in someone without wings.

"Yes, sir."

"That won't work."

"What?"

"The name."

"Won't work for what?"

"For being in a fighter squadron. Can't go around with a name like Charlene. You've got to have a call sign."

She couldn't tell if he was pulling her leg or not. She thought only aviators got call signs. "Why doesn't it work?"

"Not strong enough."

"You mean *masculine* enough?"

Her comment surprised him. "Did I say masculine?"

"Not in so many words—"

"Right. I said *strong* enough."

"It has always worked for me. What woman's name *is* strong enough?" she asked pointedly.

Woods thought for a moment. "I don't know, maybe . . . Ethel. Or Betty. Something like that. Not Char*lene*. That won't do at all," Woods said. "I'll have to give it some thought."

"Right." She drew some coffee from the urn into her Styrofoam cup. An idea occurred to her, a way to head off the problem. "A lot of people have called me Charlie in the past."

He studied her with a glint in his eyes. "No, Charlie doesn't work either. Too . . ." He struggled for the right word. ". . . Masculine." He looked at her again. "We'll just go with your name."

"Charlene?" she said, pleased.

"No, your last name."

"Pritchard?"

"Part of it. Pritch. I think that will work."

"It rhymes with—"

"Niche. Exactly. Which is what you have here—intelligence. By the way, you need to get a squadron cup. Can't drink out of Styrofoam. Bad for the environment."

"Yes, sir," she said. She looked more closely at him. "Did you used to have your ear pierced?"

"What?" he asked.

"High school, I'd bet?"

"When I was young and impetuous."

"You still wear an earring on liberty?"

"You gotta be kidding me," he replied.

"Do you think we'll be able to go to Israel?"

"Already worried about port calls?"

"I've always wanted to go to Israel."

"Never been?"

"No. Have you?"

He drank from the heavy white porcelain cup that had the Jolly Rogers insignia on it—the skull and crossbones—and gold pilot wings and his call sign, "Trey," on the other side. "Once. Another cruise. I don't know if they'll still let us go. Last time we went, there was a terrorist bomb in Jerusalem. They delayed our visit by a month, but we went. We may be far enough out that the Gaza thing won't matter at all. Plus it wasn't really in Israel. I think we'll be okay." He looked at the Intelligence Officer on the television completing his section of the brief. "Why don't you join us in the brief so you can see how it's done?"

"Thanks," she said as they walked slowly toward the chairs. She leaned over to Woods. "Who's the other pilot there?"

"Boomer. Tony Vialli."

"Why do they call him that?"

Woods put his finger to his lips so he could hear the weather portion of the brief, then turned toward Pritchard. "Came into the break at the ship supersonic once. He was late. Busted a window on the bridge. That's the kind of thing you don't live down."

"Why do they call you Trey?"

"When I CQ'd in F-14s, I got all three wires."

"What's CQ?"

Woods tried not to roll his eyes. "*Carrier* quals. Landing on the carrier to qualify in that airplane."

"What are three wires?"

"Later," he said, listening to the television suddenly. He started writing information down on a five-by-eight card.

"What kind of flight are you going to do?"

Woods looked at Pritchard with an expression of curiosity, as if the question hadn't occurred to him, and then shrugged. "Don't know. Wink'll take care of it. I'm just driving. He's the mission commander." He paused. "Have you done your squadron check-in card yet?"

"Just started."

"Don't forget to get Lieutenant Curly Crumpacker's signature."

"Who's he?"

"Lots of hats. RIO to the Air Wing Commander, Squadron Morale Officer, F-14 Simulator Officer, lots of things."

"I'll get him."

Woods nodded and sat down. He looked across at Vialli and said quietly, "Did you hear from her?"

Vialli smiled and nodded. "E-mail. Confirmed she'll be there in Venice."

"I *knew* I shouldn't have left you alone with her for even a minute."

"She's interested."

"I hope you know what you're doing."

Boomer got up to fill his coffee cup. "Hey," he said to Pritchard. "Hi," she replied.

When he returned, she asked, "You know where Lieutenant Crumpacker might be?"

"Huh?" he said. "Trey tell you to find him?"

"Yes, sir."

"I'm not sure where he is. He's awfully hard to find. Busy guy. I'd look in the forecastle." He just couldn't tell her Crumpacker was a longstanding squadron fiction used against all kinds of people who were unsuspecting, especially new officers.

"Thanks," she said, truly grateful. "By the way, what's a three wire?"

He raised his eyebrows, surprised she didn't know. "Third of four arresting wires on the flight deck. The one we aim for. Why?"

"I asked Trey how he got his call sign."

"What did he say?" Vialli asked skeptically.

"During carrier qualifications, CQ, I think he called it, he got all three wires."

"Hah!" Vialli guffawed. "How about he didn't get *any* three wires! Take *everything* he says with a grain of salt."

When the intelligence brief was concluded and the television went dark, Wink stood behind the lectern. "We're event One Alpha . . ."

&

The men walked slowly through the path in the boulders so narrow their shoulders rubbed both sides. Their black attire was hot, but caused them no more discomfort than they were used to. There was no way off the path once on it; it was a mile long and required dedication to reach the end. No one would venture down the path without knowing where it led—it was too claustrophobic. The path wound through craggy rocks that jutted upward at odd angles. At almost every step, anyone walking could be observed by someone in the right position higher up in the rocks. And there was always someone in the right position. This path had been perfected through centuries of use.

After thirty minutes of walking through the labyrinth the men reached their destination. They waited outside an opening in the stone wall that was hidden by the angle of the opening, almost going back the same way they had come. A man approached them speaking softly in Arabic.

The leader of the group, which had obviously traveled a long way, nodded wearily. "Please tell him we have returned."

"He said you should spend some time in the garden. He will call for you."

The man nodded again. Then to the others with him, "Come," he said, gesturing with his left hand, something not done in the Arab world—the left hand was for other things, and never part of conversation or polite gesturing.

They followed him into another opening in the rock face, walking in near darkness through a tunnel, wet with condensation. They could hear the underground river below them, the river that no one outside knew about, which had sustained those who had come here through the centuries—the flowing water feeding the lush gardens hidden in the inner paths of the mountain.

Coming out of the tunnel, they entered a green garden filled with waterfalls and ponds. Tired, their black robes dusty from their travels, they sat heavily on the stone ledge surrounding one of the fountains and waited. Two of the men drank from a spigot that spilled water into the fountain.

When a man appeared the group stood as one and followed him, moving across a small entrance so low they were forced to duck down. The room into which they were ushered was light and dry, its openings and doors facing a deep cavern. The only approach to the room, the central space of this invisible fortress, was through the small cave and garden from which they had just passed.

Here were thirty or so men, dressed in black like the newcomers, standing quietly around the room's walls. A man in the middle of the room sat at the table studying a map. He made one final notation and rose. Six feet tall and solidly built, his weathered face was covered by a closely cut, stiff beard that was mostly black but had a hint of brown. His eyes were black and hidden in a shadow of his heavy brow. In his forties, he commanded the attention of everyone in the room, without protest or doubt. He spoke in beautiful Arabic, addressing the leader of the group that had just arrived. "Welcome back, Farouk. Your mission was a success. The reports preceded you."

"Thank you," Farouk said. He looked directly at his leader, his gaze intense. "It went better than we had hoped. We lost no one."

"Excellent," the bearded man replied. He glanced around, making sure no ears were present that shouldn't be there. Satisfied, he continued. "You must rest and recuperate. In a very short time, I have another mission for you."

Farouk waited.

"We have located the one about whom we spoke. We must strike first."

Farouk nodded. "When?"

"Soon. And then it will be time to tell the world who we are. They must know. If they don't fear us, we will never accomplish our goals."

"We will leave now if we must."

"Not yet. Perhaps tomorrow, but today, rest, refresh. For this will be the hardest thing I have yet asked you to do." He pointed to the map on the table. "The plan is ready."

5

Woods and Wink stepped onto the flight deck and lowered their dark visors at the bright sunshine reflecting off the blue Mediterranean. The *George Washington* (CVN-73) moved slowly westward through the water away from the climbing sun. Woods handed his knee board to the plane captain who stood by the ladder to the Tomcat.

"Morning, Benson," Woods said, as he ducked under the wing to begin his preflight.

"Morning, sir," replied Airman Reece Benson.

Woods knew Benson well. He was highly regarded in the squadron even though he was only nineteen. He cared a lot about his plane and the people who flew it. He took Woods's knee board and Wink's helmet bag, which never carried his helmet, just charts, navigation books, and knee board, and climbed up the ladder to store their gear in the cockpits.

The wheels of the Tomcat straddled the centerline stripe at the very aft point of the flight deck, the round down. The back third of the plane protruded past the deck and hung over the sea. Woods checked every panel, every hole, every place where something might go wrong. He bent over and continued aft as far as he could go on each side without falling into the water. He ran his hands over the live missiles and checked the long, red safety tags that were in place to prevent an accidental firing on the deck. Woods climbed up the ladder and once on top worked his way to the back of the plane. He moved toward the twin black tails that jutted majestically into the beautiful sky, checking the exterior panels, the spoilers on the wings, and the overall airworthiness of the plane. He saw nothing to worry him. His Tomcat was pointed straight down the flight deck. The ship had increased its speed to twenty-five knots to generate more wind for the pending launch. The wind swirled around Woods as he thought of the power under his feet, the Tomcat, the carrier. He made his way forward along the back of the plane and stopped next to his ejection seat.

He pulled out the six pins that were there to prevent an inadvertent firing of the seat. They were connected by one long, red nylon strap, ensuring that none of the pins was forgotten. Woods rolled up the strap and pins and jammed them into the map case in the cockpit.

He threw his right leg over the side rail to the right of the stick that dominated the center of the cockpit, jutting up with its handle and array of buttons and switches. Bringing his left leg over, he settled into the ejection seat, adjusting the rudder pedals forward. Someone short had flown the plane last.

Benson climbed up and placed the harnesses over Woods's shoulders. Woods took each in turn and attached them to the two Koch fittings on the top of his torso harness. He then attached the lap belts on his two hip fittings and the two leg restraints to keep his legs in place in case of ejection. He pulled the lap straps tight and ensured the shoulder harness fittings were secure. The plane captain moved back on the fold-down steps seven feet above the steel flight deck and helped Wink strap himself in.

They sat in the cockpit, Wink four feet behind Woods, canopy up, arms hanging over the sides. The sunshine felt gloriously warm through their green Nomex flight suits. Woods looked at the sky for any signs of coming weather but saw nothing but clear blue sky. He gave the signal for electrical power. In short order the plane captain hooked up the electrical cord from the yellow tractor-like vehicle that also served as the huffer—the high-speed air that turned the jet engines to get them started.

"Coming down!" Wink yelled as he pushed the lever forward to close the double-length canopy.

Woods moved his arms inside the cockpit. The canopy came down slowly, hesitated, then slammed forward into the locks.

Woods gave the signal to hook up the huffer to send in high-pressure air and quickly started the two turbofan engines. He and Wink silently prepared for flight as each checked the weapons and aircraft systems.

Woods gave a thumbs-up to his plane captain, who returned the signal. The chains were removed from the plane and the chocks were pulled away from the wheels. His oxygen mask was tight on his face, feeding him pure oxygen. Woods looked over at Boomer in the Tomcat next to them, also facing forward and nodded. Vialli nodded back as he pushed the bayonet fittings of his mask to his yellow and black helmet with the skull and bones on the sides.

The yellow-shirt aviation boatswain's mate signaled to Woods to taxi. "I'm going hot," Woods announced to Wink, activating the microphone in his oxygen mask. Wink did likewise. They were both hot mike—they could hear each other breathing.

Wink turned the rear seat radio to the frequency used by the Air Boss, the commander six stories above who ran the flight deck like a dictator. The frequency was quiet. Everyone knew what to do; talking wasn't necessary.

Woods taxied forward to cat 3—one of the waist catapults on the angled deck. The two F/A-18s on the bow cats would go first. Woods watched carefully as he taxied slowly toward the plane director and onto the catapult. The yellow shirt straddled the catapult track and steam rose up all around him. There were men in different colored shirts running all around, looking at innumerable things on the airplane. If anything was wrong they would signal that the airplane was down, and they weren't going to go anywhere. A man ran up to their plane on the left side and held up a board with a number on it— 62,000. Wink gave a thumbs-up and the man took the weight board and turned it to the catapult officer sitting at the side of the flight deck with only his head showing above the deck level. The officer acknowledged the Tomcat's weight, and dialed it in to the catapult.

On the signal, Woods brought the wings out of oversweep and put them into automatic. The wings swiftly swept to their full forward position, 20 degrees back from straight out. It was one of the truly remarkable things about the F-14, that it could sweep its wings back and forth, either manually or automatically. It made the large airplane very maneuverable, and a serious fighter. Woods continued to taxi forward slowly, steering the nosewheel with the rudder pedals, and touching the brakes at the top of the rudder pedals to keep from going too fast. As the F-14 approached the shuttle the yellow shirt gave the signal to kneel. Woods hit the switch and the nosewheel collapsed on schedule. The plane crouched down and the launch bar dropped to the deck, working its way over the shuttle as they taxied forward. The yellow shirt signaled Woods to slow the plane down and he felt the familiar clunk as the bar dropped home. Automatically, Woods hit the brakes. The yellow shirt took a quick look and stepped to the side, looking down the track and at Woods. Another man crept under the plane, careful to stay out of the suction of the jet engines. He attached a hold-back bar to the rear of the F-14's nosewheel to keep it from rolling forward too soon. The bar in place, Woods took his feet off the brakes. Everything looked normal. The yellow shirt raised his right hand at the same time that he slid his left hand toward the bow of the ship. The shuttle jerked forward and put the plane in tension—pressure from the catapult—but not enough to launch them yet.

Woods put the throttles at full military power and pushed the handles outboard into the detent to keep them from coming aft on the cat shot. "Checklist," he said calmly, running through it from memory. "Fuel pressure, fuel flow, engine rpm, and TIT all good. No caution or warning lights. Full aft stick."

"Clear."

"Forward stick."

"Good," Wink replied.

"Left," Woods said.

Wink looked at the port wing to check all four spoilers.

"Right . . . and rudder."

"All good," Wink said.

"Ready?" Woods asked.

"Ready," Wink said immediately.

Woods checked his instruments once more. He put his head back against the seat and saluted with his right. The catapult officer, from his glass bubble buried in the flight deck; looked down the deck, examined his instruments, and pushed the launch button.

Woods felt the immediate jerk of the plane as it was pulled down into the flight deck then hurtled forward by the catapult. The rapid acceleration was thrilling. The shuttle pulled the F-14 from a dead stop to one hundred thirty-five knots in two seconds.

"Good speed," Wink said calmly in the same voice he always used when he was sure they had enough airspeed to fly and didn't need to eject from a cold cat shot.

Woods rotated the nose up gently above the horizon and climbed away from the carrier, banking hard left into a clearing turn to get away from the ship. An F-18 had been launched off one of the bow cats just before them and had turned to the right, away from them, for the same reason. Woods raised the landing gear and flaps and set his speed at two hundred fifty knots. He climbed to five hundred feet and leveled off.

Wink changed the radio to Strike and called to report airborne. He strained to look around and saw Boomer being shot off the catapult behind them.

When they were seven miles out from the ship Woods pulled back hard on the stick and the plane climbed quickly. The wings threw off trails of vapor as the moist air condensed under the pressure.

"Going cold," Woods said as he deselected the hot mike setting on their Internal Communication System, the ICS.

"Ditto," said Wink, throwing an identical switch in the backseat.

"Where are we going anyway?" Woods said, keying his mike with a button on the throttle.

"Overhead rendezvous at 12, then descend to tank at 6, then we're cleared into the gunnery pattern at 0845."

"Right. Two or four planes in the pattern?"

"Just us and Boomer. I think the F-18s have it after us, but I'm not sure. We have it until we run out of bullets. *Roger, Strike,*" Wink said, responding to Woods and the radio at the same time.

Woods climbed to twelve thousand feet and leveled off. He dipped his left wing and saw the carrier two miles below. As large as it was, it looked impossibly small from two miles up, far too small to land a helicopter on, let alone a 60,000 pound jet. Just as Woods set up a gentle banking turn to circle over the carrier he saw Vialli approaching him from behind. "There's Boomer."

"Tally," Wink said.

Vialli approached from inside the turn and slightly below Woods. He was doing a perfect rendezvous—not too quick, and not dangerous. As he closed to fifty feet or so, he lowered his right wing and slipped underneath Woods, taking up a perfect position on the outside of the turn, exactly as he was supposed to do.

Woods looked over at Vialli, thirty feet away, and nodded. "He's a natural," he said to Wink.

"He's still got a lot to learn."

"Don't we all." Woods put his left hand on the stick and with his right motioned for Vialli to take a trail position, farther back and directly behind Woods. Woods waited until Vialli was in position and then pushed his throttles to the stops without using afterburner. The

F-14 accelerated quickly. "Anybody scheduled to be above us over the ship?"

"Not a soul," Wink replied, smiling, looking forward to pulling a few Gs as he used his radar to scan the empty skies ahead of them.

As the plane accelerated through four hundred fifty knots Woods pulled up quickly, away from the dark blue sea to the paler blue sky. He watched the accelerometer steady at six Gs and eased off when they were pointed straight up. Glancing in his mirror, he saw Vialli right behind him. He rolled the plane over onto its back and leveled his wings to complete an Immelman, immediately pulling up again to continue climbing. Vialli was still right behind him.

"Heading 067 for 6," Wink said to Woods, reporting the course to the carrier as he changed radio frequencies back to Air Boss, the tower of the carrier. "*Morning, Boss. Victory 201, flight of two, 6 miles out for the spar,*" he said.

"*Roger, 201. Spar trailing. Cleared into the pattern. Report 3 miles.*"

"*Wilco,*" Wink replied. "Checklist," he said to Woods.

They went through the gunfire checklist in preparation for their strafing runs.

Woods looked down at the carrier now five miles away and headed for it. "Which way is she going?" he asked Wink.

"Don't know. Hold on . . . *Boss, say ship's course.*"

There was a pause, then the response came. "*Course 355,*" Air Boss answered.

Woods headed starboard of the ship so they would end up three fourths of a mile or so behind it, just the length of the cable towing the spar.

"*Victory 201, flight of two, 245 at 3 miles,*" Wink transmitted.

"*Roger, 201. Pattern clear. You're cleared in to the spar. Call when in last run.*"

"*Wilco.*"

Woods lowered the nose again and descended to fifteen hundred feet. He checked his gun sight and switches, Wink searching the air with his radar for any stray airplanes the Boss might not be aware of. Everything was clear. "Looks good, Trey."

"Roger."

"Passing through one thousand—four hundred fifty knots."

Woods made no reply. He saw the spar, a telephone pole being dragged behind the carrier, one mile away, making its own wake like a periscope. He placed the gun sight on it and continued his descent to five hundred feet, glancing over his shoulder at Vialli, knowing he would be right where he should be. Vialli was an instinctive pilot. Woods never had to tell him where to go. It was like flying with yourself in two airplanes at once. He had to admit Vialli was better than he had been himself when he was in Vialli's position, his first cruise. Woods's first squadron tour had been in VF-103 three years before. He had gone to Topgun before returning to the fleet. This was his fourth Mediterranean cruise. It was Vialli's first.

Woods flew directly over the spar at five hundred feet and looked at the carrier to his left. He trimmed the plane to fly perfectly straight and level at four hundred fifty knots, then slammed the throttles forward and pulled up hard to start the gunnery pattern.

Vialli waited ten seconds, then followed suit.

Woods pulled the nose up at a 45-degree angle then turned sharply to the left until the plane was going in the opposite direction. Out of the corner of his eye he saw Vialli, his nose also up at a 45-degree angle. Woods flew down a ways, then began a sharp turn toward the spar. "*One's in,*" he transmitted. He bunted the nose of the F-14 until his wings were level and he was pointed directly at the spar, moving his aiming point to twenty feet behind it. He was only supposed to shoot close to the spar, not hit it. They wanted to be able to use it again.

"Four-fifty, two thousand feet," Wink called out, looking at the instruments. He noted that Woods had guns selected.

Woods raced downhill at a 20-degree angle and brought the throttles back to maintain exactly four hundred fifty knots.

"*Two's in,*" Vialli transmitted behind him.

"One thousand feet," Wink said.

Woods pressed in toward the spar, then pulled the trigger on the stick and felt the Vulcan cannon in the left side of the nose of the Tomcat spool up and spit out twenty-millimeter bullets at six thousand rounds per minute. It didn't sound like a gun really, more like a very large and angry sewing machine with a cold.

The deckhands watching from the deck saw the smoke come from the nose of the plane, then saw the bullets strike the water behind the carrier in a furious white foam, then heard the report of the gun firing. The bullets were supersonic, reaching the water long before the sound.

Woods bottomed out at five hundred feet and pulled up hard, pulling five Gs as the plane strained to go skyward again. *"One's off,"* he transmitted without letting more than the required air out of his mouth, bringing the nose up high to head the other way in the racetrack pattern.

"Boomer's too steep," Wink grunted.

Woods glanced over his shoulder to his left at his diving wingman. His heart jumped. Wink was right, Vialli was way too steep. Woods watched, hoping to see some recognition by Vialli of the hole he was getting into. The Tomcat raced down toward the spar.

"He's too fast," Wink said, seeing the danger building. If Vialli got his nose too low with too much speed on the plane, it didn't matter what he did, he would be dead. He would be unable to pull out before hitting the water, and he would be outside the ejection envelope. Even if he realized what was happening and tried to eject, it would only mean that he would die in his ejection seat instead of sitting in the airplane.

Woods waited as long as he could before keying his mike for the front seat radio. *"Boomer! Throttle back! You're too steep!"*

The nose of the F-14 turned up suddenly as Boomer was startled into action by the shock of the unexpected voice of his section leader. He pulled hard and cloud-like water vapor appeared on the tops of the wings from the pressure. He leveled out at about the height of the flight deck, seventy feet off the water, still way too low, but pulling up quickly to follow Woods.

Woods shook his head and rolled back in on the spar. *"One's in,"* he transmitted.

"Two's off," Boomer transmitted, well after he should have.

"He sure dicked that up," Woods said.

"Hasn't he ever strafed the spar before?"

"Maybe not. We'd better watch him."

"We'd better tell the Skipper about that."

"No, I'll handle it."

Vialli followed Woods religiously through the remainder of the runs on the spar. They cycled through the gunnery pattern again and again, shooting their bullets in fifty-round bursts, until they were both out of ammunition. *"One's winchester,"* Woods said after his last run.

"Two's winchester," Vialli replied, following him up again.

"Victory 201, flight of two exiting the pattern directly overhead, Boss," Wink said.

"Roger, 201. Good shooting."

"Fifteen minutes till we have to be overhead," Wink reminded Woods. Wink looked back to see Vialli closing in to join up.

Woods accelerated away from the carrier and climbed to fifteen thousand feet. "Let's woodshed our wingman a little," Woods said. Without warning, he jerked his plane to the left and hit afterburner. He had waited until Vialli wasn't looking at him, and Vialli didn't notice until he was nearly a half-mile away. Vialli turned to catch up. Woods came out of afterburner and turned sharply into Vialli. *"Fight's on,"* he said over the squadron frequency, the universally recognized declaration of the commencement of voluntary air combat. Woods loved air-to-air combat, and loved taking advantage of his unsuspecting wingman. A few more times like this and he wouldn't be unsuspecting again.

6

Sami looked around the conference room. He was just starting to get to know the other members of the task force. All were members of the CTC, the Counter-Terrorism Center of the CIA. The CTC had been in operation for years on the ground floor of CIA Headquarters in Langley. There were two hundred men and women permanently assigned to the CTC, and their cubicles were separated by "streets." Signs hung from the ceiling that spoke volumes of what they were about: Abu Nidal Blvd, and Tamil Tiger Terrace, and Osama bin Lane, named after Osama bin Laden, one of their greatest and longest running frustrations.

Sami had walked through the area a few times before, but only to answer a specific question. He was not a member of the CTC. He was just an analyst from the Middle East Section who happened to research emerging terrorist groups. But Kinkaid knew about him. He had insisted on Sami and Cunningham joining the new task force.

The conference room that had been set aside for it was in the middle of the CTC, surrounded by people who spent every waking minute tracking terrorists and dreaming of the day when another one would be caught or somehow defanged.

Sami's analysis was still raw, and might be shown to be ridiculous at any moment. He was uncomfortable briefing anyone about it. He didn't even know what he believed yet. It was just speculation. But Kinkaid had looked ill when Sami had first brought his ideas to him. He had insisted he tell the task force immediately.

He wasn't sure exactly how to begin. Almost all of his work ended up in reports or memos. He had never given a brief to anyone from the DO, the Directorate of Operations, the ones who actually went out into the world and put their lives on the line to accumulate intelligence or effect things. He felt like the water boy to the football players.

The task force had assembled early. They had a 7:30 A.M. meeting scheduled, but Kinkaid had asked them all to be there at 6:30 to hear Sami. They were interested, but skeptical. They drank coffee and sat in their chairs around the large table, waiting. Kinkaid signaled Sami, who got up from his seat in the front and walked to the podium.

"As some of you know, I've been looking at emerging terrorist groups in the Middle East for a long time. My job is to recognize a new group before they know they're a group. You get all kinds, the young boys who have delusions of grandeur, people who want an Islamic state, people who hate the West, or Israel, or the ones who want money and are trying to figure out what they need to say to get that. You've heard about them all."

"Right," one of them said, encouraging him to go on.

"As you know from my preliminary memo, I read a report from NSA the other day about an intercept—"

"What kind?" someone asked.

"Cell phone."

"Where?"

"Eastern Lebanon."

"What did it say?"

"Nothing, really—"

Kinkaid didn't like the exchange and prompted Sami. "What about it gave you concerns?"

"A name."

"What was that?"

"A man was talking about a meeting. To discuss Gaza. Clearly a reference to the attack." Sami looked around and went on. "He talked about a time and place, which didn't make a lot of sense, but then, signing off, the man on the other end was talking to someone else. Like he's got to explain who he's talking about. It's a little hard to hear, they think because he put his hand over the phone, but he said 'Sheikh al-Jabal.' "

Ricketts, slouched in his chair, said, "So?"

"It's the name of a legendary leader of the eleventh century. Others later used his name to sort of carry on a tradition. Marco Polo even met his successor, who carried the same title. He called him the Old Man of the Mountains. But the name he called himself is the same name that has been passed down through the centuries, Sheikh al-Jabal. He started an empire from a fortress in western Iran called Alamut. They were called the Hashasheen."

"Hash smokers? When?" Ricketts asked, suddenly hearing the "eleventh century" part of what Sami had said.

Sami looked at his notes. "To be exact 1090."

"What the hell does—"

Kinkaid cut him off. "You think I asked him to tell you this because it has nothing to do with what we're doing?" Kinkaid's look shut him up. Kinkaid nodded to Sami.

"So this guy gets boys, twelve years old or so, and raises them to adulthood in his gardens. Big fortress, gardens, the whole thing. Calls it paradise. Then when it's time for one of them to kill for him, he just tells him he will return to paradise if he does the killing—"

"Tie it in," Kinkaid said.

Sami Haddad looked at their eyes, which showed both interest and skepticism. "The Hashasheen were formed during the Crusades. They terrorized the Crusaders, killing many of them, but staying out of the typical battles. They would sneak up on the Crusaders and cut their throats. They were the forerunners of modern terrorists. Born killers, who would gladly die for the cause, which is defined by the current Sheikh al-Jabal.

"They basically disappeared, but there have always been rumors of their existence, all the way from Lebanon, to Egypt, to Iran, to Pakistan. This is the first time since the early nineteenth century that someone called himself Sheikh al-Jabal. That time they fought for Napoleon's interests in the Middle East for money. So if this is new, and he is what he claims to be, it could be huge trouble. They have no friends. They've always been ostracized by Muslims too. They're considered heretics. So they don't trust anyone. Unless you grew up with them, you're the enemy."

Kinkaid looked at their faces. They weren't sure what to think. They'd never heard of anything like it. Kinkaid spoke first. "If for some reason this guy is the one who started the fight in Gaza, he's way ahead of where our knowledge is. We're playing catch-up. Ricketts, we got anything that can get close to these guys?"

Ricketts was more at home in a foreign country disguised as a beggar than in a conference room with a bunch of eggheads. It showed. "Not right now."

One of the officers to Ricketts's right spoke quietly. "What's this about hashish?"

"Nothing about hashish. It's what they were called, the Hashash-een. It has nothing to do with the drug—" Sami answered, but was interrupted again.

"Then why were they called that?"

"It's a mystery. Some think it is because they did use hashish. But the best explanation I've found is that Hashasheen is close to the Arabic word for guardian. These guys consider themselves not only the guardians of Islam, but the guardians of the Middle East, from invaders and infidels."

"They call themselves that?"

"Yes. But Hashasheen sounds like another word in English and other languages," Sami said. "Assassin. It's where the word assassin comes from. These guys invented assassination as a political tool."

The room was quiet as the task force members pondered what he had said.

"We've got a lot of work to do," Kinkaid declared. He looked at Ricketts. "You getting any HUMINT?" Human Intelligence, informa-tion from people. Spies.

Ricketts sat silently before answering. "A little. Nothing useful yet."

"Keep working it. Need any help?"

Ricketts shook his head.

⌇

Vialli stood in front of the church of San Marco in Venice. He looked at his watch. He had told Irit in his e-mail that he would be there at 11 A.M.; but she hadn't replied. It was now 9:30; the large square was quiet. A few people wandered around, vendors pushed their carts, and people walked to work at the shops around the square, which was nearly empty. It was cold and damp. Pulling up the collar of his brown leather jacket, he exhaled and watched his breath. It was the same color as the sky and the river to his left.

"Hi, Tony."

Vialli spun around at the sound of Irit's voice. "Irit!" he said, sur-prised. "How did you sneak up on me?" He reached for her, not sure what to do. He gave her a side hug.

She rose on her toes and kissed him softly on his cheek. "As soon as I came into the square I saw this American staring at the church with his hands in his pockets. Who else could it be?" She smiled.

"I'm conspicuous?" he asked, feigning injury.

"You may look Italian, but you look more American."

"What can I say?" he said. "Look at this church. It's made out of tile."

"It's not made of tile, it's just that the outside is tiled."

"That's what I meant." He looked down at her. "I asked Sean to come along this morning. I hope you don't mind."

"Sure. He's very nice. By the way, I have to go back to Trento by this afternoon." She saw his disappointment as soon as she had said it. "I'm sorry. I just have to get back."

"Why?"

"I just have to be back."

"No problem." He studied her face, reacquainting himself with her. She was even prettier than he had remembered, but not as tall. "I kind of wanted to go on a gondola ride, if it isn't too cold."

"Okay," she said. "We can sit close together to stay warm."

"Here he comes," he said, running down the four steps to wave at Sean from across the square. Irit followed behind him.

Woods saw them and walked down the middle of the colorful square. "Hey," Woods said to them. "Sorry I made you late."

"Actually, you're early," Vialli replied.

"Hello," Irit added.

"So what's the plan?" Woods asked.

"Do the gondola thing."

"Cool. Where do you want to go?"

"Just drive around. See the buildings, you know." Tony looked at the sky. "I just wish it would clear up. It's kind of cold."

"It's okay. Let's do it. Then we can get a cappuccino or something."

They walked back across the square toward the canal that ran parallel to the face of San Marco. Vialli said, "I spotted some gondola guys over here."

They all followed. The sky was breaking up and blue was showing through the wispy cloud cover. The chop in the canal had settled down and the cold biting wind began to grow quiet. They arrived at the edge of the water, which was nearly level with the square. "How do they keep the water from flooding?" Vialli asked.

"It does flood," Irit replied. "The city is slowly sinking and it gets worse every year."

"Nothing like sinking and being surrounded by water."

"How about this one?" Irit said, pointing to a large black gondola.

Vialli shrugged. She spoke rapid Italian to the man and they stepped in at the middle of the boat while the driver held it steady with his oar. They walked carefully to the back of the gondola and were about to sit down when a wave from a passing motorboat rocked the boat roughly. Irit stumbled, catching herself with her hand on the seat. Vialli grabbed the side of the gondola and steadied himself. He had begun to move aft again to sit down when he noticed Irit's right hand. She had only her thumb and middle finger. It looked like a claw. The rest of her hand was gone. He felt a cold knot in his stomach as he stared at it, unable to avert his eyes. He couldn't believe he hadn't noticed before—he had been with her for hours over several days in Naples and had never noticed her right hand. Vialli looked at Woods. He had seen it.

Irit quickly withdrew her hand and turned to sit facing forward. She looked into his face as he avoided her look. He sat to her left and leaned into the red padded seat back. Irit spoke again in Italian and their gondolier moved them quickly away from the landing.

They sat in silence as the boat moved quickly down the canal. Vialli found himself breathing harder than usual. He watched the passing buildings, feigning interest, to avoid looking at Irit. After several minutes passed awkwardly, she spoke to him softly. "Does it make that much difference?"

"What?" he replied.

"My hand." She looked at her feet. "I guess you hadn't seen it before." She hesitated, then studied his face. "I'm very good at hiding it. I've had time to practice. Some people who consider themselves my friends don't know, or at least don't show that they know. But most people are so shocked when they notice that they can't help reacting." She leaned forward slightly to look into his eyes. "Like you did. Will it matter? Do you think less of me?"

"Of course not," he said quickly. "How could it matter?"

"People react. They can't help how they feel, and it makes a difference. Will it make a difference with you?"

"No. I just thought you were left-handed."

"I am."

"No, I mean naturally left han . . . never mind." He looked at a house they were passing. The main door faced the canal, and there were steps leading down to the water directly in front of them. The door was three feet above the water level. "Do you have to take a boat to get to that house? I mean, when the guy goes to work every morning, does he have to take a boat?"

"Some of them do, but most either walk, or some have cars. Many of the houses have streets or alleys behind them in which they can walk or drive. Most cars aren't allowed in Venice, but some can have them. I haven't quite understood that yet."

Vialli sat quietly and watched the houses go by. "I'm sorry I reacted. I thought I was bigger than that."

Irit smiled at him. "Don't feel bad, it's natural. Most people wonder what happened to me. They think I was involved in some horrible accident, and want to pity me. But I was born like this. Nothing I can do about it. I won't hold it against you. But you mustn't hold it against me either."

"How could I hold it against you?"

"Some boys, men, that I've dated, cool on me very quickly after they notice. I think they believe I am somehow defective, or worthless . . ."

"No way—"

"Let me finish." She sighed. "I know they don't mean to, but they do. They see me as an incomplete person. It isn't intentional, but some men can't get over it." She looked down again, and was quiet.

Vialli knew she had seen his shock and dismay. He hated himself for reacting at all.

Sean was carefully studying anything that would require him to turn his head.

"There's more," she said quietly.

"What?"

Irit sat back and put her head on his shoulder. He moved his arm around her. She spoke softly. "I'm not Italian."

He pulled back slightly and looked at her. "What are you talking about?"

"I'm not from Trento. I don't even live in Italy. My cousin lives in Trento and I come to visit her once in a while. That's why I'm here. Then I travel around Italy because I love it. But I don't live here."

"Where do you live?"

"Nahariya."

Vialli looked at her uncomprehendingly, his mouth open. "Where?"

"Israel."

Vialli's mouth stayed open. He didn't know what to say. He didn't even know where to start. "Are you . . ."

"Jewish?"

"Yeah."

"Of course."

"I'm Catholic."

"I know."

Vialli stared past her at a small square that was full of shops. The light cascaded out of the shops and reflected on the wet pavement. It looked magical. Gondolas were lining up to unload. "Does it matter?" he asked finally.

"Not to me. Does it matter to you?"

"I don't know. I don't think so. I'm not very Catholic."

She smiled at him for the first time since they'd gotten into the gondola. "I'm not very religious either. My family is not Orthodox or anything."

"If we see each other would your parents be upset?"

Irit looked at him with her gorgeous eyes. "Probably."

"Does that matter?"

"A little."

"Are we going to see each other?"

She shrugged. "That's up to you. You've gotten two surprises today, and I doubt you liked either one very much. It will depend on you, I think."

Vialli sat in turmoil. "Why didn't you tell me from the first?"

"I don't know. I just thought you would find me more interesting if I were Italian. Being Israeli can be quite a burden."

Vialli considered what he had just heard. "I want to see you again."

"Are you sure?"

"I'm sure. Two people who love Italy who aren't *from* Italy? We're perfect for each other." He watched the boats that passed the other way.

Woods caught his eye. With an immediate exchange of looks Woods asked him if everything was okay, and Vialli told him things were fine. Woods focused his attention back on the sights.

Vialli spoke. "When am I going to see you again?"

"I don't know," she answered. "Where is your next port?"

"Naples I think, but it's not for a couple of weeks."

"I'll be back home by then."

He breathed in sharply. "This isn't going to be easy, you know."

"I know. Most good things aren't."

He nodded. "We're gonna be in Israel in about a month."

"I know. You told me."

"I guess that will be it. Our next chance to be together." He thought for a moment. "And after that, I won't see you again before we head back to the States unless you can meet me somewhere."

"I'd like to see you sooner." She pursed her lips. "I'm going to miss you."

He leaned over and kissed her gently. She kissed him back.

"You're amazing," he said.

She looked at him curiously. "Why do you say that?"

"I don't know. You're so . . . together. You aren't like all the silly girls I've dated. You're just . . . different."

She smiled but said nothing. "I need to get back."

"You just got here." He sat up straight as if he had just thought of something. "I'd like you to meet the guys. Want to walk with me to the hotel where we're staying?"

"I don't have time."

"Sure you do."

The gondola came to a gentle stop where they had started. They climbed out and walked to a café at the corner of the square. They sat down at a worn wooden table, grateful for the warmth.

"What'll you have?" Vialli asked.

"Cappuccino for me," Woods said enthusiastically.

Vialli looked at Irit. She shook her head. "I have to get going. I need to get the train back to Trento. I didn't really even have time for this morning, but I'm glad I came." She stood up and adjusted her coat with her left hand.

"You sure?" Vialli asked.

She nodded. "Send me an e-mail when you know where you'll be next. We'll see if there's some way to get together."

"Sure," he said. He was dying at the idea of her walking away. "Are you going to the train station?"

"Yes. I have about an hour to get there."

"I'll walk you," he said, deciding suddenly. "Okay with you?" he asked Woods.

"Sure. I'm going to go to the admin. I'll probably just crash. I'm beat."

"You sure?"

"Yeah. You going to come back here or go to the ship?"

"I'll meet you back at the admin."

"Okay," Woods said. He finished his coffee quickly and put the cup down softly on the saucer, then looked for the waiter to order another. "It was nice to see you again," he said to Irit.

She averted his gaze. "Did you hear what I told Tony?"

He nodded.

"I'm sorry."

"I'm sure you have your reasons," he said, not giving her the complete forgiveness she expected.

"There's really no excuse. I'm sorry."

"Don't worry about it." He smiled.

Vialli watched Irit, thankful for the opportunity to observe her as she talked to someone else. "I'll see you in a while," he said to Woods, walking out with his arm around her.

"Bye," she said to Woods as they went through the door.

Vialli took her left hand in his and they walked down the street toward an arching bridge that rose up over a canal. He stopped on the bridge and said, "What time is your train?"

"One o'clock."

"We've still got forty-five minutes. How far away is the train station?"

"It's a pretty good walk."

He put one hand on the bridge rail and looked past her. He knew he had to bring it up again. "You could see I was shocked," he said.

"Sure."

"I'm sorry."

"It's nothing to be sorry about. It happens."

"I expected better of myself."

"I just don't want you to feel like you have to be with me now out of pity or something. Like now. You held my hand. Why?"

Vialli was pierced. "Because I care. Why do you think?"

"So you can show me you're not holding it against me. And so you can think better of yourself."

"Come on, Irit. Give me some credit." He was growing frustrated. He couldn't say anything right. "I really do care for you. I haven't felt like this before," he blurted.

"What do you mean?"

"You're unlike anyone I've ever known." He turned toward her and touched her face. He leaned down and kissed her on the lips, tentatively, unsure of himself, not about how he felt, but about how she would respond. He was afraid. He broke off the kiss before it became a commitment. He kept his face next to hers and put his hands on her waist. She put her hands on his waist at the same time. The bridge was deserted. There was no one to be seen along the road. Two gondolas made their way under the bridge in opposite directions but took no notice of them.

"I'm sorry," he said again.

"Enough of that. We have to get past it," she said softly.

He kissed her again and felt her warmth as she pressed against him. He was glad not to have to explain himself anymore. She understood and didn't hold it against him. She was remarkable. She had forgiven him at a level beyond where he was entitled to it. He kissed her deeply. He put his arms around her and held her tightly as he kissed her, his desire for her growing with every moment.

"We need to get to the train station."

"Stay the night, here in Venice," he pleaded.

"I can't."

"Why not? You said you weren't working, what's the hurry?"

"I just can't."

He leaned back and looked into her eyes. "*Why?*"

"I can't talk about it."

"Why not? What could you possibly not tell me about?"

"It's personal."

He studied her. "You still don't trust me."

"I absolutely do."

"Then tell me."

"I can't."

"I want to spend more time with you. This just isn't good enough. There's so much to say." He kissed her again. "There's so much to do."

"I know. Next time. I promise. I have to go. Come to the train with me. Ride the train with me," she said suddenly.

"What? I can't go to Trento."

"No, just buy a ticket to one of the stops on the way, then get off, and ride the next one back. You'll be back in a couple of hours, and we can sit together for a while in the warm compartment. Maybe we'll have one to ourselves . . ." She smiled as she took his hand.

"Let's go," he agreed finally. "Sounds like just the thing."

"You got him, Wink?" Woods asked over the ICS.

"Yeah. I got him. He's trying to come in out of the weeds."

"There aren't any weeds in the ocean, Wink."

"No kidding. Come starboard hard to 005. Set four hundred fifty knots. He's still descending. I show him at one hundred fifty feet doing four hundred fifty knots."

Woods slammed the stick of the F-14 to the right and banked the Tomcat steeply, lowering the nose and starting a descent to complete the intercept. "He can't be at one hundred fifty feet, Wink."

"Why?" Wink replied as he worked the thumb wheel of the radar control handle between his legs.

"Because there's a regulation against going below five hundred feet, Wink."

"I forgot. Come port to 355. He's made a hard right turn."

The flat gray paint on the F-14 made it hard to see. That was the idea. Woods squinted as he looked down through the thick windscreen at the green diamond projected on the Heads Up Display. It showed where the bogey was; but Boomer was still too small a dot to see, even through the diamond that outlined his position. Just blue-gray water and blue-gray sky. "How far?"

"Twelve miles."

"You think he's got us yet?"

"If he does, he sure isn't acting like it. He's not coming up to get us. He's just playing bogey."

"How do you want to do this?"

"We're going to break port in about two miles."

"Roger."

"Course 357 for ten miles, angels 0, slight left to right drift. He's ten right, twenty low, closure nine hundred knots."

"No tally."

"Port hard," Wink said, his voice cool. He watched the radar track on Boomer until it was sufficiently out to the right, then called, "Starboard hard," as Woods wrapped it around in a hard right descending turn.

"Tally," Woods said as he saw Boomer dead ahead at three miles with a shadow below him on the water.

They rolled in behind Boomer doing four hundred fifty knots at two hundred feet. *"Fox two, set up another one, Tiger,"* Wink transmitted.

"That's all we have time for, 207," Tiger replied. *"Your signal is RTB, check in with Strike."* Return to Base.

"Thanks for your help. Switching button one," Wink answered.

"My pleasure," Tiger responded, a twenty-one-year-old OS-3, an enlisted man whose job it was to control intercepts from the carrier.

Woods checked his fuel and liked what he saw. He jammed the throttles into afterburner to catch up with Boomer quickly. He passed through five hundred knots and came out of afterburner as he approached his wingman's F-14. Sliding out to the left, he signaled for Vialli to join on him. Boomer touched his forehead and pointed to Woods, transferring the lead to him. Woods pulled up quickly and climbed away from the ocean, the G forces causing him to grunt automatically. Wink gave Sedge a drinking signal. Sedge signaled 5,100 pounds left.

"Strike, Victory 207 checking in, flight of two, 258 at 15, angels 5, low state 5.1."

"Roger, 207. Report ship in sight."

"Wilco."

He scanned the horizon where the Tactical Aid to Navigation needle—the TACAN—was pointing but couldn't pick out the carrier from the haze and grayness. Quickly, Wink and Woods ran through their descent checklist as they passed through ten thousand feet on their way to five.

Again Wink looked ahead through the quarter panel of the windscreen where the TACAN needle was pointing and this time he saw the *Washington,* their home away from home.

"Strike, Victory 207, see you."

"Roger, 207. Cleared overhead. Switch button four."

"207, switching," Wink said. He tuned his powerful digital radio to the Air Boss's frequency. It was silent, as it was supposed to be for a day VFR recovery. Woods lowered his tailhook as he and Boomer entered the overhead circle at two thousand feet hawking the deck, waiting for the next launch to begin. The other planes in the air were orbiting at higher altitudes, each separated by a thousand feet. When the recovery began, they would all spiral down and land in order, thirty to forty-five seconds apart.

Woods brought his flight up the starboard side of the carrier again and watched the launch in progress. Planes taxied toward the bow cats, but the waist cats were about to launch their last planes. "What do you think?" he asked Wink.

"Next time around," Wink said. "And Boomer's tailhook isn't down."

"What?" Woods stole a look. "What the hell is he doing?"

"Beats me. I've been giving Sedge the signal and he just stares at me."

Woods took his eye off the flight deck below and stole another glance at Boomer. "What's he doing way out there? We look like a couple of damned helos flying formation in two friggin' area codes." He quickly keyed the mike for the front radio. *"Tighten it up. Hook down."*

Boomer quickly closed the distance and dropped his hook, now ready to land aboard the carrier.

They began their gradual port turn and descended from two thousand feet to eight hundred. As they came into the break Woods signaled for wings aft. On the signal, he and Boomer swept the wings back on their F-14s simultaneously to 68 degrees and steadied out on the ship's heading. Woods and Wink checked the deck one last time. The deck was nearly clear and only two planes were left on the bow cats. "Let's do it," Woods said.

They flew past the carrier, Woods watching closely over his shoulder. At just the right moment, he kissed off Boomer, threw the stick to the left, and banked sharply into the break. The F-14 lay on its side in its nearly delta shape as they pulled around to head in the opposite direction from the carrier, downwind in the landing pattern. Woods put the wings in auto and they moved forward quickly to their 20-degree position, as full forward as they could go. Woods and Wink went through the landing checklist automatically as they leveled out, checking the gear, flaps, wings, and hook. When they passed the ramp of the carrier one mile to their left Woods began his controlled turn and rate of descent. They went hot mike.

Woods was one of the smoothest pilots in the Air Wing around the boat. He routinely had the highest or second-highest landing grades in the squadron. Even though he was good at it, he never took landing aboard the ship for granted. He had seen too many guys plant it on the ramp or unable to get aboard at all.

He rolled into the groove, kept the ball centered on the landing lens, and touched down hard. The tailhook grabbed the two wire and pulled it down the carrier deck as the engines screamed against it at full power until the Tomcat was completely stopped. Boomer landed next but floated over the four wires and boltered, his hook sparking as it tried to grab something on the steel deck. The F-14 flew off the angled deck and climbed into the landing pattern. Boomer looked at the airplanes in the break and those turning downwind, and tried to pick a time to turn downwind and fit into the landing pattern.

"What the hell is he doing?" Woods asked, frustrated.

"I don't think he's ever boltered in the daytime before."

"Pisses me off," Woods said as he shut down the engines and Wink opened the canopy.

They returned to their ready room and filled out the paperwork. Ten minutes later Boomer and Sedge walked in. Chief Lucas, the maintenance chief, came out of Maintenance Control into the ready room. "Two up jets?" he asked hopefully.

All four nodded.

"We've got to turn them around for the next event. Any gripes at all, sir?"

Woods replied first. "Trim button sticks, but it's not a big problem."

"What about 211?" Lucas inquired.

"ECS is really loud," Vialli replied. "When it changes the temperature it wants to get there *now*. Sounds like a hurricane."

"We can take care of that," Lucas said confidently. "What about the backseat?"

"No problems," Sedge said.

"Great," Lucas said and hurried out.

Vialli crossed over to Woods, and sat down next to him. He leaned toward him, and said in a low voice, "I need to talk to you."

Woods glanced up from the paperwork on his fold-over desk. "About how you're going *numb* on me out there?"

"No, something else."

Woods studied his face. "When?"

"Now . . . if you can."

Woods looked at his watch. "The wardroom will be shutting down. Let's go to chow. We'll just wait out the rest until we have time." Vialli's face showed concern. "Unless it can't wait. We can just go to the stateroom . . ."

"No, lunch is fine," Vialli said. "I'm kind of hungry anyway. They're having sliders—we can stuff a couple of those and then talk."

Woods handed the yellow sheet to Wink, who took it to Maintenance Control. "You want to go eat?" Woods asked him as he was walking away.

"Sure," Wink said. The four of them walked the three hundred yards from Ready Room Eight to the forward wardroom. Greasy hamburgers lay quietly in the steel pans over heated water. They each made double cheeseburgers and put them on their plates. As they went for drinks, Woods moaned when he saw the cow was disconnected and there were boxes of funny-shaped cartons in front of it. "Not German milk again," he groaned.

No one answered him. Woods hailed one of the messmen and asked him directly, "All we've got is German milk?"

"Afraid so, sir."

"When did we run out of real milk?"

"Yesterday."

"What's the matter with German milk?" Vialli asked.

Woods shook his head. "It tastes like goat's milk."

Vialli laughed. "How the hell do you know what goat's milk tastes like?"

"I'm guessing," Woods said sarcastically.

Wink sat next to him and said, "We go to sea for weeks on end and you expect someone to bring you milk out of an American cow—pasteurized and homogenized—and whine about it when you have to drink German milk someone probably paid through the nose to get trucked down to Italy just for you?"

Woods looked at Wink. "You don't have to make me sound like an ax murderer. I just like regular old milk. That's all. And eggs, and butter, and all the things people back home take for granted. Here we eat powdered eggs, no butter, no real milk, and get paid less than bus drivers, and we're supposed to be really grateful. I keep forgetting," he said, finally biting into his hamburger.

After the other officers had eaten and wandered off, Woods sat with his hands around his coffee cup and studied Vialli across the table. "So what gives?"

"I need to ask you something as a friend," Vialli began tentatively. Woods waited. "I know you're my section leader, and senior to me and everything. But I feel like you're my brother. You're the best friend I've got. Can I say that?"

"Sure. But before you go too far, what's eating you? You just about bought it on the strafing run the other day. And today you were flying formation like you were afraid of it. Your hook wasn't even down. What gives?"

"I don't know. I guess I'd rather be somewhere else."

"Who wouldn't. But if you want to get out of the Navy, you've got to wait—"

"No, it's not like that."

"What?"

"It's something else." Vialli swallowed. Now that he was actually going to say it, his courage was evaporating. "Always before, in New York, in college, I was always the tough guy. Always doggin' everybody, making life hard. But here, I don't know. It's different. I don't have to prove anything except in the air." He grinned at Woods. "Don't worry. I'm not gonna ask you for money."

"Just say it. Don't get misty-eyed on me or something."

"You're a Lieutenant, a second-tour Lieutenant, and I'm just a first cruise JG."

"So?"

"So that means you're probably a lifer and figure the Navy's your career. I haven't come to that point yet, and figure flying around in a 747 would be a pretty good job."

Woods was puzzled. "What are you trying to say?"

"Before I tell you, I need your promise you won't tell anybody about this."

Woods was starting to feel uncomfortable. He had responsibilities in the squadron that went beyond friendship. "Okay," he said after a long pause.

"It's Irit."

Woods smiled suddenly. "So you're in love. Why don't you want anyone to know?"

"It's not that. Well, I guess part of it is . . . I was in love in college once." He struggled to express himself. "You ever fall in love a lot faster than you even knew you could?"

"Just once."

"How did you know?"

"The usual. Every hour I lived when she wasn't there was like it was wasted."

"Exactly," Vialli agreed. "That's exactly how I feel."

"This is all about Irit?"

"Yeah. It is. It's the strongest thing I've ever felt. It's almost scary."

"Does she feel the same way?"

"I think so." He hesitated. "You see her hand?"

Woods nodded.

"She only has her thumb and one finger on her right hand. She's really good at hiding it."

"Does it bug you?"

"Yeah. And I can't believe it does. I always thought I was bigger than that. I was horrified."

"You'll get over it." Woods started to push his chair away from the table and get up, but Vialli put up his hand to stop him.

"I've got to see her."

"We'll be there in a few weeks," Woods said supportively.

"I can't wait that long."

"What's a few weeks?"

"I can't explain it."

"What do you have in mind?"

"I want to take some leave and go there."

"Where?"

"Israel. Nahariya."

"Nahariya? Isn't that way north?"

"I'm not sure—"

"Just *wait*, Boomer. We'll be there in a few weeks."

"I can't."

He knew Vialli was impulsive, but he also usually had good judgment. "You know better than to decide things like this just 'cause you're hot—"

"It's not like that."

Woods had his doubts. "What are you thinking about doing exactly?"

"When we pull into Naples I'm going to take leave."

"And?"

"Fly to Tel Aviv. Commercial. She's going to pick me up. I've already made the reservations."

Woods sat back. "Skipper will never approve a leave request for Israel."

"The leave request won't say Israel."

Woods immediately understood. "It'll say Naples? You're going to put *a false* destination on it?"

Vialli looked into Woods's eyes. "You don't have to put it that way, but yeah."

"I can't do that."

"I'm not asking you to. The Skipper will approve it. I'll tell him I need some time off. I'll be back *long* before we sail."

"What if we sail early?"

"I'll take the COD and catch the ship when I can. Same as if I woke up one morning on leave in Naples and saw the big gray ship had left without me."

"She know about this?"

"I talked to her on the phone the last day we were in Venice."

"She said it was all right?"

"It was her idea."

Woods shook his head. "I don't like it, Boomer. Why'd you tell me all this?"

"You're my friend. If you see me doing something really stupid you'll tell me."

"Okay. I see you doing something really stupid. I don't even know if we're *allowed* to visit Israel on our own. I don't know if it's on the list—"

"It's not. I asked Pritch."

"Don't do it," Woods said.

"Why?"

"It's illegal. It's not the safest place in the world. You're going to lose your wings if you get caught."

"I'll be back before you know it."

"I'm *telling* you not to go."

Vialli was taken aback. "Telling me meaning what? An order? You gonna *order* me not to go?"

Woods had hoped it wouldn't come to this. "That's exactly what I'm doing. I'm *ordering* you not to go."

"Oh please. It's *my* skin."

"It's mine too, now. If something happens they'll be all over me for not stopping you."

"You can say you didn't know about it."

"Just lie?"

"Sure. They won't know the difference."

"*I* sure will. I'm telling you, don't go."

"I hear you, and I'm going anyway."

"I can't let you—"

"You're really something," Vialli said, the veins in his neck straining. "You follow the rules when it suits you. But when you want to have a little fun, like *thumping* my ass in the middle of the night from a cloudbank, that's fine! Right? You're fine with breaking a few rules when it's *you,* and you think it's clever, or funny, or shows how adventurous you are. And I'm just supposed to look the other way, not report you for a *flight* violation, like I should have. But when it's someone else who wants to bend one, and not one that's gonna get us killed, just one to go visit a girlfriend, then you get all high and mighty." He was angry. "That's bullshit, Trey!"

Woods was stung. "It's completely different."

Vialli got up. "Maybe. But I'm going. If you want to tell the CO and get my ass in trouble, feel free. And if you do, I swear to God I'll write you up for a flight violation for thumping me. Just try me."

Before Woods could stop him, Vialli was on his feet, turning his back on his roommate and walking out of the wardroom.

8

Vialli stepped off the El Al Airbus 320 at the Tel Aviv airport. He looked at the California-like terrain through the huge windows and was instantly charmed by the brightness of the sunshine and the blue sky. He was in a mood to be charmed. He felt his stomach tighten when he saw Irit waiting for him. She walked up to him slowly, smiling her perfectly shaped smile. She was wearing tight jeans that just touched her black shoes and a black long-sleeved T-shirt sharply outlining her shape, its sleeves pulled up to the middle of her forearms. Her black leather belt had a silver buckle that Vialli immediately noticed. On it, in English, were the words Israeli Defense Force as well as some Hebrew writing and the figure of an Israeli fighter.

"Hi," he said softly as she approached.

She kissed him on the lips, her right hand still in her pocket. "Shalom," she said.

"Oh, oh," he said. "Do I have to learn Hebrew?"

She smiled. "Of course not. Most people speak English."

"That's lucky," he said. He glanced around the terminal, taking it all in. "Lot of soldiers around here," he said, stating the obvious. There were uniformed soldiers with submachine guns every fifty feet.

"You'll get used to them. They're everywhere. I like having them around."

"Thanks for inviting me," he said, picking up his bag. He was trying hard not to look like a Naval officer, to look like any other twenty-something man. He had even let his hair get a little longer, a little shaggier than he normally would have to soften his otherwise military look. He felt very athletic in his loose-fitting jeans and running shoes, with a T-shirt and baggy shirt over it.

"I'm glad you're here. You have any other bags?"

"I'm used to traveling in an F-14. One gym bag."

"Great. Let's go." Crossing over to his right side and walking next to him, she asked, "Did you have any trouble getting time off?"

Vialli hesitated. "Yes and no."

"What do you mean?"

"Time off, no. The Ops O—he's sort of my boss—thought it was cool I wanted to take leave in port. Trey recommended he approve it. He said I needed the time off. But they think I'm in Naples."

"I don't understand."

He had hoped he wouldn't have to tell her, especially not first thing. "The Skipper wouldn't have let me come. He'd have told me to wait until we come here on our port call. But I wanted to come now. So I told him I'd be in Naples."

She stopped. "You shouldn't have to lie to him about it."

Vialli squinted at her. "You're one to talk."

She lowered her head.

"Sorry. That was a cheap shot."

"I deserved it."

"I didn't mean to hurt your feelings . . ."

"We both probably did something we shouldn't have done," she said, smiling conspiratorially. "At least it was for a good cause."

"That's the way I see it. And what are they going to do if they catch me? Cut my hair? Send me to sea?"

She laughed and they started walking again.

He shifted his bag to his left hand and held her hand as they walked. "So how do we get to Nahariya?"

"Train. It runs right up the coast. You'll like it. It's very pretty."

"Then what?"

"My father will pick us up at the train station and take us home."

Vialli looked at her at the mention of her father. "What does he think about you having a U.S. Navy officer come visit you?"

She shook her head slightly. "He likes the American part, and the Navy officer part, it's the goyim part he has trouble with."

"The what?"

"Goyim. Gentiles. Non-Jew, but broader. Um, outsider, I guess. Foreigner, with a touch of unwelcomeness to it."

"Is it a big problem? I thought it didn't matter to you."

"It doesn't matter to me, it matters to him a lot."

"Is he one of those Orthodox Jews who wears a funny hat and has curls around his ears?"

"Tony," she said in a low tone.

"What? What did I say?"

"They aren't 'funny' hats. Orthodox Jews take their dress very seriously. They think the Torah says very specifically what they are to wear, and they comply with it. They think all Jews should. They think the way I'm dressed is disgraceful."

"It *is* disgraceful. You should be ashamed of yourself," he joked. "I wasn't trying to make fun of them, I was just wondering if your father was one of . . . of . . . those."

"No. He is not. He isn't even very religious."

"Then what difference does it make? I'm not very serious about being Catholic either. I take it you're not very serious about being Jewish."

"Of *course* I'm serious about being Jewish, what kind of talk is that?" she asked, slightly offended.

"I don't get it. You told me you weren't very religious."

"I'm *not* very religious. Being Jewish means a lot more than being religious."

"Like what?"

She looked up at him with a pained expression that he had never seen before. "Maybe later we can talk about that. It's complicated. Come this way," she said pulling him.

The train station was clean and neat and here too there were soldiers with M-16s or Uzi submachine guns. There was no place in the train station that you could be out of the gaze of one of the soldiers. On the train, they were able to get two seats together. They sat facing forward on the left side of the train. Two soldiers sat in the seat facing them. The soldiers wore very unremarkable uniforms and sat casually. Their hair was over their ears and they hadn't shaved in a couple of days. What bothered Vialli most were the machine guns resting on their laps that were pointed directly at him.

The train lurched into motion and Vialli tried to take his eyes off the guns but found himself preoccupied; he had to know whether they were loaded and whether their safeties were on.

One of the soldiers began talking to Irit in Hebrew, which Vialli had no hope of understanding. She saw that Vialli's eyes were focused on the gun of the soldier directly across from him. "I'd like you to meet Moshe Levitz," she said to Vialli. She looked across at Moshe, who was staring at Vialli. "This is a friend of mine, Tony Vialli."

"Hi," Vialli said. The soldier nodded at him and extended his hand. Vialli took his hand and shook it with conscious firmness. "You a soldier?" Vialli asked.

"No," the soldier replied, then laughed, saying something to Irit and his companion in Hebrew. "I am banker," he went on, and laughed again, followed by more Hebrew. "This is what we wear in banks here. You never know when you'll meet a bandit, like"—he looked at his friend then back at Vialli—"John Dillinger, or Bonnie and Clyde." He laughed out loud, very proud of himself. His English was good, but heavily accented.

Vialli blushed. "Sorry. Stupid question."

The soldier held up his thick hand and shook his head. "Not a stupid question, American. I am only in the Reserves. During regular time, I *am* banker!" he said, and once again broke out into laughter.

Through the window, Vialli could see the city as it went by. It was like New York on a smaller scale, and it also looked like Athens, or parts of Athens, and a lot of other places. There were children playing in the streets, cars driving generally in order—overall a rather nice place, he thought. He looked at Moshe Levitz again and saw the two small ribbons over the pocket on his mostly brown unremarkable unkempt uniform shirt. "Haven't seen much action?" he asked.

"Why do you say that?" the soldier asked, looking at him intently.

"I don't know. Two ribbons . . ."

"You are very observant, but very unknowing." He glanced down at the two ribbons and pointed to the first one. "They are both for fighting. Those are the only ribbons I could get." His eyes flashed. "There is another award, like your Medal of Honor, but most of us get that when we are . . . under the ground."

Vialli looked at Irit. "You got any other stupid questions I could ask? I'm kind of running out."

Irit smiled up at him and took his hand.

"You want to see it?" Moshe asked Vialli, lifting his weapon for Vialli to examine. "I saw you looking at it. You know how to handle a rifle?"

"Yeah," Vialli answered. "I qualified as an expert in rifle and pistol."

"Where?" Moshe asked, frowning.

"U.S. Navy."

"You were in the American Navy?" he asked, surprised.

"Still am," Vialli said, taking the rifle from Moshe. "What is this?"

"Galil."

"Looks sort of like an AK-47."

"It is sort of like an AK-47."

"Where is it made?"

"Israel. In the late sixties, Israeli soldiers had only M-16s from America. They didn't do well in sand and dust. Everyone said AK-47 from Russia—that all the Arab countries had—was better. Israel Galili, the chief weapons designer for Israeli Military Industries, decided to make an Israeli rifle that would be better than *all* of them."

Vialli felt it, weighed it in his hands, and looked at Moshe. "It's kind of heavy."

"Heavier than the M-16, but lighter than the AK-47."

"Is it better than all of them?"

Moshe considered the question. "I think it probably is. Very reliable, good weapon. Accurate."

"Does it shoot the 7.62-millimeter NATO round?"

"You do know weapons. Most shoot the 5.56-millimeter, but there are some that shoot the 7.62. Mostly the ones sold to friends in other countries."

Vialli checked the sights, and pointed it toward the window as the train rocked along. "Any other country in the Middle East use it?"

"We don't have any friends in the Middle East," Moshe answered.

Vialli aimed the rifle again and asked Moshe about the collapsible stock. Moshe wasn't listening. He was talking to Irit. Vialli lowered the gun. "What's he talking about?"

"He doesn't believe that you're a pilot. He thinks I'm pulling his leg."

"That would be bad," Vialli said, smiling as he leaned over and spoke quietly into her ear. "Tell him in Hebrew, quietly, I'm an F-14 pilot, and, given the chance, could kick any Israeli pilot's ass. Anywhere, anytime."

She looked at him, shocked, then smiled. She translated quickly to Moshe, whose smile faded as she went on.

"And tell him," Vialli said, still whispering, as he looked at Moshe, "I could kick *his* ass too."

Again she translated for Moshe. His face reddened and he studied Vialli. Then he saw the sparkle in Vialli's eye, showing that he meant it, and that he was full of mischief and good humor. Moshe smiled broadly at Vialli, sizing up his muscular six-foot-two-inch frame. Moshe spoke rapidly in Hebrew, as his friend looked on, concerned. To Vialli Moshe said, "How many men you have killed?"

Vialli stared at Moshe unblinkingly. "Don't worry, I won't kill you."

Moshe erupted in laughter and said to Irit in English, "I like your friend. He has courage. I don't know whether of a lion or a donkey, but courage he has. When he is done with his Boy Scout tour, he can come join the Israeli Air Force after he marries you, an Israeli."

Vialli saw that her neck was redder than usual. He laughed. "That's pretty good."

Irit blinked in surprise at his sudden laughter. "Why do you laugh?"

"Because I don't think you'd marry me," he said casually.

Her eyes clouded with concern and she turned toward him and spoke quietly, disappointment in her voice. "Then why are you here?"

Vialli was stung. "I didn't mean it like that. I just meant . . . I'm not . . . I don't know, I'm not the guy your father is looking for, probably. We're just getting to know each other. I didn't mean it could *never* happen. I meant it like it isn't close, it isn't imminent."

Moshe looked at her expectantly. "It's none of your business," she said sharply in Hebrew.

"Did you just tell him off?" Vialli asked, amazed.

"Sort of."

"What for?"

"Because he wants me to tell him everything we're saying—he only understands you about three fourths of the time. He wants to know everything he can't hear or understand, and it's none of his business. Don't worry. I've known him since I was a little girl. He is a banker—in Nahariya. He's going the same place we are."

Vialli gave the Galil back to Moshe and took Irit's hand.

✍

The Sheikh paced in the stone-walled room. The dripless candles that he used for illumination could fight back only half the darkness. He insisted the fortress be lit with candles to save electricity for the things that needed it—the computers and communications equipment. They ran off a portable Honda generator that was two miles away, attached only by an underground cable. It pulled air through a tube that came up under a bush on the top of the mountain. Unless someone stepped on it, it would never be found. And if it was, and they closed it down, or the generator failed, there were five others in place waiting to replace it, ready to go at a moment's notice. The generator could not be heard in the room where the Sheikh was finalizing the planning.

He looked at Farouk, his trusted lieutenant. "Do you understand it?"

"Yes. It is very clear." He was troubled. "How do we know their schedule?"

"We have received confirmation from inside."

"Why am I not able to know the source? I should know everything about this mission. What if there is interference?"

The Sheikh was growing annoyed. Farouk seemed reluctant. "You might be captured—"

"They would *never* capture me—"

"You would never intend to talk. Agreed. But there are ways. We have been over that. What is it about this that causes you to question it suddenly?"

"I am not questioning it. I want to know the extent of my authority. I do nothing without your authorization."

"You have complete authorization. Exactly as we discussed."

"Yes." He looked at the chart one last time, having already committed every detail to memory.

"And then we go to the world and tell them who we are, and who we were at Gaza, and why we are taking our stand. Now. Here." The Sheikh exhaled with deep contentment. "We will show them, and then we will tell them. It will be exactly as we planned. The first communiqué is prepared." He drank some water from a cup on the table. "Go. Make sure the men are ready. They must be strong and faithful."

"I give you my personal word."

⚜

"What did you think of my father?" Irit asked, slipping her hand into Vialli's as they strolled along the beach.

"Serious."

"Very serious. He's a good man, though."

"How come you still live at home?"

She hesitated. "Only sometimes."

"When?"

"I'm not sure what my next move is. I don't have a teaching job, and I'm not married. I sort of needed to be home for a while. They're a very stabilizing influence on me."

"Any brothers or sisters?"

"Two brothers. Both older. One's in the Army, and the other one works for Hebrew University, teaching biology."

Vialli watched the sun reach the horizon and hover for a minute. "Thanks for inviting me. I appreciate it."

They stopped along the shore of the flat turquoise Mediterranean. She smiled at him. "I didn't think you'd come."

"Why?"

"I don't know. It's a big step. I just didn't expect you to come. But I'm glad you did."

He put his arm around her and lowered his head to hers. They walked again. "So tell me about tomorrow."

"We'll take the bus to Tel Aviv in the afternoon. I've reserved a room at a wonderful hotel on the beach there, and we can go out to my favorite restaurant in the whole world. Greek. Right on the beach. They have wonderful desserts . . ."

"Greek?"

"Sure. You'll love it. I promise—"

"We should do Italian, since that's where we met."

"Good idea. I'll think about that." She smiled. "Anyway, then we'll go to a club I know, where there will be lots of people, and I'll probably know several of them. I'll introduce you as my American fighter pilot boyfriend, which will make them all jealous. We'll dance, and stay out too late, and then I'll get up the next morning for my interview. I'll cover the bags under my eyes with just the right amount of makeup and go try to impress the airline and see if I can get all the way through the interview without falling asleep. Then we'll take the bus to Jerusalem, I'll show you the Wall, the old city, the Via Dolorosa even though you're a Catholic and don't care—"

"What's that?"

"You really don't know?"

"No."

"You'll see. And then we'll come back to Nahariya."

He nodded and thought of the wonderful time ahead. He looked forward to it. "Sounds like a blast. It'll be fun just to be with you. What are we going to do tomorrow before we leave?"

"Stay around the house. Go for another walk. My parents will probably want to talk to you some more."

"I'd better be on my best behavior."

"Just think. In three weeks you'll be back again. This will be old hat."

"Old hat?"

She looked surprised. "Is that the wrong expression?"

"No." He smiled. "What will be old hat?"

"Israel. You'll know all about it. You can show your Navy friends around."

"I'd rather just spend the time with you. Alone."

"That would be fine with me," she replied.

"I don't want to share you."

"I'm glad," she said. She stopped and kissed him gently. He held her and they felt closer to each other than either expected. They were comfortable, and pleasantly surprised.

9

How come we didn't take the train?"

"We'd have had to go this morning. I didn't want to leave until later. So is Israel like you expected?" she asked over the sound of the diesel engine of the bus and the thirty school children bouncing on the seats. The bus windows were open and the two teachers were spending much of their time trying to keep the grade-schoolers from jumping out onto the Tel Aviv highway. Irit and Vialli had been riding for thirty minutes and initially found the children amusing, but were now becoming annoyed by their noise. They had hoped for a nice quiet bus ride to talk. Other than the teachers, the only other adult riding on the bus was an Israeli soldier, who sat casually behind the driver.

Vialli looked out the window at the beach and the sea. The sun had set fifteen minutes before. It was a beautiful if unspectacular sunset. Vialli had already seen more than a hundred at sea, and was growing accustomed to the sun dropping suddenly into the water. "I'm not sure what I expected, but it's smaller and more arid than I thought. It's beautiful. Reminds me of Southern California—not that I've been there. Woods's always going on about San Diego, and how beaut—" He stopped as a different look came over her face. He peered out the bus window following her gaze.

Something had caught her eye on the darkening water.

He leaned toward the window and saw several men in dark uniforms running up the beach carrying assault rifles. They were coming from rubber boats they'd pulled up on the shore. "Look like SEALs," he said.

"Why would they come ashore in Israel?"

"They *look* like them, but I'm sure they're not. Do you have navy commandos?"

"We have commandos, but I don't know if they're with the Army or Navy . . ."

"Wait a minute," Vialli said, focusing on the armed men.

"What are they doing?" There was concern in her voice.

"I don't like this," he said, jumping up from his seat. He got to the front window just in time to see three of the men cross the road a hundred yards ahead of the bus and turn and point their guns directly at the driver.

"Go around them!" he said to the driver.

"No! They are security—"

"No, they're not!"

The driver looked ahead, examining the men as he slowed the bus. He looked quickly at Vialli and said something in Hebrew. The Israeli soldier sitting in the seat directly behind the driver stood, holding his M-16 by his side as he looked out the windshield over the driver's shoulder. He didn't like what he saw.

"Gun it! Run them over!" Vialli yelled.

The soldier didn't speak English and shouted something in Hebrew at the driver. As the bus rolled to a stop, one of the armed men pointed his rifle at the driver while the other two ran directly toward the bus.

"Are there any other weapons on board?" Vialli shouted.

The Israeli soldier pulled the slide back on his M-16 to chamber a round and pointed his rifle at the approaching men.

Suddenly shots shattered the windshield on the right side of the bus. The soldier was struck by several bullets and thrown back into the seat behind the driver. Vialli tried to grab his M-16 but the soldier had the strap around his shoulder. Vialli crouched and retreated down the aisle.

The children were hysterical, screaming. The teachers were pleading with them to stay down on the floor of the bus.

More shots rang out and the window on the door shattered. The armed men yelled at the driver, who reached for the handle to open the door.

Vialli sat down next to Irit, bending over, trying to keep his head below the top of the seat. "You okay?"

"Yes. They're speaking Arabic."

"You speak Arabic?"

"Yes."

"Now what?" Vialli asked Irit, his eyes darting around for a means of escape. He looked to the back of the bus and saw there wasn't a rear door, not even a bathroom. There was no way out except through the front door or a window. He reached over Irit, grabbed the two handles of the top window, and pulled it all the way down. It left a hole big enough for him to get out of if he had to. "If they get on we're going out the window," he murmured in a low, tense voice.

She nodded, understanding. In seconds two of the armed men were on board. Vialli stood up to help Irit out the window when he saw five other men running toward them from the beach, their automatic weapons trained on the bus. They were all dressed in black jump-suits and wore black ski masks, no insignia or rank on any of them. They yelled at the people on the bus, waving their weapons wildly.

"What are they saying?" Vialli demanded, trying to understand.

"I don't know," Irit said, her face suddenly colorless, her voice hoarse.

Vialli looked at her and saw she was looking straight ahead, dead calm. He tried desperately to get his running shoe off in the cramped enclosure of the bus seat. He had double-knotted it as he always did, and grunted as he forced it off. He slid his Navy ID card inside it before furiously working it back on.

The two men in the front of the bus were yelling at the driver to no effect. He didn't speak Arabic. The driver, shaking, saw the other men outside the bus pointing their weapons at him. He opened the door again slowly as a hand reached through the broken glass and forced it open the rest of the way. The others charged onto the bus, suddenly full of men wearing black. Making their way down the aisle, they pointed their weapons at the passengers, who screamed and cowered on the floor. The men spoke rapidly to each other, trying to gain immediate control. Up front, one of the men shouted at the driver in Arabic. Another terrorist said something to the first one and pulled him away from the driver. He spoke quietly to the driver in Hebrew, and the driver nodded.

From where they were, Vialli and Irit could see everything that was happening. Irit breathed hard, trying to understand what was being said to the driver; Vialli watched the terrorists to see if they had any vulnerabilities.

One of the bigger terrorists, six feet tall and stockily built, walked back and stood next to Vialli. He pointed his rifle at Vialli's head. Vialli recognized the gun as a Galil, the same kind Moshe had shown him on the train. The bus began moving and the man grabbed one of the handles on the back of a seat to keep his balance. He shifted the gun away from Vialli's head.

Vialli stole a glance at him. His face wore a cold determined expression, a look that Vialli had seen before in street fighters who fought all the time. For fun. The ones who knew something hard was ahead, and were ready for it. Regaining his feet, the man suddenly concentrated on Irit. He spoke to her softly, with the same look in his eyes. Vialli watched her react. "What is he saying?" Vialli demanded. She shook her head as the man continued. The terrorist continued talking to Irit, still holding the gun to Vialli's head. She shook her head again and again, fear in her eyes. "What's he saying?" Vialli asked once more.

Shouting at Vialli, the terrorist hit him in the side of the head with the barrel of his rifle.

The man who seemed to be the leader came back and talked to the stockily built one, who pointed to Irit, satisfaction on his face. The leader nodded and began speaking rapid Arabic to Irit. She pretended not to understand.

The leader's submachine gun dangled from his shoulder on a sling. Vialli recognized it as an Israeli Uzi. He began calculating whether he could grab it at about the time the leader pulled a handgun out of his belt, holding it to Vialli's head with his left hand. "Get up."

Vialli was surprised to hear English. "What do you want?"

"Get up," the man repeated, swaying with the movement of the bus. The driver was speeding down the highway and the terrorists were spaced throughout the bus, covering every direction.

"What do you want?" he repeated, still not moving.

The leader brought his handgun up and hit Vialli in the mouth with the barrel, splitting his lip and shattering his two front teeth instantly. "Get up!" he yelled again.

"Thshit," Vialli cursed through the blood and broken teeth.

"Sit there!" the man insisted, pointing to the seat in front of them. Vialli rose and staggered to the seat, sitting down heavily, fighting the pain in his head.

The leader returned his attention to Irit, putting his handgun back into his belt. He unslung his Uzi and handed it to one of his men. Some of Vialli's blood was on the seat next to Irit. The leader touched it with his finger and looked at it. It was bright red. He touched her cheek with his bloody finger. He spoke to her in Arabic, obviously asking her a question. Vialli tried to figure out what the man wanted; he was concentrating on Irit, no one else. He peppered her with questions. She sat silently, staring at him.

Finally she spoke in fluent Arabic, which seemed to gratify the leader for a moment, as if he were making progress. He asked her another question, which she also refused to answer. He kept using the same word over and over again. Vialli knew he had heard the word, but couldn't identify it. The bus slowed and the leader looked out the window toward the water. Turning to the man behind him, he spoke. The man looked down at the small electrical device he was holding and nodded. Vialli tried to see what it was. He could make out four white arrows on a handset with a small window—a GPS receiver. Global Positioning System. A satellite navigation system that allowed anyone with a receiver to know his position within a few feet. They were checking a rendezvous point.

Vialli stared out at the water, but saw nothing. It was growing quite dark.

The leader turned back to Irit with more intensity. He asked her one more question, which she clearly wasn't going to answer. He nodded to two others in masks, who reached over the seat and grabbed her, pulling her screaming toward the aisle. One of the men grabbed her right arm and pulled it out. Her deformed hand was exposed for all to see.

The leader glanced at it and nodded. Satisfied. He took out his handgun, pointing it at her. Vialli leaped out of his seat, and lunged at him. He went for the man's gun with his left hand, momentarily knocking the terrorist's arm away and grabbing for the other's Uzi. Vialli was much bigger and he was quick, and his movement caught the other man by surprise. Vialli managed to get his hand on the Uzi and was pulling on it roughly when the leader reached out with his gun and struck Vialli viciously on the head. He fell back, blood dripping from a deep gash. The heel of the handgun hit him again, this time squarely in the forehead, dropping him instantly to the floor. Vialli lost consciousness as his body fell to the rough rubber mat. The leader pointed the gun at his back and pulled the trigger twice. Two bullets tore into Vialli, killing him instantly.

Irit stared, horrified. Then somehow she managed to pull away from the men holding her and climbed onto the seat. Turning quickly, she tried to jump out of the window, but the leader raised his pistol again, shooting her in the back. The impact jerked her backward, and as she fell he shot her once more, her lifeless body tumbling on top of Vialli's.

The leader moved quickly. He checked the GPS handset, glanced out at the dark water, and nodded to his men. One of them went forward and ordered the driver to stop. When the bus had come to a complete halt, the man shot the driver, who pitched forward against the steering wheel.

The teachers and the children huddled together on the floor of the bus, sobbing, terrified that they too would be murdered. The leader motioned to his men, who removed their hoods and threw them on the floor. They stripped off their black jumpsuits and adjusted the Israeli Army uniforms they wore underneath.

The leader spoke clearly in Hebrew. "Silence! The rest of you, stay behind your seats. You must remain still for thirty minutes. We will be outside on the sand. If anyone moves, we will come back and kill all of you!"

The terrorists put on the red berets of the Israeli paratroopers, and one by one left the bus carrying their Israeli rifles.

They walked up the beach in orderly fashion, looking like an Israeli patrol. A fast black rubber boat appeared. It had a blue Star of David in a white circle on the side and was driven by a man who also wore a red beret. They waded out into the shallow water, climbed into the boat, and disappeared.

⸎

Woods strode into the ready room and sat at the desk where he worked as the Assistant Operations Officer. Vialli worked for him as the Flight Officer and drew up the flight schedule every day. Among other things, he kept track of how much flight time each pilot and RIO had each month, how many arrested landings each had had, daytime and nighttime, and how many of each kind of hop each pilot had flown.

Now well past the middle of their six-month deployment to the Mediterranean from their home port of Norfolk, Virginia, the only things they needed to worry about were traps and hours. Everything else had been taken care of before the cruise.

Woods studied the greenie board behind him. He had the second-highest landing grades of any pilot in the squadron, followed closely by Bark himself and Big McMack, another lieutenant. The only one ahead of him was Lieutenant Terry Blankenship, but he didn't count. All the other pilots thought he was actually a machine and therefore he didn't qualify for admiration. Woods was proud of his landing grades, but didn't talk about it. You were supposed to act as if it was a very ordinary accomplishment and that you never thought about at all. Routine stuff. Ordinary day's work. The objective of Navy Air was to accomplish the impossible with negligible apparent effort.

Woods wanted to draft the flight schedule for Vialli for the first day out of Naples. It would be ready when Vialli got back and he wouldn't have to try to do it in the middle of the night after everyone had gone to bed, not knowing when they were flying the next day and therefore angry at him for not doing it sooner. And that's exactly what would happen if he didn't do it for Vialli. Vialli wasn't due for one more day. He would undoubtedly rush to get back to the ship the hour his leave expired, which was midnight the night before they sailed. Better to do it now, get it over with, and have Vialli owe him one. He drank deeply from his coffee cup and opened a new file on Vialli's computer, under the flight schedule macro.

The rear door to the ready room flew open from the passageway. Big walked in with his usual flourish and looked around. There were three officers in the ready room including Woods. Brillo was the Squadron Duty Officer and was sitting in his khakis at the desk at the front of the room, and Sedge was using his ready room chair as a desk to write the evaluations of the enlisted men in his division. He had the Aviation Armament division, which included the AOs, the aviation ordnancemen who handled the missiles and the bullets.

Big saw Woods and walked over to him. "Well, I guess we're hosed on our port call in Haifa," he said resignedly.

Woods glanced up, debating whether to ask Big the question he was obviously begging to be asked. Might as well get it over with. "Why's that, Big?" he asked as he typed "Event 1A" on the computer.

"Didn't you hear?" Big asked, hiking his pants up around his girth, glad to have found someone who didn't know what he and most everyone else on the ship knew.

"Why don't you tell me," Woods said, bored.

"Terrorist attack in Israel last night. It's on the closed circuit TV."

Woods forced himself not to jump up and turn on the television. He knew Big would do it for him. Big crossed to the briefing area in the back of the ready room and turned on the television overhead. Brillo had heard what Big said and turned on the larger set in the front of the room at the same time. They came to life simultaneously. Lieutenant Commander Randy Dennison, Intelligence Officer for the Air Wing, was on the screen.

Woods turned his chair around to listen as Big raised the volume so it filled the room. ". . . But we don't know yet how many were killed, or why. No one has taken responsibility for the attack. Hamas and Hezbollah have made public statements that they had nothing to do with it, and hint it may be the same people who were responsible for the Gaza crossing attack." Dennison showed a news wire photograph of a bus sitting by the side of the Tel Aviv road, its windshield shot out. "The bus was on its way from a town north of Haifa to Tel Aviv. It had numerous school children aboard and several adults. There were four adults killed, three men and one woman. None of the children was harmed. For those of you who are wondering whether this will affect our port call to Haifa in three weeks, we don't know right now. If you have any questions, dial two-two-four-five on your phones."

"Brillo!" Woods shouted. "Call him and ask if there were any Americans on board."

"Don't you think he'd tell us?"

"Do it!" Woods screamed.

Brillo looked quickly at Big as if to ask, "What the hell's up with him?" but Big simply shrugged. Brillo dialed the phone on the desk and spoke to an intelligence specialist, first class, who was covering the phone in CVIC, the carrier intelligence center. Lieutenant Commander Dennison took the call.

"Yes, sir, Ready Room Eight. Sir, we were wondering if there were any Americans on that bus in Israel."

"Why do you care?" Dennison asked.

"Just interested in our fellow citizens," Brillo said, glancing at Woods.

"We don't know. I don't have any information either way. Looks like it was just a bus trip from Nahariya."

"Okay. Thanks, sir," Brillo said, hanging up. "They don't know. School trip from Nahariya," he told Woods.

Woods jerked visibly on the mention of Nahariya. He fought the panic he felt deep in his gut. He tried to act nonchalant and drink his coffee as he looked at the flight schedule, but he realized he had been staring at it for five minutes without writing anything. He glanced up suddenly and saw Brillo and Big studying him. He couldn't shake his feeling of foreboding.

The ready room door swung open again and Bark came in carrying a stack of papers. He sat in his chair and opened the steel drawer between his legs. He dropped the papers in the drawer on top of another pile of papers and tried to shut it. The drawer wouldn't close. "Damn it!" he said, standing up quickly. He turned around and kicked the drawer. The drawer flew back and jammed, with paper stuck between the drawer and the seat bottom. Muttering, he sat down in the chair with the drawer hanging open three inches. He got up again, walked three steps to the front, and leaned down under the blackboard and sliding charts. He examined the stacks of individual mailboxes that one of the squadron's shops had created at his request. He stood on the enormous skull and bones cut into the tile in the front of the ready room. It had been his idea to bring the template of the skull and bones used to paint the huge Tomcat tails to the ready room and use it to make a tile masterpiece on the deck when the squadron retiled the ready room in Norfolk. He had purchased the black and white tiles with his own money. The pilots had cut pieces to form the skull and bones, which now lay perfectly as part of the tile floor surrounded by the yellow tile of the rest of the room, the squadron's color. He was the only one in the squadron actually allowed to walk on the skull and bones.

He looked into his mail slot as he spoke to Brillo, sitting at the desk to his left. "Mail call yet this morning?"

"Yes, sir. Petty Officer Whaley just put it all in the slots."

Bark bent over farther, looked into the back of his slot, and saw some letters. "Aha!" he exclaimed, drawing out three letters in pastel envelopes with the same writing. "She *hasn't* forgotten me!"

"Well, she may have; she may just be writing so you don't know it yet," Big said, laughing hoarsely at his own humor. He was as his name suggested. Big. He was about six four, well over two hundred pounds, with a jolly round face and thinning hair.

"Thanks for the encouragement, Big," the CO said, sitting back down in his seat. He held the letters to his nose and breathed in deeply. "Aaahhh," he said, exhaling. "Why is it that perfume fades on the body in a matter of hours, but stays on a letter for weeks, or months?"

"I don't know, Skipper," Big said, glancing at Brillo. "I've always been fascinated by that question myself. Probably some scientific explanation about that. Maybe we should write to Chanel, or . . ."

"Maybe you should shut the hell up, Big," Bark growled as he opened the letter with the oldest postmark. "As much as I love e-mail, there's nothing like a good, old-fashioned letter . . . Hey, Brillo," Bark said, stopping momentarily. "Where's Vialli? I need to talk to him about the flight schedule for the next at-sea period. He's had me on too many night hops lately. *Real* night hops. That's no way to treat your Commanding Officer. I need a few more pinkies." Pinkies were hops that landed after sunset but before it got really dark. They counted as night hops.

"He's on leave, Skipper."

"That's right," Bark replied, pulling out the two pages from his wife's first letter.

"Hey, Trey," Brillo said loudly so Woods could hear him from the back of the ready room. "When's Boomer due back?"

"Tomorrow night," Woods said. "Midnight. So, undoubtely he'll be on the last O-boat at 2359. He's probably trying to figure out whether being 'back' means ashore on the pier, or here in the ready room."

Big stood next to Brillo drinking his coffee, his other hand in the pocket of his polyester khaki trousers, still looking for people who hadn't heard the news. "Hey, Skipper, d'ya hear about that bus thing in Israel?"

Bark put down the letter and shook his head vigorously. "Could you believe that? I don't get it at all. Take a bus, drive south, kill four of the people on board and disappear? Not the usual terrorist attack at all. Sounds more like an assassination. But why kill schoolteachers? I'll tell you, those guys'll kill anybody." He shook his head in amazement. "I wonder if they'll identify themselves. Bunch of cowards." They all nodded in agreement. He started reading his letter again, then holding the open letter out in front of him, as if reading, he said, "They probably write letters to their sweethearts: 'Dear Susie, weather is great here in southern Gaza. Wish you were here. I want you, I need you. Had a great day yesterday. Read a good book, killed a few people. It was great. Please write soon. Love, Abdul.' " He rubbed his forehead with his fingers. "I just don't get it. What makes someone able to kill innocent people? Where does that come from?"

"I don't know, Skipper," Big replied. "I never have understood it. But if there's anybody who knows how to take care of terrorists, it's the Israelis. They don't take any shit from anybody. We just wring our hands and sit on our asses. If it was a bus full of Americans, I sure as hell'd be ready to hurt someone."

After the Skipper had read through his letters twice and smelled them three times, he stood up and stretched. "Hey, Trey," he called out. "You put any more thought into how to intercept those Air Force F-15Es when they come out?"

Woods looked up from his blank flight schedule. "Not really much to it, Skipper. Pick them up on our radar from about a million miles out. They'll be on the deck, thinking that going fast and low will make us not see 'em, we'll roll in behind them and shoot 'em."

"I've heard they can go almost supersonic on the deck in military power," Bark said.

Woods shrugged. "They can go supersonic all day long for all I care. Just means they won't be using their burners. Saves gas. It's not like we can't do supersonic intercepts."

Bark looked at him as if he was slow. "I just think it's pretty impressive to be able to go that fast without burner. I wish we could."

"I don't know of anybody else who can," Woods said casually. "Maybe the Concorde. Or the old F-111F. Now *that* was a fast airplane."

"Want to head down to the wardroom for lunch early? I'm starved."

Woods didn't. He wanted to be alone. He wanted to think. He wanted to stare at the blank flight schedule to hide the worry that he knew would soon showing be on his face. "Sure, Skipper," he said as they walked out the ready room back door. He needed some time. He had to tell the Skipper that Boomer had gone to Israel. But he was probably fine, and if he told the Skipper now, Boomer could be court-martialed. He probably wouldn't be; Bark would probably just put him in HAQ—House Arrest, Quarters—for the next five thousand port calls, or make him SDO for life, but it wouldn't be in his record. Take the risk, Woods thought; just don't be wrong.

10

The members of the task force had a uniformly grim look. The banter was gone.

Kinkaid spoke. "What do we know?"

Nicole White, a woman with short dark hair, sat next to Kinkaid in the conference room. Sami was in the next seat, and Cunningham sat next to him. She stood and approached the front. She had a small infrared remote control in her hand, which she pointed at her laptop sitting on the conference table next to the Sharp projector. Someone in the back dimmed the lights. She pushed a button and a map of Israel came up. There was an arrow on the map pointing to the coastal highway from Haifa to Tel Aviv.

"This is where it happened, or rather where it stopped. The bus was taken"—she pointed with a laser pointer—"here. The attackers came from the sea, apparently undetected. The Israelis are greatly chagrined about this. They thought their coastal surveillance was impenetrable. They used rubber boats, which don't show up on radar, and they apparently knew the pattern of the Israeli patrol boats off the coast. The IR sensors and other equipment either didn't pick them up or the guards watching it weren't paying very close attention. In any case, they came ashore and took the bus. They drove south twenty miles, killed four adults on the bus, including the driver, then vanished. They left two teachers on the bus, and thirty children."

"Go on," Kinkaid ordered.

Nicole called up the next slide. "Here is the bus after the attack." The photograph was from the front and showed the windshield shot out and the driver slumped on the side of the steering wheel. She silently went to the next photo, which she had scanned into her computer, and which was now incorporated into her digital slide presentation. It showed the inside of the bus and the seat behind the driver where the Israeli soldier lay. The next photo had been taken inside the bus looking down the aisle. A man and a woman were lying dead on the floor, face down. Their blood was a dark brown against the black rubber mat of the aisle. "This is the couple who was killed. We have no idea who they were. If the Israelis know, they're not saying."

Kinkaid looked at the photograph hard. "I'll call."

"Mossad or Aman?" Ricketts asked.

"Mossad," Kinkaid replied, appreciating that Ricketts knew the difference between the Israeli intelligence agency and their military intelligence arm. He had learned long ago never to underestimate Ricketts. "Who would operate like this, Nicole?" Kinkaid queried. "Why not kill everyone? Why not make demands, and play it out? Why hit and run? To show they could? Some other agenda at work? These the same people who did Gaza?"

Sami stared at the map, wondering.

One man in the back spoke. "This isn't the usual terrorist attack. They did this for a reason. The who is the why in this one."

Sami spoke. "If this is the same group as Gaza," he began, still forming the thoughts, "it's a new level."

"What do you mean?"

"These would be the first civilian targets."

"We don't know they were civilian targets."

"Well, the driver, the couple—"

"We don't have any idea who they were," Kinkaid said.

"Fair enough, but if they *are* civilians, and it's connected to Gaza, it would be the first time they have attacked civilians."

"So?"

"Other terrorist groups have focused on suicide attacks. Some of that is to be dramatic. Some of it is because they know they'll never get away with it anyway, so they may as well go out in a blaze of glory. These guys know they *can* get away with it. They're smarter and more clever. And they're showing the world," Sami replied.

"What do we make of that?" Kincaid continued.

"I think we're going to be hearing from them. They're going to want to let everyone know who they are. That's my guess."

Farouk sat down heavily in the chair across the table from the Sheikh. He was proud and content, but exhausted from the journey. "We had complete success."

"You bring honor to us. Did everything go according to the plan?"

"Yes. It went perfectly."

"What of the men?"

"All did well, except for one. He was yelling and screaming. Too charged with feelings."

"Do not take him next time."

"Of course."

"Did you find what you expected?"

"We did. We made sure."

The Sheikh closed his eyes and put his head back. He seemed to be thinking for a long time. Finally, he stood and leaned on the chair he had been sitting in. He looked at Farouk. "It is time. I will go to Beirut and show myself. They must know of us and what we stand for. Things will never be the same again."

Woods sat in the wardroom with other pilots and RIOs from VF-103. They took up almost an entire table of twenty as they sat shoulder to shoulder drinking coffee in their leather and nylon flight jackets, joking about other squadrons, other carriers, the Pacific Fleet, the Air Force, and one another. The morale in the squadron was as high as Woods had ever seen it. Bark had left the wardroom ten minutes before, which had allowed the rest of the officers to relax.

"Where's our next port call, Trey?" asked Brillo.

"Athens," Woods answered.

"What's it like?" Wink asked. He was on his third cruise, but his first two had been to Westpac, the western Pacific, on the *Nimitz*. This was his first time in the Mediterranean.

"It's really beautiful—" began Woods.

"It's not even a port," Big interrupted.

Wink looked at him curiously. "Huh?"

"It's not a port. Athens isn't on the water. Everybody thinks it is, but it isn't. The port is Piraeus, about fifteen miles south of Athens. It's a great place though."

"Who's in charge of the admin?" asked Brillo.

"Gunner Bailey," said Big, wrinkling his nose, referring to Chief Warrant Officer Ruben Bailey. He was a Warrant Officer, and therefore a member of the officers' mess. But he was more like a Chief Petty Officer, a senior enlisted man, which he used to be. He didn't have many friends in the squadron among the officers, mostly because he was very serious about his job and not prone to joking around. He was old enough to make them feel very young, yet, as a Warrant Officer, junior to the most junior Ensign. "He's got the taste of a hooker," Big continued. "He'll find some Greek motel with no running water and prostitutes all over the place. He'll crow about how much money he saved."

Woods replied, "He did a good job in Barcelona."

"Yeah, but we got arrested by the Guardia Civil right by the hotel he selected for making too much noise . . ."

"No, Big, *you* got arrested for taking a leak on him—you thought he was a *light* post."

The table erupted in laughter as Woods brought up one of the squadron's mythologically large stories about Big, the one who always seemed to be in the middle of a story if it was colorful.

Big's eyes disappeared as he laughed with the others. "How was I supposed to know? Brillo was supposed to be my seeing-eye dog. *He* allowed me to make that perfectly understandable mistake."

Brillo exclaimed, "You're going to lay that on *me*? You piss on the meanest cop in the Med and it's *my* fault? I don't think so."

Big chuckled deeply. "Anybody who wears a hat that stupid deserves to get—"

The 1MC loudspeaker system on the ship came to life. "Now hear this. Now hear this," said a young voice that they all recognized as one of the boatswain's mates on the bridge who routinely made announcements. They quieted just enough to hear whatever he had to say. "Lieutenant Woods to the flag bridge. Lieutenant Woods to the flag bridge."

Woods turned deep red. He looked at the other members of the squadron, who were looking at him. Never in his experience in the Navy had he heard of an aviator being summoned personally to the bridge, let alone the flag bridge. His heart was racing as he stood up, reluctantly, ready to go to the executioner. The smiles faded. They could tell from his face that either he had no idea what this was about, or he knew exactly. They didn't ask.

Woods walked aft from the wardroom down the starboard side through the knee knockers. They had been on cruise for three months and he had never even *seen* the Admiral. He didn't even know what he looked like and couldn't remember his name. He stepped from gray tile to blue tile, denoting his passage into flag country. He passed the Admiral's wardroom, nearly as large as one of the forward wardrooms for fifty officers. What's his name? Woods asked himself. He found the shining ladder with white painted rope wrapped around the rails and began his long climb up to the 08 level, eight levels above the main deck—the hangar deck—and five above the wardroom and the ready rooms on the 03 level.

He jumped up the last two steps on the ladder to the 08 level and breathed deeply to catch his breath. Standing in front of the closed door that led to the bridge, he was finally ready. He opened the door and stepped through the hatch, stopping in his tracks as he neared the bridge—the Admiral, the Ship's Captain, the Air Wing Commander, and Bark, his Squadron Commanding Officer, were all there. The Admiral was holding a sheet of yellow paper, which was obviously from an official Navy message.

"Here he is, sir," Bark announced as Woods approached.

"Good evening, sir," Woods said.

"Lieutenant . . ." The Admiral looked at Woods and then said. "This isn't the place to get into what I have to discuss with you. Let's go below." With that he stood up and walked past Woods out the door, starting down the ladder that Woods had just climbed.

Woods and the senior officers followed the Admiral to his wardroom. The admiral sat at one end of his table and motioned for the other senior officers to join him. He was about fifty, average height, trim build, with graying black hair combed neatly. Everything about him said that he was organized, neat, and disciplined. The messman automatically went for cups and a pot of coffee. Woods stood awkwardly in the middle of the room. "Sit down, Lieutenant," the Admiral said roughly, pointing to the seat at the other end of the table.

Admiral Joseph Sweat, former A-6 and F/A-18 pilot, with over a thousand carrier landings and a chest full of ribbons, had a reputation in the fleet as being fair and reasonable, but he wasn't known for his great sense of humor.

The messman set a cup in front of each of them and poured coffee. He put cream and sugar in the middle of the table in matching porcelain containers.

The Admiral's leather flight jacket was covered with patches from his former squadrons and centurion patches from carriers marking each one hundred carrier landings. "What do you know about Lieutenant Junior Grade Vialli?" he asked quickly, reaching for his coffee and staring at Woods with his intense eyes.

Woods didn't want to have this conversation. Whatever it was about, it was going to be bad. He prayed it wasn't as bad as he feared. "He's my wingman, roommate. What in particular would you like to know?"

"Where is he?"

Woods's heart skipped as he swallowed. "He's on leave."

"Where?"

"Naples, sir."

"Did he go anywhere else?"

The other officers were watching him closely. "I'm not sure," Woods replied finally, not wanting to meet the piercing gaze of the Admiral's blue eyes.

"Did he tell you he *might* go anywhere else? Anywhere at all?"

Woods knew the game was up. "He did mention one possibility, sir."

"Where?" the Admiral pressed, knowing Woods knew.

Woods leaned against the back of the black leather chair, trying not to slump. "He met a girl he thought was Italian. Turned out she was from Israel . . ."

At the mention of the word Israel, the Admiral's face twitched noticeably.

". . . and she wanted him to come see her. He took leave for Naples, thinking he might fly to Israel for the weekend, see her, and come back before he was due back aboard."

Bark's eyes opened to twice their usual size. "You didn't tell me?"

Woods didn't respond. He just looked at his CO with his lips pressed tightly together and nodded almost imperceptibly.

The Admiral picked up the yellow paper. "We just received this message. You should be aware of it. It's from the Secretary of Defense, forwarding a message from our embassy in Tel Aviv. Apparently one of the adults on the bus that was attacked, one of those killed, had Lieutenant Vialli's ID card in his shoe."

Woods closed his eyes and lowered his head. The pain on his face was apparent to everyone at the table. They sat in complete silence, waiting.

Finally the Admiral spoke again to Woods. "Can you think of any way someone else would have his ID card?"

Woods tried to speak, stopped, then tried again. "Can't they identify him?"

The Admiral nodded. "Probably. But they were wondering what the hell he was doing there, and asked us. Now *we're* wondering what the hell he was doing there and asking you."

"What happened?" Woods asked.

"He died in the attack."

Woods was suddenly engulfed with rage. His eyes burned as he looked around the table. None of the senior officers was affected. Bark was mad at him for not telling him Vialli was sneaking off, the Admiral was mad because he was being squeezed for allowing one of his officers to go to Israel without the State Department knowing about it, and the others were just along for the ride.

"What do you have to say for yourself?" Bark asked finally.

Woods looked at him in disbelief. He felt betrayed. "What do I have to say for myself? For not telling you he was going to see his girlfriend in Israel? *Guilty.* I should have told you and I didn't," he said, spite dominating his thoughts. "I should probably get court-martialed."

"Don't get cute, Lieutenant," the Admiral said. "We just want to get to the bottom of this. We want to find out what happened, how one of our officers could have gone to Israel without us knowing about it. We wanted to ask you how—"

"Doesn't anybody care who did this?" Woods interrupted. "Why aren't we talking about what we're going to do to *them*?"

The Admiral looked at him disapprovingly. "You're upset. That's understandable." He paused. "I want you to prepare a report on how Mr. Vialli took leave without informing his Commanding Officer of the true destination and have it ready by the end of the day."

Woods exhaled suddenly, a sound that could have been an exclamation or a laugh. He looked at Bark. "Yes, sir. I would be happy to prepare a *report*, sir." He got up and moved toward the door.

"Lieutenant!" the Admiral shouted.

Woods stopped and turned around.

"I have not dismissed you yet."

Woods stood at attention looking over the Admiral at the portrait of George Washington on the wall behind him. *He'd* go after whoever did this to Vialli.

After some seconds the Admiral said, "Dismissed."

Woods executed a perfect about-face and strode quickly out of the room. A sailor opened the door for him and shut it quietly behind him as he left.

≁

"What the hell was he doing in Israel?" Sami asked Cunningham as they walked to the conference room, for the next of what seemed like an infinite number of meetings of the task force.

"Woman," Cunningham replied, looking down the corridor for Kinkaid whom he wanted to see right away.

"Did he have permission?"

"Nope."

"No?"

"No. Told his roommate, but nobody else. The roommate didn't tell anyone until it was too late."

"He's in some deep shit."

"Good guess." They opened the door to the conference room and crossed to the coffee machine that was kept fresh by some unknown person.

"Good morning," Kinkaid said as they got their coffee. "If everyone will take a seat, we can begin. We all have work to do, so I want to keep this time to a minimum. We've got two hits, clearly well planned and well executed. No casualties to the terrorists, which sets them apart from virtually all terrorists that have come before them. They care about living through it and they have escaped without a trace from Gaza, and from Israel itself, something most of us considered impossible. Anybody got anything?"

Nicole spoke. "I've been in contact with the Mossad. They're playing it very close to the vest. I think there's more to this one than meets the eye. Official position is that they have no idea who did it or why. The one initially unidentified man who was killed we now know was a U.S. Navy pilot from the *Washington*. The carrier was in Naples. The officer, we now learn, was on unauthorized leave, apparently visiting an Israeli woman from Nahariya. At least that's the report we've gotten from the Navy. Met her on the train south of Naples, and fell for her. Went to visit her, and she's the one who was killed with him." Nicole stopped, seeing the image of what she was about to say. "They were both shot in the back. At close range."

"Assassinated," Sami said. The others listened. "So who was the target?"

Kinkaid replied, "You can't know from that evidence, but the communiqué makes it pretty clear. Sami?"

"Right," Sami said. He stood and switched on the overhead projector, placed the acetate of the communiqué on it, and turned on the light. The beautiful Arabic script was projected onto the large screen in the front of the room. "This was received this morning by several wire services and our embassy in London. You all have a translation of it in front of you." They glanced at the papers lying on the table. Some picked them up. "The translations from the wire services aren't bad, but there's more to it. First, I want you to note that this is handwritten. Beautifully. Someone took great care in writing this. There are no errors of spelling, or punctuation, or grammar, or even syntax. That implies several things: We're dealing with someone who is very educated, and very careful. My guess is that this document went through many drafts, probably before the events it discusses. It also shows that the person doesn't care if he is identified. Like English, only perhaps more so, Arabic script writing is very characteristic. You can recognize someone's hand, or style, fairly easily. My sense is that he doesn't care."

He placed a pencil on a line in the middle. "The content is equally interesting. The gist of this communiqué is that they are the ones who conducted the attack on the Israeli bus, and they also are the ones responsible for the Gaza crossing attack. They note . . . here"—he pointed to some Arabic—"that they left their American weapons in the van in sequential serial number order for easy identification. We knew that because the Mossad sent us those pictures. Those photos have not been released to the press, and those not involved in the attack would have no way of knowing about the serial numbers. This is their means of authentication."

"Or they could have inside information from Israeli intelligence," Nicole added.

"Or Palestinian intelligence," Cunningham said.

"Other than those two possibilities, it shows they were involved," Sami replied.

Sami read on to himself, then spoke. "Here's the heart of it . . . 'We are the Assassins. Israel is an intolerable sore in the region and must be eradicated. We are everywhere, but will never be seen. We will never rest until Israel is no longer. The bus attack was necessary and important. Ask Israel why, if you want to know the reason.' " He looked up. "Frankly, I'm puzzled. Why would Israel know the reason for the school bus attack? Anyway, they go on. 'The American was an unexpected gift. His presence on the bus confirms that Israel is the puppet of America and America is just the most recent Crusader to try to take over Islamic land.'" He read on to himself for a moment, then stopped. "The rest is pretty predictable, condemns the Palestinian Authority of Gaza as a bunch of traitors, condemns the West, the usual."

"So," Ricketts said. "At least they've identified themselves. And it's not the usual. Very different. The Assassins . . ." he said. He looked at Sami. "Is it signed?"

Sami looked down at the document even though he already knew the answer. He was annoyed at himself that he hadn't mentioned it already. "Yeah. Sheikh al-Jabal."

Ricketts sat up. "That's your guy, right? The one from that NSA track?"

"That's him."

11

Woods sat in the front row of folded chairs in the forecastle. It was jammed with aviators in their khaki uniforms and flight jackets, sitting and standing around the enormous anchor chains that disappeared through the deck beneath them. The entire Air Wing was there to honor Tony Vialli and to extend their sympathy to his family, or what passed for his family in the Navy, his squadron. As his roommate, section leader, and best friend, Woods was the one expected to play the unofficial role of grieving next of kin.

But Woods didn't want sympathy. He didn't want to hear a bunch of awkward phrases and silly comments like so many other memorial services. He tried to concentrate on the final words of Father Maloney, who was completing some sort of Catholic service. Vialli was, after all, Catholic, or at least close enough for a government chaplain to say whatever was usually said at these services. Woods was certain Vialli had never attended a Catholic service on the ship, and he was quite sure Lieutenant Commander Maloney couldn't have picked Vialli out of a lineup.

Woods barely noticed the playing of the Navy hymn, the plea for God to guard and guide the men who fly . . . in peril in the sky. He barely noticed the final prayer, the last words of farewell and the clatter of chairs being pushed back slightly on the hard, gray steel as the Air Wing officers got to their feet. They stood in groups, talking low and moving around aimlessly, but no one left. The rite of passage wasn't quite complete until there was some conveyance of sorrow. No one seemed to know exactly what was expected, or what was enough, but at some point enough of whatever it was was exchanged and people began getting ready to leave.

Woods had been to lots of memorial services for pilots who had hit the ramp, or flown into the water, or simply disappeared into the night. He'd made the same comments as those now standing around him. But this was all wrong; everyone was behaving as if Vialli was just another accident victim, as if fate had reached down and touched him, his time being up. *We never know when any of us is going to go . . .*

"No!" Woods yelled, stepping back from some of the pilots milling around him. "Don't you get it?" he said to the entire group, gaining attention. "We all stand around here like we're used to this. Like Tony's death was an *accident*. It's not the same!" he said loudly.

Some of the aviators looked at each other wondering if Woods had finally cracked. Too much pressure, maybe even responsibility. Rumor had it he knew where Vialli was going and could have stopped him, but didn't.

The ship moved up and down perceptibly under their feet as the awkwardness of the moment froze it in time. No one could leave. It would have been a slap in the face to Woods.

"This wasn't an *accident!*" Woods's gray eyes flashed. "He didn't have a bird strike, or run out of gas—he was *mur*dered!" He drew out the word as if speaking to someone who was not quite with it.

The VF-103 Operations Officer said in a quiet voice, "We know that, Trey. We know that." He looked around to see if he was speaking for the group. "But there isn't much we can do about it. We all feel really bad about Boomer. He was a great guy. A talented guy. But we can't exactly go after whoever did this on our own."

Woods took a deep breath. "I know," he said with exhaustion. "But we've got to do something."

"We'd love to," the officer responded. Others murmured their agreement. "And when you figure out what that is, you let us know. We're behind Boomer, and we're behind you."

Woods turned away from the crowd. The Ops O nodded to the others and the crowd began to file out the two doors around the enormous anchor chains. Woods walked toward the bow. He could see the milky gray water out of the small porthole. Waves strove to become whitecaps but fell just short. Slowly Woods realized a voice had been calling his name for some time, but he didn't want to hear more tripe about how sorry someone was . . .

"Lieutenant Woods?"

Woods glanced over his shoulder and saw Father Maloney. Great, he thought. Just what I need. He said nothing.

"Lieutenant Woods, may I have a word with you?" Maloney asked.

Woods stood silently, then grudgingly he said, "Sure. What about?"

"About Tony."

Woods thought perhaps there were some arrangements that had to be made. He had been appointed as the officer in charge of putting together Vialli's personal effects and tying up whatever needed to be done. "What is it?"

"Would you mind coming to my office, just to talk for a while?"

"What for?"

The priest smiled, then replied, "I just thought you might want to talk about how you're feeling."

Woods tried not to show his disgust. If there was one thing he hated, it was people who spent all their time talking about how they were "feeling." "Why would I want to do that?"

Maloney was taken aback by Woods's reply. "I just thought you might like to."

"You some kind of psychologist or something?"

"Not at all. I just thought . . ."

"It's kind of obvious how I feel, isn't it? Some other time, maybe," he said, walking away. In fact, he thought, it was time for him to do something about how he was feeling.

Woods went briskly up the ladders to the O3 level and straight into the blue tile. He stopped at the Admiral's wardroom and knocked loudly. He waited five seconds and knocked again. He heard a voice inside, then the door opened quickly. "Yes, sir?" a sailor asked.

"Is the Admiral here?"

"Yes, sir."

"I'd like to see him."

"Is he expecting you, sir?"

"No."

"Your name, sir?"

"Lieutenant Woods. Sean Woods, VF-103," he replied.

"Please wait while I inquire, sir," he said. The door closed quietly in front of him.

Woods stood in the passageway for a short time, but long enough to feel foolish as several sailors passed by. He knew what they thought. He was in trouble.

"The Admiral would like to know if this is an emergency, sir."

"Yes, it is."

"The Admiral would like to know if you have exercised your chain of command, sir."

"No, I haven't. And I don't plan on it."

"One moment, sir."

The door closed again, and Woods waited outside for another minute. The door opened and the sailor motioned to him. "You may come in, sir. The Admiral will see you."

"Admiral—" Woods began before he had even reached the Admiral's table, the same one he had sat at so recently.

"Hold it right there, Lieutenant," the Admiral said.

Woods looked around and realized he had barged in on a meeting of the Admiral's staff. The Chief of Staff was there, the Operations Officer, the Intelligence Officer, and others he didn't recognize. Nice move, he told himself. But he didn't care.

"What's the emergency?" Admiral Sweat asked Woods.

"It's about Vialli, sir."

"We've had this discussion. Does your CO know you're here?"

"No, sir. It's not the same conversation we had before, sir."

"You have thirty seconds."

"I think we should do something about Vialli, sir."

"Like what? His death didn't even involve us, Lieutenant. If you recall, he had to lie to his Commanding Officer—a lie which you joined—just to be where he was to get himself killed."

"We should retaliate, sir," Woods said, as if he hadn't heard a thing the Admiral had said.

The Admiral looked surprised. "How? And against whom?"

"Against the people who sent the communiqué, sir." Woods answered, words gushing out as if he were now free finally to speak his mind. "I think they said it was faxed from Beirut. Pritch even printed out the translation. Didn't you see it? I'll bet our intelligence knows who this Sheikh is, and exactly where he came from." He glanced at the Intelligence Officer on the staff, a small bookish man of about forty who made no sign of agreement or disagreement. "Once we find where they're hiding, we attack them."

The Admiral stared at him. "They thought they were killing Israeli citizens," he said.

"Not too many people would mistake Vialli for an Israeli for long."

"We don't take action on our own, Lieutenant. It's not for us to decide. You know that. It's up to the politicians."

"Admiral, couldn't we at least ask for authorization?" Woods begged.

"No."

"Couldn't we tell them we're here, that we're available, that we could do it if they wanted us to? Sir?"

"They *know* we're here, Lieutenant. The President will take whatever action he deems appropriate. Your time is up." With that, the Admiral redirected his attention to the document in front of him.

"Couldn't we at least tell them it's feasible, and we could do it if they want? Maybe put the idea into their heads?"

"I think not," the Admiral said as he leaned back and removed his reading glasses. "Look, I know how you feel. I've lost a lot of my friends in this business. I know how it pulls at you. I know how you wish you could have done something different, so it never would have happened. Especially in your situation. *You* could have prevented the whole thing by the exercise of a little leadership," he said, looking hard at Woods. "You were his superior officer. You could have *ordered* him not to go. But now you're going to have to learn to deal with it." He picked his glasses up again. "Dismissed."

Woods swiveled and began walking toward the door. Then he stopped and turned back to Admiral Sweat. "How many of the friends you lost were *murdered*, Admiral?"

Admiral Sweat remained silent, and Woods left quickly.

He opened the door to Ready Room Eight and saw a brief in progress. They hadn't missed a beat, fitting the memorial service in during the time the ship was leaving port—still in sight of port—and not yet in position to fly. Wouldn't want to interrupt the flight schedule with something as mundane as a memorial service for one of the Air Wing's pilots.

Woods had never gotten used to the Navy's cold approach to death. The first time he had seen someone killed aboard the carrier during a catapult accident, the ship hadn't even slowed down. The launch went right on and the spare was launched to replace the downed airplane. The memorial service had been a few days later, when it could be held without interfering with the flight schedule. He had been told that if they did it any differently death would loom too large and affect the pilots' willingness to put themselves at risk. He wasn't convinced.

He closed the door quietly so he wouldn't disturb the brief, removed his coffee cup from its hook, filled it, and took his seat at the desk on the other side of the ready room. He began working on the next day's flight schedule. They were going to operate in the Aegean Sea south of Athens, to a small island, Avgo Nisi. An island reserved for military use, to be shot and bombed. It was inhabited only by very scared mountain goats and sheep.

Bark saw Woods come in. He got up quickly and strode to the back of the room. Bark had the look on his face that Woods had learned to dread.

"Hey, Skipper," Woods said, trying to be nonchalant.

Bark pulled a chair up until it was touching Woods's. He moved his face close to Woods's and spoke in a low intense voice. "Don't 'Hey Skipper' me," he said, his eyes boring holes in Woods. "I just got a call from Admiral Sweat's Chief of Staff. Later this afternoon, after I fly, I get to go tell the Admiral how it is one of my loudmouth Lieutenants showed up at his wardroom unannounced, to tell the Admiral that we should launch an attack on somebody, and if not that, to at least notify the Secretary of Defense and Congress, if not the President, that the nuclear aircraft carrier *Washington* is in fact in the eastern Mediterranean and ready to attack whoever they want us to." His brown eyes bored into Woods. "That about sum it up?"

Woods tossed his black government-issue ballpoint pen down. He answered in a voice equally intense. "I was pissed, Skipper. Everybody is taking this too lightly . . ."

"Wrong!" Bark exploded, drawing looks from everyone in the ready room. He lowered his voice again. "You have no idea what anyone is doing! You've got a chip on your shoulder. We're *all* pissed. We all would love nothing better than to hit back. But you know how these things go. The people who commit these acts are usually killed. Then it becomes real sticky. If the politicos want to go after the bad guys, they have two choices. To use the military—"

"We *never* go after the bad guys, Skipper! We just tool around the Med boring holes in the sky and worrying about our next port call! We never hit terrorists. Even when we know who they are, and where they are! We might send a Tomahawk somewhere, but the most powerful country in the world just *whines* about it!"

"You can't just go after a terr—"

"Why not?" Woods argued, energized by the chance to talk about it. "Why can't we go after them? It's not like we don't know who they are. They sent a communiqué to the press, saying how happy they are that they got to kill an American in their attack! It was a big bonus for them. We should take them at their word and make them pay for it."

"We can't just take revenge against them."

"I'm not talking about taking revenge, Skipper. We have the biggest military in the world and we let these two-bit terrorists murder us or hold us hostage, and we sit around and wring our hands wondering what to do. Well, I know what to do. We know who they are and where they live. We ought to go knock the shit out of them. And we have the ability to do it right here on this ship."

"It doesn't work that way. I'm sure if the government wants to go after the terrorists, they'll send the CIA after them. There are a lot of things that happen that you and I never hear about. We need to leave it to—"

"The CIA? The *CIA*? You've got to be kidding me, Skipper," Woods said, barely holding back a smirk. "Those guys? Send some guy in with a handgun to get some terrorist mastermind? He wouldn't have a chance. We've got to hit them, and hit them hard. So they know it'll cost them if they attack Americans."

"They weren't attacking Americans, Trey," Bark replied. "They had no way of knowing there was an American on that bus. They thought—"

"Come on, Skipper! They had to know he was an American! How do we know they weren't there because of him?"

Bark stood up quickly. "That's it, Trey. I've had enough. I came here to talk to you about going to the Admiral without my knowledge. That reflects poorly on the squadron." His voice was loud enough for everyone in the ready room to hear now. "I was prepared to write that off as a lapse in judgment. But I think your head is full of bad judgment right now." He pointed to Woods's chest. "You're grounded. From right now until when I say, you're off the flight schedule. You're the SDO for life until I say so. You got that?"

Woods stood up, looking at his Commanding Officer in stunned disbelief. He didn't know what to say.

"Easy!" Bark yelled to the front of the ready room. "You're relieved as SDO. Woods will take your place. Write yourself into the flight schedule."

Easy looked at Bark with big eyes. Lieutenant Junior Grade Craig Easley was a junior RIO in the squadron. It was his first cruise. He had never seen a Commanding Officer on the warpath before. "Yes, sir," he said quietly.

Bark turned from Woods and strode quickly to the front of the ready room. He picked up the papers on his seat and moved toward the door.

Woods yelled from the back of the room, "You can't do this!"

Bark stopped where he was and turned, saying softly but clearly, "You may think you're immune from Captain's mast or court-martial. You're not. You're already over the line. Don't *push* it," he said as he walked out.

Woods moved slowly to the SDO's desk and sat in the chair recently vacated by Easy. He slid down until his head rested against the back of the chair, staring at the cables coursing through the overhead.

The phone on the desk rang. Woods let it ring. After six rings he reluctantly leaned forward and picked it up. "Ready Room Eight, Lieutenant Woods speaking, sir."

"This is Captain Clark. Chief of Staff. Is your Commanding Officer there, Lieutenant," he asked, saying "lieutenant" as if it made him sick.

"No, sir," Woods replied with no attempt at being helpful.

"Would you please find him, Lieutenant, and inform him that his appearance before the Admiral has been moved up. He will now be here at 1300. Is that clear?"

"Yes, sir. Crystal clear, sir—1300, sir. I'll tell him, sir," Woods said sarcastically, gripping the phone hard. The phone line went dead. Woods slammed down the phone, picked up a ballpoint lying on the desk, and made a note of the call on a pad of white paper.

"I am *impressed*," said Lieutenant Big McMack, who had been sitting in the chair closest to the SDO with his feet up on the safe. He hadn't moved since Woods got there. Woods hadn't even noticed him. "I can't remember when I've seen a junior officer anger so many senior officers. Nice work, Trey."

Woods looked at Big with contempt. "Up yours, Big. I'm not ready for any of your sarcastic shit right now."

"Now going after friends and peers, soon to be ridiculing strangers, women, and children."

"Did I ask for your commentary?" Woods said.

"No."

"Then keep it to yourself."

"Can't. It's like poetry. It just flows. The real tragedy for the rest of the world is that I don't have sycophants following me around writing down every word to pass my wisdom and humor to succeeding generations."

Woods gave half a smile and a begrudging snort. Then he looked at Big. "What the hell is a sycophant?"

"Sorry. No clues. You only learn new words by looking them up. If I told you, you wouldn't remember and then the next time I used the word brilliantly, you wouldn't understand it then either, again missing the moment."

"You an English major or something?"

"We've been together so long, and still you don't know me."

"What are you talking about?"

"Sorry. Another allusion. No I wasn't an English major, Trey. I am one of those rare species—a drama major, now flying for the greater good in the world's best fighters."

"Drama?" Woods said incredulously. "*Drama?*"

"That's right. Thespian. Actor extraordinaire. Writer of dramatic works, performer of the Bard, wizard of special effects on the stage."

"How did you end up here?"

"I went to college on an NROTC scholarship. That which all you Canoe U grads *wish* you had done in retrospect."

"Why do you say that?"

"Because we went to accredited colleges that had numerous women and real football and basketball. And we only had to play Navy one day a week, and we could major in things like drama."

"I thought you had to be a hard science major."

"Nope. Most do, but there's room for guys like me, with talent in so many areas. As long as we take physics, math, and the other extraneous crap that allows the Navy brass to think we're truly just misguided science majors, we can still get a full scholarship and graduate with the rest of you pinheads, only senior to you in lineal numbers, because they throw us *all* into a pool, distinguished only by grade average. And our grades are *always* better than you chumps at the boat school."

"We'll see who makes Admiral," Woods said defensively.

"You can have it. I'm going to make my fortune as a screenwriter after this gig."

"Right," Woods said, rolling his eyes. His mind was still dwelling on his sentence of death, his grounding. "Did you hear what the Skipper said to me?" he asked.

Big sat up in his chair. "I think everybody on the ship heard the last part, but I heard the whole thing, being nosy and all."

Woods looked at Big's face, trying to read him. "Was I out of line?" he asked, finally.

"Way."

"Why?"

"You said things you shouldn't have said. You challenged him, the ship, the entire political system. You could have said all that to me, but not to him, not here, not like that."

"Don't you agree?" asked Woods. "Don't you think we should do something about Vialli and not just sit around?"

"Absolutely. I'd like nothing better. But there are the right ways to approach things and the wrong ways. Going to see the Admiral was stupid. Did you really figure that because some Lieutenant comes barging in the Admiral's going to say, 'Okay, you got me. Let's launch an attack?' he asked, raising his hands in exasperation. "Without authorization?"

"I thought I'd get him to think about it. Maybe pass something up the chain of command."

Big waved his hand in dismissal. He put his large feet on the deck. "You're amazing. You're one of the coolest customers I've ever seen in the air. You never get rattled. The tougher the situation, the calmer you get, like you feed on the pressure. But down here, on terra firma, or aqua firma if I may mix my metaphors, you go *loony*. You attack the Admiral in front of his whole staff, put him on the spot without going to the Skipper, making him look like puppy ca-ca in front of the world, then when the Skipper reads you out about it, you challenge *him!*"

"I'm just thinking of Boomer," Woods said.

"Boomer's dead, Trey. You've got to start dealing with reality again soon or you'll end up like him. You're going to lose your concentration in the middle of a strafing run or something and prang yourself."

Woods sighed. "I just can't let him down. I'm going to get that Sheikh guy. One way or another . . ."

"You're not letting him down. He couldn't ask for any more."

"I don't know, Big." The speaker box behind him that was tied to the radio frequency used by pilots when landing aboard the carrier crackled to life as the Landing Signal Officer transmitted to the F-14 on final. "*Power!*" he said with authority. "*Power!*"

Woods and Big both quickly looked at the small black and white television in the corner behind Woods. It was the PLAT, the Pilot Landing Assistance Television. The camera was in the middle of the flight deck and directly below it. The lens pointed out through a very small, almost imperceptible window in the middle of the flight deck and looked up at the approaching planes. The crosshairs represented the glide slope. It was the view from the camera with the crosshairs that Woods and Big saw when they looked at the F-14 in its final approach to the flight deck. It was well below the center of the crosshairs. *"Power!"* the LSO yelled, his voice augmented by the sound of the approaching jet in his microphone. *"Wave off! Wave off!"* the LSO screamed as the F-14 went to full power trying to stop its rate of descent, finally leveling off at the same attitude, the same angle of attack, and flying twenty feet over the arresting gear.

"Geez, nice pass. Who the hell was that?" Big said.

"XO," Woods said, shaking his head.

"204, say your state," the Air Boss transmitted.

"3.9," replied Lieutenant Junior Grade Bill Parks, the XO's RIO, whom everyone called Brillo because of his wavy, kinky hair.

"Great," Big said. "What's Bingo today?" The fuel level at which the ship sent you to the nearest airfield instead of coming aboard the carrier.

"3.5," Woods replied.

"Where's the Bingo field?"

"Crete."

"One more pass, then it's tank or consequences," Big said.

"They're tanking him now," Woods said, listening to the radio chatter.

"How'd the XO get so low on gas on his first pass?" Big asked.

"I don't know. That's a question he was undoubtedly hoping to avoid. Probably trying to show some junior officer the intricacies of air combat. Something he doesn't know much about."

"Not everyone can be a Topgun instructor like you, big shot."

"Spare me," Woods said. His face clouded again. "I still think I'm letting Vialli down if I just let this go. If I let American politics take its course and do nothing, like we always do . . ."

"I don't know that it's fair to say we do *nothing*. I mean when President Carter faced the hostage crisis in Iran he waited with great intensity nigh on four hundred days. He wrung his hands effectively, and overall did an admirable job of worrying and sweating. How can you say we did nothing? And then at the end, he launched that fiasco in the desert and tried to control it from the White House. Why, never a prettier bit of 'doing something' have I ever seen. And Clinton, Car-

ter's modern protégé in the looking tough and doing nothing department, specialized in mechanical strikes by Tomahawks and invisible
stealth jet bombers. Wouldn't want to actually risk a human being. Of
course what would you expect from someone who fought like hell to
stay out of the evil military. Now as to George Bush—"

"We should do something like Entebbe, like the Israelis did."

Big shook his head and scratched his scalp. "I hate to break it to
you, Trey, but there aren't any hostages here. They did all the killing
they wanted to. And as to retaliation, you can rest assured the Israelis
will do plenty of that. Probably already have."

"It doesn't count. It's not from us. The world will still think they
can kill Americans and it won't matter. We won't do anything about
it."

"I think you need to think about something else for a while. If you
ever hope to fly again and get unchained from this desk, you'd better
start acting normal."

"You still like living in your stateroom?" Woods asked.

"What kind of a question is that? Am I being evicted? Is the land-
lord from the second deck going to come and lock me out for failing
to pay my mess bill on time?"

"No, I was just wondering—"

"*Victory 204, Tomcat ball, 4.8,*" Brillo transmitted.

"XO's on the ball again," Big said, looking over Woods's shoulder.

Woods turned around to watch the television image. The XO was
in the middle of the screen and holding the crosshairs steady as he
descended toward the deck. Woods and Big could see the horizontal
tails moving quickly to correct for minor changes in pitch and roll. The
black smoke was barely perceptible on either side of the dangling tailhook as the XO changed power to maintain his perfect rate of descent
and accommodate for minor changes in wind direction and strength.
He crossed the ramp and held his exact attitude and power setting
until the Tomcat slammed into the deck at a five hundred feet per
minute rate of descent and the tailhook grabbed the number-two wire.
The nose of the plane pressed into the deck and the XO went to full
power as he felt his wheels touch the flight deck. The Tomcat rolled
down the deck and strained against the arresting wire until it was clear
that the wire had won the tug-of-war. The XO reduced power and the
hook came loose from the wire. He taxied away from the landing area
to the bow of the carrier as he swept the fighter's wings behind him.

"Decent pass," Big said.

"Good enough," Woods replied. "I was thinking maybe you'd like to take Tony's spot in my stateroom."

Big considered the offer. "I don't know, Trey. This is so sudden," he said, smiling.

"Well, think about it."

"Isn't there someone more senior who would want it? I'm only a frocked Lieutenant. I won't start getting paid for it for a few months."

"Vialli was a JG."

"I never did understand how he scammed a spot in a two-man stateroom when he was a nugget and a mere JG."

"Sedge was supposed to take it, but he decided he wanted to sleep in the four-man. He hated being right under the catapult at the water break. Every time the cat went off after he went to bed, which was just about every night, he used to sit up like he'd been shot when the catapult hit the water break," said Woods, laughing as he recalled Sedge's reaction. "You get zero warning. We're at the end of cat three, and you can't hear it coming. All you hear is this 'BAAAM,' when the piston hits the water break. I don't even hear it anymore, but Sedge couldn't get used to it. So when Vialli came, he took Sedge's place."

"I could probably handle that," Big said. "I'm under cat two right now . . ."

"Plus there's Bernie the Breather."

"Who's that?" Big asked, his face full of concern. He didn't like there being problems with anyone, especially someone who called himself a "breather."

Woods laughed to himself. He lowered his voice. "There's this pipe that hangs down into our stateroom out of the overhead," he said, holding his fingers together to indicate a pipe of three inches in diameter. "It stops about three feet from the deck. Just hanging there. It's between our bunk beds—our racks—and the bulkhead." Woods got a twinkle in his eye. "And sometimes, not all the time, but sometimes, it makes this breathing noise. There's a valve somewhere inside it, not at the end—the end is open and pointing down at the deck— but somewhere in the lower three feet, there is a flapper valve. And the pipe breathes in, a kind of 'guuushhhh,' as it breathes in, then a 'cuh cuh cuh,' as the flapper flaps down," he said, using his hand as a valve flapping against an invisible opening in a pipe. "Guush, cuh cuh cuh. It's stealing air out of our stateroom," he said, raising his eyebrows twice and smiling mischievously. "Or, maybe, it's putting air into our stateroom. Either way, we can't figure out why, or where the pipe is going."

Big looked at him skeptically. "You're pulling my leg," he said.

"Nope. I'm not. You'll have to see it. I just wanted you to know about it so you didn't move in and then whine about it. Sedge about went nuts between the water break and Bernie."

"Sounds weird."

"It's a great stateroom. It's not like those other boring staterooms that only have regular deafening noises; we have the regular deafening noises, but we have the unique noises too."

"Okay. I'm in," Big said, shrugging. "How could I not be?"

12

Pritch searched under her seat in the ready room for something. Bark watched her struggle. "Need some help?"

She looked up. "No, sir. Thanks. Just looking for my notepad."

Bark sat down and studied the message board. Suddenly Pritch sat down next to him. "Sir," she said, "can I ask you something?"

He looked at her skeptically. "You don't like going to sea and you want to go home?"

"No, sir, nothing like that. I may be off base, so let me know if I shouldn't be asking."

He frowned in expectation. "What?"

"It's about Trey."

"What about him?"

She didn't know how to begin. "He's . . . I don't know. So upset about Boomer. I understand being upset, everyone is. But Trey is over the top. He seems so intense about it. Angry. At the government. What's going on with him?"

"You *are* off base."

"I'm sorry—"

"No, it's okay. We're like a family. We see each other every day, and we wonder what's going on with someone if they're acting odd. Well, he is. And I know it. And I've taken steps to reel him back in. We'll see."

"What's it about? Anything more than meets the eye?"

Bark lowered his voice. "I take it he's never shown you the notebook."

"Notebook?" she asked. "What notebook?"

"Pan Am Flight 103."

"What about it?"

"He has a notebook with every scrap of news or evidence or spec-ulation in it. News reports, book excerpts, photographs, his own notes trying to figure it out, you name it."

"Why?"

"He wants to know what happened, and why the U.S. didn't do anything about it. He's got all kinds of theories—"

"Like what?"

Bark thought. "Oh, I don't know. It's been a long time since I got the speech. He doesn't talk about it much. He's afraid people will take him for a fanatic or something, like one of those people who've ob-sessed about the Kennedy assassination for decades."

"Is he obsessing?"

"Probably."

"What theories?"

"Oh, let's see. I remember he said that the Libyan thing might be a red herring. Israel started planting stories about Libya being respon-sible hours after it happened, and the press swallowed it. Some group. L-A-T, or something—"

"LAP?"

"Yeah, I think so—"

"That's Israeli. Department of Psychological Warfare."

"How do you know *that*?"

"I just do."

"If you say so. Anyway, they started accusing Libya—calling jour-nalists all over the world to plant the story—then spread rumors Sy-ria and Iran were involved, and then that Iran did it as revenge for the shoot-down of the Iranian airliner by the USS *Vincennes* a few months earlier. But then it gets real complex. He loses me, but he says there was some illegal CIA group dealing drugs in the Middle East, and it was tied in to the Iran-Contra thing for funding the Contras, and that that group was on board the plane. They were called KOREA, or something like that. No, COREA, that's it. And there was an American Army hostage rescue team on board that had been in the Middle East and one of the guy's suitcases disappeared from the accident scene and was suddenly returned empty. That the COREA group had been tipped off by German intelligence that a bomb was aboard the plane, but didn't do anything about it . . . I can't remember it. I couldn't really follow it when he was telling me about it."

"He has information on all that?"

"Oh, yeah, and more. He has stuff from the attorney who represented Pan Am in all the suits from the accident. Trey wrote to him. The attorney got on the scent of all this stuff about the cause of the accident and subpoenaed the CIA, the FBI, the FAA, the NSC, and NSA. The government wouldn't give him anything. Claimed it invaded national security."

"Seriously?"

"Yep. It's all very mysterious. Then those two Libyans were sent to trial in Scotland for the thing. He just scoffs at all that. The thing that really got him though was reading in some book that Israel sent one of its Mossad case officers from London—"

"A Katsa?"

"I don't know what they're called, anyway, sent him to Lockerbie hours after the crash. Why would you send an intelligence agent to the site of an airplane crash?"

"I don't know."

"Anyway, he's got a lot of skepticism. He distrusts the Israelis, the CIA, and the general approach of the U.S. to terrorism. He thinks it's all a game to them."

"Incredible," Pritch said. "Why does he care so much about Pan Am 103?"

"His father was on it."

Pritch gasped. "Truly?"

"Yeah. He was in London on business. Coming home for Christmas."

"That must have killed Trey."

"He was sixteen."

"I had no idea." She sat quietly. "Does everyone in the squadron know this?"

"A few."

"Thanks for telling me. I wish I could help him somehow."

"There's nothing anyone can do. He's a big boy now. He just has to deal with it."

As soon as Woods turned on the overhead light Lieutenant Big McMack rolled over in his rack and pulled the Navy gray wool blanket over his large head. "What are you doing?" he asked, offended.

"Getting dressed," Woods replied. "What do you think I'm doing?"

"Do you have to do it with the overhead light on?"

"It's six-thirty, Big. Time for all good Navy pilots to be out of the rack. Didn't they teach you that as a Golden Bear Cub in Junior NROTC at UCLA?"

"I didn't get in until one this morning when you were getting your academy-puke beauty sleep."

"What can I say?" Woods replied, lacing up his black leather flying boots. "I was in HAQ for three long days, but now I'm back in the good graces of the Skipper, I'm back on the flight schedule, and I've got the second brief this morning. Not the first brief mind you, not the one that would have required that I be there at 0630; no, I've got the brief for the second event, which briefs at 0800. Which has allowed me to take a shower, to go now and get some breakfast—a five-egg omelet with bacon, ham, and cheese should do it—and then I'll stroll down to the ready room and brief for a hop in which I will intercept numerous Air Farce F-15Es trying to sink our home and get our stereos wet, and properly kick their asses." He stood up and looked at Big's general outline underneath his blanket. "Who wrote this *incredible* flight schedule?"

"You're making me sick," Big replied.

"Well, I'm off. Don't wait up," Woods said as he opened the steel door to the passageway. "Do you want me to turn out the light?" he asked. He answered his own question before Big could. "Nah, you're getting up anyway," he said, closing the door and leaving the light on.

"Trey!" Big yelled helplessly.

Woods stood outside the door for five seconds, then reached in and turned off the light before locking it behind him.

☙

Woods and Wink walked out to their airplane at 0830. It was as clear and beautiful a day as either could remember. Blue everywhere, the sparkling ocean, and the crystal clear sky, divided only by the razor-thin horizon that was visible only because of the color difference between the water and the sky.

They handed their helmet bags and knee boards to Airman Benson and stared at the ocean. Woods noticed that Wink was looking up. "What you got?"

"Intercept of an F-15," Wink replied, pointing and smiling.

Woods saw them immediately. He could hear the distinctive sound of the Tomcat's engines. "The sound of freedom! I *love* it!" The F-15 was heading straight for the ship and descending on the way. It was about three miles out and hard to see. Woods saw the F-14 to its right running an intercept on the F-15.

"Who's up?" Wink asked.

"XO and Brillo," Woods replied, naming the crew he had written into the flight schedule last night for the first hop of the day.

They watched as the F-14 lowered its nose to cut across the circle and get to the F-15 before he reached the ship. "He's doing a low yo-yo," Wink observed.

"He's a little low to try that."

They stood in their flight gear and watched the F-14 approach the F-15. Others on the flight deck were staring. It was rare for them to see an F-14 flying that fast after another airplane so close to the carrier. The sky was completely clear except for the two fighters.

The F-14's nose continued to drop toward the ocean.

"He must be doing five hundred knots," Woods remarked, growing increasingly uncomfortable with the steepness of the F-14's dive.

"At least."

"He's going to be in some deep shit if he doesn't pull up," Wink said, watching with building terror.

The F-15 was within a mile of the carrier and continuing to increase speed and move lower toward the ocean. The Tomcat's nose continued down and was now pointed directly at the water a thousand feet above the carrier and right in front of it.

"He doesn't know where he is!" Woods exclaimed; he and everyone else on the flight deck knew what the Tomcat pilot didn't.

"Pull up!" Wink screamed.

"Get out! Get out!" Woods joined in, watching helplessly.

Others on the flight deck were yelling futile instructions at the Tomcat.

The F-14 couldn't hear them. It made the sound of a breaking baseball bat as it plunged straight into the sea at six hundred knots and vanished beneath the surface.

Woods and Wink dashed madly to the bow of the carrier as the Captain tried to stop the *Washington*'s forward momentum.

The F-15 screamed overhead and banked to see the point of impact in the water. The Eagle pilot pulled up and headed back to Italy.

The sea boiled with white foam from air and jet fuel and energy where the Tomcat had just buried itself. Woods could feel the deck of the carrier shuddering as the enormous screws reversed themselves to slow the ninety-five-thousand-ton behemoth to a stop. Woods and Wink searched the water for any sign of life or of hope. All they saw were small pieces of honeycombed airplane parts floating quietly to the surface.

"They bought it," Wink said.

Woods nodded, fighting back the desire to scream, or throw up, or quit flying. "Let's go tell the Skipper," he said. They found the nearest ladder down to the 03 level from the flight deck and worked their way back quickly to the ready room. Word had somehow already spread through the ship. All the sailors in the passageway could tell the officers needed to get by and made a hole allowing them to pass.

They turned into Ready Room Eight. They knew by the long faces that word of what had happened had preceded them.

Woods looked at Bark. "The XO?"

Bark nodded, his face dark with sadness. "I need you to head up the on-scene accident investigation team."

"Yes, sir," Woods replied automatically.

"There's a helo turning on deck. It'll take you over to the *David Reynolds.* They have a motor whaleboat in the water. They're waiting for you. Recover what you can. Check for signs of malfunction or fire."

"Yes, sir," Woods said.

"Any questions?"

Woods spoke quietly. "There wasn't any fire, sir. They just flew into the water. I saw it."

"I know. We're just going to do this by the numbers. . . . How am I going to tell his wife? Three daughters."

Woods put his helmet on a chair, then wondered where his knee board was. Still in the plane, he recalled. Then what Bark had just said hit him. He remembered the XO's daughters. They had come to the last squadron party before their father left on cruise. "How old?"

"Eight, ten, and twelve."

Woods hated the senselessness of it. "It's not worth it." His frustration boiled over. "What are we doing out here, Skipper?"

Bark thought about it. "Brillo. All he wanted was to get married and have a family. Never even got the chance. He didn't even have a girlfriend." He forcibly shifted his focus. "Get up to the flight deck."

"Aye aye, sir." Woods walked quickly out of the ready room and hurried down the passageway to his stateroom, grabbing his flight jacket. He slipped it on while running toward the island and the waiting helicopter. He reached the office on the flight deck and looked around for the transportation officer.

A First Class Petty Officer approached. "You the one going to the *David Reynolds,* sir?" At Woods's nod, he handed him a cranial helmet and flotation rest and opened the hatch to the flight deck.

"Follow me, sir," he said.

Woods walked quickly after the man, heading for the SH-60, which was on the aft-most helo spot. Its rotors were turning.

The *Washington* was dead in the water, trying to stay as close to the accident scene as it could, hoping to find at least one of the crew alive. But everyone knew they were dead. The Tomcat had plunged into the ocean like a lawn dart less than a mile in front of the carrier. Everyone on the flight deck had seen it.

The sea and sky were still bright blue. There were no clouds or whitecaps in sight. The helicopter's turning blades and screaming jet engines were the only noises on the deck.

Woods stepped through the cargo door of the helicopter and grabbed the arm of the crew chief, who hauled him in effortlessly pointed to a forward-facing seat and instructing him to secure himself by the straps. The helicopter lifted off into a low hover, steadied itself, and flew off toward the west at two hundred feet.

The flight to the destroyer took less than ten minutes. Woods saw the small flight deck on the fantail of the ship and wondered if the pilot was going to set down or just dump him out somehow. He watched as they slid sideways until they were directly over the flight deck of the ship, the helicopter inching down carefully until it was hovering three feet above the flight deck. The crew chief motioned Woods to the hatch and held his arm across the opening while he watched the deck. A cord from his helmet was plugged into the bulkhead of the helicopter so he could talk to the pilots on the Internal Communication System and listen to the radio talk. He waited, pointed for Woods to sit down on the deck of the plane, and then jump down to the ship.

Woods sat and jumped the three feet to the deck, where he was immediately met by two of the ship's crew. He followed them forward as the deafening helicopter lifted away from the destroyer.

He climbed the ladder to the next deck, looking around for any signs of the wreckage on the water. It was finally quiet, the SH-60 heading back toward the carrier. A commander approached Woods and extended his hand.

"Good morning, Lieutenant. I'm Commander Bill LaGrou, the Commanding Officer. Welcome aboard the *David Reynolds*." He was accompanied by another Commander, and two Lieutenants. "This is Gary Carlton, my XO."

"Thank you, Captain," Woods said, evaluating him. His ball cap, with the name of his ship on it and gold braid on the bill, was pulled down almost to his eyebrows. Shorter than Woods, he had to turn his head up substantially to look into Woods's eyes. His hair was completely gray, almost white, and his belly strained against the web belt holding up his khaki trousers. His brown eyes searched Woods's face.

"I don't want you to waste any time. You've got to get to the accident scene right away," LaGrou said, pulling his eyes away from Woods to look toward the port side of the ship. "The motor whaleboat is ready to go. I'm not really sure what you need, but I've got a good coxswain, our corpsman, and three boatswains to go with you. If you want anything else, let me know."

"Yes, sir, sure will. Is there a radio? Some way to contact you?"

"Oh, yeah, we'll make sure you take the handheld. They told me you're supposed to bring any major wreckage you can recover back to the ship, so we can carry it to Sicily where some accident types are going to look at it."

"Yes, sir."

"And if you find anything from the pilots, the corpsman has a body bag—"

"Okay. Fine."

LaGrou hesitated. "We were supposed to drive to the point of entry, which is right"—LaGrou looked around—"over there," he said pointing to a spot aft of the ship and a few hundred yards off the port side, "and stay there. When we got here we saw some debris. We held our position but the currents and waves have moved the wreckage away from here, probably a mile or so by now. It's probably over there," he said, pointing past the bow on the port side. He lowered his voice. "Those guys from your squadron?"

"Yes, sir."

"Inexperienced?"

"No, sir. Our XO and a very good, although young, RIO."

LaGrou looked shocked, then scanned the sky. "What could have happened on a beautiful day like today?"

"That's what we're going to try to find out. I'd better get at it."

LaGrou nodded and scratched his pale face. "They just flew into the water, going straight down. They must have been going five hundred knots." He looked at Woods again.

"Yes, sir, I saw it."

"Well. Then you know how fast they were going. What would you estimate?"

"Probably about that. Maybe six hundred."

LaGrou shook his head. "I guess when it's your time, it's your time."

Woods looked into LaGrou's face. "What do you mean?"

LaGrou immediately saw that his words had carried more meaning than he had intended. "Oh, nothing, really. Just a figure of speech," he said, shrugging. "If we're scheduled to check out today, or tomorrow, there's not much we can do about it."

"I think if these guys had been paying attention, they wouldn't have bought it."

LaGrou squinted at Woods. "I'm sure you're right.... Let me know if you need anything, Lieutenant," he said again.

"Will do, sir." A First Class Boatswain's Mate indicated that Woods was to follow him. "This way, sir. We're ready to go." He hurried down a ladder and then another, finally descending the Jacob's ladder on the side of the destroyer to the motor whaleboat. Woods was right behind him.

"Good morning, sir," said the coxswain standing in the rear of the boat. "You ready?"

"Yep. I'm Lieutenant Woods," he said. "Let's get underway, and we can talk about what we're going to do as we head out there."

"Roger that," said the coxswain, increasing power on the diesel motor as one of the boatswain's mates cast off from the destroyer. Half the ship's company was on deck looking on curiously.

Woods sat back against the side of the boat, air moving across his face as they worked away from the ship. "Where's the wreckage?" Woods asked.

"Out about 310, sir," the Coxswain replied, pushing the tiller slightly away from him. "I don't see it right now, but I'm sure we will soon."

Woods couldn't think of what else to say. He knew he had to move quickly and speak with authority as if he knew what he was doing to give them confidence in him; but in reality, he had no idea how to proceed. He had never had any training in accident investigations. He hadn't even been briefed on what he was to look for other than signs of fire—charred bits of airplane, he guessed. He concluded this was simply one of those times when someone had to do something or everyone would feel more helpless than they already did. That instinct to "do something" seemed to dominate the thinking after someone has died. Sometimes knowing why or how something happened made the fact less painful, especially if blame could be placed on some mechanical defect or malfunction. Then you wouldn't have to believe your shipmate screwed up. Whatever the reason, he had to do something to make this effort worthwhile.

"There it is, sir!" one of the boatswain's mates in the bow cried out, leaning forward like a harpoonist. He pointed toward the starboard side and the coxswain steered in that direction. Woods stood up carefully and looked where the boatswain was pointing. Squinting, he covered his eyes to get a better look. He saw two dark shapes jutting out of the water, floating. Instinctively, he put his hand out to get the coxswain to slow down. The boat slowed to a crawl as they entered the area where the remains of the F-14 were. They approached the two shapes cautiously, not knowing what they were looking at or whether more might be floating under water, unseen. The coxswain turned toward the two shapes and slowed even more, to two knots. They were within one hundred yards before Woods recognized the shapes as the twin tails of the Tomcat, floating perfectly upright in the sea like shark's fins. The air and water moved quietly around the tails, touching them ever so slightly.

The coxswain inched the boat forward until he was right next to the black monsters. The boatswain in the bow grabbed the rudder of the starboard tail and pulled the boat to it. Woods moved forward and stared.

Small pieces of honeycombed metal—all sizes and shapes—floated around the tails. Woods was surprised by how intact the tails were, the white skull and crossbones staring back at them defiantly from the middle of each tail. He peered into the blue water underneath the tails for more of the airplane, but the way they were bobbing meant there wasn't much attached below the surface.

There was something odd about the top of the left tail where the red anticollision light should have been. Woods walked aft in the boat and examined the light, holding his hand over his eyes to block the sun and squinting slightly to focus. "What in the world . . ." Woods said out loud.

The corpsman stood up next to him and looked where Woods's eyes were focused. He stared for a few seconds, then said, "It's a scalp."

Woods lowered his hand, fighting the nausea in his stomach. "What?"

"It's a scalp, sir. Sure as hell," the corpsman said.

Woods raised his eyes and examined the light once more. It was Brillo's scalp, all right, sitting on the anticollision light just as if it were sitting on Brillo's head. He recognized the uncontrollable wiry brown hair. The horrific image was searing itself into his brain and he turned his eyes away. "How could his *scalp* be on the tail?" he asked.

The corpsman replied, "He stopped before the tail did. Took him clean out of his helmet. Shitty way to go. At least it was fast." The corpsman sat down quickly and pulled something out from under his seat. A body bag. He unzipped it and stood up again by the port side. "Slow down," he said to the coxswain, who couldn't have been going more than one knot. The corpsman leaned over the side.

Woods saw a large white piece of meat floating next to the boat, undulating gently and heading for them. "What is that?" Woods asked, not wanting to know.

"A back," the corpsman said matter-of-factly. "See the indentation for the spine?"

Woods felt his mind at work again, searing this new image into his memory. He couldn't stop it.

The corpsman reached down and picked up the flesh with his latex-glove-covered hand and hauled it into the boat. He put the back into the body bag and zipped it partway up. He held it at the top in his fist, like a trash bag with potting soil in the bottom. "Here comes some more," the corpsman announced. "Help me out here," he ordered.

Woods looked the other way, pretending to be interested in various pieces of wreckage until the body collection was completed.

After much effort and boatswain cursing they secured the tails to the boat as well as they could. The boat headed slowly toward the destroyer, towing the tails behind it.

Commander LaGrou was waiting when Woods came up the ladder. "How'd it go, Lieutenant?" he asked anxiously.

Woods couldn't say anything. The images tore through his brain.

"Any signs of what caused it?"

Woods shook his head and forced his mouth into an inverted crescent, as if he had no real expectation of finding anything that would give a reason for the crash.

"We'll have to detach soon and head for Sicily—they're going to set up an accident wreckage inspection sight at Sigonella."

Woods nodded absently, barely hearing the Commander.

"The bad news for you, Lieutenant," LaGrou said, "is that the helo that was supposed to pick you up would have had to get you five minutes ago to work you into the air plan." LaGrou waited for some reaction. Seeing none he continued, "So, you'll be with us until tomorrow morning at 0700. They'll send a helo back to retrieve you. You can sleep in my in-port cabin. It's very comfortable."

"Thanks," Woods said absently.

"No problem. I'm sure the wardroom will treat you very nicely. I think you'll enjoy your stay."

"Thank you, sir, I appreciate it."

The wardroom did treat him nicely. The men were even deferential. They weren't sure how to console Woods over the loss of two of his squadron mates. They wanted to ask the questions that would tell them how close he'd been to the dead men so they could know exactly how bad he was feeling, but they didn't want to be morose. So they avoided the questions, and didn't know how deeply he was affected. They all knew about the scalp though. Everybody on the ship knew about the scalp. It was one of those details that was too good not to tell someone else about, usually starting with "Can you believe it?" to set the tone of disgust and amazement.

Woods excused himself from the wardroom early, skipping the movie and free popcorn in spite of the guarantee that it was just what he needed. He went to the Captain's in-port cabin and sat on the rack. He was exhausted. He pulled his flight suit down around his waist and washed his face in the steel sink. He looked as tired as he felt. He took off his flight boots and flight suit and lay on the top of the Navy blanket in his boxers and T-shirt. The ship was moving too much for him to sleep on his side. He stared at the overhead that he couldn't see in the blackness and thought of the XO and his three beautiful daughters. All blond with curly hair. He wondered if they knew about their father yet.

Suddenly there was a quiet knock on the door. He wasn't sure he had even heard it. There it was again. "Yes?" he said loudly.

"Commander LaGrou."

He swung his legs over and pulled his flight suit on quickly. He crossed to the door in his stocking feet and opened it. "Yes, sir?"

"Mind if I come in?" LaGrou asked.

"No, sir," he lied, turning on the light.

LaGrou closed the door behind him. "Didn't mean to disturb you. I was afraid you'd be asleep."

"No, sir, just resting a little. Kind of hard to sleep."

"I'm sure," LaGrou said. He stood awkwardly. "I . . . I just wanted to make sure you're okay. They were your friends."

Woods didn't want to talk about it. Talk wasn't going to do anything. "Yeah. Yes, sir."

"Look, these things happen. People are killed every day in the Navy, just doing their jobs—"

Woods had heard that enough. "And *why*? Not why did he crash—we'll figure that out—but why are we here where he *could* crash? Why do we fly off carriers every day?"

"It's what we do—"

"So we're *ready* when we need to use force. So we stay sharp—" He stopped. "Do you have a chart that shows our position?"

LaGrou was taken aback by Woods's intensity. "Sure, in Combat—"

"I want to show you something," Woods said as he quickly sat down on the single chair in the stateroom and pulled on his flight boots. He laced them halfway, wrapped the laces around the ankles, and tied them hurriedly. "Show me."

LaGrou opened the door and headed down the passageway. Woods followed. They walked into Combat Information Center, the nerve center of the ship. It was almost completely dark. Three large screens were in front of several consoles, where officers and enlisted men sat, monitoring the huge volume of information that flooded in from innumerable sources.

"Over here," LaGrou said. They crossed to a large flat table that had a chart on top of it. "I have our navigator keep a paper chart with our position just in case all the electronics crap out at the same time," LaGrou smiled.

Woods studied it quickly. He saw the mark that showed their current position. He spread his hand out along a longitude line, then used it to measure their distance to Lebanon. "Two hundred nautical miles to Beirut," he said. He stared at LaGrou. "Two hundred miles."

"I'm not following you, Lieutenant."

"That Sheikh who killed Tony Vialli, my best friend, is eating grapes in Beirut while we're out here, two hundred miles away, picking up the pieces of two others. What were they doing? Trying to stay sharp. To stay ready. For what?" he said, raising his voice. He stared at the chart. "We keep sharpening our sword, showing everybody how sharp and shiny it is. We use it sometimes. Kosovo? Sure. Iraq? Sure. For an American Naval officer murdered by a terrorist?" He could see LaGrou was trying to control his surprise. "I guess not. We just sharpen our sword, and cut ourselves with it."

13

Kinkaid had been alarmed by Ricketts's call in the middle of the night. Most of the alarm though came from the fact that Kinkaid had complete faith in Ricketts's judgment. If he called in the middle of the night, it was for a reason. He was wily, brilliant, a master of languages and disguises, and someone who never failed in a mission. But there was a dark side as well—no respect for authority. He was known to think that those not in the Directorate of Operations, the DO, were just weak-tit parasites. He was unimpressed with electronic intelligence and "analysis," a word he used only when forced.

Kinkaid pulled up into his reserved parking spot at 4:37 A.M. His hair was still matted in the back. He had taken the time to get dressed for the day, since it was sure to be another long, frustrating day anyway.

He walked toward CIA Headquarters and shifted his travel coffee mug to his left hand with his briefcase while he put his car keys in his suit coat pocket. He nearly dropped everything he was carrying when a voice called his name from right behind him, no more than a foot away. He swallowed. "Trying to give me a damned heart attack? What the hell are you doing?" he said, turning around.

Ricketts stared at him with his hands in his pockets unsmiling.

Kinkaid growled, "Let's go inside where it's warmer. I'm freezing my ass off."

"Out here," Ricketts said.

"What for?"

"I don't want any of the other parasites listening."

"To what?"

"Our conversation."

Kinkaid put his briefcase down and took a long drink from his coffee. "Okay, what?"

Ricketts looked around the mostly empty parking lot. There wasn't anything but asphalt for seventy-five yards in any direction. "What do you want to do with this Sheikh?"

"Do with him? I want to find him. Then I want to get him."

"Meaning . . ."

"I don't know." Kinkaid frowned. "Grab him. Bring him back for trial. Put his ass in prison for a few lifetimes."

Ricketts stared down at his feet. "I may have some information on his whereabouts."

"What? You're shitting me? Where is he?"

Ricketts shook his head. "I know where he *will* be. Not where he is."

"Where? How do you know—"

"I cannot disclose—"

"I'm in charge of the task force," Kinkaid said gruffly. "You'll tell me whatever I need to know—"

"No, I won't," Ricketts said icily. "Not if it will endanger my agents."

"How would telling me endanger your—"

"I got an agreement from the Director himself when I started running agents that I didn't need to tell anyone anything I didn't want to. It's my judgment alone—"

"That's bullshit. We have to share information—"

"That's why I'm here," Ricketts replied. "But I will tell you only what is necessary, and to the others, nothing. They can do their analysis, and stare at their photographs, and drink Starbucks—"

"We are on the same team—"

"We walk to the same destination, but not together."

"What do you have in mind?" Kinkaid asked.

"I don't think we should waste our time trying to capture him. We should take him out—"

"That would require a finding—"

"I know. That's what we should do."

"No," Kinkaid said. "The Director wants him here. He wants a nice big trial the whole world can see."

Ricketts understood, even though he disagreed. "I can grab the Sheikh. I need only your approval."

"How would you get him?"

"You do not need to know that."

"The hell I don't—"

"You may ask the Director. He won't tell you, but you may ask him."

Kinkaid fought back his frustration. "When?"

"Soon."

"Do you think you can do it?"

"I'm sure I can."

"How much risk?"

Ricketts pondered, as if doing a calculation. "Much."

"Do you want to do this?"

Ricketts nodded in the darkness. "Yes."

"Do you need any help, any support from us?"

"No."

Kinkaid wasn't sure what to say. It was all very irregular. He also had served in the DO long enough to know that some of the best officers were the quirkiest. "I don't like it. I have to know."

Ricketts said nothing. He just stared at Kinkaid. The distant light in the parking lot at the top of a pole was behind him and showed only his silhouette. "You can tell me not to do it. Or you can let me put this guy out of our misery, but I can't tell you how or when."

"How about where?"

"Sorry."

"You got a plan?"

"Start of one."

Kinkaid debated with himself. He finally had to admit that results were what he wanted, and Ricketts brought results. "Do it."

*

"Want to get a slider?" Woods asked Wink and Big at the back of the ready room as the SDO set up the video projector in the aisle between the seats and aimed it at the enormous screen suspended from the overhead in the front. Movies in the Navy had long been a grand tradition. The movie would be shown at an announced time and all the officers would show up to watch it. The SDO was responsible for selecting the movie from the hundreds of videotapes available from the ship's video library and ensuring the projector was set up. He had to roll the movie exactly at the specified time. To the second. Or the Executive Officer would rail on him and he would be held in general contempt by the squadron for some unspecified period.

"Sure," they replied together. "We can get back in time for the movie. How many stars is it?"

"I'm not sure. Three, I think." The star system was legendary within the squadron. Every SDO tried to get a five-star movie. If the CO agreed that it was five stars, that SDO was taken off the SDO watch bill for an entire month. But it was hard to find a five-star movie. The categories were clear enough: a train, an Indian, female nudity, a mort (someone killed by other than natural causes), and a snake. The snake and the Indian were the toughest. One movie had a hat trick in one scene—a naked female Indian riding a horse when confronted by a snake. There was a mort, but a train never showed up so it stalled at four stars.

In the forward wardroom, several aircrew in their flight suits were spread out among the long tables. Woods, Wink, and Big stood in front of the grill expectantly. After a few seconds the messmen asked them what they would like.

"Double slider," Woods said.

"Triple cheeseburger," Big said enthusiastically.

"Single for me," Wink said, looking at Big. "Geez, Big, you're going to weigh three hundred pounds."

"I already do." Big smiled.

Wink glanced at him skeptically. "Are you kidding?"

Big leaned against the bulkhead behind him while he watched his triple cheese slider sizzle on the large flat grill. "Wink, you're amazing. If I weighed three hundred pounds I wouldn't even fit through the door. I am a svelte two-forty."

"Wow," Woods said. "Athlete."

"You going to start on me?" Big said.

One of the EA-6B Prowler pilots joined them in line. "Hey, Wink, was that you on button seventeen in marshall this last recovery?"

"Yep."

"Did you have that cloud layer right at marshall?"

"We were below it. Darker than a witch's heart."

"We were in the goo the whole time. Unbelievable."

Pritch appeared in the room, moving to the end of the line.

Three plates magically appeared on the counter. The men grabbed their food and sat down at a table.

After taking a large bite from his burger, Big looked across at Woods. "How you doing? About Boomer and all."

Pritch sat down on the other side of Big. Woods looked at her, slightly annoyed she was there, and annoyed at himself for being annoyed. "I don't know," Woods replied. "I was really bent. Nothing seems to be happening. I try to act normal, do my job, be myself, but it's like it's all in slow motion, or something. Then the XO . . ."

"I know what you mean," Big replied.

"Mind if I join you?" asked Father Maloney, standing next to Woods, a cup of tea in his hand.

Woods rolled his eyes as he looked at Big and Wink across the table. "No, please," he said, motioning to the chair next to Wink.

"I gotta go," said Big, getting up as the chaplain sat down. "Gotta go debrief."

"What?" asked Pritch. "I debriefed you an hour ago."

"Maintenance. I've got to talk to maintenance about the FM radio."

"You've got FM in your airplane?"

"There's a lot you don't know, Pritch," Big said as he bounced quickly on the balls of his feet to get his flight suit to unrumple and straighten down his legs over his flight boots.

"Me, too," said Wink, standing.

Woods was stuck. He wanted to catch the movie in the ready room, but it was obvious that the chaplain had sat down to talk to him. He didn't know the other officers at all, and he'd met Woods at Vialli's funeral service.

The chaplain sipped his cup of tea. His round, kind face was slightly red, as it usually was, as if life on the carrier was too much of an effort. He seemed very out of place in a uniform. He had a Lieutenant Commander's gold oak leaf on one collar and a cross on the other—the insignia worn by a chaplain.

Woods had always thought crosses looked incongruous on uniforms. He found the whole chaplain thing almost offensive. They tried so hard to be everyone's friend it was as if their lives didn't have any content. He was sure his opinions were stereotypical, especially since he had never had a conversation of any length with any chaplain, but he wasn't in any hurry to change that.

Woods finished his burger without knowing what to say. To talk shop, or ridicule Pritch—the thing he wanted to do most—just didn't seem right with the chaplain sitting there.

"How have you been, Lieutenant Woods?" Father Maloney finally asked.

"Pretty good, thanks, just trying to figure out where to spend all the money I make."

Maloney smiled at Pritch. "Hello. I'm Father Maloney, the Catholic chaplain aboard. I don't think we've met."

"No, sir, I'm Ensign Charlene Pritchard."

"Nice to meet you."

"Same here."

"Does Lieutenant Woods always joke with others the way he does with me?" he asked Pritch.

"He doesn't take much very seriously."

Maloney looked at Woods. "Is that true?"

Woods shrugged, waiting for the right time to make his exit.

"Have I made you angry somehow?"

"No, sir," Woods replied.

"It seems like my presence makes you uncomfortable," Maloney said.

Pritch sneaked a glance at Woods.

"Not really. Seeing you just reminds me of Vialli, and that aggravates me."

"Why does it aggravate you?"

Woods stared at Maloney. "Is there something about being a chaplain that makes you ask such dumb questions?" he said, his face reddening. He hesitated for a minute, then went on. "Sorry. He was my roommate, and my friend. He was *murdered.* Here we sit on the most lethal weapon ever designed, his murderers are a couple of hundred miles away, and we're eating hamburgers. The whole thing just pisses me off."

Maloney nodded his head understandingly. "I know what you mean. But we don't know that nothing is being done about it."

"You know something I don't know?"

"No, I certainly wouldn't know. I just meant that the government might be doing things we don't know about."

"Like what? Sending the crack CIA to find some terrorist and put a stick in his eye? Come on."

"All I was saying is we shouldn't assume we know everything when we don't."

"What's *probably* happening is that we know more about it than anyone, and nothing is being done at all. That's the most likely."

"Perhaps you're right. But we can't do much about it."

"The hell we can't. Sorry. Yes we can."

"What would you suggest?" Maloney asked, sipping his tea.

Woods's words were direct. "I think we should announce to the world that we're going after the terrorists. Launch an attack on their headquarters. They've already claimed responsibility for it. Let's take them at their word."

"We can't do that, can we?"

"Why not?"

"That would be an act of war."

"So what?" Woods replied. "What are we here for, Father? Why are we in the Mediterranean?"

"To defend NATO," said Pritch.

"From *what*?" said Woods.

"Whatever threat develops."

"Isn't attacking a Navy officer a threat?"

"Not to peace, not really," the chaplain said.

"It's a threat to every American. Terrorism is intended to make us afraid. To make us change our plans, our attitudes, and live in fear. That is a threat to peace. I think we should go after them. Quit waiting around for the politicos to test the wind. Let's go *now*."

"That would be vengeance," said Maloney.

"What's wrong with a little vengeance now and then?" asked Woods, angry.

" 'Vengeance is mine, says the Lord,' " said Maloney. "It's not up to us to exact revenge against an enemy, it's God's decision."

Woods frowned. "What does *that* mean?" he asked. "Was it wrong to take vengeance on Japan for attacking us at Pearl Harbor? Should we have left that up to God? Should we wait for a storm or an earthquake or something? I remember a lot of attacks directly ordered by God in the Old Testament. Maybe we should just be listening for his order."

Maloney realized he was in much deeper than he'd intended to get in the conversation. He also realized he had to answer. "Of course the country can respond. That's legitimate warfare. But the ship, or the Captain of the ship, can't do it on his own—that's revenge."

"I don't see the difference," Woods said. "The country acts through us. Through people. That's all we can do."

Maloney considered his words. "It is a question of authority. The *country* can act, individuals cannot."

"Doesn't it matter what they're doing or why? If the U.S. can attack, why can't we? We are the U.S."

"We can, if instructed to by the government. Even you would agree that we can't act on our own."

"I don't care who does it, as long as someone does!" Woods said, his voice loud, drawing looks from other pilots on the wardroom. "It's only the police that can stop the guy who breaks in to rape your wife? You have to stand there and watch. Call 911. 'Hello, police, there's a guy here in my bedroom. He's raping my wife, but I know I can't act on my own. Only the *state* has the authority to protect me . . . I think he's almost done . . . Do hurry . . .' That's how it's supposed to go? That's your idea of authority?"

Father Maloney didn't respond. He breathed deeply and looked down at the table. Then he said, "The use of force by an individual in an emergency is different than an act of war." He smiled a small smile. "I'm sorry. I didn't really mean to get into this. I didn't mean to make you feel uncomfortable."

Woods showed his annoyance. "I'm pretty tired of people telling me why we can't do anything about murder," he snapped. "I for one am not going to just live with it. I'm not going to stop until they *regret* having killed Vialli. Not until they've paid for it."

Maloney shrugged. "What can you do? You have to let it go."

"Why do I have to let it go? Why does everybody keep telling me that?" Woods said, his voice rising again.

"Because you can't change it. You can't do anything about it. It isn't profitable to strain at things you can't change. It only causes frustration and pain."

Woods spoke slowly, deliberately. "I will never forget, and I will *never* quit. Ever."

Pritch slid her chair back, sensing an opening. "I've got to go debrief the last recovery in CVIC. See you later, Trey. Nice to meet you, Father Maloney."

Maloney rose and extended his hand to Pritch. "I enjoyed meeting you. Are you Catholic?"

"Used to be. See you later," she said uncomfortably.

"What do you have in mind?" Maloney asked, sitting down again and sliding his chair directly across from Woods.

"Nothing."

"I miss Tony a lot."

Woods was amazed. "Father Maloney, you didn't even *know* him. All you did was preside over his funeral."

"You perhaps think you know more than you do. You should be careful. Tony was a Catholic—"

"I know that. But I also know he didn't *buy* it. He was a regular guy—"

"Are you Catholic?"

"No."

"What church did you grow up in?"

"Presbyterian."

"Do you *buy* it, as you have put it?"

Woods shrugged and nodded.

"Well, Tony did buy it. All of it. He came to our Wednesday morning mass every week. Never missed once. We talked weekly."

Woods stared at the priest, dumbfounded. "I didn't know. I'm sorry."

"That's okay. I didn't say that to embarrass you, but so you could understand that there are others who feel his loss as deeply as you do."

"I know that. I've just been a little careless lately." Woods stood up, pushing his chair back under the table. "I've got to hit the rack. It's been a long day. See you again sometime."

"Yes. Good night, Lieutenant Woods. Have a good evening."

"Thanks," Woods said as he headed toward his stateroom, knowing he'd missed the start of the movie and not really caring. He was no longer in the mood.

He closed the flimsy steel stateroom door behind him, sat down heavily in his desk chair and unlaced his boots. He dropped them on the tiled deck, standing up to take off his flight suit. He slung it over his chair and removed his yellow T-shirt. He turned on the small neon light over the steel sink, feeling the coolness of the metal through his cotton boxer shorts as he leaned against it.

He stared at himself in the mirror. He looked tired. He felt tired. He had been up almost nineteen hours. Nothing unusual about that though, he told himself. Eighteen was the norm. No, it was weariness. He couldn't do anything about Vialli and he knew it. Every time someone reminded him of it, he felt the frustration more deeply. He shook his head vigorously, and splashed cold water on his face.

He switched off the light and brushed his teeth in the dark. He couldn't hear Big breathing in the top bunk—he was probably at the movie—but Bernie was there—guush, cuh cuh cuh. At least the catapults were quiet. The last launch was over. He could hear the recovery aft, as an S-3, distinctive by sound of its relatively quiet but deep turbofan engines, strained futilely against the arresting cable.

He pulled back the white cotton sheet and gray USN blanket on the lower bunk and crawled in. He listened to the familiar sounds of the ship, as he closed his eyes. He took a deep breath, and prepared for his usual instantaneous unconsciousness.

His eyes snapped open as his heart raced. Why hadn't he thought of it before? He jumped out of bed and pulled on his flight suit, socks, and boots, zipping up his flight suit all the way to hide the fact he wasn't wearing a T-shirt. He threw open the door to the stateroom and slammed it behind him. He turned outboard, went through a hatch, and grabbed the railings on the ladder as he slid down feet first. Down another, and another, and another, until he was on the mess deck.

He stopped in front of a door and tried the handle. It was locked. Shaking the handle, he finally let go with a grunt. He looked up and down the passageway, but no one was around. He was about to walk away when he saw the sign in the middle of the door: IN CASE OF EMERGENCY, CONTACT LIEUTENANT RAYBURN AT 4765.

Woods walked aft and grabbed the closest phone. He dialed the number, letting it ring and ring. Finally someone answered. "Hello," a voice said, obviously having awakened from a deep sleep.

"Is this Lieutenant Rayburn?"

"Yeah. Who's this?"

"This is Lieutenant Sean Woods, VF-103. I need to talk to you."

"Why?" Rayburn said testily. "Can't it wait?"

"No. I have to see you tonight."

Rayburn sighed. "I'll meet you in my office in five minutes. Can you be there by then?"

"I'm already there," he said. The line went dead. He hurried back down the passageway to the office door to wait.

Five minutes went by, no Lieutenant Rayburn. Then ten. Woods paced in front of the door, waiting. He looked at his watch again, and finally heard the clanging of a nearby ladder as Lieutenant Rayburn slid to the deck.

Glancing curiously at Woods, he opened the door to his office and switched on the lights. Rayburn was short, about five six, with clipped straight brown hair. In his late twenties, he had obviously taken the time to comb his hair and put on a clean uniform. He was wearing gold wire-rimmed glasses. "Now," he asked, "what can I do for you?"

Woods offered his hand and said, "I'm Sean Woods. Thanks for coming in the middle of the night."

"What's up?" said Rayburn impatiently.

"I was lying in my rack, and I couldn't sleep." He saw Rayburn's face—he was getting angry—and decided to change his approach. "You remember the guy who was killed in the attack in Israel?"

"Sure. He was there *illegally*. Faked his leave papers. I had to review the JAG investigation to determine whether he was in the line of duty and all that."

"Then you know what happened."

"Probably better than you do."

Woods looked at Rayburn, trying to read his tone of voice. Rayburn was impressed with himself. Great, Woods thought. Just when I need some help I get an arrogant attorney.

"You're the JAG officer on the ship, right?"

"Obviously."

"So you're supposed to know the law."

Rayburn shrugged. "Some of it. The rest I have to look up, but I have a good set of law books aboard. Why, what do you want to know?"

"Mind if I sit?" he said, pointing to a chair and sitting down without waiting for a reply. Rayburn took the desk chair behind a Navy-issue steel-gray desk.

"I've been trying to think of some way to hit back for Vialli. Some way to go after the terrorists who murdered him."

"Like what?" Rayburn asked, putting his feet up on the desk.

"I've already talked to the Admiral about us attacking them, but he isn't going to do that. . . . I was thinking that we should declare war."

Rayburn realized Woods had finished. "That's it?"

"Yeah. What do you think?"

"Against *who*?" Rayburn asked, narrowing his eyes.

"The guy who was in charge of the attack, and planned it. The Sheikh." Woods's eagerness showed on his face. "We should declare war against *him*, as an individual, and maybe his group of terrorists. We wouldn't have to just issue statements about how horrible it all was and do *nothing*. I say declare war, tell the whole world the full force of the U.S. military is going after them, and then *do* it. If some country is hiding them, or letting them train there, they should know it won't matter to us. We'll go after them wherever we can find them. If someone is protecting them, they'd better get the hell out of the way."

Rayburn's expression was one of disbelief. "You got me up in the middle of the night to ask me about declaring war against terrorists?"

"Yeah. What do you think?" Woods said enthusiastically.

"It's ridiculous."

"Why?"

"The Admiral can't declare war, only—"

"I know that. I'm not saying we should declare war, I'm saying the country should declare war."

"Only Congress—"

"I know. But that's it. That's what I want to know. Where does it say that Congress can declare war?"

"In the *Constitution*," Rayburn said sharply.

"Then here's the question," said Woods, leaning on the gray desk. "Is there anything there, in the Constitution, that says we can't declare war against one man? Or a terrorist group?"

Rayburn shook his head. "You're nuts. I have no idea. You don't need a JAG officer, you need a psychiatrist. I'll call him in the morning and set up an appointment for you," he said, starting to get up.

"Come on, think about it! What's so wrong with it? It could be the very thing Congress has been looking for all these years to combat terrorism. Leave a standing declaration of war against every terrorist who attacks us. Then wherever we find them, we can go after them with the full force of the military and *hammer* them. We don't need to worry about arresting them, or playing international police. We treat them like any other soldier of any country that we're at war against. They're fair game."

Rayburn put his hands on his desk, and pushed himself up. "Good night," he said.

Woods was confused. "What do you mean?"

"Don't know how else to say it," Rayburn replied. "We're done. And next time," he added with a bite, "spare me the late-night hare-brained schemes, will you?" He motioned to Woods to leave the office as he turned off the lights, one after the other. Rayburn locked the JAG office behind them and started down the passageway.

"At least think about it, won't you?" Woods asked of his back.

"Good night," Rayburn said without slowing or turning.

14

Woods put his tray down across from Big McMack, who had gotten enough eggs, French toast, and bacon to preserve his name for at least one more day. "I've got it figured out, Big," he said as he sat down.

Big squinted at him through swollen morning eyes. "Did you take a shower this morning?"

Woods looked at him with confusion. "Sure."

"*And* yesterday?"

"Yeah. So what?"

"We're only supposed to take showers every other day."

"Probably send the shower Nazis after me," Woods remarked.

"They'll make you take saltwater showers from the fire main."

"Just like the good old Navy. David Farragut. John Paul Jones. They washed with salt water. I guarantee you."

"Yes," Big agreed. And they read books, and wrote letters, and thought great thoughts. Today's Navy officer is condemned to a life of the lowest common denominator. Men love to see breasts, so they give us these horrible movies. Anything rated R. The library is full of *Mad* magazines, and books about cars. Where is the intellectual in uniform? Where is the Renaissance Man?" Big asked, hunched over his plate, cramming his mouth with a forkful of French toast. "You've got what figured out?" he asked through his food.

"How we can hit back."

"Speak English. I do better in that. It was my minor."

"For Vialli. We can do something about it."

Big put his fork down on the table and sat back. "You still on that? Your little vendetta bit? Let it go, Trey. It's going to drive you crazy."

"No," Woods said with intensity. "We can declare war."

"Against whom?"

"Against the people who killed Vialli. Against the Sheikh."

"I hate to break it to you, Trey, but war is declared against a country. You know, 'a date which will live in infamy . . . I ask that the Congress declare . . . a state of war has existed between the United States and the Japanese Empire' and all that. You've heard Roosevelt. It just wouldn't do if he'd said, 'We hereby declare that a state of war exists against Admiral Yamamoto.' Just doesn't have the same ring."

"We can do it."

Big suddenly realized he was serious. "How?"

"I had this brainstorm last night. I was lying there and it just hit me. Like a bolt of lightning—like a vision. So I went to see the JAG officer. I told him the idea. He said he's gonna think about it. I think it struck him as something completely new."

"Well, if you get it so the *Washington* can declare war, then you're on to something."

"No. *Congress*. If they really chew on it, they might just do it. And if they do, and we're right here, we'll be the ones to go." Woods looked at his roommate with obvious enthusiasm. "What do you think?"

"I think you're nuts. You should have some French toast and fill your belly. Once you get enough fat in your system you'll be ready to fly, and then you'll start making sense."

"You'll see. You laugh now, but you'll see."

"What am I going to see? You going straight to the Admiral with this insight? He may just put you right in the brig for insubordination, sitting on the deck in your underwear with a bunch of druggies." Big smiled to himself at the image.

"*This* Admiral isn't going to do anything about it. He doesn't have the balls. He's more worried about his *prostate* or something. He's not worried about his pilots."

"His prostate?" Big said, screwing up his big round face.

"Well, whatever."

"So what are you planning?"

"I'm going to write to my congressman."

"Now *there's* an idea," Big said, rolling his eyes, his belly moving with internal laughter. "Shoot, I'll bet your congressman doesn't get more than ten or twenty thousand letters a day. Probably answers every one of them personally. He'll probably read yours on the floor of the House as one of the most brilliant ideas in American history."

"Get off my back, Big. This could be the kind of idea that changes American foreign policy forever." Woods was flush with excitement. He hadn't slept all night, and was operating on adrenaline. "We've never had a good response to terrorism. It's always covert, or half baked, or a one-time air raid. We never go after the bad guys. But in a war, that's exactly what we do. We go after the bad guy. We go after him until he surrenders or we've killed him. Capture the Flag. Out in the open, in the full light of day, with the full force of the military. Right at them, until it's over. It's time to do that with terrorists."

"Do what with terrorists?" asked Father Maloney, sitting down next to Woods and removing his breakfast from his tray.

"Morning, Father," Woods said, debating with himself whether to tell the chaplain. Why not. "Have Congress declare war against terrorists. Then go after them with the military to take them out."

"I didn't know Congress could do that."

"I didn't either. But I thought of it last night, and asked the JAG officer. I don't think there's any limitation against it. He's still thinking about it, but he didn't say anything right away."

"Hmmm," Maloney said, scooping up a forkful of scrambled eggs that had an odd green hue to them. He stopped. "Are these powdered eggs?" he asked no one in particular.

Big replied. "I don't think so. They may be sneaking in some powdered with the regular, but I saw them break mine and scramble them."

"I wasn't watching."

"They may have poured yours from the special pitcher," Big said, emphasizing "special."

To Woods, the Chaplain said, "Do you think such a war against a terrorist or a group would be a just war?"

"Absolutely," Woods answered immediately. "How could it not be? If we're attacked, we can respond. Why wouldn't that be true if the attack was only against one person?"

Maloney nodded slowly. "Have you ever studied the theory of the just war of Aquinas?"

"No," Woods answered. "But I'll bet you have."

"It comes up in my reading—"

Big stood up. "I'm out of here. This is too heavy for me." He looked at Maloney. "Sorry, Padre. Aquinas didn't write any good screenplays, so I don't know much about him." He spoke to Woods. "I'll be in the ready room."

"Okay, see ya in a minute," Woods said, wiping his mouth on his napkin. "I've got to go too," he said, rising, trying to get away from Chaplain Maloney.

Maloney continued, almost to himself, ". . . You have the seven requirements, as outlined by Grotius in the seventeenth century, which was really just a refinement of Aquinas . . ."

"I'm sure it's very interesting, but I've really got to go to the ready room. We're having an AOM in a few minutes."

"That sounds very important. What is it?" Maloney asked innocently.

"All Officers' Meeting."

"Well then, I won't keep you."

"See you later," Woods said, standing. He was about to walk away when a thought occurred to him. Turning to Maloney, he said, "You know a lot about this just war stuff?"

"Oh, I don't know. A lot is saying a lot." Maloney smiled. "Little word joke there. Um, I suppose so. I studied ethics at the Catholic University, and my area of emphasis was the ethics of the use of force, warfare, those sorts of things."

"I'm going to write a letter to my congressman telling him that we should declare war on terrorists who attack the U.S. or its citizens," Woods said. "Do *you* think it would be a just war? 'Cause if I can convince them it is, they'll have no reason at all not to do it."

Maloney regarded Woods with his pale intense eyes. "I don't know, I haven't considered it. I'll have to think about it . . ."

"I'm going to do the letter tonight, and send it off by e-mail. It'd be great if I could attach something from you, saying it would be a just war. Might just make the difference."

Maloney nodded tentatively, unwilling to commit himself.

The ringing phone startled Woods. The sound of a jet being thrown off the carrier by catapult four made him wait a few seconds before answering. "Lieutenant Woods."

"Trey?"

"Pritch?"

"Yes, sir."

"What's up?"

"I was just reading a report that I thought you might be interested in seeing."

"What kind of report?"

"The investigation into Vialli's death."

"Murder."

"Right. Murder. It gives a lot of facts about it."

"Like what?"

"I think you should read it."

"I will. But give me the heart of it."

"I don't know. I think it'd be better—"

"Just give it to me."

"Okay." She turned a couple of pages. "Four people were killed. They didn't kill any of the teachers, or the kids."

"I know that."

"They shot a soldier, the driver, Vialli, and the woman—"

"Irit."

"Right," she confirmed, surprised he knew her name. Then she remembered the story of how Vialli had met her. "Tony had been hit in the mouth with a gun butt, hit on the head with something hard, and then shot in the back."

Woods closed his eyes. "In the back?" he whispered.

"Twice. Close range. Basically assassinated."

"Why?"

"That's what nobody can figure."

Woods had tried to put it behind him. "Anything else?"

"Irit was shot in the back too."

Woods tried to control his breathing. "What about the soldier and the driver?"

"Soldier got it in the chest, and the driver got it in the back of the head."

"They were after someone."

"I don't know what to make of this."

"Who were they after? Because whoever it was, they got him."

"You think they were after Tony? And Irit just happened to be there?"

"Sure looks like it."

"But why?"

"I don't know. But I'm sure going to find out."

Sami pulled up into his parents' driveway in Woodbridge, Virginia, a beautiful, tranquil northern Virginia suburb of Washington, D.C. His father had done well for himself. He had left the diplomatic service of Syria over serious disagreements with Hafez al-Assad, the President of Syria, who had been there for two generations and had maintained his position through brutal oppression and eradication of dissent. Sami's father, Abdul Rafiz Haddad, couldn't stomach selling the Syrian propaganda internationally anymore. He had been warned by friends in Damascus that his name had been put on the list of the disloyal. He had walked out and had never been back.

Sami looked at the large, brick colonial house and grew angry as he did every time he came. His father was often critical of the United States and its declining morality, its general lack of sophistication, its materialistic culture, the ugliness and coldness of the cities, but he was always ready to take advantage of the good parts. The ability to buy a big house and own an acre of land, to raise a family in freedom, to read an Arabic newspaper *and* the *Washington Post* at breakfast, and to loudly and freely criticize the government of the country in which he lived and the one from which he had come.

Never happy, Sami thought, slamming the door on his Nissan as hard as he could and waiting for the car to stop shivering from the blow. He went to the door and opened it without knocking. He had gone to high school from this house, taking the long bus ride to St. Alban's Episcopal School at the Washington National Cathedral every day. His father, a devout Muslim, had decided to send Sami to the Cathedral school because it was supposed to be the best in Washington. He saw no irony in that.

Sami went to the back porch, where he knew his father would be. "Father!" he called out as he approached the door. His father hated being surprised. "I'm home!"

He opened the sliding door from the family room to the enormous screened-in porch and saw his father sitting in his favorite chair reading an Arabic newspaper.

"My son!" his father said, putting the newspaper down and rising from his chair. They embraced. "How have you been?"

"Well, thanks. Where's Mother?" he asked, looking around.

"In the kitchen."

Sami smiled. "Of course. Why do I ask?"

"Would you like something to drink?"

"What do you have?"

"How about some iced tea?"

"Sure. That sounds great."

There was a pitcher and glasses on the table next to his chair, and his father poured tea into one of the glasses and handed it to him. As Sami took it the door slid open again and his mother, Linda Haddad, came in. She was tall with dark blond hair, and had a gentle face. Smiling at Sami, she said, "Sami, thank you for coming," and hugged him.

He hugged her back. "Of course," he said.

"So," his father began in Arabic, "we must discuss the developments in Gaza."

Sami balked. He didn't like discussing the Middle East with his father. Too often, such talks ended in arguments. To Sami's opinionated and intransigent father, it was inconceivable that Sami might know more than he did about the place where he had grown up. Sami hadn't spent more than a few months there, total. Sami didn't dare tell him that he actually knew much more, but couldn't share it with him. This made for some awkward conversations.

"What about it?" Sami answered in English.

"What do you think of what happened?" his father countered in Arabic.

"Speak English."

"Your mother speaks Arabic as well as you do. There is nothing wrong with speaking the language of my youth."

"No, there isn't. But you live in America now, and some day you're going to have to acknowledge that."

"Ha!" his father exclaimed. "I acknowledge it every day by staying here."

Sami drank from his glass. "It is a great tragedy," he said in Arabic, "that just when the peace process was nearing completion, when Syria and Israel had finally reached an agreement, when the Palestinian state is operating—although not with great health—someone tries to stir it all up again."

His father looked satisfied. "I wouldn't put it past Syria to be behind it."

"What?" Sami asked. It had never occurred to him. "How could that be?"

"They speak peace with one side of their mouths, and pay others to destroy it at the same time. This regime is just like the one before it. They gain nothing from peace with Israel. Their power comes from conflict. They don't know how to build roads or a great economy."

"But who is this Sheikh?" Sami asked, not wanting to tell what he knew.

His father was pleased by the question. "You've never heard of the legend of the Sheikh al-Jabal? It goes back many centuries. To Hassan al-Sabbah, the first man to take the name. In the eleventh century. The founder of the Assassins. The guardian of Islam and the region. It is fascinating that someone is calling himself that today. It will inspire others."

"I guess we'll see."

"Are you working on this at all?"

"Father, you know I can't discuss my job."

"Yes, well, you speak Arabic better than anyone in Washington who didn't grow up in Syria, and better than many of them. Since you work as an intelligence agent," he said with a hint of contempt, "it follows that you study the area of my home."

"Of course I do. You know that. I am an analyst of the Middle East. No mystery there."

"But what are you working on right now?"

"Father—"

His father acknowledged the rebuff with a wave of his hand. "All right, all right. But keep one thing in your mind when you do your analysis of this attack. At the base of every tree is the root. And the root of all problems in the Middle East is Israel."

"What?" Sami asked, annoyed. "Come on. The Sheikh didn't do what he claimed? Israel did it? They attacked their own people? For what?"

"No. I meant they take positions which ensure outrage from others and then plead innocence. To gain sympathy, maybe to set back the peace process, who knows. Their brains don't work like the rest of us." He raised a hand and pointed one finger toward the sky. "Just mark my word. The root of all trouble in the Middle East is Israel. You'll see one day. Maybe not today, but one day, you'll see."

"It's time for dinner," Sami's mother announced.

"Come," his father said, putting out his arm around Sami's shoulder. "I will tell you of the book I have decided to write."

15

"Can I borrow your laptop?" Woods asked Big.

Big looked up from his desk, where he was working on a Sailor of the Month nomination. "Are you kidding me? This is my baby. This is the machine that contains all the great novels and screenplays I'm going to write."

"So can I use it? I let the Ops O borrow mine."

"Hold on. Let me get out of this," he said, saving the file. "I suppose you're going to want the printer too?"

"Yeah, that'd be great."

Big pulled out a ream of paper, carefully taking out two sheets and handing them to Woods. "Is this the Big Letter to your congressman?" he asked as Woods turned on the computer.

"Yep." Woods stared at the screen. "What do you call a congressman? Your Honor? The honorable whatever? What is it?"

"You must have been an engineering major."

"What do you call him?"

"You address it to 'The Honorable Joe Schmuckatelli at the address for the House of Representatives, which I do not know off the top of my head. Then inside, you say, 'Dear Mr. Schmuckatelli,' or 'Dear Congressman Schmuckatelli.' Nothing to it. It doesn't really matter though. No one will see it except some twenty-two-year-old puppy-dog-college-grad who has never done anything, never served his country in the military, and is destined for law school in three years."

Woods stopped typing. "You're really encouraging, you know? Everybody tells you to work through the system, and then ridicules the system as being unworkable. Which is it?"

147

"I thought you were the one who was cynical about the system."

"Sometimes. I guess I always hope that someone will do the right thing."

There was a loud knock on the door and Woods heard voices. "You expecting anybody?" Woods asked.

Big shook his head, reaching behind him and opening the door from his chair. Lieutenant Rayburn and Lieutenant Commander Maloney entered together.

"I didn't know you had your staff doing your research for you," Big said, amazed.

"What are you guys doing here?" Woods asked.

Rayburn answered first. "I just came to talk to you about some things I've found, and the padre here was hovering outside your door."

Maloney looked at Rayburn horrified. "I was not hovering. I was composing my words. I wanted to say the right things."

"He was hovering," Rayburn replied, looking at Woods. "Anyway, I found some interesting things," Rayburn said. "You got time? You want to talk about this stuff now?"

"Absolutely," Woods said excitedly. "Come on in."

Rayburn and Maloney entered the stateroom and looked for somewhere to sit down.

"Pull up a bed," Woods said, indicating his own tightly made bed, which of course was welded to the deck. They sat on the edge of the bed and leaned forward so their heads didn't hit Big's upper bunk. Woods turned his chair to face them. "I was just drafting a letter to Congressman Brown, the congressman from my district in San Diego," he said, trying to contain his excitement. "He's got to love this—he's a retired Vice Admiral. Former AIRPAC." AIRPAC was the Commander of Naval Air Forces, Pacific. "He was the one in charge of all the carriers in the Pacific, all the airplanes and all the training."

Rayburn spoke first. "I've got to tell you," he said, "I thought you were nuts. But I understood," he acknowledged. "Predictable response to losing your best friend. Then when I heard what you wanted to know I *knew* you'd lost it. But the more I thought about it, the more I thought you might be on to something." He opened the massive blue book in his hands. Adjusting his gold-rimmed glasses, he looked from Woods to Big. "I was going to show you the Constitution, and tell you how stupid you were. But when I read it again, I started thinking about it a little . . ." He fumbled with the book, trying to balance it on his lap while he flipped to the back.

"What is that?" Woods asked.

Rayburn glanced up at him. "What? Oh, this?" he said, looking at the book. "Kind of funny. Even though I'm a lawyer, I don't really read the Constitution very often. I wasn't even sure where to find a copy," he said, chuckling. "This is my Con law book from law school. The Constitution's in the back, in an appendix. First time I've pulled it out since I graduated five years ago. Never thought it'd be to see if we can declare war against somebody," he said. "Let's see," he said. "Article I, Section 8 . . . Congress shall have power to . . . it goes on for a while," he said, turning the page, "but here it is, to declare war."

Woods waited, watching Rayburn. "That's it?"

"That's it."

"What does it mean?"

"Just what it says," said Rayburn.

Woods spoke carefully. "Anything that would make it impossible for Congress to declare war against one guy?"

"I read the entire Constitution several times. I looked in every article, every section. I couldn't find anything that says you can't do it."

"Are you kidding me?" Woods asked, his heart pounding.

Rayburn put up his hand. "But Con law isn't just about reading the Constitution. The Supreme Court stopped reading it decades ago. It's about what the cases say—it's about what the Supreme Court *says* it says, not what it actually says."

"So, what do they say?"

"I have a lot of case books aboard, most of the federal cases. I looked. And I got on the Internet and looked on Lexis."

"And?"

"Never been dealt with at all. At least not that I can find. I may be missing something, but I haven't found anything that would stop Congress from declaring war against the Sheikh." He waited for a reaction from Woods. "I haven't done a complete job of the research, but I feel pretty sure if I did I wouldn't find anything. There isn't even much in the law review articles. Lots of talk about the balance of power between the President and Congress, and talk of Letters of Marque since Congress pulled that stunt a few years ago, but nothing about declaring war against a person. In fact, what I've found so far shows that not only is there no prohibition it used to be ordinary."

"What did?" Woods asked, confused.

"Declaring war against somebody by name. When you go back and look at how it once was done in England, centuries ago, they used to declare war against the king of Spain. As a person. Naming him as an individual. Sure, it was in his capacity as the King of whatever, but it named him as a *person.* So to say you can't declare war on a person is simply wrong at least historically. The question is could we declare war against Joe Smith, a citizen of England. And I haven't found anything that says Congress can't do just that if it chooses to but it kind of goes against what war is. It's sort of defined as against a sovereign country." He paused. "But it seems to me the definition is ripe for expansion. We don't get attacked by sovereign countries anymore. Our battles are against groups of people, or individuals. Seems like a great idea to me, and I don't see anything that would stop you."

"That's amazing," Woods said. "Nothing?"

"Nope. Not a thing. The more I've thought about it, the more I love the idea. This could change foreign policy forever . . ."

"See, Big! What'd I tell you?" Woods said. "It's a great idea, isn't it?" he asked Rayburn, seeking further confirmation.

"I don't know why someone hasn't thought about it before. It solves so many problems. It could add a few too, such as what to do with a country that is protecting a terrorist. But just put them on notice, and pretty soon they'd realize maybe it's not such a good idea to let terrorists run training camps there. Could shut down the whole operation. I mean if Switzerland had allowed the Nazi armies to hide in Switzerland, you think we'd have just said, okay, no problem, we'll wait? No chance. It would have been at their peril. There's the doctrine of pursuit in warfare and international law. Nixon got in trouble for bombing Cambodia, which might be similar, but hey, they didn't even declare war in Vietnam." Rayburn adjusted his bent wire-rim glasses. "I think what would really happen is that there would be a huge constitutional law argument, about whether you really can do this or not. But at least as to whether there is something out there that says Congress can't, it's not there."

Woods smiled like a little boy. "I really appreciate your help. I'll let you know when he answers. We may hear about it on the news first, when Congress goes after the dicks that killed Vialli. Thanks.

"What about you, Padre?" Woods said, looking at him, then speaking to Rayburn. "The chaplain is an expert on ethics and warfare. That kind of stuff. He was going to help me convince Congress that it would be a *just* war. Right, Padre?"

Maloney's round face flushed pink. "I didn't see my role as convincing Congress that it would be a just war," he said. "I was simply trying to analyze the situation as you described it, hypothetically, and bring my understanding of just war theories to bear . . ."

"Don't go intellectual on us. What did you find?"

Maloney was clearly uncomfortable. He debated with himself whether to continue at all, but he saw no way to extricate himself. "I am hesitant to give you my preliminary conclusions, because if you send them off to your congressman they may be used to justify decisions with which I am not wholly comfortable. I came here only to discuss them with you. Having said that . . ."

"What's the bottom line, Padre? Would it be a just war, or not?" Woods asked impatiently.

Maloney nodded. "I think it would. May I explain?"

"Did you write it down?"

"Yes, I prepared a preliminary analysis, very superficial . . ."

"Can I see it?" Woods said, sticking out his hand.

Maloney pretended not to hear him and spoke without looking at the document rolled up in his hand. "There are seven criteria. I have given some thought to each of them. First," he said, touching his left forefinger with his right, counting, "it has to be the last resort, your *last* option; this may be, I don't see any diplomatic options here. I don't know enough to say. Second," he said, continuing to count with his fingers, "it must be aimed at deterring or repelling aggression; this probably is. Third," he said, sneaking a look at the paper he had rolled up, "it must be undertaken by legitimate authority; that, I take it, is your current objective, and why Mr. Rayburn is here. Fourth, it must be a right intention, such as defending against a great injury; this might qualify, since he shows no signs of quitting. Fifth, there must be probability of success; clearly, there would be. Sixth, there must be proportionality of goals and means; that remains to be seen, depending on what exactly we did after such a declaration—"

"And?" Woods asked. "Cut to the chase."

"Lastly," Maloney continued without missing a beat, "care must be taken to protect the immunity of noncombatants; I assume that would be done. In summary, Mr. Woods, I think St. Thomas Aquinas would not consider your cause unjust. These are just preliminary you under—"

"Unbelievable!" Woods said, standing up suddenly. "How can Congress not do this? I'll tell the congressman you endorsed it."

Maloney was startled. "I haven't endorsed anything."

Woods fixed him with a gaze the chaplain had never seen before. "Not willing to put your ass on the line a little?" Woods let the silence linger for a few seconds. "That's what being a Naval officer is all *about*. You make decisions, things happen. You live with them. We don't usually get to study them forever, or argue about them with our colleagues for a decade while we sip *tea*. We decide based on the information we have. Can you do that?" He looked at the paper Maloney was carrying. "Will you let me send that to my congressman?"

Maloney handed him the paper. Beads of sweat were visible on his temples. "I hope they know what they're doing."

"*Oh*, yeah," Big said sarcastically. "Congress always knows *exactly* what they're doing. I for one have all the confidence in the world—"

"Can I send it?" Woods asked Maloney again, not allowing him an ambiguous ending.

Maloney hesitated, then nodded.

"Thanks, Padre," Woods said, smiling. "I'll let you have a copy of the letter I send out. And I'll let you know as soon as I hear back."

"Thank you," Father Maloney said. "This is a very unusual thing. I hope we can learn from this."

Woods turned to Rayburn. "Would you be willing to write a memo that says what you just told me?"

Rayburn hesitated. "I don't think that would be a good idea. I don't want to give a legal opinion to Congress without my superiors knowing about it. I don't think it would make them very happy."

Woods looked back at the chaplain. "What are you going to do, Padre, when Congressman Brown proposes this on the floor and cites you as his justification?"

"Let's hope that doesn't happen," Maloney said, feeling trapped.

"Let's hope it does. I think Brown will be on national television within two weeks. You'd better be ready."

"You're dreaming," Big said.

"I'm afraid he's right," Father Maloney said to Woods. "I think you are overestimating one person's ability to affect things. Or at least political things."

"Ideas have power of their own."

"Who said that?" asked Big.

"I did. One way or another, this country will take care of Vialli."

Father Maloney and Lieutenant Rayburn got up, ready to head out.

"Thanks for your help, you guys," Woods said.

"Sure," they both replied. "We'll see what happens," Rayburn added. "You never know."

"Exactly," Woods said, closing the door behind them. He took a deep breath and tried to decide what do to next.

Big interrupted his thoughts. "Does it matter to you?"

"What?"

"Whether it would be *right* to attack these guys, as in moral."

"What do you mean?"

"All this talk about Thomas Aquinas . . . does it make any real difference to you? 'Cause I get the feeling you're just using this stuff as an angle. To get what you want."

"What's got you stirred up?" Woods asked.

Big opened his closet and started putting on his flight suit. "I was listening to you pin the poor chaplain to the wall, and making that Navy lawyer-puke feel uncomfortable. You were working them. I just wonder if what they're saying *matters* to you or if you're just using them."

"*You're* worried about me misusing Aquinas?"

"Nope. Don't even know that much about him. So, does it matter? What they're saying?"

Woods considered Big's question. Big had a way of asking questions that made him squirm. "Yeah, it does. We've let the whole thing slide to the President, and he decides when and where we go to war. It's all wrong. My father fought in Vietnam—"

"I know—"

"—in an undeclared war. I think it delegitimized the whole thing. It may have been one of the things that caused the public to lose faith in it. Congress never voted for it."

"Come on—"

"No, you *asked*," Woods said, getting it off his chest. "So we don't operate like we should anymore. I think we should get back to that. Where we don't have to sit out here planning a strike against some guy, or group, just because the President says so. That's what a *king* would do. I'm willing to go to war, but I want it to be something the country supports. I don't want to come home and have people spitting on me like they did my father."

"Sorry I asked."

"I'm not. It's important."

Big smiled. "Maybe one day somebody will listen to you."

"Yeah, like today. I'm going to get this e-mail out tonight. I'm going to retype the padre's memo and put his name on it, and mention Rayburn, and send it to Admiral Brown."

"Admiral who?" Big asked, concerned Woods had decided to try for a truly momentous jump over the chain of command.

"Brown. My congressman. *Retired* Vice Admiral Lionel Brown. You know."

"Oh, yeah—" The phone on the bulkhead rang, startling both of them. Big reached over his head and pressed the button that released the handset and kept it from falling during high seas. "Lieutenant McMack, Ready Room Ten," he said. He listened, then frowned. "Aw, *no*," he said, closing his eyes momentarily. "When?"

He glanced at the clock on the bulkhead. "They find anything?" He waited, then nodded. "Okay. Thanks." He hung up the phone and looked at Woods, who was waiting expectantly for some indication of what had happened. Big sighed. "Gator just flew into the water."

"The F-18 guy?"

"Yeah. Their LSO. On approach, half a mile out. Just kept descending and didn't pull up. The LSOs were screaming at him. He just flew right into the water. Perfect attitude, perfect rate of descent, right into the water. Hit like a pancake. Didn't even try to eject."

Woods couldn't believe it. Most cruises resulted in one or two accidents, maybe one death. This cruise was snakebit.

"His wife is waiting for him in Piraeus. We pull in tomorrow and nobody knows how to get ahold of her."

16

Sami stopped his Nissan in front of Cunningham's townhouse. It was in one of those condo complexes where it required GPS or perfect directions to find someone's condo. All the buildings looked the same, all the stairways and doorways looked the same: the same colors, the same decorative plants, the same cars in front—junkers for those who just moved in, and the BMWs for those about to move out.

Sami leaned over and peered up the stairway for Cunningham. He checked the clock on the dash, which, much to his annoyance, continued to work and kept more accurate time than his three-hundred-dollar wristwatch. Finally Cunningham came bounding down the stairs carrying his briefcase.

Opening the car door, he slid into the front passenger seat.

"Sorry," Cunningham said.

"No problem," Sami replied, backing out into the deserted, small street that looped the entire complex. He drove off quickly. "What do you think of Kinkaid?"

"What?" Cunningham said, looking over toward Sami for the first time.

"Kinkaid."

"Too early."

"What do you think of him?"

Cunningham watched the traffic on the street they were turning on to. They never talked when they carpooled. He didn't like to think this early. "What about him?"

"You think he's doing a good job?"

155

"Sure."

"See anything that troubles you?"

"Let's hear what's eating you."

"I think he may be in bed with Israel."

"What? What the hell are you talking about?"

"Where does he go first when we need info? Israel. Where does he have a pal on the 'inside'? Israel. Too many crosscurrents at work here. I don't like it."

Cunningham rolled his eyes but tried not to let Sami see. "You're losing it. He's the most quality guy we've got. He's cool."

"I don't think so." He accelerated hard and the four-cylinder engine strained to meet his demands as they merged onto the mostly deserted freeway. "Ever hear of Mega?"

"No. What is it?"

Sami didn't answer.

17

Woods stood next to Big, anxious for the officer boat to touch shore at Piraeus. He knew they should be excited about a new port, liberty, all the things that were supposed to make his job fun. But it wasn't like that. Other thoughts clouded his mind. Vialli, the XO and Brillo, and now Gator, whom he hardly knew.

"Aw shit, Trey," Big said.

"What?" Woods replied.

"Look who's standing on the pier."

Woods looked at a woman who was carefully watching the officer boat approach the pier. "Who is she?" he asked.

"Gator's *wife*," Big replied. "She was at the Air Wing party before we left on cruise. Look at her," Big said, studying her body language. "She hasn't heard."

"Oh, no," Woods said. He checked the officer boat for anyone from Gator's squadron. "*I'm* sure not going to tell her."

"*I'm* not going to tell her," Big said, searching desperately for some way to dump the unpleasant job on someone else. He spotted the Air Wing Maintenance Officer coming out onto the deck. "Greebs," he said, calling to him. "Gator's wife is on the pier. Someone's got to tell her."

Greebs looked at them both. "Not me," he said. "Didn't even know the man."

The boat touched the pier as the coxswain reversed the engines to stop its forward progress.

Woods and Big watched in fascination as Gator's wife smiled and waited anxiously for the officers to get off the boat. She had flown all the way from the States for this port call to see her husband for the first time in three months. She was wearing a silk blouse, tight white pants, and heels. Her freshly washed black hair glistened in the Greek sunshine. She had something in her hand that Woods couldn't make out. "This has the makings of a disaster, Big," Woods said.

A Petty Officer jumped off the bow onto the pier and tied the boat off. He hurried to the stern and tied off the other line. The coxswain killed the engine and the boat settled into its place next to the pier.

Woods and Big held back, hoping someone else would recognize Gator's wife and beat them to the pier to take the poor woman aside. The officers streamed right by her and headed toward the waiting taxicabs fifty yards away at the head of the pier.

Finally, Woods and Big stepped ashore. "Hi," Woods said to her. "I'm Sean Woods." Big stood behind him, pretending to look for someone or something down the pier. "You remember Big," he said. "I think you met at the Air Wing party."

"Hi," she replied. "I'm Susan Gomez—"

"Right, Gator's wife."

"Right." She smiled. "Have you seen him? He *promised* he'd be on the very first O-boat ashore," she said. "Is this it? Did I miss it?"

"No," Woods said. "This is it." Woods hated this. He wished he had just kept walking. "Let's go over there for a minute," he said, pointing down the pier away from the taxis and the activity. He put his sunglasses in his pocket and moved away slowly.

Susan followed, but with a growing sense of foreboding.

Finally, Woods stopped. Turning to her, he met her eyes. She was stunningly pretty, but her face was full of fear. She couldn't speak.

Woods held her shoulders. "Last night, Gator was on the last recovery. He was on final approach, and got into a descent that he never pulled out of. His F-18 hit the water and he didn't eject. He was killed, about ten o'clock. I'm sorry to have to tell you this, but that's why he's not on the boat. Someone from his squadron should have been here to tell you, but they were trying to find you. I don't think they knew how to get in touch with you."

She stared at him with no comprehension, her mind refusing to accept what he had just said. "What?" she said finally.

"Gator's dead," he said. "His airplane went down."

Woods put his arm around Susan's shoulder. Susan's thin body began to shake, as she fought back the truth that would change her life forever. Tears erupted from her eyes and ran down her cheeks. "Are you sure? Could there be some mistake?"

"No, they're sure."

"Where is he? Did they find his body?"

"No," Woods replied. "They're still looking for him. They'll have people out there all day, looking for wreckage, trying to figure out what went wrong."

She covered her eyes with her hand, her diamond wedding band glimmering in the sunshine. She shuddered. "I don't know what to do," she said. "He was . . ." She couldn't finish.

At the pier, another officer boat was tying up. "Big, go see if there's someone from Gator's squadron on that boat."

"Rog," Big said. He hurried down the pier and waited for the officer boat to unload.

Woods reached for Susan and held her close to him. "I'm sorry," Woods said. Her mouth pressed into his shoulder, muffling her sobs. He stroked her hair, trying to comfort her. He didn't know what else to say or do.

Big came back with another officer in tow. "Susan, here's the XO," Big said, relieved.

Gator's XO looked at the scene and knew he had blown it. He was the one who was supposed to tell Gator's wife about her husband. He had taken the Chief's word for it as to when the first O-boat would leave. He hadn't anticipated a bunch of anxious officers talking the coxswain into going early. "Hello, Susan," he began. "I'm sorry about Gator. We don't—"

"Is he really dead?" she asked, searching his face for any glimmer of hope.

"I'm afraid so."

"But you haven't found his body. He might still be out there."

"We saw his airplane hit the water, Susan. He didn't even punch out."

"Aren't you still looking for him?"

"Yes, we are, but he isn't alive. Maybe we'll find his body, but probably not. Don't get your hopes up because we're out there looking for his body. Look," he said, wanting to comfort her, but not having any idea how to, "I'd like you to come with me. I have a place arranged. There are some things we need to do."

The XO turned to Woods and Big. "Thanks. I missed the first boat. I owe you one."

Woods spoke. "You need us for anything else?"

"No. I've got it from here. Thanks for stepping in."

"Sure," Woods said.

The two of them watched Susan and the XO walk slowly down the pier in the beautiful sunshine.

"You did good, Trey," Big said.

"We didn't have any choice."

Big hitched up his jeans and tucked in his shirt. "Oh yes we did. If I'd been by myself I'd have walked right by her. No doubt about it."

"So now we set off to go get your flokati rugs."

"Yeah," Big replied. "But I don't feel much like shopping. That sure took the fun out of the morning. Nothing like staring mortality in the face."

"How 'bout a cup of coffee?" Woods asked.

"Yeah. That sounds good." They began to walk. "You ever come close to just buying it? Flying into the water or something?"

"Once. Scared the hell out of me."

"Dangerous business, Trey."

"Keeping the world safe for democracy."

"I'm saying."

Congressman Lionel Brown liked to have his staff meetings every day at 0730. Not 7:30, 0730, just like he was still in the Navy. Admiral Brown wasn't like other members of Congress. He was a Naval Academy graduate and a retired Vice Admiral. His last job in the Navy as AIRPAC had taken him to North Island Naval Air Station in Coronado, California, the peninsula that forms San Diego Bay and sits across the water from the city. After retirement, Brown had moved to Washington, D.C., and worked in the defense industry. A beltway bandit, as they were called.

While in Washington he had been able to observe how the government operated. He had seen how military policy was made by people who had never served a day in the military. It had distressed him so much he'd decided to move back to Coronado, where he had kept a home, and run for Congress. Prior to his election there hadn't been a single former flag officer or general in Congress. He had come to Washington with one agenda item—to make sure Congress knew what it was doing in the decisions it made about the military. Nothing else mattered to him. Just defense. The Speaker had wisely placed him on the House Armed Services

Committee, and through attrition and retirement, he was now the senior member and the chairman. Considered defense-oriented, but rational, he was well regarded on both sides of the aisle.

He sat at the head of the conference table on the edge of his seat as he always did. He believed in daily staff meetings of thirty minutes to make sure everyone was on the same page. His schedule was passed around and problems that had come up the day before were identified and someone was assigned to solve each one. The meeting was over at 0800 whether all business was completed or not.

This meeting had been short, with all business completed at 0750. The Admiral was in a good mood. He pushed his thick, graying brown hair away from his forehead and put his reading glasses into his suit coat pocket. "Anything else for the good of the cause?" he asked his staff.

Jaime Rodriguez hadn't planned on saying anything, but there was time. "We received an interesting letter the other day," he began tentatively.

"Why didn't you bring it up in constituent correspondence?" the Admiral asked absently.

Jaime knew he should have. That was why he was bringing it up now. "It didn't strike me as being that important then, but it keeps coming to mind."

"What was it?"

"From a Navy Lieutenant—"

"Constituent?"

"Yes, sir."

"What's his command?"

"Excuse me?"

"Where is he? Where is he currently stationed?"

"A carrier."

"Ship's company or an aviator?"

"Um . . . I'm not really sure."

"What ship?"

"I don't really remember, sir. Sorry, I hadn't intended to bring it up. Since we had some time . . ."

"What's so interesting about it?"

"It was about this Sheikh guy. The new terrorist?"

The Admiral nodded.

"He thought he had a way of hitting back at this guy."

"What's that?"

"He thought we should declare war."

"Against whom?" the Admiral asked, amused.

"Against the Sheikh himself."

Admiral Brown looked confused. "How could we do that?"

"It's pretty interesting. He did his homework. He sent it by e-mail. He attached a memo from a priest—"

"A priest?"

"Yes, sir—claimed he had some expertise in ethics. It's an analysis of whether it would be a just war, mentions Aquinas, and Grotius—"

"Seriously?"

"Yes, sir, but he also talked to a JAG officer about the legality of declaring war against one man. The JAG guy looked at it and said it could be done. Nothing that would keep us from declaring war against one man, a terrorist, or his whole organization for that matter. Then we could send the entire military after him. Wherever he is. And if someone is protecting him, or guarding him, then international law would allow us to go through them too."

Admiral Brown looked at Jaime, his legislative director, carefully. He was clearly pleased. He loved new ideas. "A Lieutenant?"

"Yes, sir."

"A very clever Lieutenant."

"Yes, sir."

Admiral Brown glanced around the room. "What do you think about this idea?" he said to no one in particular.

Nobody said anything. Jaime finally replied, "I think it's incredible."

Brown nodded and checked his watch—0800. He stood. "Tim?"

"Vacation."

"Have him research it. This is the kind of thing that might respond to some good thinking." To Jaime he said, "You'll need to do a reply."

Sheepishly Jaime said, "Sir, I already sent a reply back to him. I sent him a form letter about terrorism."

The Admiral frowned but then he said briskly, "All right . . . Let's get on with the business of the day." Then he had another thought. "Jaime, why this Lieutenant?"

"What do you mean, sir?"

"Why did he care about it enough to write?"

"You know that bus attack? Where the Navy officer was killed?"

"Sure."

"It was his roommate."

"Want me to get your mail too?" Woods asked as he changed into his uniform in his stateroom.

Big nodded, lying there with his eyes closed.

"You should have let me help you carry those rugs. I thought that was the whole idea."

Woods locked the stateroom door behind him and headed aft toward the ready room. It was deserted except for the duty officer. Woods leaned over and looked in his mailbox. He pulled out two news magazines, a post card, a sports weekly, and two letters, one from his mother and . . . his heart skipped, one from the House of Representatives. He looked at the envelope, not sure whether to open it or bring it back to the stateroom. He decided to take it where he could find some privacy and not have somebody looking over his shoulder. He hurried back to his stateroom, slamming the door behind him. "Big! Look!" he said breathlessly.

Big rolled over and peered at Woods sideways, examining the envelope. "I can't read it."

"It's from Congressman Brown," Woods said excitedly. "I just e-mailed him!"

"Doesn't take long to print a form letter."

"You're missing this one, Big."

"Open the letter."

Woods stuck his finger under the flap and tore the top of the envelope. He opened the single sheet. "It's on his letterhead, and signed by him personally."

"Read it."

Lieutenant Sean Woods, USN
Fighter Squadron One Zero Three
FPO New York, NY 10023

Dear Lieutenant Woods:

Thank you for your recent letter. I share your concern about terrorism. It is a scourge on civilized societies. I agree it is no way to achieve even a worthwhile end; it demonstrates the inhumanity of the terrorist by his disregard for human life.

I have taken several steps to combat terrorism, both here and abroad. I have endorsed the bill recently introduced in the House by Congressman Black, which strengthens the FBI and its ability to track terrorists. I have also cosponsored the Act to End International Terrorism. That act will do two things, first, increase the ability of our intelligence-gathering agencies, including the CIA, to monitor terrorist activity abroad, and second, facilitate cooperation among INTERPOL and other international police and intelligence agencies making it easier for them to share information and planning on how to deal with terrorists.

I hope this meets with your approval. It is important that a congressman receive correspondence from his constituents. Thank you, Lieutenant Woods, for your letter and your support.

Sincerely,
Lionel Brown, Vice Admiral, United States Navy (Retired)
Congressman, 49th District of California

Woods stared at the page after he had finished reading the letter.

"He didn't even *mention* what I said. How can he write a letter like that and not even mention it? He didn't even say anything about Father Maloney's memo or the law stuff. Nothing."

"It's a form letter, Trey, just like I told you it would be."

"It *can't* be," Woods said. "This must just be the first letter, there's probably another one coming that will answer mine."

"You're dreaming," Big said.

"But it is the *perfect* solution!"

"That's got nothing to do with it. You've bought into the myth that we live in a representative democracy that is actually responsive. That's rubbish. Congressmen exist for one purpose only—to stay in office. That's why they start running for office as soon as they get in. That's all they do. Shoot, Trey, during the cold war there was more turnover in the politburo than in Congress."

"Bullshit—"

"It's true."

Woods wasn't even listening. "It's one thing to tell me my idea is stupid, or wrong. But to treat me like some Rube from Brawley writing about his check for farm subsidies . . ."

Big sat up. "You really think a *congressman* saw your letter? What have you been smoking? Some flunkie gets the letters, sorts them by issues, and cranks out whatever form letter is closest. Then they mark down your issue, which side you're on, and count them up. All you'll get out of your letter is that somewhere in your congressman's office, your letter caused some bright young college graduate with unlimited ambition to put a mark on a list that shows one of the congressman's constituents is in favor of a stronger response to terrorism. That's it."

"That sucks."

"Yep."

"Don't they want to do anything about it?"

Big chuckled. "You don't understand. You don't get the critical difference between the *ability* to do something and the *will* to do it. They don't have the political will. They don't ever step out in front—they're afraid of taking the wrong position."

Woods laid the letter on the desk and stared at it as if it bore a disease. Then he picked it up and tore it in half, then in half again, and again, until he had ripped the letter to shreds, slamming it into the steel trash can.

Big rolled over and moaned. "Anything else in the mail?"

Woods picked up the rest of the mail and went through it again. "No. Just the usual." He stopped. "Who would send me a postcard?" He examined it, then recognized the writing.

"What?" Big asked. "What is it?"

Woods whispered, "It's from Boomer. From Israel."

"You're shitting me," Big said, swinging his legs over the side of the bunk. "What does it say?"

Woods read it with an odd feeling, as if he were doing something somehow improper. "He's in Nahariya. He's in love. Irit is great . . . they're going to Tel Aviv tomorrow where she is going to interview for a job with El Al as a flight attendant. They're going to take the bus down the coastal highway . . . should be beautiful . . . very upbeat."

"That's kind of spooky."

Woods was sad, remembering the last time he had seen Vialli.

Big interrupted his thoughts. "Hey."

"What?"

"I thought she was a schoolteacher. What's she doing interviewing for El Al?"

"I don't know. I think the schoolteacher bit was when she told him she was from Italy."

Big squinted. "So what did she really do?"

Woods and Wink orbited twenty miles out from the *Washington*, waiting. Finally the Air Boss transmitted, *"Victory 200, you're cleared in."*

"You ready, Wink?"

"Hit it," he said to Woods, then to the Air Boss: *"Roger."*

Woods lowered the nose of the Tomcat and pushed the throttles to the stops.

"Passing through ten."

"Roger."

Woods checked his instruments and made sure the TACAN needle was on the nose pointing to the *Washington* straight ahead, sixteen miles away. He glanced over his shoulder and watched the wings begin sweeping back as the Tomcat passed through .7 Mach, seven-tenths the speed of sound.

"Passing five."

"Roger," Woods replied. Ten miles. He pulled the nose over farther toward the water, pushing the throttles into afterburner. He felt the burners kick in and shoved the throttle to the end.

"Passing two." The needle on the airspeed indicator moved steadily through Mach 9. *"Home base, Victory 200, 6 miles out for supersonic pass."*

"Roger, 200. Cleared in supersonic."

"I can't believe they pay us for this," Woods said. "Passing one thousand feet, going hot mike." Woods remained amazed that Bark had let him do the supersonic pass. They had done air shows for dignitaries often, and the supersonic pass was the most fun of the entire event, but it was always the Commanders or Lieutenant Commanders who got the job. This time for some reason, Bark had let him do it. The ship had offered to perform the show for Israeli dignitaries, and they had eagerly accepted. The COD had made two trips to Haifa, and the dignitaries from Israel now stood on the flight deck, watching the demonstration of the capabilities of an aircraft carrier. One weapon system they wished they had and knew they would never get.

"I'm hot," Wink said, flicking the switch on his ICS.

The F-14 slipped through the sonic barrier imperceptibly, its wings swept full aft, like a horse with its ears pinned back.

"Radar altimeter set at fifty feet."

"Cool," Wink said, leaning forward to look for the carrier so plainly visible on the radar. He saw the big gray hulk on the beautiful blue sea. The sky was lighter blue and equally smooth. They continued to accelerate through Mach 1.1.

"Home base, see you," Wink transmitted.

"No tally on you, continue . . . tallyho. You're awfully low," the Air Boss transmitted, corrective concern in voice.

"Roger that," Wink said, smiling.

In an instant they were on the carrier. They flew down the port side of the *Washington*, like a blurred image in a photograph, with no sound.

Big McMack, standing on the flight deck, was always amazed at the sight of a supersonic airplane. He had done it countless times, but seeing it from the flight deck was another experience entirely. He scanned the faces of the Israeli dignitaries as they watched the passing Tomcat. He knew the look. He knew what they were saying: "It's so quiet . . ." Just wait he said to himself, putting his fingers in his ears.

Woods and Wink looked up at the figures standing on the flight deck as the Tomcat flew like an arrow at fifty feet over the water, twenty feet below the flight deck. They passed the entire length of the flight deck in less than a second.

"You ready?" Woods asked Wink.

"Pull it," he replied, leaning back in his seat.

Woods pulled on the stick as they passed the ramp of the flight deck and pegged the accelerometer on 6.5 Gs. The silent Tomcat pulled up from the horizon and pointed straight up from the earth with no apparent effort.

Big, gritting his teeth, kept his eyes on the watching dignitaries. They were smiling. Then, just when they had forgotten it might ever be coming, BOOM! Their knees buckled and their hands went to their ears. "Too late," Big said to himself as he removed his hands from his ears and chuckled.

The Jolly Roger F-14 left thick white vapors behind it from the G forces acting on the wings. It screamed away from earth, still supersonic, climbing like a bandit. In five seconds it was passing through ten thousand feet and growing smaller.

Woods held the stick against his left thigh as he took the Tomcat spun through one aileron roll after another. The nose was exactly straight up, ninety degrees away from the horizon, the earth spinning around and around beneath them, as if suspended on a string. "Passing fifteen," Wink reported.

"Roger," Woods replied. "Who was on the flight deck anyway?"

"Passing twenty. I'm not sure. I think the Israeli Secretary of Defense and a couple of other politicians."

"Prime Minister?"

"Passing twenty-five. Yeah, he was supposed to come. Don't think he did though."

"We'll level off at thirty."

"Okay."

As they passed through thirty thousand feet, no longer supersonic but still rocketing away from earth, Woods steadied the Tomcat in level flight, upside down, then rolled upright, his throttle reduced to four hundred knots.

"*Victory 200, RTB.*"

"*Roger, 200. Air show complete, green deck. Cleared into the break.*"

"*Roger that,*" Wink said. "Let's do it."

Woods rolled upside down and pulled the nose down toward the horizon. The plane quickly descended through twenty thousand feet and headed back toward the ship. Woods glanced to his right as they straightened from their left turn. "Check it out," he said, looking over at Israel. "Sure is pretty."

"I'll say."

"You ever been there?"

"No. Passing through five thousand feet. You?"

"Once. Wings coming back. Last cruise I was on."

"What did you think? *Victory 200, five miles for the break, see you.*"

"*Roger, 200, cleared for the break. Say speed.*"

Wink glanced at his airspeed indicator. "*Five hundred.*"

"*Roger.*"

The carrier was passing underneath them and to their left. Woods banked the plane slightly to see the deck clearly. "Check that out," he said. "They've got the dignitaries standing on the flight deck just forward of the island."

"We ought to bolter just to give them something to see."

"Not today. I'm too hungry."

They waited until they had passed in front of the carrier. Wink braced and Woods snapped the Tomcat into a left bank, pulling back hard on the stick. At eight hundred feet they headed downwind, the opposite direction of the ship. Leveling out, they went through the landing checklist quickly and started their approach turn toward the carrier, the only airplane in the air.

Big watched his roommate bank toward the flight deck onto final approach. The LSOs were in place, ready to receive the big fighter.

Woods rolled into the groove and steadied on his heading and rate of descent. He was on rails. The Tomcat descended steadily and quickly toward the landing area as the dignitaries stared, openmouthed.

Wink transmitted, *"Victory 200, Tomcat, ball, 7.0."*

The LSO replied, *"Roger, ball."*

Woods watched the ball, the landing reference lens on the port side of the ship. It was perfectly centered. He glanced again at his rate of descent, his lineup, and his angle of attack. The deck rushed up and stopped the Tomcat's descent and the wire grabbed the tailhook. Woods put the throttles full forward and tried to pull away from the wire. The Tomcat rolled to a short stop on the deck. A perfect landing.

The Israeli dignitaries were stunned. They had been around the military all their lives, but had never seen anything remotely like this. They looked at the Tomcat and the carrier with envy.

18

Eight F-16 Israeli fighters appeared out of nowhere and flew over the *Washington* as it steamed majestically into Haifa Bay. They banked east and flew inland, still in formation. Woods smiled at the sight. There was nothing quite like seeing fighters fly in formation. Woods aligned his belt buckle to keep his whites pristine and perfect. He was one of the few squadron officers willing to put on his dress uniform for the privilege of standing on deck while approaching Haifa. Sailors lined the perimeter of the flight deck and every deck above it, to the O12 level above the signal bridge, their whites snapping like flags in the stiff breeze.

Small patrol gunboats of the Israeli Navy—officially not a Navy, just part of the Israeli Defense Force—cruised alongside like puppies, dwarfed even by the *Ticonderoga,* the Aegis cruiser accompanying the *Washington.*

Excitement had been building for days since the port visit to Haifa had been confirmed. The sailors had assumed it would never happen. Too much volatility. Port calls in Israel were always subject to the political winds and changed with little notice. Many of the sailors had been on cruises in the Mediterranean before and had been scheduled to go to Haifa only to have the plans change for reasons they couldn't now remember. But someone had decided that allowing events like the bus attack to vary the schedule was giving in to terrorism. And now they were in Israel.

They were excited; more than the usual excitement of a port call. Perhaps it was the recommendation to wear their uniforms ashore that so astounded them. The usual instructions were to wear civilian clothes and try not to look too American; otherwise, it was thought, people might spit on you or try to shoot you. But here, there were stories of people being asked over to dinner by Israelis *because* they were Americans. And women who *wanted* to spend time with you because you were in the Navy. That rumor alone was enough to make the sailors lose sleep.

As always in the Mediterranean, the *Washington* anchored offshore, her draft too deep to pull into port.

As soon as the anchors were lowered the boats were prepared to carry the men to liberty. Woods was in line to be on the first officer boat. Big was his reluctant companion.

Woods bounced impatiently. He had been to Israel before, but had never taken advantage of his time to see the country. This would be different. He had traded with other officers so the duty watches he was scheduled to stand weren't during the time in port in Israel. He could spend every minute of the next four days seeing the country. And finding out what had happened to Vialli.

"How are we going to get to Tel Aviv?" asked Big unenthusiastically.

"I don't know yet."

"Do you even know where we're going?"

"Vaguely. It's north of Tel Aviv on the coastal highway."

Big looked down at Woods. "Why are you doing this?"

"Have to."

"Won't change anything."

Woods nodded slowly. "I know."

"Then why do it? You've gotta get on with your life. Vialli's death—"

"Murder."

"Okay, murder. You can't spend the rest of your life obsessing about it."

"I'm not obsessing."

"Right," Big replied as the line started to move.

"I just want justice . . ."

Big scoffed. "You need to read more Shakespeare. Then you'd know justice doesn't exist."

"I'm not talking about global justice, Big. I'm talking about making the people who did this pay. That's all."

"Good luck," Big replied, stepping into the open enlisted boat being used as an officer boat. Automatically, he walked toward the bow.

Woods followed. "They never find those guys, and if they do, they can't ever do anything about it."

"That's what I'm trying to change. That's why I wrote to my congressman . . ."

"Looks to me like you've hit a wall. You didn't accomplish *anything* except to get frustrated and obsess on Vialli for a month."

The boat pulled away from the *Washington*, headed for Haifa. The white buildings of the city stood out sharply from the hills, reminding Woods of the Azores. He sat back against the seat and looked aft toward the diminishing carrier.

When the boat touched the quay the sailors jumped off to moor it firmly. The officers waited for the Air Boss, the senior officer aboard— always last on and first off—to go ashore first, then filed off after him, looking forward to what they thought awaited them.

Woods and Big stood on the shore, shielding their eyes from the sun, not sure which way to turn. Officers and sailors, conspicuous in their brilliant white uniforms and covers, congregated in small groups. Israelis in passing cars and buses stared at them, then at the enormous ship sitting in the middle of the bay.

A short man with curly black hair approached Woods and Big who were still unsure about which way to go. "Taxi?"

"You speak English?" Big asked.

"Sure. I grew up in New York. Where you want to go?" the driver asked, grinning.

Woods chuckled. "To the train station. We want to go to Tel Aviv."

"No problem. Let's go."

Having been ashore in foreign ports before, Big asked, "How much?"

"You got money?"

"What?"

"Money. You got Israeli money?"

"No. Just dollars."

"That's fine. Five dollars."

"Okay. Let's go," said Woods, surprised by the reasonable fare.

The ride to the train station took only five minutes. Woods and Big looked out the windows of the cab like the tourists they were. Haifa was a bustling vibrant city.

The people who noticed the cab also saw the white uniforms and tended to stare, more curious than hostile. Woods paid the driver and walked into the train station carrying his gym bag. Big followed. The train station reminded Woods of those he had seen in Southern California, a small station house with a lot of open space. They looked around and walked to the ticketing office.

"Hello," Woods said. "Do you speak English?"

"Little," the man said kindly, leaning his head to one side to allow him to hear better.

"We would like to go to Tel Aviv. When is the next train?"

"Left just now. Two hours more."

He moved away from the window toward Big, who was watching the people in the station. "We just missed it. Next one is in two hours."

"So we wait I guess," Big said. "Unless you want to forget about this and go back to the boat."

"No. I'm not going to forget about it. We can . . . hold it. What do you say we go to Nahariya instead?"

"What for?" Big asked, already knowing whatever he said wasn't going to matter.

"To meet her family."

Puzzled, Big asked, "Whose family?"

"Irit's. You know. The one he was with when he got killed."

"Murdered."

"Touché. What do you say?"

Big didn't like the idea at all. "Do you even know her name?"

Woods grimaced. "I'm sure I'll remember by the time we get there. Plus I'll bet everybody in Nahariya knows who she was." He shifted his weight to his other foot to relieve the pressure on the one that was killing him. His white shoes never had fit him, and he was too cheap to replace them, since they rarely wore whites.

"You ever been there?"

"No. But it isn't that far. I mean the whole country is about the size of San Diego County."

"You don't even know where we'd go once we got there."

"There's got to be some kind of hotel or something, and if not, we can ride the train straight from there to Tel Aviv and sleep on the way. What do you say?"

"I think you're nuts. But since this is your rubber room we're living in, I'm just along to make sure you don't hurt yourself. Lead on."

Woods went back to the ticket window. "Is there a train soon to Nahariya?"

The man glanced at the clock on the wall. "One half hour," he said.

"Half an hour, Big, what do you say?"

"It's your script, Trey. Whatever you want to do."

Woods turned to the man at the window. "Two to Nahariya please."

Sami was asleep and afraid. This was something new for him, to be fast asleep and have his unconscious mind yelling at him in fear. He *had* to wake up, but he couldn't. He had been pushing himself too hard lately, too many late nights, too much anxiety from everything riding on his shoulders.

Something was in his eyes. Something red. He stirred waking slightly, his eyes still shut. Redness flashed across his eyelids again and his heart raced. What the hell— He opened his eyes in his dark bedroom inside his townhouse. He sat up and looked around. The room was a mess, his clothes were on the floor right where he had left them. He was about to lie down again, when the red light moved across his face again. Sami had no idea what was going on. The red light had come from the window, through the gap on the side of the window shade.

Padding over to the window in his bare feet, he opened the shade slightly and peered out. The red light was there again. Sami grew annoyed. Some neighborhood kid had decided that climbing into a tree and shining a laser pointer into his bedroom would be great fun. What a prick—

"Sami," a gruff voice whispered.

The voice scared him. It was no kid. "Who's there? What do you want?"

"Downstairs."

The laser pointer was switched off and he heard the man climbing down the tree. Sami was confused. Whoever it was knew who he was and where he lived. Still barefoot, he went down the stairs to the front door and peeked through the peephole. Nothing. As he strained to see outside in the darkness, pressing his nose against the door, he heard a soft knock. "Shit!" Sami exclaimed, jumping back. He stood in the dark, his heart pounding. Then, turning the handle, he cracked the door open.

Someone shoved at the door, pushing it wide open, as a hand hit his chest, knocking him backward into the townhouse.

"What the—"

"Hi, Sami," Ricketts said in Arabic, reaching up to put out the porch light and then closing the door behind him.

Sami stared at him. "What the hell do you think you're doing? You trying to give me a heart attack? What are you doing here?"

"I need to talk to you," Ricketts said, still in Arabic.

"At . . ." Sami looked at his wrist, which had no watch.

"Three o'clock."

"What are you *doing* here?" Sami asked again in English.

"Speak Arabic," Ricketts said.

Sami was happy to. He continued in Arabic. "What were you doing in the tree?"

"I've been knocking on your door for fifteen minutes. There was no answer."

"So you climb in a tree and shine a laser pointer into my bedroom? Can't that make you go blind?" he asked.

"It wasn't a laser pointer."

"What was it?"

"A laser sight."

"A *what*?"

"A laser sight. From my weapon."

"*What* weapon?"

"The one I carry."

Sami stared at him. He couldn't believe his ears. "You were pointing a *weapon* at me in my bed? Loaded?"

"What good is an unloaded weapon?" Ricketts asked.

"You could have *killed* me!"

"Not unless I wanted to. I was using the sight to see if I could see you inside your bedroom. Then I thought maybe the sight might wake you up."

"You some kind of psycho?"

"I want to ask you some questions."

"Why can't you ask me at the Agency, later? Why the big, dramatic thing?"

"I don't have much time. I must use every minute."

"Until what?"

"A mission."

"What mission?"

"Can't say."

"What a surprise."

"It has to do with our friend."

Sami stared at Ricketts, suddenly realizing that the man had been speaking the best Arabic Sami had heard in a very long time; as good as Sami's father. Very learned, very articulate. Not a hint of an accent, except perhaps Arabian, as in Saudi Arabian. "What do you need to know?"

"Absolutely everything you know about him, everything you have thought or suspected. A long, rambling, illogical, speculative talk, that will give me as much help as you can give."

"When?" Sami asked, still tired.

"Now."

Sami sighed and then pulled himself together. "Coffee?"

⟶

"It sure didn't take us very long to get here," Woods said as he picked up the phone book.

"That's because it wasn't very far," Big replied, scrutinizing the Nahariya train station from the chair he was sitting in.

"You're hilarious," Woods replied.

"You still don't remember her name? Didn't Vialli tell you?"

Woods refused to look at Big. "Yeah, he told me. I just can't remember."

"How do you know she wasn't lying about that too?"

"I guess I don't."

"Come on. Let's go back to the ship. This is a waste of time."

"Hirschman. That's it!"

"How do you know?"

"I just know," he said, opening the phone book. He turned the pages quickly and then slowed. "This is in Hebrew. I figured the names would be in English." He put the book down.

"You are dumber than a post sometimes, Trey. Why in the world would there be an English phone book in Israel?"

"Excuse me," Woods said to a passing soldier, one of the many in the train station, each carrying an M-16 or an Uzi. The soldier stopped.

"Yes?" he said.

"Do you speak English?"

"Yes, a little."

"Could you find the Hirschman residence for me in the phone book?"

The soldier was young and sturdy. He stood nearly six feet tall and had short black hair under a beret. He studied Woods as he considered the request. "Sure, of course. Why do you want their phone number?" he asked.

"We just need to talk to them. Their daughter, Irit, was a friend of a friend."

The soldier slung his M-16 over his shoulder and took the phone book. He looked at the pages as he talked. "Are you off the carrier at Haifa?"

"Yes, we are."

The soldier's eyes brightened as he considered the *Washington*. "I wish we had just *one* ship like that. You Americans have twelve of them and don't know what to do with them." He glanced at them. "Is it nuclear?"

"Yes."

"What is that like?"

Big shrugged. "Just like *not* being nuclear-powered," Big answered. "You can't tell at all, except there's no stack."

The soldier studied Woods's face. "Was your friend the Navy officer on the bus?" he asked.

"Yes."

He closed the book, holding a finger in it to keep his place. "We all knew her. She was two years older than me." He grew somber. "She was one of the jewels of Nahariya. Wonderful girl, very strong spirit; I don't know the words in English. She was special."

"Tony thought so. He was my roommate. He came here to visit her and was murdered with her."

"Here is the number," he said, indicating it. "You want me to call? I don't know if her father speaks English."

"Would you?" Woods said.

The soldier dialed the phone and waited for an answer. He spoke rapidly into the receiver in Hebrew, then he stopped, and held the receiver out. "He would like for you to come to their house. Would you like to go?"

"That would be great."

The soldier spoke into the receiver again, then hung up.

"What did he say?"

"He said he would be honored if you would come to his house. He would come to get you, but I told him I would show you where they live. It is not far from here."

"Thanks. We really appreciate it. This was kind of a spur of the moment thing."

"Follow me. . . . Oh, I'm sorry, I haven't introduced myself. My name is Jesse Sabin."

"Sean Woods, and this is Big McMack."

"You named after a sandwich?" Jesse said, smiling as they left the train station coming out into the bright sunlight.

"Exactly. My parents named me Big so I could take crap from people all the time. Actually it's a nickname. My real name is Joseph."

"Ah, the favored son," Jesse said and then added, "I should warn you, Irit's father did not take her death very well." He unslung his M-16 and carried it at his side by the handle on the top of the rifle. Woods could see that the rifle's ammunition clip was in place. Jesse continued, "The family hasn't really gotten over it. Use wisdom. When you think it is time to go—"

"We won't stay too long. Thanks for the advice."

They walked for several more blocks through neighborhoods and streets filled with pedestrians and children playing, many of whom stopped what they were doing to stare at Woods and Big in their white uniforms.

The Americans and their Israeli escort entered a narrow street and stopped at a gate in a low wall.

"This is it," Jesse said. "You can go knock on the door. I have to go."

Woods and Big both extended their hands and Jesse shook them.

"Shalom," Jesse said, smiling. He turned and headed in the direction of the water.

Woods and Big went through the gate. The building was unremarkable, a slab-sided, sand-colored condominium. They knocked and waited. The door opened slowly, and a little man in his sixties appeared. He had bushy eyebrows and sad eyes, thinning gray hair, and stooped shoulders.

"Hello," Woods said cautiously. He wasn't even sure why he had come. His enthusiasm and impulsiveness had gotten the better of him. Now, here he was, about to remind this poor old man of the death of his daughter. Woods suddenly felt deeply sorry for her father. "I'm Lieutenant Sean Woods. This is Bi . . . Joseph McMack . . ."

"Come in," the man said, leaving the door open and moving toward the inside of the house. They followed him into a small living room off the kitchen. There was an unusual smell to the place that Woods couldn't identify. He glanced into the kitchen as they passed it to see if food was being prepared, but he saw no food at all. A square patio surrounded by a fence was on the other side of a sliding glass door at the far end of the living room.

The old man motioned them to the couch and sat down in a dilapidated leather chair. He breathed deeply as he studied them.

Woods didn't know how to start. He formed a few sentences in his mind, but none of them worked.

"So," the man said. "You knew my daughter."

"I spent a little time with her, but Tony Vialli—you met him?"

"Yes."

"He was my roommate on the *Washington*. I spent some time with Tony and Irit in Italy."

"Tony," he replied. "Good boy. Handsome, but not one of us . . ."

Woods looked at Big for help but got back only a blank stare. "He was a great guy. I'm glad you got to meet him. Was he here long?"

"Only couple of days. He and Irit were together the whole time." He stared at the tile floor. A woman walked into the room from the front of the house. Woods and Big stood up. "Hello," she said in a friendly voice with an English accent. "I'm Miriam Hirschman."

"It's very nice to meet you, Mrs. Hirschman."

She said suddenly, "You didn't give them something to drink?"

He answered quickly in Hebrew at which she just waved her hand. "Can I get you boys something?"

"Whatever you have would be fine," Woods said for both of them.

"How about some lemonade?"

"That would be great."

"So you met her," Mr. Hirschman said.

"Yes, sir, but I only saw her once," Big said, trying to participate.

Jacob Hirschman pointed with a crooked finger to a picture frame on a corner table by the couch. "There she is," he said.

They both looked where he was pointing. "She was gorgeous," Woods said.

Jacob nodded his agreement, smiling just slightly with the corners of his sad eyes.

The picture captured Woods's attention. He crossed to the table and picked it up. Something was different. He looked at her smiling face and her dark hair. Her hair was shorter in the picture, she was a little thinner . . . Suddenly he noticed her hand. It was completely normal. Woods looked at Jacob. "Her hand."

"Yes. It was a tragedy."

"What happened? I thought it was from birth . . ."

Jacob was puzzled. "Oh, no. Only for the last eighteen months. Since the accident."

Woods looked at Big, who was very confused. He asked Jacob, "What accident?"

"The one where her hand was hurt."

Woods waited. He had a strange feeling he was opening a door he hadn't even known was there.

Jacob shrugged. "I don't really know. She didn't talk about it."

"Did it get caught in something?"

"I don't know."

"Was she working at the time?"

"Yes, of course."

"But she was a schoolteacher. What could—"

"A what?"

"Schoolteacher."

The old man's bushy eyebrows lifted in confusion. "Why do you say that?"

"That's what *she* said."

"She never taught school," he said with finality.

"What did she do?"

"She worked for the government."

"Doing what?"

"I'm not really sure. All she ever told me is it was the defense department. It was her business."

"Was she working for the government when her hand was injured?"

"Yes, of course." Jacob paused. He spoke to Big. "So you two are pilots."

"Yes, sir," Big said. "We're stationed on the *Washington.* We pulled into Haifa this morning."

Miriam came back into the living room, bringing the lemonade. She gave each of the men a tall cold glass and then sat in the only empty seat, a cloth-covered chair with shiny spots from years of use. "It was very nice of you to come and see us," she said "We don't get many visitors in white uniforms from the American Navy."

"Thank you for having us," Woods replied. He sipped his lemonade and complimented Miriam on the flavor. "I was just telling your husband, Tony Vialli was my roommate. I wanted to come see what he saw, and visit where he went."

"That's nice . . ."

"In fact, I got a postcard from Tony just the other day. It took a while for the mail to get there. It was from Nahariya."

They smiled weakly, remembering.

"It was sent the day before he and Irit went to Tel Aviv for her interview."

Miriam looked at Jacob. "What interview?"

"With the airline. El Al," Woods said.

"She didn't have any interview." She looked at Jacob. "Did she?"

"No. What interview? What for?" he asked.

"Flight attendant."

They both looked mystified. "No, she didn't have an interview."

"Then why was she going to Tel Aviv?"

"She didn't say, really. I guess she wanted Tony to see some of the sights. And I think she had some business."

Woods's mind raced around considering the implications. "Government business?"

"I suppose."

"She still worked for the government?"

"Of course."

"And that was one of the reasons she wanted to go to Tel Aviv?" Woods drank from his glass. "Well, that's interesting. But it probably doesn't mean anything. Tony must have misunderstood her."

"Yes, that must be it."

"Well, we don't want to take up all your time. We were on our way to see where Tony and Irit were murdered," he said. The words chilled them.

"Why?" Miriam asked, her eyes moistening as her husband fought back his own emotions.

"I have to. I owe it to him."

"Not much there," Jacob said.

"You've been there?"

He shrugged.

"When?"

"When it happened."

"Were you glad you went?"

He sighed. "I'm not glad about anything. I've lost too much. You have children?"

"I do," Big said as Woods shook his head.

Jacob looked at Big. "Ever lost any of them?"

"Only in the store," Big said, smiling, then immediately regretting it.

"She was everything to me. I don't know how to say it." He drank his lemonade with a shaking hand. "She was the family. It is the only thing you leave. . . . You know what I am saying?" he asked anxiously. "When you leave the world, you leave only your family. Even then, after fifty years, nothing. But at least for fifty years, you have people. You made a difference."

Woods didn't know what to say. Then to Jacob, "Would you like to come with us?"

Big stared at Woods, his eyes enlarged in warning.

"You mean to where it happened?"

"You've been there. You'd find it faster than we ever would."

Jacob looked at Miriam, who smiled gently at him. She said, "I can't, Jacob, it's too hard for me. But you go if you want."

"All right," he said. "You stay here tonight. I will drive you there first thing in the morning. Tonight, I will tell you stories about Irit, my little girl. Our only daughter."

✧

"So?" Ricketts asked, somewhat annoyed that he had to ask at all.

"So what?" Kinkaid replied. He had gone over to the DO, out of the task force area, to find Ricketts. Kinkaid had gone to the Director to talk to him about Ricketts. He had a bad feeling about Ricketts's mission. He had to acknowledge to himself that it was probably because he didn't know how the mission was to be carried out. But there was something else about it that gnawed at him. He had asked the Director of Central Intelligence, who was in charge not only of the CIA but all intelligence, to read him into Ricketts's mission. He had refused. Not only had he refused but he said that the agreement he had with Ricketts was that no one else could be read into that mission, and Ricketts had to be personally notified if anyone else even asked to be read in. The DCI had told him that he now had to notify Ricketts of Kinkaid's interest.

The idea had made Kinkaid so angry he had almost quit the Agency on the spot. He was fed up with the distrust, the over-the-top concern for secrecy, especially when it involved an area that was supposed to be under his control as the head of the task force. It drove him nuts. He was able to extract one promise from the DCI though, one that he thought might just drive Ricketts crazy—which at this point would be okay in Kinkaid's mind—the right to decide whether Ricketts could go at all. The go, no-go decision was Kinkaid's. Just as Ricketts had implied when they'd talked in the parking lot. Kinkaid knew Ricketts had pulled that early morning stunt just to imply that Kinkaid had the power, knowing all the time that only Ricketts and the Director really had the clout to call off the mission. He had made Kinkaid lower his guard by making him think he had power he never really had. Well, now he did.

Ricketts had decided he had to go now, and he had told the DCI so. The DCI had then informed him that that decision was now in the hands of Kinkaid.

Kinkaid had found him in the coffee room.

"Tell me why it has to be now," Kinkaid insisted.

"Why should I?"

"Because if you don't, I'm not going to approve it."

"I'll see the DCI," Ricketts argued.

"He gave it to me."

"Then he can un-give it to you."

"Maybe."

Ricketts hated these games. "The location I have for our friend is only for an hour. Two at the most. I don't decide when to do this, he does. I have no idea where he'll be before or after. Just during that window. That's it. If I don't get him then, I'll probably never get him."

"You sure?"

Ricketts sneered. "You know better than that. We're *never* sure. The whole thing could be a trap. But I'm prepared to bet my *life* it's not a trap, and he'll be there. That's as sure as I ever get."

Kinkaid sighed. "Look, I know I've been hard on you. I just don't like it when things I'm responsible for are outside of my control."

"You're not responsible."

"The hell I'm not. This will come down on my head if you fail."

"I won't fail," Ricketts said.

"When we get him back here, you going to do the interrogation?"

"Personally. I'd like Sami to help."

Kinkaid was surprised. "Seriously?"

"Yes. He understands."

"I'll think about it." Kinkaid turned, then Ricketts spoke again.

"I don't have to bring him back at all."

"We can't do that," Kinkaid replied, understanding exactly what he meant.

"I can get someone else to do it."

"Nope. Bring him. We need to have a chat."

Ricketts nodded and walked past Kinkaid.

19

Woods wasn't sure what he thought he'd find, but he was sure he expected to find something: blood, marks on the pavement, empty shell casings, something. But there wasn't anything. He and Big stood there next to Jacob, the beach behind them, and stared at a very ordinary road.

"Are you sure this is the place?" Woods asked.

"Yes, I am sure. This is where they killed Irit," Jacob said, his arms folded in front of him, his voice hardening.

Woods stared at him, then at the water. "They came from the sea?"

"Yes," Jacob said. "In rubber rafts."

"Why did they do it?" Woods asked.

"It is so hard for others to understand," Jacob said wearily. His eyes met those of the American Naval officers. "They do it because they *hate* us. They hate Jews. Just like the Germans before them, and others before them; they want to kill all Jews."

"But *why*?"

"Ask them. All we want is to be left alone. This is our land, given to us by *God*. The Promised Land. They think it is theirs and we stole it from them when we became a nation in 1948. They tried to kill us then, and they try to kill us now. They will always try to kill us. So we defend ourselves. But it is never enough. They come and kill our daughters, our sons . . . ."

"I've seen enough," said Woods with finality. "We owe it to Vialli, Big. We can't just let this drop."

They walked to Jacob's car.

"What are you thinking? Another letter to your congressman?" Big asked.

"I don't know."

"Nothing we can do, Trey."

"Nobody cares. Nobody. Not Congress, not the President, not the Department of Defense, not anybody. Huge power, and no will to use it. That's us."

Big looked at Woods earnestly. "Yep. That about sums it up."

Ricketts waited to board the airplane in Athens, Greece. He was wearing a fine gray Armani suit with a dark blue shirt and a designer tie, expensive loafers, and socks with a diamond pattern. His recently grown moustache was perfectly trimmed and his hair was oiled and combed back. A shiny stainless steel diving watch showed slightly below his French-cuffed shirt. He looked every bit the rich sophisticated Lebanese businessman he was trying to portray.

The Middle East Airline's clerk took his passport and ticket. She smiled, then addressed him in Arabic. "Going home?"

"Yes. Finally."

She examined the ticket and checked his name and photograph on his Lebanese passport. "Beirut?"

"Yes."

"Are you from there?"

"All my life."

"Me too," she said. "What part?"

"On the beach. My parents managed the Sheraton Hotel, until the city became like Berlin in '45. We closed it down, and I have worked in many other hotels since. Now, I own my own hotel."

"Which one?"

"It is in Spain." He smiled warmly. "Much safer."

"Beirut is safer now . . ."

He shrugged. "My parents say so as well. I just go to visit. I will return to live, and build a new big hotel on the beach, when everyone else is out. The Israelis, the Syrians, the Iranians, everybody."

"I will come visit your hotel," she said. "I hope it is soon." She handed him his passport and ticket and he joined the line of people waiting to board.

"What are you doing here?" Big asked as he reclined on his bunk reading Tolstoy.

"Taylor put in an emergency leave chit. I had to come in to sign off on it."

"I just don't get it. This guy introduces a million characters in about fifty pages; they stand around at parties, 'interact,' have feelings, it's boring."

"What is?"

"War and Peace."

"Maybe you need to skip to the war part."

"I've been thinking about Irit's picture. What do you think?" Big asked, closing his book.

"I don't know. I'm *sure* she said it was from birth. But I don't remember talking to her about it. I can't remember if Vialli said that, or if she did. If it was just him, he might have gotten it wrong. I suppose she could just tell people that so she doesn't have to explain the accident every day. It might be too embarrassing. Maybe she got it caught in an elevator door or something."

"Right. Or maybe there's a lot more to this."

"Like what?"

"How about the whole fake interview thing?"

Woods shook his head. "That one really got me. I mean Boomer even put that in his postcard. No mistake there."

"So what the hell is going on?"

"Don't know. We just don't know enough."

"You going to the reception tonight?"

Woods gave him a weary "oh no" look. "What reception?"

"At the Air Force base."

"What Air Force base?"

"Ramat David."

"Who is that?"

"You know, Israeli Air Force, F-15s, F-16s. Guys with wings, cool guys, like us."

Woods pulled his T-shirt off and tossed it into the bottom of his closet. "I have no idea what you're talking about."

"Well, while you were out playing tourista to the Holy Shrines, the Israeli Air Force sent word to CAG that they wanted to sponsor a reception for all the aircrew in the Air Wing to come to Ramat David. We leave in two hours, by bus. You coming?"

Woods sighed. "I'd love to talk to those guys. That sounds great. What's the uniform? Is anybody else from the squadron going?"

"Whites. Everybody."

Woods made a mental survey of the state of his tropical white uniform. "Maybe there'll be somebody there who can tell us more about this Sheikh guy."

"Don't count on it."

"Never hurts to ask."

The Americans were in their distinctive white uniforms and the Israelis were in their indistinctive olive-green uniforms. All were young and vigorous, and tried to impress each other. The pilots stood in small groups and traded stories. Many of the Israelis talked of combat victories and MiGs downed; the Americans stuck to carrier aviation, which the Israelis would never experience.

Woods and Big were talking to three Israeli Captains. They were F-15 pilots and proud of it. Pritch hovered outside the group, not sure whether she could participate as a full member of the unspoken but recognized fraternity of fighter pilots. She had insisted on coming even though she wasn't "aircrew." She argued that she was an officer in the squadron and should be allowed to come. Bark thought it might be amusing to have her along.

Woods was distracted. He had to write the flight schedule for the morning's flights, some of which were to launch immediately after the *Washington* pulled out of Haifa, and he hadn't even started it. "I'm sorry, what?" he said, realizing one of the Israelis was talking to him.

"You went to Topgun."

"Not only did he go, he was an *instructor*," Big said.

"Thanks, Big," Woods said sarcastically. "I don't know what I'd do without you."

"Is that true?" the Captain asked, impressed. "You were an instructor?"

"Yeah. Two and a half year shore tour, flying F-5s and F-16Ns."

"Must be great flying."

"Best there is."

"Is Topgun a good thing for the Navy? It is just Navy?"

"Yes. It's a Navy thing. The Air Force has Red Flag; but there's nothing like the original," Woods said, smiling. "It sure made a difference in Vietnam when it started. Our kill ratio was 2:1 until we started Topgun, then it went to more than 12:1. The North Vietnamese told their pilots not to fight gray Phantoms."

"What do you mean?" the Captain asked, perplexed.

"Gray Phantoms. Navy Phantoms, F-4s. Fight the Air Force Phantoms, the camouflage ones. They haven't been to Topgun."

"Oh, of course. That's good," the Captain said. Grinning, he repeated this in Hebrew for his fellow pilots. They laughed weakly. "You think you still fly as good?"

Woods smiled. "We like to think so. We'd love the chance to see how we could do against you."

Big stepped closer as the stakes went up. "That *would* be something. Since you guys are *clearly* the best in the world—because of your combat experience—it would be quite an honor to test ourselves against you."

"It would be our honor," the Captain said to Woods. "And we would only hope to do well enough so as not to bring discredit on ourselves." He studied the white-uniformed Navy pilots carefully. "I wish we could find out," the Captain said.

At the front of the room, someone tapped on the side of a glass.

"May I have your attention please," said an Israeli officer. Woods couldn't figure out how to decode their insignia yet, but assumed the one speaking was in charge. "I am Colonel Yitzak Bersham. I want to welcome the American pilots from the *Washington,* and thank you for coming to Ramat David, our aircraft carrier that doesn't move." He smiled at his small joke. "The reason we asked you here tonight is to get to know you better, let you get to know us better, and talk about airplanes and the great traditions of aviation. We also wanted to thank you on behalf of your country, for your constant support, and for the weapons you have provided us, without which we would never have survived." He waited as the Israeli pilots clapped, endorsing his thanks.

"Please make yourselves at home, get to know our pilots, and enjoy your stay in Israel." He raised his glass and then stepped away from the microphone.

A U.S. Navy Captain took the microphone and spoke to the crowd. "Good evening. I'm Captain Dave Anderson, the Air Wing Commander of the *Washington.* We wanted to thank you for your hospitality, and for inviting us to meet you at your air base. Several of you were able to visit us on the *Washington,* and next time perhaps the rest of you can as well . . ."

Woods had stopped listening. He never liked speeches, or toasts, or any other times when people said things other than what they meant. He looked at the Israeli pilots standing next to him, then at his watch. He still had to prepare the flight schedule.

". . . and let me simply say that it is an honor to be with the second-best group of aviators in the world." The Israelis hooted and laughed at the comment, although half were behind because of the translation lag.

Commander Anderson moved away from the mile, and the officers began talking again. Woods didn't feel like making any more small talk. He toyed with going out and waiting in the bus. "Lieutenant Woods," the Israeli Captain said, "I want you to meet our Squadron Commander, Major Mike Chermak." Chermak moved closer to Woods and extended his hand.

Woods was surprised. "Your name is *Mike*?"

"Yes." Chermak smiled warmly. "Nice Christian name, yes?"

"Interesting."

"No, it is short for Micah. Old Hebrew name. There is even a book in your Old Testament by that name." He watched Woods, then recognized his name on his nametag. "So you're the Topgun instructor," he said softly. His brown eyes bore holes in Woods, making him uneasy.

"Former instructor, sir," Woods said. "Now I'm in a squadron."

"103?" he asked.

Woods's eyes narrowed. "You've done your homework."

"Skull and bones," he said.

"That's us."

"I went to your school. I am a Topgun graduate."

Woods studied him more closely. "When?"

"Oh, before your time. Class of 04/97, in F-16s."

"*That's* why you guys are so good. Navy-trained."

"How do you like the F-14?" Chermak asked.

"Best fighter in the world," Woods said quickly.

"You really believe it's better than our F-15s?"

"Depends on what you're doing. Can you shoot down six planes simultaneously?"

"No, but how often are you called on to do that?"

"Not often enough."

"What about in a dogfight?"

"We can beat anybody, except a well-flown F-15 or 16. *Really* well flown. And we'll beat him about half the time."

Chermak changed the subject. "Have you enjoyed your time in Israel?"

"Not really," Woods said.

"Why not?" the Major asked.

Woods was silent for a minute before he answered. "Because I went to see where my roommate was murdered."

The Major hesitated. Then he asked. "How did it happen?"

"He came to visit his girlfriend, in Nahariya, and was killed by that Sheikh."

The Major sighed. "He was the one on the bus?"

"Yes, sir," Woods replied, his gray eyes full of fire.

"I'm sorry," the Major said. Shrugging his shoulders, he added, "Americans don't usually get involved."

"Shot him in the back."

The Major responded softly, "I'm sorry . . . but, you know, Israelis are killed every year. In cold blood. I don't mean to minimize the death of your friend, but if it had been an Israeli man killed on that bus, you probably wouldn't have even heard about it."

"You know, you don't have a patent on suffering," Woods said angrily. "Sometimes it seems to me like you're proud of how much you've had to suffer. Well, we suffer sometimes too. Seems like it's always for someone else, but we suffer too."

"Of course you do. I didn't mean to say you don't. But you must understand, we are in a unique situation here. There have been over fifteen hundred terrorist attacks on Israel since we became an independent nation in 1948. We are a country of four and a half million people, and we are surrounded by forty million Arabs, who have sworn to kill us all and push us into the sea. Sometimes some of them deny that. But *never* all of them." He raised his glass and drank deeply. "We are in a constant state of war. Constant. They shoot rockets at us across the border, and hit schools and hospitals. They come ashore in rubber boats and murder families. They blow up buses and kill innocent women and children. And for that, they want recognition and respect."

"I didn't mean to say you were wrong, or . . ."

The Major waved him off with his hand. "I know, I know. . . . We just live it every day. You are feeling what we *all* feel, every day of our lives. We have all lost family and friends in the wars, in terrorist attacks, and in intimidation." His eyes came alive. "But now as a nation we can do something about it. We don't sit back and walk to the gas chambers like lambs to slaughter." His voice rising, he said, "Deliver those who are being taken away to death, and those who are staggering to slaughter, hold them back. If you say, we did not know this, does he not consider it who weighs the heart? And does he not know it who keeps the soul? And will he not render to man according to his works?" He paused to look for recognition in Woods. "Do you know that? It is from the Meshalim. Your Book of Proverbs, in the Old Testament, as you call it."

Woods nodded.

"Now, we do something about it. We strike back. Never again will Jews go to their deaths quietly."

"That's exactly how I feel, but I can't do anything about Vialli," Woods said. Noticing the Major's confusion he added, "My roommate."

"What do you mean?"

"I wanted to do something about Vialli. But I'm out of options." Woods spoke out of frustration. "I just wanted to *do* something."

The Major took another sip from his glass. "Like what?"

"To strike back. I wanted to go after the people who did it." Woods's eyes showed his intense disappointment.

"Do you know where they are? 'Cause I think some people have an idea of where they are. Or where the Sheikh is."

"He's in Lebanon."

Woods waited. He wasn't sure if he was being asked, or told. "How do you know?"

"We make it our business to know where terrorists are who murder Israelis. He isn't always in Lebanon, but he is right now. His headquarters is somewhere else."

"How do you know he is in Lebanon?"

"Our intelligence people are very good."

"Where in Lebanon?"

"Eastern."

"I thought when he sent his statement to the press he signed it in Beirut."

"Maybe. But now, he's in eastern Lebanon."

"You know the town?" Woods asked, wanting to get as much information as he could, whether he was supposed to know or not.

"I do know the town."

"What town?"

"Dar al Ahmar."

"Where is that?"

"If I had a chart I would show you."

"Why are you telling me this?"

Chermak shrugged. "We're on the same side, aren't we? Didn't he kill your American roommate and my three countrymen?"

Woods wondered what Chermak was getting at. Why did he feel as if he was being tested. "If you know where he is, why aren't you doing something about it?"

"What makes you think we're not?"

"Because nothing has happened. We'd know about it."

"You would know about it if we wanted you to know about it. If it was done some other way, you might not hear about it."

"I hope you hammer him."

"So why didn't you?"

"Why didn't I what?"

"You said you wish you could do something about it. Why didn't you?"

"It's not up to me. I went way out on a limb. Even went to see the Admiral, to get him to launch an attack. Kind of stupid. I could have been *court*-martialed. I think everyone was giving me a lot of room since Vialli was my roommate. Then I had a brainstorm, and wrote to my congressman to tell him about it. I had hoped our government—Congress in particular—would do something. I should have known better. They never do. They say a bunch of words and go to their next party. I guess we're supposed to just let it happen."

Except for Big, the other officers had drifted away as the conversation had become more and more serious. The Major looked around the room slowly, then back at Woods, as if considering something. He leaned forward slightly, saying on a soft voice, "May I talk to you outside?"

Woods wasn't sure. "What for?" he asked, trying to resist but without offending.

Chermak didn't respond directly. "Yes?"

"I guess so." He turned to Big, saying "I'll be right back."

Big gave him a "be careful" look.

Woods and the Major walked outside the club and into the star-filled night, from the loud cacophony of conversation to the deep quiet of the evening. It was chilly and Woods wished he had something on other than his polyester white uniform. He put his cover on his head and pulled the bill down.

The Major started down the road. "Come," he said.

Woods walked beside him on the side of the field next to the club. "What's this about?" he asked impatiently.

"Just a minute," the Major replied. "I want to make sure we're out of hearing range of the building. You never know what is attached to a building or who is inside it."

Woods frowned but didn't say anything. After a few minutes, the Major stopped. A single spotlight from a building hundreds of yards away lit the Major from behind just enough that Woods couldn't make out his face. He listened carefully over the chirping of the crickets as the Major stood very close to him and spoke softly, almost in a whisper. "What are you doing tomorrow morning?"

Woods was puzzled. "We sail early, then we'll be conducting flight ops west of here."

Major Chermak said, "Can you fly in the morning?"

"What?"

"Can you fly in the morning?"

"I told you, we'll be flying off the ship in the morning. We're pulling out."

"What time?"

"I can't tell you that. Confidential."

"What time is your first flight?" the Major asked again, undeterred.

"What difference does it make?"

"What time," the Major repeated.

Woods hesitated, then said, "I think our first launch is 0700."

"Can you be on it?"

"Why?"

"Yes or no."

"Of course. I write the flight schedule. I can put myself on it anywhere I want. But why?"

The Major checked around them slowly in each direction obviously watching for any movement.

"Can you meet us overhead right here," he said, pointing up, "at 0730?"

"*What* are you talking about?" Woods asked, his heart pounding as the implications of what the Major was asking sunk in.

"Yes or no."

"I suppose I could, but what for?"

"Tomorrow we go north. Into Lebanon. We will be after several terrorist strongholds in southern Lebanon, from where they launch their actions, including the place the rubber boats came from in the attack when your friend—"

Woods cut him off. "Where was that?" he asked sharply.

"Never mind about that. We also will be in eastern Lebanon. I will be leading that strike."

"Why eastern Lebanon if the attack was launched from the coast?"

"We're going to Dar al Ahmar."

"You're going after the Sheikh himself? The one taking credit for Gaza, and the bus?"

"The very one."

Woods felt goose bumps on his arms. "What would I do?"

"You can cover me. We are expecting the Syrians to come after us this time. We will be baiting them. Just a little."

"They're going to be sending fighters after you?"

"Yes."

"What could I do?"

"Keep them off me. I have to deliver a laser-guided bomb to our friend."

"Why don't you want your own fighters doing escort?"

"I do. They will be there. You can fly high cover, above most of the AAA and low SAMs."

Woods tried to keep his voice from shaking. "I'd never get permission."

Woods barely heard Chermak's rueful laugh. "I didn't expect you to ask."

Woods's mind was spinning. "Are you serious?"

"Very."

"I couldn't be of much help. I can't fire my missiles. Can't very well go back to the ship without them."

"There may be a way around that too."

🙚

"Are you nuts?" Big asked, quickly glancing around for other squadron officers. "This is the kind of thing that they don't think is funny. We'll be making big rocks into little rocks."

"What's up?" Pritch asked, strolling up to the two Naval officers she enjoyed being with the most. "You look like you've seen a ghost," she said to Big.

Big ignored her and, returning his focus to Woods, said, "You talk to Wink yet?"

"No. I wanted to talk to you. If you're in, we can talk to Wink and Sedge."

Big shook his head thoughtfully. Pritch looked at them in frustration. "We'd never pull it off," Big said finally.

"It'll work. There's not that much to plan. We just have to go along with them. Making it look like a regular hop from the ship will be the tricky part, but it will work. I *know* it will."

"Maybe you're not the best person to decide that."

"Let's find Wink and Sedge. I'll go over the whole thing. Then we'll decide."

Big spoke to Pritch. "Let's go."

They moved toward the back of the room where most of the squadron was congregated, waiting to return to the ship.

"Go over what whole thing?" Pritch said to their backs.

20

Big took off his white uniform and hung it in his closet. "We're sticking our heads into a noose. They don't *need* our help. If we don't show up it won't make any difference at all."

"Except we already said we would."

"I doubt they'd care," Big said, sitting down heavily in his stateroom chair.

"You having second thoughts?"

"I'm way past that," Big said. "I think these are fifth or sixth thoughts. I've done a lot of things in my life that I shouldn't have done, some of them even illegal." He leaned back in his chair, closing his eyes. "I've broken Navy regulations on occasion, when it suited me. I've even worn my belt upside down, contrary to Uniform Regulations. My being left-handed and all, it seemed like I should be able to wear it as a normal left-handed person would, not some arbitrarily drawn regulation." He opened his eyes and studied Woods's face. "But I've never done anything that qualifies as a *felony* before."

Woods stopped undressing and turned to Big. "You don't have to come if you don't want to. I'm not going to talk you into anything. You'd hold it against me."

"Of course I would. I'll hold it against you even if you *don't* talk me into it," Big replied. "Are we doing the right thing here, Trey?"

Woods closed his closet door too hard. "Tell me what right is, Big. Is it right that some self-appointed Sheikh Assassin or whoever else it will be next time, can shoot one of our squadron mates and get away with it? Is that right?"

"That's a stupid question. I'm asking about *us*, not them. What's right for us isn't decided by what they do. It may make it harder, but it doesn't determine it."

"They don't care about *anybody*! Human life is not valuable to them, except maybe for the chumps who are at the head of *their* organization. I don't see them doing the attacks themselves. Human life is valuable to *me* though. A lot. That's my point."

"I don't know, Trey," Big said. He drummed his fingers on his fold-down desk. "What do you think Father Maloney would say about it?"

Woods was shocked. "Since when do you care what he thinks about anything? Every time he sits down by us you get up and leave like he has leprosy."

"I get uncomfortable talking about religion." He chewed his lip thoughtfully. "I guess I don't like being put on the spot. I don't know what I think. It shows fast." He rubbed his mouth. "You ever think about dying?"

Woods's face showed his amazement. "What's gotten into you? Mr. Cavalier, Mr. Cynic, suddenly you want to know the meaning of life?"

"I don't know, Trey. Thinking about tomorrow, it just occurred to me."

Woods sat down. "Sure, I've thought about it. The way I see it, I'm invincible until God wants me to die, then there's nothing I can do about it."

Big reflected. "What does *that* mean?"

"I don't know. My father used to say it. I always thought it sounded clever . . . until he died. Then it wasn't funny anymore." His voice trailed off. "You gonna go with me or not?"

Big sighed resignedly. "You'd probably get lost, or screw something up. I'll have to be there to watch out for you."

Woods relaxed. "Thanks."

"Don't thank me. We may both end up in Leavenworth."

"Bring it on. Let me testify in a court-martial about how no one cared about Vialli. If we end up in Leavenworth, it'll be worth it."

"I hope you're right," Big said, climbing onto his rack for a short night's sleep. "Somebody's got to take care of these terrorists. I guess it's time somebody took a risk to do it. It's like Humphrey Bogart said in *The Maltese Falcon*," Big added. He did a Bogart voice: 'You've got do something about it. If you don't, it's bad for business, bad all around.' "

Woods thought he heard a noise and turned toward the stateroom door. He heard it again. It was a soft but determined knock. He opened the door a crack and Wink pushed it the rest of the way open and let himself into the room.

"Wink. What's up?" Woods asked.

"We can't do this," Wink said nervously. He looked around the room to make sure they were alone. He acknowledged Big sitting on his rack.

"Do what?"

"Cut the crap." Wink sat down in Woods's desk chair and rubbed his hands back and forth on the tops of his legs like a schoolboy in the principal's office. "We'll never pull it off."

"Yes we will," Woods countered.

"Too much can go wrong—"

"No doubt about it. But we *will* pull it off, Wink. You know we can do it."

"It's not the escort part of it that worries me." He was clearly struggling. "I don't want to go to *prison,* Trey, not for some impulsive, feel-good revenge deal."

"We won't go to prison!"

"We'll never pull it off!" Wink exclaimed, louder than he intended.

"Yes, we will. What's gotten you going?" Woods asked. "You said you were in—"

"I was. I've been lying in my rack staring at the overhead. I can't even swallow. Do you *realize* the implications if we get busted?"

"Of course I do. But we won't."

"Yeah. Right. Tiger has to do the fake symbols on the radar—"

"You talk to him?"

"Yeah."

"He said he could?"

"Sure. But if someone looks close they'll see the difference—"

"They won't. Nobody checks on Tiger. He's the man."

"What if they do?"

"They won't."

"And we've got to get there and back in one cycle? One hour and forty-five minutes? Are you kidding me?"

"Wink, I *showed* you the chart. You know this stuff. It's one hundred eleven nautical miles to Ramat David. How long is that at five hundred knots? Thirteen point three two minutes, Wink. You did the calculation. And how far is it from Ramat David to the Bekáa Valley in Lebanon? Sixty-four friggin' miles, Wink. How long does *that* take at six hundred knots? Six point four minutes, Wink. So far that's about twenty minutes. And to get back? Another fifteen, or twenty minutes, depending. So forty or so minutes total, add a little time for air combat. What, ten minutes? Think we can squeeze that into an hour forty five? Sure, there will be some time between, but the timing works—"

"I just don't think we'll pull it off."

"Come on Wink," Woods said. "Show some cojones. This is about Tony, not us. We're doing this for him. It's about courage, about *never* forgetting. About a willingness to hang your ass out when it's time to hang it out, and not sit around, fat, dumb, and happy, after these *assholes* murder our squadron mate."

Wink stood up and looked straight at Woods. "*No*, Trey. It's about going to *jail*. It's about doing something *really* stupid!"

Woods wasn't going to force him. "If you don't want to go, I can get somebody else to go. Easy would go."

Wink looked at Big who was sitting on his bed listening carefully. "You in?"

"With both feet."

"Why?"

Big jumped down. "For Boomer. For the kids he never had. If I got whacked like that I want someone to go take them out. I don't care who, but *someone*. And no one else is going to do it. It's up to us."

Wink struggled. "We can't even fire any missiles—"

"Yes, we can! The Major has taken care of it. I told you the plan."

"How do we know he'll actually do it? What if he's setting us up for embarrassment? And what about on the ship? Won't they know?"

"The Gunner is on board with us."

"Shit! Who else? Everybody on the ship know?"

"Just who has to. He'll take care of the missiles."

"How?"

"He's got access to the computer and the hard copies of the missile records."

"This is right on the edge, Trey."

"You coming?"

Wink stood silently. They all listened to the humming of the ship. "Yeah."

☙

Woods tapped lightly on the hollow stateroom door, leaning forward to listen for sounds of someone stirring. He tapped again, slightly louder. He looked at his watch, glowing in the low red light of the passageway—0200. He tapped once more and heard someone shuffling to the door. Pritch opened it. She was wearing a baggy flannel nightgown, her hair sticking up in all directions. "What?" she asked angrily.

"Get dressed, please," Woods said.

"What for? Do you know what time it is?"

"I need some help."

"Help? What are you talking about?"

"Get dressed, please," Woods said again.

Pritch groaned and turned back toward her bed, wanting desperately to crawl back into it. But she knew Woods—he wouldn't give up so easily. She groaned again, opened her closet, and removed the fresh uniform she had set out for morning when she would be giving the 0515 intelligence brief for the first launch at 0700. She closed the door while she dressed.

Woods leaned on the bulkhead in the passageway. He had started to doubt himself. The chance to hit back was irresistible. He had to do it for Vialli. But for the first time he hesitated. While he waited, Woods glanced down the passageway. Three knee-knockers aft a sailor was waxing the deck. Half the passageway was taped off so no one would step on the fresh wax. Woods watched him as the handle of the rotating wax buffer pushed against his ample belly, causing it to shake under his soiled dungaree shirt. He shook his head, glad he didn't have to wax floors. He had done it once, when he was a third-class midshipman on his summer cruise. That had been enough for him. Never again, at least not until he was court-martialed and busted to seaman for violating every Navy regulation known to man, international law, and good sense. The door startled him when Pritch threw it open.

"Okay," she said with irritation.

"Let's go," Woods said, moving quickly down the passageway.

"Where are we going?" Pritch asked, trying to keep up.

"To CVIC," replied Woods.

"What for?"

"You'll see."

They rounded the corner into CVIC, the carrier intelligence center, and looked into the one-way glass where the Duty Petty Officer sat. Recognizing Pritch's face, he buzzed the door and Woods pushed it open. They stepped through and heard it electronically seal behind them. Woods walked deeper into CVIC and stopped. A seaman was buffing the green tile in one corner of the large room, and another walked by carrying a piece of electronic testing equipment.

"What are we doing here, Trey? I've got to give a brief in three hours. I need my sleep."

"No, you don't. Sleep is for chumps." He turned to Pritch. "I need charts; an ONC and JNC of Israel, Lebanon, and Syria. Then I need you to pull out the Electronic Order of Battle for Lebanon and find all the SAM sights for me, and whatever we know about the AAA sights."

Pritch didn't bother to hide her astonishment. "What for?"

"It doesn't matter what for."

"It does to me."

"Then don't ask."

Pritch lowered her voice to make sure the seaman couldn't hear her. "The only reason you could possibly want them is because you're going to be flying there. But we're not flying there."

"This is one of those times in your life when it may be best for you not to know, Pritch. Just do what I say," Woods said with an intensity Pritch had never seen in him before.

Pritch walked to a metal chest in the corner. It had several long thin drawers and a flat top angled down. She pulled out a drawer close to the bottom and removed a chart of Lebanon. She opened it up and laid it flat on the top of the chest. They leaned over it and began examining the terrain. "This is Lebanon. Where are you going?"

Woods didn't even hesitate. "I didn't say I was going anywhere. This is just a research project. If I *was* interested in going to Lebanon, I might be interested in going"—he studied the chart, then pointed— "right here."

21

Ricketts checked the rearview mirrors on the gray panel truck. He was pulling a trailer with five new Honda motor scooters in it, two purple, one white, one red, and one black. The truck had tools, and various Honda parts. He entered the main street of the town, scanning every window, alley, and rooftop as he went, checking for security. He wished Dar al Ahmar was closer to the coast.

Ricketts was in favor of having a talk with the Sheikh. He was interested and willing to have a very personal conversation with him. To let him know how the Americans felt about his murder of one of its Navy officers. But he had been overruled in the DO. We want him brought back alive, for trial. Only in America. Capture murderers, take them to Washington, give them room and board and attorneys paid for by American taxpayers, have some ACLU asshole find some reason to call a press conference, and sue the government because the murderer was discriminated against somehow, or deprived of his rights, or "captured" illegally in Lebanon or where the hell ever. They always spoke with great offense and outrage.

Ricketts tried not to think about the U.S. side of the operation. That wasn't his job. His job was to get the Sheikh. And he had just the plan—*if* his agents were right, and hadn't sold him and the entire operation out to somebody else for more money. The agents who would help with the transfer were already in place. He had visited them during the night. The decoys were set, the helicopters ready, and the shooters standing by. The actual grab was the last piece, though obviously the most important.

Ricketts drove around three sheep, which were wandering through town, and manuevered his truck and trailer into a narrow street lined on both sides with two-story buildings. The motorcycle shop was on the far corner. It was small and crowded and there was no place to park in front of the shop. A large van had been waiting there and when the driver saw Ricketts coming in his mirror he pulled away from the curb. It was timed perfectly. Ricketts turned into the spot and switched off the engine. He checked his watch.

The shop didn't open until ten. Through the shop window, Ricketts could see almost all of the inventory of motorcycles, motor scooters, and mopeds. He knew that most were used, but a few were new. He also knew that the shop had been asked to bring in several new motor scooters because Assam—an elusive man whose family had come from Dar al Ahmar and who was known mostly for his apparently unlimited influence and money—wanted to buy one for his niece for her birthday. Assam had promised to personally pick it out with her, not just to send a lieutenant to do it for him. He would be in between eight and ten that morning to choose, before the shop opened.

Ricketts stepped out of the truck and stretched. He wore old Arab clothing and moved stiffly, as if he were twenty years older than he was. His dark face was covered with what looked like a one-week beard that had a lot of gray, unlike his actual beard. As he went to the door of the shop he noticed the four armed men on the rooftops of the surrounding buildings, already in place to protect their boss, Ricketts's target. Nice work, he thought to himself. They were exactly where they should be. The other six bodyguards that Assam would bring would undoubtedly go inside the shop with him. They had to. If they didn't, all would be lost.

It wasn't even seven o'clock yet. Ricketts shielded his face as he pressed against the locked glass door. He knocked loudly and shouted in perfect Arabic, "Hondas are here! Open up!"

There was no reply. He banged again, and glanced around as if concerned about waking somebody up. "Hey! You said to be here early! I'm here. Where are you!? Hey!"

Finally he heard something inside the store. He stood back and nodded expectantly. He glanced over at his Hondas to be sure someone wasn't trying to unchain them. The shop door opened. "Yes. You made it."

"Of course, I made it. I brought the motor scooters. Where do you want me to put them?"

"Right in the front of the store. Our guest will inspect them there, his niece can ride whichever ones she wants, and then we will do business inside."

Ricketts nodded several times. "Coffee?"

"Of course," the man said, indicating the inside of the shop.

They went through the door and left it standing open. In the back of the shop, the man poured steaming thick coffee out of an ornately decorated copper pitcher into a dark blue cup. Ricketts drank and took in the room. He could quickly see that everything had been prepared and all was in place. The line on the floor was almost invisible, more a line drawn in the lingering dust by a finger. He could see it clearly though, and knew the others who needed to could as well. All they had to do was get the Sheikh beyond the line toward the back of the store and they would be in business.

Ricketts looked into his agent's eyes. "Is everything ready to close the sale?"

The man's eyes flickered knowingly. "Yes."

"Are you sure our friend will come?"

"I am never sure of anything."

Ricketts poured himself more coffee. "I drove a long way with my new Hondas. I don't want to waste the trip."

"He does what he wants. If he decides not to buy the motor scooter for his niece, then that will be that. We cannot tell him what to do. We were fortunate to get the notice we did."

"Do you have any more information on when he will be here?"

"He will be here when he wants to be here."

"Before the store opens. Yes?"

"That is what he said. He might come today or another time. We will see."

"So we wait," Ricketts said, sipping his thick coffee.

"We wait."

⁂

"Here we go," Woods said, going hot mike as they taxied toward the catapult. The two Tomcats were to be the first planes to be shot off on the earliest launch of the day, just west of Israel.

Wink was studying the chart he had been given an hour before the brief. He was starting to get anxious.

The sun was rising over the horizon on a spectacular morning. The calm Mediterranean lay in peaceful surrender underneath the *Wash-*

ington, gently holding it up. The water was an uncharacteristically dark purplish blue, with occasional foam.

Since waking Pritch, Woods had been up planning the flight. He had gone over all the information the Major had given him until he had everything memorized. The schedule, the frequencies, everything.

"Tiger know what he's supposed to do?" Woods asked as he turned the nosewheel toward the catapult with the rudder pedals.

"He just hopes nobody looks too close."

"Don't we all," Woods said, his voice revealing some tension.

They taxied to the catapult and stopped. They put their hands up while the ordnancemen removed the pins from the six missiles they carried on nearly every flight: two Phoenix, two Sparrow, and two Sidewinder. The ordie gave them a thumbs-up and showed them the long red flags attached to the safing pins they had pulled from the weapons and counted them for Woods to see. Woods inclined his head, and the ordie turned away. They taxied forward and kneeled the Tomcat. The airplane was ready and so were they. Woods stole a quick glance forward to cat two; Big and Sedge were ready, wings forward, engines at full power. He watched as their catapult jerked. The nose of the Tomcat went down toward the deck, then raced toward the bow. Big rotated the Tomcat as it left the deck, sucked up the gear, and climbed away in a right-hand clearing turn. After a quarter of a mile he turned left to parallel the ship's course.

Woods felt tension go into the catapult as the shuttle pulled on the nosewheel launch bar. He hurried through the final items on his takeoff checklist with Wink. The radios were silent.

"Ready?" Woods asked quickly. "Ready," answered Wink just as quickly. Woods saluted and put his head back. The Tomcat jerked downward, then shot down the deck.

"Good speed," Wink called calmly the way he always did as the Tomcat flew off the end of the carrier.

Woods automatically raised the landing gear, pulling up and away from the carrier in his left-hand clearing turn. He climbed to five hundred feet and leveled off. He felt exhilaration; he was full of coffee and energy. The weather was spectacular, the water was beautiful, and the plane was performing perfectly. He was finally doing what he had been training to do for years. He felt calm and completely alive. He accelerated and caught up with Big, who tapped his helmet and pointed to Woods, giving him the lead. As they passed seven miles away from the ship, Woods pulled back steadily on the stick until they were climbing quickly away from the water.

Woods returned overhead the ship and orbited at six thousand feet for five minutes waiting for the S-3 tanker to arrive at its station. It felt like an hour and a half. His heart was beating rapidly and his breathing was deeper and faster than he was used to.

"Where's that stupid S-3?" Woods said, frustrated.

"He was sitting on the deck when we launched. You really think he's gonna get here before we do?" Wink replied.

Woods scanned the sky anxiously.

"Got him," Wink said. "Forty left, four thousand feet, climbing."

Woods looked to his left. "Tallyho," he said as he brought the Tomcat sharply left to head for the S-3.

"Better let him get to altitude or he'll yell at us," Wink cautioned.

"We don't have a lot of time to screw around today, Wink."

"I know that, Trey. Just lighten up."

Woods frowned under his visor and oxygen mask as he rendezvoused with the tanker. He motioned for the pilot to deploy the basket and moved quickly back when it was in place. After both the Tomcats had taken as much gas as they could hold they broke off from the tanker and headed for their air intercept station to practice intercepts.

Wink switched to button eight on the radio in the backseat, and Woods changed to the radio frequency in the front that he and Big had agreed on, Jolly Roger common—the frequency used by the squadron, but they added one digit in case anyone else was listening.

"Big, you up?" Woods asked.

"Two," Big replied.

Wink consulted his card to see what the *Washington* was calling itself and what the squadron's code name was for the day. "*Gulf November, this is Bright Sword 211.*"

"*Bright Sword 211, Gulf November, your station is 020 at 30. Who wants to go first?*"

Woods checked his clock. They had to go now.

"*211 will be the first fighter, and 207 will be the bogey,*" Wink transmitted to Tiger, the familiar voice of the controller. They had met at 0300 that morning.

"*Roger 211, squawk 3234. Take station 020 for 60. Break—207, squawk, 3353. Take station 020 at 30.*"

"211," Wink said.

"207," Sedge transmitted.

They headed out the 020 radial as they climbed out toward their stations. Big kept his place on Woods's starboard wing waiting for the signal. They approached thirty miles and Woods leveled off at fifteen thousand feet.

"*Thirty miles,*" Wink transmitted.

"*Roger, 207, you can orbit there, and 211, continue outbound.*"

Woods nodded and the two F-14s pitched over and headed toward the ocean. Wink and Sedge turned off their IFFs—Identification, Friend or Foe—and changed the Link 11 frequency that allowed automatic communication for data link from that of the *Washington* to the frequency Trey had given them of the Israeli Air Force E-2C Hawkeye, the radar plane identical to those on the *Washington.* It was orbiting somewhere in northern Israel.

"Should be getting their picture any minute now," Wink told Woods as he switched the displays in the back cockpit and Woods adjusted his own displays so he could see Wink's radar picture. They descended rapidly to the water with Big on their wing. Wink looked around for airplanes, but saw none. The radar showed no ships or airplanes in any direction closer than twelve miles.

Woods turned east, heading 086. It was 0715. They were a couple of minutes behind the rigid schedule Woods had set for them in his planning. They had no room for error. "We may be late. I'm going to push it up a little."

"Whatever you do, don't go super."

"Don't worry," Woods said, advancing the throttles to military power as he leveled off at fifty feet. The sea raced by, a dark purple comforting blur. Big stayed above Woods, long ago having learned the lesson that when flying very low the wingman should stay above the lead or risk being scraped off the ground or a tree. "Head 080," Wink said.

"How do you know that?" Woods asked without looking into the cockpit. He was concentrating to keep from flying into the sea. If he sneezed, they'd hit the water going five hundred knots.

"We've got good data link. They're showing Ramat David, and all the airplanes that are airborne." Wink leaned forward and raised his hand above the green on black screen to block out the reflected sunlight. "I'm going lead nose. No radar from here on."

"Don't turn it on accidentally, Wink. That's all we need is for someone to detect our radar."

"Don't worry," he replied. "I'll set the frequency to sniff in case I hit the switch."

"211, come south to 200, Bogey 200 at 30, angels 15," Tiger transmitted.

"Roger. 211 coming to 200," Wink replied. "Sounds like Tiger's on board."

"Think he'll pull it off using fake symbols?"

"He thought so. We'll soon find out."

"You didn't tell him where we were going, did you?"

"No. Don't want them to run out of room at Leavenworth. Less he knows the better."

"What if he doesn't pull it off?"

"We're cooked," Wink said, shrugging. "We could still say we were doing unauthorized dogfighting. Didn't want Admiral Sweat dirtying his shorts."

"Good idea."

"Radar altimeter set?"

"Forty feet."

"That should keep us dry."

"How far to the shoreline? I think I can just make it out."

"Without the radar it's hard to tell, but about fifteen miles."

"Big doing okay?"

"Yep. Sedge has his arms up on the canopy rails. Looking for birds or something. Very casual."

"Good," Woods said as they accelerated through five hundred fifty knots.

The two Tomcats with their white skull and bones painted on the tails screamed toward Israel fifty feet off the water. They cut through the smooth air like parallel daggers, their wings working their way back to a 68-degree sweep, programmed by the onboard computer as they approached supersonic.

"211, Bogey 199 for 20 miles, angels 15."

"Roger. Judy," Wink said, taking control of the imaginary intercept.

Woods's heart was pounding as it had been since they took off. His throat was usually dry when flying this fast this low, but now he could barely swallow. His palms were sweaty as he gripped the stick and throttles with his bare hands, not wearing the required Nomex fireproof gloves.

"I've got the shoreline," Woods announced, trying to sound calm.

"Come to 084," Wink replied.

Woods immediately made the small correction. In the green projection of the HUD on the windscreen, he could look right at his heading, weapons status, and altitude without taking his eyes off the terrain in front of the plane. The HUD symbols were focused at infinity, the same as looking off in the distance.

Suddenly the beach shot by underneath them, giving them a sense of speed the passage of constant blue water never did. Palm trees snapped by only a few feet under the Tomcats. Woods stole a glance sideways to see if there was anyone on the beach this early, but saw no one. They passed directly over a car as they crossed the coast highway, the highway where Vialli had been killed. Woods breathed deeply and drank in the pure oxygen. He pulled slightly on the stick and climbed to five hundred feet. He brought the throttles back and slowed to three hundred knots.

"How far to Ramat David?" he asked.

"Thirty miles or so. Six minutes," Wink said. *"Fox Two, knock it off and set up another one,"* he transmitted.

"Roger, 211. 207, head north as the fighter, 211, south as the bogey," Tiger said calmly.

"211. Roger."

"207. Roger."

Woods looked at his clock—0730. "We're late."

"I doubt it'll matter," Wink said. "Nobody gets that organized on time."

Woods could make out every detail of the houses and farms. He could see the animals' breath in the cool morning air as they moved away from the screaming sound he brought from the sky when he approached them. People looked up even though all over the country they were accustomed to low-flying jets at any hour of the day or night.

Woods felt invincible. He was completely in control and found his heart settling down, but just as he relaxed, his heart jumped into his throat. "You see what I see?"

Wink leaned over and looked forward through the side glass of the windscreen. "Holy hell, Trey. There must be seventy-five airplanes!"

"They're all over the place" Woods said, reducing the throttle to slow to two hundred fifty knots. "Well," he said with relief. "At least we're not too late."

"Directly overhead at five hundred feet? Is that where the Major said to rendezvous?"

"Yep. That's where I'm going, but there are still airplanes taking off. They'll just have to avoid us. There's quite a gaggle in a racetrack over the field at five hundred. Seems about twenty planes or so."

Woods turned slightly right to head for the group of Israeli planes circling over Ramat David Air Force Base. "Let's push and catch up with them so someone else trying to rendezvous doesn't hit us."

"Roger that," Woods said, advancing the throttles slightly. He glanced down to his left at the air base and saw two F-15s in afterburner lifting off the runway in formation. "I don't see any others. They must be the last."

"*211, come north. 207, come port, your bogey is 197 for 32, angels 25.*"

"*211, Roger.*"

"*207, Roger.*"

"*207, bogey 196 for 30 miles, angels 25.*"

"You getting a good picture?" Woods asked Wink, unable to take his eyes off the F-15s and F-16s with their blue Star of David in a white circle.

"Holy shit! It's *unbelievable,*" Wink said, hunched over his screen as if watching a show. He had the screen on the large scale with their F-14 in the middle. The Israeli E-2C Hawkeye was flying north of Ramat David, south of the Lebanon border. Wink stared at the radar picture. It was what the E-2 saw. The symbols on his screen were upside down, indicating they were data link symbols. The Israeli airplanes appeared as half circles, and the other airplanes—designated as hostile—were upside-down chevrons. Wink could see them all without even turning on his own radar.

"Look at this gaggle!" Woods remarked as he searched the sky over Ramat David. Dozens of Israeli fighters circled, waiting. F-15s, F-16s, F-4s, all ready to go to battle. Itching for the chance. Suddenly, the group of F-4s peeled off and headed northwest.

It was the second group of Phantoms. The first was crossing the Lebanese border while the real strike rendezvoused. Dozens of Top Secret Ze'ev Antiradiation Missiles streaked north into the sky from Israel—the missiles had been used only once before, and their existence had never been confirmed. Thanks to the silent Arava, the electronic monitoring plane, the ground launchers knew where to aim and the missiles homed hungrily toward the radars trying to shoot down their fellow unpiloted Israeli drones. F-4 Phantom Wild Weasels, positioned by the E-2 in southern Lebanon, raced forward on the silent signal and fired American-made HARM antiradiation missiles toward the northern targets out of reach of the Ze'evs. The drones flew directly into the SAM and AAA radar envelopes over Lebanon, looking like airplanes being flown by very stupid pilots. The operators salivated and turned on their systems to get firing solutions to shoot into what looked like a large number of Israeli planes. The SAMs flew off the rails as the radars guided the missiles toward their targets. The Phantoms rolled in with their bombs and antiradiation missiles on the SAM and AAA sites to clear the way for the real raid. All over Lebanon, in the Bekáa Valley, around bases and camps, and along the border, antiradiation missiles slammed into radars and control vans wiping out the antiair capability of the Syrians, who had controlled Lebanese airspace for years. Even those operators smart enough to detect the ruse and turn off their radars before the Ze'evs hit, soon learned that the missile remembered where the last transmissions came from.

The F-4 Phantoms that had been assigned to attack the SAM sites screamed across the border toward the bases in southern Lebanon. They carried thousand-pound laser-guided bombs, with the laser illumination provided by yet more drones circling over the designated targets.

Just then Major Micah Chermak, in the lead F-15 of the aft-most group of airplanes over Ramat David, rolled his wings level and headed north. In front of Woods, Chermak's group of eight fighters spread out into two boxes of four, five hundred feet above the ground. Woods let them accelerate ahead and signaled Big to move out to combat spread a mile and a half directly to the right and a mile behind the last F-15. There were fighters everywhere, gray, light blue, and camouflage, flying in loose formation with missiles hanging from every rail, ready for the fight.

"Here we go," Woods said to Wink as he pushed up his throttles to stay with the F-15s. They accelerated to four hundred fifty knots.

Wink studied the radar picture being steadily transmitted to them by the Israeli E-2C. "Trey, I've got six or eight bogeys on the screen, headed south toward the border. This could be a fur ball," he said.

"Are they headed for us?"

"No. The F-4s that went in to bomb all went from the east to west, and are now headed toward the coast. The bogeys are falling in behind them. I think the Phantoms are dragging them. Son of a bitch. The whole thing is a setup! They should be in front of us about fifty miles, twenty degrees right, moving right to left, about five hundred knots."

"Combat checklist," Woods said, excited.

"Roger," said Wink, reaching for the cards attached to his knee board. "Wings."

"Auto."

"Missile prep."

"On."

"Sidewinder cool."

"On."

"207, bogey 195 for 25, angels 25."

"Roger. Judy," Wink said, responding to Tiger to keep the pretend intercept alive in case anyone on the *Washington* was listening to the radio communications. His mind wanted to shut down the ruse to allow more processing time for reality, but Wink knew it would be too risky.

"Weapons select."

"Sidewinder."

"Master arm."

"Off, for now."

"Put it up now so we don't forget."

"Roger," Woods said. He reached over and flipped up the red switch. "Master arm, on."

"You ready?"

"Ready. Sure you want to do this?"

"Yep."

"Me too."

The fighters moved apart slightly as they closed on the MiGs now streaming down from Syria. Woods took his eyes off the radar picture and looked around. He could faintly see another group of twenty fighters or so east of them, and yet another group to the west. Woods had never seen so many airplanes airborne at once in his life and he couldn't believe he was flying into combat with the Israeli Air Force.

The group of fighters to their west angled northwest to intercept the incoming MiGs. The F-4s the MiGs were chasing were supersonic over western Lebanon, circling back toward Israel in what appeared to be a desperate attempt to avoid the Syrian planes. The EC-135 activated its jammers, clogging the Syrian Ground Control Intercept radar as well as its SAM and AAA radars.

"I'll bet those Syrian pilots have their fangs out," Wink said. "They think they're finally going to be able to catch one of the Israeli bombing strikes. If only they knew—but I'll tell you one thing. They're coming in force. There must be thirty MiGs coming, maybe forty, and probably others taking off. The E-2C is picking them up as soon as they're airborne. We'll have to watch the northeast."

Woods pushed the throttles forward slightly as the Tomcats fell behind the F-15s and F-16s. "They're accelerating ahead. What's the speed of the MiGs?"

"About five hundred fifty to six hundred knots."

"We'll push it up a little."

"Say hello to Lebanon. We're in their airspace now."

Woods looked around and down at the ground, still only five hundred feet below. "Looks the same to me."

"May look the same, but if we get shot down, it won't be the same, I promise you that."

"Don't even think that," Woods replied. Unconsciously, their voices had moved up in pitch.

They followed the Israelis deeper into Lebanon. No turning back now, Woods thought.

"005, for ten miles for the first of them, the rest are east and north from there, angels—they're all over the place, all above us! The E-2 is showing about thirty bogeys! I have no idea how many targets are real," Wink said.

"I see some specks, but nothing clear," Woods said, half in frustration, half in anticipation.

"Five miles. Here we go," Wink said, watching the F-15s ahead of them begin a climb. The Tomcats started uphill right behind them, going to military power to accelerate in the climb. They saw no sign that the Syrians knew they were there. They passed through five thousand feet on their way to ten.

"Check our six," Woods said.

Wink grabbed the handle in front of him on top of his radar panel, and forcibly turned around so he could see between the tails. "Nothing," he grunted. "Belly check," he added.

Woods rolled the airplane into a knife edge so they could see directly underneath them to the ground, to make sure no MiGs were doing to them what they were doing to the MiGs—sneaking up on them from below. He rolled back level and saw Big do the same thing. He checked behind Big to make sure there weren't any bogeys following him. All clear.

Suddenly Wink remembered. *"Fox two, Tiger. Set up another one,"* he said.

"Roger, 211. New heading, 005, 207, head 175."

"211, Roger."

"207, Roger."

Woods scanned the sky around him again, quickly. Suddenly it was full of white smoke as the Israeli fighters shot their AIM-9M heat-seeking Sidewinders at the Syrian MiGs head-on. Dozens of missiles streaked toward the bogeys, flying toward the targets on the corkscrew paths, which gave them their name.

"Geez, Trey! You see that?" Wink shouted.

"Fight's on!" Woods replied calmly, tightening his lap belt.

The Sidewinders tore toward their targets. Some of the MiGs saw them as soon as they were fired, others only after the missiles hit their wingmen. Two on the left pulled up in an emergency break and dropped burning magnesium flares to avoid being hit. But the heat-seeking Sidewinders were hungry missiles, especially looking up, away from the ground, at a target streaking through the sky riding a hot jet engine.

The missiles smashed into the MiGs across the sky as far as Woods could see. MiGs exploded all around and fell out of the heavens. F-15s and -16s climbed through the disintegrating MiG formations. As the Sidewinders raced in all directions, the lead F-15s broke through the first group of MiGs and went after the others. The MiGs panicked. They watched as their wingmen dropped from the sky like clay pigeons, missiles exploding in their bellies. Chermak was the first to fire a second missile. Woods watched in fascination as the supersonic missile flew off the F-15's underwing rail and silently hurled itself at a MiG-23 two miles ahead. The missile hit the MiG in the chest, right in front of a drop tank full of fuel. It absorbed the blow like a wounded animal and immediately lost speed, rolling over and heading for the ground ten thousand feet below, upside down, flames licking skyward.

"I've got MiGs to the right and left," Wink said excitedly, straining to see behind the Tomcat.

"I've got Israeli fighters everywhere," Woods said, looking carefully at the melee all around them. He checked to make sure he had Sidewinder selected and went to full power.

"There goes the Major. He's made the turn to the target!" Woods exclaimed as Chermak and three other F-15s peeled off and headed east. Woods and Big fell in behind them, slightly higher, in a position of cover and fighter escort. "How far is it to that town?"

Wink looked at the chart and at their position listed as latitude and longitude in a continuous readout on his PTID. "Thirty miles."

"No sweat. As long as a bunch of MiGs don't close in behind us and cut us off, we'll be okay."

"The F-15s are heading down. I think they're doing a pop-up delivery."

"Where do they want us?" Wink asked, growing anxious. "They must be trying to stay low on the radar. If we stay high we'll give them away!"

Woods looked around. "Let's take a low trail position on them," he said as he pushed the Tomcat over and followed the F-15s downhill. Before he knew it they were tearing across eastern Lebanon at five hundred fifty knots toward a town he had never heard of forty-eight hours before. The F-15s were flying in two sections of two, in a welded wing formation—Chermak was in the lead, the wingman right on the his wing.

Woods watched Lebanon streak by under their jet as they followed the Israeli fighters to their target. Every few miles they would see AAA, antiaircraft artillery that tried to reach the strike group. It was always poorly aimed or too far away to do any damage. They weren't heading toward a predictable target. All the known targets were protected by SAMs or AAA. But Dar al Ahmar? There wasn't anything there. No reason to be surrounded by a multimillion-dollar defense—except today, when the new scourge of the Middle East was there.

"Bogeys!" Wink shouted. "Eleven o'clock high!"

Woods headed up and to the left to meet the MiGs head on. Big moved at the same time, still flying in combat spread, one mile to Woods's right and a little higher. The two Israeli F-15s flying behind Chermak and his wingman left the low-flying strike group and went after the MiGs with Woods and Big behind them.

Tiger, sitting on the *Washington,* interrupted with instructions for the fantasy intercept, "*211 come south to 195, your bogey 193 for 40 miles, angels unknown.*"

"*Roger, 211, south.*"

"Shit," Wink said. "I wish we didn't have to keep talking to him. Come port harder, Trey," he said, trying to run the intercept off the E-2C data link symbols.

"*207 as the bogey, come north to 014.*"

"*207, Roger,*" Sedge replied to Tiger, feeling the same frustration and mounting adrenaline party that Wink was experiencing.

"Hard port!" Wink said suddenly. "Bogey, left ten o'clock, slightly high, descending left turn. There are two coming toward us, and two more after the F-15s!"

Woods threw the stick to the left and rolled the F-14 on its side. He pulled the nose of the airplane toward the MiG-23 Flogger. He sucked the pure oxygen out of the rubber mask as his body readied for the G forces it knew were coming. He checked their speed. Four hundred fifty knots. The MiG still didn't see him. He pulled 7 Gs to get the nose of the F-14 onto the MiG three miles away.

"Break right!" Big yelled over the front cockpit radio.

Woods immediately slammed the stick in the opposite direction and came back to the right. He saw the MiG-23 Big had seen. It was accelerating toward them. Suddenly a large missile flew off the MiG and headed their way. Woods turned into the missile, rolling the F-14 over on its back. He pulled toward the ground, hoping the missile would lose them in the ground clutter, praying it was a radar-guided missile.

In heading toward Woods the MiG-23 had turned right in front of Big. Big pulled gently left and put his pipper on the MiG. He listened for the growl of the Sidewinder, then heard it, louder and louder as the seeker head on the missile acquired the heat signal from the MiG. The MiG made it easy by staying in afterburner as he went after Woods.

Big squeezed the trigger on the stick and the Sidewinder flew off the wing rail toward the MiG. It was there in seconds. It hit the Flogger in the tail. The exploding warhead cut the tail off and the MiG fell toward the ground. Big looked away quickly for other bogeys, and didn't see the MiG pilot eject from the wreckage.

The missile streaking toward Woods pitched over and headed for the earth.

Woods rolled his wings level and checked around. There were no airplanes in front of them or to their right. "Where is everybody?" he asked Wink.

"211, your bogey is 190 for 39, angels 17."

"Judy," Wink transmitted quickly. Damn it. "They're all behind us. We've flown through most of the fight," he said, holding his hand up to block the sun on his screen. "About three miles behind us."

Woods started a hard right turn, and Big, reading his mind, started his own left-hand turn; they passed each other close aboard to clear the other's tail, and headed back in the other direction.

"I wish we could turn our radar on," Woods said, squinting through the windscreen.

"No way," Wink replied. "This E-2 picture is good enough."

"I sure hope these Israelis don't mistake us for a MiG-23. We both have wings that sweep."

"That would be bad," Wink agreed. *"Fox, two, set up another one."*

"Roger, 211. Head north as the bogey, 207, south as the fighter."

"207."

"211."

"This is incredible," Woods said as they headed southeast toward the F-15 fight that was continuing. There were missile contrails and smoke everywhere, white ribbons that cut across the sky in every direction. "Tallyho!" he cried. "Wink, I've got at least six bogeys. We're way outnumbered."

"Let's get back into position behind the Eagles," Wink said, looking for the F-15s that were to drop on the Sheikh.

"Roger that. I've lost them," Woods said, scanning the blue sky to his east. He jammed the stick left and right, checking for bogeys anxiously, not feeling at all comfortable about the way this was going.

"MiGs!" Wink yelled. "Left nine o'clock low. Come port hard!"

"No! The fight is to our right! We've got to support Chermak." Woods jerked the F-14 into a hard right turn and followed Chermak, who was now pulling up from the arid desert floor into his pop-up maneuver. Woods looked past the F-15 and saw the town. The F-15s formed up into a nearly vertical position as the one-thousand-pound laser-guided bombs came off gently heading up, away from the ground in a graceful arc. The F-15s continued up as the bombs flew off in their lobbed trajectory toward the building in Dar al Ahmar that was being lased by two separate F-15 laser designators simultaneously.

Woods watched the bombs fly with fascination. "That Sheikh will never know what hit him."

22

Ricketts was startled when a man he didn't recognize ran into the shop with a frenzied look on his face yelling something incomprehensible. "What?" Ricketts asked in Arabic.

"Big plane battle near. They're heading this way! Come and see!"

The shop owner looked at Ricketts as if to ask whether they should go outside.

"We've got to stay here," Ricketts said gravely, annoyed that the shopkeeper would even consider leaving the shop at this critical point in the operation. He stared at the owner, who understood and tried to find something to keep him busy until the Sheikh showed up. Any minute now.

Chermak's one-thousand-pound laser-guided bomb slammed into the Honda trailer Ricketts had driven so carefully to the right spot. The explosion, like a huge car bomb, detonated the C4 explosives that lined the inside of the van. Ricketts had set the van up to create the much needed diversion while he and the Sheikh disappeared into another section of buildings. His group was waiting to secret them out of Dar al Ahmar in a highly detailed and rather brilliant plan, at least Ricketts thought so. The guards and supporters of the Sheikh would be left to sort through the rubble and confusion for days after the Sheikh was out of the country and on his way to justice. As it turned out, Ricketts only had three-one-thousandths of a second to realize that his van had exploded at exactly the wrong time. The second American-made laser-guided bomb landed directly on the roof of the single-story building and penetrated right to the floor between Ricketts and the owner of the shop before exploding with all its force.

"Yes!" Woods said into his mask as he saw the explosions in Dar al Ahmar some six miles away. He couldn't judge how close to each other they'd really hit but what he could tell was that they were close to each other in time and proximity. Which meant they had gotten their target. It would be unlikely in the extreme for both to miss in the same direction at the same time. "They got him!" Woods said to Wink, fighting the urge to do a victory roll.

"Yeah, well, they're going to get *us* in about a minute if we're not careful. Syria has come in force, and we can't even talk to the airplanes around us. Stay off the radio, the Major said. Fine, right. But we don't know what the hell is going on!"

"Relax. We've just got to get back to Israel."

"We've got to get back to the damned boat, Trey! We're due to land in forty-five minutes and we're two countries away in the middle of the biggest fur ball I've ever seen!"

"We're heading south." Woods took in the sky around them in amazement. There were at least twenty planes, MiGs, F-15s, and F-16s, turning toward each other. Some were in afterburner, others not, some trying to escape, others trying to pursue. He didn't see any MiGs on the tail of any Israeli, but there were plenty of MiGs in deep trouble from the fighters with the blue Star of David on their sides.

"We've got to help out," Woods said as he moved sharply to the right to head toward the fight. Approaching, he could see another cluster of planes to the west, and another farther south. He selected Sidewinder on his stick.

Wink changed the display on his screen to show their plane in the center. The symbols showed planes, friendly and hostile, to the east, behind them. Wink turned to look, but couldn't make any of them out.

Without any warning an F-15 shot up in front of them from below, with a MiG-23 following it a mile behind. Woods was sure the Eagle pilot didn't know the MiG was behind him. He looked to his right at Big, went to military power, and pulled straight up to follow the MiG after the F-15. They were much slower than he was and he gained on the MiG quickly. His airspeed started to bleed off. He went into afterburner and pulled his nose up to the MiG, flying straight up away from the earth. He heard the hungry growl of the Sidewinder missile and pulled the trigger. He felt a slight shudder and listened to the characteristic whoosh as the missile raced off the rail and headed for the tailpipe of the Flogger. Woods's heart pounded, as he watched the first missile he had ever fired at an airplane fly toward it with mindless dedication. Unknowing, uncaring, unmerciful, wanting only heat, and more heat. The hotter, the more intense, the more concentrated, the better.

Woods wondered if the Syrian pilot flying the MiG knew the capabilities of the Sidewinder, knew how mean it really was, that once it locked on to your heat signature, you might as well jump out. Apparently not. The missile flew right up the tailpipe of the Flogger, disappeared in the luxurious heat of the afterburning engine, and exploded. The Flogger pitched over as if it had been pole-axed, and the pilot ejected, jettisoning his worthless airplane.

"Boola, boola!" Woods yelled.

"Nice shot," Wink replied. "Belly check."

Woods rolled the airplane completely around, still heading straight up. No bogeys threatening. "Clear!"

Woods pulled the Tomcat over on its back and brought the nose to the horizon. He rolled wings level, checked his instruments, and came out of afterburner.

"Two visuals, left nine and eleven," Wink called. "F-16s."

"Got 'em," Woods replied. Four F-15s were chasing three MiG-21s trying to escape to the north. "They're bugging out," he reported.

"Still a lot of them around here," Wink said, looking at his screen. The sweat rolled down his face even though the cockpit was cool. His hand shook imperceptibly as he held the radar control handle. "Looks like a flight of four bogeys to the west, headed this way," he said with concern in his voice. "Come starboard hard, head 275!"

Woods came hard right, and accelerated. Big saw him turning and began his own right turn. They steadied up heading west, and climbing. Big took his place in combat spread, one and a half miles to Woods's right, and five thousand feet below.

Woods strained to see ahead, looking for the bogeys. "Nothing, Wink. You sure?"

Wink looked at the screen again. "Yep. Four of 'em have broken out of the pack and are hauling east, headed right for us. Five miles ahead. Slightly right."

"I don't see anything," Woods said, concerned.

Suddenly Big's voice came over the radio. "Below us!"

Woods saw four Syrian MiGs coming up for them. He pushed the nose of the Tomcat over into a negative G dive. Dirt and dust flew up from the floor of the cockpit and settled against the canopy as they went downhill. Woods and Wink floated up against their straps, as the blood in their bodies fought to get into their heads and pop blood vessels in their eyes.

"211, come north. Bogey 020 for 45 miles, angels 12 . . ."

"211, Judy," Wink said hurriedly, cutting Tiger off.

"Two Fishbeds and two Floggers!" Woods said, sweat on his face. Two MiG-21s, two MiG-23s. Not great airplanes, but good enough to kill you.

"No other bogeys," Wink said, his voice up half an octave. Lots of airplanes, lots of bogeys, but none that was a factor right now.

Woods struggled to get the nose of the Tomcat on one of the MiGs. The two MiG-21s were in the lead with the MiG-23s behind them. Woods couldn't tell if they were flying in a box formation, a difficult formation to attack, or had just ended up in the same piece of sky at the same time. Didn't matter now. They were after *him.* The lead Fishbed on the left was directly in front of him, heading right for him, two miles ahead in afterburner. At least they aren't timid, Woods thought.

He checked to make sure Sidewinder was selected. He listened for the tone, and shot. The missile flew off at the MiG. The Fishbed saw the missile come off and immediately began a hard turn away, dropped flares, and dove for the ground. Woods watched the Sidewinder correct its flight path to compensate for the target's movement. It caught the MiG and ripped the wing off. The MiG tumbled out of control and Woods shifted his gaze to the trailing Flogger. He smiled inside his mask, then suddenly his mouth went dry. The Flogger had radar-guided missiles, and Woods didn't have any more Sidewinders. They couldn't turn on their radar. They were flying right into the heart of the envelope of the Flogger's radar missiles with no ability to shoot back. He could see the big nose, like an F-4 Phantom, with its radar probably trained on him. They could turn and run, or—"Turn on the radar, Wink!"

"We can't! They'll pick it up!"

"It's a Flogger!" Woods yelled into his mask as he waited for a missile to come off at them. "Now!"

"No!" Wink said. "Split S and we'll bug out!"

"No chance. We're too close, too low. Turn on the radar, Wink!"

"Let's close on him and gun him," Wink said, trying to think of any alternative, continuously scanning the skies for other planes. "We can't use the radar!"

"Turn it on!" Woods screamed. "We're inside three miles!"

Wink growled in his mask. "Let me do the shooting. Select Sparrow."

Woods's thumb quickly slipped to the round weapon selection button on the stick and moved it to select Sparrow missiles. Wink moved the radar out of standby, chose a radar channel out of sniff, and immediately picked up the two approaching Floggers. "Geez, Trey; they're really hauling," he said, looking at their speed—two hundred eighty-five for three miles. "Two right, slightly low."

"I've got a tally!" Woods said. "Shoot him!"

"Come starboard, easy," Wink said quietly. "Steady." His left thumb went to the red launch button on the console by his left knee. He waited until the Flogger was in the absolute heart of the head-on shot, where there would be no escape. He locked up the target with the radar, and pushed the launch button. They felt the clunk and movement of the Tomcat as the five-hundred-pound Sparrow missile dropped off the plane and its motor fired. It flew hurriedly toward its target as the Flogger shot its own missile.

Woods brought his throttles back to idle to keep as far away as he could from the Flogger missile while their own missile flew toward its target. Woods glanced over at Big, who was flying directly at the other Flogger, but hadn't fired a Sparrow. The Flogger shot at Big, and closed on him. Big rolled over and did a split S, pointing the nose of the Tomcat at the ground.

Wink's Sparrow drank in the continuous reflection of the radar energy from Flogger all the way to impact. The warhead exploded next to the Flogger and severed both wings. The plane fell toward the earth as it rolled uncontrollably.

The missile from the other Flogger followed Big down toward the ground. The Flogger was descending, following its missile down, closing in on Big for the kill. Big leveled off at a thousand feet and pulled up and into the Flogger, heading right for him. The Flogger's missile couldn't make the turn and overshot Big's Tomcat, exploding harmlessly behind him. Seeing Big coming back uphill at him, the Flogger turned hard and headed north, his big single engine in afterburner pushing him as fast as it could, his wings moving aft.

Big turned north, climbing after him. Woods fell in behind Big, looking for other planes. Two F-16s were directly above them at twenty thousand feet chasing two MiG-21s. To the west were countless missile trails and parachutes.

No, Big, Woods said to himself. Don't get pulled too far north.

But Big had no intention of flying too far north. He was going to let his Sparrow fly north for him. The missile dropped off his left wing and tore toward the fleeing Flogger. By this time the Flogger was supersonic, in full flight, its wings aft.

"Fox two, set up another one," Wink transmitted as he watched Big's missile pursuing the Flogger. The missile closed on the target, not nearly as fast as they expected; but just fast enough. The Sparrow flew by the Flogger ten feet away. The warhead exploded with startling speed and deadliness and cut the engine off from the rest of the plane. It broke in half and tumbled end over end, flames coming from its ruptured belly and lapping around the entire front end.

Big turned toward the south and picked up Woods. They climbed back to ten thousand feet and checked their fuel.

"You okay, Wink?" Woods said.

"So far. Fuel's okay, but we need to think about heading south."

"Let's get north of the fur ball, and pick off the next one that tries to bug out north."

"Roger."

Woods turned gently left and climbed to fifteen thousand feet. He kept the biggest group of tangled fighters just to his left as he closed on them.

"Right two o'clock! Way low!" Wink yelled. "Starboard hard!"

Woods brought the Tomcat around to the right pulling 6 Gs. He saw the bogeys. Under Big. Two MiG-21s running from the fight. They were low and headed lower, two miles away. Big pulled up to let Woods pass underneath him, rolled over on his back, and fell in behind his section leader.

The MiGs were only doing three hundred knots or so, but their engines were in afterburner. They had clearly decided to bug out after running out of airspeed, altitude, and ideas. They looked out of sorts, flying unevenly. Woods's fangs were out. He wanted blood. He felt the rush of the pursuit as he aimed his Tomcat at the Fishbed on the right. Its desert camouflage paint was worn and blotchy. The Delta shaped wing seemed wrong somehow, incomplete. Suddenly he realized the plane had been hit, probably by an F-15 or F-16 cannon, the same 20-millimeter Gatling gun sitting in the Tomcat, just under his left foot.

Woods pushed his throttles to the stops to close the gap. He saw Big catch him on the left. The Tomcats stayed in tight combat spread as they chased the MiGs northward.

"We'd better close them fast, Trey, or we'll be ten miles away from the strike group."

Woods nodded, glanced at his remaining fuel, and touched his afterburner to close the MiGs. "They're sitting on the deck," he commented, frustrated. "Are they in range?"

"Barely. We could take a shot, but the chances of hitting them from here aren't very good."

"Go for it," Woods said.

Wink locked up the right MiG and waited for the distance to close slightly. "Fox one," he said as he fired the Sparrow at the low-flying MiG. The Sparrow came off and guided straight for the Syrian. Woods pulled out of afterburner as the Sparrow closed the gap for him.

"If we hit the lead we may get both of them, they're so close together," he said excitedly.

Wink took his eyes off the missile and forced himself to look for other planes. He spotted a Flogger going the other way three miles to the west, but didn't think the Flogger saw them. Wink's first instinct was to call out the bogey, but he knew it wouldn't do any good. That MiG wasn't a factor. He tried to breathe easier, but his throat was so tight it felt like a balloon being tied off.

"AArrgghhh," Woods said.

"What?" Wink asked.

"Sparrow hit the ground. Went under the lead."

"We're not shooting a Phoenix, if that's what you're thinking. We'd never be able to replace that."

"No sweat."

"Better head back. Come starboard to . . ." Wink checked their position.

"Not yet."

"Why?"

"We'll gun him."

"He'll outrun us."

"Nope. He's crippled. Got a hole in his wing. He can't outrun us," Woods said as he closed the distance in military power. "The problem is, he's so low, we'd have to hit him from behind, and he's too low to do it. We'll see what he does when we get close. It'd be a brave man who doesn't do anything," he said. "Anybody behind us?"

Wink turned hurriedly, realizing he hadn't tried to look in over a minute. "Nope."

"We're less than a mile, Wink. Lock him up with the radar again. See if it spooks him."

"VSL low, selected," Wink said. "Got him," he added quickly as the radar locked on the fleeing MiG.

Woods waited. Suddenly the MiG pulled up sharply from the ground and toward Woods. "Oh, yeah," Woods said. He used the change in altitude to close the distance. He selected "gun" on the weapon-select button on the stick, and pressed the attack. The MiG was in a climbing left hand turn pulling hard.

Woods settled in behind the MiG. The G forces mounted as the MiG turned harder and harder, now apparently seeing Woods. The second MiG started up after his leader but changed his mind and stayed on the deck heading home. Woods closed the MiG, watching the computerized gun sight as it marched up his HUD toward the plane. He curled his finger around the trigger. He grunted as he held his breath and tightened his stomach muscles to help his G suit keep the blood from leaving his head. The G forces continued to mount, to 6 then 7 Gs, as the MiG tried desperately to turn into him. But his turn was predictable, and the F-14 could match it easily. Woods was about to shoot when the MiG suddenly reversed and began a hard right-hand turn, descending. Woods looked over his shoulder to see if the MiG had help in that direction, but only saw Big hovering above, protecting them.

Woods was closing too fast. He pulled back and converted some of his airspeed to altitude and looked down at the MiG in a tight right turn. He pulled over and back down toward the MiG.

"We've got to head south, Trey. Let this guy go," Wink said.

"No," Woods grunted.

"We're not going to make our recovery time!" The radar suddenly broke lock.

"I know!" he said as he pulled lead on the MiG.

Woods held his breath, exhaled in bursts, and concentrated on his pipper. "VSL high!" The radar went into a vertical scan that locked on the first thing it saw.

Wink hit the switch to make the radar scan above the nose and looked at the two green lights to show the radar had locked on. "Good lock," he reported through the crushing G forces. Wink had one hand on his leg, and the other on the radar control handle. He couldn't move either as Woods pulled harder to get the lead he needed to shoot the Fishbed.

"Bingo," Big said over the radio, stating the dreaded fact that they had run out of any spare fuel. They had to turn toward the ship now to be able to recover with the minimum fuel.

Woods pulled back on the stick and fired. The 20-millimeter bullets flew out of the Tomcat at six thousand rounds per minute. The first burst went ahead of the MiG, and Woods relaxed the pressure on the stick. He shot again and the bullets slammed into the MiG's cockpit and shattered the Plexiglas. The MiG began flying straight and level, gently toward home.

"Aren't you going to finish him?" Wink said as they pulled off and up toward Big.

"I did."

"Doesn't look like it."

"Watch him," Woods replied as he checked his fuel.

Wink watched over his left shoulder, as the MiG descended gently and slammed into the ground in a ball of flames.

Big rendezvoused on Woods's Tomcat. He looked over the airplane. He descended, crossed under the jet, and back up the other side. He scanned the plane with his trained eye for any damage or problem. He crossed back over to the other side and gave Woods a thumbs-up. Woods gave him the lead and returned the favor. Their planes were both in good shape. No damage.

He gave Big the signal to take combat spread again, and headed south. "What heading, Wink?"

"200 for 60."

"Okay. We got a little east," he said, surprised. "How we doin' on time?"

"We're sucking wind. You realize how hard it's gonna be to explain if we don't show up on time?"

"Yep," Woods replied. "Where's that MiG's wingman?" he asked.

"I don't know," Wink replied, not having thought about it before then. "Did Big get him?"

"I don't think so. I didn't see anything."

They flew south at three hundred knots toward Ramat David. Planes still cluttered the sky to the west, but it was clear to the east.

The major part of the fight was over. Israeli and Syrian fighters were heading toward their respective homes; those that were left.

"Keep your eyes open," Woods said, looking up through the canopy toward the sun for the unseen bogeys.

They crossed the border of Israel without seeing another MiG. The radar warning gear continued to indicate occasional SAM and AAA activity, but nothing steady or close to them. Wink looked up from his radarscope when he felt Woods rocking his wings back and forth vigorously. "What's up?" Wink asked, concerned, as he put his radar on standby again.

"Left ten o'clock, low," Woods replied.

Wink looked left and low and saw an airplane with its nose on them converting an intercept, rolling in on them to shoot. It was an F-15 showing no sign of recognition. Woods exaggerated his motions even more. Big, seeing the problem, and the other F-15 closing on them from the right, did likewise.

The F-15 cooled his intercept and rolled out behind the Tomcat. He flew up beside Woods on the left and examined the U.S. Navy fighter. He joined on Woods's wing, and nodded to him. Woods looked at him and nodded back. The Israeli pilot tapped his forehead and pointed to his chest. "It's Chermak." Woods held up a fist. Hold on. He pulled away from the F-15, then moved his plane like a porpoise. Big read the signal and flew over to Woods, joining on his wing, flying in formation. Woods then shifted over to the F-15, tapped his forehead, and pointed at Major Mike Chermak; no radio transmissions required, everything understood. The other F-15 joined on the outside of Big. The flight of four, two Eagles, two Tomcats, fled south toward Ramat David.

In what seemed like no time at all they were overhead the field. Micah Chermak kissed off Woods and pulled up sharply, dropping him off directly over the field in perfect position to enter the break. Woods kissed off Big, and broke left in a sharp turn. They both landed without incident, but looked at their clocks in horror as they taxied to the end of the runway.

"What are we supposed to do now?" Wink asked.

"I'm not really sure," Woods replied, removing his oxygen mask and breathing deeply. They reached the end of the runway and taxied to the right, as instructed. He pulled his oxygen mask over his mouth again to talk. "The Major said to taxi off to the right, and everything would be obvious. The only thing that's obvious to me is how conspicuous we are here. One guy with a camera on this base and we're *dead*."

"I hadn't even thought of that," Wink said, the implications chilling him. "What are we supposed to be looking for?"

"I don't *know*," Woods said, exasperated. "Wait, here comes a truck."

A camouflage truck raced toward the taxiing Tomcats and stopped in front of them. It changed directions with a quick turn, and headed back down the taxiway in the direction they had been traveling.

"Guess we're supposed to follow him," Woods said, watching the driver motion him with his arm, like a cowboy in the front of a posse.

"Where are we going?"

"I think we're about to find out."

Woods eyed his clock and drew in a short breath. The next launch from the *Washington* was in ten minutes. They were supposed to be overhead in the pattern now, preparing to recover at the earliest possible moment after the last airplane of the next launch was airborne. We'll never make it, Woods thought, feeling a sense of panic. He looked around for the ground personnel the Major had said would be waiting for them. He didn't see anyone. There were F-15s, F-16s, and F-4s everywhere getting refueled and rearmed. The camouflage truck continued past the main section of the airfield, nearly to the end of the taxiway, right by the end of the runway where they had just touched down. Then Woods saw them. A man was waving at them from a spot off the taxiway in front of the hangars. Woods stepped on the left rudder to steer the Tomcat to the left with nosewheel steering and they followed the truck into a small cul-de-sac behind the last hangar. There were several men in white uniforms with large orange Vs on their chests waiting for them with two trailers next to them. Big followed as they taxied faster than was safe, but necessary under the circumstances.

Woods spun the Tomcat around and pointed parallel to the runway. A soldier walked in front of the plane and raised his hands. Woods stopped hard, and put on the parking brake. The soldier looked over the Tomcat and gave him a thumbs-up. There were eight other men standing by one of the trailers. They stood at parade rest with sound protectors over their ears. The soldier nodded to them. They ran to the Tomcat, examined the missile rails and wing pylons, then backed away to the truck. The leader of the eight nodded to the soldier in front of the Tomcat. He put his arms up as if signaling a touchdown. Woods and Wink put their arms on the air conditioning rails so their hands could be clearly seen. The eight men turned up the canvas flaps on the trailer. Missiles were stacked on racks on both sides, Sidewinders and Sparrows.

Woods would have smiled if he had been able. As it was, he was so concerned about their time and being found out, nothing was even remotely amusing, appealing, or satisfying. Every second made them later and more anxious. Wink watched the men line up underneath a Sparrow and lift it easily off the rack. They moved toward the Tomcat, sitting there with both its engines turning. "I sure hope these guys know what they're doing," Wink commented as the one in front moved closer to the jet intake. "I'd hate to suck one of them down the intake. You have any idea how hard it would be to explain *that*?"

"If that happens, I'm just going to shut it down, walk west until I hit the Med, and keep walking," Woods replied, trying not to think of how many things could still go wrong.

Wink, on the other hand, was reflecting for a long time on each little thing that could go wrong, rolling each around in his mind, like a new candy, wondering what was inside, dwelling on each potential catastrophe with a detachment that he found refreshing.

Wink took off his oxygen mask again and breathed deeply of the Israeli air. He wiped the sweat from his face, and took off his helmet. His skull cap fell into his lap as he scratched his head. He put the skull cap and yellow helmet with white skull and bones on it back on, and reconnected his oxygen mask. He watched as the Israeli ordnancemen loaded new missiles on the rails. "You sure these are the same missiles we carry?"

"Yep. AIM-9M Sidewinders, and AIM-7M Sparrows. Same exactly."

"No difference?"

"I sure hope not. If there are, as long as they can load them on, the Gunner can take care of anything else."

"I hope we don't have scorch marks all over from the rocket motors."

Woods suddenly sat up. "I didn't even think of that," he said, looking around. He glanced quickly at Big's plane sitting fifty feet to their right, and studied it for marks. He could see black carbon where the Sidewinder had fired off the rail. "It's noticeable, but looks mostly like dirt. I don't think anyone will notice. The Sparrow didn't leave any marks. They don't fire until they eject clear."

"Let's go; they're done," Wink said hurriedly, noticing the gesturing of the soldier in front of the plane.

Woods lowered his hands and released the parking brake. Big's crew finished right behind Woods's.

"Let's go," Woods said. He looked at the Israeli ordnancemen, who were smiling. The leader saluted him and Woods returned the honor with a snappy salute of his own. He added throttle and taxied quickly away from the truck. He turned toward the runway to take off and head back to the *Washington*.

They turned left onto the taxiway next to the runway. Israeli fighters were still landing, nearly one every minute. Woods looked around anxiously. They didn't have time to hang around. No time at all. They had to get back to the ship. They had to go *now*.

Wink broke into his thoughts. "You know how hard it's going to be to explain why we couldn't get back to the ship on time when we were supposed to be thirty miles away?"

"We'll make it," Woods replied.

"You know that the next launch begins in *five* minutes and we're in the middle of Israel?"

"And we're supposed to be the first down," Woods said as the Tomcat bounced down the taxiway toward the end of the runway, receiving stares from ground crew and pilots alike. "We should be in the overhead pattern right now, circling at two thousand feet, looking cool with our wings back and our tailhooks down."

"We're not even off the ground, and we don't have enough gas to go back very fast. You realize that?"

"We'll land with a little less gas than usual, Wink."

"A *little*? We're *already* below what we usually *land* with," he said, watching the fuel gauge with horror. "We'll be lucky to get on the deck before we flame out."

"I know."

"You know how hard it's going to be to explain why we needed to tank before we land, when we're coming back from a simple air intercept hop?"

"We'll be okay."

Woods stopped at the line separating the taxiway from the runway. Big taxied up next to him and stopped. Wink looked at Sedge and gave him the signal to report his fuel state—4.5. Four thousand five hundred pounds. The amount they should be landing with. Five hundred more pounds than Wink and Woods. "This is gonna be colorful," Wink muttered.

A section of F-16s landed directly in front of them. Woods looked at the control tower, dying inside. He saw the green light the controller was shining at him and looked quickly left to see if anyone else was landing. Clear. He taxied to the left side and turned to point down the runway, ready to take off. Big taxied to the right side, just behind Woods. Woods turned two fingers quickly next to his ear, and the Tomcats ran up their engines to full military power. They didn't need afterburner—they were light. They couldn't afford the gas anyway, no matter how much they'd like to impress the Israelis, which was a lot. Woods didn't even hesitate. He did a cursory check of his instruments, skipped his usual check of the flight controls, dropped his hand to point forward like signaling a first down, and released his brakes. Big released his as soon as Woods's jet moved. They rolled down the runway together and lifted off in a formation takeoff after nine hundred feet. They raised their gear and flaps together and turned toward the Med, leveling off at five hundred feet.

Woods looked at his clock—0845. The second launch of the day was starting. The first plane of the second event on the *Washington* was being shot down the catapult right now. The Air Boss was no doubt leaning over by his window looking up, wondering where the Jolly Roger Tomcats were. All the other planes from the first launch were either in the overhead pattern, or making their way there. Soon, people would notice their absence. He advanced the throttles to full military power and headed straight west.

"What heading?"

"Don't know," Wink replied. "We're too low to pick up the TA-CAN," he said watching the needle spin aimlessly on the compass dial. "The only thing I can say is where the boat was when we left. Could be off by twenty miles or more."

"Use it if it's all we've got," Woods said.

"Head 265," Wink said. "We really should head northeast of the ship, so we're at least coming back in from the right direction when we check in."

"We don't have time for that," Woods said.

Wink watched the airspeed indicator climb through four hundred fifty knots. "We can't burn gas like this, Trey! We'll flame out!"

"You got any other ideas? You want to come strolling in after the recovery and answer a lot of questions about where we've been?"

"No. We'll never make it! I sure as hell don't want to go swimming! You know how much gas we burn at five hundred knots on the deck!"

"We'll make it. I'm sure."

Wink didn't answer. He knew it was useless. Their speed climbed through five hundred fifty knots. They flashed over the coast highway and the beach, and were quickly over the water, where they were most comfortable.

As soon as he thought it appropriate, Wink called the carrier on the radio, about fifty miles out. *"Gulf November, this is Bright Sword 211, flight of two, 020 for 20 inbound."*

"Roger, 211, don't have you, continue inbound, report see me."

"Wilco," he replied.

"Why don't you climb to two thousand feet. It'll put us at our orbit altitude and we can pick up the TACAN sooner."

Woods pulled back on the stick and the Tomcat climbed quickly to two thousand feet as their airspeed passed through six hundred knots. They flew west, minute after minute, the TACAN needle spinning, heading generally in the direction of the ship. Wink turned his radar on and scanned the sea for the big target and the airplanes above it. But there were a lot of big targets: tankers, cargo ships, and other military ships.

As if on cue, the needle of the TACAN settled and fixed on the carrier, and pointed steadily five degrees to the left. The DME—Distance Measuring Equipment—which showed how far they were from the ship, began to spin, then settled on thirty-three miles. Woods turned left to put the needle directly on the nose, and checked his clock—0850. The launch was probably half over. The Air Boss had to be wondering where they were by now. If they were much later than *now,* questions would be asked. The officer from VF-103 who had the Pri-Fly watch, standing right behind the Boss in case there were any F-14 emergencies or questions, would be asked some very hard questions about the performance of his squadron mates, which the Boss would order him to pass on to the Commanding Officer of the Jolly Rogers. All very awkward.

"211, see you," Wink transmitted.

"Roger, 211, still don't have you, switch frequencies."

"You see the ship?" Woods asked, amazed.

"No, I just didn't want Strike to be looking for us too hard."

"I think I see it," Woods said. "I'm showing fifteen miles, that should be just a couple more minutes," he said, looking down at his clock. He glanced over at Big, who was flying tight formation on him.

Wink turned on his IFF so the ship would see them. The tower frequency was silent, as it usually was on day recoveries. He looked for other airplanes, but didn't see any yet.

"I've got the ship," Wink said. "Just to the right. Looks to be heading 300 or so."

Woods came right, and headed for the carrier, five miles ahead.

"*211, see you*," Wink transmitted.

"What are you doing?" Woods yelled at Wink.

"*Calling Boss, say again?*"

Wink knew he had screwed up. "Sorry, Trey. I blew it." He realized he had called the ship on the Air Boss's frequency, something you didn't do. He had lost track. He sat silently hoping the Air Boss would let it pass.

The radio was silent as Woods and Big screamed toward the USS *George Washington* in tight formation. Woods reduced throttle to slow down from six hundred knots to three hundred fifty. They came up the side of the ship and looked at the deck. The last plane for the second event, an S-3 Viking antisubmarine plane taxied onto the bow catapult. The landing area was clear.

Woods glanced at Big, brought his right hand to his mouth like an Italian chef, and kissed him off. He threw the stick hard left and broke in front of the carrier. He pulled hard, five Gs, and took the Tomcat downwind. As they leveled their wings Woods lowered the landing gear and flaps, and went through the landing checklist with Wink.

Wink looked left and saw the S-3 shoot off the bow of the ship, and men scrambling to clear the flight deck for their approach. The white-shirted LSOs were in place, ready to wave them off if their approach was dangerous, or "advise" them if their approach needed correction.

As they flew past the LSO platform a mile away heading the opposite direction from the ship, Woods began a left turn that he would hold until directly behind the ship in the groove. He had done it so many times it was a habit.

Big was right behind them with a perfect interval. Woods rolled his wings level three quarters of a mile behind the ship, lined up with the centerline of the angled deck. The ball, the lens that showed where they were on the glide path, was centered. Woods checked his airspeed, lineup, and angle of attack, and descended steadily toward the flight deck. He made small corrections to stay on the glide path—big corrections would lead to bigger ones later. They landed just behind the three-wire. The hook grabbed the wire, pulled it up off the deck, and held the Tomcat as Woods went to military power. The plane tried its hardest to get airborne again, but the steel cable held it back and finally stopped it fifty feet short of the end of the angled deck.

A yellow-shirted sailor ran out and signaled Woods to take his feet off the brakes and go to idle on the engines. He did, and the retracting three-wire pulled the Tomcat gently backward. They rolled toward the stern for thirty feet until the cable cleared the hook. Woods raised the hook on the signal and quickly taxied forward to get out of the landing area for Big to land. They crossed the red and white line on the edge of the landing area ten seconds before Big slammed into the deck, snagged the number-two wire, and came to a stop just to their left.

They taxied toward to the bow of the ship. The yellow shirts maneuvered them just forward of the island as the ordies ran underneath the wings to safe the missiles. Gunner Bailey stood in his red turtleneck and red flotation vest supervising the entire operation. Woods and Wink put their hands up while the ordies put the pins with long red flags on them into the missiles to ensure no accidental firings. Routine. Ordinary. Happens every flight. Except the ordies weren't usually safing Israeli missiles. Woods closed his eyes, hoping they didn't notice anything different about them.

The ordies ran out from under the wings with their thumbs up. Woods looked at Bailey, who gave him a knowing thumbs-up, and the yellow shirt motioned for them to taxi forward to the bow.

Woods, Wink, Big, and Sedge walked into the ready room together, helmets and flight bags in hand. Woods surveyed the room carefully, trying to look casual, and saw the usual activity: briefing and watching the PLAT as the recovery continued above their heads. The first day out from a port was always more exciting as the aircrew were anxious to get back into the air, back into their routine of flying.

"How was the hop?" Meat asked, sitting at the SDO desk in his khakis. Second only to Big in size, Lieutenant Mark Mora, Meat, was another first tour pilot.

"Defied death once again," answered Woods.

Meat looked at Woods more closely as he sat in a ready room chair to fill out the yellow sheet. He frowned. "You guys look like you've been swimming," he said, noticing the sweat-drenched hair and flight suits. "You didn't do any unauthorized ACM, did you?" Air Combat Maneuvering, Dogfighting.

Woods tried to look disinterested. He put his finger to his lips. Meat smiled.

Chief Lucas walked into the ready room looking for them. "Any gripes?" he asked.

"None," Woods replied, looking at Wink, who shook his head.

"Nope," Big answered.

A young sailor with a green maintenance turtleneck on stuck his head into the ready room. "Hey, Chief, can you come here for a sec?"

Chief Lucas rolled his eyes, "Never a moment's peace," he said, turning. "What!" he yelled, walking next door to Maintenance Control.

He came back in five seconds later and crossed to Woods. He stood in front of him glaring angrily. "Petty Officer Wynn said the accelerometer reads eight Gs. You pull eight Gs on that hop, Lieutenant?" he asked.

Woods felt a rush of blood; he wanted to kick himself for failing to reset the needle on the accelerometer. "Guess we got carried away. Did a little tail chasing."

"Sir, that's a *down jet*. You know we've got to pull the panels if someone pulls eight Gs. You told the mechs on the roof the plane was up, sir!"

"Sorry, Chief," he said, chagrined. "I guess I forgot."

"Sir, begging your pardon, but how do you forget pulling eight Gs? We told the aircrew for the third go that they could have your jets. Now the spare'll have to go instead of the lead," the Chief said, putting his hands on his hips. "They're gonna be pissed."

"Sorry, Chief," Woods repeated.

Bark walked into the ready room in his flight suit ready to brief event four. "Hello, boys. How'd it feel to get in the air again after five days off?"

"Great, Skipper," Big said, watching Chief Lucas to see if he was going to take the opportunity to let the Skipper in on his unhappiness.

Chief Lucas scowled, and left the ready room without another word.

"What's with him?" Bark asked.

"What's for lunch, Meat?" Big asked.

"Spaghetti, and Israeli milk."

"Weird containers again?" Woods moaned, writing on the yellow sheet.

"You're still fixated on the German milk," Big said. "The Israeli milk is actually *much* worse. It tastes like Brie cheese that has been sitting out for three days with flies crawling on it. It's cold just to cover the flavor."

"Lumps?"

"What the hell is Brie cheese?" Wink asked, annoyed.

Big shook his head. "You are so cosmopolitan, Wink. You probably think eating a cheeseburger on a whole wheat bun is on the cutting edge of culinary adventurism."

"You really crack yourself up, don't you, Big?" Wink replied.

"I *have* to laugh. Nobody else gets my sophisticated humor. Living with you guys is like putting on a Shakespeare play in front of a bunch of prisoners. They just stare at you, no idea what's being said, missing the subtlety, the nuance, the turn of the phrase, the *double enten-dres . . .*"

"What the hell is a dooble ontonder?" Wink said.

"Do you actually know who Shakesp—"

"Blow it out your ass, Big. Don't give me your drama major crap," Wink said, not looking at him, writing on the yellow sheet. "You don't even know what a cosine is."

"Sure I do," said Big quickly. "It's someone who guarantees a debt for another, someone . . ."

Wink laughed out loud, joined by others, the engineers.

Big smiled, his eyes twinkling. "You guys are so easy. You think you've got a secret world that we truly educated don't know about? Cosine is so sophisticated it's from about, oh, eighth grade or so, maybe ninth if you're slow."

"So what is it then?" Wink pressed, hoping Big was bluffing.

Big glanced at Wink, sitting three chairs away from him. "You don't think I know, do you," he said, looking down at the green sheet on which he was writing a minor gripe about the throttle friction sticking. "Maybe I won't tell you."

Wink smiled knowingly. "Like I figured."

Big spoke tiredly, as if to a poor student who had heard the expla-nation before. "It's a trigonometric function of an acute angle. It's the ratio of the leg of a triangle *by* the angle, if it's a right triangle, and the hypot—"

The ready room door opened suddenly and a group of officers in white turtlenecks and flotation vests walked in. "Event one?" the leader asked.

Woods looked up and recognized the CAG LSO, the Air Wing Landing Signal Officer, the one on the platform for the recovery of the first event. He was debriefing every pilot who had landed and had worked his way aft to Ready Room Eight. "Hey, Bolt, right here," Woods said, lifting his hand.

Woods and Big stood up and the group of LSOs—and LSOs in training crossed to meet them.

"211?" Bolt asked.

"Me," Woods said.

Bolt opened his book and looked for the entry on 211's pass. Finding it, he read the comments. "Okay three-wire, little high at the start, settled over the ramp. That's it," Bolt said, looking at Woods. He didn't expect much response, having given him nearly the highest grade possible, only an underlined okay being better, but very rare.

"Thanks," Woods said.

"207?"

"Me," Big said.

"Okay two wire, little left in the groove, little nose down at the ramp."

"Thanks," Big said.

Bolt closed his book. His fine straight blond hair was a mess from the wind and jet exhaust. He looked at Woods and Big with a gleam in his eye. "How fast were you guys going coming into the break? We didn't see you in the overhead pattern, then suddenly we see you coming like your hair was on fire, enter the break, and land."

Woods glanced at Big and shrugged. "What do you think, Big, two-fifty? Two seventy-five?"

"Kilometers, maybe," Big said. Then to Bolt. "It's hard for you, Bolt." Bolt was an S-3 pilot. "You're not used to seeing that kind of speed, you know, like a Cessna or a Piper might throw at you."

"You're hilarious," Bolt said, smiling.

Pritch came in as Bolt left. Woods fixed her with a sharp glance, but Pritch avoided his eyes. "The aircrews from the first event haven't debriefed in CVIC," Pritch announced to Sedge.

Sedge turned away from the schedule board where he was looking for their next hop. "Like it matters. What are we going to say? Did four million intercepts, saw my wingman each time, returned home, and took a leak? Why do we go through this charade?"

"Not up to me, Sedge," Pritch said. "Who's it going to be?" she asked, studying all four of them.

"Come on, Sedge," Wink said. "Let's go tell the nice Intelligence Officer about our hop."

They followed Pritch out the door and down the passageway to the intelligence center. "How'd it go?" Pritch asked Wink as they walked down the passageway.

"No problem. Routine hop," he answered.

"Everybody get back okay?"

"Of course. Why wouldn't we? It was just a silly AIC hop, you know, you go outbound, then inbound, then you land. Nothing to it."

Pritch turned and examined their faces as they walked behind her.

"You expect any trouble?" she asked in a low tone of voice.

They both shook their heads, as they entered CVIC.

23

The task force members had gathered in the fusion room, where they waited for Joe Kinkaid. The computers in the room hummed from the satellite photos and data being manipulated by eager agents; a live CNN broadcast played in the back of the room, showing footage of an Israeli air strike into Lebanon. Sami watched it abstractedly. It looked so much like other strike footage he had seen he couldn't help wondering if they ever just pulled out footage of a similar Israeli air strike and showed it with a new date on it.

Now his attention focused on Joe Kinkaid, who'd just come into the room, looking more rumpled than usual. Sami could tell that Kinkaid wasn't interested in the latest news reports or anything else. He was very unhappy, and very angry. "I didn't tell you what Ricketts was doing," he began, forgoing any preliminaries.

Sami stared, wondering what was coming.

Kinkaid continued, "He was involved in an operation to kidnap the Sheikh."

Sami looked around to see how many of the task force members were in control of their expressions. Kinkaid wasn't looking for any reaction as he went on. "He had excellent intelligence of the Sheikh's whereabouts and set up one of the most creative covert ops I have ever heard of. The Sheikh was about to walk into the trap this morning, while you were all sleeping soundly in your beds." Kinkaid reached for the cigarette pack in his shirt pocket, forgetting that it hadn't been there for ten years. "Apparently the Israelis had the same intelligence we did. The air strike they conducted this morning was against many targets all over southern Lebanon, but one of the targets was the place

239

where the Sheikh was supposed to be this morning. Ricketts was standing right in the middle of it. There was some thought that the explosives Ricketts was . . . using, might have gone off at the wrong time. But we don't think so. The Israelis hit the building with two one-thousand-pound laser-guided bombs and blew it to hell."

Sami winced. He had enjoyed his evening conversation with Ricketts. It had ranged from the general untrustworthiness of the Israelis to the stupidity of Syria and various terrorist groups. They had discussed Islam, Judaism, Christianity, the future of the United States in the Middle East, and the Agency's role in the area. Sami had asked Ricketts what guided him through all the confusion. Loyalty to the United States had been his response. Not the answer Sami had expected. Ricketts had actually said loyalty to the U.S. Sometimes it was tricky, but that was his guide. And look where it got him, Sami thought.

One of the members of the task force from the Directorate of Intelligence, the same directorate Sami was part of, asked angrily, "When are the piss-ant Israelis going to start telling us when they have an operation this big going down so we can stay out of the way?"

Kinkaid agreed. "That was the first question that occurred to me too. I think their answer would be 'when are the piss-ant Americans going to tell us they're conducting a covert op we might want to know about?' I don't think we can blame the Israelis for this one." His frustration boiled over. "I mean what are the chances two countries are going to act on the same piece of intelligence at exactly the same time? Minuscule. Can't happen. But it did."

"Now what?" Sami asked.

"Now it's going to be harder than ever to get to him, and what's worse, we've probably stirred up the hornet's nest. Let's just hope the Sheikh doesn't know about Ricketts's operation or he'll blame everything on the U.S. He'll probably think the Israeli attack was our idea. Oh, and by the way, the Sheikh hadn't arrived yet when the bombs hit. They missed him, and now he knows they were trying for him, which means he knows he has an intelligence leak. It's about the worst possible result."

"Think he'll be on to Ricketts?"

"I don't think there's any way Ricketts would leave a trail. I think we're okay there. But now we've got to get smarter on how to get this guy. He'll be twice as paranoid as before."

Sami was stuck on something else. "Anybody talked to the Israelis lately? 'Cause it looks like they really wanted this guy too." Sami looked at the others. "The Sheikh had to be after the woman on the bus."

"How do you figure that?" Kinkaid said doubtfully.

"It wasn't the bus driver." Everyone nodded. "And probably not the soldier . . ."

"Well, possibly—"

Sami replied, "No way. He was"—he opened a thick file and looked for a piece of paper—"nineteen years old." He looked up. "Unless he's somebody's son, he probably hasn't done enough to piss off someone of the Sheikh's stature to make him take that kind of risk to get him. And it couldn't have been that Navy Lieutenant . . ."

"Lieutenant Vialli," Kinkaid said.

"Right. Couldn't be him. *Nobody* knew he was going to be there, including his Commanding Officer. That leaves her. What does the report say about her . . ." He read from the paper again. "Deformed hand. The report on the Navy investigation says—"

"What are you, an analyst all of a sudden?" someone called out.

"Just thinking out loud. Want me to stop?"

"Go on," Kinkaid said.

"Says she told Vialli and a Lieutenant Woods her hand was deformed from birth. Now we learn she was involved in an accident of some kind a year and a half ago. What kind of accident? I don't know. I'm just saying, maybe she's the one they were after."

"What does that do for us, though?" Kinkaid asked.

"If they were after her, the Israelis know why. And if they know why, then they know more about this guy than they're letting on. I've read what they've given us. It's something, but overall . . ." He stared directly at Kinkaid. "It's a pile of shit. They're holding back on us."

Kinkaid had stopped listening. He hadn't been able to think of anything else but Ricketts since he'd gotten the news. He had agreed to make the arrangements for the secret memorial service and to give a eulogy. It was one of the hardest things he had ever had to do. Ricketts had always been the one Kinkaid fantasized about being. Of all the people at the CIA, Ricketts did what intelligence officers were supposed to do—he actually made a difference. Kinkaid could cite chapter and verse, but he wouldn't be able to, because most of the people who would be at the service didn't even know about the mission. Over the years Ricketts had become his friend, in a thorny, challenging kind of way, the only way Ricketts knew how to have friends. He thought everything was calculated to gain some advantage, even friendship . . . Suddenly realizing that he hadn't heard what Sami was saying, Kinkaid forced himself back to the present. "I'm sorry. What did you say?"

"The Israelis—they're holding back on us."

Kinkaid mumbled, "Maybe . . ." Then he apologized again and headed for the door.

Meat erased the aircraft numbers on the grease board in the front of the ready room for the event that had just landed and began to put numbers up for the crew's briefing. The board showed the ever-changing status of the flight schedule. Woods sat in the chair in the first row staring at the television screen. Most of the other officers in the ready room were watching the CNN report too, but none with his intensity. A reporter stood in front of a pile of rubble on a clear bright day in southern Lebanon. Several people behind her, their mouths covered, were sorting through the broken stones and pieces of building. On the bottom of the screen was the name of the town, Dar al Ahmar, Lebanon.

The officers in the ready room listened with skepticism. Any time the media reported on anything military, they held onto their wallets.

". . . and here, as you can see, there has been substantial damage by some stray Israeli bombs. We have spoken to many local residents and all of them have said that there was no reason to bomb Dar al Ahmar. It has nothing of military value and is not defended by any antiaircraft guns or missiles. They are very upset that the Israelis were unable to aim their bombs correctly and killed several innocent people. According to the residents, the building was hit by two bombs almost simultaneously. It was a motorcycle sales and repair shop, selling mostly motor scooters and motorized bicycles. At the time of the attack there were approximately six people inside getting the shop ready to open for business, including one unlucky fellow who had just stopped in this morning to deliver some new Honda motor scooters to the shop. The attack occurred at approximately 8 A.M. Lebanon time, and was very short in duration. There were several other places bombed, and there were airplanes shot down, but details about the air battle are still unclear, according to what I have been able to piece together. Back to you, in Washington."

Woods tried to look nonchalant. He was so glad Israel had done it. He was thrilled to have been in combat for the first time. He wanted to shout from the highest point on the carrier, "*Got* you!" He wanted to let everyone know that Americans would always protect their countrymen. But his exuberance was tempered by Leavenworth. He knew the chances of being caught were now less—they had made it back safely and on time, and the Gunner would take care of the rest. The Gunner assured him he knew how to fix the computer and paper records so no one could trace the replacement missiles.

The remainder of the day passed unremarkably. That night Woods lay awake staring at the overhead. He kept seeing the MiG that he had gunned go down and slam into the desert, undoubtedly killing the pilot. He tried to count. That MiG pilot for sure. The Flogger pilot with the Sparrow shot . . . the Sidewinder kill, no chute. Three. He had personally killed three men. At least three. Maybe more. It was such a blur, but a vivid blur. He had never killed anyone before. He had never even started a fistfight before. Been in a few, but never of his own making. Over and over again, he could hear the whoosh of the missiles coming off the rails. Sparrow. Sidewinder.

Bernie the Breather was making its curious gushh, cuh cuh cuh sounds, matching the images of the missiles going off the rails in Woods's mind. He listened for several minutes to the mindless valve inside the pipe flapping up and down.

"You awake?" Big asked.

"Yeah," Woods answered.

They lay in the dark, unable to see each other.

"What you thinking about?"

"The strike."

"What about it?"

"Everything. Cat launch, going over the beach, the rendezvous, going north at low level, the air battle, the fight, the LGBs on the target, heading south, reloading, getting back to the boat on fumes. But most of all, pulling it off. By God, pulling it off," Woods said. "We actually did it, Big."

Big didn't say anything at first. He had his arms behind his head under his pillow. Finally he spoke. "So far."

"What do you mean?"

"A lot of people know about it, or know something about it. Somebody's going to slip."

"Nah. They wanted us to hit back as much as we did."

"All it takes is one."

"Don't sweat it."

Big wasn't to be comforted. "How does it feel to have killed somebody?"

"How do you feel?"

"Sort of cold. I expected to be upset, or feel sorry for the guy or something. It hasn't gotten to me at all."

"The only one that keeps coming back is the Fishbed I gunned. The bullets went right through the canopy. He never knew what hit him. No ejection. Nothing. Dead as a doornail. Just drifted down and hit the deck. That was it for him." Woods was quiet. "That's the one that keeps coming back."

Bernie breathed and flapped between their bunks and the bulkhead. Airplanes rushed down the deck above them, pulled off the carrier into the night by the catapults.

"Knowing what you—"

"Would I do it again?"

"Yeah."

"In a second. And we got him, Big. Vaporized him."

"The Israelis got him."

"We were there. If I could have, I would have *personally* vaporized him." Woods turned onto his side. "How about you?"

"In a second." Big rolled over. "Do you know how great a screenplay this would make?"

"I'm telling you."

"I'll start on it tomorrow."

"No, Big. You can't tell anyone about this for twenty years."

"Twenty years? I'll be *ancient* by then. Forty-six."

"Twenty years."

"Not fair," he said, rolling back to lie face up on the top bunk. "Probably best anyway. We don't know how it ends."

Woods settled into the chair in the back of the ready room just as he had hundreds of times before. Wink sat next to him, and the other four officers in the brief were scattered in the other chairs. At the prescribed time, the television came on for the brief, but instead of one of the Ensign Intelligence Officers, CAG stood behind the podium looking particularly stern. "Instead of the usual intelligence brief before the first event, there have been some developments of a serious nature that I want to discuss with you. Those of you in the ready rooms, call all your officers. I want to speak to as many at once as we can. The television will be going off right now. You have five minutes to round up your squadrons. My brief will begin in exactly five minutes."

Woods yelled to the front of the ready room, "You hear that?"

"I heard it. I need help," Easy said as he reached for the phone. "Can you start at the bottom of the list and call from the phone on the ops desk? I'll start at the top with Rocket One and go down."

Woods jumped up, threw a concerned look at Wink, and ran to the phone on the desk on the other side of the ready room. "Bottom aye," he yelled to Easy as he ran.

Within five minutes they had found everyone in the squadron but one. Word spread fast. Most of the officers had been in the wardroom eating breakfast, and those who weren't had been in their racks. They came in their flight suits to see what CAG thought was so important.

"You ever seen anything like this, Skipper?" Sedge asked casually as all the officers settled into seats.

"Never," Bark replied, annoyed the CAG hadn't talked to the Squadron Commanders first. Typical. Senior officers were always yelling about using the chain of command, except when it suited them to go around it.

"You got any hints what this is about, Skipper?" asked Easy.

Bark shook his head. He drank from his coffee cup as the television in the front of the ready room jumped to life.

CAG stood in the same place with the same grim look on his face. He was sour-looking anyway, a forty-five-year-old man with skin that looked as if he had spent his whole life avoiding the sun. He was tall and gaunt, and kept his graying hair closely cropped. "Sorry to interfere with the cyclic ops, but we have some news that I wanted to convey to all of you as soon as possible," he began.

"As you and everyone else in the world knows, yesterday Israel attacked terrorist bases in southern Lebanon. But this was more than the usual air strike. This time they went in force. They sent antiradiation missiles to take out the air defense network, they sent Wild Weasels to take on the SAMs directly, they sent special forces to attack the communications. They had jamming birds, and the E-2C airborne, and they sent their bombers against the camps and one town. They sent fighters in force. Syria apparently responded in kind, and sent dozens of its own fighters. . . ."

Woods sneaked a look at Big, who was licking his dry lips and avoiding Woods's gaze.

". . . all leading to an enormous air battle. Israel apparently was very successful in taking out the air defenses, as well as the Syrian fighters. The preliminary reports out of Israel are that over twenty Syrian MiGs were shot down, with no Israeli losses."

The Jolly Rogers looked at each other amazed, murmuring. "Ooorah," one said.

"All this is interesting, and I'd love to see the gun camera film, but there are other implications," the CAG went on.

"If you recall, this ship was in port in Haifa the day before yesterday. We went en masse"—he pronounced it "in-mace," butchering the word, "to a reception at Ramat David Air Force Base. In all likelihood we were with the very people involved in the raid. They couldn't very well tell us about it because it had probably been in the plans for weeks. The timing of our visit was just unfortunate. The problem is that someone may try to imply that we helped plan the raid. We must do everything we can to avoid even the appearance of complicity. That is why the first two events of this morning are canceled"—the aircrew moaned as a group—"and the ship is going to steam due west to put more distance between us and the Syrians and the Israelis. We don't want to be mistaken for someone participating in this melee," he said, butchering the pronounciation again.

"So, when we do fly, stay west of the carrier, ensure that we aren't approached by any unauthorized aircraft, by *either* side—we don't need another *Liberty* incident—and we'll make our way to the western Mediterranean. If you have any questions, please address them up the chain of command. Anything you want to know about the raid will be forthcoming in intelligence reports or news reports, whichever comes first. That is all," he said, removing the microphone from his shirt. The television went blank.

Bark stood up and turned to look at the squadron. "How 'bout them apples," he said, grinning. "Hey, Trey, just when you were whining, wishing someone would go beat the hell out of them, the Israelis were planning to do just that," he said, shaking his head. "I'll bet you'd give your left nut to have been on that go."

Woods nodded and laughed. "I don't know about that, Skipper. That's an awfully high price—I'd let them have *Wink's* left nut though," he said.

Bark continued, "Did you tell the Israelis it was Vialli?"

Woods nodded.

"I'll bet they were busting a gut to tell you," Bark said.

"Probably," Woods replied.

"Well," Bark said, "nothing really to be done. Can't wait to hear the after action reports. Stay loose, and don't fly feet dry over Lebanon. Course it'll be hundreds of miles away by the time we fly again." He stopped and looked around. "Any questions?"

Easy raised his hand. "What liberty incident was CAG referring to? Some sailor do something in Tel Aviv?"

Bark shook his head. "Not liberty incident, the USS *Liberty* incident," he said, emphasizing the name of the ship. "How many of you have heard of the *Liberty*?" Three of them raised their hands tentatively, hoping he wouldn't call on them for an explanation. Bark shook his head disgustedly. "You guys are pathetic. The *Liberty* was a U.S. comm ship operating off Suez in the eastern Med in 1967 when the '67 war kicked off. The Israelis attacked it and killed a bunch of Americans. Over thirty. Even though it was *clearly* in international waters and clearly flying an American flag."

The officers looked at one another. "Mistake?" one finally asked tentatively.

Bark shrugged. "Broad daylight? U.S. Navy gray ship, with U.S. flag? ID number and name in twelve-foot-high letters? International waters? Attacked by airplanes *and* torpedo boats all of whom were close enough to hit it with machine guns, and neither Egypt nor Syria has a ship anything like it?" He paused. "You tell me. A lot of people think they did it because they were afraid the U.S. was sending intel to Egypt."

"That's incredible," Big said, feeling somehow betrayed, looking at Woods, who was fighting the chill that had settled over most of the officers in the room.

"There are books on it. Read for yourself. Israel said it was a *mistake* and they were *really* sorry."

"What do you think, Skipper?" Big said, anger inside him.

Bark stared at him. "Would *you* make a mistake like that? Dropping iron bombs on the wrong ship? If you weren't sure, would you drop? And they had boats out there *machine gunning* it. Visual range."

Big shook his head.

"Me neither. I think the official U.S. policy is to accept the Israeli explanation. Well," Bark continued, "go about your business. Lieutenant fitness report inputs are due to the department heads by Friday, and in final form to the Ops O, our pinch hitting XO, by the next Friday." He hesitated as they all thought of the XO and Brillo. Woods tried to keep the image of Brillo's scalp on the airplane tail from leaping into his mind but was completely unsuccessful. "First class evals are due to you in draft from your division chiefs by the end of the month. I still need Sailor of the Quarter nominations, and we have a surprise health and safety inspection scheduled for tomorrow morning. Any other questions?"

There weren't any.

Kinkaid put the photographs up on the screen. There were three of them, the three views from the accessible sides of the building. There were white arrows on the photographs next to two individuals who were barely noticeable otherwise. It was a grainy, fuzzy photograph, obviously taken through a thermal site. "We just got these in," he said. He turned the lights down to make the room even dimmer than it already was. All they could see clearly were the computer screens, lights from the equipment, and the photographs on the screen in front of them.

Kinkaid continued, his voice tired from years of tracking people who were hard to find and harder to deal with. "These are from the embassy in Rabat, Morocco. Maybe a couple of thieves. Or, they may be something else. They were standing outside the embassy at two in the morning. They were very hard to see, because they're very good at what they're doing—"

"How do we know they're not just thieves?"

"They may be. That's what I *just* said, if you would listen," he replied annoyed. "But in this case, our officers on the ground say this is a little out of the ordinary. It's their job to spot the anomalies, and they say this is out of the ordinary. Plus, if you thought about it, thieves don't usually case an embassy. Not a good target for theft, what with Marines and all.

"I wanted us all to be aware of this. You can see what the concern is. If someone's watching an embassy, the obvious question is why and the obvious answer is to conduct some kind of attack on the building."

He showed an overhead diagram of the location of the embassy in Casablanca, another larger one of the city, and a smaller one of the blocks immediately around the distinctive three-story structure. "As you can see, the possible approaches for a truck bomb are numerous. There has been some progress made in blocking off the parking near the building, but we're not free of risk."

"He wouldn't use a truck bomb against an embassy," Sami said.

Kinkaid stared at Sami, put off by his tone. "How do you know that?"

"It's not their style."

"So that's the end of our analysis? 'It's not their style'?"

Sami was stung. "I just don't think they will. His Assassins operate based on a different set of criteria. He doesn't seem interested in large bombs that blow up hundreds of people. I think there might be some— I hesitate to call it wisdom—but thinking there. If it's a big explosion and a hundred people are killed, all we see is a pile of dead people, but it isn't really personal. So far, at least, he's gone for the dramatic impact."

"So don't worry about a large attack or truck bomb because Sami says?"

"No, sir, we should take precautions, absolutely, I'm just telling you that I don't think it's very likely."

"I'm sending out Snapshot Teams," Kinkaid said with finality. "Anybody disagree with that?"

Cunningham spoke reluctantly. "Why would he be after us? Unless he knows Ricketts was there, the only American he's encountered was the Navy officer. By accident. So why would he start on us?"

"Maybe we've been his target all along, and now he's just getting started."

Cunningham nodded. He and the others knew better than to disagree with the head of the task force, at least when he had declared what he had decided to do. And it did make sense. It was something that should be done, even if they found nothing. The riskier course would be not to send the teams, and have something happen.

⚓

Woods sat in front of the computer screen dealing with the e-mails he looked at every day. In fact, in many ways they made his day. He stayed in touch with his mother, his brother, his friends from college, and

Navy pals whom he had met at various points in his Navy career. He stared at the in box, surveying the return e-mail addresses for the new e-mails he had received. He noticed one he didn't recognize—"jaime.rodriguez@mail.house.gov." What the hell is that? he thought to himself as he scrolled down and hit Enter to retrieve that e-mail first. It came up and he read it:

Dear Lieutenant Woods:

We've never met. I am the Legislative Director on Admiral Brown's staff. I'm the one who received your letter recommending we declare war against Sheikh al-Jabal. I am also the one who sent you the form letter, saying essentially that we shared your concern with international terrorism, and that the Admiral was supporting this or that.

I've felt bad ever since that letter went out. I wanted to tell you that the form letter didn't truly reflect the interest your letter generated in this office.

You probably don't know Admiral Brown. He is bright, energetic, and most of all, willing to listen to the ideas of his subordinates. That distinguishes him from a lot of his fellow members of Congress, believe me. But he was willing to listen to you too. That's what I wanted you to know. I personally talked to him about your idea. He was fascinated. We talked at some length about whether it was possible, legal, etc. Good stuff. The staff has been talking about it ever since. He's even got some people looking into it further, including me. It just seemed unfair to let you continue to think that no one here paid any attention to it all. There are enough cynics there who think nothing that a constituent says has any value at all. I guess sometimes that does seem to be the case. But at least as far as your letter is concerned, it has stimulated a lot of thought and I wanted you to know.

Let me know if there is anything I can ever do for you. I feel like I owe you one.

Sincerely,

Jaime Rodriguez

Woods couldn't believe his eyes. He read the e-mail again and again. He sat back in his chair and stared at the screen. Suddenly he yelled, "Big!"

✦

Woods and Wink were elected by Bark to be the first aircrew to sit alert five. During the transit west, while there wasn't going to be any flying, the carrier still had to protect itself from an unexpected attack. It was one thing that all carrier Captains and Air Wing Commanders had in common—an aversion to being attacked by surprise. Pearl Harbor had changed everything. If there was even the remotest possibility of a threat, pilots sat in airplanes on alert, ready to take off on a moment's notice. With Israel and Syria having at it, it was decided to keep fighters in alert five until the flight schedule picked up again in the afternoon.

Alert five simply meant they had the ability to get airborne with live missiles and defend the carrier battle group from any attack in five minutes. The aircrew had to be strapped into their seats, airplane plugged in, sitting on the cat, alignment set, ready to go. All they had to do was start the engines and get shot off the catapult.

Woods and Wink sat in the Tomcat on catapult three in the middle of the landing area of the flight deck. The canopy was open to the warm beautiful Mediterranean day. The sun was overhead, the sea swept by at thirty knots.

Woods concentrated and moved the buttons quickly with his thumbs. He had done it hundreds of times and was ready. He knew the limited time he had, about thirty seconds. He moved buttons furiously, frustrated, an occasional curse coming from his mouth. The thirty seconds passed, and the ship's radar antenna came around again, wiping out the electronic football game he was manipulating. "Fourteen points," he called to Wink as he passed the football game back to him.

Wink grabbed it and checked the location of the rotating radar. Thirty seconds. He worked the game frantically, passing, carrying the ball and scoring, again and again. He was much better at it than Woods. He could see the radar approaching. He worked faster. The radar beam passed through them and wiped out the game. "Seventeen points!" he announced.

He reached forward with his right hand and passed the portable game back to Woods. "You cheated," Woods accused. "No way you could score that much in one pass of the radar."

"You just can't stand losing."

Woods was so intent on the game he didn't see their relief approaching the plane. The two officers began their own preflight. Each new alert crew took the opportunity to check the airplane themselves. Not that they didn't trust their squadron mates. They wouldn't have trusted themselves. When they were done, they called up to Woods and Wink. "Okay," they said. "You can come down."

Woods and Wink unstrapped, gathered their navigation information and flight bags, and climbed down to the flight deck. "All yours," Woods said. "I wish we could stay and sit in this plane longer, but I guess we can't have all the fun."

Lieutenant Commander Paulson looked at Woods with a smile. "You may not be winning this deal. There's another officers' meeting in five minutes. That's why we decided to relieve you just a little early. Now *you've* got to go."

"Ohhh, not another one. What about?"

Paulson shrugged. "CAG's on the warpath. He's running around all over the ship with his hair on fire. Something's up."

Woods looked at Wink, who was trying not to throw up. "You guys want the football game?" he asked finally.

"No thanks. I brought a book."

"You're not supposed to read," Woods said.

"I know. I'd better be careful, or they'll give me a *time out* and strap me into a seat in a small confined place for two hours." He shrugged. "What are they gonna do? Send me home? *Hurt* me," he said as he climbed into the front cockpit.

"See you guys," Wink said. He glanced at Woods and saw the concern on his face. They walked across the flight deck to the starboard side by the arresting wires and stepped onto the short ladder leading below to the O3 level. As they stepped off the ladder, Wink asked Woods, "You worried?"

Woods took longer to answer than he usually did. "I feel like a criminal hoping the police don't find the evidence I know is there."

"I still can't believe we did it," Wink said, pursing his lips as he moves through the hatch to the passageway. "But I'd do it again."

"Do what again?" asked Bark, standing in the passageway waiting to go into the ready room.

"Kick his butt in the portable football game," Wink replied quickly.

"That all you guys do on alert is play that stupid football game? You don't ask each other NATOPS and safety questions? You don't review airplane systems?" All the systems were explained in Naval Air Training and Operational Procedures Standardization manuals on which they were tested regularly. Failure meant you were grounded.

"Guilty, Skipper," Woods added. "Paulson says there's yet another meeting. What's the deal?"

"I don't know. It's CAG's show. I'm just an attendee, like you. I guess we'll soon find out. But this one's just for our squadron. In five minutes—actually, right now," he added, checking at his watch.

Woods and Wink followed Bark into the ready room. The Jolly Rogers were sitting in their assigned ready room chairs. Woods made his way to his seat in the second row. Wink took a chair farther back.

Officers were talking quietly to each other, but their attention rarely diverted from CAG, who was standing in front of them waiting for something. Nervousness was universal. No one knew why they should be nervous, but they all knew they should be.

CAG looked at Bark, sitting directly in front of him in the front row chair. "Everyone here?" CAG asked him.

"Yes, sir, except for the alert."

CAG started without any preliminaries. "You heard what I said on the television this morning. There was a large battle between Israel and Syria, and we didn't want to be anywhere near it. It was bad enough for us to have been in Israel the day before. They should have told us not to come knowing what they were going to do the day we left—but we can't change that now. The reason I wanted to talk to you, our one and only F-14 squadron, is because it has turned ugly. Israel has been sending continuous raids all day. They're not letting up this time."

The officers glanced at one another, relieved to hear it wasn't about them.

"But there has been a new development that has really got me frosted," he said, scanning the faces in front of him. "This is really about VF-103. I just hope there has been some . . . *mistake*."

Woods involuntarily gripped the armrests of his chair. He tried to continue to breathe through his nose. He could feel Wink's eyes burning holes in the back of his head.

"I was just called on the carpet by Admiral Sweat. Syria has lodged a formal protest against the United States. Actually, against *us*. Their Ambassador called on the Secretary of State this morning, in Washington, to accuse *us* of assisting the Israeli attack on the Syrian Air Force, and of actually *participating* in the attack."

The officers, murmured about how ridiculous that accusation was.

"According to Syria, their pilots reported seeing U.S. Navy Tomcats during the air battle."

The aircrew laughed nervously. Woods tried to join in with sufficient sincerity so he wouldn't stand out. He glanced at Pritch, who was standing in the corner behind the SDO desk. She looked as if she was going to faint.

"Not only do they say they saw F-14s in the battle, but they say the F-14s had the skull and crossbones on their tails," CAG said. "And there's more. Syria said they aren't basing this accusation only on visual sightings. Several of their pilots claim their wingmen were shot down by F-14s. They claim that Sparrow and Sidewinder missiles were used. A couple of pilots themselves claim to have been shot down by Tomcats."

The officers dismissed the accusation as so much nonsense. "That's not all," CAG said, frowning. "The Syrian Ambassador said that they were *sure*." He lowered his voice and took a step forward. "Their electronic warfare people identified the F-14 radar."

Woods tried not to hyperventilate. The pilots and RIOs were silent, wondering suddenly if it was somehow true, but unable to imagine how it could be.

"If anyone has anything to say, I would like to hear it," CAG said softly. He stood in front of the group and waited for someone to speak.

Woods tried not to draw attention to himself. He began to sweat, and told his body to stop sweating. He knew he couldn't look at Big, or Wink, or Sedge. Any knowing look would be intercepted by the CAG, or someone else, and all would be lost. They had never discussed what to do if found out. Lie? Lie boldly? Say nothing? Lie to protect others but not yourself?

Woods admitted to himself that he hadn't thought it through in the infinite detail he should have. They never should have turned on their radar. Just because he wanted the kill. No, he thought, because he wanted to live. Because the Flogger was coming after them and was going to kill them if they hadn't turned on the radar. He had to.

But he thought he had all possibilities covered. He had told himself that if they closed in on him, if they discovered what had happened, he would stand up courageously and announce what had happened, and tell the world that he was proud of it.

But he wasn't proud anymore. He was scared. Officers began to stir. Nobody wanted to even touch the subject, or risk being the focus of some investigation.

Bark stood up and crossed to the other side of the ready room from the CAG. He looked at the squadron. "Any of you have anything to say?" he asked, sweeping his eyes over them. "Who was on the flight schedule yesterday?" he asked.

Woods thought Bark's gaze rested a little longer on him than it did on the other officers.

"CAG," Bark said, "when was this supposed to have happened?"

"They didn't give a time. Sometime yesterday, during the air battles."

"But the reports I've read said there were several battles, going on most of the day."

"That's right. We don't know the actual time."

Bark smiled. "Well, are they saying there were Jolly Roger Tomcats there all the time?"

The other officers smiled, realizing the ridiculousness of such a statement.

"I don't think so," CAG said. "Sounds like one section to me."

Bark rubbed his chin, his brown eyes intense and thoughtful. "They say these Tomcats shot down 'several' MiGs?"

"That's right."

"How many?"

"Between four and eight."

Bark whistled. "That's pretty good work. And with missiles?"

"That's right," CAG confirmed.

"If they shot down four to eight MiGs, there should be four to eight missiles missing. Right?"

CAG thought for a second. "Right."

"Let's inventory the missiles."

"Great idea," CAG said. "Do it."

"Yes, sir, sure will," Bark replied.

CAG turned his gaze back toward the aircrews. "But I want to hear from the officers in your squadron. I want to hear from them that they *weren't there*."

"Sir, you asked them if they had anything to say, and they didn't."

CAG paced in front of the squadron. "How could the Syrians have been so wrong about seeing F-14s?"

Bark smiled. "I'd like to meet the MiG pilot that can tell the difference between an F-14 and an F-15 in the heat of the battle. Both have two tails, two engines, nice radome shaped noses, basically the same color unless you see them together—I have trouble sometimes when we fight F-15s. Easy mistake. Look at World War II—U.S. pilots shot at *American* planes thinking they were Japanese. Happens all the time."

"But why would they say the planes had the skull and bones on the tail?"

"Because we're the most famous Navy fighter squadron in the world!" Bark replied.

"Ooorah," one officer said loudly, endorsing the accolade.

Bark went on, "We've been in movies, commercials, you name it. Nearly every book you see about F-14s has our plane on the cover. Every model made of the F-14, just about, has our paint scheme on it. It's everywhere. It's probably the only one they know about. Hell, CAG, that's why VF-103 changed its name to the Jolly Rogers when the Navy decommissioned VF-84. We didn't want to see that great tradition die, so we became the Jolly Rogers."

CAG hesitated, his confidence in his information faltering. "What about the radar? They detected the F-14 radar."

"I'll bet they had the F-18 radar too, and our E-2C," Bark replied. "It's a powerful radar. Those electrons keep going—I'll bet you could pick them up on the moon." His eyes searched the room. "Who's our NATOPS RIO? Wink?" Wink raised his hand. "How far you figure an F-14 radar could be picked up by ESM? More than a hundred miles?"

Wink nodded. "Way over two hundred miles. Probably could detect it on the moon. Literally."

"They probably were being *bombarded* by F-14 electrons. No news there. We were flying all day, and radiating the entire time. No reason not to. We didn't even know about the air battle. This sounds like sour grapes to me. They know we were in port the day before. They're probably just trying to make us look bad. To tie us in. Trying to throw blame around for their rout. As if the Israelis need our help."

Maybe there was an explanation, CAG decided. He surveyed the room slowly, trying to find something that seemed out of place in the demeanor of the officers. "Well," he said to Bark, "I guess we'll know for sure if we've got a problem when that missile inventory is completed."

"Yes, sir, we sure will."

"I want CAG Ops to do the inventory."

"Yes, sir, no problem," Bark said.

CAG hesitated and then made his way out of the room. The officers breathed easier.

25

Woods sat at one of the tables in the dirty-shirt wardroom with his squadron mates.

"What do you think?" asked Easy, holding the lasagne on his fork in mid-air, his elbows resting on the table. "We now have evidence CAG has lost his mind. Do we do the *Caine Mutiny* thing and have him removed, or what?" he said, smiling.

"How could he buy what the *Syrians* say?" asked Big. "Have they *ever* said anything that was true?"

"You think he really bought it?" Sedge asked.

"Did you see his face?" Big asked. "He looked like he was going to kill somebody. All because the Syrians claimed to have picked up an F-14 radar."

"He was really intense," Easy said. "I thought he was gonna explode."

"Depends on that inventory, I guess," Terry Blankenship, the Machine, said in his usual mechanical way. "Like they're going to find a bunch of missiles missing," he added. He glanced at Gunner Bailey, who was sitting quietly at the end of the table. "Gunner, you'd better hope to hell your brain-surgeon ordies haven't lost seven or eight missiles on this cruise."

Gunner Bailey drank slowly from his glass of red bug juice, then put it down. "We inventory all the time," he said. "There aren't any missiles missing. Could have told him that," he added. He took another sip from his glass and looked knowingly at Woods, who found himself breathing easily again for the first time in an hour.

Sami held the paper in his hands and read it quickly. The Arabic flowed. It was printed neatly in the newspaper and was easy to read even though his was a fax copy. The others in the room waited for him to finish. When he finally looked up, Kinkaid spoke first. "Well?"

"We're in deep shit—"

"Yeah? Maybe *he* is. What does it say?"

"Well, first, it's in *Al-Quds al-Arabi*. That's the most authoritative Arabic paper in Europe. Published in London. They printed the entire communiqué. Very nicely done."

"What the hell does it say?" Kinkaid yelled impatiently.

"The title is: 'Declaration of War'—actually Jihad—'of the World Islamic Guardians against the Jews and the Crusaders.'" He read, then continued. "According to the newspaper it was faxed to them under the signature of Sheikh al-Jabal. The Arabic is incredible. Poetic . . . He starts off with a bunch of stuff from the Quran and the sayings of the Prophet Muhammad . . . then he says: 'Since God laid down the Arabic Peninsula and created the Arabs for the land east of Europe, no calamity has befallen this land like the Crusades, which the Europeans brought here a thousand years ago and continue to this day, now carried on with their puppets, the Jews. The Crusader-Jewish alliance has ruined the verdure of the land, eating its fruits and destroying its people; this when the nations contend against the Muslims like diners around a table of food.'" Sami motioned with his hand, indicating he was skipping the totally unnecessary. "'The facts are known to all . . .' Then he lists the three main grievances: 'First, The United States is occupying the lands of Islam in the holiest of its territories, plundering its riches, overwhelming its rulers, humiliating its people, threatening its neighbors and using bases as a spearhead to fight against the neighboring Islamic peoples. The true nature of this occupation is now made clear by the continuing American aggression against the peoples of Syria, Lebanon, and Iran.

"'Second, despite the immense destruction inflicted on the Iraqi people at the hands of the Crusader-Jewish alliance, and in spite of the appalling number of dead, now exceeding a million, the Americans—never satisfied—nevertheless tried to continue and repeat the dreadful slaughter against Iraq and now spread their death to other countries in the region.

"'Third, while the purposes of the Americans in these wars are religious and economic, they also serve the petty state of the Jews, to divert attention from their occupation of Jerusalem and their killing of Muslims in it.

" 'These crimes amount to a clear declaration of war by the Americans against God, his Prophet, and the Muslims. This condition calls for Jihad, according to the Ulema and the Sharia." Sami glanced at his listeners, explaining, "This is the *fatwa*—the ruling. It holds that: 'It is the duty of every Muslim to kill Americans and their allies, both civil and military. It is an individual duty of every Muslim who is able, in any country where this is possible, until the Aqsa Mosque'—that's in Jerusalem," he said, looking up at the now horrified faces of the task force members, " 'and the Haram Mosque'—in Mecca—'are freed from their grip and until their armies, shattered and broken-winged, depart from all the lands of Islam, incapable of threatening any Muslim.' "

Sami, chilled by the language before him, forced himself to keep reading. "He cites some Quranic verses, then continues: 'By God's leave, we call on every Muslim who believes in God and hopes for reward to obey God's command to kill the Americans and plunder their possessions wherever he finds them and whenever he can. Likewise we call on the Muslim Ulema and leaders and youth and soldiers to launch attacks against the armies of the American devils and against those who are allied with them from among the helpers of Satan . . .' And he goes on with more quotations from Muslim scripture.

"That's about it. I could explain most of the Quran references if you want. He's extreme, but I've got to say his beliefs are not that unusual in much of the Islamic world."

"Who does this guy think he is?" Kinkaid whispered furiously. "How the hell can he declare war on the United States?"

"He must buy that Syrian bit about the U.S. Navy going into Lebanon with Israel. That was more effective than we expected."

"How could he believe *that*? As if we're going to send a couple of airplanes with the Israelis. We have *never* operated with them! What would we accomplish? Some people will believe anything. So," he said to Sami, "what do you make of it?"

"Pretty simple. He wants a war with the United States."

Kinkaid gritted his teeth. "Maybe we should give him one."

Bark sat at the console in a small room on the *Washington* that controlled the PLAT cameras. It also had a station to replay tapes from previous landings since LSO's occasionally reviewed the tapes. Once in a while the Air Boss came down and watched a tape. Whenever there was an accident the station got quite a workout. But this was the first time any of the Petty Officers had seen a Squadron Commander watch a normal landing of one of his squadron's planes over and over again. Especially a three wire. They glanced at each other and shrugged. If a commander wanted to sit there all day and look at landings, it was fine with them.

Bark rolled the tape backward and forward. Regular speed, slow speed, stop action, every way he could. Woods's plane was coming back from the first hop after they'd pulled out of Haifa. Bark leaned forward, easing the cramp in his lower back from the metal chair he had been sitting on for too long. The missile inventory had gone fine. There wasn't one missile missing. That should have ended it. But Bark wanted to check everything. He had a feeling. Woods and Big had come back awfully sweaty.

He studied the images of Woods's F-14 coming aboard the ship again. Suddenly he slapped a large button on the console and froze the image on the screen. He studied it. There was a dark area, perhaps a shadow, perhaps carbon, on the Sidewinder missile rail on the left side of the airplane. But the missile was still there. They *couldn't* have shot any missiles, Bark thought to himself. Even if the Gunner has faked the missile records, that wouldn't explain how Woods had missiles on his airplane when he landed. Can't reload in the air. They sure weren't reloaded on deck. He could see them. He slapped the button again and the film continued. He stood and stretched, checking his watch. Not time for chow yet. He debated inspecting Woods's airplane. Might as well. "Thanks," he said to the Petty Officers as he stepped out of the small room and headed to the hangar deck.

Commander Whip Sawyer had enjoyed his first month as the Naval attaché at the U.S. embassy in Paris, one of the choicest jobs in the entire world. There wasn't a lot of intelligence gathering or analysis, but there was the opportunity to live in Paris. Sawyer had brought his entire family along with him on this choice assignment. His children, however, ages seven, nine, and eleven, had been nervous about the change. They had spent the last five years in Coronado, California, where Sawyer had been an Intelligence Officer on the staff of a SEAL team, and then for SPECWARCOM, Special Warfare Command. He spoke passable French, and had placed his children in French school. The children had come home teary-eyed for the first two weeks, but were now getting used to it. His wife was still unsure, but overall his family was settling in. They had found a wonderful small apartment in the fourth arrondisement, not too far from Notre Dame.

Sawyer was content. He had already discovered what he considered to be one of the best jogging paths in the world—from his apartment, down to the Seine riverbank, then along the river toward the Eiffel Tower. He could run along the Seine as far as he wanted, sometimes on the sidewalk above, where artists sold paintings and booksellers sold used books, sometimes down the stairs on the cobblestone quays along the river where the barges pulled up. It was quieter there, less traffic, and no intersections.

Sawyer had been starting his run earlier each morning so that he was now beginning in the semidarkness, although he could see well enough to keep from tripping. He dashed across the street onto the sidewalk that paralleled the river, keeping his running pace consistent, a moderate pace that would allow him to go five miles or so without overdoing it. Today he decided on the lower route and turned down one of the stone stairways to the cobblestones below. He took the stairs rapidly and headed toward the Eiffel Tower. He wanted to get in a good long run.

The Seine was beautiful in its quickly flowing darkness. Sawyer had been surprised at how clean the city was, and how few homeless people there were. He wondered how France had solved the homeless problem. But there were a few pathetic homeless winos who populated the underbelly of Paris by the river, usually under the bridges. It was one of the unfortunate realities of running on the quay.

Sawyer approached the second of many bridges. It was one of the prettier ones, although some thought it gaudy. It had gilded nudes on the side with Roman-looking soldiers beside them. There were black figures and gold ones, emphasizing the contrast, and the city obviously kept the bridge in good condition. It was a wide bridge and provided cover for several people beneath. Sawyer recognized all of them, except one. The person looked like a puddle of humanity in large clothes full of dust and leaves. An old woman's head stuck out the top of the puddle of clothing, her arm protruding at an odd angle holding a cup out to him. Her witch-like voice called to him for money. As he got closer he glanced at her again. The woman was a big lump with no obvious spine, and seemed to have no legs at all. Sawyer tried not to show his revulsion. As he reached her, he accelerated just slightly. He never saw the leg come out from under the dark mass of clothing, the strong leg of a man. Timed perfectly, it caught him in the shins as momentum carried him forward. Sawyer slammed to the cobblestones, instinctively putting his hands out in front to catch himself but he was falling too hard. He smashed his cheekbone on one of the cobblestones, lights shooting through his head as he groaned and tried to get back up. The young man who had been hidden under the pile of clothes threw off the black cape and the woman's face and jumped on Sawyer, still lying on the stones. He pulled out a knife, jerked Sawyer's head back, and cut his throat. As the blood spurted onto the cobblestones, the man rolled Sawyer's body into the Seine.

✍

Woods and Big were surprised by the loud knock on their stateroom door. It was after midnight.

Bark stormed in, closing the door loudly behind him.

Woods stood up as Big jumped down from his rack.

"Hey, Skipper."

Bark looked at them without speaking. Finally he said, "Can I sit?"

"Yes, sir, of course."

"So, I need to get the straight story."

"What straight story?" Woods asked.

"You know *exactly* what story I'm talking about."

"The Syria thing?"

"Right. Talk to me."

Woods and Big eyed each other, wondering who was going to go first. Then Woods spoke. "What is there to say?"

Bark was not impressed. He wanted this to be easy, not something he would have to work for. "Guess what I've been doing?"

Woods felt a chill race through him. "What?"

"I've been watching the PLAT films from the day of the attack."

Big tried to look casual. "What for?"

"One thing that has puzzled me. If anyone was involved in the attack, it had to be you, now that they've given us a time when this supposedly happened. But I couldn't figure out how you could have returned to the ship with all your missiles. I was checking for that."

"We had all our missiles."

"That's right."

"So what's the problem?"

"You know how when you shoot a Sidewinder it leaves carbon deposits on the missile rails?"

Woods tried not to look away from Bark's intrusive stare. "Sure."

"Can you explain to me how it is that each of you had missile exhaust on your Sidewinder rails coming aboard the ship that day?"

Woods felt trapped. He wanted to confess, to brag, to tell Bark everything. He knew Bark would understand. But he also knew Bark would do his duty. And that meant Leavenworth. "That's impossible, Skipper. Can't have missiles and exhaust at the same time. Unless the exhaust is old."

Bark shrugged. "That's what I still can't figure out. . . . Well, I thought I'd just stop by and see if you guys had any ideas." He had great respect for his two Lieutenants, but he knew they were capable of a lot of things. "Either of you have anything to say?"

"Not me," Woods said.

"The exhaust could be from the missile shoot at Roosevelt Roads," Big said. "We shot a lot of Sidewinders there."

"You think so?" Bark asked.

"Sure," Big said. "Probably was."

Bark's eyes focused on Big. "Except the two Sidewinder shooters at Rosy Roads were 200 and 201. I checked."

"Oh," Big said, feeling exposed.

"And I went down to the hangar bay and looked at your two airplanes. You know what? You can still see some faint missile exhaust marks on the rails. It's still there."

"How can that be?" Woods asked.

"I was hoping you two could tell me. Anything else you want to say?"

"About what?"

Bark frowned. "About anything."

Woods couldn't speak. Anything he would say could imply something. Finally he said, "Not really."

Bark waited, then stood up, opening the door. "See you in the morning." The door slammed behind him.

Woods waited and heard Bark's footsteps on the tile as he strode quickly down the passageway toward the ready room.

Big said, "We're busted."

"If we were busted, he would have said so. He's not sure."

"He may be very sure. He might have just been giving us the opportunity to prove we're honest. . . . I guess we aren't."

"We didn't lie."

"That wasn't a lie?"

"Not really—"

"Shit, Sean! What do you think we're doing here? We just deceived our Squadron Commander!"

Woods eyes were darkening. "Did you really think we'd go into Lebanon, or Syria, or wherever, and kill some people and not *lie* about it?"

"I don't know. It just feels so dirty. Lying to your CO is just so unbelievable."

"You'd better get used to it, Big, unless you want to go to Leavenworth."

"You're okay with all this?"

Woods wasn't okay with it at all. He had never felt worse in his life. He had broken laws, serious laws, and he had killed for the first time. Now he was falling down the laundry chute of lies and covering. "No. I'm not okay with it. I feel like shit, and I'm yelling at you because I don't know what else to do. I want to just go on with my life and be a Naval officer. I want to get back to complaining about Navy paperwork, or the night's movie. Or Bernie the Breather. . . . What can we do about it now, Big? We can't undo it."

"Nope."

"If we confess, we'll just go right to Leavenworth."

"We never should have done it."

"So what now?"

"I don't know."

"I guess we repent and go straight. We don't rob any more banks, and we don't go on any more air strikes into Lebanon."

"I'm not sure that's enough."

"It's all we've got."

Ronald Pope enjoyed his work as the Assistant Secretary of State for Middle Eastern Affairs. It was very interesting, and allowed him to travel, but he was growing tired of his job. He wanted to move back into academia where the demands were substantially less, and he could write to his heart's content. He thought a life of writing would be just the thing. His mind was full of book ideas and articles. Even driving to work with the radio on, he was thinking of what he could write about the Middle East. There was so much to say, the area was so complex and difficult. Maybe one day.

He shifted his briefcase to his left hand as he put his key in his car door to lock it. It jammed slightly and he grew annoyed. He had chosen not to get an alarm or keyless entry on his new Taurus, and now regretted it. He was sick of having to lock the door with a key. He knew he could just push the button on the inside of the door to lock all the doors at once, and then just close the driver's door, but he didn't want to take the risk of locking his keys in the car. So every day he shifted his briefcase to his left hand and put the key into the door.

"Excuse me," a man said, who suddenly appeared next to him.

"Yes?"

"Are you Ronald Pope?"

"Yes. Who are you?" His eyes darted around for help, in case he needed it. But no one else was there. He always arrived before his peers.

"It doesn't matter." The man pulled a gun with a long silencer on it out of his jacket. Pope stared at the gun. He had never even seen a silencer, but he knew what it was.

"What are you—"

The gun jerked as the man shot Pope in the stomach. He fell, his blood spilling out onto the ground. The man moved closer to Pope, now writhing and groaning. The gun barked quietly as the man shot him again in the chest. Pope lay still. The killer put his gun back in his jacket and leaned down next to Pope, shoving his body underneath the Taurus.

The club in Naples had often been used for squadron functions. The F-18 squadron had reserved it long ahead, knowing that it booked up early when the carrier was in port. The Mediterranean usually contained at least one American aircraft carrier, sometimes two. One was almost always at sea. The *George Washington* was in the eastern Mediterranean and the *Dwight D. Eisenhower (CVN-69)* was in port in Naples. VFA-136, an F/A-18 squadron, had decided to have a Dining-In, an officers-only party, where the officers wore their dress white uniforms and enjoyed the Naval traditions of roast beef, port, and toasts. It was a highly regimented, scripted event. The officers had been anticipating the night for a month, dreading it because they had to wear their dress uniforms, but looking forward to it because of the Navy mythology that rose around the dinners. Stories of great excesses and drunkenness, toasts given and regretted, food fights, general mayhem and craziness. Few had seen such things, and the legends went back several decades, even centuries, but there was always great anticipation of legends in the making.

Commander Gary Witt, the F-18 Squadron Commanding Officer, was by definition the president of the mess. He was, therefore, required to do certain things and behave in a certain way. Very savvy, he knew what was expected of him and so far he had been doing his job beautifully. He caught the signal from the Lieutenant who was acting as the Officer of the Mess with a sword on his side that it was time to parade the beef. Witt stood and asked for attention. "As you all know, it is now time for that great moment where we begin our feast by bringing in the main course for all the red-blooded Americans seated at these tables. I call your attention to the parading of the beef!"

With that the doors opened in the back of the banquet room and two large Italian waiters entered. Walking solemnly, they carried an enormous platter between them on their shoulders. A bagpiper followed them, odd moaning sounds coming from his instrument as he puffed up the bladder in preparation for playing. Finally, in keeping with the tradition, "Scotland the Brave" screamed out of the pipes. The waiters and the piper made their way slowly around the room, allowing each officer to gaze longingly at the beautiful side of beef as their eardrums were pierced by the deafening bagpipes.

Suddenly the doors on the side of the room flew open. A man in a hood and black clothing appeared with an assault rifle with a scope at his shoulder. He glanced around quickly, saw Witt standing at the head table, and sighted through his scope. Several officers cried out at the same moment so that the Officer of the Mess reached to his side for his sword, but it happened too fast; no one could stop the shooter. He fired and Witt fell forward, his head slapping against the lectern as he dropped to the floor, dead. Some of the men jumped to their feet, ready to rush the gunman. The Officer of the Mess had pulled out his sword and was moving toward the gunman when the man saw him and immediately fired three bullets into him, killing him instantly. The gunman stood quietly, waiting for anyone else to move. No one did. The pilots wanted to charge out and attack the gunman but they all had seen what happened. The man began backing up slowly, moving toward the door where he had entered. Two other gunmen, also wearing hoods and carrying assault rifles with scopes appeared, opening the two doors for the killer, and he backed out unmolested. As the room erupted in shrieks of horror, revenge, and anger, the three gunmen disappeared.

26

Presdent's going on TV in about an hour," Jaime Rodriguez reported breathlessly to Vice Admiral Brown, who sat up straight at his spotless desk, his reading glasses on.

"What about?"

"The Paris killings. He's pissed, and he's going to yell at them. No prepared speech."

Admiral Brown removed his glasses. "This ought to be interesting." He sat back slightly, and turned to Jaime. "How is that paper coming on declaring war?"

"Done. We're just polishing it."

"Same conclusion as last week?"

Jaime saw where the Admiral was going. "Yes, sir. No reason at all we couldn't do it."

"I don't know if we're quite ready for such a big move. This is the kind of thing that needs months—if not years—of analysis and discussion. . . . But maybe we don't have that kind of time." He stood up and walked around his desk. "Get Tim to get me a copy of the draft memo right now, and be ready to talk about it after the President's speech. We may have just the tool he's been looking for."

❧

Sean Woods picked up the phone that was ringing on his stateroom wall. "Lieutenant Woods."

"Trey. All officers' meeting right now." It was Sedge. He had the duty.

Woods immediately assumed the worst. He was going to be exposed in front of the entire squadron. He tried not to react like a criminal who is spooked by everything, knowing he is about to be caught, but he couldn't shake it. "What about?"

"President's going to make a speech about the Paris killings. Skipper wants all the officers to watch it in the ready room."

"What time?"

"Five minutes."

Woods had been sickened by the news of the attacks. There was no doubt in his mind who was behind the killings, and that it was his fault. If they hadn't participated in the attack with the Israeli Air Force, none of this would have happened. If he hadn't insisted on turning on the radar so he could shoot down one more Syrian airplane, they wouldn't have been sure an F-14 radar was nearby. His tracks were covered, but his conscience was not.

Woods walked quickly to the ready room. To someone who knew him it would have been clear that his usually confident stride was less so. He was carrying a burden he wasn't accustomed to.

The rest of the officers arrived about the same time Woods did. Bark was there, waiting. When most of the officers were in their seats, Bark began speaking. "Morning. The speech is in about five minutes. We'll see what the President has to say about all this. But *I* wanted to say that this Sheikh al-Jabal character is going after Americans directly. No argument like with Vialli that these people were just in the wrong place at the wrong time. He's coming after us. And after Navy officers. I—"

The image of the President of the United States came on the television in the front of the room. Bark sat down as the President's speech began.

President Garrett looked somber and angry. The officers were accustomed to hearing the President speak, but none of them had seen this look on his face. "As all of you know, there have been three brutal attacks on Americans in the last twenty-four hours. The first was the Naval attaché in Paris, attacked by someone unknown on his morning jog near the Seine. The second was closer to home, here in Washington, D.C. The Assistant Secretary of State was gunned down in the State Department parking lot. I just heard details of a third attack, equally shocking and disturbing. A Squadron Commanding Officer of a fighter squadron off the USS *Dwight D. Eisenhower* was at a squadron dinner in a club near Sixth Fleet Headquarters in Naples, Italy. Three gunmen broke in and murdered the Navy Commander and the Officer of the Mess.

"I want to extend the country's heartfelt sympathy to the families of the men who were killed. Our hopes and prayers are with them. I'm sure they wonder what kind of monsters would do such a thing. We wonder too. We understand from the same London newspaper that received the communiqué from the man who calls himself Sheikh al-Jabal that he is claiming responsibility for these attacks as part of his continued response to the attempt to assassinate him by this country working in conjunction with Israel." The President paused. "These acts, on top of the false accusations against the United States, are outrageous. This man is not only vicious, but completely misguided. He appears to be fixated on the idea that we had something to do with the attack in Lebanon that the Israeli Air Force conducted some two weeks ago. I want to state publicly and unequivocally that we had nothing to do with that raid. Nothing whatsoever."

Woods tried not to look at Big.

The President stared at the camera longer than was customary in political speeches. His fury was obvious. He was speaking extemporaneously, which was dangerous. He continued. "I want the man who is responsible for these attacks—and whoever is working with him or protecting him—to be held accountable. This country will never rest until he and his men are brought to justice for the murders of innocent Americans, military and political. He has declared a Jihad on the United States. We have done *nothing* to earn his wrath. I want to say clearly today, I personally will never rest until he is brought to justice. And I hereby obligate the United States and all its power. We will *never* rest until that justice is satisfied. Not ever.

"I will be meeting with other political leaders and military leaders to decide how best to proceed. But I want the world to know now that we will proceed. We will respond. We will ensure justice is done. Good night."

As the President's speech ended Bark stood up and walked to the television in front of the ready room. The Air Wing Intelligence Officer was on the screen, apparently in an attempt to play the ship's Dan Rather and explain what the President had just said. Bark addressed his officers. "I probably don't need to tell you that I am not one of the military leaders he is consulting. If he *were* consulting me, I would tell him to strike *now*, strike tomorrow, strike every day thereafter until this guy is buried in fifty feet of sand. We may have a special role in this. In fact, we already do. We are the ones accused of having started this with the Israelis. But we know that didn't happen. We inventoried the missiles. Woods and Big"—their hearts jumped— "have *told* us they had nothing to do with it. That means that not only did this guy murder Vialli, but he has murdered a Naval attaché in Paris, the Commanding Officer of a Navy fighter squadron and a Lieutenant serving as Officer of the Mess, and some poor guy from the State Department. These guys are really pissing me off. I just hope that we actually get to do something about it personally, and that it's not left to someone else to do it.

"I have no idea what the President has in mind, but I want us to start getting ourselves ready for whatever action is going to follow, because I believe action *will* follow. I want to make sure that our weapon systems are up, that our airplanes are all up, and every officer in the squadron is one hundred percent ready to go into combat tomorrow." To Wink, he said, "Let's do a weapons-systems NATOPS review tomorrow afternoon. I want written tests for everyone. I wanna be talking weapons, weapons delivery, weapons choice, air-to-air combat, everything we do—I want it discussed every day at every meeting, every meal, and every minute we're awake in this ready room. We will talk combat, we will talk fighting until this is done." He studied the faces of his men. "I really hope we get a chance to do something about this. I really do."

The officers stood to leave. Woods crossed to Big. "Did you hear how the President was talking about the Sheikh?"

"Yeah . . ."

"He's still a threat."

Big was startled. "You're right."

Woods lowered his voice. "That can only mean one thing. We missed. *Shit.*"

The conference room in the White House was full. The President had not waited even a day to call the meeting he had promised. Those invited had only a few hours' notice. The Chairman of the Joint Chiefs of Staff was there, the Secretary of Defense, the Director of Central Intelligence, and the National Security Adviser. Also present were the Speaker of the House, the Members of the Cabinet, the chairmen of the Armed Services Committees of the House and the Senate, the

Senate Majority Leader, the Senate and House Minority Leaders and the Vice President. No press was invited. This was not a staged photo opportunity as so many White House meetings were. This was a meeting the President had called to decide what to do about Sheikh al-Jabal.

President Garrett was from Texas. His drawl was mostly gone, but when he was angry, the drawl came out more clearly. And he was angry now. A tall, thin man with wavy brownish-gray hair, his personality was so large that it overwhelmed others who were in his presence. He scanned the room to make sure everyone was accounted for before he began speaking.

"Thank you all for coming on such short notice. I know it's a bit unusual, and I hope that you don't misunderstand what I'm trying to do. This is not some attempt at a political event. I realize we have people here from both parties and I know that might look like a publicity stunt rather than a planning session. But I want you to know right now, I am here for one purpose only—to do whatever we can to eradicate this Sheikh al-Jabal rodent from the face of the earth. He has killed innocent Americans, he has attacked us in every way, and he has declared a holy war on this country and its citizens.

"I have my own ideas of what to do about this, but I want to hear your ideas as well. I don't want to do some secretive behind-the-scenes action. I want something new." He raised his hand. "Before anybody says it, I'm not inclined to use the Letter of Marque or Rules of Capture Congress has implemented in the recent past with which we're all too familiar.

"I want to do this together. I might agree that Congress abdicated some of its authority in the past, and the Presidents of the past took more liberty with the employment of the military than they were entitled to; but I don't want the pendulum swinging too far in the other direction either. Let's work together, come up with the right approach, and execute it immediately. That's why we're all here." He waited, then had another thought. "Tell you what. Carl is here for the CIA. Anything new?"

Carl Spear, the Director of Central Intelligence, stood up. "Mr. President, there really isn't a lot more to say about this man than has already been said. You received our report, written by one of our analysts, which compares this man to his namesake of the eleventh century, and a few others since then. You know the history of the group, the Assassins, and it really isn't necessary to go into more than that at this time. . . . The thing that I might add—which may make this discussion a little more difficult but is something we all need to be aware of—is that we don't know where he is. We have some leads, and we're trying to locate him. We had a good bead on him once, but not anymore. We simply don't know where he is."

Garrett agreed. "Terrorists don't have capital cities, or Navy bases with piers and ships parked next to them, or airports with fighter jets lined up like ducks. Always one of the hardest things to do in attacking terrorism is finding the terrorists. But let's set aside that difficult issue for just a moment." He folded his arms. "Let's assume that the largest military in the world can find him. I want to know what we should do about it. I can send the military. I can do that. Presidents have been doing that for long time. I *will* do that, if it's what we agree on. But that is the question. How do we justify going into somebody else's territory with our military to get this guy?"

The Attorney General spoke. "There would be some international legal considerations that we would be wise to take into consideration before doing something like that. You might recall when President Clinton attacked Osama bin Laden by simply sending off a flurry of Tomahawk missiles into Afghanistan and Sudan. That clearly violated the sovereignty of those countries. There were all kinds of international ramifications—"

"I don't really care if there are ramifications for our attacking him in another country if we're sure he's there. It's not that that I'm worried—"

"Yes, sir, what I meant was if we can avoid some of that, it might be wise to do so."

The rest of the people in the room shifted uncomfortably. None of them had any particularly new or creative ideas on how to attack terrorism. They didn't want to say anything at this point and look stupid before they knew the way the President wanted to go.

Congressman Lionel Brown, the Chairman of the House Armed Services Committee, spoke. "I may have an idea, Mr. President."

Everyone in the room looked at him. When he spoke about the military, people listened. The President knew better than to try to argue with him about military policy. At least here. "What might that be?"

Brown had been debating whether to actually bring it up. He was afraid he would look foolish. "I'm a little embarrassed to say where this idea came from, but I've been thinking about it ever since it came across my desk. When I first heard it, frankly, I disregarded it. But it's one of those ideas that grows on you. It has definitely grown on me. In fact, since hearing about the idea, although initially rejecting it, I had my staff look into it and research it over the last few weeks."

"What is it?"

"This Sheikh al-Jabal, by his own words, has declared war against the United States."

Everyone in the room nodded their understanding. "Several weeks ago, after that Navy officer was killed in the bus attack in Israel, I received a letter from his roommate on a carrier in the Mediterranean. I'm sorry, but I don't recall his name. He was very upset. On reflection, I think I failed to give the letter the respect it deserved, probably because it came from such an unlikely quarter. What he said"—Brown hesitated, knowing this was his last chance to avoid being known for this idea, however it came out—"was that Congress should declare war against Sheikh al-Jabal. As an *individual*. And against the Assassins, as a group. He had even gotten the JAG officer on the carrier to do some research on the issue, and he saw no reason why it couldn't be done. The Lieutenent got a priest, of all things, to do an analysis of whether it would be a just war under the old just war doctrine that goes back hundreds of years. Both of those other officers supported him. This Lieutenant is one of my constituents, and frankly, I think we should give his idea some consideration, certainly more than I gave when I first heard of it.

"We declare war against countries when they attack us. At least we used to. Yet most of the attacks nowadays are from individuals, or terrorist groups. Why not declare war against *them* and use the full force of the military to go after them? Why not attack this Sheikh al-Jabal with the military which was designed to do just that? We always turn away from responding with the force of the military, and declaring war, when that is exactly what seems to be called for."

Congressman Brown watched the faces of those in the room. He smiled, knowing what was happening in their minds: crazy idea, interesting idea, clever idea, it will never work, who will support it, is it going to prevail, am I on the right side?

Brown was most interested in the President's impression. He had a lot of respect for President Garrett, and the fact that Garrett had done what only two other people in the room had done—served in the military. President Garrett had been in the Army for two years after college. It wasn't much, but it was more experience than any other President since Bush. Brown could see the surprise on Garrett's face. Not unpleasant surprise, good surprise. He was clearly stunned by the thought.

"Would that be legal?"

"I had my staff look into that. I have to give the Lieutenant credit. The JAG officer he roped into looking at this got it pretty much right. There is nothing that says we couldn't do this."

"We've never done anything remotely like that."

"Mr. President, I've been thinking about this a lot," Brown said, leaning forward in his chair. "We have lost our way in using the war powers as they were designed. We somehow got to the position where war had to be *total* war. We had to declare our intention to completely destroy another country if we were going to go to war with that country. I think that came out of World War II, where only unconditional surrender was acceptable. That wasn't the old understanding of war in this country, and certainly not the understanding of war at the time the Constitution was written."

"Is everybody tracking this?" the President asked the others.

They were interested, but not yet ready to commit to supporting the idea.

With every eye on him Brown continued. "Speaking for Congress, if I might—and without its authorization—we have lost track of our power to declare war. Congress has abdicated its role. During Korea, Vietnam, Grenada, Panama, Desert Storm, Kosovo, many other times, we have sent troops, sometimes hundreds of thousands of troops, and not once did we declare war. That is unconscionable. It stems from a misunderstanding of a declaration of war."

"You think we could do it here?" the President asked.

"I think so, Mr. President. This murderer has declared war against us, and seems intent on seeing it through. He isn't just issuing hollow threats. I think we should return the favor. I propose that we declare war against *him*. As an individual. And against his group."

"How?" President Garrett asked.

Brown stood up, unable to sit still anymore. "When the Korean War started, we had the World War II mentality. Only the stakes were higher—a potential nuclear war with Russia—but also, as I said, war was understood to mean total annihilation. We haven't declared war since. Yet fifty thousand Americans died in Vietnam. We tell their families that we weren't at war? If you go back before World War II, such as to the Spanish-American War, or the War of 1812, no one thought that it meant we were going to level *Spain,* or *England.* It simply meant that we would set a political objective attainable only through warfare, and achieve it. There was no misunderstanding about that. And *Congress* declared war. The President agreed, but it was Congress that declared that it was warfare that would accomplish the objective.

"The way to deal with terrorists today is to declare war against them. *Pursue* them with the full force of the military wherever they are. If they're in Syria—we go into Syria. The general rule is that no one can harbor combatants. We have the right to pursue those with whom we are at war. The country that protects combatants does so at its own risk."

"Are you serious?" the Attorney General asked. "You want to declare war against one man?"

"Exactly," Brown said. "It's time to go to war against terrorism. Not with the CIA, not by the DEVGROUP, or the Delta group, not by some covert cooperation with another country's intelligence arm. I mean full-out, wide-open, out-in-the-sunshine war against them. We declare war, the President signs it, and we pursue them to *hell* and back until the war is over. We don't have to live with the ridiculous niceties of the judicial system, where we have to send FBI agents to arrest them, and give them their rights, and try to drag them back to the United States for *trial.* That is one of the most ridiculous concepts ever devised in the history of combat. Imagine Genghis Khan tearing out after someone who had just burned a village in his territory, and having one of his men climb down from his horse and say to the bad guys—you have the right to remain silent, anything you say can and will be used against you in a court of law." He waited for their smiles to fade. "We *know* who did these acts. What exactly was it that Hitler had done to us in 1941? Nothing. There had been some skirmishes in the Atlantic. We waited until Hitler declared war against us, and then we returned the favor. That's what we should do here—return the favor. Declare war back." Brown suddenly felt conspicuous. He had gone on too long. The silence of those around the room seemed to confirm his fears. "Please forgive my rambling. I feel strongly about this, and I believe it is the correct course. I think we should go to the public with this as soon as we can, and tell the American people what our intentions are. I see no harm in having a wide-open debate about this today. Tomorrow. For a week. Whatever it takes, we debate it, we declare war, and we go after him."

President Garrett tried to fight back a smile. "It would be setting quite a precedent. But what would we do when the case was less clear? When people claim responsibility for terrorist acts that we believe were not actually commited by them?"

Brown thought for a minute. "There will be times when discernment and judgment call for this power being used against a terrorist group. But it doesn't mean we have to use it *every* time."

The Director of Central Intelligence was extremely unhappy. He finally could not resist speaking out. "Don't you see the problem? We could have a lingering, unfinished war forever. How do you know when it's over?"

Brown had anticipated such a question. "Would it be any worse than having a lingering unfinished *un*declared war like we *still* have with Korea after fifty years? How could it be worse than that? It seems to me that it's over when we say it's over. After we have killed or captured the rodent—as the President called him—we can declare it over. Congress declares that the war exists, and it can likewise declare it is stopped or has ceased to exist. We simply stop it when we want to, when our objective has been achieved. But let me add that I have no problem at all with an open declaration of war whenever a terrorist attacks the United States. The military *and* the CIA could be free to pursue such terrorists with a license granted in wartime against the soldiers of the enemy—the freedom to shoot on sight throughout the world, for all time. What more effective tool could there be in combating terrorism than that?"

"It seems to allow an awful lot of room for error," the Attorney General said.

Brown smiled. "Error? We seem to make more errors by the use of our intelligence assets and covert operations than all the wars put together." The DCI was enraged by Brown's comment, but the Admiral was unintimidated. "We have more egg on our face as a country from minuscule intelligence operations, than from all the bungled military operations throughout history. If that's your fear, I'll place my money on the military."

Someone in the room started clapping, slowly, but steadily. Brown was surprised and looked around quickly to see the source of the noise, which he had assumed was disapproving. Before he knew it, several others began clapping. Brown was shocked, but he was also as excited as he had ever been in his short political career. It was all coming together, his military background, his leadership in the House, and his lifelong willingness to stick his neck out for the right thing.

The President stood up. "We'll need to think about this, won't we?"

Brown could tell the President was surprised and caught off-guard. He should have called Garrett's Chief of Staff. The President might have bought into the idea, and even made it his own. That was probably why he hadn't—he wanted the idea for himself. To become respected and well known. What a petty political thought, Brown quickly realized. As if the idea was even his. He had stolen it from a lowly Navy Lieutenant.

"Admiral," the President said, "I appreciate your willingness to throw that idea out here. Took a lot of courage to do that. I think you've given all of us plenty to think about, and I think some of my advisers are waiting to tell me a lot of things you don't get to hear. So rather than spend a lot more time in this meeting, unless someone has a better idea than that"—he looked around the room—"I'd like us all to retreat to our respective offices and chew on this. I think it is worthy of consideration, and that is what I plan to do."

27

The Squadron Duty Officer gave Woods a knowing look. Woods stared at him, confused. The SDO pointed toward the rear of the ready room. Woods glanced back and saw the chaplain. "Oh, man, what's he doing here?"

The SDO shrugged. "Beats me."

"Hey. What's up?" Woods said to Maloney as he approached.

The chaplain spoke softly. "I thought perhaps you would like to talk."

"About what?"

"Just about all the things that have happened."

"What things?"

"The attack that went north, the accusations, and now the retaliation and the President's speech. I think more things may come from this as well."

"So why would I want to talk to you about that?" Woods was feeling more than a little uncomfortable.

"Is there someplace we can sit down?"

Woods looked around the room and saw two or three officers watching him, trying not to show that they were. "Sure. Let's sit right here," Woods said, indicating the briefing area. "What is it?" he asked, not really wanting to know.

"You don't think much of me—"

"Sure I do. You helped a lot with the letter to my congressman."

The chaplain measured his words carefully. "Did you fly into Lebanon and Syria with the Israeli Air Force?"

"What? Where'd you get that?"

"Did you?"

"I've been through this with the CAG. I'm not going over it again. If you don't get what happened, I can't help you. Thanks for your interest, but I've got a lot of other things to do. Anything else?"

"I'm surprised that you're unwilling to answer a simple question."

"Where do you get off coming in here and grilling me about something that is ancient history? And even if I did go with the Israeli Air Force, so what?"

"If you did, it probably was illegal."

"Illegal where?"

"Illegal here. On the carrier. Under U.S. law."

"Probably. So what?"

"I was just remembering how important it was to you that the declaration of war be within the law. You asked the JAG officer to do research on the law so that you could get it right. He kind of stuck his neck out for you, and I'll bet you sent his information to your congressman, didn't you? Since I never got a copy . . ."

"Yes, I did. I meant to tell him about it . . ."

"You asked me to do the memo I did on what would constitute a just war. All intended, I suppose, to make the declaration of war 'legal.' So it struck me as odd, that if in fact you were willing to go with the Israeli Air Force and attack another country, how it was that you came to such a position. If you did, I thought you might be having . . . some problems of conscience. That is why I am here."

Woods stared at the chaplain. He didn't know what to say. His conscience *was* bothering him. Even what Big had said had kept him up all night. He had never seen himself as a liar, or someone who deceived his superiors and peers. But he wanted to stay out of Leavenworth. He had to. "How's *your* conscience? What have you done wrong lately? Done anything dishonest in the last two weeks?"

"A very fair question. I probably have been dishonest in the last two weeks. And if I had, and I remembered, I would hope that I would confess it, and seek forgiveness from the person I had deceived. That seems to be the right course. Wouldn't you agree?"

"Look, Padre. When I get a pang of conscience, when I need to talk to someone about it, maybe I'll call you. Okay? Until then, I got other things to do."

The chaplain stood up. "I understand completely. I hope that you don't feel my visit has been intrusive. I'm concerned about you.

Whenever I've seen you in the wardroom, you seemed to be deep in thought. If you'd like to talk about some of that with me, I'm available anytime."

Woods's icy exterior warmed a little. "Fair enough."

Lionel Brown found himself in a position he never expected. Word of the meeting at the White House had leaked out before he even got back to his office. The Speaker was jealous of the bomb of publicity that had gone off all over D.C. surrounding the Admiral's "idea." The Director of Central Intelligence was livid, for reasons that Brown couldn't quite fathom, but the phone calls and the general media were full of enthusiasm and encouragement. He was the man of the hour. All the television shows wanted him yesterday.

Jaime Rodriguez, the Mexican-American legislative director for Admiral Brown, was in heaven. He loved his boss, and would do anything for him, primarily because Jaime thought he had found the Holy Grail: A politician who wasn't owned by special interests and was willing to think outside the box. And Brown listened to Jaime when he expressed his opinions instead of flipping through his Rolodex, something the last congressman Jaime had worked for had done.

Jaime was waiting for Admiral Brown when he came back from the White House. He had already watched the report on CNN that had claimed that Congressman Admiral Brown, as they always called him, had recommended to an unprecedented gathering that the country declare war against Sheikh al-Jabal and go after him wherever he was. The option they had been looking for for thirty years had been laid in front of them by a retired Admiral.

Actually, Jaime smiled, it had been laid in front of them by a Lieutenant who might be in just the right place to make it all happen. Jaime wanted to make sure Lieutenant Sean Woods got his chance, if there was any way in the world to pull it off. "Admiral!" Jaime yelled as Brown walked into the office. "Congrats!"

"Thanks, Jaime," Brown replied as he removed his soaked suit coat and tossed it on the small couch across from his desk. The press was waiting for him to come back into the hall as he had promised.

"Admiral," Jaime intruded.

Brown waited for the next question.

"I've got some ideas on how we can, um, return the favor to our constituent."

Brown liked it. "Always thinking, Jaime, that's what I appreciate most about you."

Sami didn't like going to the Association of Arab-American Business-men's meetings, the AAAB. They were well attended and the people he met there were, for the most part, interesting and intelligent. What he didn't care for about the meetings was what they did to his father. He strolled around with his chest puffed out, going on at length about the good old days in Syria and in Egypt, where he had spent time. He even managed to mention Saudi Arabia and Tunisia, emphasizing the position he'd held on the Syrian Ambassador's staff. He was the life of the party with some of the best Arabic bona fides. But the scene never failed to make Sami uncomfortable.

Sami slipped into the front seat of his father's Mercedes and closed the door softly.

"You're late," his father scolded.

"I'm busy. I shouldn't even be going."

"You must go. If *you* don't look out for Arabic concerns for your generation, who will?"

"There seem to be plenty of people who are quite happy to do that for me," he responded tiredly.

"Don't you care about your heritage?"

Sami glanced over at his father as he drove into downtown Washington. "We have this same conversation every time we go to these meetings. Let's just skip to the part where you tell me you expected better of me."

His father switched to Arabic. "You need to treat your father with *respect*," he growled.

"I do respect you. You know that."

"Then be the good son you should be and enjoy the meeting and your heritage."

"Yes, Father."

"You never come to the Mosque."

Sami bit his tongue, but it didn't prevent him from saying, "We haven't had *this* conversation in probably three weeks."

"So what's the answer?"

"I don't like going."

"Why not?"

"I don't want to talk about it."

"What *do* you want to talk about? Your work? What is it you're working on anyway? Helping the U.S. help Israel?"

"What? Where did that come from?"

"Have you seen how they are causing the latest problems? I'm sure you have, with all your inside information. All your big secrets. You must see much that gives you concern about Israel, if they let you see those things, unless you've brainwashed yourself into ignoring the obvious."

"What has got you so hot tonight?"

"The latest news. I can't help wondering what is behind all the curtains." He made a sharp right hand turn into the parking lot of the Hyatt Hotel. "You see behind them, maybe. Maybe you see who is pulling all the strings. Frankly, Sami, I agree with Sheikh al-Jabal. He, or those like him, have been around for nine hundred years. I don't agree with the way he is doing it, and I'm not in favor of the Nazir Isma'ili sect that he comes from. I am not in favor of murder, or terror—"

"How can you agree with—"

"Let me finish!" he said, stopping the Mercedes. "I agree with their position against the Crusaders and the Jews. They don't belong there."

He turned off the car and got out. Activating the alarm, he looked at Sami across the roof of the shiny black sedan. "Don't ever forget what Muhammad said: 'Let there be only one religion in Arabia.' And Arabia is the entire Arabic world. Don't *ever* forget that, Sami."

Sami followed his father, walking a few steps behind him, feeling like a tethered goat. When they entered the large ballroom, ornately decorated with flags and banners from Arabic countries, it was full of people, mostly men in suits. Sami's father headed straight for a group he recognized. As the most recent past president of the Association of Arab-American Businessmen he knew nearly everyone there. Reluctantly, Sami joined the circle.

The conversation immediately turned to the Sheikh. Everyone had something to say. All, of course, had heard of the Hashasheen, and several knew the basic historical origin of the Sheikh and his followers. And they had also heard the Washington rumors, that the United States government was considering declaring war against him as an individual. There was general scorn and derision over the idea, and many commented that it was of course only an Arab who would receive such individual attention, unprecedented in history. It was just another example of the general anti-Arab sentiment of the United States.

Sami didn't say anything. He tried to figure out how long he had to wait until he could make an exit.

One of the men addressed Sami. "So, Sami, you still work for the CIA?"

Sami hated the question. "Yes, more or less."

The man smiled. "We need men like you at all levels of the U.S. government."

Sami drank from a tall glass of water a waiter had just brought to him.

"Are you able to make any headway?"

"In what way?"

"In protecting Arab interests. What else?"

"I protect the interests of all Americans."

The man frowned but quickly smiled again. He glanced at Sami's father then back at Sami. "Don't you think our interests are different? What we're here for?" he asked, indicating the entire room of people.

"Different in some ways, sure. But not for what I do."

"Don't you find that often there is a certain derogatory mind-set about Arabs? About Islam? Is it in the CIA?"

"I'm really not free to talk about my work," Sami replied.

"Yes, but people come to conclusions that are different if someone you're thinking about, or studying, is an Arab. Am I right?"

"I don't know—"

"What about this Sheikh?" the man pushed. "Does anyone explain his roots? His history? What he means in our countries?"

"Like I said—"

"Yes, yes." The man laughed. "Never mind. Too Top Secret. I understand. Let me ask you this instead," he said, leaning toward Sami. The rest of the small circle listened carefully. "Can we count on you to be fair to the Arab cause? To what we stand for?"

"I'm fair to every cause."

"Then you should have no problem at all in *promising* me, all these men here, all of the members of the Association of Arab-American Businessmen, that you will personally be fair to the Arab cause in whatever you do in your Top Secret job. Okay?"

"Sure."

"Say it."

"What?"

"Say you will be fair to the Arab cause."

"I will be fair."

"To the Arab cause."

Sami took another sip of his water and noticed his father staring at him from his left. "To the Arab cause."

The man smiled and lifted his glass to Sami in victory and camaraderie.

The idea had swept through Washington. As soon as President Garrett had gone on the record publicly as supporting it, the only opposition was from those who felt it degraded a declaration of war so much as to render it useless, like turning a firm pine baseball bat into a plastic Wiffle-ball bat good only for playing the make believe backyard game forever thereafter, never fit to return to the big leagues. But its supporters had won the day in two furious days of debate, mostly on live television with appearances by harried law professors and scrambling politicians. Most of the politicians had lined up in the idea's favor and the opposition was sounding limp and bitter. Admiral Brown was the public hero, and the mysterious Lieutenant who had come up with the idea was the unknown hero. Admiral Brown had acknowledged him, but had refused to name him. He was painfully aware of how easy it was to find people, and the last thing he wanted was for Lieutenant Woods, or someone in his family in the States, to be the next victim of the Assassins. The press pressured him, but Brown balked, unwilling to identify him.

But now Brown's time had come. The President had asked him to present the resolution for a declaration of war before a joint session of Congress. And the President would be there to sign it as soon as it passed. He stood looking over the packed House floor.

Brown waited for the minor conversations on the floor to die down. He had the attention of everyone in the room and he began with the usual introductions, then, "This country has declared war six times. But there have been more times when the United States has sent its armed forces into combat and never called it war. We have done our military a grave disservice by asking them to do the work of the politicians, without the politicians having the nerve to call it what it is. We have put the burden on men and women of our country to risk their lives when we were unwilling to risk our political lives. The result has been the divorce of warfare from the people. The founding fathers put Article One, section eight, into the Constitution, stating that Congress has the power to declare war. Congress, not the President. It has exercised that power before, but not since World War II. Since then, Congress has been afraid. We have fought all over the globe, sending the members of our armed forces to their deaths in defense of American interests, and have not declared war once.

"The reasons for this are obvious. We did not want to declare war against a small country and have that country believe that we were going to annihilate it. We did not want to declare war against a large country, whether cold war or hot war, thereby causing World War III and a nuclear exchange. Those fears are understandable. It can be debated whether or not it was right to fight without declaring war from the end of World War II until the end of the cold war. But from this point forward it *must* be done differently. War must be declared by Congress, the representatives of the people of the United States of America. Without the participation of Congress, the war powers become just another arrow in the quiver of the Executive Branch. The war power is probably the greatest power that can be held by any government. To allow that power to migrate to the Executive Branch and be held by the President results in our taking one large step toward monarchy. Such a step is not only intolerable, it is unthinkable. Yet, it is exactly the step we have taken.

"But it can be undone. Congress must reestablish itself with the power that it was given by the founding fathers.

"I say all that by way of background. I am bringing such a request before the House now. I hereby request that the United States declare war against Sheikh al-Jabal and his group of murderers, his empire of Assassins, those who have harmed Americans, those who have participated with those who have harmed Americans, and anyone else found with them. This is the time of limited war. Not based on geography, but based on people. Not about conquest of territory, but of fear, and of terror. We are ready for this war, and will prevail. We will bring to bear all the force that the United States has, and we will never rest until we are victorious in this endeavor."

Sami turned off the television in the task force room. "Looks like he's dead serious. I think it's a great idea."

Cunningham was less enthusiastic. "Seem to be an awful lot of international law implications here people aren't dealing with. How do you declare war against an individual? The whole idea of war is against another *country*, a sovereignty."

"And what do you do if all the people who are waging war against you, killing all your people, are not found in any particular country?"

"I don't know. It just doesn't sound right to me."

"Some people think the whole nation-state concept is basically dead anyway. All the major countries that were formed from consolidation or takeover are falling apart. Look at Russia, Yugoslavia, China, the United States."

"United States?"

"Just seeing if you're listening. But it's only a matter of time here too."

Kinkaid interrupted the banter. "You know what *we* have to do, don't you?"

Cunningham and the others nodded. "Find him."

"Exactly. We have to provide the geography for this new kind of war. We'd better know where he is. We'd better have someone to go to war against. When we give this target a place, the war is going to start in earnest. And if we don't find out where he is, the entire thing is going to stall out and we are going to look really stupid. Anybody know what happens to the people who make the President start to look stupid?"

Sami raised his hand and changed the direction of Kinkaid's point. "I've been thinking."

"What?" Kinkaid replied, annoyed by the interruption.

"Remember when I said he might be living in the same places as the old guys did?"

"Same kinds of places?"

"I'm wondering whether he's gone back to the *identical* places where the original Sheikh lived."

Kinkaid stared at Sami. "Could he?"

"I don't know. I just thought of it. We should do some work to locate them, and get some imagery."

"Where are they?"

"One is Alamut."

"What?"

"The only one I know of for sure is Alamut. It's a mountain fortress that is almost completely inaccessible."

Kinkaid looked around the room wondering what everyone else was wondering. "Where is it?"

"Western Iran."

"Iran?"

"Yeah."

Kinkaid hesitated, not liking this information at all. "You realize the implications if these guys are in Iran?"

"Makes it harder."

"Uh, yeah. Of all the guys that you don't want to dick with, those would probably be at the top of the list. They have no sense of humor at all."

"It's a long shot. I doubt he's using Alamut anyway."

"We've got to find out. You know the location?"

"I can get you a picture."

"You got a latitude and longitude for our satellites to look?"

"I'll have it to you by this afternoon."

"Do it."

~

The Sheikh was extremely pleased. They had performed better than he had hoped. They had not yet had even one casualty, and had inflicted on the world a mass panic and concern for the future for not only the Middle East but for all Americans worldwide. The Sheikh sat in his dark, stone room inside the fortress. He was surrounded by those who had grown up yielding their will to his. He operated with a group of men around him, his staff, although he didn't call it that. There were six or seven near his age—forty-five—whom he thought had enough wisdom to manage the men underneath them.

He worked closely with his inner circle, on a daily basis. They sat around him now. No one spoke. They were reveling in the glory of their success, and their newfound world fame. The Sheikh finally broke the silence. "Allah has been very good to us. We have succeeded in everything we have tried." The group nodded, agreeing with his sentiments. "But the war has just now begun. The United States has declared war against us. That is fair and just, as we have already declared a Jihad against them. By doing this, they have given us even greater recognition and power than we ever could have hoped for. No country has ever done this to one man before, this declaration of war that the West does. They have recognized me as their threat, large enough for their entire government to declare war against me. A larger threat, one must assume, than Korea, and Vietnam, and Iraq. This is a great honor and a great sign that they are afraid.

"But they do not understand us. They do not know who we are, or what it is that we hope to achieve. They do not understand that we have already achieved much of what we hoped to achieve. From this point, it can only get better. We must execute the rest of our plan to draw the entire region of Palestine into the bath of fire that we will create to eradicate the Jews, America's puppets. The PLO has gone soft, all for the pitiful Gaza Strip and part of the West Bank. Although they are our brothers, they have failed.

"Now the Americans have, as I told you they would, walked directly into our trap. They have obligated themselves to come into our land. But they don't know where we are."

The youngest of the inner circle had been listening closely. His face showed concern. "They will find us. They almost succeeded in killing you at Dar al Ahmar."

"That was my error. I deviated from my rules to help a member of my extended family. It will not happen again. Our circles are tight. Our intelligence is good. We have those in the right places who tell us the things that we need to know. Our locations have not been discovered. But we must now execute our plan. If I am right, the Americans will attack, and when they do, they will attack our protectors, who also hate us."

He reached down to the table in front of him and picked up a cup of strong coffee. He drank from it. "Then the bath of fire will truly begin."

Woods, Wink, and Pritch stood in CVIC and stared at the charts of the Middle East that covered an entire corkboard wall. Other aircrews were poring over the same charts, checking out the latest intelligence now represented by marks for SAM sites, navigation points, outlines, and other points of interest. Woods spoke to Pritch without looking at her. "This would be a lot easier if we knew where we were going."

"Yes, sir. We're working it."

"We who?"

"Your entire intelligence community at your service, sir."

Woods winced. "The same professionals who didn't know this guy existed a month ago."

"Yes, sir. We'll find him."

Woods didn't respond. "Can't even plan anything. No route."

"Think of it as a challenge, sir—"

"Quit saying 'sir' all the time."

"Yes, sir. At this point all we can do is become familiar with the area." She put her hands on her hips as she gazed at the charts. "I think it's helpful to chart the SAM sites, for example. I'm in the process right now of updating Syria and Lebanon, and particularly the Bekáa Valley."

Woods's face showed his surprise. "You think we're going to the Bekáa Valley?"

"I don't know," Pritch replied. "A lot of things seem to happen in the Bekáa."

"This guy have any ties there we know about?"

"Not directly. But as you recall, Dar al Ahmar is in the southeast part of the Bekáa. They're trying to figure out all this guy's ties around the world." She looked around to see if anyone was listening to their conversation, as if it made some sort of a difference.

She continued. "The FBI is working with the CIA to try to find out where this guy has his money, his contacts, his false documents, any people in place in the United States, anywhere they can find anything. They're pulling out all the stops. Plus the usual analysis, imagery, you name it. I've never seen anything like it."

"I guess that's good."

"It's good unless you're him. I would bet that we find him, and pretty quickly. Think of how much easier it is to look for someone than to be looked for. It's a lot easier to shine a flashlight into the dark than to try to be invisible when someone else shines his light."

"You got that right." Woods returned his attention to the charts. He studied the Bekáa Valley. "If he's there, he'll be under a SAM umbrella on the way in and on the way out."

"Looks that way."

"What are his ties to Lebanon? What was he doing in Dar al Ahmar in the first place?"

Big strode quickly into CVIC. He saw Woods and came to where he and Pritch were standing. "Hey," he said. "What's up?"

"Just checking out the charts. Trying to break the code on where we'll be going," Woods replied.

"Sure," Big said, studying the charts. "Hell, Pritch, these charts make it look like there are more SAM sites than people. What is up with *that*?"

"We're working the problem, sir—"

"Shit, Pritch," Big said. "We've already declared war! You telling me we don't even have a target? We're going to look stupid again. For once in their lives the politicians step up to the plate, and Intel can't get their shit together to find out where the target is?"

"We're trying, sir."

Big was getting frustrated. "You buying this preplanning a hundred routes?" he said to Woods.

"I hear ya," Woods replied.

"I'm not going to plan nonexistent strikes. I'll wait till we have a real target."

Lieutenant Commander Randy Dennison, the Air Wing Intelligence Officer, yelled at them from across CVIC. "You guys hear?"

"Hear what?" Woods asked.

"Syrians say they found a missile casing from the big air battle with the Israelis. They're claiming it's an American missile."

Woods tried not to look surprised or show his inner panic. "What do they mean by that?"

"They say it's different from the Israeli missile casings that they have. There's some different writing on it."

"That's a dead issue," Big said. "They're still trying to make us look bad. Pretty desperate. I wonder what they did to it to make it look American. Probably put 'This missile is American, fired by an American fighter at a Syrian without authorization' on it."

Dennison walked over to them. "Could be interesting if the missile is truly different."

"Interesting in that it might help us see how clever and deceitful they are. We weren't there, Commander. And if *we* weren't there, there sure wasn't any other carrier or American airplane nearby." Woods hoped his bravado disguised the panic that was about to engulf him.

"If the missile has a number on it, it can be traced," he said, smiling. "I guess we're about to find out."

Pritch tried to get back to the planning. She didn't even want to know about the missile. She wasn't ready for her world to crash down around her, which is exactly what would happen if the missile they found had an American serial number on it. She was sure she'd be exposed at some point. She had begun to think that not being fully informed about the entire operation wouldn't get her out of it. Yet she couldn't tell Bark about Woods. It would ruin him, and she had grown very fond of him, fonder than she would ever acknowledge. "What exactly is the plan for the strikes?" she asked Big and Woods.

Woods replied first. "The *Eisenhower* battle group is on its way. They are supposed to be here tomorrow—"

"From Italy?"

"Right. Naples. Where the CO of VFA-136 was shot."

"It's ironic," Big said philosophically. "They murdered an officer off each carrier. Makes the revenge knife just a little sharper."

Pritch studied the pilots. "What did we ever do to him?"

"We're the Crusaders of the Middle Ages, conquering the Middle East in a different way. They used horses and soldiers, we're using Israel and diplomacy." Big pushed his sleeves up. "These people construct these bizarre dead-wrong theories, and go kill people based on them. They are so far from reflecting reality that it causes you to wonder if there isn't something else at work."

"Are we going to have some kind of briefing where we discuss who will be doing what?" Pritch asked.

"There's supposed to be a joint strike planning meeting when the *Eisenhower* gets within helicopter range. Big and I are on the strike planning team. I'm not sure if the meeting will be here or on the *Eisenhower*—"

"Think I could go?" Pritch pleaded.

"I doubt it. Why would you want to?"

"Because I need to know what's going on."

"We'll see."

28

Sami strode into Kinkaid's office and looked at his boss anxiously. Kinkaid glanced up from a pile of papers he was leafing through. "Right in the middle of this crisis, I have to do paperwork. What you got?"

"I've been searching every library I can find. Every historical reference I know, anything else that would help. I found some histories of the Isma'ili sect, the one these Assassins came from. I think I found something."

Sami walked over to the table and spread out an Operational Navigational Chart of the Middle East. Then he laid several reference pages he had copied on the corner of the table. "Check this out," he said, handing a copy of a photograph to Kinkaid, who took the picture and studied it. "What's this?"

"Alamut. The very place we talked about. The fortress of the Old Man of the Mountains, where these guys have operated for centuries, off and on. The same place referred to by Marco Polo, of all people. This is the actual place."

"Where'd you get this?"

"It was in a book I found. Looks to me like the fortress has been improved since it was last abandoned. I think we have to consider the possibility that he went back to the place where his namesake originated."

"When was this photo taken?" Kinkaid asked, his curiosity aroused.

Sami brought the photo close to his face to study the unusual numbers at the bottom. "It doesn't say. But I think it was taken in the 1930s."

"There's no photograph of this fortress after 1930?"

"I sure haven't found one."

"Maybe it's time to get some new imagery," Kinkaid said. "Where is this place?"

Sami leaned over the chart and studied the northwestern part of Iran. He checked the piece of paper on which he had written the latitude and longitude. "Right . . . here," he said, putting his finger on the brownish area on the chart, some of the highest mountains in Iran.

"Shit, Sami. Talk about inaccessible. We could never get anyone in there. And worse than that, it's in Iran." Kinkaid pondered the problem. "We've declared war against this guy, but we haven't declared war against Iran. Ever since that declaration of war went out, they've been yelling about how they are going to go ballistic if we set one foot on their land or do anything contrary to their sovereignty. Typical Iranian bluster, but still . . ."

"We can at least get some imagery. If he's there, maybe we'll be able to figure it out. If he isn't there, we'll know to look elsewhere."

"Like where? Could he be somewhere else?"

"Yes. Those were even harder to locate than Alamut. According to the stuff I found, this guy, or the ones who came before him, went everywhere. Egypt, India, Pakistan, Syria, Lebanon, even Jerusalem. Everywhere. But it's still a small group that is generally thought of as political, even in Islamic circles. There are several other mountain fortresses that may be tied to this guy. Left over from the Crusades. Some were built to stave off attacks that were sure to come from their Muslim neighbors. I finally came up with two others that I think are candidates. I could only dig up a picture of one of them, and we'll need to track the others."

Kinkaid was pleased. Although it wasn't hard information, it was a good start. It certainly gave them something to work toward, and at least a place to focus intelligence gathering. "Let's find the two. You can keep looking for more in the meantime. What do we know about them?"

Sami picked up the stack of papers on the table corner. "The first one isn't too far from where Ricketts got it."

"Dar al Ahmar?"

"Yeah." Sami recalled the laser sight dancing on his eyes. "Sure would have made things easier if he had just kidnapped the Sheikh."

"And he'd still be alive. . . . I had forgotten he was even there. How could I have forgotten that?" he asked Sami, but more to himself. "That

guy gave his life for his country, and nobody'll ever know. Except us."
He paused.

Sami thought maybe it was time for him to leave when Kinkaid spoke
again. "We should have known about the Israeli air strike. We could have
coordinated with them to take out this Sheikh guy before he did more
damage. Not only did we not coordinate, we didn't even know about
their plan. So we took a risk, sent one of our best men to snatch this guy,
and he gets obliterated by a bomb that we should have known was on its
way. Just three weeks ago, I was sitting in this same room with Ricketts
planning his operation. And now he's dead. And I had *forgotten* about
it." Kinkaid sat down heavily. "How do you get to the point, Sami,
where the immediate takes away your friends and their memories?"

"When you still have to finish it. Once we've finished it we can
think about it more. He sure wouldn't want us to stop now."

"That's what's really ironic about it," Kinkaid said. "The Assassins
didn't kill Ricketts. The Israelis did."

Sami waited. "Would you like to see the other two locations?"

"Yeah."

"The first one is in Lebanon. It's about eighty-five miles northeast
of Dar al Ahmar. It is not as high as Alamut, but it's difficult to see—it's
built into the side of a mountain as opposed to sitting on top of the
mountain. Very hard to find, according to the accounts I have read. In
any case, it is right . . . here." He pointed to an area in eastern Lebanon
southeast of the Bekáa Valley.

Kinkaid studied the position. "Conveniently located under the SAM
umbrella of the Bekáa Valley."

"Exactly. The other one is in southeastern Syria, also in the mountains. There aren't many references to it, even in the Isma'ili documents."

Kinkaid knew what had to be done. "I'm going to get the best
possible imagery of all three of these positions immediately. The two
carrier battle groups are supposed to rendezvous today. We need to
get imagery to them as soon as possible. The President wants this war
under way. He's scared to death of having declared war against one
guy, not knowing where that guy is. According to the Director, it's his
one fear—we've declared war against one guy who then eludes us for
years.

"Maybe we should declare war only against countries. At least you
always know where they are."

"Well, if this goes sideways, and Syria and Lebanon and"—he

glanced down at the chart with Alamut marked on it—"Iran get as mad as I think they will, we may soon have a real war with real countries and we'll know exactly where they are. And they'll know exactly where we are too."

Bark waited in his flight jacket at the front of the ready room. Woods sat in his chair going through the large metal drawer that was under his seat. It stuck out between his legs. He pushed aside various notes, Navy instructions, and copies of *Approach* and *Naval Aviation News* to find a blank writing pad. He finally found a mangled white one and pulled it out. He tried to bend the corner of the paper back so it looked slightly closer to a flat, respectable writing pad.

Bark spoke to Woods. "Trey, you ready?"

"Yes, sir. Just getting some paper."

"You have the charts Pritch did with the SAM sites?"

"Big was going to bring those."

"Where is Big?"

"He stopped by the stateroom to get his laptop."

"We're supposed to be at the helo in five minutes."

"Yes, sir. I know." Woods looked at his watch and glanced at the SDO's desk to see if anyone was on the telephone. He walked quickly to the desk and dialed his stateroom. Big answered. "Big, you coming?"

"Yeah. I'll be right there. I was just looking at something that made me have to go clean out my drawers."

"What's that?" Woods asked, trying to stay casual as he watched Bark for any sign of anger or suspicion.

"The photographs from Syria that claim to show the American missile that shot down one of their jets."

"Really," Woods said. Bark was growing impatient. "Bring it along."

"Roger that."

"Are we dead?"

"Not sure."

"Okay. See you in a minute." Woods hung up the phone.

"Dead about what?" The Squadron Duty Officer asked.

"He's afraid we won't get to go on the strike. He figures Lieutenant Commander and above only. Too much glory to be had." Woods sat down and scribbled on his notepad. He hated the feeling of things closing in on him.

The ready room door flew open and Big strolled in with his laptop and notebook. "Sorry, Skipper."

"Let's go," Bark said. The three of them left the ready room, heading to the flight deck inside the island. They donned cranial helmets and flotation vests and went out to the waiting SH-60 that was turning on the flight deck. The helicopter crewman directed them to their seats. They strapped in and immediately began looking for a way to escape if the helicopter went into the water. Some other pilots, in addition to Wink and Sedge, were already in the helicopter. They all knew what the others were thinking, because jet pilots always thought the same thing when they got in a helicopter—they had just increased their chances of being killed.

Jet pilots, as a rule, would rather walk than fly in a helicopter. The pilots who fly supersonic jets for a living and sit in ejection seats all day believe helicopters to be much more dangerous than their jets. One fact had settled deep into the psyche of jet aviators in the Navy: In one year in the nineties more jet pilots were killed as passengers in Navy helicopters than in jets. It was the kind of statistic that had been remembered and repeated for years because of its mythological significance. It was reinforced by the unpleasant training they all had endured—being strapped into a simulated helicopter, blindfolded, dropped into a deep swimming pool upside down, and told to escape from the sinking helicopter while holding their breath underwater.

Finally they heard the rotor blades bite more heavily into the air and the SH-60 rose from the flight deck of the *Washington,* climbing away quickly from the ship and heading toward the *Eisenhower,* sixty miles away. In World War II when aircraft carriers operated together, they generally stayed within sight of each other. It allowed for their antiaircraft guns to support each other. In the modern Navy, carriers operated within visual range of each other only for photographs.

This would be the first time since Desert Storm that carriers had worked together in combat. The aviators were excited. They would get to do their two favorite things: fly fast and blow things up. They could only hope that some country would get mad enough to send up its Air Force. If that happened, they would get to do what they all dreamed about—shoot down another fighter who didn't want to be shot down. They yearned for the opportunity, usually unspoken, to prove themselves against an enemy.

The eastern Mediterranean was cloudy but still mostly sunny. The customary haze obscured the horizon though the visibility was six or seven miles. The SH-60 made it to the landing pattern of the *Eisenhower* in less than thirty minutes. During the transit the F-14 aircrew had been silent. They weren't hooked up to the helicopter Internal Communication System and, other than yelling, had no way to talk. Nothing on this flight was important enough to lose one's voice over. For the most part they'd sat quietly, bobbing in response to the helicopter's movements, lost in their own thoughts.

Except Woods. He was fighting the urge to hyperventilate. He was thinking about the picture in Big's flight suit pocket. Woods couldn't see it, he couldn't even bring it up or ask Big how he might have come into possession of such an interesting photograph when no one else seemed to be aware of it. What would he say if it was their missile and it could be traced? The photo might be virtually unanswerable proof. If so, not only would it show they did it, it would show they lied about it and constructed an elaborate scheme *with others* to hide the fact. Pritch would be at risk; so would Tiger, Big, Sedge, Wink, and the Gunner. Even the Ordnance Handling Officer. Woods knew the Gunner couldn't gundeck the missile records by himself. They were kept on hardcopy and on the computer. The Gunner must have called in a big favor with the OHO. His neck would be in the noose too, and Woods hadn't even met him. Going to Leavenworth had seemed so noble a risk to take to avenge Vialli, but as the actual possibility on the aura of reality, he found the idea shockingly unattractive. He forced himself to think of something more pleasant, like the helicopter losing power, banging off the flight deck, and landing upside down in the sea. That was something he could take action about, or sink his mind into for a few seconds.

He couldn't help thinking of his Navy career. He used to wonder whether to retire in twenty years as a Captain, or in thirty years as an Admiral. Now he thought of his Navy career in terms of hours, or maybe minutes.

He felt the helicopter settle slowly onto the flight deck. He thought of the strike planning ahead, of the two carrier battle groups working together. Whatever came of his first adventure into Lebanon, this was invigorating. This was how it should be done. He almost smiled as he thought of his congressman's speech asking for a declaration of war. Exactly what Woods had thought he should do. If it had been done a little earlier, maybe he wouldn't have gone into Lebanon on the Israeli raid. Maybe the State Department guy and the Navy attaché and that Squadron Commander and the Officer of the Mess would still be alive. Maybe the Sheikh would already be dead. Never know now, Woods thought.

Their helicopter was the last one to arrive at the conference. They went quickly through the hatch into the island of the *Eisenhower* and down the passageway. Even though none of them had ever set foot on the *Eisenhower* they knew the way perfectly—it was identical to the *Washington,* both Nimitz-class carriers. They climbed quickly down the ladders to the wardroom on the second deck. It was set up for a presentation with an overhead projector, computer projector, charts, and a lectern with a microphone.

Woods and Big moved toward the rear of the large wardroom and sat down with other junior officers. Wink and Sedge followed Big and Woods. Bark went forward and sat at the table reserved for the Squadron Commanding Officers.

The excited conversations of aviators from both Air Wings filled the room with a buzz. They had been selected by their squadrons to be involved in the planning of the strikes. The best minds in the squadrons. The most experienced. Almost all were graduates of Topgun, or Strike University, where strike warfare and air combat were taught in the deserts of Nevada by Navy instructors.

The aviators, or Airedales as they were called in the Navy by non-fliers, were ready to go. They just wanted to know what the targets were. Not that they cared. Knowing that they were going after the terrorist who had taken it upon himself to attack Americans and kill their fellow Naval officers was enough for them. Each person in the wardroom thought declaring war against an individual was one of the greatest ideas they had ever heard of. No more dark, covert operations. This was using sharpened military instruments as they were intended to be used. The Navy pilots felt as if they had been asked to a prom.

The ship's messmen had set up food in the wardroom. There were several stations, like salad bars. Many of the officers grabbed trays and went through the lines.

"Hey! Trey!" an officer called as Big, Sedge, Wink, and Woods made their way to the back of the line.

Woods looked around. It was Terrell Bond, a friend of his from flight training, who was now an F-18 pilot on the *Dwight D. Eisenhower.* "Tear! What's happening?" he said, extending his hand.

"How'd you get stuck with this job?" Bond asked.

"Yeah, stuck. I *begged* for this. Our big chance to go after this Sheikh guy." Woods introduced his squadron mates.

"Hi," Tear said.

"How's it going?" Big asked. "How'd you meet Woods? You guys in the brig together?"

Bond laughed. He was tall and good-looking with a perfect smile. His dark black skin looked like obsidian. "Seems like it. We were at Meridian together." Meridian was the Navy jet training base in Mississippi.

Big replied, "At least you didn't get stuck with him in the same squadron. I don't know how I'm ever going to get rid of him."

Tear looked at Woods. "It'll be nice to turn this Sheikh into dust, but you already had the chance, didn't you?"

Woods frowned. "Huh?"

"That foray into Lebanon that everybody in the world is talking about. Wasn't that you?"

"Where'd you hear that?" Woods asked, chilled.

"Hell, it's all over the fleet. I think one or two of our guys are in e-mail contact with your girlfriend."

"Hey, bite me," Woods replied.

"So," Tear pushed. "How was it? You going to get your picture on the wall at Topgun for four kills?"

"I don't know what you're talking about."

"Yeah, okay. Cool. One day?"

"If there were anything to tell you about, I would be happy to tell you about it. One day."

"I hear you. Let's hurry through this food shit so this killex can get started." Killex, short for "killing exercise," Navy lingo for an event. A screwed-up event is a flailex. A bombing exercise is a bombex. Waiting too long is a sitex.

They finished putting food on their plates and worked their way through the salad and sandwich bars. They nodded at other officers they knew, some well, some just as acquaintances. Navy Air was a big family, but a family nonetheless.

As they walked with their trays, Big said quietly, "Shit, Trey. *Everybody* knows."

"Don't say a word, Big. If we let on, even hint at it, we're dead," Woods admonished.

"*They know!*" Big said.

"Cool it. Don't panic. They can smell panic."

They took their food to a table closer to the front, where Tear had been sitting with four officers from his squadron. They set their trays down and sat facing the front of the wardroom. Tear addressed his buddies. "Guys, this is Sean Woods—we were at Meridian together—and some other guys from his squadron, Big McMack, Sedge, Wink." The pilots greeted each other and Tear introduced the officers from the *Eisenhower*. "This is Dale Hoffer, known here as Dull, Stilt Wilkins, and Ted Lautter."

They all shook hands, each checking out the other for patches, rank, and pecking order.

They discussed who was where in the fleet and who was going to what job ashore in the next year as they downed their food. Woods watched a Captain he didn't know approach the podium. "Who's the 0-6?" he asked.

"Our CAG. Bill Redmond, or Red Man as he is known."

"I've heard of him. He's legendary. F-18 guy. Didn't he bag a MiG-29 over Yugoslavia?"

"That's the one."

"Good guy?"

Tear shrugged. "Typical Captain. More interested in making Admiral than making us safe, or even getting to know us. Kind of an asshole. Rep in his squadron was that he was a screamer."

"Hold on," Woods interrupted. "Here we go."

The overhead lights dimmed as Captain Redmond looked out over the audience and waited for complete silence. Between the two Air Wing Commanders, he had been picked to lead the strike planning effort because of the primary criteria in the Navy for deciding who is best qualified. His lineal number. His name was higher on the captain's list than the Air Wing Commander from the *Washington*. So he was in charge, and the brief took place on his carrier. No one thought anything of it. That was always the way it was done. Admiral Sweat, who was truly in charge, wanted to go to the *Eisenhower* anyway. The Captain of the ship was his former Chief of Staff.

Red Man reviewed his notes and began his presentation. Very tall, he was thin, almost bony, with square shoulders, a large head, and graying blond hair. "Good morning," Redmond said. "For those of you who don't know me my name is Bill Redmond. I'm the Commander of Air Wing Seven. I want to welcome those of you who came over from the *Washington* strike team and from Air Wing Seventeen. I'm not sure we had to do it this way, but I'm glad we did. We need to make sure we're all operating off the same sheet of music so we can support each other and not run into each other at the wrong time. There's already enough room to screw this up and I don't want that to happen because we don't understand each other."

He touched the space bar on a computer on the lectern and a large chart of the Mediterranean came up on the screen behind him. "Let me get right to the point. We will be planning a series of strikes that I hope we can launch within the next twenty-four hours. As I said, I *hope* we can. As you know, the United States has declared war for the first time since December 8, 1941. Some people think that this act is out of proportion, like hitting a fly with a sledgehammer." There was some snickering from the audience. "Why that is bad if your objective is a dead fly escapes me. I, for one, believe that some flies deserve to be hit with sledgehammers. So let's not worry about that. Our job is to be the sledgehammer, and make sure it hits the right spot.

"As you can see, I have a chart of the Med here. Our current location is at 33° 51' N, 86° 45' E. Right about"—he turned to look at the screen and touched a spot with the pointer—"here." He placed the pointer on the table next to him. "The real issue though, is where are we going to strike?

"What is our target? We're not attacking Syria, or Lebanon, or Jordan, or Iran, or Iraq, as countries, but our targets may be in any one of those countries. It makes our mission doubly sensitive with far-reaching political implications. Especially if our target decides to hide out in a city. We can't control all the political impact, but we can do some things. We must do everything that we can to minimize damage to any person or property other than that belonging to Sheikh al-Jabal."

"Here we go," Woods whispered to Tear. "Right after they tell us what a tough, butch sledgehammer we are, they start telling us not to hit anything *too* hard. Typical."

The Air Wing Commander touched the space bar on his computer again and a chart of the Middle East came up. "Most of you are familiar with the countries in the Middle East. Many of you have been ashore in Israel, but I doubt if many of you have been ashore in Syria or Lebanon. I know I haven't. We will be having extensive briefs on each country from our intelligence people this afternoon. We will be discussing their orders of battle, their political responses to our declaration of war, and the best guess of their responses if we in fact strike a target on their territory. But at the end of the day, it will be a crapshoot. We'll be told either to go, or not. And if we are told to go, we will go, regardless of whether it will make someone mad or not. They should have thought about how good an idea it was to allow the Sheikh to operate out of their territory before now. In any case, before we get into the countries, I've asked Commander Glenn Healy to give you an overall intel update." He looked to his side and Commander Healy took the cue and came forward.

He was the Air Wing Seven Intelligence Officer. "Good morning." His audience replied in kind.

"I wish I could stand up here and give you the latitude and longitude for every place where Sheikh al-Jabal is likely to be. We could just strike them all simultaneously and be assured of success. But this is a war unlike any war before it. We are after one man and his organization. That, by definition, is not a geographic war. It means that we're not after SAM sites, ships, ports, cities, military bases, or roads—the usual targets of wars. In some ways, that makes it almost impossible. In other ways, it makes it somewhat easier. We do not have to destroy an entire country to accomplish our objective. We must simply find our target and destroy it. Or him, I should say.

"I want to show you the most recent intelligence that we have, and one additional point of interest. According to the CIA, as of one hour ago, these are the three targets that they believe to be the most likely." He hit the space bar on the same computer Red Man had used and a closeup map of eastern Syria and northern Lebanon came up.

Woods and Tear sat up, suddenly aware that there might actually be content to this brief. "Shit hot," Tear said as he watched the screen in the front of the wardroom intently.

"Two of them are on this map, the third is east of here, in Iran," Healy continued.

Woods and Tear glanced at each other. Iran? Too far. No fun.

"The way that these sites have been determined is admitted by the CIA to be extremely speculative at this time. In fact, they didn't want to give me this information at all until I insisted. They said it was preliminary, uncertain, and as likely to be wrong as right at this stage. It is based on a historical analysis of the group of Assassins back over several hundred years and the fortress from which they were known to operate. The CIA apparently has some hot young analyst who thinks he understands how these Assassins operate. He believes they are duplicating the historical model—to perpetuate the mystique—and may be operating not only out of the same areas but the *exact* same fortresses. I don't know whether that's true or not, but until we get more imagery or other confirmation, we can use these at least as a starting point.

"Let me show you the first one. It's in northwestern Iran, and is called Alamut. I don't know whether we in fact will go into Iran. I have my doubts, but until we know for sure, we have to at least list it as a target. It may be a target for a B-2—it's a long way from the Mediterranean for us . . ."

"Why should Iran get a free pass?" Tear asked Woods in an angry whisper. "Seems to me like they may deserve it more than anybody else on that map. They've been jabbing us in the eye since I was born. . . . Pisses me off . . ."

"This is an old picture, but you can see the castle of Alamut, which was built in the eleventh century and is still there. We're obtaining imagery on this castle today and should receive the photo within the hour.

"The other two sites are more intriguing, although less historic. One is in Lebanon, southeast of the Bekáa Valley." He brought up another slide in his PowerPoint presentation, which showed the location on the chart very specifically. It was surrounded by rings of various sizes. They represented the effective ranges of the SAM sites in the area, most of them overlapping. "As you can see, if this were to be a target, it is under the SAM umbrella that protects the Bekáa Valley. That could be a very nasty place to go, *if* those who control the SAMs decide to shoot them at U.S. planes and I think we should assume that they will. This one is called Teru'im. What I find particularly intriguing is that it is near Dar al Ahmar, which both the United States and Israel identified as where the Sheikh was supposed to have been on the day that the Israeli attack took place. That attack, as everyone knows, is the one by Israel—and someone from the F-14 squadron from the *Washington* actually participated in!" Healy smiled at Woods and Big, who wore their Jolly Rogers patches on their shoulders. Every eye in the wardroom was on them. Woods couldn't believe he had been confronted in such a public way. Fear and a conspicuous bafflement froze him. All he could think of was the photograph in Big's pocket. The Commander probably had a copy too. "Isn't that right Lieutenant?" he asked Woods.

Woods finally realized that the Intelligence Officer was smiling and got himself under control. His reply was loud enough for everyone in the wardroom to hear. "It was a *great* flight. There we were inverted, supersonic—"

When he went into "there we were," everyone in the wardroom knew Woods was signaling the beginning of a "war story" generally divorced from the truth. They laughed, stopped listening—as he had hoped—and turned their attention back to Commander Healy. He brought up the next slide, which was a copy of the photograph that Big had folded up in his flight suit. Big gasped and shifted in his seat to cover the sound. The photograph showed the curving side of a missile. "As you can see, this is a copy of a photograph provided to the world press this morning by Syria. It shows the United States missile that was used to shoot down one of the Syrian MiGs. This was offered by Syria as proof that our friends from VF-103 were in fact leading the strike into Lebanon and shot down one of their planes with an AIM-7M Sparrow missile. They got it right. This is a casing from a Sparrow missile." He waited as the officers leaned forward to get a better look at the casing. It was white, and was from a missile about six inches in diameter. Woods could clearly make out some English letters on the casing and a part of a number. The Intelligence Officer surveyed the wardroom. "Do we have any of the Ordnance Gunners here?" He waited. "I was hopeful someone could tell me which one of VF-103's missiles this is. I'm sure we have enough of a serial number here to trace it back. Right, Lieutenant?" He smiled at Woods again.

Woods found that he could barely breathe. "Yes, sir. No problem. I'll get our Gunner right on it so we can find out which one of our missiles landed in Lebanon."

Commander Healy went on. "I think the Syrians have forgotten that the AIM-7 missiles we use are identical to the Israelis'. What do they expect to find on the ground? A missile casing with Hebrew on it?" He turned again to the screen. "Let me show you the next potential target. It's in the southern part of Syria, east of Lebanon, and is also in the mountains. We don't have a picture of this site because there aren't any. According to the CIA, the likely position of that fortress is here." He brought up the next slide, a close-up of southeastern Syria. It was covered with SAM site range circles. He studied it with the rest of the wardroom for a moment. "If we do go after this target, and Syria fires on us, it would be as bad as the Lebanon site southeast of the Bekáa Valley. We'll have to work hard at SAM suppression.

"Keep in mind, if we go into Syria, they may very well consider it an act of war. They may respond militarily, not just with their diplomats yelling at us. Those are the considerations that I'm sure are being evaluated in Washington, but I want you to be aware of them as well. What could that mean? Well, what would our first move usually be? To go after the SAM sites, right? SEAD, your favorite mission—Suppression of Enemy Air Defenses. Well, who's the enemy? The Sheikh? What air defenses does he have? What if he's in Syria, and the air defenses belong to Syria? We're not at war with Syria. Do we hit the SAMs of a country with which we are not at war? Do we let the SAM sites sit there and lock us up, and just *hope* they don't actually shoot at us?"

Red Man couldn't resist. "The President warned Syria to stay out of the way."

"True enough, sir, but we have to consider the possibilities—"

"Just tell them not to lift a finger to defend this guy."

"That's exactly what they have been told, sir. But what will they do?"

"Don't know."

"Me neither. So we need to be aware of the SAM sites even though we'll probably not be able to hit them—unless, of course, they shoot at us. Just a heads-up, sir."

There was a murmur of discontent from the aviators in the wardroom. Red Man stood up next to Healy. "I understand your concerns," he said, facing the two Air Wings. "They're the same as mine. It puts us at risk. However, as is often the case, political concerns outweigh safety. I know what you're thinking—someone else's politics, and our safety. But that's how it is. Get used to it. Our objective is to conduct precise, effective strikes and get this thing over with. That's why we're here. I want to have potential routes planned into and out of each country in such a way that we can keep our exposure to a minimum. Don't get me wrong. I'm going to ask for permission to strike the air defenses first, I just don't expect to get that permission.

"Thank you, Commander. Later this morning Commander Healy will be going over the Order of Battle for Syria, Jordan, Iraq, Iran, Israel, everybody. You need to have in mind what all their capabilities are in case any of that comes into play. As I said in my message yesterday, I want to do some group planning. We'll go to CVIC, and break into the three groups that I have already outlined. I am confident that you brought your charts with you and have already begun thinking along these lines. The PFPS and TAMPS," the two flight planning programs commonly used on the carriers, "are up and we've had extra computers loaded and moved into CVIC so several of you can work at the same time. I want numerous potential routes for each potential target before we leave here at four o'clock today. Everyone understand?" He waited. "Very well. Any questions?"

A Lieutenant Commander toward the front raised his hand. "CAG, do you have any idea when we might launch?"

"Could be within eight hours, could be a week. Depends on how good and how quick our intel is on locating this guy. Once we know, or even suspect, we will launch. And it will almost certainly be at night." He looked around. "Any other questions?"

No one said a word. They wanted to do something: plan, figure routes, calculate fuel consumption for various weapons load-outs, any-thing—anything except sit around and wonder where the Sheikh was. If they didn't find him, this was going to get embarrassing quickly.

"Very well. Let's get to work."

"Sir, what about the Air Force?" Tear asked.

Red Man replied immediately. "Good call. They're trying to make this into an Air Force event. As always, if there is something going on, they offer to preposition their forces and fly the rest of them around the world, refueling them twenty-four hours a day. But so far, this is going to be a Navy war. The President is doing what I think is the smart thing, saying that the war is narrow and short, against one man, and will be over as soon as that man is finished or surrenders. We don't need the entire United States Air Force to go after one man. In fact, it looks like overkill and says we may have some alternative objectives in mind. If we leave it as a carrier battle, with the strikes going from here, it will appear like a very minor skirmish against a terrorist. That gives the President great comfort, although it may give the rest of the world only minor comfort. In any case, so far at least, this is a Navy war."

"Oorah," someone said from the back.

Red Man smiled. "We're going to go after a very bad person and kill him dead if I have anything to say about it. We will be sending as many strikes as we need. Maybe even more than we need. But we will get this guy. I promise you that."

29

Sami noticed Kinkaid's hands. He was using them for emphasis, which he rarely did. This late night meeting was different, and everyone on the task force could feel Kinkaid's excitement.

Kinkaid pointed his miniature laser pointer at the brand-new imagery. "Look there, and . . . there. Recent construction. And how about this? Consistent use of the footpath." Bringing two images up on a split screen, he said, "We compared some recent IR imagery. You can see the warmth of the path compared to the ground next to it. It's either human or animal use. Not many animals around there. This is the Lebanon fortress." His smile was one of relief, not triumph.

"The second group of images is of the fortress in Syria." He glanced at Sami. "Mr. History here is the one who predicted this would be the most likely to be used. So far he has been dead on. Must have inside information."

Sami bristled at the implication. Then Kinkaid surprised him.

"For those of you who don't know, Sami came up with these through an amazing analysis that will go down in Agency history as one of the most clever and creative—especially if it turns out to have been true.

"In any case," Kinkaid said, clicking on the next picture, "this one also appears to have had recent use. The imagery isn't as good, but it's good enough to conclude that the place is active, as is . . . this one," he said, moving to the next slide. "If you look closely you can see the same evidence of recent use—"

"But by whom?" one of the analysts asked. "If we're going to list this as a bombing target based on it being 'active,' I wouldn't feel comfortable. The last thing we need is the PR fiasco that would come from bombing some old fort that homeless people had moved into for shelter—"

"Hold that thought," Kinkaid replied confidently. He put up the next slide and the members of the task force leaned forward to get a clearer picture in the darkened room. "This is the mother ship. Alamut. It is believed by some that the Sheikh is at Alamut in Iran. We need to at least consider it. It would be harder than hell to attack, and more likely to stimulate one of our sworn enemies than attacking a terrorist base in Syria or Lebanon. In any case, you can see that this fortress is in awfully good shape for being as old as it is. *Someone* is there. No historical preservation society in Iran. If you look close, you can make out the labyrinthine approach to the fortress. The approach is so deep in a crevice that we couldn't get good IR to see whether it's being used." Kinkaid brought the lights up. "Those are the fortresses. They show use and probably are our targets."

"But—"

"Exactly. How can we be sure?" He pulled out a piece of paper from a file sitting on the table. "Those of you who don't know me very well don't know my background. I was once a member of the DO." Where Ricketts had worked until recently. "I worked in various countries. One of them was Germany. Thirty years ago now. It was during the Munich Olympics."

So, Sami thought. Now we learn. He watched Kinkaid's face cloud as he recalled the events of those days. It had affected him deeply. That was clear to everyone in the room.

"In this business you build and maintain relationships. Some endure," he said shrugging, "others don't. I've known one man since then who has been a friend. You've heard me mention him on occasion. I've never explained why we are able to communicate like we do. He was involved in that investigation. His name is Efraim. We shared many hours together in Munich and elsewhere, and became close. We have spoken many times since then. He tells me what I need to know, and I tell him what he . . . needs. Always unofficial or unclassified. Just a heads-up, if you will. Sure, once in a while we trade actual intelligence. With approval," Kinkaid said quickly, "and *some*times it has been helpful."

Kinkaid waved his piece of paper. "This is one of those times." He walked around the podium and leaned on it, looking very casual and chummy, unlike the other people there who were becoming less comfortable the more Kinkaid went on.

"You recall how all this started? Navy officer from the—which ship was it?"

"*Washington.*"

"Right. Ran off to Israel. With an Israeli woman . . . Efraim called me back this morning. I had asked him for a reality check on these fortresses. I wanted to know if they had come to the same conclusions from a different direction."

"Did he know about the Sheikh before Gaza?" Cunningham asked.

"Yes."

"Why didn't they tell us about him?"

"No need to know. They didn't think the Sheikh was going public anytime soon. And they thought that Israel would be the primary target. Unless they see us being implicated somehow, they wouldn't necessarily share that kind of information with us."

"We might have been able to intervene—" Cunningham said.

"Let me go on. Here's the crux of the matter. As part of their attempt to close in on him, they found what they believe to be his primary base of operation. Alamut. He has a free pass from Iran and goes as he pleases. They're very happy with his work, and they're prepared to overlook his ties to the Isma'ili sect with which they are not terribly friendly.

"The second most used operational base is the one Sami identified in eastern Lebanon, in Teru'im. Makes perfect sense as it's the closest one to where the Israelis attempted to take him out by that air strike. According to their best information, that is where the Sheikh himself has one of his headquarters.

"The third location is exactly where Sami predicted it would be— southeastern Syria. In other words, they confirmed exactly what Sami came up with in his analysis. Coincidence? I don't think so. I think it means Sami was right. So, the question becomes whether this information is good enough to list them as targets for air strikes for the Navy."

Kinkaid put up a large-scale map of the Middle East. "Now that you know everything I know, is this good enough information for targeting? Because if it's wrong, you know who's going to eat it."

The members of the task force sat silently—there was almost too much to consider. Sami spoke first. "Did you tell your Israeli friends about our theories before they told you what they did?"

"Good question. Are they just giving back to us what we already know? Good intelligence trick. But no, I had not told Efraim about the three fortresses you identified. He came up with the identical information without knowing that I expected them to do just that. Anything else?"

They all had concerns, but no one wanted to express them, because they weren't sure they could defend them. There were concerns. Feelings.

"Well?" Kinkaid asked, waiting. "Good targets?"

Still no one spoke. Several glanced at Sami, who was studiously staring at his hands.

"Then if no one objects, I'm sending these off as good targets."

No one said a word.

"Done," Kinkaid said as he gathered the folders together.

"We the fighter or bogey?" Woods asked Wink.

"Bogey. We're supposed to be taking the 290 radial at sixty miles." Woods stared at the TACAN needle, which pointed to the carrier on a compass. He tried to study it to figure their heading to the 290 radial sixty miles away.

"Head 323," Wink said before Woods could make the calculation.

"Roger," Woods said. "Show off."

Wink ignored him. "You think we'll ever get to go after these guys? I mean, we've declared war, are we ever gonna like, *do* something about it?" Wink asked.

"I think they're worried about stirring up Syria or Iran. Those guys don't need much of an excuse."

"I think it's time to stir them up. They let terrorists operate from their country but they don't want anybody coming after them on their territory? They can eat shit."

"I think their time is about up."

"So what the hell are we going to do about it?"

"Maybe we'll go sooner than you think."

"*I'm* ready to go. They should target where they think he is right now."

"Air Force is sending all kinds of airplanes to Sicily, Aviano, Italy, England, you name it."

Wink chuckled. "Typical Air Force. The closest they can usually get is about five thousand miles away. Except for Desert Storm, when

Saudi Arabia invited them in, gave them hotel rooms, and perfectly built bunkers. Country club all the way. I tell you, if I hear one more person say we don't need aircraft carriers . . . Where the hell are all those bases the Air Force built? Are they flying out of that wonderful Air Force base we built for our friends the Libyans? Oh, yeah. Never mind. Or maybe we should be flying out of one of the big Air Force bases we built in Iran for our good friends. Oh, yeah. Never mind. Or maybe we could fly out of our good NATO ally base in France. Oh, yeah, never mind. Or if we were in the Pacific, we could use the Air Force base in the Philippines. Oh, yeah, *they* threw us out too. For every one of those bases we built it's like taking an aircraft carrier and sinking it. About the same cost. Except with the Air Force, they just hand them the keys. Not only the keys to the base, but the officers' club, golf course, barracks, tower, electronics, and for good measure, sometimes we throw in the airplanes too. Somebody ought to do a damned study of how much we've given away supporting the Air Force pilots and their blue dickies."

"You crack me up, Wink. You must have gotten turned down by the Air Force."

"I did. I wanted to go to the Air Force Academy. Cool-looking chapel. But that's got nothing to do with it. The whole idea of flying B-52s around the world is just ridiculous. Their objective is not to win a war—their objective is to *look* like they're winning the war on CNN."

"*Victory 203, turn to 110 as the bogey.*"

"*Roger,*" Wink replied.

Woods brought the Tomcat around. When he reached their radial and DME he started in as the bogey on the first intercept of the night.

"So who's going to be on the first attack, if it ever goes?" Wink asked.

"You're finally going to be happy that you fly with the Assistant Operations Officer. The guy who writes the flight schedule. You're not worthy, Wink. The first flight is an attack on the fortress in Lebanon. The *Eisenhower* is going to attack the Syrian fortress. Looks like we're on the first strike, carrying two-thousand pounders."

"You mean it's on?"

"Yep."

"Shit hot! How come you didn't tell anybody?"

"Just got the word. Bark is all over this. I think we might be on Bark's wing, maybe even leading the strike. He wants to fly with the LANTIRN god."

"We're going to be leading the strike?" Wink said, suddenly concerned.

"Victory 207, contact 290 for 33."

"That's your bogey."

"Judy."

"Looks like it," Woods replied, trimming the airplane so it would stop flying slightly nose down.

"When do we go?"

"Tonight."

"I gotta go plan! We've got to get ready."

"You just said you were ready."

"I want to be *really* ready."

☙

Cunningham walked by Sami's cubicle and saw him staring at his computer, deep in thought. Cunningham rapped his knuckles on the aluminum frame of the cubicle. "You awake?"

"Yeah, hey," Sami said, sitting back, his expression troubled.

"What's up?" Cunningham asked.

Sami hesitated. "I don't know. Ever since Kinkaid told us about his Israeli connection, I've had an uneasy feeling. Things haven't been adding up."

Cunningham sat down heavily in the chair by Sami's desk. "Don't go paranoid on me," he said.

"Check this out," Sami said, pointing at the screen.

Cunningham leaned forward and looked at Sami's computer. "What?"

"The Syrians say they found a missile casing, and showed it to everyone. Remember? That picture of a torn missile with a partial serial number?"

"Sure."

"Then everybody wanted to know the story. So the Raytheon guy holds a press conference—"

"Right. Live. We all watched it."

Sami glanced back at the screen. "And he said the entire lot that missile was part of was shipped to Israel."

"Right. Confirmed what we had been saying all along."

"Look. This is the actual shipment list. They *didn't* all go to Israel. Eighty-five percent went to the U.S. Navy, seven percent or so to the Air Force, and seven percent to Israel."

"You sure?" Cunningham asked, peering at Sami's screen to see if he was reading the numbers right. "Okay, so the one Syria found was from the seven percent shipped to Israel."

"Maybe. But the Raytheon guy said *all* of that lot was sent to Israel."

"They probably just didn't want people getting carried away. Syria may have faked the number anyway. Maybe they got hold of the list you're looking at and picked that lot because it had the *fewest* shipped to Israel. They're trying to make it look like the Navy did it."

"And how the hell are they going to get this list?"

"Maybe a CIA analyst of Syrian descent sent it to them—"

"What the hell does that mean? That really *pisses* me off! If you've got something against me—"

"Whoa," Cunningham said, smiling. "Just pulling your chain. Relax."

"That was a cheap shot. You think it's easy being an Arab in this place? Everybody thinks I'm a terrorist. I don't need any shit from you—"

"Sorry. Look, I wouldn't trust Syria to know a telephone number even if they got it out of the phone book. I'd *know* they were wrong. Everything they say is a lie. It's just a matter of how big a lie it is. Everything comes through the government. Everything is calculated to deceive for a purpose. So I don't know what's going on with this number, but I'm sure as hell not worried about it. If we treat everything Syria says as a lie, we're usually okay."

Sami indicated the computer screen, angered by his friend's generalization. "Looks like we're the ones lying this time."

"I wouldn't worry about it if I were you. There are plenty of people here who can worry about missile casings. We have a big enough problem trying to find the Sheikh."

"But it all comes down to that. Kinkaid is relying on Israel to give us the inside information. *I* don't trust *them*. I'm not buying this."

"So don't. But it's not our job to follow the missile claims from Syria. What do you think, one of our planes went into Lebanon like some gunfighter and shot down a bunch of Syrians?"

"Maybe."

"Oh, come on. You probably believe in UFOs."

"Why is it so hard for you to believe?"

"Because things like that just don't happen."

"You don't know that."

"I hope it *did* happen! We should do it more often. I'm all for blurring the lines. I like the idea of the terrorists looking over their shoulders all the time. I'm happy as hell we've declared war against this Sheikh guy. It's time to turn his lights out. I frankly don't care whether our guy went up there illegally. They murdered one of our Navy officers—"

"He was in the wrong place at the wrong—"

"They shot him in the back!"

"I still think—"

"Keep your eye on the ball, Sami. We've got enough to worry about already."

"I got a feeling there's more here than meets the eye."

Cunningham stood up. "Always is, Sami."

Sami's phone rang. Cunningham waved and left the cubicle as Sami picked up the phone. "Yeah?"

"Sami."

"Father."

"I am sorry to interrupt your day. You know I don't like calling you during your work."

"It's okay. No problem. What's up?"

"Something has happened that I wanted to tell you."

"What?"

"Remember the man who was talking to you at the beginning of the meeting the other day?"

"Sure."

"I didn't introduce you. I apologize for that. His name is Hussein Gamal. He called me this morning."

"What about?"

"He is one of the most influential men in the United States. He is from Lebanon originally, and now runs a large construction company. Biggest in Washington. He called me—just this morning—and said he was impressed by you."

Sami knew how much it meant to his father to impress rich people. "Great."

"And he said he wanted me to ask you if you would ever be willing to consider leaving your government job to come work for him. On his personal staff. Can you believe it? He said he didn't want an answer now, he just wanted to tell you that he expected your salary would be at least double what you make now. At least. Could be more. What should I tell him?"

Sami actually allowed the thought to rest in his mind for a short time. It was not altogether unpleasant to consider being able to afford a new car, and maybe even a new house in the expensive Washington area. "That's nice of him, but he doesn't even know me."

"He knew you enough to be impressed."

"Tell him thank you, and someday in the future maybe I'll consider it."

"Excellent. I will tell him. I will call him back today and tell him that. I am proud of you, son."

"Thanks," Sami said.

"He also told me to remind you of your promise."

"I figured."

"Don't take it lightly, Sami. Don't disregard what your friends say."

"I don't, and I didn't. You don't have anything to worry about."

Dinner on the *Washington* had passed unremarkably, but the aircrew were growing restless. Bark called an AOM in the ready room for 1900. They were all there early for the first time in anyone's memory. Bark's expression spoke to them of pending action.

At exactly 1900 Bark got up from his chair. He glanced toward the back. "Petty Officer Griffin, would you please hang the sign on the rear door?"

Griffin crossed to the door and hung the DO NOT DISTURB—MEETING IN PROGRESS sign on the outside.

Bark nodded, ready to begin. Woods noticed that Bark was wearing his "lucky" flight suit. It was the one he had been issued as a flight student in Pensacola. He had worn it in every airplane he flew and every squadron he had been in. It was getting frayed and faded, but that didn't deter Bark. He knew a good thing when he saw it.

Bark's voice was loud. "We're going in. We've got the targets."

Excitement was visible on the faces of the Jolly Rogers.

"Strike Ops is deciding what strike package to take right now. I've been lobbying for the only medium attack capability in the Navy. That would be us. I want them to have us as the go-to strike, and use the F-18s as bomb trucks directed by us. We'll see. I think we'll be on the first strike, but it's not settled yet. The important thing to know is that we expect to go tonight.

"The Admiral tells us that additional forces are inbound to this area from all over the world. The Army will be sending an airborne division to Italy, the Air Force is sending several squadrons of fighters and light attack to Aviano, but we still don't know if Italy will sign off on attacks from her territory. This isn't a NATO deal, so I have my doubts. Plus some of the countries like Syria, and maybe Iraq, will whisper in Italy's ear and tell them how unwise it would be for her to support this misguided war of America's. So we'll wait to see. So far though, Italy hasn't tried to tell us what we can do from our own carriers." Bark smiled. "The first stage of this war will be Navy strikes, and we're it. We'll be going after the fortress in Lebanon."

"They expecting any opposition?" Lieutenant Commander Paulson asked.

Bark shook his head. "No way of knowing. But when Israel went north into Lebanon to go after this guy, who came to his defense? Syrian Air—"

"Bring them on—"

"That's why the initial strikes—2200 tonight—will be Tomahawk launches. First airplanes will launch immediately thereafter. The Tomahawk missiles are destined for certain structures, and certain SAM sites in the area—"

Big interrupted. "We're going to attack Syrian and Lebanese SAM sights? They're not *in* this fight, are they?"

"That's one of the problems. Seems wise to assume that any SAM site in the area is going to be trained on our fighters. It'd be foolish in the extreme to fly over a hot SAM site and just figure they're not going to shoot at us."

"But won't Syria and Lebanon say we've attacked *them* if we attack their SAM sites?"

"That's been the decision. I am both surprised and pleased. I was afraid we'd head into these strikes and just hope they didn't shoot at us. Now they almost certainly will, but we hope they won't have much capability left to do it. Anyway, we can discuss the politics of it another time. The initial strike will be by Tomahawks against their Air Defense Command and Control, and some fixed SAM sites, then we'll go in. That's the plan, and that's what I'm here to talk about.

"A lot of things can go wrong with this operation. Let's concentrate on what we need to do. I've asked Pritch to get the latest intelligence photos of the targets."

On cue she stood up and moved to the front of the room. Pritch's briefings were well regarded and listened to carefully. It was obvious to everyone she took her job very seriously. She spent her off hours researching things she didn't understand very well and deepening her knowledge of those things she did understand. It made her briefs much more reliable.

She nodded to Petty Officer Griffin, who turned down the lights. "We're going to spend some time getting familiar with the target. I say 'target' because it is likely we will be participating on strikes on only one target. For the whole Air Wing."

30

Sami stood before the clerk. He outranked her in terms of who had a higher GS number, but she had what he wanted and would give it to him only if she was satisfied he was entitled to it.

"It's an old file," he pleaded.

"It doesn't matter, sir. It is still classified, and you're not on the access list."

Sami had to get the file. He couldn't steal it—that would be impossible—and he could end up in prison just for trying. "What is the code word of the program?"

"Sir," she said, in the prim tones of an old-fashioned schoolteacher, "you know I can't tell you that."

It suddenly struck him. "You're aware of the Gaza Task Force?"

"Yes, sir, of course."

"I'm on it," he replied.

"Okay."

"Have you seen the order?"

"Yes, sir, I have it right here."

"Read it," he demanded.

"I don't need to. I've already read it."

His face glowed. "Then you'll recall that it gives the members blanket clearance for all research and investigation files dealing with the Middle East, with a few exceptions that are in specific categories. Right?"

"Yes," she said, not following.

"Well, this file deals with the Middle East. And it's not in the category of excluded matters."

"I don't know that it deals with the Middle East—"

"Well, look at it!" he said, exasperated. It had better deal with the Middle East, he thought. He turned his back on her so she could examine the first page of the file.

"You're right, sir," she said. She slid the file across the counter to him. "Sign this," she said, handing him a checkout card.

He signed the card quickly and gave it back to her. She studied it and smiled at him. "Have a nice day," she said.

He turned quickly away, anxious beyond measure to read the file. He put it under his sweater vest and went straight to his cubicle. Glancing around to make sure no one was approaching or likely to interrupt him in the next fifteen minutes, he took the file out from under his sweater, opened it, and read the cover: MEGA INVESTIGATION. TOP SECRET.

Woods pushed against the weights as he strained to beat his personal record of bench-press repetition. He tried to get to the weight room on the 03 level at least five times a week. It had been three days since he had been there, and he was itching to get back to his schedule. He often found himself at the weight room after midnight, when it was not only uncrowded, but unrushed. Sometimes sacrificing sleep for conditioning was not a good trade, especially when he had to fly, but he found lifting weights reduced his stress.

They had already planned the strike down to the last second, but he needed a forty-five minute workout before he got ready for the brief. The workout helped him keep his mind off all the things that could go wrong.

He wasn't the only one. The weight room was crowded with sweaty men and two women, two S-3 pilots who worked out every night. Woods was slightly put out because he had to wait for each station.

As he finished his fifteenth bench press, he lowered the weights slowly so they didn't drop. Sweat rolled down his cheeks as his red face relaxed. Grabbing his towel, he stood up and moved to the next station. He waited for the S-3 pilot to finish and then put the pin in the weights for the leg press.

"Lieutenant Woods?"

Woods hadn't see the man come in, but he recognized the voice. Great, Woods thought. I am *not* up for this. Not turning around, he placed his feet on the metal plates to begin his first leg press. He pushed hard and the large column of weights moved upward. Finally, Woods nodded toward the chaplain, just one inch short of rudely ignoring him.

"I'm sorry to bother you," the chaplain said, unfazed.

Woods didn't say anything. He pushed the weights up with his legs, his hands solidly gripping the handles on either side of the seat. Straining against the weights, he held his breath and tried not to grunt.

"Your roommate, Mr. McMack, told me I could find you here."

"What's up?"

The chaplain stood awkwardly, watching Woods. "May I talk to you?"

"I'm going to keep going, if that's okay. But say what you want to say." He pushed against the weights again.

"I've been thinking about our last conversation." He waited for Woods to reply, but Woods was silent. "I have some concerns I'd like to discuss with you."

Woods let the weights he was holding up with his legs slam down. The sharp sound was like a rifle shot that sent a bolt of fear through the chaplain. "What?" Woods said.

The chaplain walked around the station so that he could look at Woods. "Do you remember what we talked about?"

"Look, Father, if you've got something to say, let's hear it."

"Yes. I'm sorry for the intrusion. I've been thinking about what has happened. I simply wanted to ask you one question."

"What's that?"

"I'm concerned about what we're doing."

"We who?" Woods said.

"The U.S. I'm concerned about how we got into this war."

"Why?"

"If someone from this ship went into Lebanon without the country knowing it, without authorization, and it led to an official declaration of war, it may not be, well, it might not be a just war, or the right thing to do. That would be deceitful."

Woods wiped his face and closed his eyes momentarily. "I'm not following you."

"When you sent my memo to Congress, we told them how just it would be to declare war. But the actual reason Congress gave for going to war was not for the attack on Lieutenant Vialli, but for the other attacks: the attaché, the Navy commander, and the State Department man. And those attacks were in response to their belief. You, or someone like you went into Lebanon with the Israelis. Wouldn't that make the war unjust? Wouldn't the declaration of war by Congress based on deceit be fraud?"

"No," Woods replied quickly. "We should declare war against this guy for killing Vialli. That's all this is about. Tony Vialli. They killed him, and now they're going to pay for it. Simple as that." Woods got up from the leg press and walked around the chaplain to the next station. He sat on the bench facing out. "And now they've killed other Americans. I don't understand how you can even say that," Woods said.

The chaplain stood in front of him, refusing to leave until he satisfied some apparently unquenchable desire to talk this through. "Remember how Germany invaded Poland?"

"What?"

"World War II. Remember? Germany invaded Poland in 1939."

"Of course. Everybody knows that."

"Well, that's what brought England into it, and started the real fighting. Remember how it started?"

"Sure. Germany invaded Poland and beat the hell out of them."

"Yes, but *why* did Germany invade? What was the supposed reason?"

"Don't remember." Woods checked his watch.

"There was an attack on German soldiers around a radio station on the Polish border. Twenty or thirty soldiers were killed. Pictures of the dead bodies with their German uniforms were circulated. Hitler was outraged and said he would defend Germany. He invaded Poland the next day."

"Okay," Woods said.

"His response was justified?"

"Maybe, I don't know—"

"Hitler *staged* the entire thing," the chaplain said. Woods was interested, but he didn't get the point. "The dead Germans were prisoners. Hitler murdered a bunch of prisoners, put them in uniforms at the communications station, and declared that an outrageous attack had occurred. He deceived his own countrymen, the Poles, and the world. He used it as the pretense to start World War II."

"I gotta keep going here. What are you getting at?"

"If someone from this ship performed an illegal action and our declaration of war is the result of that, we're in the same boat as Adolf Hitler."

"It's not the same at all," Woods said.

"Why not?"

"Because the Sheikh *murdered* Vialli."

"How do you know that?"

"Because the *Sheikh* said so!"

"What if they were there for another reason, and Vialli attacked them? After all, they didn't kill the children."

"Right. Unarmed, Tony attacked a bunch of innocent terrorists who just wanted to ride on the bus." Woods had heard enough. He was losing patience with this attempt to cast the American action in a cloud of moral ambiguity, where, for once, Woods believed it didn't belong. "Now I get it," Woods continued, trying to keep from saying too much. "You just make up a scenario to justify doing nothing. Well, I'll tell you what. I am going to do something about it. You can watch and you can wring your hands. You can complain that it didn't all line up perfectly, but things in human history rarely do. We're doing the right thing here. This was going to happen eventually anyway. So we're going to go after this guy, and we're going to go all out. If anything else comes of it— if World War III results—then at least we know who our enemies are. Let's get it over with."

Woods stood up, took his towel, and left the gym without looking back.

Sami was surprised to see Kinkaid at the agency cafeteria. He'd never seen him there before. It was close to personal enjoyment and Kinkaid seldom did anything for fun. He only ate for fuel. The caffeine was simply the stimulant that allowed him to work ungodly hours without collapse.

He waited in the checkout line behind Kinkaid. "Hey," he said to Sami, finally noticing him, "What brings you here so early?"

"The espresso. They guy who runs the machine is actually Italian, and knows what he's doing."

"You mean it matters?" Kinkaid smiled as he paid the clerk. "I thought the idea was just to make it as bitter and awful as you could, and then sell it to people who have spent a long time convincing themselves it tastes good."

"No, no," Sami replied enthusiastically. "There is a huge difference.

Lots of factors. Probably the most important are the quality of the coffee beans and the freshness of the coffee when it's handed to you. He does a great job."

"Well, good," Kinkaid said. "You got a minute?"

"Sure," Sami shrugged, a little concerned. He paid for his espresso and followed Kinkaid to the corner of the room, where they sat at a small round table. "What's up?"

"I don't know," Kinkaid said, taking a drink. "I try to read people. Sometimes I'm right. I'm getting the feeling that there's something eating you about our task force. Something's going on in there," he said, pointing to Sami's head.

"I hope there's something going on in here," Sami said, trying to make his response sound lighthearted. He wasn't ready to talk about things yet, but he did have serious concerns.

"So what's going on?"

"Nothing, really."

"Horseshit," Kinkaid said with such force that it caught Sami completely off guard.

"What?"

"That's horseshit. Don't try to blow smoke at me, Sami. Something's bugging you. What is it?"

"You really want to know?"

"Yeah, I really do."

"I don't trust the Israelis."

Kinkaid was surprised. "Huh? What do they have to do with any of this?"

"They might be behind the whole thing."

"What whole thing?"

"The whole stinking mess. The whole thing may have been just to get the United States more deeply involved. To do their dirty work for them."

"What the hell are you talking about?"

"Think about it. A nice Navy Lieutenant met a beautiful girl who turned out to be Israeli. She lured him back to Israel, where he was promptly murdered—"

"So was—"

"You wanted to hear it, let me finish," Sami said more abruptly than he'd intended. "He got killed, then something happened in Lebanon that may have involved a Navy plane. I'm not sure what happened there, but let's assume one of our pilots went on his own private revenge attack with the Israeli Air Force. That sure as hell was with their consent, and would almost certainly have been their *idea*. No doubt. Then this Sheikh guy got all pissed at the U.S. because we were on the attack, which the Syrians claim to have figured out all by themselves, and his guys start attacking U.S. citizens all over the damned place. Now we declare war against him and are figuring out how to get back at him and take him out. Exactly what Israel wanted."

"They couldn't do it themselves? You think they're afraid of this lunatic?"

"He's not a *lunatic*," Sami said, shaking his head. "Trust me, he is no lunatic. He may be wrong, and misguided, even evil, but he's not a lunatic."

"So who attacked the bus and killed this Lieutenant and his girl-friend?"

"You saw the reports. Men in Israeli Army uniforms."

"So the *Israelis* attacked the bus and killed their own people?" Kinkaid exclaimed. "*You're* the lunatic! Don't go irrational on me, Sami! I can't afford to lose you."

"I'm not being irrational. I'm thinking about angles you may not be. You have to look at *all* the angles, Joe. All of them!"

"And then the Sheikh cooperated and took responsibility for the attack? Where are you getting this stuff, Sami? Get off it before you stink up the whole place."

"If the order comes from high enough, the Mossad would do anything."

"I'll see you at the task force meeting," Kinkaid said disgustedly. He got up and walked out of the cafeteria.

Sami hadn't even touched his espresso. He had sounded stupid, like some conspiracy theorist. He hadn't thought it through all the way. Still, it was possible.

✍

The *Washington* Battle Group steamed northward two hundred miles off the coast of Lebanon. Woods and Wink had waited anxiously for the final word. They were sure that at some point, someone would cancel their flight. That's what always happened. When it came time to pull the trigger, politicians and Admirals wanted everything to be perfect, and it never was. So they had waited, certain the strike would be called off at the last possible moment.

They went up the small ladder that rose from the catwalk to the flight deck, leaning backward into the wind automatically as they moved aft toward the fantail and their waiting Tomcat. Woods glanced up at the night sky through the dim red floodlights that lit the deck. He could see the stars faintly. A perfect, crisp night for flying.

Wink started around the Tomcat counterclockwise as Woods began his preflight clockwise. Woods looked for leaking hydraulic fluid the way an ER doctor would look for blood. Both red, and both would mean death if the bleeding wasn't found. Only Woods had to look for his in the dark. It was one of the most important things in his life tonight. The fluids inside the titanium and composite skin were more important to him now than the blood running through the veins of a lot of people in the world.

Woods wanted the people who had killed Vialli so much he could taste it. Their mission was to drop laser-guided bombs on the fortress where they thought the Sheikh was most likely to be. He wished he could ride one of the bombs like Slim Pickens in *Dr. Strangelove*— but without dying.

Woods walked underneath the F-14 and saw the dark shadows of the GBU-10s underneath. The ordies had already placed the laser guidance noses on the massive, two-thousand-pound bombs.

Wink stared at the bombs. "Know what I like about these bombs?" he asked Woods.

"What?" Woods said.

"They just make shit go away. Just vanish. That's so cool."

Woods smiled at Wink, who was being much more talkative than usual. "Probably should be carrying the GBU-24s, though."

Wink agreed. "Bunker busters. Maybe on our next hop."

"We'll see."

Woods ran his bare hand along the underbelly of the Tomcat and turned on his mini Maglite flashlight now and then to check for the telltale red hydraulic fluid. He went as far aft underneath the F-14 as he could until he came up to the edge of the flight deck. He shone his flashlight as far back as the light would reach out where the tail of the plane was hanging over the water that was eighty feet below, examining it carefully.

He turned back, going forward, until he was by the left jet intake. Now he was in a hurry. He could feel the tension building throughout the ship as launch time grew closer. No one had canceled it. It might actually happen.

He slipped into the front cockpit and Benson hurried over to stand next to Woods on the access step. He reached over, grabbing the shoulder harness fittings and handing them to Woods, one at time. Benson connected Woods's G-suit to the environmental system that fed air in direct proportion to the G forces experienced.

"All set, sir?" Benson asked, already knowing the answer.

"All set, Benson. Thanks. Wish us luck."

"Be safe, sir," Benson said.

"Roger that," Woods answered, checking the switches in the cockpit of the Tomcat and pulling the elastic strap of the knee board around his right thigh.

Wink watched Benson climb down and fold the ladder up into the Tomcat. Wink checked both sides of the plane and looked up at the large canopy that stuck into the sky at a forty-five-degree angle. "Clear!" he announced in a loud voice.

"Clear," Woods said.

Wink pushed the handle of the canopy forward and it closed.

The engines were turning beautifully, the engine instruments hovering in the middle of acceptable ranges. Woods signaled Airman Benson, who disconnected the huffer and power cable. Wink ran through his checklist carefully. Woods's hands darted back and forth, instinctively moving switches and knobs until the cockpit was set up perfectly and the systems all checked out. He could almost do it without thinking, a risk he was particularly aware of tonight. His mind wasn't worrying about cockpit switches—he was thinking about SAMs and the Syrian Air Force, which would like nothing better than to be able to engage him, and ideally, ask *him* a few questions.

He put his feet on the top of the rudder pedals to hold the brakes as Benson took the tie-down chains off and moved the chocks away from the wheels. Benson glanced at Woods and Wink and saluted sharply. Woods returned his salute in the dark, then saw that the yellow shirt was ready to start him taxiing toward the catapult.

"Hot mike," Woods said as they moved toward the bow catapult. He glanced down at the clock on his dashboard and saw that it was ten minutes before the time for his launch. It was also five minutes before the scheduled launch of the Tomahawk missiles. No one knew what Syria would do. All they had was a warning from the Syrian Ambassador to the United Nations. He had called a press conference immediately after the declaration of war by the United States and had told the Americans in unequivocal terms that any attack on Syrian soil would be perceived as an act of war against Syria. This had given the politicians some pause. The reaction in the VF-103 Ready Room had been: Excellent! Come on up.

Woods squinted at an enormous flash that lit the horizon to his left. As he watched, a fireball climbed into the sky and suddenly another, then another, all of them coming from the vertical launchers of the destroyers that surrounded the carrier. Five more glowing, burning missiles flew up from the ships and headed east after the first.

"Holy shit," Wink said, almost speechless as he too watched the Tomahawks head inland. "We're really going to do this."

"Sure looks like it. You ready?" Woods asked, his heart racing, now in full sprint. The Tomahawk launch had caught him off guard, a let's-go-to-war exclamation point.

"Ready."

"Lights on." Woods flipped the light switch on the outside of the throttle with his left hand and the exterior lights of the F-14 illuminated. It told everyone on the flight deck they were ready. The aircraft suddenly jerked down and was ripped forward accelerating almost instantly. They were pulled along the length of the catapult and thrown off the bow of the carrier at one hundred thirty-five knots.

"We're flying," Wink said, his eyes locked on the altimeter and airspeed indicators, watching for any sign of loss of altitude or speed. He wanted to make sure that he had enough time to eject if they started down. He had about three seconds to make the decision if things went badly.

"Gear up. Flaps up," Woods said as he threw the levers. More Tomahawks flew up into the sky from a distant destroyer, the last group of the unmanned land attack missiles that would get there long before the Air Wing and soften up the approach to their targets.

Woods heard Fungo, Lieutenant Commander Lyle Tourneaux, the Admin Officer who was also Bark's RIO, call airborne as Bark flew the second Tomcat into the dark sky three miles behind.

Wink checked out the systems and turned on all his sensors. The radar was picking up everything in the sky. The huge wattage output of AWG-9 radar was unparalleled in aviation. It could pick out a bomber-sized target a hundred twenty miles away, and calculate launch solutions on twenty-four targets at once. It displayed them all on the PTID, the clear and understandable display screen in the backseat.

He trained the radar around to the starboard side of the Tomcat as they completed the turn waiting for the rest of the airplanes in the strike. The radar swept over Syria. Go ahead, Wink thought. You want F-14 radar energy to talk about? Have some of this. He looked anxiously for the fighters that might come from Syria to stop them. Nothing but airline traffic.

Woods glanced at Wink's radar picture, which was repeated on his Visual Display Indicator. "Looking for Syrian fighters?" he asked.

"You can always hope."

"The day Syria sends fighters up after American planes at night will be the day you and I have simultaneous heart attacks."

"Don't think they'll come?"

"You heard the intel brief. I don't think they've even flown at night, let alone *fought* anybody at night. Plus after we hit their SAMs and blow up the Sheikh they'll be able to bluster about it. If we whack a bunch of their fighters to boot, they'll just look stupid."

"So all we need to worry about are the long skinny ones without pilots."

"Right. The SAMs."

Simultaneous flashes illuminated the horizon.

"Look at that! SAMs trying to hit the Tomahawks. Good luck."

"I *love* that!" Wink exclaimed. "One stupid missile trying to shoot down another stupid missile!"

To his left Woods saw Bark rendezvousing on him from across the circle. Woods and Bark both had their anticollision lights off for the night hop. They could see each other only by the green, rectangular formation lights. Bark slid toward Woods expertly at exactly the right closure rate. Woods eased his turn a little to make the rendezvous even less difficult. "Bark's joining on us," he told Wink, who had his head buried in the charts and mission planning.

"Roger," Wink said absently, and then looked at the time. "We've got to head inland in ten minutes."

"Rog," Woods replied. "How's your data link picture?"

"EA-6B's ten miles ahead. The two F-18 HARM shooters are on his wing." The EA-6B was to jam every radar of consequence on the way in and out for the strike. The F-18s were waiting for a fire control radar—a surface to air missile or AAA to turn on. "Looks like the guys off the *Eisenhower* are ready to go into Syria. Everybody's in place."

As Bark slid under Wood's F-14 and moved out to his right, Woods saw the sky being peppered with tracers and glowing missile flames. "Check that out."

Wink's eyes shifted from his radar and his navigation to focus inland. "That's where we're going."

"Combat checklist," Wink prompted.

"Okay," Woods replied. He started reciting the checklist from memory.

Wink knew that Woods had the checklist memorized but he always turned to the written checklist he carried on his knee board. He didn't trust himself or anyone else to remember everything when combat approached. He swore by the adage that when the balloon goes up, 90 percent of your brains go to your butt to squeeze it off as tight as it will go.

Woods pushed the throttles forward to military power and started the F-14 up to their ingress altitude of forty thousand feet to avoid most of the SAM envelopes.

The LANTIRN pod under the right wing of the Tomcat was the key to the strike. The F-14 had proved itself to be one of the best night attack fighters in the world once it had learned to use the LANTIRN pod. It stood for Low Altitude Navigation and Targeting for Night. When night-vision devices were worn the LANTIRN allowed the F-14 to fly very low, very fast, and drop bombs at night with deadly accuracy.

Woods leveled off at forty thousand feet. Bark, on his wing, had taken a trail position, flying loosely behind Woods, headed inland.

"Ten seconds," Wink said.

"Roger."

Wink watched their symbol cross over the way-point on his PTID exactly on time. "Three, two, one. Take heading 083," Wink said.

Woods steadied the Tomcat on the new heading.

"Set five hundred fifty knots," Wink said.

Woods pushed the throttles forward to the stops, short of afterburner. Wink studied the display on his PTID as he watched the EA-6B and the F-18 HARM shooters fifteen miles in front. They were at thirty thousand feet, hunting SAM radars. They would head down the corridor for the attack and hope that Syria, or Lebanon, or the Hezbollah, or whoever ran the SAM sights surrounding the Bekáa Valley, would be unwilling to allow the Americans to just strike with impunity, unable to resist turning on their SAM radars at least to see what was coming. As soon as the radars went on, the EA-6B would lock on to their position, then launch their HARM missiles or the F-18s would launch theirs. Even if the radar shut down, the missiles would remember where they were. It was a very hungry missile.

The radios were silent. The Tomcat passed through five hundred knots to five hundred fifty. The air streamed by their two-thousand-pound bombs so quickly that it made a slight buzz, or hum, underneath the plane.

Woods felt odd being in the lead with his Commanding Officer on his wing. It was all because of Wink, the top RIO in the squadron, the one who was without a doubt the best at running an attack with the LANTIRN system, the one sure to put the bombs on the target. Everybody knew it, including Bark. So Wink was taking them in and showing them where to go.

"Feet dry," Wink called as they passed over the beach of Lebanon and headed inland. "Good thing we got that stealth paint," he cracked.

"You wish. See any airplanes?"

"Negative."

"Push over in ten minutes."

"Glad Lebanon's small."

Wink's voice suddenly raised slightly in pitch. "We've got a SAM site at nine o'clock lighting us up. Fire control radar."

Woods quickly lowered the left wing to look for a SAM launch. Nothing but darkness.

"See anything?"

"Not yet. They're just tickling us."

"EA-6B should be reading him. Bomb switches set?"

"Yeah. We're set. LANTIRN system checks good."

"Everyone else in position?"

Wink checked his PTID. "Yes. We're set—" Suddenly a very distinctive warble pierced their ears. "SAM launch, SAM launch!" Wink cried.

Woods searched the sky. "Where?"

"Two o'clock!" Woods dipped his right wing and looked beneath the plane. He saw a red ball tearing up from the ground toward them. It was the missile motor burning as it pushed the weight of the surface-to-air missile uphill.

"Chaff!" Wink urged.

Woods hit the white button on the stick with his thumb and fired off a preprogrammed series of chaff. Underneath the tails at the back of the airplane small cylinders of tightly packed metal foil fired down from the F-14. They immediately burst into small clouds of falling metal strips to attract the radar's attention away from the Tomcat, which made an excellent radar reflector in its own right.

The best radars, though, looked not only for reflected energy, but reflected energy that moved. The chaff stopped dead behind the Tomcat, as the airplane continued forward. If it was a newer radar, or upgraded, it would track the plane through the chaff release. Woods turned to his left to put the missile directly on his right wing as it continued to climb up after them. It had nothing else on its mind except to have a collision with Woods and Wink. As soon as the missile was ninety degrees off, Woods rolled the Tomcat over on its back and pulled down hard toward the earth. He leaned harder still, using the added acceleration of gravity to move them down quickly, to achieve the maximum possible change in position from the missile. As the nose of the Tomcat dropped and the missile peaked and headed down after them, Woods rolled level and headed up in a 7-G pull away from the earth. Woods watched the missile continue to close on them.

"They're still locked on!" Wink said grimly.

A bright flash lit the horizon in front of them. Woods tore his eyes from the missile momentarily to see whether an airplane had fired on them. It was a missile, but from the EA-6B. A HARM—a High Speed Anti-Radiation Missile—luxuriating in the energy that was guiding the SAM toward Woods. The HARM raced down toward the source of the energy, ready to explode on the transmitter. The HARM gave the SAM site operator two choices—leave the radar on and eat the HARM, or shut down the radar, and lessen his chances of dying.

Wink watched the strobe on the ALR-67 radar warning indicator that showed where the SAM had come from. They maneuvered up, then down, as the missile continued to track them, but then suddenly diverted its attention from the Tomcat, appearing to lose interest. Woods watched the missile fly straight again. "Strobe?"

"Gone," Wink said, glancing down at the indicator. "We're clear."

"He saw the HARM coming," Woods said, steadying out on his original course.

Bark rejoined in loose trail on Woods's wing and they pressed on toward the target.

"Fifteen miles to the target," Wink announced, forcing himself to walk through the bombing run. "Everything looks good."

"*SAM! SAM! SAM!*" someone yelled over the radio. It chilled Woods and Wink, who had yet to settle down after their close call. They both jerked their heads around searching for a new SAM. Wink checked the radar warning screen but it was uncluttered with fire control radars.

Wink called to Woods. "Come starboard hard to 070. Beginning release run." In the backseat he checked the switches on the AWG-15 weapons panel to ensure he hadn't changed the drop settings for the bombing run.

Woods responded immediately to Wink's request. "How's the LANTIRN system?" he asked, concerned about the high G maneuvering the pod had endured during the attempt to evade the SAM.

"Sweet. I've got a good picture." He looked at the infrared image on the screen. "Clear as a bell. It made it easy to pick a target. There it is, Trey. The fortress, bigger than shit. One minute," Wink warned, watching the precalculated release point timer count down.

Woods checked his switches and prepared for the release.

Wink was focused on making the bombing run perfect. He didn't know what the bomb would do by way of damage, but he sure could say where it was going to hit. "Three, two, one." Woods pressed the release button on the panel and the two laser-guided bombs dropped off the Tomcat and headed silently toward the earth.

As soon as Woods felt the release, he pulled up and left, ensuring that the laser designator stayed on the target.

"Good release!" Wink exclaimed. The hop was all worth it now to Wink. They had done their job, and Bark was dropping right behind them. "Good target," Wink said, seeing the image of the crosshairs on the exact place where he had designated the bombs to hit, just at the base of the fortress, calculated to do the most damage to the structure. "Five seconds to impact," Wink said. He stared at the image waiting anxiously for the explosion. Suddenly the screen lit up at the same time the sky did five miles away when the two enormous bombs slammed into the centuries-old fortress in Lebanon.

"War's on," Woods said as he headed toward the Med.

"Home base, 263 for two hundred thirty."

"Roger that. Let's get out of here," Woods said.

31

S ean Woods sat in the ready room chair in the briefing area and fought to stay awake. He had been operating on adrenaline for so long that when the excitement of flying in combat waned, he was left more exhausted than he would have been otherwise. He'd been up for twenty hours. He had flown the first strike into Lebanon and was about to fly on the last strike of the night. He could smell himself. He waited for 0230, for the brief to start for his next hop. His launch time was 0430.

The sorties after his first had been met with even more resistance even though they had expended as much effort hitting the SAM sites as they had the fortress. They had suppressed the SAMs somewhat, but not enough to satisfy those who were about to fly over them again.

His eyes were scratchy. They seemed to be the focus of his existence as he closed them to capture some moisture. We should have used more Tomahawks, he thought. But he also knew they cost a million dollars each, and one laser-guided bomb was only fifty thou, assuming of course that the zillion-dollar F-14 that was dropping the fifty-thou bomb didn't get shot down.

Wink sauntered back from the front of the ready room and sat next to Sean. They didn't speak. They knew each other better than brothers. They knew the things to look for in the other that might be a sign of a problem, especially a problem that might cause a flight to be unsafe.

Big and Sedge sat down as the spare crew just as the Air Wing Intelligence Officer came on the closed circuit TV.

"Morning," he said curtly, obviously as tired as the aircrew were. "The next event will be the final night's strikes against our target. Moving quickly to what you probably want to know about first—the battle against the SAMs we've been waging all night. We've had great success. As you know, one of the problems with mobile SAM systems is that they are mobile. The ones that have been brought in by Syria, contrary to our expectations, were used more frequently and were more capable than what we had been led to expect. The Syrians have apparently shipped a number of their SA-6s into the area as well as SA-13s. Although we've had success, we think they're still focusing on the western approach to the target. We've recommended to most of you who will be going feet dry that you change your approach to make it farther to the north to actually make the final bombing runs from the east to the west . . ."

"We got time to change our route?" Woods asked Wink, concerned.

"Already did."

"When?" Woods asked, surprised.

"When you were snoring in your ready room chair like a dying calf," Wink replied.

Woods swallowed and confirmed the dryness of the back of his throat. He hadn't even known he'd been asleep. "I was preoxygenating. Loading up on extra air, for the hop. Makes your brain clearer."

Wink rolled his head toward Woods and looked at him without saying anything. Woods just stared at the screen.

The Air Wing Intel Officer went on, unaware of the various distractions in the ready rooms of the aviators that were watching him. "Let me show you the SAM sights that are currently operating." He turned to a chart of the target area with the telltale red circles. "The new ingress corridors are clear. We don't expect any SAM activity until you reach the target areas." He went on to describe in general the mission for each airplane on the event.

"As to the success we've been having against the target, we haven't had a chance to do much BDA," referring to Bomb Damage Assessment, "as it is still dark. What we can tell is that we've been hitting the target, and hitting it hard. We'll have to wait until light to get a better feel for whether we're having the success we hope for."

When the intelligence brief was completed, Woods went to the podium in the back of the small briefing area in the ready room to finish the section's brief for the hop. He leaned on the podium. "This is it. Last hop of the night. I'm tired. You probably are too. We have to set that aside. I think adrenaline is going to be as important as JP-5 tonight," he said, referring to the jet fuel used by the Tomcat. "We've got to stay alert. We need to start thinking supersonic now, to make sure we don't miss anything. Pritch has given us updated charts." He moved the sliding map board to reveal a detailed chart of all of Lebanon, prepared with tremendous detail. There was a large white box on the lower right corner of the chart. It said: "Current as of 0217."

"Kudos for Pritch," Wink said, pleased.

Woods went on with his brief. "If in fact the SAM sites are where they're shown, this should not be too tough. Many of them, though, are mobile SAMs. They could be moved, but it seems unlikely to me that these guys are going to drag SAM sites around in the middle of the night to any great extent. I think our chances are pretty good to stay free of them.

"Our load-out is the same it's been all night: two GBU-10s, two Sparrows, and two Sidewinders. We've got up-LANTIRN pods on both birds. Wink and I will be in the lead.

"We don't expect any fighter opposition." He paused. "But sometimes you get what you don't expect. The Israelis got plenty of fighter opposition when they went into Lebanon a while ago—to an area not far from where we've been going. We've heard. So we'll see. Don't assume anything. It's unlikely they'll come after us because it will be dark. Let's go."

✍

Skate Wilson didn't like the setup around the Rabat embassy at all. Since the arrival of the Snapshot Team he had spent his time finding the best observation posts and angles for the evening's work. None of it met with his satisfaction. They were too close to many other buildings. Very easy for a sniper or bomber to set up. Even for a mortar, if someone were so inclined, a dangerous and deadly weapon that terrorists hadn't used since the IRA tried to take out 10 Downing Street from a few blocks away with a mortar in the back of a van with a canvas top. Clever, but ultimately unsuccessful.

After circling the entire inside of the building several times like a cat, Wilson reluctantly chose the best of several bad locations for his team members to position themselves with their equipment. He set up a heavy tripod and opened a case to remove the enormous lens of a nightscope. He was screwing the tripod into the base of the scope when the door opened behind him. Wilson watched the door as he continued what he was doing. It was the American Ambassador to Morocco himself.

"Hello," the Ambassador said to Wilson in a friendly tone. "I figured you're the one in charge of this surveillance thing."

"Yes, sir."

"What are you looking for?"

"Anything out of the ordinary at all."

"Don't you think they will be expecting us to look for them?"

Wilson adjusted the scope and tested its balance on the tripod. It was perfectly weighted so the attachment point was exactly in the middle and moved easily and precisely. "Probably."

"But it still makes sense to do this?"

"Does to me."

"Why did they pick this embassy? Do you know? I mean there are a lot of embassies out there. Why this one?"

"You mean why are we here?"

"Well, yes."

"Teams have gone to several embassies. But here . . ." Wilson closed the case for the site and placed it out of the way. "Probably because of the photographs."

"Those pictures the Marines took?"

"Right."

"Really? Hmm. I didn't think they showed very much."

Wilson wasn't going to humor him. "Probably right. They didn't show much at all."

"Well then, this is really just an exercise, isn't it?"

"You bet, sir."

"How long do you think it will take to find this Sheikh person?"

The Ambassador was beginning to annoy Wilson. Politicians generally did. He didn't answer, intending his nonresponsiveness as an insult.

The Ambassador didn't pick up on the insult. His thoughts were elsewhere. "Well, I believe they already have it narrowed down, and will be dropping some big bombs on him soon, if they haven't already."

"That will take care of it then." Wilson thought of Ricketts. Laser-guided bombs. Right. Easy mission. No problem. Over tomorrow. "That how you think these people work?"

"I think in this case, it may well end the whole thing. This seems like an operation run by one man. If he's gone, that may very well end it."

Wilson pulled a second tripod out of a nylon bag and started to extend the legs. "You ever heard of this guy before?"

"No. No one had before he started killing people."

"The Old Man of the Mountains goes back nine hundred years. There's *always* someone to replace him." Wilson adjusted night-vision goggles over his eyes. The Ambassador suddenly looked ominous— Wilson could see his dilated pupils. He looked like a zombie. Wilson directed his attention outside, through the crack in the gauze curtains. The side streets were clearly visible.

"Well, I guess that's right," the Ambassador said a full ten seconds after a normal response would have been due.

Wilson saw someone move toward a doorway in an alleyway beside the embassy. He took off his night-vision goggles, reached for the huge night-vision scope, and pointed it toward the doorway, where a man stood, his face covered. Wilson transmitted on the lip mike that trailed a cable to the radio on his belt. It was digital and secure. *"Suspect at 26/33, grid 6. Get the locals out there."*

He heard a double-click on the radio in response. Wilson waited. The man appeared to be expecting someone. He should have moved long ago. Wilson wanted to check his watch but didn't want to take his eye off the suspect, who still lingered in the doorway, extremely cautious. Wilson's attention was drawn to movement through tiny side streets two blocks away. Two police officers approached the quiet street carefully. Wilson listened to the sounds of rhythmic cars throughout the city as the two walked toward the doorway brushing against the stucco along the wall of the building as they approached.

The Ambassador interrupted his thoughts. "So how long you think—"

"Just a minute," Wilson said as the two policemen the Ambassador couldn't see cautiously neared the doorway. Wilson watched them as the sounds of distant cars interrupted the silence with their unceasing honking even though there was no other traffic below.

The policemen gripped their automatic rifles as they crept along the wall ten feet from the opening. Suddenly they charged the doorway, rifles ready. Wilson watched the fuzzy green images, horrified, as they stepped in front of the doorway and pointed their weapons at the unidentified man. The policemen were thrown back into the street, the fire from the silenced machine pistol surprising Wilson as much as it did them. He could hear their weapons clatter to the stone street as they fell backward.

Wilson stared helplessly as the intruder, his face still covered, walked confidently away from the embassy down the narrow street. He transmitted on the encrypted radio, *"Race, you there?"*

"Here."

"Get on the Sat phone. Tell them we've got contact and our friends know we're onto them. We will pursue, but likelihood of capture or significant intel is low. Tell them to get out as many Snapshot Teams as they can. This guy is taking it to a different level."

The next morning on the *Washington* found a lot of very tired aircrew anxious to know whether the war was over or just beginning. Syria had started the day by going apoplectic about the American attacks. It was a violation of their sovereign statehood. A violation of international law. An act of war against a country that had done nothing to the United States. The outrage must stop.

The Air Wing Intel Officer was conducting an unscheduled brief over the ship's broadcast closed circuit television system to all the ready rooms showing the BDA, based on satellite images and reconnaissance flights that had gone in at dawn.

Every ninety minutes, airplanes off the *Washington* and the *Eisenhower* had gone all night, attacking the targets in Syria and Lebanon and the surrounding SAM and AAA sites. The bombs had mostly been on target, but determining how much damage had actually been done was difficult. They also now had evidence that several mobile SAM sites had been moved to the areas around the targets during the night and might be operational within twelve hours.

"As you can see, we've had numerous hits with our laser-guided bombs on the fortresses that were our targets last night. The damage is obvious, here, and . . . here, and on the side, there. It is impossible to know how much internal damage has been caused. These hills are very hard. The bombs didn't penetrate very deeply, and if he is underground, we surely didn't get him."

The Air Wing Intelligence Officer put up a video image of Marines landing their helicopters on a field and running out of them. "This is the video provided to the news media in the States to show on their news programs. It is what is likely to happen next, according to all sources. The President believes the only way to truly get the Sheikh is to put troops on the ground and go after him. That is why the Marines are preparing to go to both fortresses on the ground within the next forty-eight hours.

"Additionally, the Army has flown the 82nd Airborne to Sigonella, Sicily, and told them to prepare for a drop into Syria."

The Jolly Rogers couldn't believe their ears. If Syria was angry about some bombs being dropped on an old fortress in the mountains, the response to landing American troops on their soil would be volcanic. Syria would be required to respond. How could they possibly just let Americans walk into their country with armed troops?

"We will continue to try to soften the fortresses, but the assessment of the intelligence community is that ultimately it will be necessary to put troops on the ground. To ID the Sheikh, if for no other reason. How will we know we've gotten him if we don't ID him?"

"Any indication of what Lebanon or Syria might do?" asked a voice off screen.

"Well, they have told us in no uncertain terms that they believe everything we're doing violates their sovereignty, and their territorial integrity. This will simply make it worse. The idea of CNN broadcasting footage of Marines landing on Lebanese or Syrian territory and walking toward the target is almost sure to make them try to take action earlier rather than later. But so what? I think the thought process is that they have been harboring terrorists for years, decades. They have supported, directly, the murderers of many hundreds of people. They are now protecting and shielding perhaps the most vicious self-appointed murderer of the new millennium. I think it is fair for the United States to ask whether Syria, or anyone else, is really intending to stand on behalf of the Sheikh.

"The sixty-four-thousand-dollar question, of course, is where *exactly* is this Sheikh? Everything I've seen"—he looked off screen for confirmation, and nodded—"seems to tell me that we don't really know where he is. His most probable locations are where we've been going. Plus, of course, the target in Iran, which we haven't yet attacked."

Kinkaid sat in his office and studied the Bomb Damage Assessment reports on the fortresses the Navy had hit all night. He didn't hear the STU-III phone as it rang repeatedly. One of his people walked by his office and came back to look at him, wondering why he wasn't answering his phone. Kinkaid saw him, and then heard the phone. He picked it up. "Yes."

"Joseph. How are you?"

Kinkaid immediately recognized the deep voice, the heavy accent. "To what to do I owe the honor, Efraim?"

"Greetings, good friend. I wanted to talk about the events of last night."

Kinkaid settled back in his chair. His mind shifted out of idle, where it had been for hours. He knew he would need all his faculties for this conversation. He stood up as he held the receiver to his ear. "How have you been?"

"Well. I wanted to talk about the strikes."

"You and I have never failed to get someone we went after, have we?"

"We have had some success."

"I don't think we've ever failed, have we?"

"Just once. Cypress."

"I'd forgotten. Did he ever surface?"

"Never. We think they might have killed him just so we would always think he was out there."

"Well, that would be just as good then. Other than him, we've had success."

"Yes. It pays to have friends on whom you can rely, Joseph."

"The problem with great friendship in our business," Kinkaid said, "is that the greater the trust, the greater the exposure to betrayal. Like a marriage."

Efraim paused, considering what Kinkaid had said. He had thrown large pieces of ice into a conversation Efraim had tried to start warmly.

Efraim hesitated. "There is something you want to say to me."

"This thing has come together in a very . . . curious way. I need to know about it. I need to know about the woman, Irit. What was she doing with the Navy Lieutenant?"

"Why?"

"It is what started all of this."

"Started? How?" Efraim asked, puzzled.

"It was the Sheikh's first move."

"No, it wasn't. Gaza was."

"Okay, second move, but part of the plan. So who was she?"

"She was Israeli."

"We know that. Who did she work for?"

"I'm not at liberty to say."

"Why's that? She must have been with the Mossad then, or you would say," Kinkaid pointed out. "This whole thing is very real now. Not just intelligence people talking among themselves. We have declared war on this man, and we have attacked his strongholds in sovereign countries. Some of it is based on what *you've* told us, and you won't tell me what may have started the whole thing? That strikes me as odd."

Efraim waited.

"What was she doing in Italy?"

"She was on vacation."

"Truly?" Kinkaid replied with doubt. He listened carefully to Efraim's reply, which came after just the slightest hesitation.

"That is my understanding."

"Let me be clear," Kinkaid said. "Was she targeting an American Naval officer as a possible source of intelligence information?"

"Of course not, what a ridiculous thought. Joe, you have been watching too many Hollywood movies."

"Really. Let's talk about Jonathan Pollard."

"An unfortunate incident. We had nothing to do with that. I was unaware of it until it was too late. We don't spy in America."

"Sure. What about how she met this Naval officer."

"I don't know much of their meeting."

"It was on a train. Supposedly circumstantial." Kinkaid tried to listen to the tones in Efraim's voice. "I don't believe in coincidences. Do you?"

"Yes, absolutely. A lack of belief in coincidences is the beginning of paranoia."

"So convince me that her meeting him was a coincidence. Not only that they just happened to meet on the train, but she then lied to him about who she was."

"Of course she did. She would not be free to talk about her position. Do you? When you go to a party and someone asks you what you do, do you say, immediately, I am in Director of Counter-Terrorism at the CIA? Don't be ridiculous."

"So you admit she was involved in intelligence and that's why she didn't tell him the truth?"

"I admit nothing of the kind."

"It's more than that, Efraim. She said she was Italian."

"Just playing the game. Flirting. I'm sure."

"Really. It has got a paranoid officer on my task force thinking. His theory is that she was sent to Italy—Naples, of all places, not exactly a prime Italian tourist destination—to make contact with an American Naval officer. The objective was to somehow entangle the United States more deeply in the Middle East. The most paranoid officer has a really odd theory. Like to hear it?"

"By all means," Efraim said guardedly.

"She was sent to Italy to lure Tony Vialli—or someone like him—to Israel. Once there, he would be assassinated."

"By whom?"

"Israel. The attack on the bus was done to look like an assault by the Sheikh you had been tracking. Such an act of terrorism would make the U.S. furious. You expected us to respond by going after him, which you were either unable or afraid to do. You wanted the United States to be at war with the Sheikh, or at least almost at war. You knew we would go into places that you either wouldn't or couldn't. You wanted us to fight your fight for you."

"Afraid?" Efraim laughed humorlessly. "We're not afraid to go *anywhere*. We're the ones who bombed Iraq's nuclear reactors while the world condemned us. We're the ones who flew our F-15s to attack PLO camps in Tunisia by air refueling long-range. We are the ones who found the PLO number two and killed him in his home in Tunisia. We flew to Entebbe and attacked those who were holding hostage an airplane full of Jews. Afraid? That's ridiculous."

"So you deny it?" Kinkaid said, feeling awkward about pressing a theory he didn't accept.

"It is ridiculous and offensive. And it is impossible."

"How's that?"

"Why would we kill our *own* citizens? And the Sheikh has publicly claimed responsibility for the attack."

"I thought you might say that. In fact that was the very question I wondered about. But I've been thinking about it."

"And what is your answer, Joseph?"

"I don't have one. I don't think you'd kill your own people, but there are a lot of things that still surprise me in the world. And the Sheikh? Lots of groups take responsibility for every terrorist attack, and any kind of document can be forged. If he hadn't claimed responsibility, maybe we would have gotten some of that helpful intelligence from you telling us that you had figured it out, and he was the one responsible. I would have been very grateful to you, I'm sure."

"So not only are we vicious, and murder our own innocent people, we're stupid as well? We wear our own uniforms so nobody will think it's us? And if it doesn't work, we'll just lie to you about it?"

"No, you wear your own uniforms so when asked you can say, 'What do you think we are, stupid?' "

"Yes. Well, I think we've gone as far as we can down this ridiculous road. It is simply untrue, and it's outrageous. I can't believe that you, of all people, have spent even one minute of your busy time thinking about such a story. You must listen to our thirty years of friendship."

"So you deny it?"

"Yes. Absolutely I do. Her meeting of the Lieutenant was a coincidence. I assure you. I cannot explain why she claimed to be Italian. Maybe she thought if she told him she was Jewish he wouldn't be interested. Young love. Who knows? But I assure you, there was nothing to do with us. Her work had nothing to do with recruiting an American for any reason at all. Her current job dealt more with a specialty she had, as an Arab linguist."

"Why were they going to Tel Aviv?"

"She was interviewing for a position with El Al. Just as she told the Lieutenant."

"She was getting out?"

"She had had enough. Since the accident."

"Maybe you're being deceived yourself."

"It is not possible."

Kinkaid cradled the phone receiver against his shoulder. He glanced at his Styrofoam coffee cup sitting on his desk. The cup was full and the coffee was stone cold. "You know about the missile."

Efraim replied, "The Syrians."

"Yes."

"The missile was yours."

"Exactly. The story Raytheon put out was bogus. Or at least partly bogus. They didn't tell the full story."

"Hard to explain," Efraim said.

"You've heard the . . . rumors?"

"That the Syrians are right?"

"Yes," Kinkaid replied.

"There's always a first time."

"If an American plane went into that fight, it was with Israel's consent."

"That would be crazy," Efraim said in an unconvincing tone.

"Not if your objective is to get us drawn in. My paranoid officer thinks that is exactly what happened. It *was* the objective."

Efraim was growing frustrated. "Aahh, Joseph, you *are* crazy. We don't need you to do our dirty work for us. All we need is your money and your weapons. We fight our own fights."

"The Mossad is not completely trusted in this town."

"Nor the CIA in this one."

"It sure could look like the whole thing was a setup. You got an American killed, then, through your Air Force, convinced his room-mate to go on a secret raid into Lebanon. Either way you win. If he gets caught, it's fine—it shows the U.S. is deeply involved already. If he doesn't get caught, you work to get the U.S. in deeper."

"I think we need to spend more time completing our current goal. Getting the Sheikh. That is something we know, and we can agree on. Am I right?"

"Yes."

"I believe I may have some additional information that will prove particularly valuable, and it is why I called. Perhaps it can convince you that our friendship will not be wrecked by a wild-eyed young Turk in your shop."

"What information?"

"The Sheikh's location."

Kinkaid winced. He had been too direct with Efraim, to the point of offense. He was calling to give Kinkaid the very information he had wanted. Now he didn't know if he could rely on it. "Do you know?"

"I can tell you later on in the day, if things go as I hope. It is dependent on a certain communications link. If things go as planned, I should be able to tell you."

"I would like that very much. I'm sorry if I offended you."

"No. It sometimes must be done, even among friends. We should be able to stand a few storms. It cleans the oil off the streets."

"Shall I wait to hear from you?"

"Yes. I must go. Shalom."

"Shalom."

32

I have the information, Joseph. If you still want it. If you think it is reliable."

"You have the Sheikh's location?"

"Yes. I can't tell you how—"

"You sure as hell can, and you will. If you think I'm going to try to sell this to our people, and ultimately the President, I need to know where this information came from and how reliable it is."

Efraim breathed deeply. "After we spoke I sat in my office and stared out the window for many minutes. I was shocked beyond description. Not only that you would believe what you said of Israel but that you would believe it of me. That we would plot to have the United States do our fighting for us and trick you into it. And not just trick you in any way, but by murdering our own people."

"We have longer arms than you. And stronger. And when we get angry, we will accomplish our military objective. You know that. But before we talk about the Sheikh, tell me about Irit."

"I asked them to find everyone who ever knew her. All the stories are the same. She was on vacation by herself. No one had the objective of recruiting an American. I have confirmed that."

Kinkaid wasn't satisfied. "Is Israel above spying on the United States?"

"There used to be people here, you know some of them, who would not think twice. But we believe in the building of a relationship founded on trust. We do not do it anymore. There were a few rogues who had that in mind. They're long gone. This is a new era. Ever since Ehud Barak, who was with Aman—military intelligence as you know—

he has brought a greater sense, of, shall we say, maturity, to everything we do. We want no more mistakes. No more miscalculations. Everything we do, even covert, is reviewed by at least three levels. I have read the reports on the raid. There were no Israelis dressing up as Assassins dressed up as Israelis to fool everyone."

Kinkaid wished he could see his friend's face. He had enough experience to know how people in the intelligence world lie to you. They look you right in the eye and defy you to disbelieve them. "Thank you for checking."

"Yes, of course. It was very difficult. Some wanted to know the origin of the request. I of course had to tell them, and they . . . didn't know how to react. To laugh, or to become furious. They all felt that we need to be on the same side of this one, and it would be very smart for someone sympathetic to the Sheikh to sow doubt between us. They wanted me to ask you about your young Turk. He of the wild eyes. Is there any chance he is sympathetic to the Sheikh? Or at least the greater Arab cause?"

Kinkaid felt as if he had been struck in the gut. "How could that be?"

"What is his name?"

"I can't disclose names of task force members."

"I am about to disclose information to you so sensitive it could put someone's life directly at risk and you won't tell me a name?"

"Let's just say your point is well taken."

"How so?"

"He is Arabic."

"From where did his family come?"

"Syria."

There was a long pause on the scrambled phone line. "Be very careful, Joseph. Friends who are close to you can wield the sharpest knives."

"I will be careful."

"I must ask you to be sure not to tell him the source of the information on the Sheikh that I am about to give you. You must give me your word he will not be allowed to know."

"He's a member of the task force."

"Take him off it. Or create a new compartment. Code word access only. And make sure he's not on the list for access. You must do this for me."

"That could create real problems for me."

"I am not going to risk a man's life because someone is holding something against us." He waited for Kinkaid to interrupt him but Kinkaid was quiet. "You have brought up Pollard before. Tell me, did your Turk bring him up or did you think of Pollard on your own?"

"We both brought it up."

"As I thought."

"Look, I'll make sure he's out of the loop. That's all I can do."

"Your word is good enough," he said reluctantly, hinting of additional reservations. "But if he does somehow get his hands on it, and the information makes it into the wrong hands, it could result in . . . it could have bad results."

"Of course," Kinkaid replied. "Tell me everything you know."

"We spoke of targets last time. Three."

"Yes. The three fortresses."

"Exactly. You have accepted them as legitimate targets, and have been bombing two of them all night—"

"Yes—"

"All except one."

"The one in Iran."

"Yes. The oldest and most important. Alamut. Why have you not attacked there, Joseph?"

"Too far, too hard, and we doubted he would be there when he seems to be staging out of Lebanon or Syria. And our overhead imagery didn't make it look like a place that saw a lot of activity."

"Then you have missed him."

"He's at Alamut?" Kinkaid asked, dismayed.

"He is."

"Are you sure?"

"We're sure. Very sure."

"How can you be so sure? Our satellites don't show anything that gives us that confidence, Efraim. Tell me what gives you such confidence."

"First, you must answer something. If I tell you this information, do I have your assurance that you will use it? I *despise* wasting good intelligence. Too many times, we have gathered information, only to watch the politicians urinate all over it in a big play to advance their own careers. Tell me about the people above you. Are they willing to go into Iran and get this Sheikh? Because if they aren't, I will save the intelligence for my people alone. They know what to do with it."

Kinkaid hesitated. This piece of information could make his career.

He could ride off into the sunset knowing he had brought to the United States the single most important piece of intelligence information in the last decade—the exact location of the one of the most hated and feared terrorists ever to attack the country. He had already promised to cut Sami out of the loop—even though he had no intention of doing it—after the Sheikh. Now he had to *promise* to attack Alamut. Whatever that meant. How could he promise that politicians and the military would do something about anything? And what if they didn't? What was Efraim going to do about it? Not tell him the information? That couldn't be it, because he would already know it. "Yes. They have the nerve. I am sure."

"Can you guarantee they'll pursue the Sheikh? I need your personal assurance, Joseph."

"They will go after him. The only thing keeping them from it now is they don't know where he is."

"But you already know Alamut is a target, and it has not been attacked. They are afraid to go into Iran."

"Not at all. I've already given you our reasons. It was just easier to start with the others."

"I remember your President sitting for four hundred or more days while Iranians held American diplomats hostage in Tehran. Were you afraid of them then?"

Kinkaid laughed to himself. "President Carter had a different way of handling these kinds of things than our current President. He'll go."

"Very well," Efraim concluded. "There is someone on the ground within visual range of Alamut. The Sheikh arrived at Alamut yesterday morning, local time. He went directly into the mountain fortress and is currently there."

"We haven't seen any foot traffic to that fort at all."

"Nor will you. They know your satellite schedule. They are also masters of camouflage."

"How do they know our satellite schedule?"

"Most of them are on the Internet. You type in your latitude and longitude and they tell you when visible satellites will be overhead—"

"But not all of them—"

"And you know of other sites that are trying to do the same for all satellites. There are many people out there who believe intelligence gathering is illegitimate and they try to expose us in whatever way they can. You know all this."

"I didn't think the sites had made it that far, that's all."

"Maybe they haven't. . . . Does your young Turk have access to the satellite schedules?"

Kinkaid thought about it, and realized Sami did have access to the overhead imagery schedule. To a great extent, he was the one who had requested it. "Probably."

Efraim said nothing.

"Where is he likely to be in the fortress? Do you know the structure, how it is organized inside?"

"Yes. We had someone inside—"

"The same person?"

"It doesn't matter," Efraim said, cutting off Kinkaid's inquiry. "The approach is impossible on foot. Tell your people not to send Marines, or airborne troops. They would be able to surround the mountain, and that is all. They could never approach the fortress. The approach is too narrow for even a mule. There are many turns too tight. Only a walking man can approach, and only one at a time and very slowly. And the entire path is guarded by men who hover above you. No one could possibly approach uninvited and live."

"So we bomb him out."

"Ah. That is not so easy, my friend. This is the problem that has confounded us. We cannot send anyone in. They would be killed. With certainty. We cannot send our Air Force, because they could only cause a disturbance. Our bombs cannot reach where they need to go."

"You have the same bombs we have. Are you saying we can't bomb him out?"

"That is exactly what I am saying. His primary room, a large, round room with a stone floor covered with beautiful Persian rugs, is deep inside the fortress. Below what you can see."

"Inside the mountain?"

"Yes. We estimate he is one hundred feet under the surface of the mountain."

"A hundred feet?"

"Yes. Approximately. It could be less or more I suppose, but he is deep inside the mountain."

Kinkaid was stumped. How do you attack someone a hundred feet under the ground? "That's deeper than our Strategic Command Headquarters in the mountains of Wyoming."

"That I wouldn't know."

"We can't drop a nuclear weapon on one man."

"Obviously."

"So how does one attack him?"

"That is what we have been unable to figure out."

"I'll leave it to the experts. If I give them his location, I have done my job."

"That is exactly what I said to my people." Efraim was about to hang up. "Remember what I said, about who knows this information."

Kinkaid bristled. "I heard you. But you have already killed one of ours."

"What do you mean?" Efraim asked, concerned.

"Your Air Force went into Lebanon to get the Sheikh, to drop laser bombs on a motorcycle shop."

"There were many targets in the area—"

"One of which was the motorcycle shop at Dar al Ahmar."

"Perhaps."

"When you dropped your bombs to get the Sheikh, one of my men was there to kidnap him. He would have succeeded. Your bombs killed him instead of the Sheikh."

Efraim didn't know what to say. He had never heard anything about Americans being killed in the raid. "I had no idea. Why didn't you tell me you had someone there, Joseph? We could have worked together."

"Yes. Perhaps I should have."

"It is good that we have talked today. We must talk more. Avoid these things in the future. We must work together to stop this killer. That must be our focus. I'm sorry for your man in Lebanon. If only we had known." He paused. "But at least one of your planes escorted the strike that killed your man."

Kinkaid was stunned. He didn't know what to say. "It's *true*?"

"Joseph."

Kinkaid closed his eyes. "I don't want to know."

⌁

"They *found* him?" Woods asked enthusiastically.

Bark nodded his head with a gleam in his eye. "CIA."

Woods laughed. "The CIA? They couldn't find their ass with both hands."

"Maybe somebody told them."

Woods wanted to know. "So, where is he?"

"That fortress in Iran."

Wink's face sobered. "That Alamut place?"

"Yes," Bark replied. "Northwestern Iran."

"How far is it?" Woods asked. "Where's Pritch?"

"CVIC, I suppose."

Woods looked at Bark. "Are they sure?"

"They're sure." Bark handed him the message they had just received. No one else in the squadron had seen it. "They canceled the ground strike into Syria."

"Must be pretty sure," Woods acknowledged. "How we going to get him?"

"Long way. We're the *only* ones who can get there and put ordnance on target and get back."

Woods glanced at Wink and saw the look he was hoping for. "We'll go," Woods said too quickly.

Bark replied, "You've been flying a lot."

"We can hit it, Skipper. You know that. We will *not* fail."

"May not matter."

"Why?"

He handed him the message. "Guy's buried underground. A hundred feet. We could drop bombs on top of him all day long, and it wouldn't touch him. I'm sure we're not going to send TACAIR into Iran to make a big bang and accomplish nothing."

"Solution to that's easy," Wink said.

They all looked at him.

"Unscheduled sunrise."

"Like we're going to nuke him," Woods said.

"It'd take care of the problem," Wink said, shrugging.

"We'll figure something out," Woods said. "We'll start the planning, figure out the tanking, how far it is . . ."

"Don't assume you're going—"

Woods and Wink headed out the ready room door immediately and down the starboard passageway toward the CVIC. They stepped over the knee knockers deftly and maintained as quick a pace as they could sustain without running into the sailors coming down the passageway in the other direction. They reached CVIC and went immediately into the large central room. There were several Intelligence Officers and aircrew in the room looking at charts and computer screens. Woods scanned the room quickly for Pritch. She was in the corner, studying a chart on the wall.

"Pritch!" Woods said as they walked over to her. "You hear they found the Sheikh?"

"What?" Pritch said, confused.

Woods handed her the message.

She read it. "Where'd you get this?"

"Just came in. Five minutes ago."

She memorized the latitude and longitude listed on the message, handed it back to Woods, and looked at the wall chart. "This is the same fortress we were thinking about before," she said. "Is this the same lat/long?"

Wink shrugged. "Don't know."

She put her finger on a mountain ridge in northwestern Iran. "Right here."

Woods moved closer to the chart and looked over her shoulder. Wink stood on the other side of her. They wanted to know the same thing. Exactly how far it was from their likely launch position. Woods took out his black, government-issue ballpoint pen. He placed it on a longitude line and counted the latitude lines that were each one nautical mile apart all the way along the pen. He picked a spot in the Mediterranean off the coast of Syria, and began moving his pen toward Alamut, counting the pen-lengths to the target. Wink counted on his own. Woods stopped with his pen overlapping the target point. He glanced at Wink.

"Four hundred fifty miles," Wink said, thinking already of flight profiles, fuel requirements, and ordnance load-out.

Woods replied, still staring at the chart for approach points and the likelihood of a direct, straight-in flight like the one his pen had just completed. "One way." He measured the distance again.

Wink did likewise.

"You know what this means," Pritch interrupted.

"What?"

"I don't see anyway we can do this."

"Why not?" Wink asked.

"Look at the last paragraph of this message," she said, handing it to Wink. "They expect him to be seventy-five to a hundred feet underground. We'll never get him."

Wink concentrated. "Got to be some way . . ."

"We'll never send troops on the ground there to get him. Never happen," Woods said.

"I don't know that. It might very well happen," Wink replied.

"So we're out of it?" Pritch said, sounding disappointed.

"Not if we catch him on the surface. Make him come out some how."

"How we going to do that?" Woods asked. "Stick a garden hose down his hole and flush him out? Play 'whack the gopher'?"

"I don't hear anything smart coming from you."

"I'll think of something," Woods promised.

Those in CVIC turned their attention to the television, which was tuned to CNN. They watched the Syrian Ambassador to the United Nations read his prepared statement.

"Yesterday, as night fell on the peace-loving people of Syria, the United States launched an unprovoked attack into the sovereign territories of Syria and Lebanon. These attacks killed innocent civilian women and children. Syria defended itself with surface to air missiles and AAA, shooting down three American warplanes."

"Bullshit!" Wink said. "They cannot utter *one* friggin' sentence, without some *bull*shit lie falling out of their mouths—"

The Ambassador continued. "These attacks cannot go on. The United States may not conduct war on a country with which it is not at war without retaliation. Syria will respond, and will respond in kind. We will not tolerate American aggression. We will not tolerate our people being killed in cold blood. We expect apologies from United States, reparations, and promises not to intrude into our airspace or our territory.

"The Americans are becoming bullies of the Middle East, where they do not even belong. They have not been invited by anyone, they have not taken reasonable steps, and now they have killed innocent people. Now of course we know the true facts."

He stared into the camera. "Even before these latest attacks the Americans had shown their contempt for Syrian and international law by attacking Lebanese and Syrian positions, by shooting down Syrian pilots, and bombing a Lebanese town in cooperation with the Israeli

Air Force. This was because an American Navy officer was with an Israeli Intelligence Officer when she was attacked and killed.

"The Americans know this. Now the world does. The American Naval officer was acting in cooperation with an Israeli intelligence agent. He was in Israel to plan attacks on Lebanon and Syria by the United States Navy, the attacks we are now seeing. They were conspiring to do the very thing that they later did—the U.S. Navy joining with the Israeli Air Force and secretly flying into Lebanon and attacking innocent civilians. Perhaps America has been cooperating with Israel and flying its airplanes on these strikes for a long time. Perhaps we were the stupid ones and simply did not know it. We will have to review the reports of our pilots and those who operated in Lebanon and Syria to see if they have spotted American forces before. We, of course, know that the Israelis operate American equipment. They fly American jets, and drop American bombs, and shoot American missiles. All given to them by the Americans. It is said that the Israelis buy their equipment, but the Americans give the Israelis three billion dollars in foreign aid every year, just enough money to buy all the military equipment that they need. From America of course.

"So America sells its own equipment, or gives it, to Israel, then conspires with Israeli intelligence to ensure that American Naval forces fly off their aircraft carriers and into Lebanon and Syria to attack our people. But when called to task, when called to account, they lie, say they weren't there, and then use it as an excuse to do more of the same."

A few of the journalists were becoming impatient and wanted to ask questions. But the Ambassador was not slowing down even for a second. He had things to get off his chest and he was determined to do so. Unlike most diplomats who made speeches at times such as this, this Ambassador seemed truly to believe what he was saying.

"So the Americans claim that there is a new terrorist organization operating out of Syria, Sheikh al-Jabar. They of course have no evidence that he has ever even been to Syria. They claim he is operating out of Lebanon. Once again, they have no such evidence. They then, without provocation, use these excuses to attack the self-defense capability of Syria and Lebanon.

"Perhaps we now understand. This is the big chance that America has yearned for for so long to come into the Middle East in force. CNN shows us that the Marines are coming. It looks like the Sheikh is right. The Americans are the next Crusaders.

"I want to make the Syrian position extremely clear: If one American sets foot on Syrian soil, or Lebanese soil, we will respond with force. If the Americans think they have a fight now, they haven't seen anything yet."

The journalists were lining up for questions. The Ambassador's dark countenance served him well in discouraging people from asking the obvious questions.

"That is all. I will not take any questions. Go ask the Americans all the questions. Ask them why they are attacking innocent people and when it is going to stop." He turned quickly and walked away from the shouting journalists.

"There it is," Pritch said.

"They can ask *me* those questions," Woods said, dead serious. "We will never stop until the Sheikh is dead. Simple as that. At least I won't."

If the *Washington* had a Main Street, it was the main deck. Post office, barbershop, ship's store, cafeteria-like ship's mess, chiefs' mess, berthing compartments, XO's office, ship's admin offices, legal office, supply office—where you could get paid—just about everything you could want.

Woods walked forward to the chiefs' mess. He looked around at the sea of khaki. All men in their thirties or forties. The red ordnance shirt stood out among the khaki ones. "Gunner!" he called. He had thought he might find the Gunner here. As a former chief, he still identified more closely with the chiefs he had left behind than the officers he had joined in the wardroom.

The Gunner looked up from his table, surprised to see Woods. "Yes, sir," he replied. He stood up slowly, reluctantly, from the table and crossed over to the door. Woods could go into the chiefs' mess if he chose to, but he knew better than to go in unless invited. "Figured you'd be here."

"Yes, sir," the Gunner said in his unique, disinterested way. He was clearly unhappy about being interrupted.

"I need to talk to you."

"Yes, sir," the Gunner said. He put his hands on his hips and waited for Woods to talk. The chiefs around the mess watched the conversation with mild interest. They knew Woods was one of the good officers. He didn't lord it over his chiefs, which was the main test of a good officer from their perspective. Let your chiefs do their job and yours will be easier.

"Let's go to your shop," Woods said, almost in the tone of an order.

The Gunner heard the tone and realized something was up. He gave a quick head movement to his friends to let them know he was leaving, turned out the hatch, and headed aft on the starboard side of the carrier. They went up two levels to the 02. The ordnance door was painted black and yellow in squadron colors and had a drawing— painted ordnance red—of a falling bomb on the door. A laser-guided bomb, for those who cared to examine the painting—and a good rendition, for those who really looked, with the fins, laser guidance system, and a good trajectory.

They stepped inside the shop and closed the steel door with a slam. Two ordnancemen, Petty Officers in their red long-sleeved cotton shirts, their cranial helmets up on top of their heads, ear protectors off their ears, stood quietly in the shop looking tired and worn. Their shirts had the cast of three days of dirt and grime. They had been up all night preparing the Tomcats for the night strikes about to start. So far, they were very pleased with performance of the F-14's of VF-103. All the bombs had come off the racks when they were supposed to, and had been placed on target with no casualties. They were keeping a running tally of how many pounds of bombs were being dropped.

Gunner sat down at his desk. As the Warrant Officer of the Ordnance Division, he was in charge of all the weapons for the Jolly Rogers: the 20-millimeter cartridges that went into the Gatling gun in the nose of the Tomcat; the Sidewinder, Sparrow, and Phoenix missiles that went on the aircraft for air to air combat; and all the bombs that were loaded on the belly. He pushed his dark brown hair from the side where it grew across his shiny head to the other side where it lay. It looked ridiculous, but no one would ever even think of telling him that. He was far too serious to ever be ready to hear that his combover hair look was silly. He regarded Woods with skepticism.

Woods sat in the metal and vinyl chair and glanced around the shop. Woods was envious. The idea of having a tight group of men and women working for you in a small shop with a narrow focus, where you could measure success on an hourly basis, where you knew exactly where you stood all the time, was attractive to him. It was an oasis from the world of ambiguity.

Woods watched the ordnancemen eat candy bars as they studied the air-plan ordnance loads for the night launches. The Air Wing commander had decided to fly all the strikes at night so that some fool with an AK-47 didn't connect with a wild shot on one of the Air Wing's jets.

The calendar on the wall above the steel desk was the latest *Sports Illustrated* swimsuit calendar. The more lurid calendars had been taken down long before under protest because of the addition of women to the ordnance shop. It had changed everything but women were now so commonplace that no one commented. If people felt unhappy about their presence, they kept that opinion to themselves. They all knew what they were supposed to think, and that's what they said whenever asked.

"We're not getting these guys," Woods finally said.

"The Sheikh's guys?"

"Right."

"Bombs aren't doing the job?"

"Not even close."

"That figures though, don't it? You can't blow up a whole mountain. You got to have a target that you can hit. They can probably blow up the building, his fort or whatever, but not the whole damn mountain. I guess he's buried. I just wish we knew where his headquarters were."

"We do."

The Petty Officers glanced at him, eavesdropping. Interested.

"Got the message this morning. They know where he's hiding."

"That shit-head. I'd like to just pinch his little neck with a big set of tweezers." He touched his hair to see if it was falling. "So where is he?"

"In their fortress in Iran."

"Okay."

"You've seen the BDA photos, right? Two-thousand-pounders are hitting exactly where we're aiming. All we're doing is turning big rocks into little rocks. We're bombing the hell out of the sides of couple of mountains, but I don't think we're getting through. Maybe ten or twenty feet deep, but not deep enough."

The Gunner shrugged. "Don't know what they expected. Those things can't penetrate granite, or even dirt. At least not very far."

"Exactly. But it's worse."

"What's worse?"

"The place where he is hiding is the fortress in northwestern Iran. Called Alamut. They think he's buried in that mountain seventy-five to a hundred feet."

The Gunner turned down the corners of his mouth in disapproval. "Can't get down there with what we got. Never happen."

"Exactly. That's why I came to you."

"I just said we can't—"

"I think I've got a solution," Woods said. His eyes were intense in the dim light. "We need to get ahold of a couple of GBU-28s."

The Gunner sat back. He looked at the overhead as he called up the picture of the massive weapon. "Designed for another one of our pals, Saddam Hussein. Made out of an eight-inch howitzer barrel packed full of explosives or some shit. Never seen one, but sure would like to."

"That's it. That's the one."

The Gunner smiled, showing his uneven teeth. "That ought to do it. Who'd carry them?"

"I would."

The Gunner felt another felony coming. "How? The F-14's never been certified."

Woods said, leaning forward, "Can we get one of them?"

"Air Force bought a hundred fifty of them in 1995 or '96. I think two F-111s dropped a couple in Desert Storm and blew Saddam's bunkers to hell. But he wasn't there. After that, the Air Force convinced *somebody* they needed a warehouse full of these things." He smiled. "We ought to be able to get a couple."

"Where are they?"

"I think Eglin, but I'll find out. But nobody'll let us drop 'em if they haven't done the flight tests on it."

"They *did* do the flight testing. When I was an instructor at Topgun they did some flight tests at the Pax River. A couple of us were allowed to observe. I flew on the wing of the guys who did the drop."

The Gunner wasn't impressed. "It's not in the confidential supplement." The supplement was the big yellow F-14 manual that contained the weapons information on the F-14. It was the bible for the operation of the Tomcat with various weapons systems.

"The Air Force said it was going to be an Air Force weapon. They didn't even want us doing the flight tests. They said the Navy didn't need to pollute their system carrying around the GBU-28. But it passed the flight tests. Trust me." Woods watched the Gunner's face. The Gunner was deciding whether to believe him. Woods hadn't expected the Gunner to think he was lying about it. He had never even considered he might be losing credibility with those who knew him best because of what he had been willing to do to get the Sheikh.

The Gunner stood. "I know the guy who runs the ordnance shop at Eglin. You know what this means, don't you?"

"What?"

"The Air Force is already pissed. They feel like they've been cut out of the pattern. An air war is under way without them being in the lead. They don't let that happen. They've got more PR guys than we have sailors. They've got more videotape recorders then we have airplanes. Any time anything is going to happen, they want to lead. You know that."

"Right—"

"So I call this guy at Air Force ordnance. If I ask him to get a couple of 28's ready for immediate shipment to the carrier Battle Group, what will go out is that the Navy is about to do a surgical strike. Everyone knows what the only important surgical strike would be in this war. They know we're going after the Sheikh. They would also know that we've found him—which they may know already. I don't know. Anyway, they will immediately load two, or three, or fifty GBU-28s aboard a B-2, fly it halfway around the world by refueling it thirty times, and say that this is a routine Air Force mission. You *know* that's what will happen."

"So how do we get around it?"

The Gunner put his Jolly Rogers navy blue baseball cap on and pulled it down over his forehead to accentuate his hard look. "I think we plan the mission, and then execute it. If something stops us that's just the way it goes. If they don't stop us, then we'll get our shot."

"Are you going to help me?"

The Gunner hesitated. He looked at the two Petty Officers hovering nearby. "Give us a minute," he said loudly.

The Petty Officers put the air plan on the counter and walked out of the ordnance shop, closing the door behind them.

Gunner Bailey stood there looking at Woods. "You've already asked me to help you once. I did something I never should have done. I faked some missile records. Which wasn't easy. The ship's records are kept by the OHO. I had to call in a couple of big markers. Way big. He was not pleased, especially after the fact when CAG's hair is on fire and it looks like the biggest damn international incident any of us has ever seen—"

"Look, Gunner, let me—"

"Let me finish," he said. "I did that, because I thought Lieutenant Vialli got a shitty deal. I was willing to help you. But I don't like this one bit. I love the Navy. The Navy is my life. More than my family. And I don't want anyone shitting all over my career for his own reasons. I helped you once, but I'm not sticking my head in another noose. If this is another scam of yours, count me out."

Woods was stunned. "Gunner, I appreciate what you did. It was risky, and we pulled it off. But this isn't a scam. It's totally legit. If we can locate some of these bombs, we'll put in an emergency requisition request, all aboveboard, all with the Skipper's approval."

The Gunner looked into Woods's eyes for any sign of games. "I'll see what I can do. I'll get on the e-mail right away." The Gunner's demeanor changed. "You need to get on the horn and keep the Air Force's fat assess out of this. This is *our* fight. If you got any strings, pull them now."

Woods immediately thought of Jaime.

President Garrett looked every bit as serious as the Syrian Ambassador did. He began speaking slowly, "I generally do not comment on remarks by diplomats of foreign countries. However, this time I could not let the Syrian Ambassador to the UN's comments pass unnoticed. He has accused us of conspiracies and evil intentions. I will not allow him to slander our country. We are currently at war. True, it is only against one man and the group that follows him. One man and his group of terrorists, Assassins, and murderers. A group whose objective is to kill Americans. Doesn't matter whether these people are armed, combatants, military, or even Department of Defense. It is despicable to attack unarmed civilians as they have. But more significantly, the Sheikh declared war against the United States. Unlike many times in the past, we decided to respond directly to this challenge to our country. It was the right decision and we will see it home.

"But Syria is a different question altogether. The implication by the Syrian Ambassador is that we have no business responding to terrorism with a declaration of war. The second implication is that they can harbor and protect the terrorists that they feel like protecting with impunity. Even one who has declared war against the United States. They are very wrong about that. They may try to protect him, but they will be unsuccessful. We will come to wherever Sheikh al-Jabar is hiding, with whatever force is necessary to get him. It doesn't matter to me whether the result is capturing him, or killing him. What does matter is that we seek justice for the people of this country that he has attacked. If Syria stands between us and him that is not our problem. It is not a condition of our making.

"The Ambassador pretended not to know that Sheikh al-Jabar has been operating out of Syria. Such a position is disingenuous in the extreme. The Sheikh is the current head of the Isma'ili sect of the Muslim religion that has been operating in eastern Syria for hundreds of years. The Assassins, as they are known, have been known to reside in Syria for hundreds of years. To now claim that this particular group of Assassins is unknown to Syria is ridiculous.

"He also knows that the Syrian government has done nothing to limit or stop Sheikh al-Jabar from operating from Syrian territory.

"For Syria to assert these positions on the argument that a U.S. Naval officer was meeting with an Israeli intelligence agent to concoct a scheme for joint operations is outrageous. Navy Lieutenant Tony Vialli had simply fallen for a pretty woman, and had gone to visit her in Israel. That is well known. He was in the wrong place at the wrong time. If she was an Israeli intelligence agent, that is news to me, and I'm sure would have been news to him as well.

"He was told, and other officers aboard the ship from which he operated were told, that she was a schoolteacher. It is my understanding that she was going to Tel Aviv to interview with El Al airlines. That has been confirmed to us by the airline itself.

"Syria still claims that United States Navy fighters off the USS *George Washington* accompanied the Israeli Air Force on a strike into Lebanon. That is false. It is wrong, malicious, and false. The missile they showed to the world as proof was in fact sold to Israel years ago. They know that."

President Garrett paused and looked at the camera with an intense stare. "What matters now is that terrorists operating from Syria continue to murder Americans. In fact, he seems to have raised the ante with his most recent bloody attacks on innocent civilians. We will raise the ante too. If it means sending American ground troops into Syria or Lebanon, or wherever he is to be found, we will do that. If countries are concerned about American troops landing in their territory, then they should get Sheikh al-Jabar out of their country. It's as simple as that."

The President looked at his audience, and said coldly, "If that makes Syria unhappy, that's fine. This war is not about happiness, it's about justice and retribution. We will not be stopped."

Woods didn't have much time to do what he wanted to do. He also wasn't sure how to do it. He first had to convince his Squadron Commander, then the Air Wing Commander, then the Admiral, then the Chief of Naval Operations in the Joint Chiefs, that an F-14 off the *Washington* should be the one to drive a knife through the Sheikh's heart. All in due time. First he had to figure out if it could be done. The Gunner was working on getting the bomb. Woods didn't think he'd pull that off, but on the off chance that he did, they had to hit the target. Dead on. No near misses. This was one shot only.

The thing that worried him, other than going into Iran itself and the distance involved, was how to laser designate the hit point. He knew Wink would be fine and that they would hit whatever they had their laser designator on. But to penetrate into the Sheikh's quarters they would have to hit the sweet spot. And they didn't know where that was. Woods had reread the message about locating the Sheikh. The message had hidden implications. There was only one way they could know for a fact that the Sheikh was there. Someone was there. On the ground. Woods turned back and headed directly toward CVIC. He had to find out.

He looked around for Pritch. He saw her in the corner studying the charts. "How do we *know* he's there?"

Pritch looked up from her work and smiled at him. "Nice to see you too, Lieutenant. I'm fine, thanks."

"How do we *know*?" Woods repeated.

Pritch wanted to help. She had begun to identify with Woods. She wanted to tell him everything she knew, but she couldn't. "I can't tell you."

"Why not?"

"It's classified."

"I'm cleared."

"No, you're not."

"I've had a Secret clearance since I joined the Navy."

"You and every other officer in the Navy, sir."

"I had Top Secret at Topgun."

"*Top* Secret doesn't do anything, Trey. This is *code* word. SCI."

Special Compartmentalized Information. A clearance wasn't good enough. You had to have a need to know, and only then were you "read-in" to the project and given the code word of the program. He pressed on, calculating other directions through which to get the same information. He lowered his voice. "Do we have somebody on the ground? Some snake-eater?"

Pritch resisted. "Even if we did, if it's compartmentalized, I couldn't tell you about it."

Woods's frustration got the better of him. "How the hell am I supposed to fly a mission into Iran if you won't tell me the source of our information? How do I know whether to trust the information or not?"

"You're supposed to trust me."

Woods paused. He realized he actually did trust her. It was the rest of the world of intelligence he didn't trust. "You have any idea how many people have been killed by relying on intelligence reports? You realize what a total failure intelligence usually represents?"

Pritch winced. "No. Maybe you shouldn't worry about it."

"I'm not going to be one more sad memory who relied on intelligence and was killed for it."

Pritch remembered his notebook. "How do you see yourself being killed because I won't tell you the source of the information?"

"Because I'm going after the Sheikh, either by myself or with a small strike force. If I don't know whether your information on his location is any good, I may be doing something too dangerous to be worth the risk. Maybe I'll let somebody else be the hero." He was torn. "He may not be there at all."

"He's there."

"How do we *know*?"

"We just do." She could see his frustration.

"So why don't I get to know how we know that?"

"Because you might get shot down."

Woods hesitated. That was why he and every other Naval aviator had gone to SERE school—Survival, Evasion, Resistance, and Escape. There they'd taught you how to be a prisoner of war, how to resist giving away any information, but always knowing that if in fact you encountered dedicated torturers, they *would* get the information from you at some point. He lowered his voice and looked directly into her eyes. "I still have to know. It's critical to the mission."

She was startled. "Why?" she asked as an aircraft flew down the catapult over CVIC, causing the ship to shudder. Neither of them noticed.

"The best way to penetrate this target . . . would be to have someone on the ground designating the exact impact point with a handheld laser designator. Otherwise, we are more likely to miss the impact point then hit it, because it won't be obvious from IR. Just another point in the dirt." He studied her face for any sign of the answer. "So do we?"

"I can't say."

"This is ridiculous!"

"I just can't."

Her answer caused him more concern. "What do you mean, can't?"

"That's all I'm going to say." She considered. "You want someone on the ground to lase the target."

"Yeah. Exactly."

"I'll ask."

"Ask who?"

"The people that I have to ask."

"This is nuts! Speak English! Can it be done?"

"I don't know. I'll ask."

"How are you going to do that?"

"By sending a back channel message."

"One of those Top Secret messages. The ones I don't get to see."

"You make it sound sinister."

"No, it's just stupid." He was growing tired of the resistance he met at every turn. What was supposed to be a team too often felt like a series of bureaucracies. "I need a yes or no."

"I'll find out, Trey. Trust me, for a change."

34

inkaid stood by his STU-III telephone waiting for Efraim to return his call. The rest of the task force continued to work furiously. The latest bold murders had increased the already frenetic focus of the members of the task fore. Outrage permeated every move and thought. Their progress, though, was still halting and uncertain. The Snapshot Teams had seen no other activity near American embassies since the one in Morocco. That didn't surprise Kinkaid. He knew that the odds of an embassy being attacked directly were low. Even the people they had seen were probably only casing the embassy to observe its personnel.

The STU-III rang at exactly the appointed minute. Kinkaid glanced at the other members of the task force who listened on the special speaker he had rigged to the phone. He wanted them all in on this momentous phone call. "Good morning, Efraim," Kinkaid said. "How are things?"

"We are enjoying watching the United States attack our common enemy. It is the joy that you have been experiencing for years. When Israel attacked your enemies."

Sami's face showed his general disagreement.

Kinkaid spoke while looking at Sami. "Sometimes, but often they are not our direct enemies."

"Oh, yes, they are. You misunderstand how closely tied our interests are."

"I have something else in mind to talk you about today. Do you have time to discuss it?"

"I always have time for you, my friend."

"Your man on the ground."

"I do not know what you mean."

"At Alamut."

Efraim hesitated. "That is a very sensitive matter. I regret having told you about it."

"I don't think you do. I think you wanted me to know about him."

"What is your question?"

"I told you we would act. You didn't believe me."

"You are going to strike?" Efraim asked, surprised.

"Yes."

"What is the plan?"

"I've been asked to present a question to you."

"This discussion should perhaps be between others, at a higher level."

"The higher levels have asked me to ask *you* directly."

"What is the question?"

"Does the person on the ground have the ability to do laser illumination on the target?"

"You ask too much. If I say yes, you will ask if he would laser designate for your strike."

"Of course."

"Then we would be working for you. In your war."

"Exactly. You told me not to ask about our pilots doing your bidding before. Maybe it is time to return the favor."

"If in fact such a thing happened . . . perhaps *letting* them go *was* the favor. We don't need the help of the United States, or of a Navy Lieutenant who is avenging the death of his friend who was only chasing a woman. Do not insult us."

Kinkaid hadn't anticipated Efraim's response. He had no leverage to bring to bear. He waited. The line hummed quietly. The entire room of Americans stared at the speaker on the table, waiting.

Efraim finally spoke. "Perhaps it could be done."

"Will you?"

"Ah. We get to the ultimate issue. I'm afraid it is beyond my ability to offer. I would need to ask others. It could only happen once, if at all."

"I assumed he was well hidden."

"No one is undiscoverable."

"Efraim, I need to hear back from you immediately. Our aircraft can do it by themselves, but the precision required in this mission would benefit greatly from someone on the ground. If you can't do it, let me know. We may drop in one of our own people to do it."

"I would recommend in the strongest possible terms that you not do that. It could compromise your mission and ours."

"The Navy has its own people who could be there in less than twenty-four hours—"

"Yes. Your DEVGROUP, I suppose. Do not do this."

Kinkaid smiled at the others in the task force. "Then make it so I don't have to."

"We will see."

"I need to hear back from you in less than an hour. If you're not willing to help, we'll be launching our own people immediately, but even that will not be ideal. They don't know what's inside the hill. Now, if you're willing to share a diagram with—"

"I will let you know as soon as I know."

"Thank you, Efraim."

"I haven't said that I am willing to help. You are beginning to make me regret I said anything to you."

"You will not regret it in the long run."

"I will call. And, Joseph, please make sure your Turk knows none of this. It cannot get into the wrong hands."

Kinkaid glanced at Sami, who sat with his hand over his chin, listening to every word. "I will await your call."

The line went dead and Kinkaid put the receiver back on its cradle. He looked at the room full of CIA officers.

Cunningham spoke. "They owe us. Ricketts."

Kinkaid nodded. "Efraim will remember him later."

"We're still just doing their dirty work," Sami said.

"How?" Kinkaid asked, exasperated.

"Maybe they want us to go after him in Iran because they couldn't. They've *known* about him. Who knows, maybe for years. They failed to take him out, which they wouldn't hesitate to do, if they *could* have. They tried in Lebanon, and missed again. Maybe rather than attack the Sheikh in his fortified positions, they just lateraled the whole thing to us." Sami played with the blank notepad in front of him. "This whole reluctance to let us use an agent on the ground to laser the target? I don't buy it. They'll do it. Guaranteed. It was the plan all along. If we called, they'd be there for the final stroke. I think their guy is on the ground for this very purpose. Always has been. You'll see," Sami said, standing. He leaned against the wall and put his hands in his pockets defensively. They were all listening. "They got to where we are now, except they thought it through first. Instead of just bombing the fortresses to dust, they realized they'd never get it done. They knew they couldn't penetrate this guy's cave. They don't have the GBU-28. They don't have the weapon. But we do."

"The what? What kind of bomb did you say?"

"GBU-28."

The others in the task force looked at one another. "What the hell is that?" Cunningham asked.

"Penetrates a hundred feet. It was designed to get Saddam Hussein. They dropped two of them during the Gulf War."

"How do you know that?"

"I read *Jane's Defence Weekly* like all the rest of you should."

"Whatever. But they couldn't just *ask* us for a couple of these magic bombs?" Cunningham asked sarcastically. "We only give them what, three billion dollars a year? Come on."

"Sure they could have asked. And we would almost surely have given it to them. But then they would have had to fly into Iran. They have *never* flown into Iran. They want *us* to do it, because if Iran blows up, we can handle it. *They* might not be able to. This is going perfectly according to their plan."

The others sat silently. Kinkaid saw their faces. He realized Sami was gaining converts. "I think you've read too many novels," he said, trying to be lighthearted.

Sami was undeterred. "If you think Israel's above using us, or *anybody,* you're mistaken. Don't forget the *Liberty* incident. Not only will they use us, they will *kill* us if it serves their purposes."

"That was an *accident,*" Kinkaid protested.

Cunningham and the others laughed out loud.

Kinkaid blushed. "That is the accepted position of our government."

Sami couldn't believe his ears. "Why do we give them the benefit of the doubt?" he asked, looking around the room at the rest of the task force. He was angry. "Why them? Why do we disregard the Syrian Ambassador to the UN, and believe everything this Efraim tells us?"

"Experience."

Sami stood up, agitated. "Experience? Israel has stabbed us in the back many times. They have spied on us, tricked us, used us, lied to us. Hell, they lie to themselves! What about the Mossad guy—I forget his name—who claimed to have a big spy inside Syria, and took out money to pay this guy for like twenty years, all about the Golan Heights, all kinds of stuff, then someone finally checks on it when he says Syria is about to go to war against Israel, and they find out it was all total bullshit. Guy made it all up and faked the reports. That was a Mossad guy!"

"They have been our friend in the Middle East—" Kinkaid replied.

"You are too close to this Efraim," Sami accused. "You aren't *objective* anymore."

"Watch it—" Kinkaid warned. The rest of the task force was staring in disbelief. "We're all tired, and saying things—"

"Tired?" Sami asked. "I'm not tired, or at least not so tired that I don't know what Israel is about. They are out for themselves. *Always.* If we are in the way, they will do whatever they need to do to us."

Kinkaid looked at Sami in a new light, remembering Efraim's warning. "Perhaps you are biased—"

Sami smiled ironically. "It always comes down to that, doesn't it? I have an Arabic name, so I'm biased. So all the Jews in the CIA are biased *for* Israel? Will you say that?"

"That's ridiculous—"

"Yet you accuse me—"

"Because of what you are saying, and how you are behaving. You are being irrational."

"Jonathan Pollard, an American Jew, is in jail for spying on the U.S. for Israel. Right?"

"Yes, but—"

"That isn't my imagination. He was paid by Israel to steal secrets from this country. They targeted us. To spy on us."

"They expressed regret—"

"For getting caught!"

"It was an unusual circumstance. I'm sure those wounds have long been healed."

Sami was discouraged and showed it. "No, they haven't. Not as long as he's in jail, and they keep bringing his name up every chance they get. He's their boy." Sami headed toward the door. "And he's not the only one." He waited for some reaction to show on Kinkaid's face. It did. Just a twitch and a glance away. "And you know it."

"Too many novels," Kinkaid said.

Sami's intense face showed he didn't think it was a time to be lighthearted. "No. Not novels. But I have read of the Mossad's espionage in the United States. I've read of their penetration of the highest levels of the United States government by *Mega.*" He stopped when he saw the look of horror on Kinkaid's face.

"You know about Mega?" Kinkaid whispered. The tension in the room was remarkable. No one breathed. "How?"

"By reading books I get at Barnes and Noble," Sami replied. "Is there some truth to it?"

"There have been rumors."

"I'll say," Sami said. "And there's a file three inches thick about the investigation conducted jointly by the FBI and the Agency to find this Mega. But the investigation was conducted by *idiots,* and they never found him. They have several documents in Hebrew, and the translations are wrong—"

Kinkaid smiled weakly, "So now you speak Hebrew?"

"Of course I do, ancient *and* modern. I've studied all the Semitic languages. If you had ever read my résumé you would know that."

Kinkaid was angry. Sami was lashing out recklessly. The entire task force was at risk of being sidetracked. "That was a long time ago. Mega was never found. It isn't known if he really even existed."

"No, the investigation was *called off!*" Sami said loudly, moving aggressively toward Kinkaid. "Because right when they were closing in on the answer, certain information was brought up about a certain President's proclivity to rendezvous with a certain intern. It was made known that the Mossad had *tapes* of their conversations. Suddenly the order came to shut down the investigation into Mega."

"That's nonsense! Where did you get that?"

"Didn't you ever read the Starr report? Monica Lewinsky *testified* that President Clinton told her that a 'foreign embassy' was taping their calls!" He looked for recognition. "Shit, Joe! Who do you think she was referring to? And right after that the Mega investigation was closed down!"

"So what are you saying?"

"Just that there is someone in the highest levels of the United States government who has Israel's interests ahead of ours. Do I need to recite for you the Jews who have held high positions in the government in the last eight years?"

A chill descended into the room. Sami had crossed the line and everyone knew it.

"So. That's it," Kinkaid said.

"No, that's not it. I am not anti-Semitic. But if you were looking for someone sympathetic to Israel, do you think you might be more likely to find such a person among the Jews? Have you never heard of their Sayan network around the world? Jews who are citizens of other countries that just 'help out' the Mossad when asked?" Sami suddenly remembered what Efraim had said. "And what is this about a young Turk? Information has been withheld from me, a member of the task force because I am Arabic?"

"He had concerns—"

"So you did what he asked and went behind the back of one of your own officers?" Sami yelled.

"I put him on the speakerphone and let him say it to your face without his knowing it." Kinkaid said, trying to control his anger. He knew he had let Sami go way too far, and in the wrong setting. He couldn't have handled it much worse. Now it was poisonous. "I didn't keep *anything* from you. You're out of line, and you're injecting issues where there aren't any. I want to get this agent on the ground to laser for our pilots. The request came from us! Our pilots want the help, and I'm going to try to get it for them. And I'm telling you and everybody else here exactly what I'm doing. So you had better keep doing what you're doing and cool it about intrigue and espionage. We've got a job to do here, clear?"

"Yeah, it's clear. But Mega is still in our government. And this whole thing may have been schemed by Israel."

"So back to that. They murdered their own people to set us up?"

Sami shook his head. "How do you *know* who the other dead people were on that bus, Joe? You can't even see the woman's face in the photos of her in the bus. And you can't see her hand! Did you even notice that? We have *no idea* who she was!"

Kinkaid took a deep breath. "That's not what happened." He scanned the faces of the task force members. Several were clearly looking at him in a completely different way than they ever had before. Sami had damaged him. "Enough speculation. What we do know is where the Sheikh is. We need to help the Navy get him. Everybody agree with that?"

They nodded.

"Then don't get sidetracked with *corrosive* speculation about ridiculous theories." He stole a hard look at Sami. "And if anybody has a problem with me, or how this is going, come see me." Kinkaid left the room.

The rest of the task force stood silently, looking at one another. Cunningham broke the silence. "This Mega thing for real?"

Sami nodded.

"Who do you think it is, or was?"

Sami didn't know how to answer. He stared at the door that Kinkaid had just walked through. "Nothing says Mega isn't inside the Agency."

✍

Bark stormed into the ready room. The junior officers in the ready room wanted only one thing—for him not to be looking for them. "Trey!" Bark yelled as he quickly and expertly scanned the room for his target. He saw him in the back preparing the next day's flight schedule. He strode to the back of the room, his steel-toed boots loud on the tile, not waiting until he was closer before beginning the conversation. "What the hell are you doing?"

Woods waited for some additional information that would help him learn how he had screwed up this time. "What do you mean?" he asked defensively.

"You asked the Gunner to submit an *emergency* weapons request?"

"No, sir, he offered to contact Eglin, Skipper. He said he knew the guy in charge of the Air Force ordnance."

"*Shit*, Trey! You've got to make requests through official channels! And that's after you've talked to me about it. You continue to make me look like dog shit in front of CAG. I'll probably get a Fitrep that says 'Marginally competent. Unable to control the lunatic officers in his squadron.' I *heard* about this from CAG! You know how that makes me feel? Do you?"

"Well—"

"Exactly. Tongue-tied. Like some little shit-for-brains who walks around apologizing for things all the time. I don't like apologizing for *anything*, Trey! You got that? I don't like there being anything that needs apologizing *for*! These days seems I'm *always* apologizing for you! You want to explain all this to me before I put your sorry ass in HAQ again?"

Woods was tired of getting beaten up for trying to do his job. "We're slamming our heads against the wall, Skipper. You've seen the BDA photos. We're just blowing up rocks—"

"Then *that's* what we do until we're told to do something diff—"

"Yes, sir, but I had an idea."

"The 28."

"Yes, sir. Why not? It's made for this!"

"Maybe. But who the hell do you think you are contacting the Air Force? *What* were you thinking about?"

"I thought the Gunner was going to contact a friend of his at Eglin. Unofficially. E-mail. I thought he was going to check on availability. How practical it would be. See if there are any around, and if they could get shipped out here. I didn't think he'd make an official request." Woods began to breathe more normally. He tried to relax, but one look at Bark's face as he stood over him with his hands on his hips would deter the most ambitious. "If I had come to you the first thing you'd have wanted to know is whether it can really be done. Are the weapons there, can they be shipped, how long would it take. I was trying to find out first whether it was a stupid idea. If it was, I didn't need to bother you with it. I never intended—"

Bark was not humored. "It's never your bright *ideas* that get you in trouble, it's your disregard for the chain of command. You see senior officers as a nuisance. You—"

"No, sir—"

"Shut up! Let me finish. You see senior officers as functionaries. They do their jobs, but aren't courageous or smart like you. You use the chain of command only when you want someone to do something for you. Never to filter your brilliant ideas and tell you that they're bullshit. Which some of them are. All of us have bullshit ideas, Trey. That's why we have to tell them to others in the Navy, to keep a stupid idea from becoming something that kills us. Senior officers make mistakes too, but they've got a lot of experience and usually a staff to help them. You don't have a damned staff, Trey. Quit acting like you run the show here. It's what keeps you from being a 4.0 officer. You're 4.0 in almost everything. But when it comes to doing things the way they should be done, through proper channels, you're about 2.0. You following me?"

"Yes." He purposely didn't add the "sir." It was his small way of registering a protest. He pushed back a little. "Do you want me to tell the Gunner to stop asking?"

Bark sat down in the chair next to Woods. He didn't want to acknowledge that Woods's latest renegade idea had any merit, but he also knew it did. It annoyed the hell out of him to admit it, and he knew he would even have to ask about it. He had no choice. "What's the status?"

"Gunner is supposed to hear back within the hour. He contacted him by e-mail. He'll get the gouge."

"Who did you have in mind to carry this pig of a bomb?"

"Me. Us."

"We're not certified."

"The testing was done. I saw the results. Tom Stenner did the testing. You know him? He's at the RAG now." Stenner was an instructor pilot at the F-14 RAG, the Replacement Air Group where new pilots and RIOs were taught to fly the Tomcat.

"Sure. TPS grad." Test Pilot School, one of the most highly respected jobs in Navy Air.

"Exactly. He said it's heavy and tricky, but drag, fuel, and performance characteristics were the same as if carrying two two-thousand-pounders. I e-mailed him this morning to make sure I wasn't hallucinating. He still had the test specs on his laptop in a PowerPoint presentation. He sent them to me in his return e-mail." Woods opened the desk drawer slowly. He pulled out the copy of the PowerPoint presentation he had printed out and handed it to Bark. "Here it is."

Bark glanced at it and handed it back to Woods. "When did he do the tests?"

"Five years ago."

"Anything since?"

"No, sir. Wasn't ever funded."

"F-18 ever drop it?"

"No, sir. Never been done."

"So if anyone's going to do it, it's got to be us."

"Yes, sir. Exactly. And I've done the flight planning."

"Shit, Trey, there you go—"

"No, just to see if it can be done. See if we can get there."

"Get where?"

"Alamut."

"That's in Iran."

"Yes, sir. Four hundred fifty miles one way."

"And then what? Drop it into a mountain?"

"No, sir. Drop it exactly where it needs to be."

"How?"

"Our LANTIRN may be able to do it. But the best way is to have somebody on the ground."

"I'll bet you have a plan."

Woods lowered his voice and glanced over his shoulder. "I figure somebody's already on the ground."

"Where do you get that?"

"Reading between the lines on the message we got, watching Pritch's face when I asked her—"

"Good—"

"The only way anyone could *really* know the Sheikh is there is if they had *seen* him. There's no way a satellite is going to tell us that that one person is there." His eyes grew darker as he moved closer to Bark. "Someone's looking at him. Either one of ours, or someone friendly. Either way, he may have the ability to lase the target for us."

"Dare I ask," Bark said, with deep annoyance, "what you have in mind this time?"

"I asked Pritch to push the question uphill. Find out if what I suspect is true."

"*Damn* it!" Bark exclaimed. "You don't *screw* with intelligence, Trey! They don't even like people to *ask* whether they have someone on the ground. They don't want *any*one to know if they do."

"That's what she said. But I thought this might be the one time where intelligence is actually good for something."

"Don't hold your breath."

Woods nodded. He could feel his Commanding Officer relax. Bark was on his side again.

The SDO interrupted them from the front. "Skipper, Commander Chase is on the phone for you."

Chase was the Strike Ops Officer, the one in charge of final strike planning and targeting. He was also in charge of the ATO, the Air Tasking Order that designated when and where everything that flew went. It had airplanes, ordnance, fuel, and target information included on one document. When the Air Force arrived to join the fight, they would be on the ATO and would probably control it.

Bark stood and stepped toward the front of the ready room, then turned back. "Anything else I should know?"

Woods hated the timing. "I stopped to see him to ask him the feasibility of a two-plane strike on the flight plan tomorrow night."

"Tomorrow?" Bark asked, shocked. He walked toward the SDO's desk muttering under his breath. He stopped again and spoke to Woods. "Don't do *anything*, or talk to *anybody* about this, until you talk to me about it." Bark hesitated as something occurred to him. He looked at Woods, his eyes brighter than they had been one minute before. "I want you and Big to plan on going. If it's going forward, I want to see the final planning before we approach anybody. And I want Wink doing the planning. At least I can trust him not to fake the gas figures."

Woods watched Bark walk away. He had gone from being furious with Woods to handing him the biggest, most important mission the squadron had ever flown without any explanation. Woods pondered what it meant, but finally quit, accepting the gift horse for what it was.

35

The image of laptops next to candles was startling, but not to the Assassins. They had long ago learned that their leader, the one who called himself the Old Man of the Mountains, believed that the future of Islam lay in the combination of old and new, of historic traditions and the use of technology. They knew how to live in the desert like Bedouins, and in the cities like the cosmopolitan Arabs they could become. Their dedication to their cause was complete. They were able to travel through the world with whatever appearance best suited them. They were Assassins, but much of what made them so deadly was being chameleons of the desert.

The Sheikh sat in the chair he preferred near the large table on which he liked to work. It was lit by candles that flickered against the uneven stone ceiling carved into the hill above. He looked at his lieutenants, gathered in front. The Sheikh wanted to speak to them as a group. He didn't do it often, but when he did, everything else stopped. He stood and walked slowly back and forth behind his chair on the dark, worn Persian rug. His beard was oiled with a substance that remained a mystery to those with whom he spent every day. The Sheikh was a strong, energetic man who demanded absolute obedience and received it. He could also be warm and engaging, but rarely smiled.

The Sheikh waited until he was finally satisfied his men had not only given him their faces but their minds. "The Americans continue to bomb in Syria and in Lebanon. They try hard, but do not know what they are doing."

Farouk, his brightest lieutenant and recognized by all as a future leader in whatever they became, spoke quickly. "Do you think they know we are here?" He was permitted to raise questions that none of the others would have been allowed to ask.

"They try to photograph our mountain with their satellites," the Sheikh said. "But the satellite cannot tell one black robe from another. They know that some of us are here, or were here when the photographs were taken, but they don't know whether I'm here now." He thought about the difficulty America had caused herself by going after him by name. "It is me they want. They took my bait. And now we are in Iran, the country which cares as deeply as any other to protect Islam. They don't agree with us, and wish we would not cause trouble. But if it is necessary, Iran will protect us from an attack. So the Americans may come, but it will be costly."

Farouk continued to ask questions in spite of the clear desire of the Sheikh to speak uninterruptedly. "But they *must* come. They will look weak if they even think we are here and don't pursue us. They have declared war."

"Perhaps. But they do not have the ability to get us where we sit. Their bombs will be as useless here as in Lebanon and Syria. Allah has created strongholds which can absorb all of America's bombs without endangering us. These are strong mountains."

Farouk knew the answer to the next question, but couldn't help himself. "Do you want us to continue with the plan?"

"Yes, it is time to execute the next phase. We have let the world know who we are and what we require. We have made the most powerful country in the history of the world turn its entire power against one man. They are afraid for every person who works for their government. We have succeeded beyond where we could have hoped. And they haven't injured even one of our people."

His lieutenants were pleased. They too wanted to continue. They had feared he would back away from full execution when the United States became so deeply involved. They now realized it had been the Sheikh's plan all along—a plan designed to entrap the Americans.

The declaration of war had troubled the Sheikh initially, but he came to see it as recognition that he was as powerful as any country. It was intoxicating to the Assassins, who now had the worldwide stature they had wanted.

"We must also, of course, be ready for men on the ground to come here," the Sheikh continued.

Two of his lieutenants looked at each other. They had considered this possibility in the initial planning. The Sheikh had dismissed it as so remote as not to be worthy of discussion. The one who had brought it up then had been given a look of pure scorn. One of them spoke, trying to disguise his surprise. "Army forces? Paratroopers?"

The Sheikh shook his head slightly. "Possibly. But unlikely. I think Special Forces. Remain alert."

"We are ready for them."

"Do not underestimate the enemy. The largest mistake all people in history have made in fighting America is that they underestimate them. People assume the Americans are soft because they smile too much, and because their culture is corrupt." He breathed deeply, as if considering something slightly unpleasant. "Their military has always demonstrated more courage than almost any other and to my knowledge has never lost a battle against a force of equal size. They are not to be taken lightly."

Farouk replied automatically, "Allah will be with us."

"Allah is always with us. But that does not give us a guarantee of immortality on earth. He does not say we will not be killed. We must all be prepared to go to Paradise."

Farouk looked down. "It would be an honor to die for our cause."

"Such an honor is not something to be sought. It may come, and is accepted with gratitude. But to behave in such a way that ensures your death shows you do not trust Allah to take care of you as he wills. It is not for us to say when we die. It is for him alone. We conduct ourselves with the belief," the Sheikh said, raising his voice just enough to emphasize his point, "that everything we do will be met with the success our planning shows we should have. We expect to go on forever. And so we shall." The Sheikh looked for another man. "Salim, is the radio ready?"

Salim nodded enthusiastically. "Yes, sir. I checked it just one hour ago."

"Very well," the Sheikh said. He had developed a way of communicating that made it almost impossible to track him. His men had found a new laser telephone under development in Israel. The designers were Palestinian, and even though the phone was only in research and not yet near production, they had allowed the Sheikh to have four of them. It worked with laser energy that was able to change amplitude much like an AM radio.

The Sheikh and Salim walked up the dark circular stairway, lit only by burning candles. Their black robes brushed against the khaki-colored dirt and sandstone that the stairway had been cut through.

They climbed until they were finally in the fortress proper, the sunlight filtering through the openings in the walls as they headed toward the westernmost part of Alamut. There were five or six other Assassins waiting for the Sheikh on the top of the highest level of Alamut, standing next to the laser phone.

"Satellites?" the Sheikh asked one of them, a dark dour man.

"Clear for another hour."

The Sheikh picked up the handset. It was impossible to intercept the signal unless you were standing between the sender and the receiver, and even then, only if you had the correct logarithm could you make any sense of it. It was as secure a means of communication as existed. His assistant aimed his laser phone at the receiver's post, ten miles away, where it was copied and relayed to another laser receiver ten miles farther away. When the signal reached its final destination, it was passed to the Sheikh's brother in the code in which it had originated. The only three people who had the code were the Sheikh, Salim, and the Sheikh's brother. Once it was decoded, the Sheikh's brother would walk across town and have a private conversation with the person to whom the communication was directed.

The Sheikh began speaking softly in quick, short sentences.

They stood in CVIC around a square chart table. Six aviators in their long, green Nomex fire-resistant flight suits and scuffed, black leather flight boots. They all had looks of intense concentration and excitement. Other aviators from other squadrons walked across CVIC looking at the charts, the latest information on SAM sights, and other strike planning information. Pritch stood behind the six Jolly Roger fliers.

Bark was clearly in charge of the group. He looked at their bright, eager faces then said, "If we're going into Iran, the plan has to be perfect." He stared at the chart that covered the table. It was an ONC, an Operational Navigational Chart, that when folded out was four feet square. It showed the area from the eastern Mediterranean to the Black Sea to western Iran where it met Syria and Turkey. Pritch had placed the most recent information on Syrian and Lebanese SAMs directly on the chart. The red circles, representing ranges of SAMs in question, overlapped in many areas. AAA sites were noted by large red dots and Syrian Army positions were done in the traditional infantry notation understood by very few on the ship. Bark spoke again. "Trey set up the plan, along with Wink. They think it will work. I think they're right. You are the best flight planners in the squadron. I want us to give this plan a murder board. Shoot it full of holes. Tear it apart. Ask every question that comes to your mind. I want it to be the best possible plan."

"Sir, do we have any indication that we can get the 28s in time for them to make a difference?" Blankenship, the Machine, asked.

"They're already on their way," Wink said excitedly. "The Gunner reached deep. Or someone did. It's like someone from Washington picked up the phone and *told* them to make this happen. Either that, or the Gunner must have incriminating photos of the Air Force pukes at Eglin. They couldn't get them to us fast enough. They're in the air on a C-17 right now. Two of them. There's a COD waiting for them in Signonella after the ordies in Signonella build the bombs. They'll come to us as all up rounds. The COD OIC has stripped the inside of the COD of the seats. ETA is 2200 tonight."

"Shit hot," one of the officers said, smiling.

"The Gunner also said that Eglin is shipping five of them to the Air Force B-2 base in Missouri," Bark added. "If we don't smoke this guy the Joint Chiefs are going to let the batmobile carry the bomb. Let the big boys take care of the problem, after the good little Navy boys have had their fun. But *someone* has told them to let us go first." Bark had an idea suddenly. He looked at Woods. "You e-mail anybody else today? Anybody in Washington?"

Woods made a face, as if it was a silly idea, and said nothing.

"Air Force," Blankenship said. "Always got to stick their nose in everything. This is *our* fight. They went after our officer."

"Frankly," Bark said, "I think that's why we're going to get a shot at it. The Air Force would never let us do it without elbowing us out of their way if it was up to them."

Wink replied. "Right—until the B-2 dropped its highly accurate laser-guided bombs on the Chinese embassy in Belgrade, it had never seen combat. And that was with all those hot Air Force targeteers working the problem."

"Trey," Bark said, "run through the plan."

"Yes, sir." Woods picked up the chart and crossed to the sliding corkboard. He took the left side as Big stood at the right. The two men pinned it tightly to the board. "One of the keys is to make sure Iran doesn't know we're coming. We recommend that we launch with a diversionary strike. We need to keep up the impression of focusing on those two targets, and keep pounding them. But on one of those sorties, two Tomcats will peel off and head east. Way east. We go down to the deck and do a Night Vision Devices low level in the weeds all the way." He took a pointer and showed where they would peel off. "As you can see, we avoid the SAMs most of the way to Iran and back. We'll have to go through them on initial ingress and egress, but once into Syria, it should be clear sailing." Woods looked at the chart as if having some new thoughts. "Then we drop these five-thousand-pound hogs and egress north and west," he said, pointing to the chart, tracing the route that had been drawn in pencil including time on target and times over each way-point.

"Load-out?" the Maintenance Officer demanded.

"Each Tomcat will have one GBU-28. That's about five thousand pounds. Limit ourselves to two Sidewinders each—another four hundred pounds—download the Phoenix rails, and we'll both carry tanks. On the way in we'll refuel feet dry as far east as we can sell it as part of a diversionary strike, and immediately on return, once feet wet. The four-hundred-fifty-mile transit will just allow us to pop-up and drop the 28s, then return low level. There isn't much room for error."

The MO scratched his chin. "That doesn't leave you any afterburner at all."

"True."

"Fighter escort?"

"We want to minimize our radar signature. Four or five planes are much more likely to be seen."

"We ought to at least think about some dedicated fighters. Never know who will show up."

"You think the *Iranians* are going to show up?" Woods asked, implying the answer with his tone. He continued, skeptical. "They'd have to know we're coming, or be awfully quick to get someone airborne. Their closest fighter base is Isfahan, and that's three hundred miles away. Then they'd have to find us and intercept us at two hundred feet over the desert. At *night*. I like those chances, especially compared to sending in four big fighters instead of two."

"Fair enough. We can think about it."

"Anyway, there's the route. We'll pop up to altitude for the drop about a half-mile apart. If things go according to plan we'll have somebody on ground lasing the target for us." Woods glanced over his shoulder at Pritch. "Any word yet?"

Pritch shook her head. She was extremely uncomfortable, unhappy with Woods for even bringing it up.

Bark looked at the other officers. "Anybody see any problems with this plan?"

"Fuel," Blankenship said. "How can you go into a mission like this and not have fuel for any afterburner? Too tight."

"We've got to get in and out undetected."

"You can't even get shot at by one SAM. You can't touch your burners at all. I don't like it."

"The only alternative is to send a tanker with them part of the way on the route—"

"Never happen. They'd all be sitting ducks."

"Exactly. That's why we ended up where we did. There's no other choice. The plan kind of wrote itself."

"Anybody else?" Bark asked.

"Who's on the ground?"

"We're not going to talk about that," Pritch interrupted.

"Tell me how *sure* you are it will happen. How reliable is this . . . ground unit."

"*Un*sure, sir."

"Well, that doesn't give me warm feelings. Fly a million miles in the dark on the deck with night-vision devices so someone or something that we're 'unsure' about will be there to finish it for us? How much of this plan is based on the guy being there? 'Cause if it were my skin at risk, I'd be real unenthusiastic."

"We don't even know if . . . someone will be there. It is a possibility. I wouldn't count on it."

"So what if he isn't? Can the LANTIRN god here," Bark said, indicating Wink, "put it down the guy's throat?"

Woods and all the others looked at Wink. He was the only one who could answer the question with any confidence. Wink thought about it for what seemed to those waiting like a long time. He knew the mission hung on his answer. "We'll hit where we're aiming. I can guaran-damn-tee you that. The problem is knowing where to aim to put it in the Sheikh's ready room. I'd say the chances of getting him if we do it ourselves are low."

Everyone stiffened slightly as the Air Wing Commander strolled into CVIC. Bark spoke first. "CAG. Good morning."

"Well," CAG said noncommittally, surveying the people before him and quickly scanning the chart. "What have we here?"

"Strike planning," Bark said, with a hint of a defensive tone. "Contingency strike planning."

"Into Iran, I see." He looked at Woods.

Woods held his tongue. He really wanted to say something clever, but he didn't want to torpedo his plan or his career right now.

CAG wasn't really expecting a reply. "I'm surprised Washington signed off on this. Flying a GBU-28 out here on a day's notice to be dropped by aircrew that have never dropped one before? Incredible. Who do you know in Washington?" He stared at Woods, still not expecting a reply. CAG examined the chart. "It really isn't a bad idea," he said, looking at Bark. "That's what separates Navy Air from everybody else, you know?" he said, suddenly taking ownership of the idea, especially if it was going to be successful. "Flexibility. Adaptability. Better than the Air Force. For us, when things change, we make new plans. Better plans. Change to make it work. It entails some risk. But to succeed in this life, you've got to take some risks. Right, Lieutenant?"

"Couldn't agree more," Woods replied, fighting back a smile. "What do you think of the route?"

CAG looked at the chart again and studied the pencil lines. "How far?"

"Four hundred fifty miles one way."

"Low level?"

"A lot of it. After we peel off from the diversionary strike."

"Diversionary strike?"

"Yes, sir, a regular strike on the fortress in Syria. We pull away from them and get down on the deck and head east."

"NVDs?"

"Yes, sir, once we get down on the deck, we'll be on the goggles all the way in."

"Hell of a long time."

"Yes, sir, it is."

"What's the longest you've ever flown on NVDs?"

"Couple of hours."

CAG wanted no part of that kind of flight. "Damned things give me a headache. Like looking through a drinking straw. Narrows your field of vision too much. Keep up the planning, Bark, I want you to show me the final plan. Nobody goes unless I sign off on it."

"Aye, aye, sir," Bark replied as CAG walked toward the TV studio section of CVIC.

"Sami, my office!"

Sami jumped when he heard Kinkaid's voice from over the padded cubicle wall. He knew he had said too much, but he hadn't even said everything he felt. He didn't care if Kinkaid fired him. He didn't want to be a part of the charade of being the American arm of Israel's military. He stood up and walked straight into Kinkaid's office. He closed the door behind him so hard it slammed loud enough to make both of them jump involuntarily.

"Sir—"

"Shut up," Kinkaid said, silencing him.

Sami waited, his anger building.

"You were way out of line."

"I was just saying what I was thinking—"

"And that justifies it?"

"It's my obligation as an officer—"

"Your obligation is to do what you're *told*! What do you think you're doing running around reading old investigation files and dreaming up grand conspiracy theories? Who do you think you are?"

"I'm not making it up. It's what makes it all make sense."

"You don't even know what you're talking about! I've been doing this since before you were born! And you stand there in front of a task force I've put together and insult the Agency, insult me, imply there are spies in our house, and I'm just supposed to take it because *you've* got it all figured out?"

"I wouldn't put it like that—"

"I'll bet you wouldn't. I should end your little career for that stunt. You'd have no future in Washington, I'd make sure of it." He studied Sami's rigid face. "Why are you so suspicious of the Israelis?"

"They're untrustworthy."

"Sami, they've done things you could only imagine doing. You've read a few things, and think you know the whole picture. They sent men into the desert alone in the Gulf War to find Scud sites for *us*. They ate lizards for days to find where the launches were coming from."

Sami smiled. "For *us*? Those Scuds were being shot at Jerusalem! What did you expect them to do? They seem to think the big favor they did for us was by letting us fight *that* war for them too! We begged them to stay home, while we risked our lives for them! They got praise from our government for being willing to do nothing. It was bullshit!"

"They give us intel that you don't even know about."

"Like what?"

"You're not cleared—"

"Of course. So tell me the great stuff they've given us that I *am* cleared for."

"They've given us entire SAM systems they captured. It gave us a great advantage." Kinkaid waved his hand. "I don't need to defend them."

"They look out for their own interests. Period."

"We all do."

"Not true. We have helped a lot of other countries when there was no direct benefit to us."

"And they have helped us. Just take my word for it."

"In another 'unofficial' exchange between you and this Efraim guy?"

"Sometimes. Sometimes in more official channels."

"For every one of those—and I'd love to be able to check them—there are two where they've either stolen from us or hurt us."

"No—"

"Like Pollard—"

"Don't go banging that damned Pollard drum again, Sami. I'm tired of it—"

"Do you know how many documents he stole for Israel?"

"Sure, a lot," Kincaid replied.

"How many?"

"I don't remember, exactly. It was a long time ago."

"Five hundred *thousand* pages of classified information."

"Like I said, a lot."

"You know how he came to find Israelis that were interested?" Sami asked.

"It doesn't matter—"

"A party in New York. Big party for the Israeli pilot who bombed the Iraqi nuclear plant. Big hero. Our boy Pollard makes contact and starts pumping out the Secret and Top Secret documents to the Israelis."

"True," Kinkaid acknowledged.

"But you know what they did with them?"

"Read them."

"After they read them."

"What?"

"They wanted to make the Soviet Union happy so it would release more Jews to emigrate to Israel. They gave the documents to the KGB."

"That's never been proved—"

"So they're our *friends*?"

"Intelligence can be dirty business."

"Like the *Liberty*."

"Sami—"

"That's right. Don't look at history. It doesn't matter. Joe," he said, "we're targeting an old fortress based mostly on my historical analysis of something that goes that go back nine hundred years." He smiled ironically. "You won't even look back thirty years?"

Kinkaid eyed his telephone as if waiting for it to ring. "The *Liberty* was a mistake. We've already talked about that."

"What about their nuclear program?"

"What about it?"

"How did Israel get the uranium for it?"

Kinkaid didn't reply.

Sami studied his face. "See, you *do* know. Rich Jew in Pennsylvania faked 'losing' two hundred pounds of it from his manufacturing plant after the Israelis visited. He had given *millions* of dollars to Israel before that. They denied it, if you can believe that."

"What's the point?"

"If it is to further *their* interests, they'll sell out the U.S. so fast it will make your head spin."

"Why do you care so much?"

Sami stared at his boss and leaned against the closed door. He stood there silently. "Back to that, huh? The young Turk."

"Haddad. That's your last name. Any relationship to Ali-Haddad? The most radical group of the PLO in the 80s?"

Sami's mouth dropped. "What kind of question is that?"

"Just showing you how faulty apparently logical thinking can be."

"I can't believe you even said that." Sami sank into the chair in the corner of Kinkaid's office. "I've spent my entire time here studying Arab terrorists. Trying to anticipate them, to defeat them. And now you accuse me of *being* one of them?"

"I'm not accussing you of anything. I'm just showing you how you can go off track with seemingly straight thinking." Kinkaid became reflective. "It goes back to Henry Kissinger."

Sami looked at him with deep confusion. "What does?"

Kinkaid sighed and closed his eyes. "America made a deal with the devil. The Red Prince. The most effective PLO terrorist ever."

Sami's face reddened. "Ali Hassan Salameh."

"You know of him," Kinkaid said, surprised.

"Also known as Abu Hassan. Of course I do. He married Georgina Rizak, the Lebanese Miss Universe."

Kinkaid smiled. "I'm impressed. He had targeted the U.S. We got wind of it. Based on Kissinger's instructions, we talked to him."

"How could we *talk* to him?" Sami asked, amazed. "He was the mastermind behind the '72 Olympic attack!"

"We made a deal. We agreed not to pursue him if he would leave American citizens and property alone. He agreed. Not only did he agree, he became one of our best sources. Not about the PLO, but anybody else was fair game." He paused and waited for Sami to look at him. "We knew where he was. Often. But we *never* told the Mossad. And he was number one on their hit list for years, until 1976 when they got him without our help."

Sami was shocked. America had made a deal with the most cold-blooded killer he had studied. He had never known. "That *is* dealing with the devil."

"We did what was in *our* interests. Just like we're supposed to."

Sami wanted to say something else. There was so much to say, so much to think through. "But that's where you met Efraim, at Munich. Chasing the Red Prince."

"Yes." He could see the light going on in Sami's head.

"And the whole time, you knew who it was and where he was and had made a deal with him."

"He came to this very building. Often. Came up the elevator, just like you do. Had coffee with the Director."

"Impossible!"

"Not impossible."

"And the whole time, Efraim was trying to find him? To kill him?"

"Yep."

"And you never told him."

"No, I didn't. He must know it now. Kissinger published it in his memoirs."

"Maybe now it's payback time."

"I don't think so," Kinkaid said, obviously having already thought of that. "I wanted *you* to know that I know what I'm doing. I know everything you know about Israel and a lot more. And I know a lot more about what we have done, and haven't done."

Sami relaxed noticeably. "It's not pretty, is it, this intelligence stuff."

"Sometimes it's beautiful. And other times, it's very ugly indeed."

"I just don't want our pilots to fly into a trap."

"Neither do I," Kinkaid said. "You need to know that I take all that, and more, into account. It's all a matter of judgment. It's why my hair is getting gray. *Your* job right now is to determine whether the Sheikh has another place. Somewhere he might flee to before we get him. We have to anticipate."

"Sure," Sami said. "I don't think there is any other place, but I'll give it some thought." He turned to go, and stopped. He looked back at Kinkaid. "I misjudged you. I'm sorry."

"There's one other thing you should know."

"What?"

"Pollard wasn't recruited by the Mossad."

"Right," Sami said, unbelieving. "It was LAKAS or something like that."

"LAKAM," Kinkaid corrected him. "*Lishka le Kishrei Mada.* The Hebrew acronym for the Israeli Defense Ministry's Scientific Affairs Liaison Bureau."

"And the Mossad had nothing to do with it."

"Actually they didn't," Kinkaid said, smiling.

"You buy that?"

"Yes."

"Whatever," Sami said, unconvinced again.

"But remember when we confronted Israel about Pollard they protested that the Mossad never spies in the U.S.?"

"Yeah."

"They do."

"The Mossad?"

"Al. Hebrew for 'above.' A secret group within the Mossad unknown to even the vast majority of the Mossad. They operate in New York, Washington, D.C., wherever they want. Active spying."

"You're kidding me?"

"No."

"Why are you telling me this?"

"Because you are right. You can't believe anything they tell you."

"And?"

"And our objective isn't to *believe* them, it is to line up things so their interests are the same as ours. Then when they act in their interests it is to our benefit. So let me do that and quit trying to out-think me."

Sami was reeling. "I had no idea."

"Exactly. But I like your tenacity. I like your hunger for the truth. Just give the rest of the people in your family the benefit of the doubt until you have a really good reason not to. It's the only way you'll survive in this business."

36

The Gunner stood on the flight deck in his khaki pants, red Jolly Rogers ordnance shirt, and red flotation vest. He had his goggles on and his helmet was strapped tightly under his chin. He took being on the flight deck very seriously. He had seen too many people killed, friends who had walked into turning props, been sucked into jet intakes, cut in half by a broken arresting gear cable, or simply blown over the side by invisible jet exhaust, never to be seen again. Most of it had happened at night, when there wasn't any moon, like tonight.

But the Gunner was so excited about the ugly plane that was taxiing to a stop in front of him he could be forgiven for paying just slightly less attention to the constant dangers. He was surrounded by his ordnancemen who were as excited about the COD in front of them as he was. A new weapon to an ordnancemen was like Christmas to a young child.

Gunner Ruben Bailey's division wanted to be there to see the COD and its cargo, but he had kept the number of men down—limited to those he needed to move and load the cargo.

The Gunner and the red-shirted ordnancemen stood just forward of the island. The COD, the last airplane of the recovery, stopped directly in front of the island.

The plane captain hurried to the wheels and put the chocks in place to keep the aircraft from rolling, then grabbed the tie-down points and secured the plane to the deck with heavy, steel chains. She hurried back out to where the pilot could see her and gave him a thumbs-up, then brought her hand across her throat while pointing at the number-two engine, telling him to shut it down. The turboprop engine shuddered quickly to a stop and she gave the signal to shut down the other one.

The Gunner and the rest of the ordies moved around to the back of the COD. The ramp came down slowly, finally touching the deck. The Gunner and his men hurried into the belly of the plane, where two GBU-28s were exposed for all to see—ready to go, an all up round, as they called it, assembled by the Navy ordnancemen on the Naval Air Base at Sigonella, Sicily.

None of them had ever seen a bomb this big. This long. It was almost 20 feet long and smooth, almost polished smooth. It looked just like it should—an eight-inch Howitzer gun barrel. Eight inches of course being the size of the shell that could pass through it. The barrel itself was ten inches in diameter. The ordnancemen were impressed. The bomb was painted a flat, dark, olive green, as most bombs were, but the surface was smooth, unlike most bombs which were rough. It was high-quality steel and all business. The ordies at Sigonella had put the wings on the bomb—the airfoil group, as well as the CCG, the Computer Control Group—the guidance in the nose, as well as the strong back, the part that allowed it to be connected to the airplane.

The Gunner studied the wheels of each dolly with his flashlight, measuring the numerous nylon straps with his eyes. After assuring himself that they wouldn't roll, he ordered his men to break it down. The Gunner yelled to leave no doubt about what he had said.

Four of the Gunner's ordnancemen grabbed each MHU-191 skid on which each bomb rested and began carefully moving the bombs out of the plane, tying one down to the flight deck with steel chains. The ordnancemen gathered around the other bomb, pushing the massive weapon slowly down the rolling flight deck to the waiting F-14.

✦

Everyone on the task force agreed Kinkaid was worn out. He hadn't slept in three days. He stared at the computer screens in the task force's room, but saw nothing. They had made no progress toward finding the men responsible for the open murders of Americans in Italy, Washington, Paris, London, and Naples and Kinkaid was disappointed with their performance. The murder in Washington had officially been handed over to the FBI, but the unit assigned was based at Langley, a rare example, though more common now than ten years before, of coordination between two services who had a history of rivalry.

But all the fusion, all the cross comparison of data from numerous sources had come up empty. They had no idea who the murderers were. At least as individuals.

"Joe. Phone."

Kinkaid took the handset. "Kinkaid."

"It is Efraim."

Kinkaid recognized his voice before he heard the name. "Efraim, how are you? What's the answer?"

"Right to business, is it?" Efraim asked, sounding disappointed. "Answer to what?"

"You know exactly what I mean."

"I've been working on your behalf only to be greeted by unfriendliness?"

Kinkaid sighed. "Sorry. I'm just tired."

"War can do that to you. It makes many people tired. I too, am tired."

"So, what's the answer?"

"I've been thinking about what you've said, or what your young Turk has implied. I'm troubled. But it has made me wonder. What if the United States is getting Israel to do *its* dirty work?"

"Oh, hell, Efraim. What are you talking about? I don't have time for this."

"Maybe the United States does not want to risk its counterterrorist Special Forces operatives. Maybe it wants to risk Israel's, instead. Is that possible?"

"No. It's not possible. It's stupid. If we need do it ourselves, we will. I thought it would be the *best* way, in fact. As I recall, you are the one who discouraged me from sending one of our people."

"Yes, I expressed my concerns. I fear I am becoming as paranoid as you, my friend."

Kinkaid waited for Efraim to go on. He wasn't going to beg.

"We'll do it, but it has to be on our schedule," Efraim finally said.

"What is the schedule?"

"Tonight."

"We're going to have to work fast."

"It must occur at four local time. When there is no moon."

"Local, meaning at the site of the target?"

"Yes."

"What is that Zulu time?"

"Three hours ahead of London."

"How will our pilots know if your man is in fact designating the target?"

"They will know."

"What if he's not there?"

"He's already there."

"Thank you, Efraim." Kinkaid was in fact grateful, but he was also uneasy. Too many unknowns.

"You are very welcome. Consider it a payment for the tragedy that befell your pilot in Israel. Our chance to give you your vengeance. An eye for an eye."

"Tell your person to do as described unless I contact you. Can I reach you at this number for the rest of the evening?"

"Yes. I will be here all night."

"Good luck."

"Thanks," he said, hanging up. Kinkaid looked at Sami, who was listening very carefully. "Maybe we've earned our keep after all."

Sami nodded. "If he's really there."

The sun was just setting west of the fortress at Alamut. It was a day like so many before in the mountains of northwestern Iran. The men who followed the Sheikh were doing as he had demanded, searching far and wide for any hint of those who would do them harm or to find the first indication that the Americans were on their way. The Sheikh knew the Americans would come. It was a question only of how and when.

Farouk and the squad of Assassins in their black head gear and flowing robes worked their way over the hills five miles from Alamut, across the valley floor. They had climbed over these rocks thousands of times as boys, and now as young men. They knew these hills intimately.

They were fatigued from the month of turmoil that they had been through. They had intended to stir things up, but hadn't expected to generate a war. They fought their fatigue and tried to maintain their intense focus during their search, but they knew there was no one here. They would have seen them approach. There was no place for an army unit to hide in this rocky terrain. Farouk slid down an enormous boulder and landed at its base. He looked around carefully, his AK-47 slung over his shoulder.

The second squad member slid down the same way, and the rest followed. The last man slid down the huge rock face slightly more to the left than the others had. As he neared the bottom his boot scraped against the rock next to the boulder and he heard a different sound. Farouk noticed it too. He looked at Farouk, who nodded. Farouk watched him unsling his AK-47 and point it at the second rock. Farouk motioned for the remainder of the squad to spread out while the eager young Assassin walked carefully toward the rock and touched it with his hand. It was cloth. Amazingly rock-like–looking cloth, but cloth nonetheless. The man pressed it and the cloth bent under his pressure. Whoever had somehow constructed a fake rock out of cloth, it wasn't a friend.

Farouk motioned for his men to stand back and fired at the rock. The bullets tore through, leaving small black holes where they had passed through the thin cloth. He waited. Nothing happened. One of the Assassins went forward and placed his face against the cloth trying to see through one of the bullet holes. He was thrown back from the cloth as several M-16 bullets struck him in the face.

Bullets tore through the fake boulder in both directions as the Assassins returned fire at the unseen enemy. Another Assassin fell to the ground screaming in agony from a bullet that had torn through his jaw, the others continued to fire wildly at the boulder.

Inside the man changed clips on his M-16 and waited for them to come closer, listening to the cautious footsteps. He knew he had no hope of escape, but he also had decided long before coming on the mission that he wasn't going to be taken alive.

Farouk knew he had to be aggressive. He indicated to the other squad members that they prepare to fire together. They all pointed their rifles at the boulder and Farouk gave them the sign.

The man inside began firing methodically through the cloth just before the Assassins. When another Assassin fell the squad fired back with a fury. Inside the cover bullets ripped through the man's body, throwing him backward. His M-16 clattered against the rock floor of the hideout. Farouk raised his hand to tell his men to cease firing; they waited in silence.

After a few minutes, he approached the decimated shell. He and another man finally tore it from the ground and looked inside. The dead man lay on the ground surrounded by food, electronic gear, weapons, and other items that the squad did not recognize.

They moved closer carefully, their rifles on him, making sure he was dead. Once certain, they looked around to see if there was anyone else, examining a few nearby boulders for another camouflage cover. Farouk was proud of their success in killing the spy, but at the same time he was worried. Someone knew about Alamut. There could be others. The Assassins searched the man's gear but nothing had any identification marks. The man on the ground was a mystery. No rank, no uniform, no identification of any kind. He could have been be from anywhere.

He had sandy hair and a fair complexion. Probably American, they thought. Special warfare, dropped by the Americans in preparation for an attack on Alamut. The Sheikh would be pleased that they had found him but concerned by the implications.

They opened a bag and put the man's gear in it. A nightscope, an infrared scope. Farouk examined one particular device carefully. He had no idea what it was and like everything else its identification marks had been removed. He placed it in the bag with the rest of the dead man's things.

Farouk studied the hideout and wondered how the man had gotten there. No parachute, nothing to show how he had arrived, or how he hoped to leave, or when. He ordered one of his men to carry the dead man.

The Assassin threw the heavier man over his shoulder effortlessly. The man's blood ran down onto him and he tried not to show his disgust. The other squad members picked up their own dead and they began their long hike back to Alamut.

Everyone on the carrier knew about the coming mission. They knew about the bomb, who was going to deliver it, and how. The men and women involved in that evening's other strikes understood that theirs were secondary, or even diversionary. They didn't care—in fact they were excited about it.

In VF-103 it was different. The squadron realized that Woods and Big with Wink and Sedge were the tip of the spear that would pierce the ground and the heart of Sheikh al-Jabal. Tonight victory meant the death of one person.

The early strikes had already gone and had reported heavy SAM fire with new AAA sites near the targets. It had been the hairiest night so far, which was discouraging since so much effort had been put into SEAD, the Suppression of Enemy Air Defenses.

Although the rhetoric had picked up, the Syrian Air Force had stayed on the ground.

Woods's event was set to brief at midnight. Bark had decided to address all the aircrew fifteen minutes before the scheduled brief, and had called all the officers together. They were tired but enthusiastic.

"I won't take much of your time, but I wanted us to gather together for a minute before this squadron launches a mission never before flown by a Navy plane." He glanced at his watch. "Their brief will begin in about fifteen minutes. We are finally going to strike what we hope will be a fatal blow against the terrorism of Sheikh al-Jabal. He has killed our squadron mate and other innocent Americans, including a State Department official who was locking his car when he was murdered, a Naval attaché in Paris, out for a peaceful morning jog, and the Commanding Officer of an F-18 squadron and one of his Lieutenants. The Shiekh is a cold-blooded murderer. If I had the chance to cut his throat, I would do it in a *second*.

"*Seriously*. I don't want to sound bloodthirsty, but I see no reason for this man to continue living. If it were up to me, he wouldn't. And, amazingly, it is up to us. Actually up to Trey, and Big. And the LANTIRN gods, Wink and Sedge."

Wink smiled, fighting his apprehension.

"I wanted each of us to tell them how much we are behind them. We will do our very best to make it happen tonight, whether we are on a strike mission, on decoys, doing maintenance support, or just praying. Whatever we're going to do, we will do it. The Jolly Rogers will make it happen. So Trey, Big, Wink, Sedge, we're with you. Do us proud." His listeners fell silent and not sure what more to say, Bark ended it. "Dismissed," he said abruptly, and walked out of the ready room.

The sudden end of Bark's talk caught the squadron off guard. They weren't certain whether to stay and slap Woods on the back, or go about their business. The opinion quickly formed that work was in order, not celebration or conversation.

Odd little speech, Woods thought. Bark puzzled him. Most of the time he was a straight-ahead, no-nonsense, you-always-know-what-he-wants kind of guy. But every once in a while he would do or say something that made the whole squadron wonder if they understood him at all. But most Squadron Commanders were on the verge of losing it at one point or another—there seemed to be something inherent in the job that made them nearly come apart. Woods wondered if Bark's difficulties were his fault. From the moment he had allowed Vialli to go to Israel without telling Bark, he had dropped in his Commanding Officer's regard. He knew it. He could feel it on an almost daily basis. What had started as a trusting relationship, with Bark as his mentor, grooming his protégé, someone in whom he saw himself, had become a cool senior/subordinate relationship. And Bark seemed to be taking it hard. He couldn't identify with Woods anymore. Some invisible line had been crossed that couldn't even be discussed. To bring it up would be to acknowledge too much. It had come to the point now where Bark didn't trust him. But Bark also knew Woods was the right one to go. He was best suited for the job—he had the most training, and perhaps the very thing that had finally driven Bark away, reckless abandon. During his big speech about showing support for our guys going in harm's way, Bark hadn't looked at him once.

Woods and Big walked to the back of the ready room. They were alone. "You still up for this?" Big asked.

Woods looked around. "We've got a couple of minutes before the brief. Let's go out on the catwalk."

Big followed Woods directly outboard on the starboard side through the darken-ship black vinyl curtains onto the catwalk. They walked up to the steel grating and stood leaning on the railing. They could see the white foam of the water through the grating beneath them as the *Washington* steamed north through the Mediterranean. Seeing water race under their feet was unsettling to those who weren't accustomed to it. Woods glanced out toward the dark sea and thought about their mission.

"So," Big said.

Woods waited. They could hear the sailors preparing the flight deck for the launch behind them. "You ever thought of Bark as stupid?"

"No."

"Ever known him to leave anything unfinished?"

"Never," Big said, surveying the stars over the black water.

"He knows what happened in Lebanon."

"He didn't seem too sure."

"Big," Woods said, "he saw the missile exhaust on our airplanes. He saw the PLAT tapes."

Big shrugged. "He didn't seem too convinced."

"He knows it wasn't from Roosevelt Roads."

"What are you saying?"

"He could send us to Leavenworth with one phone call."

Big thought about it. "So why hasn't he?"

"A lot of people in his squadron would go down. He doesn't know who. But he knows there had to be somebody in ordnance. And doesn't know who else."

"So why has he laid off?"

"Redemption."

"Huh?" Big asked.

"If we get the Sheikh and make it back, we've redeemed ourselves in his eyes. If we *don't* come back, we got what was coming to us."

"That's pretty calculated."

"Yep."

"What do you think? You still glad we went to Lebanon?"

Woods had thought of little else for weeks. It had haunted him. "It was stupid," Woods said. "And reckless. But isn't war made up of basically stupid acts? Things rational people would never do, given a choice? It seems like you have to get yourself into a position where you feel like you have no choice. Then you just do the inevitable. It's a game your mind plays with you. I was absolutely convinced if we didn't do something, no one would."

"Would you do it again?"

"No."

"What about now?"

"Now we're at war. It's the difference between dying as a soldier and dying as a criminal."

"You're just as dead."

"One's with honor."

"What difference does *that* make?" Big said with a small, sarcastic chuckle.

"I don't know. I just know it's different." Woods listened to the water hiss against the side of the carrier. "I used to think I knew it all. Not anymore. I just need to do my job and do it as well as I can."

"Which tonight means flying into Iran," Big said, smiling. "And you think Bark is setting us up?"

"No. He's just given us an incredible opportunity which also happens to come with just enough rope to hang ourselves."

"All the freedom we want to pull off our little scheme, on the off chance it will make up for last time." Big shook his head as he thought of all the implications and all the machinations. "My wife will be so pissed if I don't come back. Especially if she ever gets the whole story."

"She'd lose it. Does she know about Lebanon?"

Big shook his head.

"We're taking a big risk tonight."

"It's worth it. I still want to get this guy. And this time it's legal. How about you?"

"Chance of a lifetime."

"Trey, if anything happens to me, tell—"

"No chance. You're going to have to tell her yourself."

Big smiled. "Let's go brief."

"Yeah." Woods glanced at the sky and the sea for one last time. "You know, if Leavenworth is waiting for us when we get back, I'd rather not come back."

"According to your own paranoid theory, if Bark is setting us up, if we get the Sheikh, all is well."

"That's the theory. But we can't very well ask him, can we?"

"No. But we can sure try to get the Sheikh."

"There it is," Woods smiled.

The squad of Assassins, candlelight dancing off their dirty faces and weapons, entered the cave room. Twenty or thirty men surrounded the Sheikh, sitting in his usual chair. The squad carefully lowered their fallen comrades to the floor and folded their hands on their chests. The blood of the dead men glistened on those who had carried them.

The man carrying the unidentified enemy stood motionless, not sure whether to put him down. As everyone watched, he finally walked to the corner and dumped the body onto the floor unceremoniously. The Sheikh rose more quickly than usual. "What has happened?"

"We found one of the invaders."

"Three of our men were killed?" the Sheikh asked.

"We discovered a spy—very well hidden. He shot through his covering." Farouk pulled out a piece of the cloth covering and the aluminum frame from under his robe and handed them to the Sheikh. "It looked like a boulder. Even from one meter away."

The Sheikh examined it. "Ingenious," he said.

"Only by touching it could we tell the difference."

"But you found him. You are to be rewarded. . . . As to these men," he said, indicating the fallen Assassins, "they have their reward." The Sheikh touched each of the dead men on the forehead. He turned to the heap in the corner. "Bring him over here into the light," he said to the two men closest to the dead intruder. They grabbed the dead body and dragged him to the center of the room. The Sheikh stood over him, studying his face. "Did you search him?"

"Yes. We did."

"Did you find anything?"

"No. There is no identification of any kind."

"Then he was certainly a spy. No uniform, no identification, not even an indication of what country he is from." He thought about the spy for a while, standing stiffly, his hands behind his back. "What did you find in his hideout?"

"Much," the leader of the section said. He crossed to the table, moved several charts aside, and reached into the bag he had hauled back from the dead man's post. The first thing he took out was the sniper rifle.

The Sheikh took the rifle and held it, recognizing it instantly. "Remington five hundred. The sniper rifle preferred by the American Special Forces." He took the next item handed him. "Night-vision binoculars. Very expensive," he said, holding them in his hands. He lifted them to his eyes, flipping the switch to activate them. He glanced around the room and then turned them off. "The best I've ever seen. What else?"

"There was much ammunition, small arms, this device—" He handed a small unit to the Sheikh.

The Sheikh examined it, turning it over and back again. "There was a plate on the side of this that gave the manufacturer's name. It has been removed." He put the device on the table and stood back, watching the faces of his men to see if anyone recognized it. To his disappointment, no one did. "This is a laser designator." They recognized the name. They knew exactly what that was, and what it meant. The Sheikh told them anyway. "He was here to designate us as a target for an airplane," the Sheikh said, staring at the small device. He looked at the dead man. "He was certainly with the American Special Forces. We have acted just in time. The Americans are on their way. . . . We'll see what they can do without their spy. And we will be waiting."

Woods attached the clip to his helmet and carefully removed the ANVIS-9 Night Vision Devices from their case. Wink, Big, and Sedge did the same right behind him. Woods expertly attached the binocular devices to the clips and folded them down in front of his eyes. "Lights," he said to the para-rigger waiting by the switch. The lights were turned off inside the paraloft and it went completely dark. Woods flipped the small switch on the side of the lenses and the interior of the loft was clear in various shades of green. He crossed to the Hoffman box and gazed into its openings. He adjusted the four lenses on the goggles until he could see twenty/twenty inside the box. The others followed suit. Big was the last to focus his lenses. "Lights," he said, and the four detached the goggles from their helmets and placed them in the carrying cases.

Woods walked toward the Tomcat, stopping when he caught a glimpse of the GBU-28 under the plane. It was as big as a small airplane, and heavier than many. He stared at the bomb, then glanced at the Gunner. "Big mother," he commented as he handed his knee board to Airman Benson.

"Yes, sir," Gunner Bailey replied, very pleased with his men that they had been able to load the bombs without incident.

Benson took Wink's helmet bag and climbed aboard to set up the cockpits. Woods and Wink split up to do their counterrotating preflight and started down each side of the Tomcat. They checked the bomb repeatedly, studying the red arming pennants the ordies would remove on the catapult. Finished with that part of the check, they climbed up and strapped in.

The night weather had taken a turn for the worse, the sea rougher than it had been in many days. The other aircraft on the diversionary strike were to launch after them, except for the dedicated S-3 tanker, which would go off cat four just before they took off. Woods and Big were to take all the fuel their planes could hold.

In the darkness, Woods released the parking brake and moved forward slightly. The yellow shirt directing him moved his wands slowly, then crossed them quickly. Woods hit the brakes and felt the launch bar drop over the catapult shuttle as he had hundreds of times before. The yellow shirt saluted and passed him to the catapult officer. Woods found himself reassured by the familiarity as he thought of going down the catapult, accelerating to one hundred thirty-five knots in about two seconds carrying a howitzer barrel filled with high explosives under his belly, and being the first person in history to do it.

The catapult officer faced Woods, raising her right hand slightly and slid her left hand quickly to the bow of the ship. The shuttle moved forward and grabbed the Tomcat's launch bar. She signaled to run up the engines. Woods went to full throttle and finished his cockpit checks with Wink. They were ready. Woods moved the throttles and flames shot out of the F-14 as the engines went to afterburner. Flipping the switch, Woods turned on his exterior lights. The catapult officer saluted, signaled, and the catapult fired.

Woods, Wink, and their howitzer barrel rocketed down the catapult track, the acceleration throwing them back in their seats harder than usual. The Tomcat reached the end of the catapult stroke and they were pushed forward. The ship was done helping them fly.

The wheels cleared the deck and the aft half of the Tomcat rotated downward, lifting the nose of the plane above the horizon. Woods quickly scanned the instruments.

"We're flying," Wink called from the backseat after watching the airspeed indicator carefully.

"Head 076," Wink said.

"Roger," Woods replied. He put the Tomcat into a gentle right turn as they continued to rise. The rest of the strike group launched behind them and climbed after them.

They could see the formation lights on the other airplanes heading east with them. The two carrier Battle Groups had switched targets for the night so Woods's flight could be better camouflaged. They wanted to be seen on the radar of whoever was watching with the airplanes heading east. After that they would simply vanish. It would take a truly special radar operator to pick them out of the clutter once they peeled away from the group.

The radios were silent as the ten airplanes broke over the beach together. There had been some talk that Syria was going to actually send up fighters against this strike, but so far, no sign.

The pilots in the formation had been briefed by the Air Wing Commander, who had chosen to personally lead this diversionary strike. He had been a lukewarm convert to the strike plan against Alamut. When he found out there would be "someone" on the ground to laser designate the exact spot, and that the Air Force had actually parted with two of its private reserve of perfectly aged GBU-28s, and that the DOD had actually signed off on letting two untested Tomcat crews carry them into Iran, he figured who was he to stand in the way? A great military leader, like a great politician, is great sometimes because he discerns a trend and gets in front of it.

Some of the pilots were hoping that the Syrians would in fact have the nerve to fight them tonight. Down deep, not one of them believed they would, but there was always the hope. . . . The idea of air combat at night with lights off was almost too exciting, especially against someone who didn't practice. For those not accustomed to night fighting it was disconcerting and disorienting. The chance of a mid-air or of shooting down the wrong airplane in the general pandemonium was extremely high. It was not an environment into which the poorly trained strode happily.

"Any bogeys?" Woods asked.

"Negative," Wink said. The PTID was blank except for the strike aircraft. They crossed over the Syrian border and accelerated to five hundred knots. Woods glanced down to see if he could make out the coastline. A few small towns glittered below, but nothing substantial.

He couldn't tell where the Mediterranean stopped and Syria started. It was one great sea of blackness, with a few lights in the easternmost part.

The strike group continued east, deep into Syria. On a radar it would look as if the strike group had gone far inland to begin the attack from the east to avoid the SAMs. As they approached the break-off point Woods flew over to the S-3 tanker that was escorting the strike just to refuel Wink and Big. Tankers rarely went overland, but without getting fuel at the last possible moment, the Tomcats would never make it back to the ship.

"Hundred knots of closure," Wink called.

Woods retarded his throttles slightly as he closed the distance. "Fifty."

Woods raised his right wing to slow the closure and increase his turn. He was a few hundred yards from the tanker. He controlled his rate of climb, closure, and turn instinctively as he rendezvoused on the tanker.

"Ten," Wink said quietly.

Woods joined on the tanker's left wing, slightly below, perfectly. He never took his eyes off the plane. He'd done it hundreds of times, even at night, but he was always careful. He glanced quickly left to confirm that Big was on his wing, right where he should be. Big had been in loose trail, a quarter mile behind. He had gone off the catapult just seconds after Woods and had followed him the whole way.

The S-3 tanker pilot signaled, and Woods flipped a switch. The refueling probe climbed out of the right side of the Tomcat and made its customary loud noises as it rose hard and rigid into the two-hundred-fifty knot airstream. Woods slid back and approached the S-3 from behind. The refueling basket bobbed along at the end of the long invisible hose waiting for the Tomcat to pull up. Woods lined up behind the S-3 and accelerated straight ahead. The probe caught the basket and drove home, hitting right in the center. The basket squeezed the probe and the green light flickered. Good seat.

Woods pulled the throttles back slightly to enable him to fly formation on the tanker ahead of him. He glanced down at the fuel indicator. No change. He looked at the lights. Good green light over the drogue. "What's up?" he asked Wink.

"Don't know. I'm showing no transfer. Push it up a little. Give him a little slack."

Woods adjusted his speed to drive the drogue toward the tanker, then away. No change. They weren't getting any fuel. "Tell 'em."

Wink transmitted, *"No transfer. Check your switches."*

"Switches are fine. Pull out and try it again."

"Arrr," Woods said as he pulled the throttles back a little quicker than he needed to. The Tomcat slowed and the drogue came free. He accelerated again to catch it, and approached the drogue exactly the same way as the time before. "If we don't get fuel, we've got to abort. We can't get back without it."

Wink didn't reply. He didn't have to. He looked at his fuel indicator. They were already behind where they expected to be in their fuel specs. The bomb must have more drag than they had calculated.

Woods plugged in again and got another green light from the drogue. Then an amber, a red, then green again. He watched the fuel indicator stop decreasing and reverse itself and head up. "Good transfer," he said to Wink.

"Roger," Wink said, relieved.

They watched the digital fuel readout march upward until the Tomcat was completely topped off, over nineteen thousand pounds of fuel. They had replaced all the fuel they had used in start-up, taxi, takeoff, and climb. As Woods backed away from the basket, banking to his right and coming up to the right side of the tanker, Big moved over quickly to top off. When he was done he pulled out and joined on Woods's right wing. They pulled away from the tanker and banked right, toward the remainder of the strike group.

The planes on the strike had reached the point of separation. They split up to approach the target from different directions, making the air defense calculations immeasurably harder for the defenders—not just one piece of sky to look for.

The breakup was Woods's cue. "Goggle up," he said to Wink. They took their NVDs out of the cases and clipped them to the brackets on their helmets, folding them down and turning them on. Woods could now see everything, the horizon, the mountains, the puffy cloud twenty miles away, and every airplane within ten miles. Everything was green. He immediately pushed the nose of the Tomcat over and headed toward the deck, watching his instruments carefully to ensure he stayed under thirty degrees of nose-down attitude. The airplane felt heavy and sluggish. Wink turned his radar to standby. They were going in totally EMCON, emissions controlled—no electronic signals emanating from the plane at all—until near their target. They didn't want anybody picking up on them heading toward Iran with their radar blasting away, detectable for hundreds of miles.

He eased the stick back to slow his rate of descent as they neared the ground—gullies, bushes, and rocks were now clearly visible. He pulled harder and brought the nose up to the horizon, steadying out two hundred feet above the ground. Low enough that no radar would pick them up outside of thirty miles or so, and high enough that he was unlikely to hit most obstacles. They had the wires and cables of each area emblazoned on their chart.

Big joined on his wing in comfortable trail formation about a quarter of a mile behind him and slightly higher.

The radar warning detector was quiet. No surface to air missiles or AAA were trained on them as they started their race through eastern Syria. The Tomcat bounced slightly as the desert air rose from hills causing minor turbulence.

In the back, the LANTIRN god was fine-tuning his picture from the FLIR, the passive forward-looking infrared that was such a significant part of the LANTIRN system. It was working perfectly. Wink settled into his navigation and was comfortable with everything he saw. One of his favorite things about LANTIRN was it had a self-contained GPS unit that confirmed its position from satellites. It gave them their position three dimensionally.

"How we looking, Wink?"

"Coming up on our turnoff," Wink replied. "See the bridge just to the right?"

"Yeah."

"Stand by." As they came upon it Wink called, "Come port to 065," and Woods turned northeast toward the mountains of Iran.

Woods pushed the nose of the Tomcat over slightly following down a hill as he stayed at two hundred feet above ground level. He increased his speed to five hundred fifty knots. Wink had his head buried in the infrared LANTIRN system and watched for any sign of the launch of a surface-to-air missile or AAA. Wink glanced at the green-glowing radar warning indicator by his right knee. It was completely quiet.

Woods checked his fuel. They were below their consumption ladder again, burning more fuel than they should be. He checked his speed and fuel flow again. The fuel flow was slightly higher than projected. His calculations had been wrong. Bark had told them to check their fuel carefully. If they weren't close, they were to abandon the mission. The last thing Bark said he wanted was to lose two Tomcats from fuel starvation. They were already burning through their Bingo fuel—the cushion they relied on when returning to the carrier to fly to a nearby airfield if they couldn't get back aboard. Wink checked their projected time on target with the LANTIRN system.

"Crossing into Iraq," Wink reported.

"This just goes from bad to worse, doesn't it?" Woods replied. He glanced at his engine instruments, the fuel flow, the turbine inlet temperature, the wing position, and engine rpm's. Everything was as smooth as silk. "You see Big?"

Wink grabbed the steel handle on top of the radar panel in front of him and twisted around to look between the tails of the Tomcat. "Yep," Wink said with some difficulty due to his contortions. "Got his formation lights. About a quarter mile behind us. Stacked right." He glanced at his PTID again. "Time to target is thirty-six minutes."

"Roger," Woods said. His hands were beginning to sweat inside his gloves. The green landscape flashed by smoothly. The desert air was mercifully quiet with few pockets of turbulence or intense heat rising into the cool night sky.

"Approaching way-point three," Wink said. He had chosen an intersection as the way-point, something that they could check visually to make sure they were on course. "Stand by to come port to 049. Check for intersection."

"Roger." Woods watched the distance to the way-point count down in tenths of miles. He strained to see an intersection. He hadn't even seen a road in thirty minutes. The desert had a way of rejecting roads unless they were well maintained. He had a feeling the chances of this intersection being well maintained were not high. He scanned the horizon for anything suspicious. There were no signs of life at all.

"Mark. Come port, 049," Wink said crisply.

Woods banked the F-14 left and pulled up slightly to make sure the turn didn't bring them closer to the ground. He checked the radar altimeter, the only emission they were making that might be detected by the enemy. It was a small radar beam that was projected directly down, beneath the Tomcat, to measure its height above the ground with amazing accuracy. The accuracy would cause the numbers to jump around even if they were level because of the changing elevation of the ground. He steadied on the new heading. Woods had found himself watching the sky even more carefully after they'd passed into Iraq. He couldn't believe they were flying through Syria, Iraq, and Iran all in one night. He started to wonder how smart his plan had been. It was fraught with potential for disaster, not the least of which was the longest night low-level he had ever flown. He wouldn't put it past Iraq to try to come up and stop them. Not that he was worried about Iraq's ability to find them and shoot them down at night with one of its fighters, but he didn't have enough gas for even one turn with a fighter.

The air grew unfriendly as they entered a mountain valley. They started bouncing noticeably in the mountain air. Woods was worried about maintaining his heading and altitude without running into something. He followed the valley through the jagged rocks and tried to maintain his course, beginning to breathe audibly.

"You okay?" Wink asked.

"Yeah."

"Entering Iran," Wink announced casually.

Woods was busy scanning back and forth with his night-vision goggles. His field of vision was much more limited than usual. He had to turn his head to see the gullies and valleys that were flashing by. He saw what looked like a tent settlement directly ahead and wanted to pull up to avoid them, but he had to stay low. He held his altitude and flew right over the dark tents. He could only imagine what those in the tents thought as they were awakened in the middle of the night by nearly instantaneous and overwhelming jet noise from one hundred feet away. Their animals probably all had heart attacks.

"We're getting close, Trey. Thirty miles out. We'll start up at ten miles."

Woods climbed over a small hill and pushed the nose over to stay low to the ground.

"Twenty miles," Wink said, his excitement growing. "Oh, *shit!*" he added. "I'm getting a SAM indication. An SA-6!"

"They're waiting for us," Woods said. "We've got to stay low and do a pop-up bomb run."

"We can't! We told them it would be a mid-altitude drop! Our laser guy is waiting for us to come in high!"

"No *way*, not in the middle of an SA-6 envelope. I just hope like hell the laser guy keeps that laser on target or this is all for naught."

Both their voices had risen as the intensity and speed of the mission had tripled and their brains tried to make innumerable calculations simultaneously. Woods looked to his right and forward in the direction the SA-6. He was surprised to see snow reflecting on the top of the mountains. He pushed the airplane over and flew lower to the ground, his radar altimeter bouncing around due to the unevenness of the ground, but hovering mostly around fifty feet.

The two F-14s raced through the long valley, hugging the ground on their way to the point where they would pull up and lob their enormous bombs at Alamut, a flight they had flown many times in practice, but never with a five-thousand-pound bomb underneath.

They came to the end of the long valley and stared at a small mountain right in front of them. Woods aimed the Tomcat a little left of the peak and pulled up slightly to match the rising terrain. He maintained his altitude above the ground as he climbed up the mountainside, the accelerometer needle showing negative two Gs as the Tomcat headed down the other side of the small mountain, still close to the ground. Woods checked their fuel one last time. They were now two thousand pounds low. It was getting critical.

The Tomcats bottomed out after the hill and headed across another small valley toward Alamut.

"The SA-6 is still tickling us from right nine o'clock," Wink said, as he checked their bombing solution. "Just over that hill."

"Let me know if he locks us up," Woods said.

Just as they steadied at fifty feet above the deck on the valley floor Woods pulled back on the stick to climb up the next summit. They headed up the hill, which was steeper than they had initially thought. As they reached the top of the ridge line Wink slaved his LANTIRN to the GPS latitude and longitude for Alamut. The forward-looking infrared immediately locked onto the fortress ten miles ahead as the Tomcat continued to climb. "Holy shit," Wink exclaimed. "There it is!" he marveled. "Clear as day." He worked his target designation crosshairs to where he thought the illumination should be. He glanced up at the clock on the instrument panel that he had double checked before launch and looked at his digital G-shock watch. They both said 0358. "Laser should be coming on any minute. One minute to drop. Weapon systems check good—GBU-28 selected." He looked at the infrared image and studied the fortress as they prepared to utterly destroy it. It was strange to be looking up at a target. But the target stood clearly on the top of the steep mountain, large and solid against the cool night sky. He placed the targeting crosshairs right where he thought the laser energy should be coming from already. Nothing. "Thirty seconds!" he called.

Big was right behind him with Sedge seeing exactly the same thing. A perfect FLIR picture of the fortress, and a clear crosshair on his designation of where he thought the 1.06 micron ground laser designator energy should be. But he too, saw nothing. Someone hadn't kept his promise.

"We're going to have to light this guy up ourselves," Wink said, trying not to panic. The SA-6 indicator was warbling in his ear. The SAM targeting radar had them. "Chaff!" Wink called. "I'm going active on our laser!" Wink's hands flew to the switches.

Woods watched their airspeed drop off at an alarming rate, down through five hundred knots, then four hundred as they climbed through five thousand feet, three-fifty, as they approached ten on their way to fifteen thousand feet. Woods tapped the burner to get the rate of climb back where it needed to be, knowing he couldn't afford the fuel.

"No!" Wink yelled, feeling the burners light off. "An IR SAM will see us!"

"We've got no choice, Wink!" Woods said. "We'll fall out of the sky."

"Fifteen thousand feet!" Wink said. They were going to toss the bomb in a high parabola so it would have the right angle and energy to penetrate. "Still no laser. I'm going active!" he said too loud as he flipped the switch that would ensure their failure—the entire mission turned on someone on the ground guiding the bomb into the underground hideout. At best, Wink was just guessing.

Wink watched the crosshairs remain steady on the target point he had selected. "Three, two, one, pickle!" Wink called as he released the bomb while they were still climbing steeply. They could both feel the airplane jump up as the enormous bomb dropped off and headed toward Alamut. The computer had calculated the right release point to lob the bomb the correct distance. Once heading down, the wings on the silent bomb would maneuver it to hit at the point of the reflected laser energy. "Let's get out of here," Wink called. Woods pulled the Tomcat hard left and brought the nose down through the horizon as they sought the safety of lower altitude from the SAM energy that continued to illuminate them.

Woods banked even harder, almost rolling upside down in the darkness.

"Keep it illuminated!" Wink screamed.

Woods glanced at his display to keep the line representing his maximum bank angle and aim point on the screen. They passed back through ten thousand feet toward the safety of the ground, then five thousand feet.

Wink stared at the aim point on his FLIR display on the PTID waiting for the impact of their huge bomb. But a new sound in the small speakers tore his eyes away. His head jerked to see what the new fire control radar was. "AAA has us locked up!"

Woods's instincts worked faster than Wink's mouth. He had already nosed over hard to get down to the lowest possible altitude. He hit the white button on the left side of the stick to release a chaff program. Small canisters of metal were ejected by shotgun-shell-sized blasts out of their receptacles in the back of the F-14 to deceive the radar. As soon as they hit the airstream they formed a cloud of reflective metal the size of an airplane to encourage the radar to lock onto the aluminum instead of the real plane.

But the mobile ZSU-23-4 below them was too hungry to be deceived by chaff. It was a nasty wheeled vehicle that carried its own radar and four-barreled antiaircraft battery. It was the most feared ground antiair weapon in the world. The Iranians had the Russian upgrade, which detected a sudden deceleration—chaff instead of an airplane—and didn't take the bait. The 23-millimeter bullets leapt into the action for which they had been waiting all night. They raced up from the four barrels toward Woods's F-14. The red tracer bullets tore into the LANTIRN pod, then into the belly of the F-14.

Woods pushed the nose over harder and banked left, not caring whether the target was still illuminated. More bullets ripped into the tail of the F-14 and the left engine exploded. The left wing buckled at its root and bent up as the left tail came off entirely.

"Eject! Eject! Eject!" Woods shouted as he reached for the ejection handle between his legs.

Wink reached for his ejection handle at the same time and both pulled. The canopy locks were blown off by detonation cord and the canopy flew up and back off the airplane. Wink's ejection seat rocketed up the rail as the airplane slowly began to come apart and plummet toward the earth. Woods's seat fired 1.2 seconds later. The Tomcat broke into pieces as Woods cleared the burning hulk. Twenty-three-millimeter bullets continued to rip into the pathetic airplane as it looked for a place to die.

Before Woods could even focus on what was happening he felt a jerk in his crotch as his parachute's ballistic spreader deployed the silk and grabbed the air to slow his descent. He swung back and forth and steadied slightly. He looked around for anything recognizable. Suddenly an F-14 flew by not five hundred feet away. It flashed its lights to acknowledge his presence. It was Big. He had dropped his bomb and was keeping Alamut illuminated. Woods's night-vision devices had been ripped off his face in the ejection and he couldn't see much else. He looked toward Alamut and saw the mountain in the distance, maybe three miles away. He heard a deep rumbling explosion, then another, but saw no flash or fire. Woods jerked involuntarily in his parachute, trying to drive his five-thousand-pound bomb deeper into the hidden fortress, into the face of the man who had killed his best friend.

Woods searched the sky for Wink, also mindful of where he was going. Nothing like parachuting into the valley of the Assassins right after having bombed the hell out of them. He hung helplessly under his parachute, horrified by how long it was taking to get down to the ground. He unhooked his oxygen mask. His breath came quickly as he drew in the cool night air, his mask hanging off his helmet. Without warning he suddenly slammed into the hard-packed ground and tumbled head over heels, skidding to a stop. His parachute filled with the small late night breeze and began to pull him again. He tried to release the shoulder harness fittings but had trouble getting his gloved fingers under the covers. Struggling to lift the flaps, he finally worked his hands into the fittings and released the parachute. It drifted away from him, driven by the wind.

Woods knew he had to hide, but he couldn't move. He was overwhelmed with a sudden sense of failure. Suddenly, he knew how it was going to end. He had succeeded only in arousing the Sheikh, who would now come and find him, torture him, and kill him.

He scanned the ground around him for Wink. He couldn't see anyone. He looked in amazement at the place where his Tomcat had plummeted. It was between him and the mountain fortress of Alamut, burning away in the darkest part of night. The base of the mountain on which Alamut sat seemed mysteriously quiet. The deep explosions had produced no visible evidence of damage.

"Trey!"

Woods's heart jumped as he heard his name. He looked behind him. "Wink!"

"You okay?"

"I think so," Woods, said standing up for the first time. He reached into his survival vest and pulled out his 9-millimeter Beretta.

"Put that thing away!" Wink said as he limped toward Woods. "You'll probably shoot me."

"We gotta get out of here," Woods said. He put his gun back in its holster in his survival vest. "This place is probably crawling with men looking for us. We've got to get to the hills and radio for help."

"I can't," Wink replied.

"Why not?"

"I tried to use my radio when we were in our chutes. I dropped it."

"You didn't have it on a lanyard?"

"No."

"Nice preflight," Woods said.

"Your radio okay?"

"I sure hope so." Woods looked down at his survival vest, unzipped the large pocket, and felt for his Motorola PRC-112 radio, which was in its place. He was reassured. "We've got to move. They probably saw us come down." As they started to walk he noticed Wink was limping. "You okay?"

"Yeah, just twisted my knee on the landing. It hurts, but I can walk on it."

They suddenly heard loud shooting from a mechanized large-bore gun.

"Holy shit!" Wink whispered as they kneeled next to a boulder. "That's the guy who got us," he said, alarmed. "He's on the other side of this hill!"

Woods pulled out his radio. He had to make a move. He turned it to the SAR frequency, 282.8, plugging it into his helmet so he could hear it without it making any audible noise. He pressed the transmit button. *"Big! You up?"* Woods waited for a reply. Nothing. *"Big! You up?"*

"Yeah. Chasing snakes. You okay?"

"Yeah. Both on the ground safe. We'll be doing a little E&E." Escape and evasion.

"We're out of here. Stay out of sight. We'll send someone back for you."

"When?" Woods asked, feeling foolish as soon as he asked the question.

There was a pause as Big tried to imagine a way to convey a time to Woods without someone else who might be listening knowing immediately what the time was. *"Stay up on this freq. Out."*

"Roger, out," Woods replied.

"What did he say?" Wink asked.

"He's okay. They're heading back. He said they'd send someone to get us."

"Like who? An H-60? They can't fly this far."

"I don't know." Woods slipped the radio back into his survival vest. "I don't know," he repeated.

"When?"

"That's what I asked him."

"And?"

"He said to stay on this freq. Come on. We've got to get out of here."

Big couldn't believe what had happened. He kept his Tomcat level on the way out, turning as little as he possibly could. He didn't want to know what might happen if he tried to turn with the left wing tip of his Tomcat shot clean off. What the hell had happened? He was frustrated with himself, with the Navy, with intelligence, with the Sheikh, with everything and everybody. He tried to contain his rage as he flew away from danger toward safety. They had gotten satellite imagery yesterday at last daylight. There wasn't any AAA. There hadn't been *any* air defense anywhere near Alamut. There were no soldiers, no AAA, and no SAM sites. There was no indication anyone knew they were coming at all. Now they were heavily defended by well-handled air defense systems. Unbelievable.

They passed out of Iraq into northern Syria. He couldn't stay as low as he wanted anymore. His Tomcat was too hard to handle. It felt unhappy with three feet of its left wing gone. It wanted to roll left and yaw. He'd been able to control it with trim so far, but he couldn't hug the ground all the way back in his condition. He climbed to three thousand feet and slowed to three hundred knots, there for any competent radar operator to see from a hundred miles away. They needed protection and help. They had to risk being heard and located by the Syrians.

Sedge called the E-2. *"Blue Door 32, this is Watchmaker 09."*

"09. Blue Door 32. Go ahead."

"Go secure," Sedge said.

"Roger, secure."

Sedge looked down to his left and turned the dial on his secure UHF encryption box. *"32, you up?"* Sedge asked.

"32's up. Go ahead, 09."

"They were waiting for us. They got our wingman. He went down at the target site, just southwest of the mountain. He landed in the valley—the airplane crashed just short of the base of the mountain. Alert whoever is in charge of SAR." Search and Rescue.

"Roger, 09. Say your posit."

Sedge looked at his PTID and read off the bearing and range to where the carrier was when they left. *"We're 083 for 230 from home base."*

"Roger. You inbound?"

"Affirmative, but we've been hit. We may not make it."

"You need assistance, 09?"

"Just have a SAR chopper near the coast in case we can't make it to the ship. We're missing about three feet from our left wing."

"Wilco. You see any chutes at the target?"

"Affirmative. Two good chutes, and positive radio contact with them on the ground."

"Roger. We'll check on what SAR assets are available."

"Roger, 09 out."

Wink rubbed his knee. "We can't stay on this hill with the ZSU on the other side. When they find our chutes, this'll be the first place they look. We've got to get to the hills on the north end of the valley. Probably a mile across. It's our only chance."

Woods hated the idea of walking across the floor of a valley with no trees, no rocks to speak of, and some unknown number of people looking for them. But Wink was right. If they stayed where they were, they would certainly be caught. His desire for self-destruction had faded as quickly as it had come.

They headed across the small valley floor to the hill north of them. Their intention was less to ease their chance of getting picked up than to find a place to hide. Elevation seemed to indicate safety for some reason.

Woods thought back to his SERE school days. They had thrown him out into the California desert at Warner Springs in northern San Diego County, and made him—and forty or fifty others—survive with nothing. No food, no shelter, and no chance of being rescued. They taught you to eat prickly pear cacti, and live in the desert, and where to find water in dried-up riverbeds. They taught you to move at night and stay hidden during the day. They taught you to be able to resist torture and how to be an effective prisoner of war. He had really hoped never to have to use that part of his training.

Woods whispered to Wink over his shoulder. "Didn't the parachutes blow this way?"

"Yeah," Wink said quietly, looking around. "But they won't expect us to go in the same direction."

They walked as quickly as they could, Wink wincing on every other step, and crossed the dusty valley floor to the distant hill where they hoped to find a place to hide out until whenever they were supposed to be picked up. Woods didn't like not knowing the plan. As impulsive as he could be, he always operated on a plan, even if it had been his plan only for a few minutes.

They reached the base of the hill and Woods stopped to look at it. His eyes ran over the entire visible face of the hill, checking for anything unusual, or any signs of life. He saw nothing. He took off his helmet and breathed the cool air deeply. "You think the ZSU was here all the time?" he asked Wink. "Think the intel people just missed it?"

"They weren't on the satellite photos. We looked at them ourselves."

"They may have just been camouflaged."

"No way. They weren't there."

"That means they were brought in last night."

"Right."

Woods put his skull cap in his survival vest to keep from dropping it. "That means they knew we were coming."

"How would they know that?"

"That's what I want to know."

"What about the SA-6?"

"We never saw an SA-6, did we? Just the radar."

That had never even occurred to Wink. "A radar but no SAMs? Why?"

"Cheaper. And to drive us down. We'd have been above the ZSU's range otherwise. If we see a SAM radar, we stay low and fly right into the heart of the ZSU envelope."

"That's pretty shitty," Wink said, grimacing. His right knee was swelling up from the impact with the ground.

"Come on," Woods urged. They started up the hill. It was steeper than they had expected and there were large boulders over the entire face that made an assent in the dark very tricky. Woods pulled himself through a crevice between two rocks and stood up straight on the uphill side.

They both glanced over their shoulders toward Alamut, which remained silhouetted against the night sky. "Looks intact." Woods said, disheartened. He continued to climb the rocks heading for the top. The hill turned out to be more of a mountain than a hill. It was twice as high as Woods had thought when he'd seen it from across the valley floor. He looked back down from where they had come. Where they had been standing, Woods saw flashlights. He squinted. He could see several men standing around examining the ground for tracks. "They're onto us."

"Shit," Wink said.

"We gotta find us a hiding place right now," Woods said, surveying the surrounding area quickly. There were hundreds of boulders, but not one tree or large bush. Just hard ground, and harder rocks.

"At least they don't have dogs," Wink said. "At least I hope they don't."

Woods stood looking at a rock formation above them. He stepped toward it tentatively. "This way," he directed.

Wink limped along behind him. They knew if they didn't find some place to hide in the next five minutes they'd be dead in ten.

39

Big tossed his helmet bag in the ready room chair and searched the room quickly for Bark. He saw him standing by the SDO desk on the phone.

"Big!" Bark said, covering the receiver with his hand, still listening to the telephone. "What happened?"

"ZSUs were waiting for us."

"E-2 says Trey and Wink got out."

"Yes, sir. Two good chutes. I talked to them on the ground."

"Admiral wants to see you. Sedge, you come too."

Sedge threw his helmet bag onto the chair next to Big's. They both had sweat running down their chests and their hair was matted and sweat-filled. They had never been through anything like what they had just experienced, the best and worst of flying. Bark finished his phone call and motioned them to follow him out the back door of the ready room, turning left to walk up the starboard side of the carrier to the blue tile—Admiral's country.

Bark banged hard on the steel-reinforced door into SUPPLOT—Supplemental Plot—where the Admiral operated and monitored what was going on. A Petty Officer opened the door and ushered them in. The three Jolly Rogers stood next to each other behind Admiral Sweat, who was watching his three large projection screens showing the entire Middle East and every airplane, ship, and submarine in the area. The Air Wing Commander was next to him.

The Admiral had dark circles under his eyes and had clearly been up all night. He had gotten as little sleep as anyone on the ship over the last three days. The entire operation and all the implications were on his shoulders. He turned around in his high-backed leather chair and studied the three of them. He was in no mood for small talk. What was supposed to be an easy mission had turned into a possible POW problem, the worst possible result. "What the hell happened?" he demanded.

"The low level and the approach to the target were no problem," Big said. "No hostile forces, no AAA, and no SAMs. The airplanes were sweet, although there was more drag with the GBU-28 than we—"

"Tell me about the shoot-down."

"Yes, sir. When we broke across the Iranian border everything was fine. We were going through the valleys. As we got closer, and pulled up over a hill, we started getting tickled by an SA-6 radar—"

"I didn't think Iran had SA-6s."

"We didn't either. Woods was in the lead, and did what I would have done. We were to do a gradual climb to a high-altitude drop— above any ground fire threat. But if we had pulled up high and cruised in, we'd have been in the heart of the SA-6 envelope. So we stayed low and did a pop-up mid-altitude attack. We looked for the laser designator from the ground, but he wasn't there. We did it ourselves." Sedge picked up the story.

"And just kind of did the best we could at aiming, did our own laser," Sedge said awkwardly.

Big continued. "The SA-6 radar was on us, but no missile. We were releasing our bomb, heading back down to get out of the SAM radar. All of a sudden we got lit up by a ZSU radar. They tore into Trey. His wing folded over and his tail came off. Burst into flames and headed down to the desert floor. They jumped. The ZSU then tried for us and got three feet of our left wing, but we made it out. We raised Trey and Wink on the radio when they were on the ground. They're okay, Admiral."

"How come we didn't know they had ZSUs protecting this fortress?" he asked of no one in particular. "Did the satellite imagery show anything?"

Big responded quickly. "No, sir, we reviewed all the photos before taking off. There was no hint. They knew we were coming. They moved some air defenses around the fortress at the worst possible time."

The Admiral considered the implications of that statement for a moment. "We'll get them out."

Big volunteered. "I'd like to fly cover for the SAR effort, sir. I owe him."

"Relax," the Admiral said. "We've been in touch with the Air Force Special Operations Command. They've got some people at Aviano who are ready to go."

"The Air Force?" Big asked.

"It's their mission, and they're ready."

"When would they go?"

"That's one of the things they wanted us to ask you. Do you think they can survive out there until nightfall?"

"They don't have much choice. They'll find somewhere to hide until dark. But I don't know how you just fly in and pick up two guys sitting right next to a ZSU-23 that will be waiting for a SAR effort."

"That's the Air Force's problem."

"Let us fly fighter cover. Let's put ten F-14's overhead Trey and take on all comers."

"That's not the way we're going to do this," the Admiral said. "It's out of our hands. You guys go get some rest."

"Aye aye, sir," they replied. They turned to leave the darkened room when the Admiral stopped them.

"Did you get the Sheikh?"

Big shrugged. "Not a chance. The laser wasn't there. We had to do it ourselves. We had to jink away to keep from getting our asses shot. I don't know if they even hit where we were aiming."

"They did," Sedge said. "But we don't have any idea if we aimed right. Probably just blew up a bunch of dirt."

The Admiral's response had a flinty edge to it. "That's the problem with declaring war against one person. If you bomb him and blow him into the next reality, how do you ever know for sure you got him? How the hell are we going to prove we got this guy?"

"We've got to get out of sight," Woods said, thinking of the Assassins making their way toward them.

Wink sat on a boulder and rubbed his knee. "I sure hope I don't have to get arthro. My knee is killing me."

"What'd you do to it?"

"I'm not sure. I just hit the ground hard. You know they tell you to look straight ahead so you don't know when you're going to hit and you don't brace for the impact?"

"Yeah."

"I'd like to meet the guy who had that idea. I'd probably have been fine if I'd been able to prepare for the impact . . ."

Woods suddenly noticed an overhang behind them that seemed to curl around and underneath a large boulder. He quit listening to Wink and scrambled onto the boulder to examine the crevice. It might be big enough for a man to get into, but it would be tight. He looked up into the sky. The stars were disappearing. Sunrise was approaching.

He slid down the boulder and sat next to Wink. "I think we're going to have to get in between these two rocks. It'll be tight."

"Think we can fit?"

"We'll have to take off all our flight gear—"

"We can't leave it out—"

"No, we'll drag it in with us."

Wink was skeptical and crawled onto the boulder and stuck his head into the crevice. He pulled his Maglite out of his survival vest and shined it into the crack.

"Are you out of your mind?" Woods cried. "Shut that off! They can see that for ten miles!"

Wink quickly turned it off and put it back where it had been. Not only had he just told everyone where they were, he had ruined his own night vision.

"So, now that you've illuminated it, can we fit in it?"

"I don't think so."

"Great," Woods said, feeling a quick flash of nausea. "You'd better try. Otherwise, we're going to be sitting ducks." He looked for the men crossing the valley. He couldn't see anybody. "They're already at the base of this hill," he announced to Wink's back as he watched him try to slide into the crevice.

Wink struggled to slide into the hole, fearful he would get into a position where he couldn't get back out.

Woods watched him anxiously. Woods never saw the hand come around his head from his right that quickly covered his mouth. His arms flailed as he was dragged backward off the boulder and onto the hard ground.

Two enormous, dark gray MH-53J Pave Low helicopters came over the horizon. They slowed as they approached the USS *Saipan* and positioned themselves for a vertical descent. The *Saipan* was a helicopter and VTOL—Vertical Takeoff and Landing—carrier that carried the Marine amphibious helicopters and Harrier jets.

The sailors on the *Saipan* watched the approach. The MH-53Js were like many other H-53 helicopters flown by the Navy and the Marine Corps. They saw those all the time. But these helicopters looked different. They had bulges and bumps where the other helicopters didn't, and they didn't have Navy or Marine markings.

The first Pave Low slowed as it neared the flight deck. The sailors strained to see the markings on the helicopter. There weren't any they could see. The yellow shirt on the deck signaled the lead pilot where to put the enormous six-bladed helicopter. The pilot was very cautious; he had landed on ships before and knew he had to be careful.

The pilot maneuvered the Pave Low gently over the flight deck twenty feet above it and steadied directly above the landing spot. The Air Boss watched it with some trepidation. The Air Force was out of its element at sea. The Navy didn't trust the Air Force to get anything right when it came to ships. But the fact that they had found the ship put them in good standing with the Air Boss. His hand was on the radio transmitter ready to call out at the smallest deviation from procedures.

The Pave Low III settled gently onto the deck, directly on the spot designated. Its landing gear compressed as the screaming plane's weight shifted from the rotor blades. The deck crewman signaled for the pilot to shut down his port engine as another sailor put wood chocks in front of and behind the wheels.

The second Pave Low approached the *Saipan* along the same path. Its spot was aft of the first one, and it settled onto it as effortlessly as the lead had.

All of a sudden the deck was quiet. The rear access ramp of the Pave Lows opened and the pilots and aircrew stepped onto the flight deck. They looked around, then headed for the island.

The sailors had started to turn away when the rest of the occupants began filing out—men in dark jumpsuits with no insignia or markings. Like the aircrew, they proceeded into the island and disappeared behind them, followed by another group carrying large boxes. The Air Force was coming aboard, completely self-contained. All they needed was gas.

Woods was flipped onto his stomach, his face pushed down hard by a hand over his mouth. Suddenly he could feel warm breath on his cheek. A man whispered in his ear in gruff, accented English, "Don't make a *sound!*"

Woods stopped struggling and listened. Suddenly the man was gone. No one was holding him down. He sat up quickly and looked around in the still, dark morning. Reaching inside his survival vest, he took out his 9-millimeter Beretta. He rose and started toward Wink.

As Wink finally freed himself from his aborted attempt to test the width of the crevice he had been eyeing, he too, was grabbed from behind. He panicked and fought as hard as he could as the strong arms pulled him backward, down the large boulder to the dirt. They tumbled off the last edge of the boulder and landed next to Woods.

The man grabbed Wink by the head and whispered loudly in his ear, "Stop struggling!"

The man, who had dark curly hair and a short beard, crouched next to them in unremarkable olive, army-like clothes. "You must be quiet," he whispered.

"Who are you?" Woods asked. Woods tried to place the man's accent. It was distinctly Middle Eastern, but he couldn't identify it. Young and vigorous, the man was clearly not a shepherd or local farmer.

"Put your gun away!" the man said when he realized what was in Woods's hand. "We must move."

"Why should we go with you?" Wink asked.

The man looked at him, understanding. "You don't have to. But they will find you."

"Who will?" Woods asked.

"The Assassins," he said quickly. "The ones coming from the valley to get you."

It was good enough for Woods. He put the Beretta away. "Where are we going?"

The man didn't respond. He unslung the M-16 that had been hanging across his back. It had a large clip of ammunition and looked well worn. He motioned for Woods and Wink to follow him.

The man worked his way through the rocks silently, Wink and Woods stumbling along behind him.

As they moved between large boulders making for the other side of the hill, Woods pulled his radio out of his survival vest and checked to make sure it was on the SAR frequency—282.8. The man turned and grabbed the radio from Woods's hand, nearly pulling Woods off his feet by the lanyard attached from the radio to his survival vest.

"What do you think you're doing?" Woods said.

"Do not turn on."

"Why not?"

The man considered the question unworthy of response. He gave the radio back to Woods and began walking again.

Woods stayed put. "I wasn't going to transmit, just *listen*."

The man replied over his shoulder. "They will hear you!"

"It plugs into my helmet," Woods replied. He was growing annoyed at the man who had apparently decided to tell them exactly what to do, and expected them to go along.

Woods glanced over his shoulder at Wink, who shrugged. The radio was silent except for the hint of static that reassured him it was working. He followed the man blindly while playing with his radio. He couldn't have retraced their steps if called upon to do so.

"We're here," the man said.

Woods looked around at the boulders. The sun was approaching the horizon and giving off just enough light to make the mountain and its numerous boulders visible. "Where?"

"Here you will hide. With me."

Woods studied the terrain, then stared at their escort. "So you're the one. What the hell happened?"

"What are you saying?"

"You were supposed to put the laser on the target."

"There's no time for talk now. First we must get out of the open," the man insisted.

Wink had had enough. "Who are you? How are we going to get out of the open?"

The sky was lightening. "We must hurry!" he said, suddenly reaching out to pick up the bottom of a rock. Hinged on the uphill end, it came up easily. The fake boulder was five feet tall, six feet long, and five or so feet wide. Underneath was a large flat area.

Woods and Wink stared at the space, invisible a minute ago.

"Get in," the man ordered.

The space was large enough for all three. Woods and Wink hesitated, but seeing no other choice, they ducked under the frame and sat down on the dirt underneath. The man lowered the frame behind him and sat next to them. He put his M-16 on the ground near him and took a deep breath. Woods whispered to the man he couldn't see in the near darkness, "So what happened?"

"My partner was the laser."

Woods was stunned. "You're with the Mossad?"

The man considered, then responded, "I am Israeli."

"So what happened?"

The Assassins found him yesterday. They stumbled on him and then killed him."

Woods wondered if it was true. "Why didn't *you* do the laser?"

"He had the equipment. Different hill. Different mission."

"Did they get his equipment?"

"Yes. But don't worry—it was untraceable. And he had no identification. There is no way they will know he was Israeli."

"I'm sorry." Woods was now just able to make out his outline.

"They are on the hill now, looking for us. They will be checking the boulders. We must wait. . . . Do you think your people will come for you?"

"Tonight."

In the darkness the man reached behind him into something that looked like a duffel bag and pulled out a submachine gun. He handed it to Woods, then pulled out another M-16 and gave it to Wink. "Here. Be ready to use these," he whispered. "If they find us, we will start shooting them right away. We will fire, open the rock, and rush out."

"Are you sure?"

"I cannot be captured. If you want to surrender now, go ahead. If you stay with me, you must fight."

Woods pressed his lips together anxiously. "I don't even know how to work this."

The man looked at the weapon he had given Woods and took it back. "Here," he said, picking up the M-16 he had put down next to him. "You know how to use this, don't you?"

"Yes," Woods said. He looked at the rifle for a moment. "This is the safety here, right?"

"No, here," the man said, indicating. "When it turns dark again we can begin preparation. One of us at a time can sleep today. You first," he said, pointing to Wink.

Wink nodded. The last time he had fired an M-16 had been seven years before in summer training. Naval officers weren't required to stay current with rifles.

On the ground Woods noticed what looked like a sophisticated electronics box surrounded by black foam. It had numerous digital displays and readings. "What is that?"

"No more talking," the man said as he looked outward. Following his glance, Woods and Wink realized that the day had grown lighter and that now they could see out of the boulder. It was like a one-way mirror.

40

Big stood in the back of the *Saipan*'s CVIC, staring at the men before him. Bark had asked Big to become personally involved in the final stages of the mission planning for the combat SAR that was to get Woods and Wink out of Iran and he had just gotten off the helicopter that had brought him over here from the *Washington*.

The SAR team had taken over the CVIC of the *Saipan*. They had their own computers set up in the corner of CVIC in a square, like a small room. The pilots and mission planners were busy clicking through various computerized charts, SAM site disks, and satellite imagery that could be seen on the monitors.

The Pave Low aircrew were identifiable by their USAF wings on black patches on their flight suits. No names, just Air Force wings. There were Velcro spots on the flight suits from other patches they had apparently left at home.

The men in the black jumpsuits wore nothing to identify them. No rank, no unit patches, nothing. Nonetheless, Big had no doubt who they were—Special Forces commandos who would be going in on the Pave Low helicopters to get Woods and Wink.

Big didn't know what he was supposed to do. He had been asked to come meet with the Pave Low pilots, but they didn't seem to be in a briefing mood.

The pilot in command of the lead Pave Low, the mission commander, saw him and got up from his computer. Approaching Big, he said, "You must be Lieutenant McMack."

"Yes," Big said. "What's your name?"

"Doesn't matter." The Air Force MH-53J pilot took a round container of Skoal from his flight suit pocket. He tapped it lightly, took off the round top, grabbing a pinch of it and sticking it between his lower lip and gum. It gave him a slightly swollen look and muffled his speech. Slipping the Skoal back into his flight suit, he spit into a small V-8 juice can that he picked up. "You were there last night," he said.

"I was the wingman."

"Tell me about it."

"What would you like to know?"

Three other Air Force officers joined them, and they all took chairs in front of a large chart of the area hanging on the wall.

"How'd you get shot down? Who got you?" the Captain queried.

"A ZSU. I think there were two of them. They were waiting for us."

The Captain spit into the can again and examined Big. "I heard you got lit up by an SA-6."

"We did."

"How do you know it wasn't him that got your wingman?"

"I saw the tracers go into his airplane, and I got hit. You can look at the bullet holes in my wing."

"Where were the ZSUs?"

Big stood up and moved to the chart, studying it carefully. "Here— this was our target," he said, his finger on the site. "It was Point Whiskey on our chart. We came in from this direction," he indicated, "got lit up by the SA-6 through here, and decided to do a pop-up drop instead of coming in higher. We didn't want to get hit by the SA-6."

"Me neither," said one of the pilots.

"All we ever got was a search indication from the SA-6. He never locked onto us."

"Did they ever launch a missile at you?" This from the Captain with the Skoal.

"Not that I saw."

"How do you know there was an SA-6 there?"

"We saw his radar."

The Captain pondered. "There's a theory that some ZSUs have an SA-6 radar transmitter that it uses to light up planes to drive them down. Doesn't have any SAMs at all, only the radar. They carry it around just so pilots will see the SAM radar and head lower to get away from it, right into the ZSU-23's envelope. They're waiting for you.

Then when you're in range, they light you up with their real radar and knock the shit out of you."

Big raised his eyebrows. "Who the hell would think of that? That's not very friendly."

"Not at all. Downright mean," the Captain said. "But if it's true, it makes this easier. We sure don't want to go into an SA-6 site."

They were all quiet, staring at the chart. The Captain broke the silence. "You see anything that makes you think there was an SA-6 there other than the radar warning?"

"No."

"See the imagery from today?" the Captain asked.

"No."

One of the other officers got up and retrieved several printed photos from a desk near one of the Air Force computers, handing them to the Captain, who asked, "Get these loaded into the computer yet?"

The pilot nodded. "All set."

The Captain gave the photos to Big, who examined them carefully. "Yep, this is the place. Right there is the fortress—Alamut. You can see it. You can even see where our two bombs went in. . . . All for naught. Whoever was supposed to be there to laser designate for us wasn't. Assholes. Anyway, we were on our own. Probably missed him by a mile."

"Where were the ZSUs?"

"The one that got us was right here, at the base of this small mountain."

"Where was the other one?"

"I never got a good fix on him. I think he was off to the east, over here."

"And where did your wingman go down?"

"Last I saw their chutes, they would have come down about . . . here. Yeah, there's the smoking hole . . ."

"Right by the ZSU."

"Basically. Yeah."

The Captain studied the photos. "I don't see any SA-6 site, or any other SAM. If our intel is right, which I don't like to count on, then our only problem will be these ZSUs and maybe some men on the ground."

"That's about how I see it. Who says the ZSU has an SA-6 transmitter?"

"National assets."

"Oh."

"We also have had it confirmed by the same people who failed to show up to laser designate for you. We're told he was there. They don't know what happened to him, but they assume the worst."

"They got him?"

"Don't know. Sounds like it. We're told there hasn't been a SAM anywhere near there in a week."

"I don't know," Big said, sitting down again. "I don't trust them. There wasn't supposed to be a ZSU there either." Big looked at the three men in the dark jumpsuits. In a low voice, he asked the Captain, "Who are those guys?"

"Doesn't matter—what freq did you talk to your wingman on?"

"SAR common—282.8."

The Captain nodded.

"Think you can get them out?" Big asked.

"If they're still there, we'll get them."

The sun had set. It would be totally dark in another hour. The camouflage was fuzzy brown now and hard to see through. Woods was about to go stir crazy. He was tired of sitting silently and urinating in a jar. He was sickened by the pungent copper smell of the filthy Israeli who was doing his best to save their lives. He ran his hands over the M-16 that had been sitting on his lap for what seemed like forever. If you added up all the time in his life he had held an M-16 it wouldn't be one tenth of the time he had held one today. And the only thing it had done for him today was remind him that at any minute, with virtually no warning, he could be the victim of a close-range fully automatic shootout. It had been a constant reminder so that any thought he might have had of rest or sleep was simply ridiculous.

He couldn't be quiet any longer. He whispered so lightly he almost couldn't hear himself, "What's your name?"

The Israeli shook his head. It wasn't time yet.

Woods wasn't to be deterred. "What's your name?" he asked slightly louder.

"Shut up!" the man whispered back. "Stay quiet!"

Wink glanced at his watch. It was 2000. "No, it's time we made a plan," he said quietly.

The Israeli sat up and looked at his luminous watch. "Keep it down. They are still around here."

"What's your name?" Woods asked again.

"Zev. That's all you need to know."

"Sniper?"

"What? Why you say that?"

"The case," Woods said, pointing to an area behind where Wink was sitting hunched over, his legs uncomfortably beneath him, his swollen knee becoming more painful.

"Yes."

"For the Sheikh?"

He nodded. "One shot only. Can't miss. I get him, they get me. That's how it would have happened."

"So now what?"

"Doesn't matter."

"Why doesn't it matter? Aren't you still going to try to get the Sheikh?"

Zev's eyes got big. "You don't know?"

"Know what?"

"What happened."

"What are you talking about?"

"You have made my job unnecessary."

Woods looked at Wink, who was unwilling to accept what Zev was clearly saying. "How?"

"Your bombs were well placed."

"We *got* him?" Wink asked.

"I heard it."

"Heard what?"

"The bombs go into the Sheikh's quarters."

"Heard?"

"Yes. The Sheikh is dead."

"How did you hear?"

He looked at the box surrounded by foam. "We have a transmitter in the Sheikh's living quarters. Very sophisticated long range, with an antenna on the outside of the mountain."

"What? How?"

"Doesn't matter."

"Are you sure?"

"Quite."

Woods closed his eyes and put his head back. They had done it. They had gotten the Sheikh. He looked at Wink who was smiling to himself. "We got him," he said to Wink. Wink put out his hand and Woods slapped it gently. Woods took a huge, deep breath. He thought about what Zev had said. "How did you get a transmitter into Alamut?"

"It was very difficult . . ." he said pensively. "When do you think your people will be here?"

"Dark, I would guess. Don't really know. Why don't you come out with us?"

Zev pondered the offer. "I think this place is not very safe anymore. The Assassins who are left are now without a leader. They will respond by doing what he would have wanted them to do, and that is looking for you. It would be best to leave. I have a way to get out, but it would take some time. I will come. If there is room."

✍

Batman. The perfect name for an airfield in eastern Turkey. The Turks had initially refused to allow the Air Force Special Forces to stage out of their bases for the rescue. The Syrians had raised such a firestorm of protest everyone was lying low, not endorsing, or participating, or allowing the Americans to use their territory to conduct attacks. It had stymied the Air Force's initial participation, but they had gone back to Turkey with the request. A simple one—let us conduct the rescue from Turkey. Through Turkey. The thing that had made the difference was that it was a rescue. They had agreed. The C-130s could launch out of their bases, and the Pave Lows could fly through their airspace on their way to Iran. Turkey had no love for the Sheikh and what he was doing. They saw him as creating terrible instability and jeopardizing peace in the Middle East. There was always someone to jeopardize peace.

Turkey's decision had given the entire operation a boost. The idea of flying through Syria and refueling over the Syrian desert somewhere had not offered the Air Force great comfort. They would have done it, but it would have been more colorful.

The four dark gray Air Force C-130s shuddered next to the runway at Batman. They had made two flights earlier in the day, all routine, all intended to make sure that if anyone was watching, they would never know what exactly these airplanes were doing there other than flying randomly into the Turkish mountains and coming back.

The C-130s were the same dark color as the Pave Low helicopters: flat, blotchy dark gray with nearly indiscernible markings. They waited next to the runway as the sun set behind them. The first MC-130P Combat Shadow taxied onto the runway and ran up its four massive turboprop engines, the airplane straining against its brakes, longing to fly. The MC-130P rolled down the runway, starting slowly and picking up speed smoothly. As it reached rotation speed the pilot pulled back smartly on the yoke and the Shadow climbed steadily into the sky. As the first lifted off, the second MC-130P taxied onto the runway, and followed the first into the sky. The two tankers were the first airplanes airborne on the night's mission. The Air Force Special Forces MC-130P Combat Shadows were designed for one thing—to refuel Special Operations aircraft on high-risk missions in difficult situations, the ones that flew too low to the ground. It was all they did, and they did it well. It wasn't just anyone who could fly a C-130 at five hundred feet above the ground and refuel an invisible helicopter at night.

The next airplane to take the runway, an AC-130U, had unusual bulges and shapes, clearly not to make it fly better or have more lift. Someone who didn't know the Spooky might have thought it was an electronic countermeasures airplane to jam enemy radars. But those who knew it and its predecessor the Spectre knew the bulges meant business. Gunfire. Three barrels projected out of the left side of the airplane. The largest barrel, farthest aft, was the 105-millimeter how-itzer. Just forward of that was the 40-millimeter cannon, and farther forward still was the 25-millimeter Gatling gun. The Spooky had the most highly concentrated firepower in the world. More per square foot than any other fighting vehicle or ship. It could put as much firepower on a point on the ground as an entire battalion of infantrymen.

The targeting and firing solutions could be calculated immediately by computer and the guns trained by the Fire Control Officer sitting at a console in the BMC—the Battle Management Center. The Spooky could find its target through infrared sensors or ALLTV—All Light Level TeleVision, a television system that worked in all light, or radar—the same radar that was on the F-15E. The guns could shoot through clouds. They also had the capability of jamming anybody on the ground who tried to target them. The pilot simply flew in a left-hand circle around the ground target while the guns pounded away. It was a fright-ening sight.

The first Spooky rolled down the runway and was airborne in less time than the two tankers. It maneuvered quickly once airborne, more agile than the heavy MC-130Ps.

In the settling darkness, the second Spooky, its lights on, followed the first. It appeared to be taking off on a routine training mission. No one at Batman knew where it was going or why. It climbed up into the cloudless deep purple sky and headed toward the other three small dots in the sky. The four airplanes rendezvoused sixty miles south of Batman and headed east into the Turkish mountains.

Aboard the *Saipan* the lead Pave Low pilot, the mission commander, stepped up the ramp in the back of the helicopter and headed toward the cockpit. The *Saipan* had moved north of its original position off the coast of Syria. It was just south of Turkey off the northwestern corner of Syria.

The Captain had downloaded the latest satellite imagery, updated locations in the mission planning computer, and put the information on a 3.5-inch disk. Just behind the pilot's seat, he placed the airplane's computer—the DMU—into its cradle and the diskette into its drive. He and his copilot began their preflight checklist.

The power was connected and the pilot called for an intercom check from the rest of the crew. Everyone was ready. The six enormous blades started to turn slowly, then with greater speed. The second Pave Low matched the first as they both worked steadily through their start-up checklists. Several people watched from Vulture's Row. They had observed thousands of helicopter takeoffs and landings on the *Saipan*, but they had never seen the Air Force Special Forces anywhere near them. They had never had men on their ship wearing flight suits with no markings, gently rejecting inquiries about who they were or what they were doing there. They had never had men with small automatic weapons and no insignia smile nicely at them and say nothing.

But the word had spread quickly through the ship at the scuttlebutts. Everyone in the fleet knew an F-14 had been shot down, and that it was the Air Force that had the mission of deep combat SAR. Word was that the F-14 was down inside Iran. The idea horrified most of the sailors. Being shot down was bad enough, but being shot down in Iran . . . they didn't want to think about it.

When the lead Pave Low pilot was ready he eased the plane off the flight deck slowly. The long blades bent upward as they took on the weight of the helicopter and beat the air to lift it. Once aloft, the helicopter dipped over the side of the flight deck and down toward the water, the second Pave Low right behind him. Forty feet off the water, they turned and headed northeast toward Turkey. They had no intention of being high enough for any radar to pick them up more than a couple of miles away.

Inside the Pave Low, the flight to the coast of Turkey was quiet. The back of the helicopter was crowded with Air Force commandos sitting quietly, holding their weapons, passengers just for a while. They could only wait. The pilot had the multifunction displays—MFDs— adjusted to see the IR imagery in front of him, and the computerized map display in the middle. It was a full-color TV-like screen that displayed a detailed map of Turkey, with a computer-generated helicopter on it showing exactly where they were to one-hundredth of a mile.

The copilot pointed to the coast ahead of them. They were on course and on schedule. To the minute. The two Pave Lows descended as they crossed the beach at an obscure, unremarkable, and uninhabited point on the Turkish coast. With their lights out it was impossible to identify them in the gathering darkness unless someone was using a nightscope or infrared, highly unlikely at such a remote and unpredictable spot. One of the reasons the Special Forces went at night was because it often meant that the one with the best sensors won.

The Pave Lows turned east and headed into the heart of the Turkish mountains toward Iran.

41

The helicopters thundered across the harsh Turkish terrain, the sky now completely black. Moonrise wasn't for another two hours. They had achieved the condition for Special Operations that they always wanted: EENT, End of Evening Nautical Twilight. It took 99 percent of the world off their threat scope. It meant the average soldier, farmer, or adolescent with a slingshot could never just aim at them. They would never see them. The only ones who would see them after EENT were those with technology: radar, IR, low-light TV, or night-vision devices.

The Pave Lows streaked toward the mountains of eastern Turkey and their rendezvous. The Captain turned on the radar and activated the terrain-following function. The vector came up on the screen and the pilot followed it into the valley.

The copilot checked their fuel consumption against the prediction. They were within a hundred pounds of where they expected to be. On the ICS, he spoke to the Captain. "You see 'em?"

The pilot responded immediately. "Two tallies."

Approaching the rendezvous, the Captain slowed to one hundred knots. He picked his tanker, the lead, and climbed to five hundred feet. They had practiced tanking with the MC-130Ps many times, always at night, always on night-vision devices; but they hadn't practiced much in the mountains of Turkey. The terrain was as difficult and remote as it was possible to get. It made the backside of the moon look attractive. The Combat Shadows had picked the rendezvous spot during one of their several recent training missions. It was a valley with enough room to fly in a good six-mile circle yet be completely protected from detection by the mountains all around.

The MC-130P saw the Pave Low coming and turned on its formation lights for the rendezvous. The pilot of the lead plane climbed and extended the refueling probe past the spinning rotor blades. He waited until the Combat Shadow tanker was ready and drove his probe home to refuel. He was very conscious of the catastrophe that resulted the last time the United States tried to rescue hostages from Iran. Jimmy Carter had ordered it. The H-53s had landed to refuel. No problem. Except on taking off one of the helicopters had run into one of the refueling planes, causing death, destruction, conflagration, failure, and embarrassment. The pilot would make sure that didn't happen this time.

Iran was America's long-running tar baby. Everything that happened there turned out badly, including a U.S. Navy Aegis cruiser shooting down an Iranian airliner because it thought it was under attack. The Captain still remembered the images of the bloated bodies floating in the Persian Gulf carried worldwide on CNN.

The other Pave Low plugged into the second MC-130P. The helicopter bounced slightly in some turbulence sending a wave up the refueling hose, not enough to cause a problem, but the pilot tried to steady the Pave Low to make sure the hose didn't rupture. If they couldn't refuel, they couldn't get back.

The commandos in the back were becoming restless. They had checked everything three times and were tired of waiting. But waiting was part of their training. They tried to sit quietly, most staring straight ahead as their airplanes took on the fuel they would need to make it home.

In less than ten minutes the two Pave Lows were ready. They backed out of the refueling baskets and turned together toward the east, with the Captain in the lead and his wingman behind him.

They knew they were less than forty minutes away from the scariest sixty seconds of their lives.

✦

Farouk was furious. Their operation was in shambles. The Sheikh was dead, and Farouk was the only one of the council who had survived—he had been out watching for other intruders as the Sheikh had insisted. It was all on his shoulders now, but for what? To become the Sheikh? Perhaps to call himself the Sheikh? Who would know he wasn't? He could take the name and carry on the lifelong mission, but he knew he didn't have the leadership skills, the knowledge of the inner workings of the teachings of the Isma'ilis. He also knew that the men who had done this were out there. The Iranians had shot one of the planes down, and the pilots were on the ground. Farouk understood that the one thing he must do now was to find them and capture them. To get hostages to embarrass America.

He realized now that they had miscalculated. They had found one American spy with his laser designator, but there must have been two. How stupid he had been to conclude the one spy had been operating by himself. He had been so pleased with himself when they'd found the one that he hadn't checked the area thoroughly for other camouflaged boulders. But there had to be at least one more. How else could they have known exactly where to drop their bombs to penetrate the mountain like that? There had to be someone else on the ground.

He knew something else as well—that when there was a downed U.S. airman, they would come to get him with airplanes. Fine. Come. The few handheld SAMs the Assassins had been able to accumulate had survived the attack. He and his men would be waiting.

Woods almost lost his footing as they climbed over the rocks above their hideout when his head was suddenly filled with static. His radio had come alive with a voice, but he had missed the words. Then he heard the voice again, clearly this time.

"Watchmaker 08, this is Sidewalk 71, inbound to Point Whiskey, ETA fifteen minutes. How do you read? Over." The lead AC-130U Spooky was in charge of the operation until the Pave Lows arrived. The helicopters were to be TOT, Time Over Target, fifteen minutes after the gunships. It would give the gunships fifteen minutes to clear out any opposition to the rescue attempt. It was also the job of the Spooky to find the downed aircrew.

Woods turned to Wink. "They're on their way. Fifteen minutes out from Point Whiskey."

"How do you know they're on our side?" Zev asked suspiciously.

"They used our mission call sign, Watchmaker."

"Who is it?"

"Sidewalk somebody."

"Who is that?"

"Beats me. American voice, though."

Wink moved more quickly. "I don't remember anybody on our call sign assignment sheet named Sidewalk," he said. "Do you?"

"No, but it changes every day. We've got to get higher on this hill so they can get us."

Zev wasn't so sure. He looked around in the dark, shifting the backpack that was full of his gear. He had left most of it behind under the boulder. "How do you *know* they're Americans?"

Woods hadn't thought about it. "How would the Iranians know about Point Whiskey?"

Zev was unconvinced. "What is that?"

"Alamut. Our target."

"Did you have a chart for your flight?"

"Sure."

"Did it mention this Point Whiskey?"

"Sure. It was marked."

"Where is this chart now?"

"It went down with our airplane. Burned up."

"You know for certain it was burned? You think the Assassins didn't search the wreckage? How do you know they didn't recover it?"

Woods was tired of trying to imagine how horribly wrong things could go. He knew an American voice when he heard one. "You're paranoid. I guess we'll just have to take the chance."

"And what of your mission call sign? You never transmitted it before?"

"I don't think so," he said, trying to remember.

"What about your wingman?"

"Nope." Woods transmitted, *"Sidewalk 71, Watchmaker 08, read you loud and clear."* He looked at Zev. "What exactly is your prob—"

The radio spoke in his ear again. *"Watchmaker, state your posit."*

Woods turned to Zev. "What's our distance and direction from Alamut?"

"We are 265 for five thousand three hundred meters. But you must *not* transmit this on a radio."

"I've got to give them our position!"

"You think they don't speak English? They'll know where we are!"

"These are Americans."

"You think the Assassins don't know what your rescue frequency is?"

Woods couldn't believe that they could have someone inbound and this Israeli was seriously not going to let him give them information. He regarded Zev with new skepticism, suddenly realizing he didn't *know* whether Zev was an Israeli or not. He didn't know anything about him at all. Zev might be one of them, there only to lure in the SAR attempt just to shoot them down and give them more hostages and problems. He could be one of their guards, an outpost to find people just like him. He looked at Zev's large sniper-like rifle skeptically. What if he did what Zev didn't want him to do? He thought of the Beretta in his survival vest and reached for it, holding it in his right hand with the radio in his left.

"What are you doing?" Zev asked, amazed.

"I want to be ready if they sneak up on us," Woods replied.

"You Americans," Zev said.

"Wink, you still got the authentication table?"

"Yeah," Wink replied immediately. "In my G-suit pocket."

"Give it to me," Woods said.

Wink pulled open the flap and reached inside his shirt pocket. It was empty. He checked his leg pocket. It too was empty. "It's gone."

Zev asked Wink, "Did you have a radio too?"

"Yeah."

"Where is it?"

"Lost it. I tried to talk to Big on the way down in the chute, but the landing jarred it out of my hand."

Zev started walking again. He had heard enough. He spoke to Woods angrily. "How do you know the Assassins aren't using *his* radio to talk to you? Or even the Iranians? They could be one hundred feet from us right now! You behave like a Boy Scout . . ." he grumbled.

Woods didn't know what to do. If it was the SAR team, and he didn't identify himself, it would cost them their only chance to get out of Iran. If it was the Assassins with Wink's radio, they were dead. He lifted the radio to his mouth and pushed the transmit button. "*We are 265 for 5,000 meters from Whiskey.*"

"*Roger. Copy. Nice to hear from you. Any injuries?*"

"*Negative. Minor knee damage to one.*"

"*Are you both ready to go?*"

"*Affirmative. There are three of us.*"

A pause. "*Roger. Who's the third?*"

"*We'll tell you when you get here.*"

"*You number one alphabetically?*"

"*Negative. Number two.*"

"Stand by." There was a long pause while Woods, Wink, and Zev walked quickly around a series of small rocks. *"Number two, state the name of your first dog."*

Woods grinned. *"BJ."*

"Roger. Authenticated. ETA 5 minutes. Move to a good LZ."

Woods's relief was instant and complete. *"Roger! We're on the move. Be advised, there's at least one and maybe two ZSU-23s nearby."*

"Roger. Copy."

Woods stuck the radio into the chest pocket of his flight suit and zipped it closed until only the antenna and cord for the earpiece stuck out. The radio was slightly heavy against his chest. "It's them. No doubt about it. They used the SAR authentication," Woods said. "We've got to get to where we can be picked up."

"How authenticate?" Zev asked warily.

"Name of my first dog."

"You don't think the Assassins could have thought of that?"

"No, I don't," Woods replied, "because I made up the question on my SAR card that they're reading from. If they'd asked any *other* question I would have known it was a setup."

"This way," Zev whispered, heading up the rocky hill and slightly away from Alamut.

⚓

The pilot of the AC-130U felt his gut tighten as they approached the target. They had fifteen minutes to suppress any air defense in the area, but one in particular was of such great concern to him that he had almost vetoed the operation. He had read the report of the SA-6 radar lighting up the F-14s before the lead was shot down. The wingman had reported a clear indication of an SA-6. Clear, he had said. But no lock-on, no fire control radar, just the SA-6 in the search mode. Odd. Then they revised their approach to go in lower, and they got hit by a ZSU. No SAM site on the imagery, but that didn't surprise him. The SA-6 was every bit as mobile as the ZSU-23. Good camouflage could beat good imagery. The SA-6 might still be there. Or, as the latest intelligence insisted, it was a new tactic of the ZSUs. Carry an SA-6 search radar, all the planes will panic and get down on the deck to avoid the SAM envelope, and fly right into the ZSU's waiting bullets. That's what was said to have happened to the F-14s. He didn't buy it. At least not at first. American intelligence claimed to have HUMINT— human intelligence—that confirmed that. Still. If they were wrong, and there was an SA-6 site nearby, this mission might be about to lose some very nice people and a very expensive airplane.

He glanced at the IR screen, then the ALLTV screen, the all-light television that could see just about anything in all light conditions. Nothing. "Any ESM?" he called on the ICS to the EWO, the Electronic Warfare Officer.

"Negative. Nothing, yet."

He spoke to the crew over the ICS. "We're approaching the target. Everybody ready?"

"All ready," came the reply.

The Spooky flew at fifteen thousand feet directly over the small mountain where Woods and the others stood. As soon as they were on the other side of the mountain the ZSU saw them. Its radar instantly started doing the calculations necessary to shoot down the huge target in the dark.

"I've got an SA-6 radar!" the EWO shouted. "I've got a ZSU radar!" he yelled even louder.

The sensor operators in the back of the Spooky checked the direction of the strobe for the two radars. They were coming from the same place. The ALLTV operator zoomed in that direction and saw the wheeled, lightly armored ZSU, its four barrels distinct in the contrast. "Good picture of the ZSU," he called calmly.

At the right seat in the Battle Management Center in the back of the Spooky, the Fire Control Officer watched the television picture. He had seen enough. "Keep looking for the crew. We've got a target," he said, selecting the 105-millimeter gun for the first salvo. He checked the status of the gun and it was ready. The airman had loaded the fifty-pound shell into the side-pointing gun long before. All three guns were pointed at the ZSU. He fired the 105-millimeter howitzer cannon and the four-plus-inch round blasted out of the plane down toward the ZSU faster than the speed of sound. The Fire Control Officer then selected the 40-millimeter cannon and began firing down the same track. The crosshairs on the ALLTV were locked on to the ZSU. The cannon screamed as its nearly two-inch-wide bullets ripped downhill at the ZSU. They watched the first 105 shell hit the ground slightly above the ZSU. Suddenly on the ALLTV they saw the tracers from the ZSU's 23-millimeter four-barrel cannon coming back at them, screaming uphill faster than the speed of sound.

"Jammin' him?" the pilot asked the EWO.

"All over him," came the reply.

"Any SAMs?"

"Just that SA-6 radar, still in search."

"It's bogus," the pilot said, relieved.

"We're getting another ZSU radar, bearing 140," the EWO reported.

"That's number two's target.

The second gunship flew past the first, headed southeast to take on the second ZSU. The gunships set up parallel orbits around each ZSU. It allowed them to keep a constant bearing on the target for firing, a consistent pylon turn around the target. No escape. Just an old-fashioned gunfight: Keep shooting until one of you is dead.

"Any sight of the aircrew?"

"Nothing," the sensor operators said. They were checking every hill nearby with the IR, but couldn't find anyone.

"*Watchmaker, you got a glint patch?*"

"*Affirmative.*"

"You got him?"

"No, sir, nothing."

The glint patch was a small patch worn on the flight suit underneath a squadron patch. It Velcroed to the flight suit, and made it visible to infrared or ALLTV, by showing up as a strobe. "We should have it by now," the sensor operator said, concerned.

⚓

The first thing they heard was the shell slamming into the earth.

"What the hell—" Woods exclaimed as they dived to the ground. "What was that?"

"Gunship," Wink declared. "I'd bet anything. One of those Hercules things, with guns out the side."

They heard a supersonic crack and glanced up to look for some muzzle flash, but could see nothing in the dark sky.

"I thought they'd be coming with helos," Woods said, worried.

"They're probably on their way. They sent the bouncers first, to clear the floor. Come on," Wink said, standing, as the gunfight began below them in earnest. They could see red tracers racing up into the black sky, into pure emptiness, as far as they could tell. But the sound of the returning fire was growing louder. It sounded as if the Spooky had all three guns going as they heard another airplane fly overhead and another ZSU light up the sky to the southeast.

One more 105 shell hit the ground in the valley below them, almost making them miss the distinctive sound of an AK-47 bullet glancing off a boulder ten feet away.

❧

The Captain of the Pave Low studied the new image on the screen in the middle of the cockpit. A digital picture of their location and the terrain around them in a 3-D format, it showed all the hills, mountains, valleys, and changes in altitude of any kind in the terrain. He had decided which of the hills was the most likely to be the one where the downed aircrew were hiding. It fit the range and bearing of the call the Spooky had gotten from them. What he wasn't sure about was the location of the ZSU.

The Captain continued straight for the hill, his night-vision devices illuminating the darkness in front of him. His rotor wash was stirring up pebbles and sand below him as he strove to get as low as he could without his landing gear hitting the ground.

He glanced again at the computer screen. Seven minutes until they were over the target. He spoke softly into his intercom to have the loadmaster in the back alert the commandos. "Seven minutes."

❧

"Watchmaker, you got a firefly?"

"Affirm," Woods replied, as Zev looked through his massive night-scope for whoever had just shot at them.

"Light it off, we still don't have you."

"Wilco," Woods replied, reaching into the side pocket of his survival vest. He pulled out the 9V battery and the small black box, maybe two ounces, and hooked it up. Another bullet whizzed by them.

Zev aimed carefully through his scope and pulled the trigger on his Remington 500 sniper rifle. "One dead," he announced coolly. "Many more behind him. Maybe five hundred yards away."

❧

"Got him!" the ALLTV sensor operator said. He saw a streak from the firefly coming from the top of a hill, lower than the one they had been searching diligently with all their sensors. He zoomed in on the hill with the IR sensor as the TV stayed locked on the ZSU, which was now moving. Its operators realized that if they were to have any chance at survival they had to get away from this invisible airplane with too many guns. They could shoot wildly without directing the fire while on the move, but at least that way they might live to shoot another day.

In the lead Spooky, the Fire Control Officer watched the movement with comfort. He smiled to himself. You can run, but you just die tired. The ZSU could no longer shoot at them effectively. In the back the airman tossed the brass shell casing from the 105 into a large square box bolted to the ramp of the airplane, then turned quickly and grabbed another of the fifty-pound shells from the rack and slammed it into the breach of the howitzer.

Suddenly the IR sensor operator exclaimed, "Multiple bad guys closing in on our airmen!" He had seen the whitish figures on the dark green background moving up the hill toward the figure with the streak from the firefly. "We've got to get some fire on them."

Through his night-vision devices the Spooky pilot watched the distant men scramble over the boulders toward the Americans. "Get the 25-millimeter on them!" he cried.

"Redirecting the 25-millimeter to antipersonnel!" the Fire Control Officer declared, training the Gatling gun on the men who could now be seen clearly on the ALLTV. The officer began firing the 25-millimeter gun at eighteen hundred rounds per minute, its maximum rate of fire.

Woods ducked as the 25-millimeter rounds began raining down on the hill five hundred yards from them, splintering rocks and sounding like the Indy 500 with all the cars crashing into each other.

Zev was watching through his scope. "They are stopping those that aren't getting hit. That will at least keep them there." He looked at Woods. "Where are the helicopters? We must get out of here!"

42

The first ZSU-23 locked on to the Spooky quickly. It erupted again and its 23-millimeter cannons lit up everything around, making the valley look like a small room filled with anger and flame. The sky fired back as the Spooky rolled high over the hill and zeroed its battery of angry guns on the ZSU. The darkness was full of muzzle blasts on the ground and in the air as the antiaircraft battery and the mobile airplane hammered at each other.

The Spooky quickly got the upper hand, its jammers confusing the ZSU's radar. Each time the radar would lock, the electronic counter-measures of the Spooky would pull it off, directing the ZSU's bullets elsewhere. The 105-millimeter Spectre cannon pumped shell after shell out of the airplane at the armored vehicle. The howitzer was accompanied by the blinding fury of the 40-millimeter gun next to it.

Woods, Wink, and Zev crouched behind a massive boulder and listened to the gun duel between the meanest antiaircraft gun in the world and the meanest airborne gun platform in the world. The bullets flew back and forth, thousands of rounds of steel flying along the same path, like a bullet freeway.

The howitzer blasted out shell after shell. Suddenly a 105 round found its mark slammed into the turret of the ZSU. The vehicle and its barrels erupted in flames and explosions, causing a blinding white flash on the TV and the IR.

The pilot in the lead Spooky radioed the second plane. *"Scratch one ZSU. How you coming?"*

"Seconds away. We'll get him."

"Yours a nonfactor for the evacuation?"

"Concur."

"Roger. Break, Grommett Niner Six, you're cleared in. Call when 1 mile out."

The Captain of the lead Pave Low heard all he needed. "Grommett Niner Six is in. Wilco," he called. They were two miles away. He started the dark gray ship up the hill toward the Americans.

The gunfire had increased. Those Assassins who had survived the onslaught of the 25-millimeter gun from the dark sky had found safe spots from which to shoot. They were firing their AKs on automatic now, knowing this was their one and only chance. They wanted to do it for the Sheikh.

The Fire Control Officer in the Spooky could see the muzzle blasts from their AKs with his IR and TV. The ZSU was dead. He turned the 105- and the 40-millimeter guns on the intruders. "Bringing all to bear," he announced. Everyone in the Spooky, all on the same ICS, nodded as the three guns began firing at their maximum rate of fire at the twenty or so remaining Assassins.

Woods couldn't believe his ears. The noise of the shells hitting the mountain and the boulders was like the Indy car wreck now joined by two or three train collisions. Shells slammed into the rocks all around the Assassins, shattering the boulders and anything near them. Jagged splinters of rock flew out for hundreds of feet as the shells hit again and again, without stopping: no pause, no mercy, just an unrelenting, unceasing rain of steel and terror.

"One mile out," the Captain declared as the Pave Low climbed up the backside of the mountain, his wingman one mile behind him. He called Woods on the radio. "Watchmaker, Grommett Niner Six coming up your backside. Are you armed?"

The men on the Spookies stopped shooting when they saw the Pave Low approach the top of the hill. They began a new pylon turn, keeping the remaining Assassins on their scopes, ready to shoot again as soon as the Pave Lows were out of harm's way.

"Affirmative!" Woods cried through the din.

"Put down all your weapons, now," the Captain ordered.

Woods couldn't believe his ears. A few Assassins were now only two hundred yards away. "Say again?"

"Put down all weapons—"

"They're shooting at us!"

"Roger, sir, we'll be doing the shooting for you."

Suddenly the Pave Low screamed up over the backside of the hill and hovered directly over Woods, Zev, and Wink at twenty feet. The two gunners from the Pave Low leaned out the doors on either side of the Pave Low and began firing 7.62-millimeter Gatling guns in the direction of the hidden Assassins.

Woods, on one knee, put his Beretta back in his survival vest. "Put your gun down!" he yelled at Zev, who hesitated.

Suddenly four large, thick ropes toppled out of the helicopter hovering above their heads and the commandos, wearing helmets and night-vision goggles, zipped down the ropes and hit the ground. The first ones to touch down began shooting from automatic weapons as they charged toward the remaining Assassins to set up a perimeter around Woods and the others.

The commando leader went directly to Zev and threw him to the ground. Zev resisted and reached for his rifle. Another soldier picked up the sniper rifle and held it away.

Woods was suddenly thrown to the ground from behind, his helmet pivoting slightly as his head hit the dirt. He felt himself being turned onto his stomach, the roar of the helicopter lessening as it pulled away. The gunfight was now just men against other men. Wink was tackled next, and Woods heard him cry out, "Shit! My knee!" One of the men muttered "Sorry, sir."

"You Lieutenant Woods?" someone asked Woods.

"Yeah, what are you holding me down for—"

"Should have been two people here. When we have too many people we sort it out later."

"There's no need for this—"

"Give me your hands, please," the commando leader said. He pulled plastic handcuffs out of a hidden pocket and expertly cuffed Woods's hands together behind his back.

"Who are you?" Woods asked.

"We're here to get you out." The leader glanced over at his men who were giving Wink and Zev the same treatment. They nodded at him. He spoke to Woods. "I'm gonna go find a place to get the helicopter back in here to get us out. Stay here."

Woods tried to sit up, but it was difficult and awkward. He could hear the Assassins' bullets ripping over their heads, the commandos returning fire furiously at the remaining men.

The commando leader returned to where Woods, Zev, and Wink lay on the dirt near the top of the hill. He spoke into a lip mike. "Let's go!" Two commandos each grabbed the bound men and headed quickly toward the top of the hill on the other side, in view of the flaming ZSU. The Pave Low came in low and fast, stopped in mid-air in a thundering nose-high maneuver. The enormous helicopter settled down toward the ground slowly as the Assassins suddenly realized what was happening and turned their attention to the chopper. Their AK-47 bullets banged harmlessly into the armor plating on the side of the plane as the commandos hurried toward it, their three captives in tow.

The Captain touched his landing gear down on the uneven hill but kept the helicopter in a hover so the gear wasn't called on to absorb the weight of the ship. He lowered the ramp. The commando captain ran the last few feet to the chopper and handed Woods over to the commandos waiting inside. They grabbed him by the arms and pulled him hard up the ramp into the belly of the screaming helicopter. Zev was next and was hustled inside unceremoniously.

Inside the helicopter the waiting commandos yelled at Woods. "We need you on the deck, sir," pushing him down to the hard steel floor of the chopper covered only with a Kevlar blanket. Woods went down reluctantly but quickly, and the commando put a plastic tie around his ankles. He then lashed Woods to the deck through several hard points in the helicopter. Woods couldn't move at all. He could see Zev across from him receiving the same treatment. "I'm sure glad I invited *you!*" Woods yelled.

Farouk refused to give up and let them get away. He was tired of firing from his protected position while the Americans were near success. He knew he must be courageous. He stood up and aimed at the helicopter a hundred yards away, firing continuously.

The commandos pulling Wink had moved more slowly out of concern for his tender knee. They'd reached the ramp and were handing him over to the men inside when the commando on Wink's left was thrown to the ground by the force of several of Farouk's AK-47 bullets hitting him in the back. He cried out as he fell. Wink's body jerked as he was hit and he lurched forward. The waiting commandos quickly pulled him up into the helicopter and shouted for the medic.

The gunner in the Pave Low saw Farouk clearly through his night-vision devices and turned his 7.62-millimeter Gatling gun on him. He pulled the trigger and walked the angry fire hose of red tracers into Farouk's body, watching as the bullets tore into him. He then turned his gun on the handful of remaining Assassins, who stayed hidden and fired occasionally by extending a weapon from behind a boulder.

Thankful for his bulletproof flak jacket, the commando who had been hit by Farouk's bullets stood up and climbed aboard the helicopter, "You okay?" the commando leader yelled. The man nodded.

Zev looked at Woods and pointed with his head toward Wink. Woods saw them working on Wink, trying to stop the bleeding from his back. "Wink!" Woods shouted, trying to move across the deck to get closer to his friend. "Wink!" He strained against the lines holding him down and tried to get free. "Get these lines off me!" he yelled furiously.

The helicopter lifted up from the landing zone as the bullets continued to plink off the side of the behemoth and its armor plating, moving quickly to its left and heading down the side of the mountain ten feet above the boulders. Wink wasn't moving.

"Wink!" Woods yelled again, his eyes growing damp.

"What?" Wink replied, his voice full of pain.

"You okay?"

"No. Those mothers shot me in the back. It hurts like hell," he said.

The medic turned toward Woods. "He took a couple of ricochets in the back." Quickly slicing through the plastic ties binding Wink's wrists behind his back, the man began cutting away his flight suit. "No organs though," he said as he examined the wounds. "He should be okay."

"Thank you, God," Woods said as he relaxed and quit fighting the lines holding him and the plastic ties around his wrists and ankles.

The second Pave Low crested the top of the mountain and hovered just off the ground as the first one had. The commandos still on the ground began a slow calculated movement toward the helicopter as they continued to receive opposing fire from the three or four Assassins now remaining. They returned fire, much more accurately, accompanied by the guns of the Pave Low. They made it into the helicopter one by one until there were only four men on the ground returning the Assassins' fire. On a radio signal from the pilot the rest of the commandos dashed up the ramp into the armored chopper and it lifted off the top of the mountain, its guns still firing their angry red tracers at the small muzzle flashes coming their way.

As the helicopter rose, the Assassin who had been lying next to Farouk saw the shoulder-fired SAM that Farouk had been about to use. Dropping his AK-47, he stood up to use the missile, but as he did so the helicopter dropped below the summit, out of sight. Suddenly, it was quiet. The Assassin lowered the SAM in frustration.

"Two's clear," the pilot of the second Pave Low transmitted.

The Fire Control Officer in the Spooky orbiting above the hill had been watching the fight on his ALLTV. He had kept his crosshairs on the Assassins the entire time, not willing to shoot with American forces so close. His mouth suddenly went dry as he saw one of the Assassins stand and aim a shoulder-fired missile in his direction. He had waited an eternity for the second Pave Low to call clear. He was ready and fired the 105 at the man, the shell missing by many feet. "Shit," he muttered. He directed the other two guns on the Assassins and put them on maximum fire as the airman in the back loaded another fifty-pound shell in the 105. The bullets rained down, but not before the Assassin fired his missile at the black sky raining death down on him.

The missile flew out of the tube at the end of a red-hot rocket motor just as a 40-millimeter shell tore the man apart. He dropped as the rocks around him splintered and severed the other two remaining Assassins.

"SAM! SAM!" the IR sensor operator screamed into the intercom aboard the Spooky.

The pilot of the Spooky reached behind him to his left and grabbed a handle hanging on the bulkhead with a long cable attached to it. He quickly squeezed one of the buttons and several flares dropped out of the back of the AC-130U as the pilot pulled up into a steep climb. The copilot was already pushing the throttles to their stops. As the flares lit up the sky around them, they climbed away and took a steep left turn to put the climbing SAM on their beam. The pilot pushed the yoke forward and the Spooky went into a steep dive.

Behind them the SA-7 missile continued to climb, but it was more interested in the flares than it was in the diving airplane. It slammed into one of the brightly burning flares and expired five hundred yards behind them.

The Spooky pilot leveled off, climbed back up to altitude, and headed west. *"One's off,"* he transmitted.

"Two's off, we're right behind you."

The Pave Low carrying Woods and the others came to the valley floor and headed west and north, going at the helicopter's top speed.

One of the commandos bent down and untied Woods from the deck. He helped him sit up. "You okay, sir?"

"Yeah," he said.

"Where's your ID, sir?"

"In my wallet in my pocket. Chest pocket. Left."

The commando reached into the pocket of Woods's flight suit. He pulled out the wallet and saw the ID in the plastic window. He shined the flashlight on it, then on Woods's face. "What's your Social?"

"Five six three, three three, five seven seven eight."

The man reached behind Woods with a knife and cut the plastic ties on his wrists and feet, then undid his handcuffs.

"Thanks," Woods said. He rubbed his wrists and crawled aft to Wink. "You okay, bud?"

"Yeah. It hurts, but I'm okay." He rolled slightly toward Woods. "I want a Purple Heart. Think this qualifies?"

"Has to."

Wink nodded. " 'Cause if it didn't, I was going to write to that congressman of yours. He'd make it right."

"I'm sure he would." Woods smiled. "Let me know if you need anything." He stood up and staggered to the bench seat. The crew chief strapped him in. It was loud inside but smoother than he had expected, only an occasional bump as they flew along close to the desert floor. The Pave Low beat its way quickly toward Turkey, and safety.

Woods leaned his head back against the bulkhead as he sat motionless. Zev's hands were still handcuffed and bound together as he lay on the deck. Woods rubbed his eyes. He hadn't realized how tired he was. He thought of sleep, but he wanted to be completely aware of everything that happened the entire way back to safety. He looked at one of the commandos and pointed to Zev, still lashed to the deck like a menacing shark. "You going to let him up?"

"No, sir. No idea who he is."

Woods wasn't buying that. He found the commando captain. "Let him up," he said, pointing at Zev.

"Don't know who he is, sir."

"I'll tell you who he is," Woods shouted angrily. "He saved our lives on the ground back there. He hid us out for a day and put his own life in danger. He was the one who told us we *succeeded* in getting the Sheikh, and if we hadn't, he'd have done it himself. Now let him up!"

"I'll let him off the deck, but I'm not going to undo his hands."

"Fine," Woods said.

The man crossed to Zev and unleashed the lines holding him down.

Zev nodded gratefully and joined Woods on the bench seat. The crew chief tossed Woods a helmet, which Woods put on Zev's head. He strapped Zev into the seat next to him. As the helicopter bounced through some rough air, Woods and Zev put their heads back against the bulkhead and closed their eyes. In spite of Wood's determination to stay awake, he dozed off.

He was jerked from sleep when his feet flew up from the deck of the Pave Low as it pitched over toward the ground. His boots slammed back to the deck when the helicopter pulled up and banked hard right, in a desperate attempt to escape something. Wink slept and Zev looked confused. The crew chief studied something Woods couldn't see. A Lieutenant came down from the cockpit and strapped into the seat across from Woods. He looked grim.

"What's going on?" Woods yelled to him.

"Fighter. They didn't see him coming. He didn't turn his radar on until the last second. Now he's all over us."

"Fighter? Syrian?" Woods asked, his mouth dry.

"Not sure. They're working the ESM gear to identify him now."

"What about the gunships? Can they help?" Zev asked, overhearing the conversation.

"No, they're air to ground only. No help at all against an airplane." They're just hoping he doesn't see them."

"So what do we do?" Zev asked.

"Not much. Try to evade him."

The crew chief listened in his helmet, then crossed to the Lieutenant, grabbing hard points of the helo to avoid falling. He spoke into his ear, then crossed back to his station.

The Lieutenant looked at Woods. "It's an F-14."

"What?"

Woods reached for the buckle to his seat belt. "Get him on the radio! It's one of ours! Try guard 243.0!" Woods said, shouting and trying to stand. "It's probably someone from my sq—" He froze. "It's Iranian," he realized.

"Iranian?" the Lieutenant yelled.

"Only other country in the world that has them," Woods yelled back.

"Great," the Lieutenant said as he made his way back to the cockpit to relay the good news.

Woods ran up to the cockpit, tearing up the three steps to the elevated area where the pilots sat. He had to get to the pilot to help him evade. If he didn't do it just right he could fly them right into oblivion.

The helicopter jerked madly back and forth and then tried to slow to a near hover right on the ground to let the F-14 go by. Woods grabbed a steel bar next to the ladder keep himself from falling down into the cargo area. The helicopter went left and right, spinning on its axis as it tried to avoid the F-14's deadly 20-millimeter Vulcan cannon, the Gatling gun that could fire six thousand rounds of heavy ammunition a minute. The helicopter had no ability to defend itself from a fighter. Woods looked for an extra headset so he could talk to the pilot on the ICS when a flash to their right made him cover his eyes.

"What the hell was that?" the copilot yelled as Woods peered out the window over his shoulder.

Woods smiled. "Missile impact. Somebody got him."

"Who?"

The Captain replied, "Fighter. F-18s from the *George Washington* staged out of Batman. They were supposed to cover our egress. You know any of them?" the Captain asked Woods.

Woods smiled as he thought of Terrell Bond bagging an Iranian F-14. He would be impossible. "Yeah, I know them."

"Tell whoever that was that I owe him a case."

"I guess that means I owe you at least two cases."

"Two cases should just about do it."

"You just let me know when and how to deliver it."

"I sure will."

"Are we in Turkey yet?" he asked, examining the screen in the middle of the cockpit.

"In about two minutes."

Woods began to relax for the first time since the cat shot off the carrier. They might actually make it home. He turned and headed down the ladder to the cargo area.

Woods sat next to Zev. "Is your name really Zev?"

"No."

"You sure we got the Sheikh?"

"Yes," Zev said. "I am sure."

"You heard it?"

"Yes. Almost made me deaf."

"How did you get a bug into that mountain?"

"*I* never could have."

"Who did?"

"One of our best."

Woods was curious. "Who?"

"Doesn't matter."

Woods wanted to know, but he looked straight ahead and said nothing.

Zev spoke. "A woman." He paused. "Spoke Arabic and Farsi. She made herself an Iranian farm girl bringing fruit for them from a distant valley. They let her into the fortress to deliver food. Several times."

"She was one of you?"

"The best I've ever seen."

"Was she with the Mossad?"

"I can't really say—"

"Why not?"

"I talk too much. Comes from sitting in the desert by yourself for days without talking to anybody."

"Was she with the Mossad?" Woods asked again.

Zev looked at Woods for a long time before he spoke again. "*Kidon.*"

"What?" Woods asked, leaning forward.

"*Kidon.* Special unit for . . . assassination."

"An Israeli assassin?" Woods was amazed. Then he went cold. "Was her right hand mangled?"

Stunned, Zev said quickly, "How do you—"

"Irit," Woods said breathlessly, as too much came to him at once.

Zev tried to imagine how a U.S. Navy Lieutenant could possibly know her name. "She was preparing a . . . gift for the Sheikh. It went off before she was ready. It ruined her hand."

Woods stared. "*She's* the one they were after on the bus."

"They found out."

Woods had to know. "Where was she going when she was killed?"

"Tel Aviv."

"To interview with El AI?"

Zev's eyes strained through the darkness to see if Woods was joking. "No. She was coming to help plan our next mission. To see *me.* We are . . . were in the same unit. Twelve of us."

"Not to interview?"

"No."

Nothing was fitting together. "Why was she in Italy?"

"She went there often. Vacation."

"I met her there."

"You met Irit?" Zev said, his surprise now complete.

"She and my roommate were seeing each other."

"The American Naval officer?"

"Yeah."

"Ah," Zev said. "Now I see." He frowned thoughtfully. "So your bombing strike was personal. You against the Sheikh. For your roommate."

"You too. For her."

"It was my fault. They never should have found her."

"I've got to know one thing, Zev."

"What?"

"What was Tony Vialli doing in Israel?"

"Who?"

"My roommate. The Navy officer."

"With Irit?"

"Right."

"I never knew his name. He came to visit her."

"Did someone else want him there?"

"Just the opposite. She was afraid his coming would draw too much attention to her. I told her he should not come. It was a risk to be seen with him." Zev was quiet for a long time, remembering Irit and all she had meant to him, and to his team, a look of profound sadness over his barely visible face.

"So why did he go?"

Zev looked at Woods and shrugged. "Because they were in love."

Acknowledgments

I would like to express my gratitude and admiration to Commander Sam Richardson, USN, an F-14 pilot and the Commanding Officer of VF-14. He was kind enough to read the manuscript and give me excellent guidance. I would also like to thank Commander Dave Pine, USN, Commanding Officer, and the officers and sailors of VF-31, the Tomcatters, and the F-14D squadron aboard the USS *Abraham Lincoln*, who treated me like a member of the squadron during my visit there. I am also grateful to Captain J. J. Quinn, USN, and the men and women of the USS *Abraham Lincoln* for allowing me the run of the ship and helping me remember what carrier life is like.

I am also greatly indebted to the fine men and women of the 16th Special Operations Wing of the United States Air Force at Hurlburt Field, Florida, and in particular those in the 20th Special Operations Squadron who fly the MH-53J Pave Low III helicopters, and the 4th Special Operations Squadron who fly the AC-130U Spooky. Their advice and assistance were invaluable.

The Book of

Editor Janine Amos
Designer Ruth Hall
Picture Researcher Deborah Brammer

Illustrations by Victor Ambrus
Bysouth and Hayter Associates
Ruth Hall

GREAT MYSTERIES

by Christopher Maynard

Purnell

CONTENTS

Photographic Acknowledgements

Aldus Archives 11, 22 (bottom), 34. Barnaby's Picture
Library 67, 98. BBC Hulton Picture Library 77. Janet
and Colin Bord 71, 79. Brotherton Collection (University of Leeds) 23. Mary Evans Picture Library 18, 22
(top), 37, 40, 104, 107, 109, 116/117. Fortean Picture
Library 29, 56, 114 (top and bottom). *Illustrated
London News* 32, 84, 85. Keystone Press 106, 111.
Mansell Collection 81, 88, 113. Tony Morrison 80.
Popperfoto 13 (top). Royal Geographical Society 28
(bottom). *St Petersburg Times and Evening Independent* 48. Syndication International Ltd. 13 (bottom),
20, 35 (top and bottom), 39, 46, 74, 101. Trustees of
the British Museum 68. Trustees of the British
Museum (Natural History) 28 (top). Zoological Society
of London 10.
Endpapers: Anthony Weir/Janet and Colin Bord.
Title page: Fortean Picture Library.

Front endpaper: Alignment of stones in Co. Cork,
Republic of Ireland.
Title page: UFO photographed in Oregon, U.S.A.
Back endpaper: Stone circle in Co. Kerry, Republic
of Ireland.

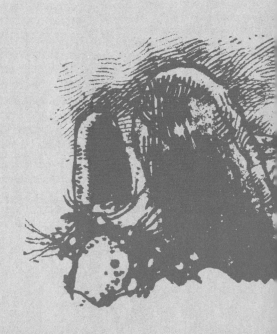

MYSTERIOUS CREATURES

Monsters

Monstrous creatures are known to people the world over and play an important part in folk-tales and legends everywhere. The unicorn and dragon of myth are popularly regarded as fabulous beasts born of human imagination, but could they have a basis in fact? And what are we to make of sea monsters? Are these creatures merely fictional—or do they lurk today in the unknown deep?

Dragons

According to legends of the Middle Ages, the typical sort of dragon that a knight was expected to battle with was a hideous reptilian monster. Although few dragons were ever bigger than a man on horseback, their gruesome looks and violent natures made them seem larger than life.

The dragon was a heavy beast. His stubby legs barely raised his belly from the ground as he half-lumbered, half-slithered along. He supported himself on feet armed with long, razor-sharp claws. High on his back was a pair of stunted bat-like wings. Although these seemed far too small and flimsy to support his weight in the air, the dragon was claimed to possess amazing flying abilities. His body ended in a long, coiled tail with a barb at the tip. It would writhe and thrash about dangerously as the dragon fought and

was a formidable weapon in its own right. The dragon's hide was covered with leathery scales, like that of a crocodile, and it served as an effective natural armour against arrows.

The most frightening part of a dragon was the great head. Like that of a serpent, it consisted mostly of a great gaping set of jaws supported by a snaking neck. The jaws were lined with dagger-like fangs, and when parted they revealed a long forked tongue. The dragon's small eyes were said to include every colour of the rainbow, and to change shades according to its moods. The patterns in them would whirl and swirl, and it was believed that to look into the eyes of a dragon was to court madness. Above all, dragons were famous for their ability to snort flames from their nostrils as they battled with their enemies.

Descriptions of dragons were not confined only to myths and legends. There are also accounts by people who claimed to possess specimens of the real thing. One writer of the 1500s described a small Ethiopian dragon that he owned as having two clawed feet, two ears, a pair of wings, sharp teeth and a long, flexible tail. Its skin was completely covered with dark green scales, save for its throat and

Dinosaurs may have served as models for the dragons of myth (top), while a flying pterodactyl (above) looks like everyone's nightmare of a dragon. The horned dragon (left) combines the most gruesome features of both.

belly which were a light shade of yellow. Although we may find it hard to believe that this description refers to a real, fire-breathing dragon, there are enough details here to suggest that the writer may have been describing another kind of reptile actually in existence. There are several species of flying lizards in southeast Asia that are able to glide from tree to tree on 'wings' that consist of a webbing of skin stretched over a fan of bony ribs. For a mind primed to believe in dragons, it would be easy to mistake a real-life flying lizard for a small, immature specimen of a dragon.

Dragon lore, however, is by no means confined to the Middle Ages. Dragons are some of the oldest and most widely known monsters in history. Accounts of them first crop up in Babylonian times about 3,000 BC. They are also found in the Old Testament of the Bible and in Greek mythology where they appear as the guardians of temples and sacred gardens. The ancient Greek dragon was quite different from the dragon of the Middle Ages. This creature had great wisdom, the ability to foresee the future and great strength. These qualities made him an ideal candidate for the role of protector of sacred places.

But whether sinister and destructive or kind and well-meaning, the question as to whether dragons have any real basis in fact remains to be resolved. There is an uncanny likeness between dragons and certain dinosaurs. Species like the giant Tyrannosaurs were dragons in every sense

(except for their inability to fly or breathe flames). Their leathery hide, clawed feet, long tails and huge jaws crammed with giant teeth make a perfect model for the dragons of mythology. Even the ability to fly crops up among some distant relatives of the dinosaurs, the pterosaurs. These creatures had long toothed jaws and bony bodies that were supported by a wingspan sometimes several metres wide.

However, knowledge of dinosaurs is fairly recent and in the ancient world they were unknown. Yet there is no reason to assume that a few relics could not have survived the great catastrophe that wiped out dinosaurs 63 million years ago. They may have managed to cling to a precarious existence long enough to fuel the imagination of early human beings and originate the legends of the terrible reptilian beasts we now know as dragons.

Dragon legends could also have been kept alive by encounters with existing lizards such as the Komodo dragon of Indonesia. This giant reptile attains a length of over three metres when fully grown, and is known locally to steal chickens, lambs and goats from farms and villages.

Although it is hard to accept that any one kind of reptile could ever have been the source of thousands of different dragon legends, the group as a whole, and this includes their ancestral cousins the dinosaurs, has too many similarities with dragons to be able to dismiss the obvious connections.

Monsters of the Deep

It was a quirky feat of seamanship, courage and endurance that took two British soldiers, John Ridgway and Charles Blyth, across the Atlantic Ocean in 1966 in a small rowing boat. Their voyage was not without danger, but perhaps the oddest drama of all took place one quiet night when the monotonous rhythm of rowing had lulled both men into a state of drowsy peace. Out of the dark came a strange swishing sound. Suddenly a huge writhing shape emerged, glittering with phosphorescence and heading swiftly straight towards the boat. It looked to

Above: **Legends of the sea are full of references to eerie monsters whose existence has so far been impossible to disprove.**

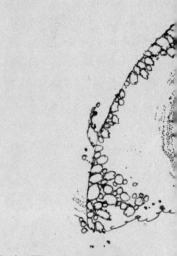

Left: **The Komodo dragon of Indonesia is the nearest thing to a dragon that exists today. it is even big enough to steal goats from local farmers. This reptile is shy, but frightening enough in appearance to fuel the dragon legend.**

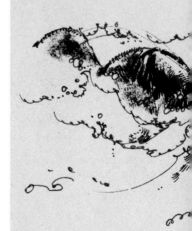

be almost ten metres in length and seemed set on a collision with the frail craft. At the last moment it dived and passed beneath them, then vanished into the gloomy night with a great splash. The amazed seamen were frozen with terror and at first quite unable to believe what their eyes had witnessed. The creature bore no similarity to any of the whales or sharks they had spotted previously. There was only one possible explanation—they had met a real sea serpent.

Encounters with such gigantic monsters of the deep are by no means rare.

One Belgian zoologist, Bernard Heuvalmans, has made a study of almost 600 sightings collected over the past 350 years. More than half of these were convincing enough in their detail to be classed as genuine 'sea serpents'.

One of the most dramatic brushes with a sea monster is described in an account that comes from Newfoundland, dated 1873. One day, the crew of a small fishing boat began to examine what looked like a mass of floating wreckage when it suddenly proved to be alive. A huge beast lunged at them and flung its tentacles around the boat. It began to submerge and drag the boat down with it. Frantically, one crew member seized an axe and began chopping at the thick, snake-like arms. The monster eased its grip and slipped back into the deep, but not before the fisherman had managed to sever one tentacle. The crew returned to shore safely with a trophy that was a good six metres long. Upon examination, it turned out to be the arm of a giant squid.

Other squid, of equally stupendous

Above: **The coelacanth, a prehistoric fish believed to have died out millions of years ago, was found to be still living off the coast of South Africa in 1938. Man's exploration of the oceans has, for most of history, been confined to the shallow coastlines. There is a good chance that other 'extinct' creatures still survive in the oceans' depths.**

Left: **Descriptions of deep sea monsters bear a striking resemblance to several kinds of ancient marine dinosaur. Myths of the sea which refer to such beasts raise the possibility that they survived until recent times. Many refer to sea monsters of stupendous proportions, yet whose bulk is easily hidden in the vast unknown of the sea.**

11

proportions, have been encountered from time to time. A specimen with tentacles measuring 11 metres long was captured off the coast of Spain in 1964, and an even larger beast was landed near New Zealand in 1887.

There is no way of being certain just how big a squid can grow. However, scars made by squid have been found on the heads of sperm whales (which feed on them). The marks seem to indicate that some squid reach an incredible length of 25 metres.

Giant squid account for many of the sightings of serpents that have been recorded at sea. But there are many tales of deep sea monsters that cannot be satisfactorily explained in this way. The only possible conclusion is that there are other, as yet unknown, creatures that lurk in the deep.

The world's oceans are so large that it is difficult to find anything sensible to compare them with. They cover over two-thirds of the entire globe, an area double the size of all the continents. Their average depth of 3,000 metres is more than twice that of the Grand Canyon. At their deepest—11km— they could hide Mount Everest with ease. Within this vast region, it would be easy for any number of unsuspected animals to survive without ever being known to man.

Such was the case with the coelacanth. In 1938, a bizarre looking fish was netted in deep waters in the Indian Ocean. This odd-looking creature proved to be a coelacanth, a fish thought to have become extinct over 70 million years ago. Other specimens have since been caught. They prove that a 'living fossil' was able to survive

Above: **The huge sea monster that surprised the crew of a small Newfoundland fishing boat in 1873 proved to be a giant squid.**

in a quiet and remote corner of the world for aeons without ever making itself known to science. No doubt there are still other 'living fossils' in the oceans. If nothing else, the regular sightings of sea monsters indicate that there are many deep-sea secrets still to be revealed.

Freshwater Monsters

Aquatic monsters are not confined only to the sea. There are many reports of incredible beasts that have been spotted in rivers and lakes. Some are simply updated versions of folklore creatures such as kelpies, mermaids and water-sprites. However, there is a steady stream of lake serpent reports that share an uncanny physical likeness yet which come from regions as far apart as Chile, Ireland and New Zealand. The beasts are described as having small heads set atop long snake-like necks. When swimming, they hold their bodies in such a way that, from above the surface, it often appears that they have several humps. They are known to throw up a considerable wake, showing that they move at a good speed as they cruise along the surface. The beasts all live in remote areas and make their homes in lakes that are especially deep.

By far the most famous freshwater beast of all is the Loch Ness Monster. The earliest record of this creature is found in the diaries of Saint Columba, a Christian missionary who went to Scotland over 1,400 years ago. He reported seeing the burial of a man who was said to have been bitten to death by a giant monster while he was swimming in the Loch.

For many years, sightings of the fabled monster were few and far between. But in 1933 a new road was built along one side of the Loch. Almost at once, the number of sightings rocketed. To date, over 3,000 people claim to have seen the monster, and many intriguing photographs have been taken.

Loch Ness is a peculiar sort of lake. It is a giant trench of icy water that stretches in a straight line for 38kms. A third of it is more than 200 metres

deep—this is twice the average depth of the North Sea. The shoreline plunges steeply into inky blackness, and its cold waters make it a rather unattractive place for swimmers and bathers.

The point of general agreement in practically all sightings was that the monster had a long serpent neck, a small head and an extended body with two pairs of flippers. These descriptions match surprisingly well with that of an extinct marine dinosaur—the Elasmosaur.

It was not until 1960, however, that people began to take more than just a passing interest in the Loch Ness Monster. A number of books and

Above: **Photographs of the Loch Ness monster show it to be a massive, long-necked beast rather similar to the Elasmosaur, an extinct dinosaur.**

Below: **This blurred underwater photograph shows a long-necked flippered beast swimming through the gloomy waters of Loch Ness. The picture, taken in 1975, created a sensation when it was released.**

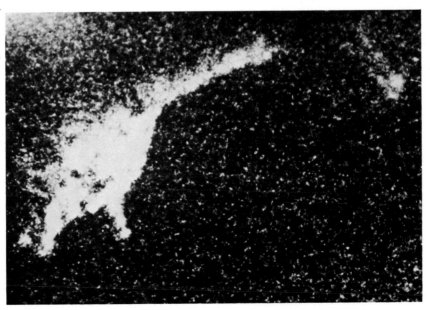

articles appeared and were followed soon after by groups of serious monster hunters arriving at the scene to scour the Loch systematically.

The results of their efforts were inconclusive. But they did produce a number of curious and tantalizing photographs. Although none was of an especially high quality, they all showed something large and dinosaur-like splashing about in the Loch. Then in 1972, and again in 1975, an American research team created a sensation by collecting some underwater photographs that showed what appeared to be the blurred and dim shape of a great oval flipper and a large streamlined body. This team used a camera linked to an electronic flash which was set to go off at regular intervals. This produced enough light to see a short distance into the murky Loch waters. The camera was also hooked to a sonar unit that registered any objects on its screen as they drifted into range. Yet even these highly technical and sophisticated pieces of equipment could not offer conclusive evidence for the existence of the monster. To this day the mystery remains unsolved.

Mythical Beasts

The folklore of the ancient world is full of stories of fabulous creatures that had supernatural powers and were immortal. Many were as dangerous to human beings as they were hideous to behold. Some were beasts of pure myth; others bore a startling resemblance to creatures that have roamed the Earth at one time or another. In either case, few people ever claimed to have seen these mythical monsters in the flesh.

Of all mythical beasts, perhaps the best known is the graceful unicorn. Ancient Greek legends tell of it having the body of a white horse, a purple head, blue eyes and a single, twisting horn arising straight out of its forehead.

A unicorn's horn was thought to have magical properties. If ground into a fine powder, just a few grains were claimed to protect people from many diseases, poisonous substances

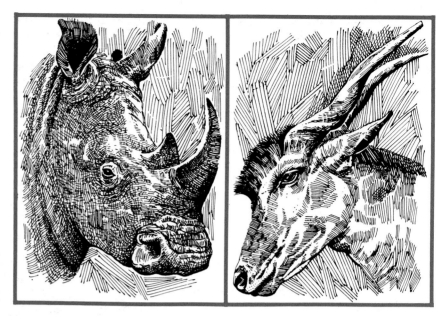

and from convulsions. Not surprisingly, people showed great interest in obtaining even minute amounts of this miraculous cure-all. Since no one had ever seen a unicorn, let alone been able to trap it, it was left to the legends to describe how to go about obtaining some of the horn. A young and beautiful girl had to venture into the remote parts of the world where the unicorn lived. In order to tame the creature she would have to remain alone in the forest until the beast approached, attracted by her sweet scent. It would then allow itself to be led away to the king's palace, where the horn would be cut off.

Needless to say, this was not a method that produced a good supply of unicorn horn. However, this did not stop a small and expensive trade in horns and powder from developing, especially in the Middle Ages as European travellers ventured farther afield. The true source was the narwhal, a small whale that lived in Arctic waters. It had a tooth that grew into a long, spiralled 'tusk'.

While there has never been any evidence that the unicorn, as it was described, ever existed, there are

Above: **Two creatures that could have inspired the myth of the unicorn are the eland and the rhinoceros.**

Below: **The mythical unicorn. According to ancient legends this graceful creature had a single, twisting horn endowed with magical properties.**

14

several kinds of antelope, such as the eland, that have spiralling double horns emerging from their foreheads. The unicorn seems to be a mixture of these graceful creatures and the sturdy rhinoceros, perhaps based on a confusion of various travellers' tales. As for horns having magical properties, those from the snout of the rhinoceros are claimed to have special powers in many parts of the world to this day.

On the other hand, the chimera was a beast for which there can be no claims to reality. It is one of a large group of mythical beasts that were assemblages of various different and unlikely creatures. The chimera had the hairy body of a lion, the head of a goat and a tail that was a writhing serpent. Like a dragon, it was able to belch forth deadly flames. According to Greek folklore, the chimera was born in a volcano in Lycia, a province of southern Turkey. There it regularly devastated the neighbouring country-

stump with pitch, as soon as a head was cut off, to stop a new one sprouting.

The question begged by all these legends is whether or not the creatures they describe have any basis in fact. At first thought, the beasts are so incredible that it seems unlikely that nature could ever produce anything so bizarre. Yet one only has to imagine

side until it was killed by the hero Bellerophon.

A similar sort of impossible beast was the hideous hydra. This grim creature lived in a shallow pool in a remote swamp. The stench of its breath was so terrible that it is supposed to have withered all plant life in the area. It had the body of a serpent from which sprouted a thicket of nine heads. Legends describe how Hercules was given the task of killing this monster. To his dismay, he discovered that this was far from easy. Every time he lopped off one head with his sword, two new ones grew in its place. In the end, he was forced to cauterize each

what the effect of seeing an elephant or whale for the first time would be to understand how easy it was for such legends to arise.

Perhaps the best example of a mythical creature which is likely to have had its origins in the world of real animals is the roc. This strange bird appears in the legend of Sinbad the Sailor, famous throughout the Arab world.

Sinbad was a citizen of Baghdad who went on seven great voyages around the Indian Ocean and the seas of south-east Asia. During one trip, his ship was wrecked by a gigantic, eagle-like bird that attacked it by dropping great boulders on to the vessel. The

Above: **The chimera of Greek folklore was an entirely imaginary beast. It appears to be an unlikely assemblage of various creatures.**

Above (left): **As this illustration on an ancient Greek vase shows, the mythical hydra bears a striking resemblance to the octopus.**

bird, which was a roc, was so big that its wings blotted out the sun like a passing cloud as it flew by. It had legs the size of tree trunks. When hungry, this great bird of prey would seize a fully-grown elephant and fly away with it to devour it in peace. Its eggs, according to Sinbad, were like huge white domes.

The roc does not only appear in the legend of Sinbad the Sailor. Marco Polo also refers to it in his travel diaries. Like the Arabs, he also claimed that it lived off the east coast of Africa.

During the Middle Ages, the time in which these stories and accounts were set, there really was a giant bird that lived in Madagascar and which fitted the description of the roc in several ways. The great ostrich-like Aepyornis survived on the island of Madagascar for centuries after similar giants in other parts of the world had died out. This flightless giant grew to a height of 270cm and is described as laying an egg the size of a football. We know that these eggs could hold about nine litres of fluid, for sailors used them in which to store their rum. The Aepyornis became extinct in the 1660s, no doubt due to being hunted by man. Except for the mistake about its ability to fly, it could well have been the inspiration for legends about a race of giant birds such as the roc.

Death of the Dinosaurs

Nearly 400 years ago, a French doctor by the name of Mazurier discovered evidence for what he claimed was an ancient race of giants. In a part of south-east France known as the Dauphiné he found a grave of gigantic bones. A skull emerged that was fully two metres long from front to back and which had eye-sockets the size of dinner plates.

Mazurier stoutly maintained that these bones were the remains of a giant human being. He even went so far as to claim that the grave bore the inscription 'Tuetobachus Rex', the name of a king of the Gauls from the second century BC. In fact, what Mazurier had stumbled upon were the bones of a mammoth. His mistake in identifying them was pardonable though, for at

the time few people suspected that such beasts had ever existed. Any finds of big bones, be they mammoths or dinosaurs, were generally thought to belong to giants and dragons.

Nowadays, we fully accept that beasts of a truly stupendous size at one time roamed the world. The biggest measured 30 metres from nose to tip of tail, while the heaviest weighed as much as a small herd of elephants—a good 50 tonnes or more.

But today, the only creatures to qualify for this league of giants are whales, for the dinosaurs disappeared long ago. From time to time there have been rumours of survivors, but there

has never been any real evidence that they still roamed the world after the great catastrophe that hit them 63 million years ago.

To the best of our knowledge, dinosaurs flourished for about 150 million years—a hundred times longer than any form of human beings. They

spread to every part of the world except Antarctica, and evolved into a bewildering variety of different forms. Some were land dwellers, others lived in the seas, while some had the ability to fly. Those in colder climates had furry coats and thick manes to stay warm. For the same reason, flying dinosaurs, like the pterosaurs, were covered with fur while other kinds had feathers. The giants were all warm-blooded. Many were highly active hunters and able to chase swiftly after their prey. The most advanced forms had excellent eyesight and finger-like claws with which to seize and grip their victims. Wherever they spread they ended up dominating other forms of life—including mammals.

Despite this success, an immense catastrophe managed to wipe out every last dinosaur. It is hard to imagine the extinction of an entire branch of life, but this has happened twice before in the history of the Earth.

Once, about 500 million years ago, there was a decimation of a group of sea-dwellers called trilobites. The second time, about 230 million years ago, almost half of all known species vanished from the fossil record.

So, although it is not unknown for an entire group of animals to die out, what is especially notable in the case of the dinosaurs is the speed with which they vanished. We do not know for sure how long it took them to go. Some people estimate several hundred thousand years. Others say days. But by geological standards, both are no more than the bat of an eye.

There is no evidence that tells us exactly what catastrophe hit the dinosaurs. Some scientists have suggested that they were overcome by the rise of egg-stealing mammals. Others have argued that they were 'poisoned' by new kinds of plants, or that an epidemic of some new disease wiped them out. But there were simply too many different kinds of dinosaurs living in too many places for any one of these reasons to have been sufficient to kill them all. Besides, not only dinosaurs died out during this great catastrophe. Many species of egg-laying mammals, reptiles, sea creatures and types of flowering plants were also killed off.

But there are possibly two disasters that might have had such a devastating effect: a supernova explosion or a collision with a giant comet or meteorite. If a giant star exploded (became a super-

nova) within 100 light years from us, it could bombard the planet with a dose of radiation that would be especially lethal to all large and advanced forms of life. It would also disrupt the atmosphere in such a way as to cause temperatures to plunge dramatically (this second result would also occur if a massive meteorite ploughed into the Earth). The destruction the searing radiation had begun would be finished off by the drop in temperatures. Dinosaurs without fur or feathers would be especially vulnerable. On top of this, the massive destruction of other animals and of plants would mean the loss of the dinosaurs' food supply. In the end, it may have been the piling of catastrophe on catastrophe that simply proved too much.

Man–like Creatures

Legends abound with all kinds of references to giants and 'little people', while stories of vampires and werewolves are a fascinating part of our folk-history. But how did such fantastic tales originate? Is there perhaps a greater substance to these ancient legends; a mixing of a fearful reality with unreality?

Giants

According to folklore, giants were some of the original inhabitants of the Earth. Halfway between monsters and human beings, they tended to be cruel and brutal. The giant in the fairytale 'Jack and the Beanstalk' is typical of this type, being a cannibalistic ogre of the worst sort. Giants were feared and hated. Fortunately for human beings, they could easily be outwitted. Heroes who met them in battle usually triumphed by the use of cunning rather than simple strength.

In ancient Greek myths, giants also had supernatural powers. One legend tells of their revolt against the gods of Mount Olympus. They were only subdued after a bloody war in which Hercules and the mighty god Zeus also had to join the battle.

In old Norse myths, giants were the enemies of both gods and human beings, just as in the Greek legends. The god Thor often found himself in battle against them and one hero, by the name of Beowulf, became famous for his encounter with the horrible giant Grendel.

Grendel was terrorizing the lands of

Below: **Late in the 19th century a young Austrian giant was exhibited to astonished crowds in Paris. His size, however, was due to a medical condition known as gigantism in which the pituitary gland, which controls the body's rate of growth, ceases to function properly. Such giants usually die at a relatively young age.**

a ruler called Hrothgar. He lived in a remote marshy corner of the island of Zealand, off the coast of Denmark, and emerged from there to attack King Hrothgar's men. He would steal into the great hall where everyone lay asleep after an evening of feasting and singing and would snatch up several men. He carried his victims back to his lair and there devoured them. His taste for human flesh led him to raid regularly, each time making off with another handful of the King's men.

One day Beowulf arrived at the King's court saying he had heard of his plight and would slay the giant for him. When Grendel arrived the next night, Beowulf seized the giant and hurled him about so violently that he ripped off one of the giant's arms. Grendal crawled away badly wounded and soon after died, freeing King Hrothgar and his people from the terror that had plagued them.

But giants do not only figure in ancient myths. According to a medieval folk-tale, the Belgian port of Antwerp owes its name to an encounter between humans and a giant. Long ago, the River Scheldt was blocked by a giant named Antigonus. He straddled the mouth of the river and destroyed any ships that tried to enter the harbour. Finally he was defeated by a hero who managed to cut off one of the giant's hands and hurl it across the river. The words 'ant werpen' describe this act of 'flinging the hand' over the River Scheldt, and from this action came the name of the city. In Antwerp today there stands a 12m high statue of the giant to commemorate this legend.

Above: **The typical giant of folktales was a huge bad-tempered ogre with a liking for human flesh.**

In the United States, a fabled giant of the 1800s was the good-natured prankster named Paul Bunyan. He was a giant logger of the north woods of Minnesota who, together with his giant pet ox, Babe, performed some of the most amazing feats the logging world has ever seen. They included straightening out a river that was so crooked and twisting that logs invariably ended up in mountain-high jams, and running a huge logging camp that was so big that the cook's stove alone covered an acre of ground.

It may be hard for modern people to

swallow the notion of giants with supernatural powers but in the past their existence seemed very hard to dispute. In the first place, the occasional finds of huge bones in the earth appeared to prove that an ancient race of giants once lived on the planet. It was not until relatively modern times that it was shown that these bones were dinosaur fossils. In the second place, there were cases of human beings who grew to such an enormous size that they could only be regarded as giants. It followed that such a person would

have much greater powers than his fellows.

The dividing line between very tall people and giants is vague at best. The average height of a fully-grown western male is 170cm, and anyone over 200cm is exceptionally tall. There are basketball players of between 215cm and 220cm who are extremely big—yet they are not called giants. They are people in good health, and who expect to live as long as the rest of us.

There are, however, those who suffer from a very rare disease called gigantism. It not only makes them grow to an enormous size, it also affects their physical appearance and the length of their life. Gigantism results when the pituitary gland, which controls the body's growth hormones, ceases to function properly. The main affect is to make sufferers grow to an extreme size and for their body's proportions—especially hands and faces—to become enlarged and altered. A typical pituitary giant was Robert Wadlow, a young American who grew to an incredible 260cm. In Switzerland in the 1800s another giant of 260cm was known, while in Russia a man of 285cm was recorded. All these giants tended to be physically weak and rather poorly developed. Almost all died at an early age, usually in their 20s, from infections that their weakened bodies could not resist.

Vampires and Werewolves

In 1732, a small village called Meduegna, not far from Belgrade, was visited by a five-man investigative unit from the army to examine stories of a strange, supernatural terror that was plaguing the community. Several years earlier, in the spring of 1727, a soldier of fortune had returned to Meduegna, his birthplace, after years of wandering abroad.

As far as the villagers knew, he was a pleasant, honest person, although from time to time he showed certain signs of unease and stress. However, he readily readjusted to his old village and soon married the pretty daughter of one of his neighbours. She, however, could not help remarking on his

Above: **The grim reputation of the 15th century Hungarian nobleman, Vlad the Impaler, provided inspiration for the legend of Count Dracula. The grisly ways in which he tortured his victims, and the legends that grew up about him drinking their blood and devouring their flesh, were a model for later vampire stories.**

Left: **Jan Van Albert, 283cm tall, standing next to a man of average height.**

occasional bouts of despair and finally drew from him the cause of his troubles. What haunted him was not the fear of death, but something even worse. For, he explained, he had once stayed in a town where a vampire had visited him. Fortunately, he had managed to flee from the creature, but at the back of his mind there still remained a lingering terror that he was not completely free of this ghoulish spirit.

Although his wife was appalled by his story she encouraged him, and together they convinced each other that the vampire encounter was truly a thing of the past.

Some time later, the former soldier was killed in an accident as he fell from a hayrick. Within the month, neighbouring villagers became alarmed as they began to claim they had been visited by the 'living' body of the dead man. Worse still, several of them soon died in quick succession. The panic-struck inhabitants demanded that the dead soldier's body be unearthed and examined. Forty days after it had been interred it was dug up in the presence of two army surgeons. As the coffin lid was pushed aside, onlookers could see that the body was partially turned to one side, and its mouth encrusted with blood. The corpse was as freshly preserved as if it had been buried the day before. The horrified onlookers plunged a wooden stake through its breast. At once a fountain of blood gushed forth and the body groaned in agony. Afterwards, it was burned and the ashes were reburied.

Although the notion of blood-sucking ghouls is ancient and widely known, the vampire legend as described in this story is typically European and contains all the classic ingredients of European vampire folklore. Germany has a particularly rich vampire tradition as does Hungary, Poland

and the Balkan countries. An elaborate folklore of vampires began to grow up. Vampires, it was thought, were either the victims of earlier vampires or perhaps the spirits of people who had been so wicked in life that they were unable to rest once they were buried. Their bodies did not decompose in the grave but stayed in suspended animation.

By day vampires rested quietly in their graves. They could not emerge since sunlight would cause them to shrivel up and disintegrate. At night, however, they rose and sought out the living to suck their blood. When they struck they usually aimed for the blood vessels of the neck.

In south-eastern Europe outbreaks of plague were closely linked with vampire mass-panics. People infected with disease were often thought to be the victims of vampires. According to legend, the result of a vampire's bite is that the victim feels drained and listless. Afterwards he falls ill, becomes deathly pale and dies. These symptoms correspond closely with many of those experienced by plague victims, and was one reason why 'evidence' of vampire activity was so widespread. Entire villages would barricade themselves indoors at sunset and cower there until daybreak. They used all sorts of charms to protect themselves; the most common being the use of garlic which was strung about doors and windows to keep the vampires out.

Today the vampire legend still survives, although it is heavily influenced by Bram Stoker's best-selling novel *Dracula*. The book was first published in 1897 and has since given rise to many related stories. The name 'Dracula' was probably inspired by an historical figure of the 15th century, Vlad V of Wallachia. He was also called Vlad Dracula ('son of the dragon, or devil'), and would punish his enemies by impaling their bodies on stakes.

The factual basis for vampires is thin. There are few accounts of maniacs with a lust for human blood. However, the fear that the dead will return from the grave to visit the living is universal. It is one reason why burial rites are so elaborate—they ensure that the dead are sent out of the world of the living properly and will make no attempt to return. Vampire legends

are also made more dramatic by known cases of premature burial in which the 'corpse' proved to be alive but in a coma. Some people have woken in time to escape being buried alive. But for others it was too late; they struggled and died in their coffins, unseen and unheard. A few, being dug up, would have shown all the signs of a vampire with their distorted and blood-stained features.

The notion of the werewolf is so common in European history that the phenomenon has its own special term —lycanthropy. It is a much older tradition than vampirism and has been well-described by writers as far back as the Romans. They claimed that werewolves were men or women who could change themselves into wolf shapes and then roam about at night hunting for human flesh to devour.

It was often believed that a magic potion had to be taken to transform a human into a werewolf, and that such a person would have to stand in the moonlight, naked except for a draped wolf skin, reciting a special charm. The change began as the palms became

Above: **Victims of a condition in which the body becomes covered with hair reinforced the legend of werewolves.**

Below: **Vlad the Impaler would punish his enemies by impaling their bodies on stakes.**

covered with hair and then gradually the rest of the body too.

Cases of mentally deranged people acquiring the habit of growling, running about on all fours and even attacking others with their nails and teeth are not unknown, although this is about the closest any human being will ever come to being a wolf. However, odd-looking strangers, especially those with heavy body and facial hair, could also have contributed to werewolf fears. Of course, the wolf is one of the few animals in Europe that is known to attack human beings. Stories of these attacks would add yet more fuel to the werewolf legend.

Little People

For some reason, the British were among the first to take spirit photography seriously. In 1918, the Society for the Study of Supernatural Pictures was set up in London to study the evidence that had been collected in this field. Among its eminent leaders was the famous author and spiritualist Sir Arthur Conan Doyle. The Society examined thousands of photographs featuring various supernatural items. Although many were rejected as being dubious, others were examined and certified as being authentic.

Nevertheless, there was considerable doubt concerning the two schoolgirls who claimed to have photographed fairies with an old-fashioned box camera. The girls, 16-year-old Elsie Wright and her 13-year-old cousin Frances Griffiths, insisted that they often met and played with fairies in the remote countryside surrounding the Yorkshire village in which they lived. In 1920, Sir Arthur Conan Doyle examined these pictures and became convinced that they were real. He declared that the evidence they provided marked 'an epoch in human thought'.

Despite the wave of hostile criticism that greeted his findings and the photographs themselves, both girls stood by their story and continued to do so for the rest of their lives. As recently as 1971, when interviewed by a television team, they insisted that the

photographs were genuine. Four years later, in 1975, they again stated publicly that their original story was true.

Belief in fairies, or the 'Little People' as they are often called, is worldwide. The Icelanders have a tradition of a mysterious dwarf race that is said to have existed since biblical times. In Ireland there are stories of a species of fairy folk called the Sidhe, meaning 'people of the hills'. The much more widely-known Leprechauns are a subgroup of the Sidhe. Even in the New World, far from European influences, the Indians had legends of tiny people. The Cherokee, for instance, told of a race of dwarfs, some of whom were friendly to humans while others were hostile and dangerous.

Oddly enough, in almost all these accounts the Little People were described as having a grotesque appearance. The dainty fairies of children's stories are quite a recent variation. By and large, the Little People looked like miniature but malformed

Above: **The first fairy photograph taken by Elsie Wright in 1917.**

human beings. The dwarfs of Scandinavia, for example, known as Dvergar, were said to be dark-skinned, heavily bearded, with small bodies, short legs and tiny, bird-like feet.

The kingdom of the fairies was supposed to be similar to that of human beings in many ways, while the behaviour of fairies was more or less the same the world over. They married, declared war on each other, feuded and had families. But they also stole newly-born babies from humans, and replaced them with their own wizened offspring.

In northern Europe, the dwarfs of the forests were supposed to be highly intelligent. They lived under the earth where they mined gold and silver. If captured by human beings, they were always able to buy their freedom with huge amounts of precious metal.

Belief in a race of dwarf people is so widespread that some anthropologists have suggested that there might be an underlying truth in these legends. Some believe that fairies are in fact a 'folk memory' of ancient pygmy inhabitants of lands that were later overrun by taller people. A hundred years ago the British scholar David Ritchie proposed that fairies or Little People might be very small Stone Age survivors who had been driven into hiding by the Iron Age Celts who conquered the country. They took refuge in caves and underground burrows from which they only dared to come out at night. This might explain

the legend that the Little People were terrified of any object made of iron. A curious coincidence, perhaps, is that until fairly recently prehistoric stone arrowheads found in fields were popularly known as 'elf arrows'.

Another possible explanation of Little People in our midst is the UFO connection. There are accounts of UFO spacemen that are not at all dissimilar from those of fairies. They are often described as elf-like creatures with large, oddly-shaped heads, stunted bodies, pointed ears and short legs. Like the Little People, space visitors are also claimed to have supernatural powers.

Perhaps somewhere between the Little People and UFO visitors are the gremlins that were reported by airmen during World War II. They claimed these dwarf-like creatures appeared inside their planes or on the wings. Later in the same war, another grotesque type of gremlin known as a spandale was sometimes reported by pilots flying high-altitude planes.

Although most of us assume that the Little People are merely creatures of folklore and imagination, it is remarkable that they should be reported almost everywhere in the world. Perhaps a shy and ancient race of dwarfs does survive deep below ground, or perhaps the fairy folk are miniature visitors from another planet. Certainly it seems that the legend of the Little People is too well documented to be totally unfounded.

Above: **Some people claim that an ancient and shy race of dwarfs, like these three blacksmiths, continues to survive deep below the ground.**

Below: **In Scandinavia, dwarfs were described as being hairy, dark-skinned folk such as this old man of the forest.**

Human Ancestors

In the evolution from ape to human being, man's forefathers passed through various intermediate phases. We have always assumed that these prehistoric ancestors are long dead and gone. Yet, disturbing reports of strange half-man, half-ape creatures living in remote corners of the world raise the possibility that survivors still exist.

The Missing Link?

In the years that followed the 1917 revolution, Russia was plunged into turmoil and civil war. Various rebel forces fought the new Soviet armies across the vast open spaces of the country. During the winter of 1925, one such unit of rebels was being hounded through the snowy Pamir Mountains of Central Asia by the troops of a Soviet major-general named Topilsky. One morning his troops reported finding the unshod footprints of a human being in the snow. Nearby, around the mouth of a cave, were further signs of human life. Suspecting that fugitive enemy soldiers had holed up there, Topilsky's men surrounded the cave. Hearing sounds of movement from within, they opened fire. To their amazement, the cries of pain that they heard were followed by the sight of a naked, wild figure staggering into the open and collapsing dead in the snow.

Topilsky and his men were puzzled by the creature they had shot. At first glance they mistook it for an ape since, except for its face, hands, knees and feet, it was totally covered with hair.

Yet they all knew that no apes lived in the high, cold country of the Pamirs. On further inspection they found that it had many traits of a normal human being. Although its hands and feet were wider than average, the legs and arms were of normal length and proportions and the teeth were regular and even, like those of any healthy adult human. The dead creature also had wide cheekbones which gave it a vaguely Mongolian look. However, its heavy brows, sloping forehead, flat nose and massive lower jaws were quite unique and puzzling to the soldiers who crowded around the body.

Some were convinced it was human, others that it was a type of ape. In the end Topilsky himself settled in favour of the first notion, and as a mark of this had the corpse buried beneath a cairn of rocks.

To any student of human evolution, Topilsky's record of the event has a very familiar quality. His descriptions sound exactly like those found in textbooks describing Neanderthal Man. The only difference is that he was talking about a fresh corpse whereas the books all refer to fossils more than 40,000 years old!

Nearly all anthropologists agree that Neanderthal Man vanished between 30,000 and 40,000 years ago when they were wiped out by Cro-Magnon invaders. Cro-Magnons are our direct ancestors and physically resemble us in every way. They suddenly appeared on the scene in Europe, arriving from the east, although their exact origins remain a mystery. Until their arrival, Neanderthalers had settled successfully throughout Europe and much of western Asia. They lived by hunting and fishing in hundreds of small communities. How it happened that they should vanish completely in the short space of a few thousand years has never been explained. Perhaps, however, their conquerors were not as efficient as has been assumed. Isolated pockets of Neanderthal descendents might have managed to survive and cling to life in remote parts of the world.

One academic who took this view was Professor Porshnev of Moscow. He argued that many sightings of primitive wild men have a great deal in common, no matter whether they came from ancient Greece and Rome, Europe of the Middle Ages or central Asia of today. These wild human beings are quite likely to be descendents of ancient Neanderthal groups. Because of their almost total isolation, Porschnev adds, they have lost nearly all their tool-making and hunting skills and have dropped back into a more primitive way of life than that of their flourishing ancestors more than 40,000 years ago.

In central Asia and Mongolia, these wild-men have long been known to the locals as almas. Although there is little concrete evidence as to who or what they are, the chance that Topilsky's victim—perhaps the only human ancestor ever to have been killed by a bullet—was an alma, and that almas are Neanderthal relics, cannot be dismissed.

A study of alma sightings made by Dr. Kofman of the USSR in the 1960s

Above: **This drawing of a bust made in 1914 shows what Neanderthal Man was thought to look like at the time.**

Below: **A family of Neanderthal hunters seen at the mouth of the cave in which they made their home.**

showed that the descriptions all mentioned the heavy brows, receding chins, flat noses and heavy jaws which we associate with Neanderthal Man. In no way does Topilsky's record differ in any important detail. The only serious doubt concerns the almas' way of life, which is recorded as being very primitive, almost ape-like. Quite possibly, these wild-men may be even more primitive than Neanderthalers, perhaps remnants of an even older, earlier group of human ancestors.

The Abominable Snowman

In the autumn of 1921, a British climbing expedition to Mount Everest, led by Colonel Howard-Bury, was making its approach when it spotted a number of oddly-human figures high up in the distance. As the climbers watched through binoculars, the dark shapes crossed a snowfield and then vanished from sight. The following day the expedition ascended to about 6,500 metres and found a trail of giant footprints. Each print was about three times the size of an ordinary human one. The Sherpa porters at once announced that these were Yeti tracks. However, Colonel Howard-Bury decided they had been made by wolves and had merely become enlarged and distorted as they melted in the sun. But the report he sent back caused an immediate sensation in the world press, and it gave zoology a new and unlikely name—the abominable snowman.

The Himalayas form a great chain of forbidding peaks and bleak plateaux, which stretch nearly 3,000 km from Afghanistan to Tibet. This is one of the highest and most remote regions in the world and a perfect setting for a legendary race of huge and mysterious beasts that seem to be a cross between apes and human beings. These creatures, most widely known as Yeti, have been part of local legends for centuries. Although they are said to be shy and no danger to people, locals do claim that they will raid farms from

27

time to time to steal goats or kill yaks. They are said to kill the yaks first by smashing their heads and then tearing them apart to eat the choicest morsels of meat. Despite these amazing claims, Yetis remained unknown to the rest of the world until the 1921 Howard-Bury expedition.

Since then, there has been a steady trickle of sightings and freshly-discovered tracks. For the most part, these reports have produced little hard evidence. Many are mistaken identifications of wolf and bear tracks, while all the Yeti 'relics' so far discovered have proved to be clever fakes.

However, it has been possible to build up a sketchy picture of the Yeti. It seems to be a huge beast about two metres tall, with an upright, shambling walk. It is covered from head to toe, except for its face, with long, reddish-brown hair. It feeds mainly on roots, leaves, berries and moss. Though obviously very powerful, it is also shy. On most occasions it seems to stay by itself, although pairs are sometimes seen together. For the most part it ignores human beings entirely.

By the end of World War II, interest in Yetis had faded considerably. Then, in November 1951, a report appeared that was to baffle even the most ardent disbelievers. Another Everest expedition came upon a trail of strange footprints high up at 6,000 metres on the Menlung Glacier. The men who found it, Eric Shipton, Michael Ward and Sherpa Tensing, were all accomplished climbers and knew the region well. But the footprints were like nothing they had ever seen before. They formed a

trail about 1.5 km long across the snow and were made in a way that would only be possible if the creature was walking on two feet. Shipton laid his ice-pick next to one print and photographed and measured it. The footprint was 33cm long and 20cm wide. It was of a naked foot that had a very long and thick second toe. Otherwise,

it looked like a human print in a number of ways. The trail also crossed a crevasse, which shows that the beast was powerful enough to leap it while still in an upright position.

Scientists who have studied the photograph have been puzzled. Although it is neither human nor ape, it bears no resemblance to any other creature known to live in the Himalayas. More than any other single piece of evidence, these prints have made it impossible to dismiss the Yeti as nothing more than an amusing local legend.

The Bigfoot

Bluff Creek Valley is a remote, heavily forested region of northern California. In the summer of 1967 two men visited the area on horseback, hunting for signs of a creature known as the Bigfoot. Suddenly, in the distance, they picked out a great hairy beast crouching by the bed of a dry stream.

Both horses panicked and reared, and their riders were thrown to the ground. One of them, Roger Patterson, recovered quickly and had the wit

Below: **This scalp of a Yeti from the monastery of Khumjung proved to be a fake. It was in fact made of goat skin. Unfortunately, the few other relics of yeti that have been preserved have all proved to be fakes as well. To date, there has been no concrete evidence that such a creature exists.**

Left: **This baffling footprint of a Yeti, with an icepick alongside to give a sense of scale, was discovered by Eric Shipton at Mount Everest in 1951.**

to snatch up his 16-mm film camera and start filming as he approached the creature. The Bigfoot, which was a female, rose and made off swiftly towards the trees. For an instant, she seemed to pause in flight and glanced back at the two men who had surprised her. Then, turning, she plunged among the undergrowth and vanished.

The film that Patterson had been lucky enough to obtain was extraordinarily precious. Until then, all the photographs taken of a Bigfoot had been of such poor quality that they proved useless as evidence. However, this short piece of film was in colour and of a quality sufficient to permit detailed examination.

The creature was a female, as its two large furry breasts show clearly. It had a conical head, a neck so short as to be almost invisible, and wide, heavy-set shoulders. Its entire body was covered with dark auburn hair and it stood about two metres tall. Judging by the impressions made by its footprints (which were 38cm long), it weighed around 225kg.

Much like the high country of the Himalayas, the forests and mountains of western North America are little-known and sparsely populated regions. Legends of a creature that sounds like a close cousin of the Yeti have been known here since before the arrival of white men. The Indians knew these beasts as Sasquatch.

Over the years there have been dozens of Bigfoot sightings and literally thousands of footprints have been spotted. In general, the descriptions all

Above: **Sightings of the Bigfoot in the western forests of North America confirm that it is a huge, hairy creature that strides around on its hind feet like a human being. Fleeting glimpses of this legendary beast have been recorded by local inhabitants ever since white people settled in the area. Before then, the Indians also told of great hairy beasts that lived in the remote woods.**

agree that the Bigfoot is a huge beast with the general form of a human being and which walks upright with a long, swinging gait. Although human beings have an average adult height of 1.7 metres, that of the Bigfoot ranges between two and three metres. Its footprints are flat and, on average, about 40cm long. The entire body is covered with shaggy brown to dark auburn hair.

It is widely agreed that the Bigfoot makes a high whistling sound when it calls and that it has a terribly strong and unpleasant gamey smell. It is known to munch berries and leafy twigs, to eat fish, small game and even large elks, and to raid dustbins and dumps for scraps of human food. However, it seems to show no aggression towards humans.

As with the Yeti, the evidence for and against the Bigfoot is confused. The short film of Roger Patterson's is believed by some to be a hoax—albeit a brilliant one. They claim the Bigfoot is really a tall actor dressed in a gorilla suit. Yet others accept it as powerful evidence that an unknown form of life, somewhere between the ape and human, survives in remote parts of America. If this is indeed the case, then science will have a great deal to explain. Our present ideas about the evolution of human beings may have to be radically revised.

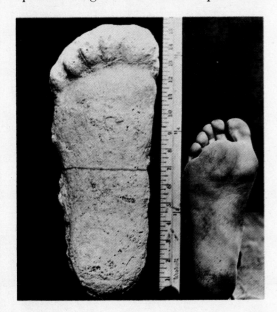

Left: **A Bigfoot's print taken from Bluff Creek, California in 1967 as compared to an average sized human footprint. The size of the print and the depth of its impression in the ground would indicate that the creature weighed well in excess of 200 kg.**

29

MYSTERIOUS MAN

Strange Powers

There is nothing mysterious about the fact that human beings can walk, talk, hear and see. Our physical abilities and mental powers are well-documented and clearly defined. But what are we to make of people who possess the ability to float in the air, to sense water underground and to know about faraway events even as they occur? Such powers have been well-documented too, yet they are by no means easy to explain.

Levitation

Levitation is one of the most difficult powers to explain, for it violates the laws of gravity in every way. But one thing about it is certain, it is definitely not the most elegant activity to practise. In 1852, a Mrs. Cheney of Barr, Massachusetts, was attending a spiritualist seance when her right hand began to rise off the table. As it floated upward it gradually hauled Mrs. Cheney out of her chair and into the air until she was left dangling heavily, like a fish on a line, between the ceiling and the floor (see illustration right).

In another instance a few years later, Daniel Home, the famous medium of London amazed his friends with one of the most spectacular exits ever witnessed outside the theatre. Concentrating his mental energies, he rose from the floor and disappeared through an open third floor window. He then seemed to hover outdoors in mid-air before returning to the room through the same open window and landing feet first.

Levitation and flying are twin themes that crop up in folklore and legends again and again, and they refer to objects—such as flying carpets—and animals as well as to people.

From ancient China comes the story of the two daughters of the Emperor Yao who taught a young man the art of flying. In gratitude, he married both of them when the Emperor died. From ancient Greece we have the myth of Daedalus and Icarus who escaped from capitivity by fashioning wings of feathers and wax and then flying to their freedom. Unfortunately, Icarus soared too near the Sun. As its heat melted the wax, the feathers came loose and he plunged to his death.

Much more recently in history, stories of flying witches became popular, while in Tibet the famous lama, Milarepa, was occasionally seen by his people flitting across the skies.

In these legends, the ability to levitate and fly is directly attributed to the powers of gods, holy men and the forces of evil. By and large, such accounts are nothing more than fantasies based on the universal human desire to fly.

But as the first two reports in this article show, there are cases of levitation that are of a different order altogether. In the first place, they appear to be derived from psychic powers, not supernatural ones. In the second instance, they have been widely observed and accounts of them come from numerous independent witnesses. It is these cases of levitation that stretch our credulity to the limits for they seem to suspend the very natural laws by which we make sense of the universe.

By all accounts, levitation seems to be an ability that anyone can learn. Long ago in Tibet it was a technique taught to a senior class of cross-country foot messengers to help them cover long distances with a minimum of effort. The practice, known as *lung-gom* or trance-walking, was learned at certain monasteries. The messengers trained by spending a secluded two or three years learning breathing exercises and intense mental concentration. A master of the art of *lung-gom* was able, as one European witness recounted, to sit in cross-legged meditation and then, with a jerk, lift his body off the seat and float in the air.

The most unnerving aspect of levitation is the excellent quality of the witnesses to these events. Leading writers, scientists, politicians and clerics have testified to watching genuine instances of people floating in the air. Often, they themselves refuse to accept the contradiction between what their senses tell them and what their reason holds to be impossible. But they do not deny what they have seen.

Even more astounding is the evidence presented on film and in photographs. In 1936, the *Illustrated London*

News published a series of pictures that were taken by a British planter and some friends in southern India, and which showed a yogi giving a performance of levitation in front about 150 people. At the high point of his act the yogi floated horizontally in the air for about four minutes, balanced only by one hand resting lightly on a cloth-wrapped stick. Apart for this pole, there was no other form of support. Even the sceptical European onlookers were unable to prove to themselves that there had been any kind of trick involved in this feat.

Could the yogi really have supported his entire weight with only one hand and the stick—or had he managed to overcome gravity?

Above: **If the ability to levitate is not a trick, then it implies that there is some way of overcoming gravity using only powers of the mind. Certainly there is no evidence of physical support in this photograph, other than one hand resting lightly on a draped pole.**

Neither the first feat nor the second is physically possible, to the best of our knowledge. But the photographs are sworn to be genuine, so something of this sort is precisely what must have happened.

We can only surmise that the best of our knowledge is simply not good enough. Perhaps it is possible to cancel gravity. After all, we still do not know exactly what the gravitational force is or how it is generated. Science is only familiar with its effects. Since this is still the case, there is no logical reason why gravity cannot be tampered with. The real mystery is why it seems so relatively difficult to do.

Dowsing

In the early years of the American oil boom a curious character, known as the 'oil smeller', travelled to Texas and Louisiana carrying a mysterious black box which was nicknamed a 'doodle bug'. The oil smeller was in fact a dowser. He would walk over likely ground muttering curious incantations and then suddenly halt. His 'doodle bug' had communicated to him the presence of oil, and therefore the correct place to drill a well.

During the same period, another class of dowser, known popularly as the 'water witch', used a similar technique for detecting underground flows of water on American farms. Carrying a forked stick with both hands, the base directed downwards, he would march back and forth across the land until the stick began to dip. The dowser counted the number of dips and, multiplying by three, would work out the actual depth of the subterranean stream. Alternatively, though this was a much clumsier method, he would suspend a ring on a length of thread inside a glass of water. By counting the number of times the ring struck the inside of the glass he could calculate the depth at which underground water would be found.

The methods used by American dowsers were introduced from Europe where they had been in existence possibly since prehistoric times. We know that the art was familiar to many

ancient peoples, including the Scythians. From Nineveh there comes a clay tablet discovered by archaeologists which depicts a dowser goddess called the 'Mistress of the Magic Staff'. In the Old Testament, Moses may have been dowsing when he struck the rock and waters gushed forth.

Nearer to our own times, we find dowsers in 14th century Germany and Hungary using this technique to find coal. They would hold a forked hazel twig in their hands with its point facing upwards. When it dipped, this was an indication of an underground seam of coal.

The dowsers of this and later periods were subject to considerable harassment by church authorities who regarded their inexplicable powers as highly dubious and most probably connected with the devil. Even in later centuries, the dowser's art could never be separated from its aura of magic

Above: **Dangling a ring in a glass of water is one method of dowsing. It can be used to determine how far underground a flow of water lies.**

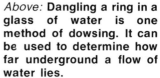

Left: **'Oil smellers' were dowsers who were said to be able to sense the presence of oil by using a mysterious black box.**

33

and the occult. This is perhaps one of the main reasons why scientists have refused to take it seriously. Their reluctance was only increased during the 18th century when a number of experimenters suggested that there was a mysterious force called 'animal magnetism' that explained this wild talent. They claimed that the force, which acted as a mutual attraction between one body and another, existed in all living things. From this premise it was argued that human beings could be sensitive to the presence of other living creatures in ways that went far beyond the normal five senses. The suggestion that there existed an unknown type of energy only antagonized the scientifically minded still further. Inevitably it held back the serious study of the dowser's art.

In spite of an officially critical attitude to dowsing, however, it has nevertheless been used by a number of governments in recent times. During World War I, the Austrian colonel, Karl Beichl, located lodes of ore in Serbia with a dowser's rod. Utilizing the same technique, Major Otto von Grave found water beneath the sands of the Sinai Desert. According to reports, Israeli geologists now use dowsing methods when searching for water in the Negev Desert.

Fortunately, a few eminent critics of dowsing have been tempted to study the phenomenon in an effort to highlight their reasons for dismissing it. The results have, in some cases, come as a surprise and have prompted some sceptics to think again.

Professor Tromp, a Dutch geologist, devoted many years to the testing of wood and metal divining rods and has published his results in the book *Physical Physics*. He recognized that some human beings do indeed appear to be sensitive to underground waters and are able to register the slight changes that this produces in local magnetism through their skin. The affect on the nervous system is such that the muscles move slightly causing the rod or branch to twitch. As far as he could tell, it did not matter what kind of dowsing instrument was used. Wire, metal rods, whalebone, wood and pendulums all seemed to work equally well.

A more difficult kind of dowsing to

explain is that carried out away from the field. By suspending their instruments over maps some dowsers have been able to discover the location of water, metal and even stolen objects. According to the book *Crime and the Occult,* police called upon a dowser to help them find a knife used to murder a person near the city of Antwerp. The dowser suspended his rod above a map of the district. Within moments, the twig began to twitch above the street where the murder weapon was later found.

As there is as yet no real explanation of the remarkable success of dowsers the subject has a tendency to be placed in the area of magical and occult phenomena, or to be seen as branch of extra-sensory perception. Dowsing is quite possibly an intuitive process that by-passes ordinary states of consciousness. As such it is no more mysterious than the homing instinct of pigeons, for which there is still no truly adequate explanation.

From the study of many cases of dowsing, however, it has become apparent that the type of dowsing object used is of very little importance. It is the dowser, and not his forked stick, who is the key to the puzzle.

Faith Healing

A group of patients filed quietly into their doctor's waiting room to find themselves facing a large tub filled with iron filings and 'magnetized water'. Poking from the tub were a number of long rods. Each patient took hold of a rod and, while music

was played, was encouraged by the doctor to sink into a state of trance.

Soon several people were seized with convulsions. Others began to babble incoherently as their frenzy grew. Exhausted finally, they lapsed into a deep coma-like sleep from which they later awoke feeling refreshed and cured of their physical symptoms.

The doctor was Franz Mesmer, and his healing methods were extremely fashionable in Paris in the last quarter of the 18th century. So unusual were they that they attracted a great deal of professional attention from other doctors. His healing sessions were investigated by such leading figures of science as Benjamin Franklin, Guilottin, Lavoisier and Pinel, all of whom were unable to deny that they seemed to be highly successful. The one thing they found hard to comprehend was that Mesmer could achieve physical cures by working with his patients' *minds*. It is this approach that lies behind all forms of faith healing.

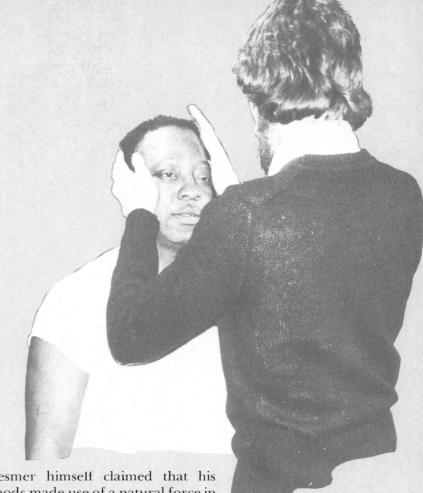

Mesmer himself claimed that his methods made use of a natural force in the universe which he termed 'animal magnetism'. His patients, he claimed, had low reserves of the force and it was his purpose to put them back in touch with it. He did not claim to be a faith healer in his own right; it was simply that his methods borrowed many of the techniques associated with faith healing and had much in common with the practices of traditional medicine men who were said to be endowed with miraculous healing powers.

Since prehistoric times, witch doctors of one sort or another have all practised forms of the mental medicine we now refer to as faith healing. They would lead their patients into trances by a combination of elaborate rituals that included incantations, songs, dances and drugs. Once in a state of trance, the patients would be highly suggestible. It was then that the medicine man would identify their disorders and command all disease to leave their bodies. The patients then sank into a coma from which they awoke feeling well again.

Spiritual healers today still use the same general techniques employed by medicine men of pre-civilized societies, although their style of operation has

Above: **This Irish faith healer is the seventh son of a seventh son. According to legend this gives him wonderful healing powers. Up to 5,000 people a week flock to his clinic to be treated. He treats his patients by laying his hands on the afflicted parts of their bodies and letting the healing power flow from himself to them.**

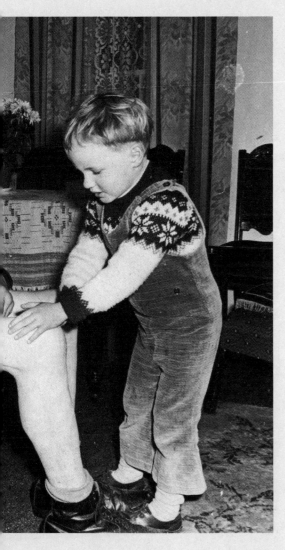

Left: **A four-year-old boy possessing the healing-touch places his hands on an old man's bad leg. The power to be a faith healer can fall upon anyone. It does not seem to require any special knowledge or training. For this reason, it is thought by some that the true source of faith-healing lies more with the sick person than the healer.**

far less elaborate ritual to it. Healers such as Oral Roberts in the United States and Harry Edwards in Britain conduct ceremonies that closely resemble religious gatherings, in which they make provision for their audience's spiritual and physical needs. Men such as these see themselves as mediums for the power of God. It is through them that the faithful can draw on God's spiritual healing power and use it to be cured.

Although the record of success by faith healers is high, the established medical profession tends to dismiss it for the most part, possibly for no other reason than that it undermines doctors' own monopoly of healing. Of course there is also the problem of finding a way to evaluate faith healing, for as yet there is precious little understanding of the way in which the power works.

In the eyes of conventional medical practitioners, a treatment which cures physical disorders by acting only on the mind is a mysterious treatment indeed. Yet experiments have shown that when one half of a group of patients was given real pills and the other half dummy ones, 30% to 50% of the latter half showed signs of recovery. Here there was no question of using faith healing techniques, yet a stunningly high success rate was achieved among people who *thought* they were being treated by doctors.

It is obvious from studies such as these that the role of the mind is crucial in curing the body. The best examples of this are the seemingly miraculous cures claimed by faith healers—cures which take the medical profession by surprise, yet which

cannot be disputed. We have good evidence that faith healing *is* successful, what remains unknown is the way in which the mind can exert such an irresistible control over the body that faith alone can heal.

Body Control

All human beings feel pain. But as scientific studies have shown, one person's hurt may be another person's agony for the quality of pain is a highly subjective thing. Some people have such a tolerance for it that their insensitivity verges on the superhuman. On the other hand, there are people whose susceptibility to pain is so great that it appears to belong to the realm of the impossible.

Pain can be generated by the body's nervous system as well as by external agents. There are cases, known as phantom limb, in which people with amputated arms and legs swear that

Above: **There are reports of one young woman who was beaten with a nine-kilo hammer to no ill effect. Her religious state of trance seemed to have created an extreme insensitivity to pain. Although the batterings she received caused her body considerable harm, she seemed to take no notice of them.**

they can still feel sensations from the missing part. They may complain of shooting pains in the non-existent limb, pains that may reach such an agonizing intensity as to become almost unendurable.

By contrast, some people are virtually insensitive to pain. In France, in the 1730s, there flourished a religious sect known as the 'Convulsionaries'. During their religious ecstasies the Convulsionaries went into a trance-like state that gave them extraordinary resilience to pain. A case was recorded of a young woman who was beaten with a massive nine-kilo hammer to no ill effect. In another instance, a 17-year-old girl proved able to withstand the efforts of several strong men to push great metal spikes into her neck. Try as they might, they could cause her no harm while she was in her religious trance.

Exceptional resistance to pain is by no means a supernatural power. It can be achieved in much more disciplined and less dramatic ways. The great Egyptian fakir, Rahman Bey, became famous throughout the world for the extraordinary powers of self-control he attained after years of rigorous self-discipline, study and meditation. On several occasions in the 1920s he demonstrated his amazing powers by inserting long metal skewers into his chest or cheeks and by cutting his body with a sharp knife. Not only did he not flinch or cry out, he did not even bleed. No matter how serious his wounds appeared to be, they closed up and healed within minutes.

In 1934, an even more astonishing demonstration of physical invulnerability was displayed by an Indian yogi before a panel of eminent, but absolutely baffled, scientists at the university of Calcutta. The yogi drank sulphuric acid, then washed down nitric acid and carbolic acid and finished off with a snack of broken glass. Then he at once placed himself into a trance to offset the lethal effects of this diet. He survived the ordeal and was totally unharmed.

Other holy men, or medicine men, who possess magical powers can show similar degrees of physical resilience. In many parts of the world there are people who can fire-walk. They stroll in bare feet over red-hot coals or glowing white stones that would char any normal footwear. Yet they emerge from the fire with no ill effects. The famous 19th century medium, David Home, could place his head in a blazing fire and 'wash' his naked face in the flames without even scorching his eyebrows. Similarly, there are voodoo masters who are able to stir boiling water with their hands or juggle, bare-handed, glowing hot balls of iron. The trance-like state they first enter somehow protects them from any harm although medically it should be impossible for them to be unaffected by the experience.

Common to all these cases is the need for this state of trance or holy ecstasy to create the incredible insensitivity to pain. In some inexplicable way, the normal physical state of these people is transformed and they discover that they possess what appear to

be superhuman powers.

There are, however, certain ways of controlling the body that seem far more sophisticated than falling into a trance. They appear to have a certain scientific quality to them as they single out one faculty to be controlled and then proceed to deal with it systematically and deliberately. Controlling such obvious functions as breathing or the flexing of muscles is straightforward; athletes do it all the time. But unconscious functions such as heartbeat, pulse, blood pressure and body temperature can also be altered dramatically, although it takes enormous powers of discipline and self-control.

An Egyptian fakir named Hamid Bey was able to vary the pulse in his left wrist (where it reached 102 beats a minute) from that in his right wrist (where it stayed at 84 beats) with this sort of self-control. More dramatic, perhaps, are the yogis who can slow their heartbeat and breathing to such an extent that, to a layman, they appear to be dead. They may remain in a torpid condition for as long as several days. The most astonishing demonstrations of this are carried out by the yogis who allow themselves to be buried alive for two or three days

—and who have lived through the ordeal.

Such sorts of miraculous feats have been witnessed far too often by respected researchers for them to be denied in the way they once were. The problem for science, however, is to make sense of human capabilities that border on fiction and the miraculous, for they seem to violate our entire understanding of the physical universe. So far, the greatest discovery has surely been a negative one; we have merely become aware of the limitations of our knowledge.

Prophecy

For more than ten years prior to the assassination of the American President John F. Kennedy in 1963, omens of his tragic death in the form of prophetic dreams, intuitions and visions were being received. Mary Tallmadge, a New Jersey woman, foresaw a scene in which the President was standing by a coffin. Nearby, the Stars and Stripes was flying at half mast. The clairvoyant Mrs Jeanne Dixon, who is now world-famous for her remarkably accurate prophecies, saw a vision of threatening clouds gathering in the sky above the White House. In 1956 she predicted that a blue-eyed president, a democrat elected in 1960, would be killed.

Nobody seems to have a clue how prophecy works. It is an intuitive power, not one that can be learned or even used with any great degree of precision. The reason some people

Left: By entering into a trance-like state firewalkers are able to endure the intense heat of the firepit.

Below: Prophecies often take the form of visionary dreams such as this scene foretelling the death of President Kennedy.

employ crystal balls or go into trances is to prepare themselves for the moments when their powers begin to work—the rest is trusting to intuition.

In ancient times, the powers of prophecy were accepted without question by the vast majority of people. Prophets themselves were held in high regard. At Delphi, in Greece, the high priestess of the shrine to Apollo (who was known as the Pythoness) would inhale sulphurous fumes and fall into trances. In this state she would reveal the mysteries of the future in the form of riddles.

Prophecy has long been an important part of everyday life in the more primitive communities, also, such as the Indian tribes of North America. Captain Jonathan Carver, an early explorer, was told by an Indian prophet that a famine affecting his tribe would be relieved at a certain time and on a certain day. Exactly when predicted, another tribe appeared and delivered supplies of food. In a like manner, the Plains Indians had medicine men who could forewarn of the arrival of strangers during their prophetic trances.

One of the most famous prophets in Europe was Nostradamus, who died in 1566. He became renowned first in France and then elsewhere for the accuracy of his predictions concerning his own time and also centuries in the future. He accurately told of the death of France's King Henry II in a tournament, and predicted the execution of King Charles I of England by Parliament, the rise of Napoleon and even of Adolf Hitler in the 20th century.

So far, it has been impossible to give prophecy a scientific basis since premonitions are usually reported after the event. It was for this reason that a Premonitions Bureau was set up in Britain in 1967 to undertake research into the subject. By 1970 about 1,000 predictions had been received covering everything from rail disasters to events relating to the royal family. A similar society has since been founded in New York to study common elements in prophecy and other intuitive forms of knowledge.

Turning to traditional explanations of the ability to divine the future, we find a common belief that a person's soul or mind could free itself from the body to journey into the future. The visions experienced during such trips were of events yet to unfold. What this implies is that the future already exists, although in a different dimension from our own. It is as if time had many levels—past, present and future—all running parallel to each other. However, it is only in trances or dreams that people are able to penetrate the barriers between these dimensions. If we

Left: **The predictions of Nostradamus were so cryptic that many have several different interpretations. Yet their inaccuracies or vagueness have never seemed to shake the confidence that people have in the powers of prophecy.**

Below: **The classic technique of the fortune-telling gypsy is to gaze into her crystal ball, a performance which is supposed to focus her powers. This ritual serves to concentrate her thoughts upon the forces of the supernatural with which she wishes to establish contact.**

were ever able to understand the universe to the extent where we could move between these various dimensions at will, then exploring the future would become a reality. Prophecy might then be seen in a new light as the first tentative and haphazard step towards travelling in time.

Extra Sensory Perception

One September evening in the year 1759 Emmanuel Swedenborg, the world-famous Swedish scientist and seer, was dining with 15 fellow guests at the home of William Castel, an English resident at Gothenberg in Sweden. Suddenly Swedenborg left the table and hurried out of the room. On returning shortly afterwards he announced to those present that he had just had a clairvoyant vision that a great fire had broken out in Stockholm, even though the city was over 480 km away. Two hours later, at eight o'clock that evening, Swedenborg sensed that the conflagration was at last under control. As it turned out, everything that he had spoken of that evening proved to have taken place exactly as he had described it.

The five senses with which we are endowed—sight, hearing, touch, taste and smell—are unable to receive impressions of the kind that Swedenborg experienced that evening. Yet to a greater or lesser degree we all possess a sixth sense by which we receive information and which does not involve our five main senses. This ability has been described by Colin Wilson, the writer on the occult, as 'faculty X'. Others refer to it as ESP.

The full range of this sixth sense is exceptionally wide. It refers to a host of phenomena that includes dreams which foretell the future, visions received while wide awake, the intuition of hidden dangers and the ability to sense events that are far removed by distance. For purposes of simplicity, ESP is often described as including three main sorts of phenomena—clairvoyance, precognition and telepathy.

Clairvoyance is the psychic condition in which people become aware of objects and events without using their normal five senses or their powers of reasoning. They may receive a detailed vision of a faraway disaster, just as Swedenborg did, or may suddenly become aware of the place where a lost object lies hidden after falling asleep in a state of anxiety and concern for its whereabouts.

Precognition is an awareness of events before they actually occur. It is much more complex than simple prediction, which is a combination of existing knowledge and intelligent

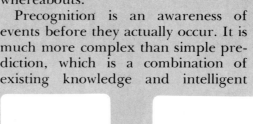

guesswork, for it describes an event in great detail rather than simply indicating that it will occur. Very often, people who have precognitive dreams will awake with a vivid memory of an event, say an aeroplane crash, that will only take place some time after. Or they may dream of an unfamiliar place which they then, quite by chance, find themselves visiting many years later.

Telephathy, another category of ESP, is one of the most common psychic experiences. It is a form of direct contact between two individuals during which they share information, even though they have used no conventional physical means of getting in touch. Telepathy may work over great distances. It is often linked with situations of distress and often both parties will react to an event that only one of them has experienced directly.

Most people can provide examples of ESP either from their own personal experiences or from those of others. For example, how many times has the phone rung and one has known who the caller is, despite there having been no prearranged agreement or even expectation of the call? Similarly, people may often sense a forthcoming success or failure long before it actually happens.

Above: **Zener cards, with their five symbols of a cross, star, circle, square and waves, were first used in packs of 25 to test the extra-sensory powers of people in laboratory conditions. The subject was seated in one building and the tester in another where he turned over the cards one by one. It was expected that scores of 60 out of 300 would be achieved. In fact, scores of over 110 were recorded. The chances against this were a million to one.**

Attempts to place the study of ESP upon a scientific basis have met with varied success. In the late 1920s, Professor J. B. Rhine of Duke University in Ohio conducted thousands of experiments into clairvoyance using Zener Cards. Statistically, the existence of clairvoyance was established but, regrettably, the ability to obtain consistent results with such tests of ESP was almost impossible and considerable controversy has continued to rage about the subject.

However, we can be certain that some sort of mysterious sixth sense which functions beyond the realms of traditional science certainly does exist, even though we are still unable to measure it or even reproduce it at will. As any scientist will admit, many important discoveries have been made through a flash of inspiration. ESP, it seems, is one of the most active of all the faculties we possess.

People of Mystery

Every now and then, people whose presence is completely unexplained crop up in history. Who they are, where they come from and what peculiar activities they are engaged in is quite unfathomable. Some seem to surround themselves in a deliberate shroud of secrecy. Others seem innocent enough, yet around them there develops a web of rumours and legends that cannot be explained. It only serves to enshrine their mysterious origins.

Kaspar Hauser

Late in May 1828, as the narrow cobbled streets of the German city of Nuremberg swarmed with people enjoying the Whit-Monday holiday, a strange young man appeared who was to transform the life of the town and ignite a blaze of speculation and rumour throughout Europe. The first to spot him was a bootmaker who was startled by the tattered figure hobbling unsteadily on stiff legs through

Unschlitt Square with a bewildered look on his young face. The lad seemed about 16 or 17 years old, but could give no coherent reply to any of the questions asked him.

The letter of introduction he clutched in his hand led to a captain in a local cavalry regiment. But the officer could make no sense of the dazed youth either. The lad seemed completely disoriented. He tried to pick up the flame of a candle with his fingers, he was confused by inanimate objects and mistook clocks for living creatures. Cooking smells made him ill, while any food other than bread and water nearly made him faint. The only words he could say when questioned were 'Don't know'. However, when given a

Above **The ragged figures of Kaspar Hauser as he first appeared to the world in Nuremberg.**

41

pencil and piece of paper, he was able to write his name—Kaspar Hauser.

The letter of introduction proved to be a forgery. The cavalry captain, now convinced that the boy was either an imbecile or a primitive savage, handed him over to the police where he was placed in a cell and at once seemed to become more relaxed.

Kaspar Hauser became an overnight sensation with the people of Nuremberg. The curious gathered to look at him as if he were an animal in a cage. They watched him sit in his peculiar stiff-legged way, wolf down his bread and water and defecate publicly without the least sign of embarrassment. A doctor sent to examine him by the local courts came away convinced that he was perfectly normal but had somehow been forcibly kept in a childlike state. This diagnosis seemed remarkably accurate for Hauser soon began to make rapid, indeed spectacular, strides in learning to be 'human'.

Six weeks after being discovered he was able to speak fluently and also read and write. He could dress himself, and handle eating utensils and other tools. By July he was able to write out a public statement that explained something of his early life. As long as he could remember he had been penned up in a tiny, gloomy dungeon. As it was too low to stand up in, he spent all his time sleeping on a straw mattress or

sitting upright against the walls. No sound or light reached him, and the temperature never changed. He had no sense of time, of day or night, or of the world outside. When he awoke, there was always fresh bread and water in his cell. Sometimes the water would be drugged and he would wake up to find that he had been washed and changed and that fresh bedding had been put into his cell. He lived this way for a long time—he could never say how long—and never set eyes upon another human being.

His isolation came to an end one day when a large and powerful man entered his cell and began to teach him his name and to say the words 'Don't know'. Soon after, Hauser was taken outside. He went into such a state of shock that he could never remember the details of the jail or the route he had taken from it to Nuremberg.

The public statement made Hauser a sensation throughout Europe. Visitors flocked to look at him, while an intense excitement about his mysterious past gripped everyone. Many maintained that he must be the nobly-born victim of a conspiracy to keep

Above: **Hauser claimed to have spent his entire life shut up in a small dark cell.**

Below: **A portrait of the boy clutching the letter of introduction with which he arrived in Nuremberg.**

Left: **The coat he was wearing at the time of his death, along with some of the drawings he made soon after his arrival in Nuremberg.**

him from his rightful inheritance. There were suggestions that he might be heir to the throne of Baden, a small German principality. Others were more sceptical and felt there was something of the charlatan about him.

By now, Hauser had been released by the police and was being cared for by a Professor Daumer, a local teacher and philosopher. His progress continued to be remarkable and within a year he produced his autobiography. However, it added nothing new to his original statement about himself.

Then, in October 1829, Hauser was found unconscious and bleeding on the floor of Professor Daumer's cellar. He claimed that he had been the victim of an attempt on his life, although the circumstances were slightly suspicious. While some people believed that the attackers were his original jailers, others argued that the wounds looked as if they had been self-inflicted.

Over the next four years, Hauser lived in Nuremberg and travelled widely in Europe. Finally he settled near Nuremberg in the small town of Ansbach. There, on 14 December 1833, he was mortally wounded in the town park. He staggered home with deep stab wounds in his lungs and liver, claiming that a tall stranger dressed in black had knifed him. According to Hauser, the man had led him into the park promising to explain about his past and give him news of his mother. Once there, the man offered him a wallet, but when he reached to take it a knife was plunged into his chest. The police checked his story, but found only one set of footprints in the snow. They were Hauser's.

Three days later Kaspar Hauser died. Although a local police chief was convinced that the attack was faked (he believed that Hauser had stabbed himself), he failed to extract a confession from the dying man.

Some people maintain that a mystery as full of unexplained questions such as this could only be a fraud passed off on a gullible public. Perhaps, they suggest, Hauser staged it to draw attention to himself and feed his hunger for fame. In any event, the city of Nuremberg basked in the publicity it received through him.

Hauser's bizarre story, and the circumstances in which he died have never been satisfactorily explained, and his short, spectacular life still remains a puzzle today.

Count St Germain

One of the great mysterious figures of history is Count St Germain, a nobleman whose legendary career impressed and perplexed the royal courts of Europe in the 18th century.

The earliest reference to St Germain is from 1710 when the Countess von Georgy and the composer Jean-Philippe Rameau met him. They described him as being between 45 and 50 years old. Although he appeared on the scene quite suddenly and made an instant and dramatic impact on everyone, his origins remained a mystery. By all accounts he was very

Below: **Count St Germain was renowned at the Court of Versailles for his brilliant and witty conversation. Although some viewed him with hostility because of his shadowy background, none could deny his brilliance.**

rich, although his tastes were far from lavish—he was a vegetarian and shunned alcohol. His wealth seemed to come from the splendid diamonds he owned, and his knowledge of precious stones was highly sophisticated. He claimed to possess the skill to melt them down and the ability to improve their quality, and he even maintained he could enlarge them.

In 1743 the Count appeared at the court of Louis XV at Versailles where, though a complete stranger, he made an immediately favourable impression. From then until 1760 he became a leading light at the court, plunging into its delights and intrigues with great zest. Although some people viewed him with hostility and claimed that he was a foolish eccentric, none could deny his brilliance. He set up a small laboratory at the court where he conducted experiments in physics and chemistry. He invented new methods for curing leather and dying cloth and, it was claimed, could turn iron into a metal that was as lustrous as gold and equally easy to work. He was fluent in several European languages, Latin, Ancient Greek, Arabic and several eastern tongues, composed music and played the violin and piano with exquisite skill. He had an impressive knowledge of philosophy and politics, and was also a dazzlingly witty and brilliant conversationalist. The French philosopher Voltaire paid him the

Left: **Count St Germain led a remarkable wandering life. The record of his appearances, a few of which are pinpointed on this map, show that he roamed as far as Persia and India. Closer to home, his travels led him to almost every major court in western Europe.**

compliment of calling him a man who knew everything.

Count St Germain's sojourn at Versailles was also marked by a restless need to travel. He visited the court of the ruler of Persia, made at least two trips to India, travelled to North Africa and Russia and roamed about Europe with an extraordinary energy, involving himself in a host of scientific and political activities.

The greatest mystery that overshadows him, however, is not his brilliance but his longevity. He chanced to meet the same Countess von Georgy of 1710 again in the late 1750s. She was astounded to find him looking as youthful as when she had last seen him, 40 years before. By the 1770s, although he was being described as a man in his sixties, he remained exceptionally vigorous and continued to travel widely.

Then, in February 1784, he is reported to have died. A year later, old friends of his and many others witnessed him attending a conference of occult groups in the German town of Wilhelmsbad. Shortly before the French Revolution he returned to Versailles, there to warn Louis XVI and Marie Antionette of the impending storm. In 1789, he went off to the court of the King of Sweden on further political business.

About this time, St Germain seems to vanish from history, although unsubstantiated reports refer to him appearing here and there until much later. The last time someone claimed to see him was in 1820 when one

Left: **Count St Germain was a mysterious figure, despite being a very public man and given to appearing at royal courts throughout Europe. The source of his great wealth never became known, nor were his home and background ever revealed.**

Madame d'Adhémar insisted he visited her. If this were true, it would have made him at least 150 years old!

Throughout his life St Germain did nothing to deny the rumours of mystery that clung to him. These were only compounded by the close links he had with such secret societies as the Masons and the Rosicrucians. He also claimed to have had occult experiences and to be familiar with ancient wisdoms and powers. Even such renowned masters of the occult as Cagliostro, Mesmer and St Martin came to him as students.

Although the possibility that St Germain was a charlatan cannot be ruled out, he was nevertheless an extraordinarily able and talented person. Unfortunately, his brilliance in no way illuminates his life. It serves only to pile mystery upon mystery.

Wild Children

In October 1920, a group of nervous villagers near Midnapur in West Bengal quietly encircled an abandoned anthill in which it was known that a family of wolves and two wild children had made their lair. As the hunters began to dig, two adult wolves dashed out of a tunnel and broke free of the ring. Soon a third wolf—a female—emerged and lunged at the men. Then, instead of fleeing, she stood her ground and refused to let them approach. Sensing she would attack again, the archers in the group fired and killed her instantly.

When the diggers tore the den apart they found the children huddled in terror with two wolf cubs. One seemed about 18 months old, the other about 8 years. They were taken to a religious orphanage in nearby Midnapur. Within a year of being found the younger child died, but the elder, a girl who was given the name of Kamala, survived for another nine years.

In the beginning, Kamala behaved exactly like a young wolf. She moved about on all fours and when she ate would squat down and bolt her food using only her teeth. Very slowly, she learned to eat with her hands and speak a few dozen words of English. But progress was slow—it took three years before she was even able to stand upright.

The wolf children of Midnapur were in no way unique. Since the 14th century there have been almost 60 cases of wild children discovered in various parts of the world. As far as can be determined, all these children had been abandoned or had become lost in the wilderness at a young age and had managed to survive by adopting a natural, animal-like existence. Some lived as solitary creatures, but many had been adopted by apes, gazelles, wolves and other beasts. Such

Below: In West Bengal, a family of wolves were known to be guarding their young and two wild children in a den inside an abandoned anthill. When a group of villagers attempted to rescue the youngsters, one wolf refused to flee and defended her lair until she was shot.

'adopted' children, although they were physically healthy, often behaved as if they were wild beasts themselves, running about on all fours, growling and howling, urinating and defecating freely, eating raw food and so on.

Such children fascinate us, but not only for their ability to have survived in the wild. It is their uncivilized, almost prehuman, state of existence that excites our curiosity. Is this, one wonders, the natural condition of human beings if they were to live with no society to shape them? Do we all have a semi-savage side to us which has become so deeply submerged by culture that we no longer recognize it? Unfortunately we cannot experiment with ourselves; by the time we ask such questions it is already too late in our development. But perhaps there are clues in the way wild children have readjusted to human society.

have contributed to the poor recovery rate of these children following their return to civilization. Many died within a short time and few ever learned to speak more than a couple of words. Often as not, the youngsters found themselves treated as freaks or as imbeciles by their 'saviours', who found it difficult to understand and cope with their aggressive behaviour.

One notable exception is the wild boy of Aveyron, in central France, who was found running about naked in the wilderness in 1799. He was trapped up a tree by a group of hunters who captured him and brought him back to Aveyron. He appeared to be about 12 years old and had evidently been living on nuts and berries in the woods.

Although one leading French psychologist of the time declared the boy to be an incurable idiot, he was lucky to be entrusted to an exceptional

Above: When the Bengalese villagers tore open the anthill, they found two human children huddled together with a pair of wolf cubs inside the wolf den.

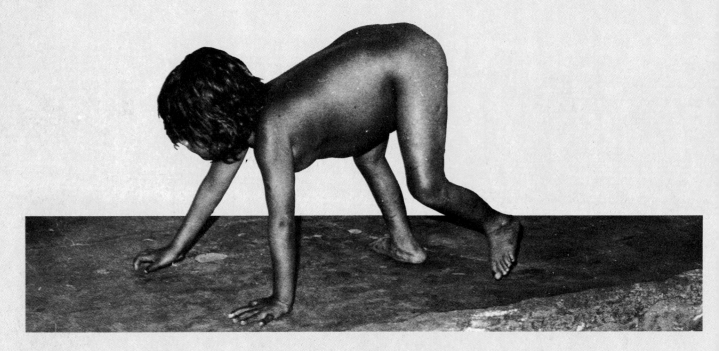

In 14th century Germany, a boy who had lived naked with wolves for about four years was found in a forest. His food, which was the same as that eaten by the rest of the pack, was devoured raw. He slept in a hole in the ground with the others and, like them, moved about on all fours. His adaptation to a wolfish way of life had gone so far that after returning him to the world of humans his captors had to strap boards to his legs to make him stand upright again.

Harsh methods such as these may

teacher of the deaf and dumb who thought otherwise. Jean-Marc Itard took over the care of the boy, Victor, as he was named, and his advanced methods were a great success. Victor learned to speak simply and grew up to be a pleasant, easy-going person who lived to the age of 40.

The fact that Victor's development never progressed past a subnormal state has been used as evidence in the argument which views wild children as youngsters suffering from the condition known as autism.

Above: This eleven-year-old boy was found living wild in the jungles of southern Ceylon where he had been adopted by a family of monkeys. It took months of living among humans for him to learn how to walk in an upright position.

46

no way to explain how he could have survived in such a hostile environment. His skills of adaptation seemed truly exceptional, well beyond the limits of what a 'normal' human being would consider possible. Nor does the autistic argument explain how such a child would have acquired the behaviour of a gazelle. Unlike autistic children who show no wish to communicate, this boy was extremely sociable.

The notion of a human successfully becoming animal-like to any great extent seems far-fetched, but from the evidence to date it is hard to rule out the possibility.

This strange disorder of the mind begins in childhood and affects language development and social communication. Some believe that 'wild children' are really autistic children who have been abandoned in the forest by their parents. It is an argument that is hard to dismiss, but cases such as the following raise a host of new doubts.

During a long trek across the wastes of Spanish Sahara, the French anthropologist Jean-Claude Armen discovered a set of strange tracks among those belonging to a herd of gazelle. As he knelt in the hot sand he realized that he was looking at traces made by tiny human feet. They were widely spaced and seemed to match perfectly the rhythmic bounding of the gazelle.

After shadowing the animals for several days he managed to attract their attention without frightening them off. At last a boy of about ten years approached him and began to sniff the anthropologist. The child had lively, inquisitive eyes, was powerfully built and in excellent health. He screwed up his nose like a gazelle and had the same habit of twitching his ears at the slightest sign of anything suspicious.

Armen watched as the boy sniffed at bushes and berries and at balls of dung, leaped and jumped about, and finally began to lick Armen. In this and countless other ways, the boy was entirely at home with the herd. He shared the animals' food, had adopted their body language and was accepted in every way.

If the child was subnormal, there is

People in Flames

For the Carpenter family, the summer of 1938 provided the opportunity to take an excursion on the sheltered waters of the Norfolk Broads in eastern England. But the holiday aboard their small boat was to be cut short tragically, for Mrs Carpenter was to become the victim of a macabre phenomenon known as spontaneous human combustion. For no apparent

Below: **For no apparent reason whatsoever, Mrs Carpenter's body became enveloped by flames. Her agony was shortlived, for before the eyes of her terrified family she swiftly burned to death. The cause of this appalling phenomenon has not yet been established.**

reason, Mrs Carpenter suddenly seemed to catch fire. While her husband and children watched in horror, flames and bluish smoke erupted from her body and quite soon she was completely reduced to ashes. Inexplicably, the rest of the family and the small wooden boat were completely unharmed.

It is inconceivable that a human body could burst into flames without in some way being set alight. The fact that there was no other fuel about to keep it burning is equally mysterious.

Mrs Carpenter's death was a bizarre and rare event, but it was not unique. Another mysterious case is that of Mrs Euphemia Johnson, a 68-year-old London widow. Neighbours discovered her charred remains on the floor of her home, scattered amongst the clothes she had been wearing at the time she was burned to death. Yet the clothes themselves were virtually unaffected by the fierce heat that had reduced her to ashes.

In the case of Mrs Mary Reeser of St Petersburg, Florida, the heat of her conflagration also affected other objects. She had been burned to ashes while sitting quietly in a favourite armchair. This time, the chair and a nearby lamp were also incinerated. All that was left were some charred springs and the blackened metal frame of the lamp. Of Mrs Reeser, who had weighed a hefty 80 kilos, only four kilogrammes of ash were left. Close examination of her remains also revealed a fragment of spine and a skull that had shrivelled to the size of a fist. Only one foot was left untouched; and it was found still inside the slipper she had been wearing.

Studies of the way in which bodies burn during cremation indicate that at a temperature of 1,150°C a body which is burned for 12 hours still does not reduce as completely to ash as that of Mrs Reeser. Human bones will shatter to small pieces after this treatment, but they are still recognizable as bones. It is simply not known what kind of raging inferno could have turned an 80-kilo woman into four kilos of ash in so short a space of time. Whatever it was, the heat must have been incredibly fierce. Why it did not spread to the room as a whole is totally puzzling. Lastly, there was no sign of a fuel that

could have burned the body so efficiently. In other words, Mrs Reeser's body became its own furnace.

There is no rational explanation for this and similar mysteries, even though there are over a dozen known cases of spontaneous human combustion. Information about them is poor, but it seems that in most cases the flames were accompanied by oily, bluish smoke. The fires raged fiercely and briefly, soon reducing the bodies to a powdery ash. Yet in all cases, clothing, nearby objects and even parts of limbs were left relatively untouched. There are no physical laws known to science that could account for such events. The mere fact that they occur at all serves as a reminder of how little we still know of the universe.

Above: **Police inspect the remains of a chair in which Mary Reeser was sitting at the time of her death in 1957. The heat from the flames that consumed her was so intense that it reduced the armchair to a small pile of ash.**

Transports of Mystery

In 1774, the Italian monk Alphonse de Liguori fell into a deep trance while fasting in his cell. After a period of unconsciousness, he awoke claiming that he had just returned from the deathbed of Pope Clement XIV, a journey which would have taken four days from the monastery of Arezzo where he lived. His astonishing story was at first dismissed as a dream, but was later confirmed by papal attendants who swore that during the Pope's last hours the monk had been with them, had spoken to them and had even helped with the last rites.

The ability to vanish in one place and reappear more or less instantly in another has been claimed by various magicians and mediums, although they have never offered any substantial

The monk seemed to be simultaneously in his cell and by the bedside of the Pope many miles away.

evidence of being able to perform this feat. But the phenomenon, known as teleportation, is well documented. Even so, it is such a bizarre and inexplicable oddity that it falls into a category of events that cannot be rationally explained. The theories that try to do so prove to be as far-fetched as the phenomenon itself.

Apportation, the process by which objects vanish mysteriously or appear out of nowhere (this happens most commonly at seances) is a variation on the teleportation theme. Bilocation is stranger still. In this event people are teleported and yet remain in their original location at the same time. Father Liguori was once such case. He was present at the side of the Pope in one form while his body remained in his cell.

There is a long tradition of people who have vanished mysteriously and reappeared elsewhere, unable to explain how it happened. One of the most spectacular teleportations, in terms of distance, took place in 1655. In that year, a man was burned at the stake by the Spanish Inquisition for practising sorcery and committing an 'outrage against the natural order of the universe'. It appears that at one moment he had been going about his business in Goa, the Portuguese colony in India, and the next found himself back home in Portugal!

Stranger yet are the frequent visits that Mary of Agreda made from Spain to Central America. In the 1620s, she claimed to have travelled through the air to the New World more than 500 times, there to convert the local Indian tribes to Christianity. Although the tales this young nun told of her journeys were fascinating in their detail, they did not impress her superiors. Not only did they disbelieve her, but they were also convinced that she was prey to all sorts of hysterical fantasies.

Meanwhile, in Central America, a certain Father Benavides who had the official task of converting heathen tribes kept encountering Indians who had already heard of Christ. These Indians all claimed to have been visited by a mysterious nun who journeyed through the region handing out rosaries and crosses.

In dismay, the monk complained to the King of Spain and to the Pope. But

there was nothing they could do for they knew of no other person empowered to convert Indians in Father Benavides' territory.

On his return to Spain he heard of Sister Mary's extraordinary claims and visited her out of curiosity. To his amazement he found that her knowledge of Central America was both accurate and wide ranging. She could describe the Indians' way of life and their customs in the most minute detail. Yet sworn statements from her convent superiors maintained that she had never left the place during the periods she claimed to have been in Central America.

To add a further layer to this mystery, the diaries of other European explorers in this part of the world also mention a mysterious nun who visited tribes throughout the length and breadth of Central America. Though impossible to explain rationally, or at least in any way we know about, Sister Mary's teleportations are certainly some of the best documented examples in history.

It seems unlikely that there is any supernatural or demonic side to teleportation. The events are too random and disconnected for there to be a masterplan. It is hard to find any link between long distance examples, like the man from Goa, and the case of a girl who, in 1883, was repeatedly transported from inside her locked home to the freedom of her front garden.

Another explanation is that teleportation is a instance of UFO abduction. This is as good a theory as any except that no teleportees have ever claimed to have travelled by spaceship, nor is there a shred of evidence to suggest that they have.

Perhaps what is involved is some sort of warp in space and time that makes it possible to pass from one place to another instantly and without seeming to travel at all. Teleportees certainly have no sense of time passing or even of travelling swiftly. They are hardly ruffled at all by the experience. It is only the realization after the event that gives them a shock.

If this is indeed what teleportation is all about, then the most important thing we have learned from it is that the journey from one dimension to another is a smooth trip.

Left: **Sister Mary of Agreda claimed to have been teleported from Spain to Central America on hundreds of occasions in the 1620s. There she set about converting the local Indians to Christianity. Yet back in Spain her superiors were incredulous. They thought she was the victim of mad delusions.**

Above: **Mary of Agreda, whose strange teleportations are probably the best-documented examples in history.**

Prester John

In 1165, an extraordinary letter was received by several European rulers including, among others, the Pope, the Holy Roman emperor and the emperor of Byzantium. The letter was a message from the legendary Prester John—a Christian king whose domains were believed to lie somewhere in central Asia along the route to India. In it he extolled his kingdom as a nation of fabulous wealth and power, where peace and justice prevailed and his people prospered in a land of natural abundance.

As well as being a glowing introduction to the physical and social attractions of his kingdom, the letter also declared Prester John's intention to lead an army into Palestine from out of the east and there to defeat the Moslems and sweep them from the Holy Land.

His message was welcome news to every Christian, and especially to the Pope. Unfortunately, the letter was a fake and whoever contrived to write it remains a mystery to this day.

Nevertheless, at the time, this first direct contact between the fabulous kingdom of an unknown Christian monarch, living somewhere deep inside Asia, and western Europe created a sensation. It prompted Pope Alexander III to write to Prester John in 1177, soliciting his support. Although the letter was entrusted to the Papal physician, he vanished soon after his departure to the East and was never heard from again. However, efforts to establish contact with this legendary ruler continued on and off for another 300 years.

The earliest references to Prester John are found in an account made by Bishop Otto of Germany in 1145. He described a tale, passed on to him by a Syrian bishop, of a great victory that Prester John had won over the Persians. His mighty army had defeated theirs and had gone on to overrun their capital. After this, Prester John had led his forces west with the intention of marching on Jerusalem and liberating it from Moslem rule. Unfortunately, his advance had been halted at the Tigris, for he had no boats in which to cross the river.

Although there are no firm historical documents proving that such a person as Prester John ever existed, the account of his campaign against the Persians had a substantial, if jumbled, element of truth to it.

During this same period, a Mongol khan did indeed defeat the Moslem ruler of Persia to found the short-lived Karakitai Empire in the central Asian region, today known as Khazakstan. The rulers of this empire were called Gurkhans. It is quite possible that the name could have been rendered as Yuhanan in Syrian (Bishop Otto's story came from a Syrian), and from which the western Johanne or John is but a small step. In addition, many of the nobles of the Karakitai Empire were Nestorian Christians. It is they who may have given substance to the rumour of powerful Christian forces somewhere inside Asia.

The Nestorians were a breakaway sect of the Orthodox Christian Church. After their split from the church in the 5th century AD they had flourished throughout the Middle East and their teachings had spread as far east as India and China.

In 12th century Europe, knowledge of the Far East was very sketchy. At a time when the dividing line between fact and rumour, and rumour and wishful thinking was highly blurred, there is no reason why the activities of the Mongols on the eastern borders of the Persian Empire could not have been the catalyst of the Prester John saga.

Though the earliest references to him were a fanciful mixture of fact and fiction, they only served to promote his legendary status. During the Middle Ages he was believed to be the ruler of a mighty Christian kingdom that lay somewhere to the east of Armenia and Persia. Such an immensely wealthy and powerful man could become an invaluable ally in the Crusades to drive the Moslems out of the Holy Land.

Throughout the 13th century, repeated efforts were made to establish contact with Prester John. A growing number of missionaries and adventurers began to travel to the East to search for him. Marco Polo, for example, made vague references to the region of Asia where his kingdom lay, although

he never went there himself.

However, as it became evident that only the Mongols controlled most of central Asia, the rumour circulated that Prester John had been defeated in a great battle and had shifted his capital to his kingdom's outlying provinces in Africa. At this time, Europe's understanding of world geography was still so vague that the leap from India and central Asia to Africa seemed perfectly reasonable. The two regions were considered to be more or less adjacent.

This time it was East Africa that became the focus of the search, for it was known, via Ethiopian monks who pilgrimaged to Jerusalem, that a Christian kingdom called Abyssinia existed somewhere in this region. Toward the close of the 14th century the first Europeans reached the area. Their reports of splendid churches and a line of emperors with an ancient

tradition behind them revitalized the hunt for Prester John. As it turned out, the ruler of Abyssinia was not Prester John. Nevertheless, he showed himself willing to ally himself with the Pope against his chief Moslem enemy, the Sultan of Cairo.

The Portuguese, who had a direct interest in developing their spice trade with India and in ousting the Arabs from the Indian Ocean, also were keen to ally themselves with this Christian empire, whether Prester John's or not. In 1493, an ambassador named Pedro de Covilham reached the court of Abyssinia with a letter from King John II of Portugal. But by now, concern with politics and trade was replacing the hunt for Prester John. As European knowledge of the region widened, interest in the legend waned. By the end of the 16th century, Prester John had faded into little more than a curiosity of history.

MYSTERIES
OF AIR, LAND AND SEA

Flying Saucers

Mysteries with a long history begin to lose the edge of their incredibility after a while. They become confused with legends and folktales. For this reason, a mystery that overlaps with the frontiers of science is especially fascinating. Although it may raise as many questions as it answers, there is always the possibility that it fills a gap in our knowledge of the universe. Such is the case with 'flying saucers'.

In the infinite vastness of space, it is likely that there are other forms of life. And there is no reason why some of these should not be more advanced than human beings. If this is true, then might it not be expected that they contact us? Or is it possible that they have done so already?

UFO Sightings

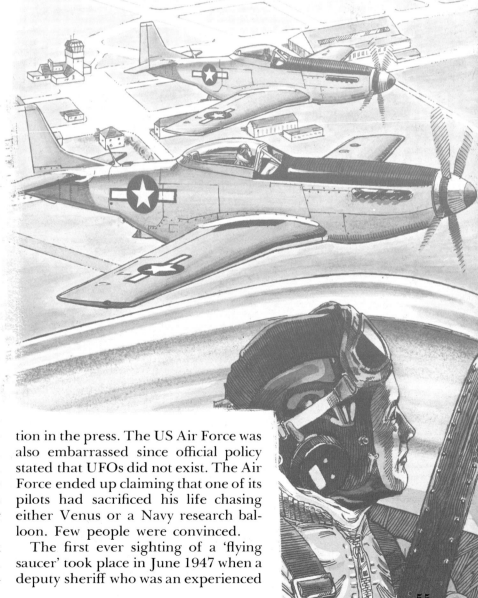

On 7 January 1948, the Kentucky Highway Patrol offices in Louisville, Kentucky were inundated with hundreds of phone-calls reporting a huge, circular unidentified flying object (UFO) in the sky. Some of the worried callers claimed it to be as big as 60 to 90 metres in diameter.

The Highway Patrol contacted the nearby Godman Air Force Base where, as it turned out, the base commander and control tower operators had also seen the UFO. As a flight of F-51s was approaching the base at the time, they were requested to give chase. Three set off in pursuit. Shortly after, one of the F-51s, piloted by Captain Thomas Mantell, radioed that it had sighted an enormous metallic object and was climbing after it. This was the pilot's last message, for then both the pilot and the UFO vanished.

Later that day, the wreckage of the F-51 was found scattered over a wide area and with it Mantell's badly burned body. It appeared that he had blacked out from the lack of oxygen as he climbed to meet the object, for his plane carried no special breathing equipment.

The crash of the F-51 was the first occasion of a death connected with UFOs and it naturally created a sensa-

tion in the press. The US Air Force was also embarrassed since official policy stated that UFOs did not exist. The Air Force ended up claiming that one of its pilots had sacrificed his life chasing either Venus or a Navy research balloon. Few people were convinced.

The first ever sighting of a 'flying saucer' took place in June 1947 when a deputy sheriff who was an experienced pilot spotted a flight of nine brilliant metallic objects while searching for a crashed plane in the Cascade Mountains of Oregon. His simple description of these unidentified craft, which he estimated to be moving at about 1,600 km/h, included the comment that they flew like saucers being skimmed across water. This led to them being immediately baptized 'flying saucers'.

Since then, thousands of similar reports have been lodged. Many of them are obvious hoaxes. Others are mistaken identifications of aircraft, balloons, clouds and other natural phenomena. The sheer variety of these sightings makes one suspect that to a great extent they are the work of human imaginations. UFOs have been described as clusters of multi-coloured lights, brilliant fireballs, and as endless variations on cigar, saucer and hat shapes.

The behaviour of these infernal flying machines has been just as bizarre as their appearance. They seem to be able to defy every law of aeronautics by flying sideways, backwards and upside-down with equal ease, and by being able to hover in mid-air or accelerate at high speed with minimal effort. They also seem able to alter their colour, their size and their shape without trouble. Even their physical substance is suspect. Some will cause bullets to bounce back, others seem to absorb them or let them pass through as if they were nothing more than mirages. On top of this, UFOs are able to appear and disappear at will.

It is possible, however, to detect a few general trends in the shapes of UFOs over the years. At the turn of the century, when powered flight was in its infancy, UFOs were never described as sleek spaceships. It was most common for people to describe them as airships, a design which represented the most advanced form of aircraft at the time. Since World War II, however, the tendency has been toward metallic, rocket-powered craft. The modification in the types of UFOs people report over the years seems to reflect the change in what they expect to see. This could be an indication that UFOs have a certain psychological dimension to them, yet no purely psychological phenomenon would leave evidence as

concrete as in the following case.

In August 1950, the business manager of an American baseball team spotted two silvery discs which turned and banked over the stadium where he worked. He grabbed his camera from his car and began filming the strange objects until they vanished into a clear blue sky. The developed pictures showed exactly what he described. In no way could they have been a figment of the imagination.

Close Encounters

Studies of thousands of UFO sightings collected from all over the world have shown that whatever these objects may be, and we still have no satisfactory explanation of them, they are definitely tangible with a physical substance.

However, the problem with UFO reports is that they are so jumbled it is hard to compare them. For this reason it has been helpful to grade them according to their nature and the quality of the information they provide. The highest grade reports are those known as 'close encounters'. These are

Above: **This UFO, looking like a giant cigar racing across the sky and trailing a cloud of vapour, was photographed by a farmer in Peru in 1952. The poor quality of the picture makes it hard to pick out details of the mysterious craft.**

cases in which witnesses make a visual sighting at a range of 100 to 150 metres or less. Close encounters may be further subdivided into three categories.

The first kind are close-range sightings in which it is possible to make out details of the UFO's shape as it hovers low or rests on the ground. A close encounter of the second kind is similar to the first but also includes physical evidence of the UFO's presence. This may take the form of scuffed marks in the earth, broken branches and scorch marks in the undergrowth. Stalled cars, severely shocked animals and people with burns and bruises are also considered as evidence.

The most bizarre of all, however, are encounters of the third kind. These involve sightings of UFO creatures and meetings between them and human beings. Some people claim to have come across UFO crews in the process of carrying out some kind of research, which includes the collecting of water, rock and plant samples and the abduction of animals.

A typical close encounter of the first kind occurred off the coast of Brazil in January 1958. The crew of a Brazilian hydrographical research ship witnessed a high-speed object shooting through the sky towards the small island of Trinidade. It flew a short

distance inland, circled a high mountain peak and headed back out to sea. The object, which seemed to be about 36 metres long, looked like a miniature version of the planet Saturn with a flattened ring around its equator. It was a dark grey colour and was surrounded by a greenish vapour that was quite distinct in the night sky. It appeared to be travelling about 1,000 km/h. One member of the crew was able to take four photographs as the object passed the ship. They form additional evidence to the sighting by over one hundred crew members, but go no further in helping to suggest what the UFO might have been.

In contrast to this, a typical encounter of the second kind involves a far greater degree of interaction between the UFO and its observers. In March 1977, two British textile workers were shaken by their encounter with a giant, black, cigar-shaped UFO that was covered with moving lights of red, orange, green and blue. As the men drove to work, the UFO descended slowly from the brow of a hill. It then stopped and hovered in

Below: **Two textile workers on their way to work in northern Britain were shaken to find their car being shadowed by a giant UFO that was covered with moving lights. The strange craft seemed to observe them from a distance before losing interest and silently drifting away.**

front of their car, causing the engine to cut out and the headlights to dim. After several minutes the strange object rose and drifted leisurely away to the south. Both witnesses were so upset by the encounter that they suffered from headaches and loss of appetite for several days afterwards.

Close encounters of the third kind are by far the most bizarre UFO events of all. They are the rare occasions when human beings make direct contact with 'UFOnauts', the intelligent creatures who appear to operate UFOs. In some instances, these encounters have consisted of the two sides merely observing each other. In others, people claim to have been on board, an experience more like being kidnapped than being politely invited.

A particularly eerie encounter took place late in May, 1974 on the road from Salisbury, Zimbabwe to the border of South Africa. As a married couple drove through the night they noticed a flashing blue-white light in the distance that seemed to be winking on and off with a slow steady rhythm. Shortly after this, a bright halo of light enveloped their car and the interior

temperature began to plunge so that even with the heater on full and wrapped in coats and blankets the couple still shivered with the cold.

Then their Peugeot began to act very strangely of its own accord. Suddenly, the headlights failed, the brakes ceased working, the steering wheel locked, and the fuel gauge showed that the tank was empty. Yet the car began to hurtle along at 190 km/h! Alongside, but still in the distance, the UFO continued to follow.

The couple were only able to stop when they reached the town of Fort Victoria. Though shaken, they were unable to find anyone there who had seen anything strange or had noticed whether the night was especially cold.

Resuming their journey at 5.30 am their strange experiences began once more. Again the car began to move at more than maximum speed and again they lost control over it. Shortly after 6 am they slipped into a semi-conscious state from which they only awoke at 8.30 am at the border crossing into South Africa. Although two hours had vanished from their lives, the car clock showed only 7.30 am, while the odo-

58

meter registered less than a dozen kilometres of the 290km run from Fort Victoria to the border.

Later, with the help of psychiatrists, the couple were able to piece together some of their experiences during the missing two hours. It seemed that several vague figures suddenly materialized in the back of their car as if they had been beamed there. During the entire period of contact with the UFO they hovered there and, as in a nightmare, took on whatever shape the two humans imagined them to have. Through the same beam that sent the shapes, the two humans could also 'see' the interior of the UFO. It had three levels, one for the engine, a middle living area which also contained communication equipment, and an upper level for navigation and flight control. Movement between the three levels was through a vacuum shaft.

Although the couple's description contained an incredible amount of detail, its nightmarish quality makes the account difficult to examine. Both humans had a very jumbled and hazy memory of what had occurred, but the physical evidence of the car's behaviour makes it easier to accept that something strange did take place.

If encounters such as this one were to continue, it might be possible to build up a clearer picture of UFOs and the creatures that travel in them. But until more concrete evidence emerges, the question as to whether there is other intelligent life in the universe remains unanswered.

UFO Visitors

Accounts of the creatures that travel inside UFOs are so bizarre and confusing that they sometimes seem quite ridiculous.

One early evening in October 1973, two Missouri men were surprised by a lozenge-shaped craft gliding across the water as they fished from a riverside jetty. The object floated inches above the surface, gradually drawing nearer until it stopped immediately in front of the fishermen. Three creatures emerged. They were vaguely human in shape, looking a bit like deep-sea

divers in helmets and bulky suits. One fisherman fainted while the other became immobilized by the huge luminous eyes of the creatures. Both humans were taken aboard the UFO for what seemed to be a medical examination. Then they were dropped back on the pier and the UFO disappeared in the settling gloom of night.

Other encounters with UFO visitors have yielded descriptions of tall giants, clothed in silvery material and having immense, piercing eyes and a humanoid form. From Quebec, in Canada, there comes an account of a meeting with a round-headed, round-shouldered creature less than 1.5 metres tall. It had no nose, mouth or ears, but its eyes were huge and had a phosphorescent glow. The woman who saw it spoke of the creature as having an enchanting beauty!

By all accounts, it would seem that the Earth is being visited by numerous races of UFO creatures and not just a single species. Yet, within this mixed bunch there are some which appear to have a common background.

In North Carolina, in September 1973, there was a flurry of reports of a

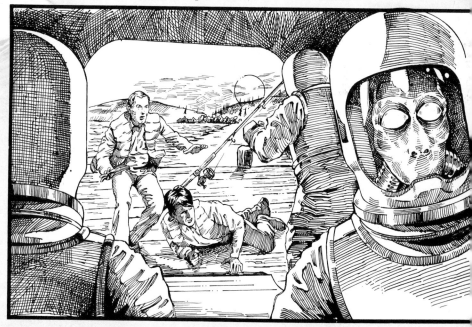

giant, one-handed creature with long hair, pointed ears and a grey face. It was said to be dressed in dark clothes and was seen to move along with great 15m bounds. This creature bore a striking resemblance to the group of UFO visitors known collectively as 'men-in-black'. Witnesses describe them as sinister-looking men clothed

Left: **Near to the Zimbabwe-South Africa border in 1974 a man and his wife were enveloped by a bright light that interrupted their all-night drive. It caused the couple to drift into unconsciousness and to lose two hours from their lives; two hours during which their car continued to travel, having collected some uninvited passengers.**

Above: **Two men from Missouri in the United States were immobilized and taken on board a strange UFO to be examined by its mysterious occupants. The reason for this bizarre abduction was never made clear to them.**

in dark shoes, dark suits and dark glasses. They seem to be bent on destroying all signs of UFO visits, especially photographs and any physical evidence, and seem to have the psychic ability to read people's minds and cause them to have hallucinations. Despite their menacing air, they often act as if they were confused by humans, and seem strangely ill at ease.

Although UFOs as we have described them are a very modern phenomenon, some students of the subject claim that this is not the first time in history that the Earth has been visited by interplanetary travellers. They claim that evidence of earlier visits exists, and that some of it is thousands of years old.

In Central America there are Mayan tomb figures which are said to show man-like beings ready to be launched by rocket. In the Sahara Desert are rock paintings which have the same big-eyed, dumpy shape and goldfish bowl head of so many reported UFO visitors today. Statues from Japan show similar goggle-eyed and helmeted creatures. There is even a school of argument which claims that ancient encounters with aliens were so traumatic for our ancestors that they became the basis of many of our legends of gods and heroes and strange creatures that could fly through the air.

The behaviour of UFO visitors is just as varied and as bizarre as their looks. Some appear to be studying the planet in a careful and systematic way. Some seem bent on terrorizing human beings and animals. Still others wander about clumsily as if in a daze.

The strangeness of their behaviour seems to add to the nightmarish quality of so many encounters. One might expect UFOnauts to first announce themselves publicly. Instead, they appear to be visiting our planet almost in secrecy, landing in isolated areas, and then vanishing as quietly as they arrived. It is as if these visitors were intent on confusing human beings deliberately. One suggestion that seems to offer some explanation of their puzzling behaviour and the variety of their physical shapes is that they present themselves to human beings as hallucinations. If this were the case, then their appearance would be partly affected by what people expected them to look like, and so their shape would change from event to event and give rise to the impression that Earth was being visited by a whole army of different aliens, not just one race.

UFO Powers

By all accounts, UFOs behave in ways that seem to flout everything we know about the laws of nature. They also seem to have uncanny side effects on machinery and on the human beings who come into close contact with them.

Whatever the propulsion systems of these strange craft may be, they seem to have the ability to hover, climb vertically and dart back and forth at incredible speeds. They can corner in mid-air as if on rails and reverse direction instantaneously without losing speed. It is as though UFOs have a mass so small that gravity has little effect on them. If this is the case, it would explain their ability to dart about in every direction without appearing ever to lose speed.

One example of this extraordinary manoeuvrability was reported by two Californian police officers who witnessed a UFO plummeting to Earth at very high speeds and in complete silence as if its engines had cut out. Tens of metres from crashing it reversed direction neatly and continued at the same pace without having slowed in the least. Were an aeroplane to try this it would have to start braking and turning well in advance. If, for some reason, it managed to make such a sudden turn, the enormous strain imposed by gravity would cause it to break up.

As well as seeming to be indifferent to gravity, UFOs are apparently able to operate in unlikely environments. Certain unexplained phenomena at sea may well be spacecraft from distant galaxies.

In 1962, as a group of French fishermen watched what they assumed to be an experimental submarine bob to the surface, it unexpectedly rose up, circled silently a few times changing colour and then shot off into the night.

UFOs have also had startling effects

on the world with which they come into contact. The powerful magnetic field that seems to surround them causes electrical objects to behave mysteriously. Radio reception is drowned by static, lights flicker and fade and car engines come to a sudden stop.

During a short drive one evening in 1976 near Winchester in England, Joyce Bowles and Ted Pratt were surprised by a UFO. As they came around a sharp bend in a country road their nearly new car began to shake and shudder. The steering wheel locked completely and then, adding to their helplessness, an unknown force pulled the car sideways through the air to land on the grassy shoulder of the road. Immediately ahead, both occupants could see a large cigar-shaped object lit up by their headlights. Not until the UFO had departed could either of them start the car again.

Stranger still are the effects UFOs seem to have on human bodies. Many subjects of close encounters experience physical reactions afterwards, such as splitting headaches, weeping eyes, blotchy marks and sores. One New Jersey man whose car was followed by a UFO developed a recurring illness every month. It lasted three or four days each time, during which he complained of chills, soreness and fatigue. As a result, he lost 16 kgs over a period of six months before finally recovering.

Perhaps the most extraordinary power of all exhibited by UFOs is the

Left (inset): **It is thought that records of former visits from UFOs exist in the paintings and carvings of people of long ago. This statue from Japan is claimed by some people to depict a creature inside a kind of spacesuit.**

Left: **Sometimes people who have witnessed UFOs claim that they are later harassed by menacing men-in-black. These sinister beings seem bent on destroying the evidence of the UFOs' visit. They also make clumsy attempts to intimidate the witnesses and seem to have an uncanny ability to read people's thoughts.**

Below: **A group of French fishermen watched in amazement as an underwater craft, which they took to be a submarine, rose into the air and silently flew off into the night.**

ability to interfere with the laws of space and time. This occurs most commonly in cases where subjects have been abducted.

In the rugged border region between Chile and Bolivia, a Chilean army patrol chanced upon an unidentified object in 1977. As the army approached to investigate, the commanding NCO disappeared. He was not swallowed by the Earth, or drawn up into the sky—he simply vanished. His men were dumbfounded. For the next fifteen minutes they searched high and low until, suddenly, their commander reappeared and collapsed in shock. When queried, he was unable to remember anything that had happened to him. Yet, during his short absence, his watch had run forward five days and he had grown a stubbly beard that matched this lapse of time.

Whatever forces emanate from UFOs, they obviously have considerable power. It would appear that they have the nature of strong electromagnetic radiations, judging by the effects on man-made objects. But the form which these energies take, and the way in which they are generated, remains a mystery—as does everything else about UFOs.

UFO Research

Before the 1950s hardly anyone took the subject of UFOs seriously. However, as interest grew and studies of early reports left a great deal to be explained, the first real investigations began. At first few scientists were curious, or if they were they found that there was too little data to undertake any substantial examinations.

Two leading civilian groups that were established early on to look at UFOs seriously were the Aerial Phenomena Research Organization (APRO), founded in 1952, and the National Investigations Committee on Aerial Phenomenon (NICAP) set up in 1956. Between them today they have over 12,000 members in all fields of science and technology who gather raw data and collate it into UFO reports for their central files.

However, it was some time before public clamour was able to spark off any serious official response. Eventually the US Air Force mounted an investigation that came to be known as Project Blue Book, prior to its demise in 1969. Unfortunately, the project was more of a political football than a serious forum of study. The Air Force tried to dismiss UFOs as simply natural or, perhaps, man-made phenomena, an approach which produced such wildly implausible explanations that the project's credibility was seriously undermined.

As it turned out, the Air Force attempted to sweep the whole subject under the most convenient official carpet it could find. For example, a panel of American scientists who met for several days in 1953 to study 20 case histories found that its final report was kept secret. Not until 1967 did the findings of the Robertson Committee become general knowledge. Officials seemed to deny and discredit UFO reports at every opportunity. The trouble with such a cavalier dismissal of UFOs is that it made little attempt even to consider the more serious reports. There are far too many sightings that simply do not justify this kind of blanket dismissal.

In 1956, at the US Air Force station of Bentwater in Suffolk, England, radar trackers picked up an object moving off their screens at 8,000 km/h. Half an hour later another high-speed object appeared. An hour after that a new blip showed up from the east travelling at 3,200 km/h. Observers outdoors saw streaks of blurred light pass by overhead while the crew of a low-flying cargo plane in the area (at a height of 1,200m) saw a source of light pass at very high speed beneath them.

At nearby Lakenheath, other units were also tracking the objects on radar.

Above: **After vanishing for no more than 15 minutes, a Peruvian army soldier reappeared with a five day growth of beard on his face. His watch had run forward a similar length of time. He had no memory of what had happened to him, other than that he had been investigating a strange object while on patrol.**

A military jet was detailed to take a look. The pilot came close enough for his radar to home in on the target when, without warning, the UFO slipped out of range and positioned itself on the jet's tail. No matter how much he turned and swerved, the pilot was unable to shake off the UFO. He was finally forced to call off the chase and return to base. The entire episode was watched by several ground radars too, yet there has never been an adequate explanation of what took place that August night.

In 1967, in response to growing public pressure, the US Air Force set

aside half a million dollars to conduct a two-year investigation by a team of scientists. Again charges flew back and forth that the committee was set up only to bury the topic once and for all. When the Condon Report appeared in 1969 it concluded that nothing valuable had been obtained from the study of UFOs so far and that further investigation could not be justified. Nevertheless, the committee found that fully one third of the reports studied could not be adequately accounted for. Since this time, the Air Force has abandoned the field of UFO study to others.

As far as anyone can tell, the UFO phenomenon seems impossible to study closely. Yet it is equally impossible to dismiss. The main criticism of the assumption that mankind is being shadowed by other intelligent creatures concerns the assertion that they are extra-terrestrial. Astronomers are quick to point out that no UFOs have ever been spotted in space or seen entering the atmosphere. But there may be other explanations. Some believe that UFOs may have come from another dimension in time—a world parallel to our own. Others feel sure that the 'UFO people' have been here all along and have only taken to using flying saucers to hoodwink us at a time when we are on the verge of travelling into space ourselves.

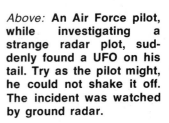

Above: **An Air Force pilot, while investigating a strange radar plot, suddenly found a UFO on his tail. Try as the pilot might, he could not shake it off. The incident was watched by ground radar.**

Lost Worlds

The belief that a glorious civilization once existed somewhere on Earth has been the source of innumerable legends. Usually it is described as being a place of perfection, where a race of human beings, who excelled in beauty, knowledge and wisdom, lived in splendid peace and prosperity. In one form or another, the power of this dream has never faded. To this day, the search for the lost worlds of a former golden age continues to exercise a powerful fascination.

The Legend of Atlantis

Around the year 355 BC the Greek philosopher Plato wrote of a long-lost island called Atlantis. According to Plato, the island was vast and fertile and its inhabitants a highly advanced race. Plato's description was based on a legend that he believed originated in Egypt, but the puzzle of Atlantis continues to fascinate and intrigue us today.

In his writings, Plato described the wealth and power of the Atlanteans, who had conquered most of the known world. Yet, according to legend, they were eventually overpowered by the men of Athens and, soon after, their splendid island kingdom was obliterated by violent earthquakes and floods. In a single night and day the entire continent was swallowed up by the sea.

Since the time of Plato, the legend of Atlantis has attracted the attention of historians, geologists, archaeologists, occultists and mystics of every description. A recent estimate claims that over 5,000 books have been published on the subject. One work in particular that has provoked much speculation is Ignatius Donnelley's book *Atlantis; the Antediluvian World.* Donnelly, writing in the 1880s, maintained that the continent had existed in mid-Atlantic and had formed a bridge of land between the Old World and the New. He also argued that the people of Atlantis were the ancient race whose culture had been the source of all the civilizations we know today.

Unfortunately, Donnelly's proposition that Atlantis still exists in mid-ocean as a sunken mass of land has been conclusively rejected by geol-

Left: **Plato's description of Atlantis was based on an already ancient legend that originated in Egypt.**

ogists. They have shown that the mid-Atlantic Ridge, a chain of undersea mountains stretching from Iceland to the South Atlantic, has been formed by material thrown up from deep within the planet's interior. It is one of the youngest geological regions on Earth and not, as has been claimed, an ancient sunken continent.

Currently, a far more widely-held view is that the legend of Atlantis is in some way linked with the civilization of Minoan Crete, which flourished over 1,000 years before the time of Plato. Crete, at the time of the Minoans, was the home of a magnificent Bronze Age civilization. From their capital at Knossos, the Minoans controlled a fleet of ships that dominated trade and travel throughout the eastern end of the Mediterranean. But, in about 1500 BC, Crete suffered a devastating calamity. At this time, the neighbouring island of Thera tore itself apart in perhaps the most enormous volcanic explosion ever known to man. Crete, a mere 160 km to the south, was hit by the shock wave of the explosion, then by violent earthquakes and finally by tidal waves and a choking rain of ash that covered villages and fields to a depth of at least 20cm.

The explosion would have been heard in Egypt and people there might possibly have witnessed the cloud of ash that was hurled into the atmosphere. In any event, reports of the catastrophe would have circulated throughout the region.

Although the immediate effect of this stunning calamity is hard to gauge from this distance in time, the fact that

Egyptian records of their contact with the Minoans cease within a century of the event would seem to support the notion that the volcanic disaster and the downfall of the Minoans were closely linked events. Therefore, the Atlantis legend picked up later by Plato may well have grown from a confused account of the natural disaster that ruined Minoan Crete.

Perhaps, however, it was not Plato's intention to present a straight history in his telling of the legend. He may also have been describing a country of the mind; a civilization that represented a bygone golden age which had been lost forever. It was not his purpose to argue where and when Atlantis existed. The fact that he could use it as an example of the perfect kingdom was sufficient in itself. And it is this aspect of the legend that continues to fascinate people throughout history, just as much as the how and where of the island's disappearance.

Below: **The tremendous volcanic explosion of Thera created tidal waves that swept through the eastern Mediterranean. The coast of Crete, a mere 160 km away, was devastated. Later a rain of ash and cinder blanketed the entire island.**

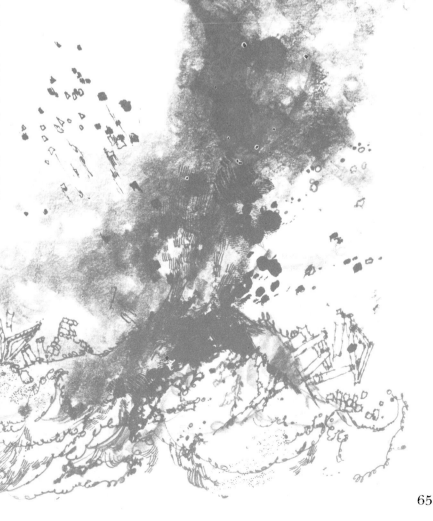

Shangri-La

In 1933, James Hilton's adventure novel, *Lost Horizon*, was published and became an immediate best-seller. The story told of two pilots who became lost during a flight through the Himalayas. They managed to make a successful emergency landing and, by a stroke of luck, were saved from death in the bitter cold by the discovery of a thriving native community in a remote and unknown mountain valley.

The lost world into which the pilots had wandered was known to its inhabitants as Shangri-La. To the outsiders, it seemed as if they had stumbled into a second Garden of Eden. A ring of towering peaks checked the blizzards that raged outside, creating a pocket of clear weather. Hot springs warmed the fertile volcanic soil, which the natives of the valley had transformed into a great well-tended garden, and the air was fragrant with the scent of blossoms and flowers.

Shangri-La was a place of such tranquillity and peace that it seemed as if time here had come to a virtual halt. Much to the astonishment of the outsiders, the inhabitants all lived for hundreds of years, yet they still kept their youthful looks. As well as near-immortality, they also had attained an extraordinary wisdom about the secrets of the universe which enabled them to live in harmony without resorting to strict laws and harsh penalties. They possessed remarkable powers of clairvoyance too, that allowed them to read the future with great insight. All in all, they appeared to be a race of perfect human beings.

The story of Shangri-La became enormously popular because of the romantic ideal to which it appealed. It described a world that was uncorrupted and untouched by the ugly side of human nature. It represented the kind of golden age that has been the dream of countless people over the ages. Some have argued that such an era actually existed long ago, in Atlantis for example, but that human beings have since fallen from this state of grace. Indeed, what gave Shangri-La its special attraction was the slight possibility that it really might exist, for

there are ancient legends about places in remote parts of the far east that sound very similar to Hilton's Shangri-La. Traditionally, they are claimed to be located somewhere in the vast wilderness that stretches from the Himalayas in the south to the Altai Mountains of Mongolia in the north.

In Buddhist myths, this lost paradise was known as Shambhala. Its people were supposed to have attained exceptional abilities through an intuitive wisdom that was the key to the workings of the universe. It gave them access to powers so extraordinary that to outsiders they seemed like feats of pure magic. In Tibet, there were holy men who spoke of this mythical Shambhala as being a place to the north, where high sheltered valleys were watered by hot springs and where a luxuriant vegetation flourished.

A number of old Chinese legends tell of a valley where a race of immortals live in perpetual peace. In India, too, there are references to a race of

Below: **In James Hilton's story of Shangri-La, a lost world high in the Himalayas was accidentally discovered by Europeans when their plane crash-landed nearby. The inhabitants of the valley seemed to have found the secret of eternal youth and possessed an ancient wisdom that gave them the power to read other men's minds.**

perfect people who dwell somewhere to the north of the Himalayas.

In purely geographical terms, the possibility of the existence of such a perfect community in this part of the world cannot be denied. Between them, Mongolia and Tibet form a vast continent within a continent. They make up an area of Asia that is bigger than all of western Europe. It is a remote and inhospitable region, a land of windswept plains that are cut off from the rest of the world by ranges of high mountains. There is plenty of room here for a lost community to survive for years without being discovered.

There is a second consideration that also makes this part of the world a likely setting for some kind of a Shangri-La. The nomadic herders of this region have a long tradition of religious mysticism and quasi-supernatural powers. The lamas of Tibet are famous for their extraordinary spiritual exercises. They are able to endure the most

numbing cold, clothed only in the flimsiest of garments. They are also said to have uncanny powers of levitation and to practise the art of trance-running. During this feat they half-float and half-bounce across the rugged terrain with an astonishing swiftness that enables them to cover over 20 kms in half an hour.

However, there is another interpretation of the Shangri-La legend that steers completely away from the idea that it has a specific location in central Asia. This view, often heard from theosophists, is that Shangri-La is a place with no tangible form. Rather, it is a country of the mind. Buddhists also speak of their Shambhala in similar terms. It represents the mental state at which people may arrive after prolonged training and discipline. This state of perfection requires a spiritual journey every bit as arduous as the one which might be needed to find Shangri-La, were it actually to exist. It is this elusiveness, coupled with the continued possibility of eventual success in finding it, that has made the search for Shangri-La such a compelling and enduring myth.

Above: **Lamas of Tibet are famous for their extraordinary mental and physical powers. Some are even said to be able to levitate. They use this ability to move about the countryside with extraordinary speed in a form of trance-running, called *lung-gom.***

El Dorado

The legend of a fabulously wealthy tribe of Indians living in isolated splendour somewhere in the jungles of South America has fascinated European explorers for centuries. One of the last great expeditions to find this fabled city set out as recently as

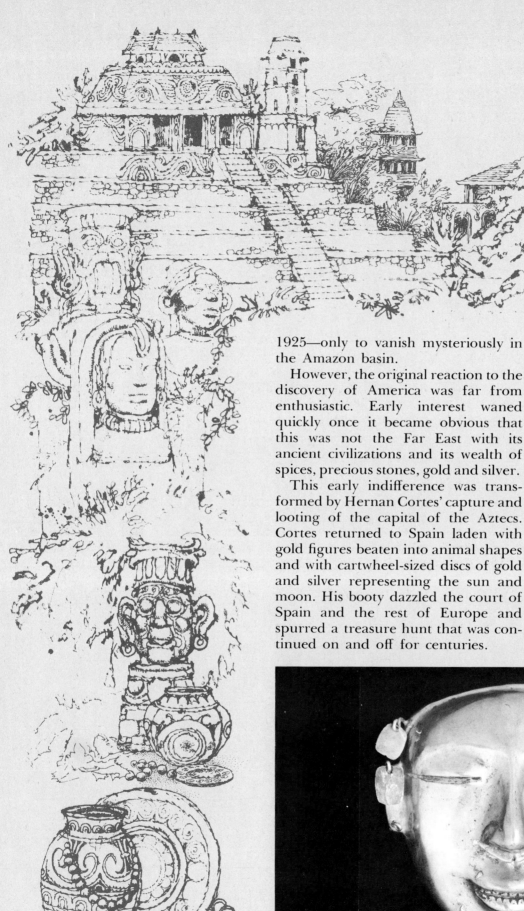

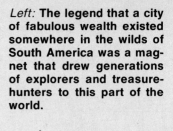

Left: **The legend that a city of fabulous wealth existed somewhere in the wilds of South America was a magnet that drew generations of explorers and treasure-hunters to this part of the world.**

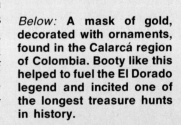

1925—only to vanish mysteriously in the Amazon basin.

However, the original reaction to the discovery of America was far from enthusiastic. Early interest waned quickly once it became obvious that this was not the Far East with its ancient civilizations and its wealth of spices, precious stones, gold and silver.

This early indifference was transformed by Hernan Cortes' capture and looting of the capital of the Aztecs. Cortes returned to Spain laden with gold figures beaten into animal shapes and with cartwheel-sized discs of gold and silver representing the sun and moon. His booty dazzled the court of Spain and the rest of Europe and spurred a treasure hunt that was continued on and off for centuries.

Below: **A mask of gold, decorated with ornaments, found in the Calarcá region of Colombia. Booty like this helped to fuel the El Dorado legend and incited one of the longest treasure hunts in history.**

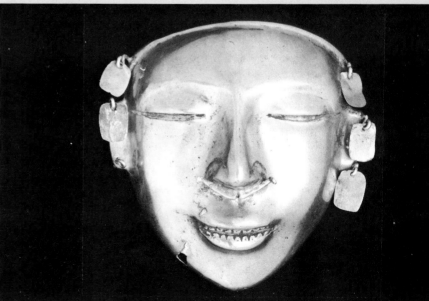

In 1529, the post of governor of Venezuela was given to Ambrosius Dalfinger. Almost his very first act was to set off on an expedition to explore his newly-acquired possessions.

Six months later he reached the great inland lake of Maracaibo where he met Indians wearing ornaments—armbands, ear and nose rings—made of fine gold. They explained that these pieces of jewellery came from a tribe far away in the interior.

According to the story they told, these Indians were so wealthy that they painted their chief with gold dust during his coronation ceremony. This story of a man of gold—known to the Spanish as *El Hombre Dorado*—entranced all who heard it and rapidly acquired a semi-legendary status. It drew generations of fortune hunters to the wilderness of central southern America, like moths to a flame. In time, the El Dorado legend became linked with that of a fabulous lost city deep in the jungle. It was claimed that its great temples were surrounded on all sides by statues of gold and silver and that almost every decorative object, from the sacred to the mundane, was made from a precious metal. The discovery of ruined temples and cities in the wilds of the Yucatan and Guatemala only served to keep the lost city of El Dorado myth alive for centuries.

A second expedition of Dalfinger's set off in 1531 in search of the treasure that he believed was there for the taking, somewhere in the interior. The expedition spent over two years on the march, during which time 135 of the original 170 men were either killed or died from fever and exhaustion, without any notable success. Dalfinger himself was shot and killed by a poisoned arrow.

However, the governor's immediate successor, Georg Hohermuth, was undaunted by his predecessor's failure. He led an appallingly difficult expedition that lasted three years and resulted in the loss of 300 men. Though he penetrated as far as southern Columbia, he failed to find the fabled source of gold. The most he obtained were odd trinkets he could loot from the tribes he encountered along the way.

In 1536 yet another fortune hunter

set out to find El Dorado. Led by Gonzalo de Quesada, a minor Spanish official, this force of 800 men took a year of struggling through the heavily forested highlands of Columbia to reach the region where present day Bogota lies. It was here that the legend of El Dorado had its source, although few Europeans of the time realized this. During the coronation of their chief, the Indians of the region would smear his body with clay and completely cover it with gold dust. This 'man of gold' was then immersed in Lake Guatavita until the gold washed off. The rite was an offering to the gods and to the tribe's ancestors in return for them bestowing the new chief with the powers of leadership.

However, Quesada met with initial disappointment here for, although he could find plenty of evidence of gold, no storehouse of treasure awaited him. The Indians obtained their supplies by placer mining the swift streams that ran down the mountains. They then cast it or beat it into a wide range of ornaments. There was a lively trade in these precious objects with other tribes in exchange for emeralds (which were found in abundance in the mountains), salt and other goods, but there was no great central store of treasure.

At last, in June 1537, Quesada came upon the mountain village of Hunsa where, his Indian sources claimed, a huge supply of gold could be found. With 50 of his original force he stormed and captured the place. To his amazement, the village did contain

Above: **The chief of a tribe near Lake Guatavita in Columbia was smeared all over with gold dust and clay as part of his coronation ceremony. The accounts of this 'maŋ of gold', or El Dorado, fuelled the legend of a fabulously wealthy ruler and kingdom somewhere in South America.**

69

a hoard of gold. Almost every house was filled with plates of beaten gold, bags of gold dust were stored everywhere, and the inhabitants literally dripped with beautiful rings, bracelets and amulets. In the home of the chief was a throne that was encrusted with gold and emeralds.

Though the value of his find was virtually incalculable, Quesada was never convinced he had found El Dorado. Later in life he mounted another two expeditions, neither of which was a success. He died a disappointed man in Bogota, in 1579.

What kept Quesada's imagination fired was that the El Dorado legend had assumed proportions that were far greater than were ever warranted by his discoveries and those of other Europeans. The belief that a city of gold existed somewhere in the wilderness of South America so entranced the early explorers that nothing they found ever came near to their expectations. The jungle civilization which they were seeking was so vast and luxurious that even a place like Hunsa could not quell their appetite.

Rumours of a lost city continued to flourish for hundreds of years. Even today, when the wilderness has been photographed and surveyed by satellite and plane, the possibility of a lost city overrun by the jungle cannot be completely ruled out. What is unlikely, however, is that such a place would be a fabulous storehouse of treasure. But the search continues.

The Court of King Arthur

The tale of King Arthur and the Knights of the Round Table is one of the best known in the folklore of Britain. The story tells how young Arthur came to the throne after miraculously withdrawing a magic sword from a stone, an act that had defeated men far older and more powerful than he. He proceeded to unite his people and, as leader of an army of famous knights, to win a series of battles that checked the waves of barbarians that were streaming into Britain from across the North Sea. He took control of a large part of the country and brought about a period of peace and prosperity.

King Arthur and his queen, Guinevere, reigned in splendour from their castle at Camelot. Here the king was surrounded by his entourage of knights, whom he organized into the Order of the Round Table. His chief advisor was Merlin, the legendary magician.

The legend of King Arthur has a tragic ending. One of his followers, a knight called Modred, proved to be a traitor who led a rebellion against Arthur. In the bitter fighting that followed, both Modred and the king were slain at the battle of Camlaun. After his death, the kingdom was swiftly overrun by foreign invaders and it soon vanished from history without a trace. But the memory of King Arthur has been kept alive by legends that have survived to this day.

For years, the question that has perplexed historians is whether there is a grain of truth in the Arthurian legends. Try as they might, they have never been able to uncover a shred of concrete evidence for his existence. The locations of his birth and death are not readily identifiable from modern

Below: **Excalibur was the name given to the sword that King Arthur drew out of a stone into which it had been driven. This unique feat was a magic sign indicating that he, alone, was suited to be the king of his people.**

time soon elevated him to the status of a great king, whose domains included much of western Britain. The stories were also populated with great heroes, with men who had magical powers and with fantastic beasts. Wherever the Celts survived in any number, these legends of a wonderful lost past lived on.

It was only in the 9th century that a Welsh monk produced the first written reference to King Arthur. He described him as a great war-leader who united the other kings of the Celts in a common struggle against the Anglo-Saxon invaders.

Then in the 12th century, a remarkable change took place. The Arthurian myths, which had so far been the property of the Celts, were rediscovered and adopted by English folktellers. They grafted a great medieval romance on to the original story and introduced such themes as the quest for the Holy Grail and the splendid royal court where Arthur's warriors —the Knights of the Round Table— engaged in noble and chivalrous deeds.

So it is through two levels of myth that one must examine the legends of King Arthur for shreds of evidence that the tales have some basis in reality.

Most commonly, Arthur's place of birth is given as being Tintagel, a location on the coast of Cornwall. Here today are the ruins of a medieval castle that was built centuries after Arthur's time. Yet excavations of the site have

Left: **According to the legend of King Arthur, he reigned from his court at Camelot, somewhere in the west of Britain. But there has never been found any trace of this splendid capital of his, leading some people to speculate that the legend is entirely mythical.**

place names. Nor is there a surviving written record of his life, nor any tomb or ruined castle that bears his inscriptions. All we have to rely on are ancient legends that have been handed down by word of mouth for centuries, and which have been retold and re-written endlessly. Whether these make for an accurate record is the subject of much debate.

The Arthurian legends are set late in the 5th century AD, soon after the Roman Empire in the west collapsed. After the legions had abandoned Britain, the native Celts continued to put up such a successful resistance to the invading Angles, Saxons and Jutes who arrived from the continent, that they were able to fight them to a standstill for a time. During this brief period, Britain attained a remarkable degree of unity and peace, and these years came to be thought of as a golden age in the folklore of the Celts.

It is highly probable that the skills of a great leader were needed to achieve even such a short-lived success. Whether this man was King Arthur or not is impossible to tell. Whoever he was, the stories that were told after his

Below: **King Arthur is said to have been born at Tintagel in Cornwall. Today, the ruins of a medieval castle are all that stands here. But excavations have shown that the place was occupied much earlier in history, possibly as long ago as the fifth century.**

revealed the remains of much older buildings and of pottery dating from the late 5th century. It would seem that an important building once stood here. Although there is nothing to link it with Arthur, it does not conflict with any of the legends of his life.

In much the same way, Cadbury Castle in Somerset may have associations with Camelot. Excavations late in the 1960s showed that a great hill-fort stood here in Arthurian times. Its 6m-thick walls of stone were topped with breastworks of timber, while watch towers and a mighty gatehouse completed the fortress. Again, although there is no link between it and a person called Arthur, it would nevertheless have taken a leader of considerable strength and resources to build such a place. The most telling point about Cadbury Castle is that there is no rival to it in size dating from the 5th century anywhere else in the west country.

In the end, whether Arthur ever existed or not is almost immaterial. It is perhaps more appropriate to query the existence of a great warrior, an 'Arthur-like leader', at this time in British history, who was able to unite his people and lead them successfully against the invading outsiders. If there was such a figure, then surely he would have gained the same stature among his people as the King Arthur of the legends. After his death, folktales and stories would soon have been embellishing his exploits, gradually creating the mythical figure with which we are so familiar.

The great problem with studying legends is to know how to take them seriously, without accepting them literally. It must be admitted that the only evidence we have of King Arthur is legendary, not concrete, but it is a legend firmly entrenched in British history. It still tantalizes us today.

Riddles of the Past

Our knowledge of the past goes back, in a patchy way, almost 5,000 years. Therefore, when an object from the prehistoric past emerges, it is usually shrouded in mystery. And if it shows signs of spectacular intelligence we usually react with disbelief, for we seem reluctant to credit our forefathers with greater skills than our own.

The Pyramids

Along the dusty rim of the Nile valley a line of 70 pyramids, stretching over 75 km, gazes impassively down at the river. By far the most impressive of all these monuments are the three pyramids of Giza, which include the Great Pyramid of Cheops, the largest and most impressive ever to be built. The Great Pyramid was constructed about 2500 BC for the pharaoh Khufu (known to the ancient Greeks as Cheops). Though erosion has gnawed away some nine metres of stone from the summit, its majestic bulk still rises 138m above the desert.

There are few other buildings to

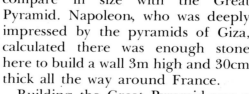

compare in size with the Great Pyramid. Napoleon, who was deeply impressed by the pyramids of Giza, calculated there was enough stone here to build a wall 3m high and 30cm thick all the way around France.

Building the Great Pyramid was a formidable task. According to the Greek historian, Herodotus, whose description was written 2,000 years levered into position on the site. As the pyramid grew, passages and burial chambers were cut into the mass of solid rock.

The four faces of the Great Pyramid are aligned with the four points of the compass. The main entrance is on the north side and from here a network of passages, many of them false and misleading, wind into the pyramid and to the burial chamber, where a huge granite sarcophagus lies. This is where the mummified body of the dead pharaoh would have been placed.

The geometry of this, the most famous tomb in the world, is incredibly complex and the skill with which its giant limestone blocks were fitted together quite astonishing. It is this

Below: **The pyramids were most likely built by an army of unskilled workers who were farmers most of the year and labourers during the months when the Nile flooded their fields. They would have been directed by a group of skilled engineers and craftsmen.**

after the building was completed, it took 100,000 labourers more than 20 years to finish the work. For this reason, the pyramid was started early in a pharaoh's reign so that it would be ready to receive him by the time he died. Along with the main pyramid, a complex of tombs for leading nobles and courtiers was also built. In addition, a great causeway was raised linking the pyramid with the Nile and a riverside temple there that guarded the ceremonial route of approach.

There is no evidence of any sophisticated pieces of machinery being used to build the pyramid, such as pulleys or capstans. The great blocks of limestone from which it was made, weighing as much as 15 tonnes, were hauled into position by rope on sledges and rollers. They were pulled up ramps and then

superb quality of workmanship, combined with the pyramid's enormous size, that has made it an object of endless puzzlement and speculation.

Although most Egyptologists accept that the Great Pyramid is the tomb of an especially rich and powerful pharaoh, one group of pyramidologists (often referred to as 'pyramidiots' by their critics) claim that there is much more here than meets the eye. They have spent considerable time and energy since the middle of the 19th century studying the occult and mystical nature of the Great Pyramid.

At one time it was suggested that it was one of the legendary storehouses of the Old Testament, used by Joseph of Egypt to hold the harvest of the seven good years that preceded the seven years of famine. Another suggestion claims that the ancient Egyptians could never have undertaken such an enormous project and that it was built by a forgotten race of 'supermen'. Recently this idea has been updated by the notion that these were intelligent beings from outer space. Even more bizarre suggestions assert that the pyramid is a landmark for flying saucers, that it marks the centre of the world or that it is the model of a giant water pump!

Pyramidologists have also been fascinated by the geometrical precision with which the Great Pyramid was built. Into it they have read signs of a system of ancient secret knowledge. This lost wisdom of the Egyptians has enabled them to calculate the diameter and circumference of the Earth, using as standards of measurement the angles and dimensions of the pyramid, and also to establish the value of π, the ratio used to obtain the area and circumference of a circle. They have also claimed that the position of the blocks embodied a cryptic mathematical code of the history of the world, as well as prophesying great events of the future.

By far the majority of these elaborate claims for the Great Pyramid can be quite readily dismissed for there is little doubt that, like the other pyramids, it was built as a tomb and a monument to a famous leader. The hidden location of the burial chamber and sarcophagus, the antechambers filled with treasures of every description ready for the pharaoh to use in the after-life, and the maze of false passages to mislead tomb-robbers all point to this use.

Above and below: **The Great Pyramid at Giza was built as a magnificent tomb to the pharaoh Cheops. Inside, in the burial chamber, his personal possessions were stored for his use in the afterlife.**

74

But there is one great mystery that has never been answered, not even 4,500 years after these great structures were erected. No mummified body of a pharaoh has ever been found in a pyramid. Even where archaeologists have entered pyramids in which the burial chamber and sarcophagus were tightly sealed and obviously intact, and where there was no sign of grave-robbers having either come or gone, they have never yet found a body. Possibly the pharaohs were buried elsewhere, and their pyramids were a deliberate bluff to divert the attention of tomb-robbers. Perhaps the pyramids were only monuments to the dead, and not tombs at all. Or perhaps the bodies may still be there, hidden in another, as yet undiscovered, part of the pyramid. If this is the case, then the ancient Egyptians were more than a match for modern archaeologists, and the pyramidiots may not be quite so far from the truth after all.

King Solomon's Mines

When European explorers first encountered the mysterious ruins of Zimbabwe in the wilds of eastern Africa in the second half of the 19th century, they were astonished to find that a busy city had once flourished here. Though they were completely baffled as to the origins of this fallen empire, they refused to consider that it might ever have been a native civilization.

Numerous explanations were put forward, including the rather far-fetched notion that the ruins had something to do with the biblical legends of King Solomon. Here, it was claimed, thousands of miles from Palestine, was where Solomon had sent his fleets to fetch his treasure of precious metals and stones. This romantic explanation of Zimbabwe struck the right note and it was soon taken up by popular adventure writers of the time, who fanned the public's interest in the legend of King Solomon's mines to an unprecedented degree.

Unfortunately for the ruins of Zimbabwe, archaeologists later showed that the city reached its height during the Middle Ages, more than 2,000 years after the reign of Solomon in the middle of the 10th century BC. However, interest in the fabled treasures of King Solomon did not wane. Amid wide speculation, it continues to this day.

During Solomon's long rule the kingdom of the Hebrews enjoyed the greatest power and wealth it was ever to attain. It dominated Palestine and straddled the major trade routes between Africa and the Middle East and the links between the sea routes of the Indian Ocean and the Mediterranean. Solomon established close ties with the sea-faring Phoenicians, married a daughter of an Egyptian pharaoh and had political links with dozens of neighbouring kingdoms. The strategic position and military strength of his empire brought him enormous wealth.

Below: **King Solomon's strength as a politician and military leader made his kingdom the hub of trade in the Middle East. It also made Solomon enormously wealthy.**

75

Trading expeditions were encouraged by land and by sea, and the travellers would return to his capital at Jerusalem bearing precious metals, exquisite stones, spices and incense, ivory and all manner of exotic products. The wealth that he received in this manner was quite staggering. Descriptions of Solomon's temple in Jerusalem tell of it being filled with carved pillars and statues and decorated with treasures of bronze, copper and gold.

the gold came, for archaeologists have identified ancient gold mines in Saudi Arabia that may have been worked during Solomon's time.

Just as likely is that the gold came from further afield. Joint expeditions with the Phoenicians lasting for three years were known to have been made. The fleets' cargoes of apes, negro slaves, ivory, peacocks and other exotic creatures certainly suggest that they pushed far into the Indian Ocean.

Long-distance voyages of this sort

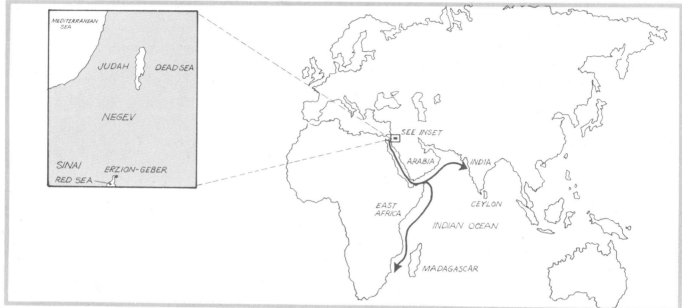

While some Bible scholars have cautioned that descriptions of Solomon's treasure were overstatements made by people honouring the glory of his reign, much of it can be accounted for. A great deal of his riches were in copper and bronze. At the time, there were copper mines in the hills of the Negev Desert between the Dead Sea and the Gulf of Aqabah, as well as smelting works at Ezion-Geber on the shores of the Red Sea.

But the Bible is vague and unhelpful as to the source of his gold. The clues it gives are oblique, for although it provides the name of a location (Ophir) there is no mention of its situation, other than to say that ships would sail there to fetch the precious metal.

One well-established fact is that Solomon's merchant navies ranged far and wide to trade. Moving south along the shores of the Red Sea they picked up spices and incense, such as myrrh and frankincense, from Arabia. It has been suggested that it is from here that

were by no means unknown in the ancient world. Around 600 BC, for instance, Phoenician sailors in the employ of Egypt were supposed to have sailed right around Africa, setting out from the Red Sea and returning by way of the Pillars of Hercules and the Mediterranean. An account of this epic journey comes from Herodotus of Greece, although he himself was sceptical that such a feat had ever occurred. However, epic journeys of this kind open the possibility that King Solomon's gold came from anywhere along the coast of Africa.

Looking to the Mediterranean where the Phoenicians traded along its entire length, their voyages to Spain would have put them into contact with the mines that supplied silver to much of the ancient world. Their close alliance with Solomon would quite naturally have made them a main supplier of his fabled treasure.

Unfortunately, Solomon's death was followed by the division of his empire,

Above: **The source of King Solomon's legendary hoard of gold has never been found. It is known that there were copper mines in the Negev Desert which he controlled, but as for the gold nobody knows. One possibility is the east coast of Africa where his fleets sailed to obtain ivory, spices and slaves.**

and Israel and Judah were formed. The power of the old kingdom waned rapidly and, not long after, Jerusalem was attacked by an Egyptian pharaoh and the temple was looted and destroyed. Solomon's wealth disappeared, and with it vanished any evidence that might have solved the riddle of the origins of his gold.

Engineers of Stone

Scattered along the Atlantic coast of northwest Europe are hundreds of mute stone monuments whose meaning has for centuries confounded those who have investigated them. These are the relics of a people so ancient that not a single record of who they were and where they came from survives. The Stone Age engineers who built them left no signs of cities, roads or waterways, or any other marks of civilization. All we know of them are their scattered megaliths—the giant stones carefully positioned in puzzling geometric patterns.

For years archaeologists dismissed the ancient inhabitants of northern Europe as primitive tribesmen who lived in small, scattered groups, hunting and fishing but without even the skills to farm the land. Their supposed lack of learning and writing, coupled with the fact that they did not know of the wheel or even keep draught animals, only deepened the mystery surrounding the giant monuments.

Although investigators in recent years have determined the approximate age of these Stone Age megaliths, and have even been able to suggest how and why prehistoric people should have built something on so vast a scale, it has not been possible to discover where they acquired the skills to do so. In fact, it has remained impossible even to establish who they were.

One thing that has been evident for years, however, is that the megalith clusters all had something to do with astronomy. The positioning of the rocks in relation to each other formed patterns by which the movements of constellations, planets and the Sun and the Moon could all be measured. The megaliths also indicated that some form of organized religion, most likely a worship of the Sun, flourished in northern Europe over 3,500 years ago, and whose oldest signs go back at least some 5,000 years.

But what is most striking of all is the scale of these monuments and the effort in manpower and time their construction must have represented in a Stone Age community. At Carnac, in Brittany, more than 3,000 stones were erected in neat parallel rows to make a pattern that stretches for hundreds of metres. Not far distant is a toppled stone column, the Grand Menhir Brise, that once towered 17 metres high and which weighed 340 tonnes.

Left: **Under King Hiram I, the fleets of the Phoenicians and those of King Solomon set out from the Red Sea port of Ezion-Geber on trading expeditions lasting as long as three years. Their return with exotic cargoes would indicate that they sailed far into the Indian Ocean, along the coasts of East Africa and India.**

Below: **At Carnac, in Brittany, hundreds of stone megaliths stand in long symmetrical rows and mark this area as a place of worship for the people who lived here 5,000 years ago.**

At Stonehenge in south-western Britain, there is a famous circle of rocks that was cut from quarries in the hills of Wales some 215 km away. The rocks were shipped by water and then were dragged more than 30 km across land to their final position at Stonehenge. It has been estimated that the task of hauling the largest slabs of stone, which weigh 26 tonnes and more, took over 1,000 men, moving them at a rate of less than a kilometre a day.

Studies of the monuments have shown that the engineers who built them had a knowledge of astronomy that was far greater than ever suspected of any prehistoric people. They had the skill to measure the orbits of the Sun and Moon and would have been able to predict their eclipses as well as determine the exact point of midsummer and midwinter. They were even able to measure something as minor as the slight irregularity of the Moon's orbit that causes it to appear to stand still in its orbit every 18.6 years.

Detailed examination of hundreds of megalithic sites in Britain by Dr Alexander Thom of Oxford University revealed that they were laid out in precise circles and that they were designed as astronomical observatories of extraordinary accuracy. Thom argued that these constructions could only have been built in this way because their engineers had a remarkable knowledge of applied geometry. For example, they made use of right-angled triangles in laying out the patterns, even though this is a method thought to have been first used in the eastern Mediterranean world and formally described by the Greeks some 1,000 years *after* Stonehenge and other monuments were built.

Another academic who has studied the megaliths closely observed that their builders seemed to have had a use of mathematics that rivalled that of the ancient Egyptians. Yet despite this, the builders of Stonehenge left no lasting records of themselves or of their knowledge. Like the Incas of Peru, they lacked the ability to write. Their knowledge must have been passed on entirely by memory, with each generation learning everything by heart.

Yet this still does not answer the question of where these ancient Euro-

Below: **The alignment of the giant stones at Stonehenge was deliberate. The site was first used as an observatory to track the movements of the Sun and Moon by Stone Age astronomers nearly 5,000 years ago. The position of the stones is such that they register both the summer and winter solstice, the Sun's most northern and southern swing from the equator.**

peans first learned to build such fantastic monuments, nor even where they came from and who they were. In any case, by the time the Romans arrived on the scene some 15 centuries after Stonehenge had been completed, they found that the Druids who lived in Britain had no memory whatsoever of the people who had built Stonehenge and other megalithic structures. The original builders had vanished, and the secrets of their great system of observatories were buried with them.

Geometry of the Giants

According to Erich von Däniken, author of the bestselling book *Chariot of the Gods,* the network of gigantic straight lines and animal-like patterns that criss-cross an area of dusty desert in southern Peru, near the town of Nazca, was made by travellers from space who visited the Earth thousands of years ago. Von Däniken maintains that the lines were makeshift landing fields, constructed for their spaceships. The patterns, he adds, are the work of native Indians, who later embellished the original runways in an effort to enduce the space creatures (whom they worshipped as gods) to return.

Although von Däniken's flying saucer explanation sounds far-fetched, the mere fact that it has been seriously considered highlights the mystery that still surrounds these desert drawings. They are some of the most puzzling prehistoric constructions ever to have been discovered. Yet from the ground they are not at all impressive. Up close, they seem to be a random jumble of lines that have been made by removing the thin layer of dark stones that covers the whitish soil of the region. The lines that are created in this way are so shallow that even on foot they are hard to make out. From a few metres to one side they are almost invisible. To see them clearly, one must straddle them and look lengthways along the line of direction.

Their true impact can only be made out from a distance; indeed, the main reason they escaped notice for so long

Above: **Stonehenge, the largest and most complex of the prehistoric stone monuments that dot Europe, remains shrouded in mystery to this day, more than 3,500 years after it was completed.**

is that they are simply too big to see. It is necessary to fly high above the Peruvian desert to discern the true scale of the lines and patterns. For this reason it was not until 1939, when local pilots began to report fantastic shapes in the desert, that anyone realized what these white markings actually were.

The questions that were at once raised, quite naturally, were who had built these giant geometric patterns and how. The clue to the first was found in the various designs of the birds, monkeys, spiders and insects that intersperse the long straight lines. The people who laid them out seem to have been the ancestors of the Nazca Indians who live in the region, for the desert shapes closely resemble the styles of the creatures that they embroider on their textiles.

The way in which the lines were produced poses a bigger problem. No one has any idea how a prehistoric people, who left no traces of any civilization, managed to lay out a series of immense designs with a skill that even modern engineers would find hard to duplicate. Their straight lines run with perfect accuracy for many kilometres, crossing gullies and hills with hardly the slightest deviation. The astronomer Gerald Hawkins noted that these lines never stray more than two metres in the kilometre from true, a degree of precision greater than can be measured by modern methods of aerial surveying.

A suggestion has been made that the ancient engineers designed these great patterns in much the same way as their embroideries, only in this case their cloth was the Earth itself and each stitch became one pace (or some other suitably large unit of measurement). Dr Maria Reich, a mathematician who has devoted herself to studying the Nazca desert geometry, suggests that the figures were worked out on scale plans and then transferred to the ground, using stone markers and rope to make measurements and to reproduce the right proportions. In this manner, the same patterns as appeared on their textiles could be accurately reproduced on a giant scale. However, the instruments that were used by the Indians to check their progress have long since been lost and forgotten. We will never know for sure

how the work was undertaken.

One intriguing theory suggests that the ancient Nazca might have had the same view of the shapes as modern airmen. Some of the designs on their textiles are of shapes that look like kites and soaring balloons. Others show men or gods in the act of flying. This, together with the fact that their cloth had a very fine and tight weave, (much closer than even parachute silk), led members of the International Explorers' Society to the idea that the ancient Nazca might have had the ability to build giant observation balloons.

In 1975 they put their ideas to the test by making a simple hot-air balloon, using only cloth similar to the old Nazca textiles. Filling it with hot air from a fire, they were able to lift a small reed gondola and two pilots a considerable height above the desert floor—high enough in fact to make out the giant shapes with ease. Such a contraption would most certainly have

The Great Flood

One of the most widely occurring myths in history is that of a great flood which once inundated the entire world. This deluge was supposed to have destroyed all mankind except for a select few who survived to carry on the species. In some form or another the myth can be traced among the Indians of North and South America, the pygmies of central Africa, the Hindus of India, the Aborigines of Australia and among numerous peoples in south-east Asia.

In the Old Testament version, which comes from ancient Hebrew traditions, Noah and his family were warned by God of the coming disaster. They prepared to save themselves by building an enormous wooden ark and filling it with specimens of every kind of animal that walked, crawled and flew. Noah's contemporaries ignored all warnings of their impending doom and when the deluge came they were wiped out by waters which covered even the highest mountains. When the rains had ended and the floodwaters had subsided, the ark came to rest on a mountain top. Noah, his family and the animals emerged to repopulate an empty world.

Other flood myths bear a remarkable similarity to the Biblical one. One Hindu legend tells of the hero Manu who was rewarded for saving the life of a tiny fish found in his bathing water. The fish instructed Manu to prepare a fully-equipped ship for

helped the original engineers to oversee the production of these complicated patterns.

The one question, however, that may never be answered is the reason why the Nazca built these geometric shapes in the first place. Whether they were motivated by religious considerations or simply took the opportunity to display their skills as surveyors by creating lasting monuments is impossible to tell. Either way, their achievements make it necessary for modern archaeology to reconsider the technical skills of prehistoric societies. Though lacking the writing, tools and organizational development of such early civilizations as the Egyptians and Mesopotamians, they were nevertheless able to undertake massive engineering projects of a scale and accuracy that still impress us to this day.

Left: **One remarkable theory about the way in which the vast Nazca patterns were constructed involves manned flight. The theory claims that the ancient engineers in charge of the work used hot-air balloons as observation posts from which to direct the workers on the ground. This idea is based on figures in Nazca textiles that resemble kites and balloons. In 1975, two American investigators built a balloon on the same designs as these figures. Its flight was a success, and from their lofty vantage point they could indeed make out the giant patterns in the desert.**

Below: **This medieval woodcut from Germany shows the traditional Biblical version of the flood. After the rains had stopped, Noah's ark came to rest on a mountain peak, the first land to reappear as the waters receded.**

sailing. When the flood that was to cleanse the world came all living things were destroyed except for Manu and the seven women he had taken on board with him. The fish, which turned out to be a god in disguise, finally guided Manu to a high mountain peak where he landed and set about recreating mankind.

In the Amazonian jungles of South America there are Indian tribal myths of the great flood which describe its warning signs in great detail. The Sun and the Moon were transformed into varying shades of blue, yellow and red, while the Earth began to rumble and heave. Soon after, the entire world was plunged into darkness and a torrential downpour of rain began. As the waters rose they drowned all human beings. Only two managed to escape the deluge and it was they who began the task of repopulating the entire planet.

These, and dozens of similar accounts of a catastrophic flood that engulfed the world, form a remarkably consistent pattern. They all describe warning signs given to a few members of a society and which most other people chose to ignore. This is followed by some kind of catastrophic upheaval and great flood, from which the few chosen people escape by ship or by climbing to a very high place. In time, the flood subsides and the survivors make their way to dry land, where they proceed to found a new race of human beings who eventually re-populate the world.

These astonishingly similar accounts raise the question of whether there was ever a real catastrophic event that could have given rise to such legends or whether all the tales merely refer to smaller floods that were local events.

Within historic times we have had no experience of any geological phenomenon that could possibly qualify as a world-wide flood. By and large, geologists discount the almost universal distribution of flood legends by pointing out that inundations occur in most parts of the world.

In particular, they describe the catastrophic effects that tidal waves may have. Triggered off by earthquakes, they sweep out of the sea and advance considerable distances inland with enormous violence. Not only may there be no advance warning of tidal waves, they may also hit a number of places more or less at the same time as they radiate from the earthquake. It would not be surprising if one tidal wave episode gave rise to a host of legends among people scattered thousands of kilometres apart. But as geologists point out, even the greatest tidal wave could not reproduce the effects of a world-wide flood and is unlikely to give rise to such similar legends on all continents.

Not surprisingly, floods which derive from other causes are also far too common to become the stuff of great myths. Most societies have devised ways to escape or deal with them, and would hardly be likely to mistake a rain-swollen river for the end of the world.

If we examine the legends more closely, however, we find another intriguing element that is common to them all. This lies in their description of the flood's origins as being almost supernatural. Some speak of it having been caused by the gods, others describe a turmoil in the heavens and on Earth that preceeded the deluge. All seem to suggest a single catastrophic event within historic times.

In the end, the most likely geological

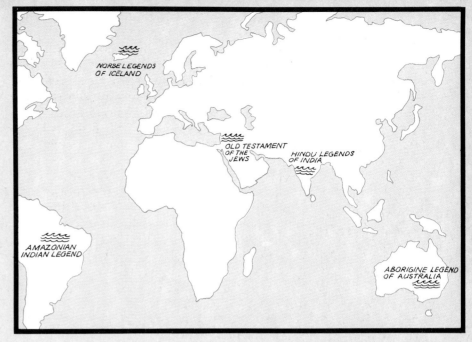

event that could have been interpreted as a universal flood, and which has occurred within recent prehistoric history (say the last 10,000 to 15,000 years), is the close of the last Ice Age. Between 10,000 and 8,000 BC the great icecaps that blanketed North America and Eurasia melted, rapidly releasing enough water to make the level of the sea rise dramatically.

Normally, this would be a gradual process with the land being slowly inundated over a period of centuries. But in recent years evidence has accumulated to show that something very near to a flood actually did occur as the ice melted. In 1975, cores drilled from the deep sea floor of the Gulf of Mexico yeilded evidence of a rapid rise in sea levels some few centuries after 10,000 BC. The waters rose as much as dozens of metres a year. The ensuing widespread inundation of low-lying regions must have trapped and wiped out countless animals and humans.

Around the same period, there is growing evidence that something strange and devastating also occurred

Above: **This map shows how widespread are the many legends of the deluge. The universality of these legends indicates that there may be considerable substance to the events they describe.**

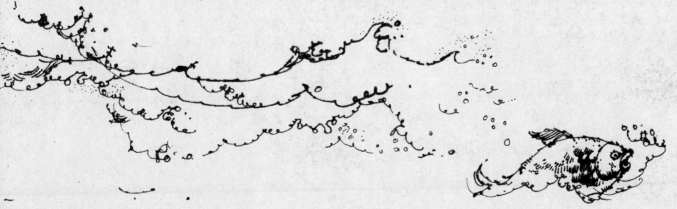

on the planet. In North America and also in Siberia there are signs in the fossil record of a sudden and extraordinarily violent extinction of millions of animals. In a very short time, such hardy creatures as mammoths, sloths, sabre-toothed cats, tapirs and countless others became extinct.

It is as if a single violent event took place which wiped out much of the animal life in the northern hemisphere and also triggered off a rapid melting of the ice, resulting in floods that affected most parts of the world. Whether the catastrophe was volcanic or extraterrestrial, (a comet strike or a near miss by another planet), is impossible to tell. Even though such an event is recent when reckoned in geological times, in terms of human societies it is incredibly ancient. The only records we have are the age-old legends of a great flood which wiped out much of the known world.

The Stone Giants

In the middle of the Pacific Ocean, thousands of kilometres from the nearest mainland in South America, lies a small patch of volcanic rock called Easter Island, (its name comes from its discovery by a Dutch sailor at Easter, 1722). It is not on any trade route, has little commercial importance and its nearest inhabited neighbour is some 1,800 km away. Yet this remote place has become the subject of worldwide attention due to the hundreds of giant stone statues that are randomly dotted about the island.

These carved giants, which weigh more than 20 tonnes and tower up to nine metres, depict only the head, or at the most the head and torso, of highly stylized human figures. Many of the heads are capped with slabs of red stone as if they were wearing hats. They stare impassively toward the horizon with their distinctively elongated faces, and look for all the world as if a race of stone giants had poked their heads out of the ground from caverns deep within the bowels of the Earth.

The history of the statues and the people who originally carved them is

obscure and their meaning is shrouded in ambiguity. The very remoteness of Easter Island ensured that its secrets remained undisturbed for many years. It was not until 1956 that any effort was made to examine the island's history in a systematic way.

In that year, the Norwegian explorer, Thor Heyerdahl, arrived along with a well-equipped archaeological

Above: **The scale of the Easter Island statues is truly gigantic. They may exceed 25 tonnes in weight and, as this horse and rider show, they tower above the surrounding landscape.**

84

expedition to study the islanders and try to learn how these relatively primitive people, who had never numbered more than a few thousand, had been able to cut and carve so many statues of such monumental proportions, and how they had managed to haul them to their resting positions all around the island.

Heyerdahl found the islanders to be friendly and gregarious. Though outwardly Catholic, they still retained many of their old superstitions and traditions, a great stroke of luck as far as the expedition was concerned. They had a deep-rooted belief that every person had an invisible guardian spirit, or *aku-aku*, whose magical powers served to protect him and grant him knowledge and power among his fellows. Heyerdahl used these beliefs to his own advantage to gain the confidence of the Easter Islanders and

simple rafts. However, this did not explain satisfactorily the presence among the small dark-skinned majority of a few who were almost white in their complexion and who had flaming red hair.

The islanders described their ancestors as being two different peoples; the long-ears and the short-ears. The long-ears were the original rulers of the island, and it was they who carved the statues that honoured their dead kings. It was the long-ear ruling class who possessed the white complexion and the glossy red hair that the expedition noted among the islanders. The traits bore a remarkable similarity to the legends of the South American Indians which described tall, bearded, red-haired gods who arrived out of the east. Yet the legends provide us with no explanation of whom the long-ears were or why they were moved to begin

induce them to speak about their past.

Heyerdahl surmised that the islanders were of Polynesian origin, although there is no remembrance in their legends of having lived elsewhere, and that they had arrived from the west in canoes or on rafts. He also suspected that there may have been contact with South American Indians who came to the island aboard

erecting giant stone statues. As further evidence of their mysterious origins, blood samples of the fair-skinned Easter Islanders showed them to have no similarity whatsoever with Polynesian or American Indian blood groups. It is as if the long-ears had landed at Easter Island from another part of the world altogether.

At some point in the past, according

to the islanders, the short-ears had arrived. At first they had been ruled by the long-ears. Later they rebelled and during the bloody civil war that followed many of the original stone statues were overturned. Since then, the production of stone statues had ceased, although the knowledge of how to carve them had not vanished.

The statues were sculpted from great blocks of volcanic rock, hewed from quarries with crude hand tools. They were then trundled into position on wooden sleds. The red stone 'hats' that decorate many of the statues were described as top-knots, and seemed to be an obvious reference to the red hair the long-ear ruling class possessed.

However, despite all Heyerdahl's careful research, his findings were rudely dismissed 13 years later by Erich von Däniken who argued that they did not explain convincingly how simple natives could have carved and raised megaliths of such size. His own explanation of the statues was that a small band of extraterrestrial beings became stranded on Easter Island after some sort of mechanical trouble with their spacecraft. To wile away the

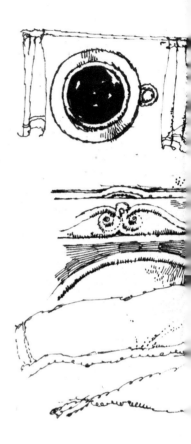

time until their rescue, and to leave the local population with mementos of their stay, they took to carving hundreds of vast figures from the volcanic stone they found here. The unfinished ones were left behind when the spacemen were rescued and, since their completion was beyond the ability of the islanders, they remained in that state to this day.

The two most damaging objections to this bizarre theory were provided by Heyerdahl already, back in 1956. In one instance, the Norwegian explorer was shown by the mayor of the island and a dozen others how to raise a fallen 25-tonne statue, using only wooden poles and stones. In another display of their skills, a handful of islanders carved the rough outlines of a new statue in three days, using only traditional stone tools and water with which to soften the rock.

While Heyerdahl was able to show that it was the islanders themselves who had carved the statues, he was unable to resolve the question of who the original Easter Islanders were and where they came from. The stone giants still keep their secret.

The Haunted Sea

The sea is a potentially violent and forbidding place. Over the centuries it has claimed the lives of thousands of people, often under mysterious circumstances. Such a setting is an ideal one to encourage legends of haunted ships, deep-sea monsters and strange, unexplainable phenomena. There are even regions of the ocean where events so bizarre occur that it is claimed the laws of time and space do not apply.

The Mary Celeste

On December 5, 1872, Captain David Moorhouse of the brigantine *Dei Gratia,* while en route from New York to Gibraltar, sighted the 280 tonne brigantine *Mary Celeste* wallowing eccentrically at sea, her sails still set, some way between the Azores and the coast of Portugal. He took a launch to investigate her peculiar behaviour and, to his astonishment, found the ship to be completely deserted.

The *Mary Celeste* was in good condition, however. Everything on board was in its place and all personal effects had been left behind as if the crew had abandoned ship in a hurry. There

were toys on the captain's bed where his two-year-old child had been playing. The crew had left their coats and oilskins and even their pouches of tobacco. There was a good amount of drinking water on board and enough food in the ship's stores to last half a year. The cargo of 1,700 barrels of commercial alcohol was untouched. Although some water had made its way into the hold, it was not nearly enough to make the ship unseaworthy. In any case, the pumps still worked well. In spite of the signs that the ship had been in a storm—the deck cabins were battened down with planks and the compass was smashed—she had not been hurt in any grave way.

Captain Moorhouse placed a skeleton crew aboard the *Mary Celeste* and she sailed on to Gibraltar. There a court of inquiry examined the mystery of the abandoned ship but without being able to solve the riddle of what had happened. In the end, the salvage money was awarded to the crew of the *Dei Gratia*.

To this day, the fate of the *Mary Celeste* remains one of the most famous maritime mysteries of all time. Although it appears she had been abandoned, there was not the slightest evidence of what had caused the crew to leave the ship. Even the log remained undisturbed, and the last entry, which was made 11 days before she was found empty and drifting, contained nothing unusual.

The only facts to strike a bizarre note were that the forward hatch was found open and on either side of the bow above the waterline two grooves, some two metres long, had been made. One lifeboat had been launched and the ship's navigation instruments and papers were missing. There was also a mark on the ship's rail as if from an axe and some brownish stains, that turned out not be be blood, on the captain's sword.

The investigating naval court struggled vainly to get to the bottom of the mystery. It considered the possibility that a sudden crisis had overwhelmed the crew's ability to handle the ship, that piracy or some other form of violent attack had occurred and even that an outbreak of illness or madness had seized the crew. Other, more farfetched explanations, such as an attack by a sea monster, were dismissed due to the complete lack of evidence.

Above: **When sailors from a passing ship boarded the *Mary Celeste* they found her to be virtually undisturbed. There was no indication that the crew had panicked and fled the ship or that some terrible catastrophe had overtaken her. Indeed, in the captain's cabin there were still toys scattered on the bed where his young child had been happily playing.**

A suggestion that appeared highly likely at the time, and which still does, is that the ship was abandoned in panic in the belief that she was imperilled and somehow on the verge of sinking. For example, the fear that the cargo of 1,700 alcohol barrels was about to explode could have led the captain, his wife and baby and all eight crew to take to the lifeboat while keeping a towline to the *Mary Celeste*. A sudden squall might have snapped the line and capsized the lifeboat, killing all on board.

Equally, the crew might have abandoned ship in the belief she was about to run aground against rocks in the Azores or perhaps they tried to investigate an uncharted island on which they became stranded when the *Mary Celeste* drifted away.

Another line of thought is that the ship was the scene of some terrible act of violence. There were suggestions that the crew tried to drink the alcohol in the cargo hold and then went beserk in their drunken rage and killed everyone. Although one of the casks in the hold had been damaged, anyone trying to consume commercial alcohol would have made a better job of poisoning himself than getting drunk. In any case, there were no signs of a violent struggle on board the ship. The possibility that the captain and crew decided to abandon the ship when they found, or pirated, another vessel with a more valuable cargo might account for the good condition in which they left the *Mary Celeste,* but it is not supported by any record of another ship being hijacked in the same part of the Atlantic in 1872.

At the formal inquiry it was also suggested that the *Mary Celeste* might have been attacked by the crew of the *Dei Gratia* who flung everybody into the sea. Although some members of the court of inquiry favoured this theory, it does not take into account the fact that the two captains were good friends. In any case, the commercial value of the *Mary Celeste*'s cargo was not especially high.

A final attempt at plausible explanation lies in the theory that some form of poisoned food or outbreak of a strange and terrible illness drove the crew, in a mad frenzy, to throw themselves overboard.

Because none of the reasonable

explanations of the mysterious fate of the *Mary Celeste* seemed to provide the answer, the door was flung open for all kinds of far-fetched theories. It has been suggested that the crew were kidnapped by spacemen, sailing as they did through the Bermuda Triangle. Another idea is that the captain, who was a deeply religious man, went into a zealous fury, during which he slaughtered the entire crew as a sacrifice to the Lord, before plunging into the sea himself. Equally far-fetched is the notion that an underwater explosion wreathed the ship in poisonous gases which drove the crew over the side in a frantic effort to escape.

Even now, more than a century after this strange episode, there has been no answer to the mystery that hangs around the crew of the *Mary Celeste*. The only thing one can say with any

Above: **This photograph of Captain Briggs as a young man yields no clues as to the nature of the misfortune that overtook him and his ship. He was known to be a very religious man and an experienced sailor, and as a part owner of the ship there is no reason why he should have wanted to abandon her in a seaworthy state in mid-Atlantic.**

certainty is that she was a jinxed ship. Six of her many captains died while on duty. The ship continued to sail the Atlantic until 1885 when, as part of an insurance swindle, she was run on to a reef near Port au Prince in Haiti and then set on fire. However, even this ignominious venture proved unsuccessful, for the swindle was discovered and it brought about the bankruptcy of all involved in the deception.

The Bermuda Triangle

Every year dozens of craft are lost at sea. In the coastal waters of the United States alone, the toll of disappearing ships hovers around 25 a year. Some are the victims of navigational error or of mechanical failure. Others are destroyed by turbulent weather conditions. But once in a while a ship or plane vanishes in mysterious circumstances, often without leaving a trace of wreckage. It is these sorts of inexplicable events that stir our imagination and become the material from which legends are born.

Researchers into bizarre and incredible phenomena have identified a number of places in the world where a disturbing number of mysterious events have occurred. They refer to these regions as 'flap' zones, for it is as if a flap, or tear, in the normal fabric of the universe occurs here from time to time, causing the ordinary laws of time and space to be flouted. In flap zones, strange electrical storms are encountered while compasses whirl crazily as if trapped in swirling magnetic fields. Here too, UFOs are sighted, while physical objects vanish and time seems to stand still.

The most famous flap zone of them all is the Bermuda Triangle. Vincent Gaddis, the writer who first coined the name in 1964, described the region as a place that has far more than its statistically fair share of mysterious events. The Bermuda Triangle describes a vast area of the Atlantic Ocean whose corners are in Bermuda, Puerto Rico and the southern tip of Florida. However, some people use the name much more loosely to mean the region of ocean that extends east to the Azores and south as far as Trinidad.

Ever since the 16th century the Bermuda Triangle has been a place of heavy traffic. It lay across the main routes of the Spanish bullion fleets, of slave traders and of the rum merchants who roamed the Caribbean. Today, the US Coast Guard estimates that about 150,000 ships of all descriptions pass through the region every year as well as thousands of commercial and private planes. Although one would expect a fair share of accidents amid such a volume of traffic, the outstanding thing about the Bermuda Triangle is that so many of the accidents defy logical explanation.

One especially baffling incident involved the navy supply ship *USS Cyclops* which, in March 1918, disappeared with 300 people on board while en route from Barbados to Baltimore. The *Cyclops* was last seen steaming out of Barbados harbour heading south —the opposite direction from Baltimore—and was never heard of again. A week and a half later she was declared overdue after failing to show up at her destination.

A major search was launched, for the navy refused to believe that a ship her size and equipped with radio could sink without leaving any traces, or at

Below: **The Bermuda Triangle is a notional region of the Atlantic Ocean covering hundreds of thousands of hectares. The points of the mysterious triangle rest on Bermuda, Florida and Puerto Rico. This region has become legendary in recent years for the exceptional number of curious incidents that have been recorded here affecting shipping and aircraft.**

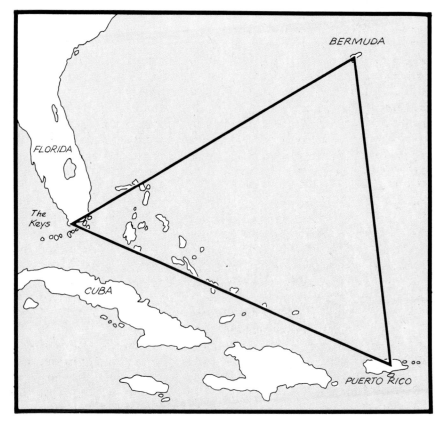

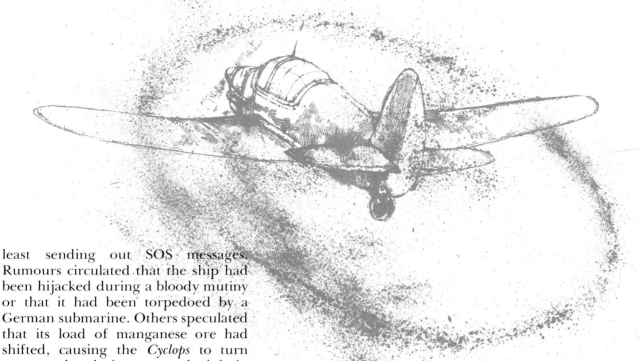

least sending out SOS messages. Rumours circulated that the ship had been hijacked during a bloody mutiny or that it had been torpedoed by a German submarine. Others speculated that its load of manganese ore had shifted, causing the *Cyclops* to turn over or break in two and sink in seconds. But a thorough investigation turned up no evidence of enemy activity in that part of the ocean, nor was there any indication that bad weather had been the cause. The mysterious lack of survivors, debris and radio signals utterly baffled the navy. Their ship seemed to have been swallowed up by the sea without a trace.

Other cases of lost craft in the Bermuda Triangle are made even more mysterious by the fact that everything up to the moment of disappearance appears to be normal. In January 1948, the airliner *Star Tiger* signalled ground control, shortly before arriving in Bermuda, to say that it was on schedule to land. Then the plane, and all 31 passengers on board, vanished forever. No SOS was ever broadcast and no wreckage was ever found. Almost precisely a year later its sister plane, the *Star Ariel,* was lost during a flight from Bermuda to Jamaica. Like the *Star Tiger,* it too radioed shortly before vanishing to say that the weather was good and that the flight was proceeding as normal. Again, no trace of the plane was ever found.

The fame of the Bermuda Triangle does not rest solely on episodes of vanishing ships and planes, or even on the bizarre instances in which a vessel has been found intact but with the entire crew missing. The area has also accounted for a stream of reports describing unexplainable navigation difficulties. The circumstances of these reports may not have been fatal, but they serve to reinforce the legend of the region.

Navigators on planes and ships have frequently found that their instruments began to behave strangely for no apparent reason. In December 1975, for example, a US Coast Guard cutter lost all power to its radio and navigation gear while at sea. Simultaneously, crew members spotted mysterious greenish lights, rather like flares, dropping from the sky, although there is no indication that a ship in distress was anywhere nearby at the time. The cutter's instruments were checked, but no physical cause of the breakdown could be discovered.

Yet more bizarre is the case of a small aircraft whose pilot decided to inspect an enormous ring-shaped cloud as he flew over the Bahamas in December 1970. Entering the cloud for a brief look, he found that his navigation equipment began to malfunction as his compass swung wildly. Then his radio and electronic instruments stopped working. When he finally landed he found that he had

Above: **In December 1970, the pilot of a light aircraft flying in the region of the Bermuda Triangle departed from his course to look at a strange ring-like cloud. Once inside it, his electronic and navigation equipment either ceased working or else ran wild. Upon landing, he found that time had been affected, too. He had mysteriously and inexplicably lost 30 minutes compared to the rest of the world.**

inexplicably lost 30 minutes of flying time during the trip.

In a somewhat similar case as this, a Boeing 727 commercial jet vanished from the radar screen at Miami airport for ten minutes. Upon landing safely, the pilots were surprised to find that every watch on board the plane was ten minutes slow. This, and the radar blackout, corresponded exactly to the length of time it had taken them to fly through a cloud of light fog on the way in. In some strange way, the fog seemed to have created a time warp.

If magnetic and temporal anomalies such as these are true, then there is something very strange occurring in the Bermuda Triangle that has still to be explained. Either the Earth's magnetic properties are far from being fully understood or there are other, unknown, forces at work.

The Flying Dutchman

The Indian Ocean is the setting for one of the most famous sea legends of all time. One version of the story describes how the 16th-century Dutch master mariner, Captain Vanderdeken, attempted to sail round the treacherous coast of the Cape of Good Hope. He ran straight into a howling gale that kept forcing his ship back, yet the captain refused to give way, even though his action imperilled the ship and his passengers. Vanderdeken simply laughed off their terror and instructed his crew to put on more sail. When the crew tried to make him change course he killed one of their number and threw him overboard. Then he carried on strolling about his ship smoking, drinking and swearing, daring the heavens to stop him and boasting that he would round the Cape even if he had to sail until the Day of Judgement.

At this point, a strange shape materialized on the ship's deck and filled the rest of the vessel's company with terror. The captain boldly threatened the figure with a loaded pistol, but in trying to shoot it he managed to blow off his own hand.

As punishment for his behaviour, the deity condemned him to sail the seas forever, never again putting into port or setting his feet on dry land. Vanderdeken was transformed into a malevolent phantom and his ship became an ill-omen to all who chanced to see her.

This legend of the *Flying Dutchman*, as Vanderdeken's ghost ship became known, seems to have originated late in the 16th century. It probably stemmed from the real-life incident involving a Dutch ship which vanished without a trace during a voyage out to the East Indies. Sometime later, other merchantmen began spotting what they believed to be the missing ship as they rounded the Cape of Good Hope. Regardless of the weather, the ship always seemed to be rolling and heaving as if in a violent gale. As they neared her, they realized with astonishment that it was a phantom vessel, a ghost of the missing ship.

Although it is hard to assess the degree of truth in these sightings, they have been confirmed over the centuries by numerous other sailors. All

Below: **The *Flying Dutchman* is the name of a legendary ship whose captain, it is claimed, was condemned to sail the sea for all eternity in punishment for his blasphemous behaviour and his taunting of the Almighty. This romantic legend is not pure fiction, however. It has a basis in certain mysterious disappearances of ships in the 17th century.**

agree the *Flying Dutchman* resembles an East-Indiaman with a great carved stern and high poop.

Interestingly, there is another version of the source of the *Flying Dutchman* legend, based on the renowned sea captain, Bernard Fokke, who left Holland in 1650 bound for Indonesia. His departure was on Good Friday, an ominous sign according to many people. Fokke's ship never arrived at any of the scheduled ports of call. Yet a year later she was sighted in the Indian Ocean in particularly rough weather. The approaching ship hailed her, but was astonished to see Fokke's craft suddenly vanish. Over the years, other claims to having spotted Fokke and his ship have occurred and they have always been in the same stormy conditions.

The sea has been a source of countless myths and legends. Some are pure fabrication; others have a substantial basis in fact. However, they soon become embellished by retelling and by becoming intertwined with existing sea tales. In the case of the *Flying Dutchman,* the original facts have become greatly exaggerated and elaborated with time. The story is so tantalizing that it has cropped up in novels, in poems and even as an opera. There is also an extensive lore of *Flying Dutchman* sightings which is almost as gripping as the original story itself.

Late in the 1890s, the steamship *Hannah Regan* sank in the vicinity of Okinawa in the Pacific, after losing a propeller and being battered by stormy weather. Her crew all died in the wreck, or shortly after. But the news that she had sunk soon attracted salvage hunters, for it was known that a million dollars in gold bullion was aboard when she went down.

A tug from San Francisco steamed out to try its luck with the wreck. The captain of the tug later described the encounter. One night, after the tug's crew had been at work for some days, he went for a stroll on deck before going to sleep. Not too far from his ship, easily visible in the bright moonlight, he spotted a large shadow on the water. As he watched, it approached him and he realized that he was

Above: **Sightings of the *Flying Dutchman* are said to be premonitions of disaster. Soon after a crew member of a San Francisco tug sighted the phantom vessel in the South Pacific near Okinawa, the little tug became the focus of disaster. Several of the crew were killed in diving accidents and a lucrative salvage operation had to be abandoned.**

looking at an old 16th-century sailing ship. She seemed to be labouring in heavy seas, for she rolled and pitched, even though the sea was flat and calm that night. The strange craft seemed on the verge of colliding with the tug when the captain realized that he could see right through it, yet at the same time make out all the details of her tattered rigging, her decks, which were awash with water, and the fact that she was sinking by the stern. The ghost ship passed him by silently and then sank into the sea and vanished.

Aside from the tug's captain, nobody else had seen or heard anything. But soon after the bad luck that always followed a sighting of the *Flying Dutchman* struck. Several of the tug's divers were killed as they tried to enter the wreck on the seabed. The captain was obliged to abandon the *Hannah Regan* and her precious cargo.

In recent years, reports of the *Flying Dutchman* have continued to crop up from time to time. But by now its associations with bad luck have become so strong that it is proving hard to distinguish whether it is the sighting of this ghost that so terrifies sailors or whether their own terrors are so strong that they actually hallucinate the ship from pure fear. In either case, both as a phantom and a legend, the *Flying Dutchman* lives on and continues to roam the sea to this day.

Sea Phantoms

Tales of ghosts and the sea abound throughout the world. Despite the generally sceptical attitudes we take toward such matters nowadays, there is still a tendency for people to accept that ghosts are as much a part of the sea as the fish. Maritime phantoms may be the product of hallucinations, or tricks of light, or perhaps there is an explanation that has escaped us entirely so far. But the fact that the lore of sea ghosts is so rich indicates that this is a subject which we should not be too quick to dismiss.

Below: **The ghostly figure of a dead lieutenant was supposed to haunt the submarine UB-65 during World War 1. Apart from the ghost, the unlucky craft was plagued by a chain of mysterious accidents that continued to trouble her throughout the war.**

Wartime provides a particularly suitable climate for experiencing ghosts for it contains all the elements of exhaustion, strain, anxiety, confusion and death in which ghostly encounters flourish. One especially bizarre case revealing this concerns a German submarine during World War I.

In 1916, the submarine UB-65 lay awaiting completion in its yard in northern Germany. Already during its construction it had acquired a reputation for being an unfortunate vessel. Accidents had killed five of the men who had worked on the UB-65 and had injured several others. Unfortunately, submarine crews were highly superstitious, even more so than regular sailors, for theirs was a nerve-wracking type of craft in which to work. Such men regarded accidents as bad omens and became very reluctant to board a vessel that was supposed to be unlucky.

But the needs of war were pressing and the submarine was launched without any fuss. Then, during her sea trials, she encountered more trouble. One sailor, possibly rattled by what he knew of the UB-65's history, threw himself overboard and drowned just as the craft was preparing to make its first dive.

The captain was determined to continue the mission as if nothing had happened, but he soon realized his mistake. Try as he might, he was unable to make the craft surface at the end of its first dive. Salt water began to leak into the submarine and drip into the batteries, causing them to smoke and discharge clouds of choking fumes. Finally, the submarine broke surface with her crew half dead from suffocation and on the verge of panic.

It is hard to imagine why any sailors continued to serve aboard the vessel, for her history of bad luck was appalling. By this point, a spell of duty with her must have seemed like a sentence to sure death. Not surprisingly, the effect of this state of affairs soon became a self-fulfilling prophecy of doom.

Back in dock, the UB-65 was being loaded with torpedoes when one exploded and killed six men, including a young lieutenant. In one sense this incident was the last straw. Soon various members of the crew snapped under the strain and began seeing ghosts. Two men swore that the spectre of the dead lieutenant had made its way on board the vessel. Some weeks later, as the craft cruised on the surface to recharge its batteries, the ghostly lieutenant was spotted standing in the bows. He was spotted again as the submarine returned to base, just a few moments before an enemy air attack on the harbour resulted in the death of the captain.

In an effort to put an end to the submarine's succession of disasters, a chaplain was called in to exorcize the ghost. But a few months later two more of the crew committed suicide, and later during the same voyage the submarine was damaged severely in battle and forced to limp back to port. The last that was heard of the unlucky vessel was that late in the war it was finally abandoned by its crew and left to explode and sink at sea—ghosts and all.

The story of the UB-65 touches on many of the reasons why there is such a strong tendency to encounter ghosts at sea. The ocean can be a cruel and menacing place. People are well aware of the perils of being at sea and have heard enough about storms and wrecks to know what might await them. When this is combined with that certain degree of disorientation one feels when travelling in a ship, it is easy to see why the human mind might begin to imagine things, and ultimately to see things, too.

Added to these psychological reasons are the physical ones. Tricks of the light, fog, low clouds, waterspouts and the ever-changing motion of the waves combine to create images that play tricks on human eyes. In such circumstances it is quite easy to 'see' all manner of strange things, especially if one is inclined to be superstitious.

For example, in 1925, when two crew members aboard an oil tanker were overcome by fumes in a hold, they were buried at sea as is the custom. Some days later, other members of the crew began to report seeing the heads and faces of their two dead shipmates in the water whenever they peered over the railing of the craft. Although the captain and officers at first refused to believe their men's claims, when they finally took a look they too became convinced. The captain had the presence of mind to photograph the faces that were appearing regularly in the waves beside the tanker. But when the pictures were developed they showed nothing more than waves and spray, even though the crew members swore they had all seen faces in the sea.

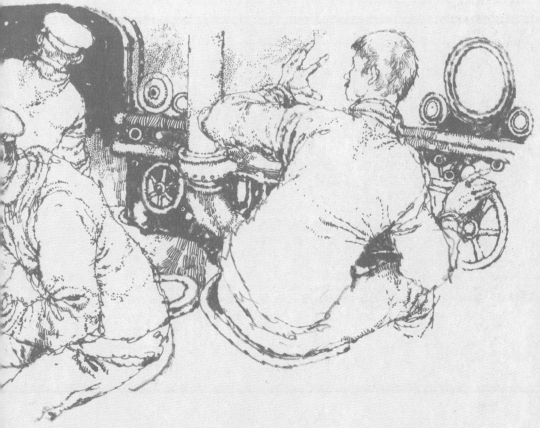

Left: **Crew members began to panic as the string of bad luck continued unabated. Some of the men swore they had seen the phantom of the dead lieutenant, who had been killed by an exploding torpedo as it was being loaded on board.**

95

SUPERNATURAL MYSTERIES

Holy Wonders

There are many religious phenomena—miracles, holy relics and the like—which have always been shrouded in mystery and which continue to baffle us to this day. In the past, people took them to be signs that supernatural beings and forces were at work in the universe. To modern, science-oriented ways of thinking, such interpretations have become increasingly difficult to accept. Yet they still defy rational explanation. For the present, we must live with these mysteries, continually seeking answers to some of the most intriguing questions of all.

What are Miracles?

In the ante rooms of the Papal apartments in the Vatican, a Dominican monk nervously awaited an audience with Pope Urban VIII. The Master General of his order stood impatiently beside him, trying at the same time to calm his excited junior. Finally, as the two were ushered in to see the Pope, the monk became so totally overwhelmed by the occasion that he floated into the air! Not until his Master General had ordered him to land was the Papal audience able to continue. Yet neither Pope nor Master General were much surprised by the event, for the monk, Joseph of Copertino, had quite a history of flight, levitating in moments of religious rapture. It was precisely this ability that most interested the two senior clerics.

The monk was eventually to become known as Saint Joseph of Copertino and his well-documented history of flying was to include dozens of reliably witnessed occasions. Indeed, his career as a friar in the 1600s was something of an embarrassment to the church authorities. He was moved from one monastery to another because of the excitement he caused. At one monastery he was even barred from singing in the choir because his ecstatic delight caused him to soar above his fellow monks—a distraction they were unable to tolerate while in full voice.

St Joseph of Copertino was by no means unique in his defiance of the laws of gravity. There are a number of other saints who were famous too for their ability to levitate, while others possessed equally miraculous powers, such as bilocation. Bilocation is the ability to be present in the flesh in more than one place at the same time. Although this is somewhat hard to substantiate, there are records of people being observed by separate witnesses in places that were days apart by the means of transport then employed.

Miracles such as flying and bilocation have long been accepted by the Catholic Church, although such amazing powers are also recognized by other religions. Buddhist monks and Hindu holy men, for instance, are famous for their ability to change shape, fly, become invisible, walk on water and through fire and generally make a nonsense of the laws of nature. But before one leaps to the conclusion that strong religious beliefs might cloud any ability to assess such phenomena critically, it is necessary to be clear about what constitutes a genuine miracle.

By the term 'miracle', we usually mean an event that is unique and which seems to defy the impossible. Miracles have no obvious natural causes—nor do they have any obviously supernatural ones. They are not a proof of God or the supernatural. Even within the Catholic Church they are only taken as the sign of a person's faith and saintliness, not as proof that he is actually a saint. After all, the Devil is credited with the same sorts of miraculous powers.

Before the Church will accept a miracle, it carefully checks and documents the circumstances that surround it. In 1738, Pope Benedict XIV established the following criteria for defining miracles that involve healing. Firstly, the cure had to be instantaneous and lasting. Secondly, the illness had to be diagnosed as incurable. Lastly, the process of the cure had to be scientifically inexplicable. Guided by these strict rules, the Church has always rejected the vast majority of the cases submitted to it for examination. At Lourdes, the world-famous centre of pilgrimage and healing in France, less than one per cent of the hundreds of cures that occur there are ever classed as true miracles.

As a result of the Church's scrutiny of the evidence, an impressive documentation of healing miracles has been built up over the years. The earliest cases come from the Bible. Christ and the prophets were famous for the miraculous cures they performed upon the sick, the dying and even the dead. The prophet Elijah is described as bringing a widow's dead son back to life, while Christ himself healed numerous lepers, cripples, blind and disease-ridden people.

Unfortunately, medicine of the time was relatively primitive in its ability to diagnose and treat illness and so it is rather difficult for science today to evaluate these miracles. This is why modern miracles are so very fascinating, for records of certain cases do exist that provide us with detailed up-to-date medical evidence, and still leave us puzzled.

In 1963, Vittorio Micheli, a young Italian, fell seriously ill with a rapidly swelling tumour in his left pelvis. It soon became a massive growth that

Above: **Saint Anthony of Padua was renowned for his faith-healing powers. Here he cures a man's leg by the mere laying of his hand on the afflicted limb.**

Left: **The French town of Lourdes is a world-famous centre of pilgrimage. Many miracle cures have occurred here which remain completely beyond explanation by present medical knowledge.**

invaded the bone and muscle and caused his left leg to shrivel and hang lifelessly at his side. The tumour was monitored by doctors as it gradually destroyed the entire hip joint. In May 1963, Micheli decided to visit Lourdes in a desperate gamble to try any cure—even a miraculous one. To universal amazement, the holy waters worked. A month later he was able to move about and soon after he shed his plaster cast and crutches and began to walk normally again.

While his case did not fall within the Church's definition of a miracle, the cure was indeed nothing short of the miraculous, especially from the viewpoint of medical science. Aside from the X-rays and biopsies that recorded his illness and cure, no other form of medical intervention was attempted —for the simple reason that there was nothing doctors could do. His case was reported by the *Journal of Orthopaedic Surgery,* and is freely admitted to have utterly baffled all the medical experts who studied it.

Miracles like this abound, and are especially common among faith-healers. Yet they seem to violate the laws of nature in every way and thus, for some people, they simply cannot exist. For such sceptics, even the most overwhelming evidence is suspect; and they have a point, for it is impossible to prove, or disprove, miracles. The difficulty in assessing them is that they cannot be repeated at will and studied in scientific surroundings. On the other hand, a less rigid attitude towards miracles accepts that they do occur, even if there is no way to explain what they are. They could be natural, but for the moment unknown, phenomena, or they could be supernatural. As yet there is no way to tell.

Holy Relics

A chair, a cloak or a staff that was once owned by a great religious teacher of the past possesses enormous value in the eyes of his followers, no matter how crude or homely the object may be. In some mysterious way, it is as if the object had become infused with the great person's virtues. His followers cherish it, not only for the links it forms between he and them, but also for the miraculous powers it is said to possess in its own right.

The relics attributed to holy figures such as Christ, Mohammed and Buddha, exert a tremendous fascination. These fragments of cloth, wood, metal and stone have become the objects of widespread cult worship. They are often claimed to have magical healing properties and the power to protect the faithful who truly believe in them.

An enormous number of relics have, at times, been claimed to belong to Christ; slivers of the cross on which he was crucified, the nails that held him to the cross, thorns from the crown placed on his head, fragments of his robe and so on.

There are far too many relics for all

Below: **This elaborate casket, or reliquary, supposedly holds a relic of St Thomas Becket. It is an object of great veneration for such relics are thought to be infused, in some way, with the holiness and powers that once belonged to the great religious teachers of the past.**

of them to be genuine. Indeed, it was once estimated that if all the pieces of the Cross claimed to be real were bona fide, they could build a battleship. And of the 32 nails that exist today which are claimed to have been used in Christ's crucifixion, no more than three or four were actually needed to do the job. But real or fake, faith in them has never wavered. All remain potently charged with the holy powers possessed by Christ himself.

In fact, so strong is the belief in holy relics that it is claimed their powers can be passed on to other objects. In the 6th century, the Empress of Constantinople wrote to Pope Gregory the Great asking that he send her the head of St Paul which the Church of Rome had in its keeping. The Pope refused. But he did send the Empress a piece of cloth that had touched the saint's head and which had thus become a holy object in its own right. The cloth had become miraculous, too. Observers claimed that when it was cut blood flowed from it.

The early Middle Ages was a time of fervent belief in religious relics. Every church or monastery worthy of its name aimed to obtain a relic of some description. There was a sound reason for this, too. Belief in the miraculous powers of religious relics was at the core of most people's faith. A priest could be sure of his authority if he could support it by claiming to own a genuine relic.

Not surprisingly, the demand for relics far outstripped the supply, and providing them led to a booming business in fakes. The faithful were sold the bones of the saints, hairs from Noah's beard, pieces of the Ark, feathers from the wings of the angel Gabriel and even more far-fetched articles. There were in circulation literally dozens of crowns of thorns, spears that had pierced Christ's side and nails that had held him to the cross.

But despite the dubious claims for their authenticity, holy relics continue to survive as objects of veneration to this day. They seem to satisfy a deep need that never questions their validity. In addition, many have proved themselves in a way that cannot be denied. There are many examples of people who were healed after visiting and worshipping a sacred relic. While

it is difficult to prove that the relics themselves brought about the cure, the mechanics of faith-healing have never been satisfactorily explained in medical terms. Still we remain puzzled—although the results are there for all to see. We may doubt a relic's authenticity, but we cannot easily dismiss the miraculous powers claimed for it.

Above: **This elaborate casket of the 13th century once stored a religious relic, believed to be linked with the life of Christ. In the Middle Ages, dozens of similar reliquaries were scattered across Europe in churches and monasteries.**

The Turin Shroud

Holy relics are revered because in some way they represent the power and glory of great religious figures. But in a few instances relics are outstanding in their own right because of the questions posed by their very nature. One such relic is the Holy Shroud of Turin.

The shroud, it is claimed, is the cloth in which the body of Christ was wrapped after he had been crucified by the Romans nearly 2,000 years ago. It is a slim, rectangular sheet, 4.5 metres long and 1.1 metres wide, of a delicate linen twill woven in a herringbone pattern. Along both sides of its entire length are a row of scorch marks and burns—the result of a fire that nearly consumed it in 1532. In the middle of the shroud are a number of faint 'stains' that resolve into the light sepia image of a human figure when examined closely. They show a man lying with his arms crossed over his abdomen. The image is flecked with spots and reddish stains. These marks correspond well with those that a crucifixion would have made and also

Right: **This photographic negative of one section of the Turin Shroud shows the image of a long-haired and bearded man. The rest of the shroud is marked with stains that indicate he was wounded by crucifixion. By implication, this is the face of Christ himself. The heated argument that still rages as to whether or not the image is real remains unresolved, despite a recent detailed scientific examination of the shroud.**

with the wounds that Christ is supposed to have sustained in the last stages of his life.

The most astounding feature of the entire image, however, is that it is a negative—exactly the same image would have been formed if a camera had taken a picture of the original figure. The parts of the body that would have been darkened shadows in real life (the sockets of the eyes, the gaps between the fingers) show up on the shroud as light areas, whereas the light parts of the original body do not show up at all. A positive image of the figure was seen for the first time in 1898 by the photographer Secondo Pia who took the first photographs of the shroud. As he took his glass-plate negative from the developing bath he was amazed to find that he was not looking at the usual photographic negative, but at a clear *positive* likeness. The image was startlingly life-like, a portrait filled with expression and character.

The shroud we know today first appears in history in a small French village called Lirey, late in the 1300s. At the time it belonged to a family of minor nobility named de Charny. We are not sure how they acquired the shroud, but in all possibility it fell into their hands during the Crusades.

An electron microscope test of the shroud revealed pollen grains native to the uplands of Turkey and Lebanon. This evidence that at some point in its life the shroud had been in the Middle East is further supported by a crusader's account of 1204, telling of a holy shroud in Constantinople with the face of Christ imprinted on it. Whether or not this was the Turin shroud is impossible to prove as it vanished soon afterwards.

The great problem in tracing the origins of the shroud is that at various times there have been 43 different contenders to the same title. All, save for the one in Turin, have since disappeared or been destroyed, but it has been impossible so far to determine which, if any, was the one we know today.

In 1578, the Duke of Savoy acquired the shroud from the de Charny family and it was moved to Turin. Today it is kept in Turin Cathedral where it is carefully stored in private, being revealed only occasionally to the public.

During the 20th century, the shroud's importance as a venerated object has been totally overshadowed by the mystery its origin and authenticity poses. This transformation from religious relic to historical curiosity is a direct result of the photographs taken by Secondo Pia, and the disturbingly well-defined portrait they revealed.

The fact that the image is a negative raises a mind-boggling question, for it virtually rules out the possibility that the image is man-made. It is unlikely that any forger in the Middle Ages would have had the technical ability or knowledge to produce a negative image. In any case, a material as light and flimsy as the shroud is extraordinarily difficult to paint on; it would take the skills of a master-forger to do so, and the paint would probably have flaked off again as soon as the cloth was folded.

Further studies of the shroud in 1973 also revealed that the reddish 'bloodstain' marks did not contain any haemoglobin. They also showed that no pigment had seeped into the spaces between the fibres, which is what would have been expected if the image had been made of paint, blood or any other staining liquid.

On the positive side, scientists trying to determine whether the figure could be that of Christ have come up with findings that are highly significant. The 'bloodstain' marks do indeed correspond with the kind of injuries a crucifixion would cause. The nail wounds are not in the hands, as icons and paintings of the Middle Ages generally show, but in the wrists. This was where the Romans actually drove them, since a nail through the palms would never have held a body to a cross. The Romans also used whips into which twin pellets of metal were fastened. The dumb-bell shaped marks on the body of the image correspond to the shape of the lash marks Christ would have received when he was scourged.

As near as can be determined, the figure on the shroud seems to have died in a manner identical with Christ as reported in the scriptures. The signs all point to a crucifixion preceded by a scourging.

In 1978, a major study of the shroud was conducted. The image was scanned to find out what chemicals made up the stains, infra-red and ultra-violet photographs were taken, an X-ray test was carried out and countless other pictures were taken for computer analysis. The results of these tests have been recently revealed —but in the final reckoning they only serve to deepen the mystery. They seem to rule out the possibility that the shroud was faked, while attesting to its great age. What they do not answer is how the image was formed or of whom it is. The Holy Shroud of Turin, unfortunately, still guards its secrets— unless, of course, we return to accepting it as a miraculous, but utterly baffling, religious relic.

Wounds of Christ

As the choir of monks, having celebrated the Feast of the Stigmata of St Francis, filed out of the church, one of their number stayed behind, quite lost in the ecstasy of his devotions. Suddenly an agonizing sensation filled his body and caused him to scream with pain. His brother friars rushed to his side only to find that he had collapsed on the stone floor and was now lying unconscious in a pool of blood. On his hands, feet and along his left side five terrible wounds had appeared.

Padre Pio Forgione was a Capuchin friar who, for many years, lived a secluded life in an Italian monastery. He was to become one of the most famous and celebrated stigmatics in history. His marks, or wounds of Christ as they are sometimes known, first appeared in 1918 as World War I drew to a close. For the next 50 years, until his death in 1968, Padre Pio was to bear his great pain with extraordinary resignation and courage.

Padre Pio had always been an exceptionally devout monk, even to the point of undermining his health with long fasts and other rigorous devotions. In his youth he experienced many visions and related psychic

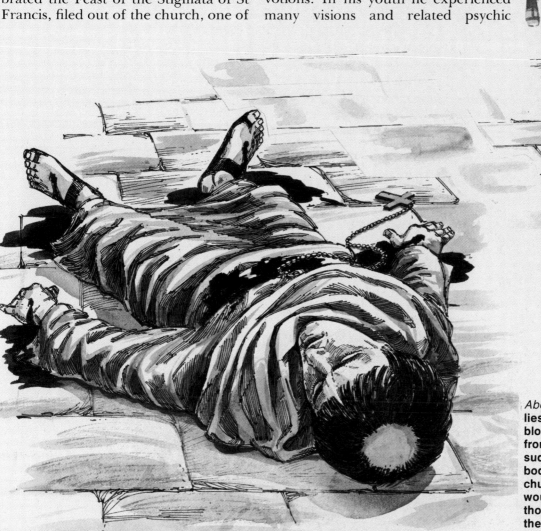

Above: **Padre Pio Forgione lies in a pool of his own blood that began seeping from the wounds which suddenly appeared on his body while he was leaving church one day. The wounds corresponded with those inflicted on Christ at the time of his crucifixion.**

phenomena. However, this hardly seems much of a clue to the origins of his holy wounds.

The word 'stigmata' refers to the wounds suffered by Christ during the period of his arrest, trial and execution. It also has a wider meaning that describes the marks or wounds that exceptionally devout believers may sometimes bear on their bodies. These wounds resemble those that Christ is said to have received, and also occur on the same parts of the body. On Padre Pio, the lesions appeared. on both hands and feet and the wounds were closely examined by doctors and by the friar's religious superiors. Those in his hands were described as being round holes that all but pierced the flesh from the palms through to the backs. One observer claimed that he could almost push his finger completely through the wound. In addition, there was a massive fissure on Padre Pio's left side which seemed as if he had been pierced by a spear. It was covered by a thick scab, but nevertheless bled regularly and heavily, reportedly yielding as much as a cupful of blood and liquid a day.

The notion that wounds can appear spontaneously on a human body without being the result of any outside agency seems quite incredible. That these wounds should appear in exactly the same place in different people, and that they should correspond with those of Christ in the scriptures sounds

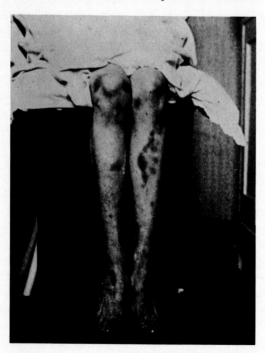

extremely improbable. It is as if someone were making a mockery of the laws of nature.

The Catholic Church, however, officially accepts stigmata, although it does so with the greatest suspicion and not without lengthy investigation. It maintains that they are a 'gift' from the supernatural that allows a person to identify directly, and in the most minute detail, with the sufferings of Christ. The wounds are not just surface marks on the body. They are the outward sign of a person whose spirit has achieved an extraordinary degree of faith and piety and who is in a state of great grace.

Were stigmata to appear in someone who showed no such signs of holiness, the Church would dismiss them and claim they were the marks of the Devil, designed to mislead the faithful. This definition would also rule out stigmata that arise from physical illnesses or any kind of psychological disturbance.

But medical science had found it hard to accept the Church's teachings on the subject without asking additional questions. Fortunately, studies of this phenomenon have yielded a wealth of detail—even if it has been very difficult to interpret.

Medical examinations of stigmata have shown that the blood which flows from them is remarkably clean and fresh. It contains no signs of disease. Nor do the wounds, which may be so severe that they pierce through the hands and feet completely, show the

Left: **The stigmatic, Georges Marasco, displays the nail marks that appeared on his feet during Easter in 1923. Such marks are said to correspond to the wounds inflicted on Christ during his torture and execution.**

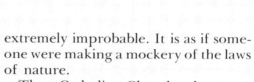

signs of inflammation that one would normally expect. They do not seem to heal in the normal way. Some close up and vanish practically overnight, while others remain raw and open for months, or even years. Still others disappear and reappear at regular intervals. In particular, there is a rhythm that seems to reach its greatest intensity during the period of Lent, then abates for the rest of the year.

Over 300 well-documented cases of stigmatism have been studied, and of these a curiously high proportion are female, although it is hard to tell why this should be so. Stigmata seem to coincide with various trance-like states of consciousness, during which the victims may have detailed visions of the wounds actually being inflicted. The visions may be of Christ himself. As his body is beaten and punctured, so their own bodies are wounded, too. On other occasions, it may take weeks before the marks become apparent.

One explanation of stigmatization is that it may correspond, in some way, to the medical condition of hysteria. Here, a person is torn by a conflict between the conscious and unconscious self from which there is no immediate form of release. There are cases where this conflict has been so intense that it has led to people going 'spontaneously' blind or becoming paralysed. Perhaps stigmata are a particular variation of this condition—one which has strong religious overtones. At best, however, this is only a very partial explanation of a religious mystery that all but defies belief.

Left: **Teresa Neumann was an extraordinary stigmatic who would begin to bleed profusely from her wounds every Friday. Yet by Sunday she had fully recovered and the marks had vanished entirely. The wounds occurred in exactly the same place as those which had afflicted St Francis.**

Below: **The spectre of a woman that entered the bedroom of a young girl and gripped her hand tightly turned out to be that of a former servant who had been seduced and spurned in the same house. She eventually killed herself and her ghost continued to haunt the place for many years after.**

The Spirit World

The idea of life after death is nowhere more strongly reinforced than by accounts of wandering ghosts and phantoms that survive long after the human beings from which they originate have died. These spirits, and others such as poltergeists and demons, often seem to be linked with violence and great emotional turmoil.

Ghosts

October evenings at Alderton Hall in England, the home of the television actor Jack Watling, can be chilling. It was here, some years ago, that his daughter Debbie awoke to find her hand being gripped by a sad-faced spectre, a young woman about 20 years old. Debbie tried to snatch her hand away, but the ghost clung to it tightly a

moment longer. Then it turned, glided into the wall and vanished.

Further enquiries established that in the 1600s a young servant girl had been seduced in the same room by the squire who then owned the house. Later, he spurned her and, in despair, she committed suicide in a nearby forest pool. To this day, her ghost returns from time to time to haunt the scene of her betrayal.

One of mankind's most deeply entrenched beliefs is that human beings can take the form of intangible spirits, or ghosts. By ghosts, we usually mean the apparitions of dead people, although there are also many accounts of living people appearing as spectres. In addition, not all ghosts are visible; some can only be heard.

Most authorities agree that there are four main groups of haunting spirits. Those known as 'crisis apparitions' are the phantoms of the living. They are

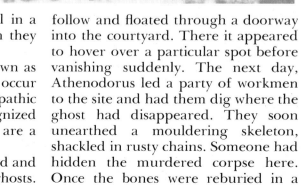

seen at times of great upheaval in a person's life, for instance, when they are seriously ill.

There is a second group known as 'communicating' ghosts. These occur when individuals project a telepathic vision of themselves that is recognized by someone else. These ghosts are a kind of psychic double.

Spirits of the dead are the third and most widely known group of ghosts. Some are passive. They linger mournfully around the site of their former lives, often as penance for some crime they committed when alive. Others are

more active; they visit the living, trying to inform heirs or relatives about hidden money and wills or of some wrong-doing that must be set right.

Spectres of murdered people are often active ghosts. They guard the buried body and act restlessly whenever a living person appears, as though trying to draw attention to the crime.

The earliest example of psychic research on record involves one such case. It took place over 2,000 years ago in ancient Greece. Athenodorus, an Athenian philosopher who had a great interest in the spirit world, volunteered to spend a night in a house that was said to be haunted in order to resolve the mysterious goings on there. During the night he heard the clanking and rattling of chains, and soon beheld an emaciated old man who seemed to appear from nowhere. The spectre beckoned Athenodorus to

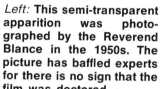

Left: **This semi-transparent apparition was photographed by the Reverend Blance in the 1950s. The picture has baffled experts for there is no sign that the film was doctored.**

follow and floated through a doorway into the courtyard. There it appeared to hover over a particular spot before vanishing suddenly. The next day, Athenodorus led a party of workmen to the site and had them dig where the ghost had disappeared. They soon unearthed a mouldering skeleton, shackled in rusty chains. Someone had hidden the murdered corpse here. Once the bones were reburied in a cemetery, the hauntings ceased.

The fourth, and largest, group of ghosts consists of suicides who have been denied a burial in consecrated ground and whose spirits are therefore unable to rest. They continue to haunt the scene of their death until released from bondage by the prayers of an exorcist.

According to researchers into psychic events, ghosts have regular patterns to their activity, and may follow them slavishly for tens or even hundreds of years. They seem to take the same route or always occupy the same site in a house. This may explain their ability to pass through solid objects. If a former route is blocked over the years, or a doorway or hall moved, the ghosts will not register the change. They will continue on their original route year after year.

There are many examples of hauntings that have continued for a long time. The ghost of the English queen, Anne Boleyn, who was put to death by

her husband Henry VIII, continues to haunt to this day. A similar sort of case is linked with the White House. Various presidents have sensed the presence of the murdered president Abraham Lincoln. Harry Truman was awakened one night about a year after his inauguration by two raps on his bedroom door. He heard mysterious footsteps in the corridor, which on investigation proved to have no known human source. The corridor had been empty of all living persons. Years earlier, at the beginning of the century, President Theodore Roosevelt claimed to have seen Lincoln's ghost shamble past with its deeply furrowed face saddened and downcast.

Most ghostly hauntings occur indoors, usually in people's homes. It is not an unknown experience for sleepers to be woken up by a spectre standing at the foot of their beds. But such ghosts are not always alarming. They may be comforting figures known as guardian spirits. They most often materialize when the sleeper is in a state of great anxiety or is very ill.

There are a number of other kinds of ghosts as well, including some very unpleasant kinds that are associated with death. One case, noted in Dr J. C. Barker's book *Scared to Death,* was of a Gurkha soldier fighting in Malaya in World War II who collapsed in terror after seeing his mother's ghost. He claimed that the ghost's appearance was an omen of his own death. Shortly after, he was found dead in his bed.

Above: **A phantom priest, that was invisible to the naked eye at the time this picture was taken in Arundel Church in Sussex, England, showed up on the developed print much to the photographer's surprise. Again, there was no sign to show that the film had been tampered with at the time of developing. Yet there is no natural explanation of the ghostly figure that can be seen here.**

Above left: **The violent manner in which Anne Boleyn was put to death led to a legend arising that her ghost still roams the Tower of London. According to one popular version, the phantom strolls the Tower with its head tucked underneath its arm.**

Left: **The Athenian philosopher Athenodorus followed a noisy old phantom in chains to its resting place in the courtyard of the house which it was haunting. Digging there, he found the grave of a person who had been murdered.**

Equally unpleasant is the Doppelgänger, a pyschic double of a living person. When one's Doppelgänger is seen, it is a sign that one is very near to death.

There can be no doubt that belief in ghosts stems from the ancient idea that every person has a soul that continues to exist after the body has died. In certain circumstances, usually when death has been violent or tragic, the soul becomes earthbound. It is unable to leave this world for the next.

Many ghost stories are probably folklore, or tall tales which are passed on from one individual to the next. Typical examples are the phantom coaches of the British countryside, and the ghostly hitch-hikers who thumb lifts from passing cars outside American cemeteries, then vanish into thin air once they are aboard.

Of the many attempts to explain ghosts logically, the idea that they are hallucinatory has many supporters. Certain sorts of illness are associated with visions, and dying persons are known to conduct conversations with long-dead relatives who are invisible to all but themselves.

A further explanation, which involves a range of telepathic forces, is that individuals who have met their death in tragic circumstances may imprint their emotions upon the place where they died. Later, people who are very sensitive may detect these psychic forces, which become transformed in their minds to visual images. This may explain why it is so rare for two people to see a ghost at the same time and in the same place.

But do ghosts really exist? The proof seems unlikely to be found in the near future, despite the sophisticated scientific methods that are being used by modern ghost-hunters.

Poltergeists

In 1958, the house of a family living on Long Island, near New York City, became the focal point for a series of extremely disturbing events which continued day after day. Bottles were observed floating around the bath-

room, while boxes of food and detergents leaped up and down on the kitchen shelves. Equally strangely, a number of religious objects, including a crucifix, became damaged as if some unseen power had attacked them. The evil spirits which were believed to be responsible for the disturbances failed to respond to the prayers of the exorcists who were called upon to help. The mystery also eluded an investigation carried out by the local police. Eventually, after several weeks, the uproar diminished and finally ceased. It was never repeated.

It should be noted that in the family where this occurred were a brother and sister both around the age of puberty. As we shall see, this is a common feature in many kinds of poltergeist phenomena.

Top: **Elenore Zëgun, a young Rumanian girl, was the focus of violent poltergeist activity in 1926. The attacks left her body scarred with mysterious tooth and claw marks.**

Above: **In this case of poltergeist activity, the famous psychic researcher Harry Price fastened the windows with tape to rule out any chance of trickery.**

The term 'poltergeist' (from the German 'polter' meaning crash or disturbance and 'geist' meaning spirit) became familiar to the public in 1926, following an investigation by the well-known British psychic researcher Harry Price and others into the strange case of Elenore Zëgun. Elenore was a young Rumanian girl who was said to have been attacked by a vampire-like devil. She was staying with her grandparents in their cottage near the Rumanian village of Talpa at the time when objects began to move of their own accord. Windows were smashed and mysterious tooth and claw marks appeared on her body. Exorcism was attempted to relieve her distress, but it proved a failure. The attacks continued until 1928, when Elenore reached puberty. Then they suddenly ceased.

Similar baffling phenomena have been reported all over the world. A thorough study of poltergeist activities was made by two leading psychic researchers, Hereward Carrington and Nandor Fodor, in their book *The Story of the Poltergeist Down the Centuries*. The book examines case after case over the past two thousand years, of which the following are typical examples. In AD 355, stones were hurled about inside a house in the Rhineland region of the Roman Empire. Occupants of the place were flung out of bed by some unknown force. At Glenluce, Scotland, some 1,300 years later, an invisible presence in a house tore the occupants' clothes to shreds. In 1944, lumps of coal in a Canadian school began to jump and dance about. Two years later, there were reports from Houston, Texas, that a piano had begun to play itself in the home of one terrified family.

In summing up their research, Carrington and Fodor noted that 330 of the cases they examined could not be associated with fraud in any way. The evidence for the genuineness of these cases was often 'striking', they claimed.

The presence of an hysterical person in a house also seems to stimulate poltergeist activity. In the 1840s, Mary Jobson of Sunderland, England, who had become deaf, dumb and blind as the result of an hysterical seizure, became the victim of a particularly spiteful attack. Floods of hot water

would pour on to her from the ceilings of her home and, as is common with poltergeists, mysterious knockings were also heard.

Poltergeist activity occurs with such frequency that serious attempts have been made to find a rational explana-

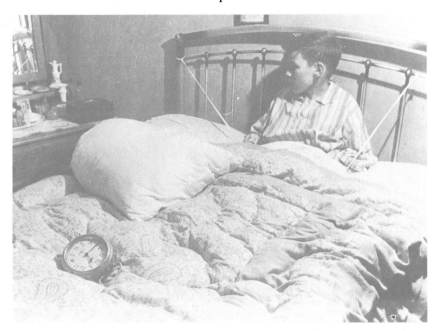

tion for the phenomenon. According to one theory, poltergeist behaviour is a form of telekinesis (the movement of objects without known physical cause). Telekinesis is believed to result from psychic energy emanating from the human body. Spiritualists, however, take the view that a person who becomes the focus of poltergeist activity is acting unconsciously as a medium for a disembodied spirit that has been roused into violent activity. This was thought to be the reason behind the bizarre series of events that took place at John Bell's farm in Tennessee. In 1821 his home became filled with the sound of knocking, while furniture began to be dragged from room to room. The voice of an invisible being was also heard crying out, claiming to be a once happy spirit that had since been disturbed and made wretched. The uproar only ceased after the farmer became ill and died, the result of a mysterious poisoning.

However, poltergeists with a message as poignant as this are very rare. By and large, it has been noted that the voices of poltergeists are either flippant or meaningless, as might be expected if they came from a low-grade elemental spirit.

Below: **Alan Rhodes was a young boy who became the focus of serious poltergeist activity. Although the boy's hands were tied, the alarm clock in this picture was hurled on to the bed from across the room.**

Below: **In the north of England in the 19th century, a woman named Mary Jobson became the victim of frequent poltergeist attacks. She was repeatedly drenched by floods of hot water which poured from the ceiling of her home.**

One possible reason why poltergeists seem linked with teenagers and hysterical persons is suggested by the writings of the famous psychologists Sigmund Freud and Joseph Brewer. In an article called 'Studies in Hysteria', they refer to an hysterical person's urgent need to release his pent-up energy. The same needs could equally apply to youngsters at the crucial years approaching puberty. However, the process by which this surplus energy could make inanimate objects move about remains unexplained.

Before dismissing this whole theory as an interesting but frivolous academic exercise, it is a good idea to consider the rituals of puberty carried out by primitive peoples all over the world. In numerous cases, young boys and girls are kept apart from the rest of the community until the time of puberty has passed. The reason is that they are thought to emit a powerful energy which could endanger those with whom they come into contact.

Although we still regard poltergeists as ghosts or malign spirits bent on upsetting us, we cannot dismiss the strong associations between poltergeist activity and unknown forms of energy which appear to be generated by certain people. It seems that a great deal still has to be explained about the range of uncanny powers which human beings possess.

Demons

In 1491, the citizens of the small provincial town of Cambrai, in the north of France, were appalled to discover that nuns of the local convent were suddenly showing signs of superhuman strength. Others barked liked dogs and a few also began to prophesy the future.

Church inquisitors rushed to investigate the strange goings on. Their finding described how the nuns had been possessed by demons sent into them by a fellow nun, Jeanne Potiers, a witch in disguise. She was arrested at once and taken out of the convent to her death. Shortly after, the other nuns regained control of their minds and bodies and the convent returned to normal.

Scenes like this, which were a common feature of life in the Middle Ages, have once again become common events in Western Europe and the United States. They reflect the current revival of the age-old terror of demons and evil spirits.

Belief in dangerous spirits is found all over the world. If we look back to the dawn of history we find that powerful supernatural forces, both good and evil, were once thought to influence almost every aspect of human life. Good spirits brought happiness, hunting success and plentiful supplies of food and drink. Evil spirits, it was believed, threatened both individuals and the community as a whole with

Above: **The possession of a group of nuns in France in 1491 was halted by Church investigators who traced the source to one nun who, they claimed, was a witch in disguise. Her removal from the convent ended the outbreak of crazed behaviour.**

ill-fortune, disease and premature death. They were thought to cause the terrible storms which ruined crops, bring about famine and drought, and provoke attacks by powerful and war-like neighbours.

But demons were only spirit forms. As such, they were invisible and possessed no physical shape of their own. However, they would try to capture and use other forms of life, including human beings, for their own vile purposes.

Demons could take on any shape or size, but were usually horrific in appearance. In India, the Hindus were tormented by Pretas, monsters with skulls for heads, huge bellies and the ability to spout fire. They usually haunted old cemeteries. Typhon, a hideous demon of ancient Egypt, was held to be responsible for the blistering winds which blew from the Sahara Desert. This demon has since given its name to those winds known as typhoons. The Aztecs of Central America believed in a devil known as Tezcatlipoca, who had the power to make corpses come to life. Disguised as a limbless blob, this demon was blown about the countryside by the wind, inflicting death and disease upon anyone unfortunate enough to meet it. In Ireland, there were demons of death called banshees, said to have one nostril and one tooth apiece. Occasionally they were spotted by river banks washing blood-stained clothing. But banshees were more often heard than seen, their terrible wails foretelling a death in the family to which they were attached.

However, it was the invisible demons who entered the bodies of human beings undetected that caused our ancestors the greatest distress. They could creep into a human being without he or she knowing it, entering through the mouth, nostrils or ears. This explains the origin of our habit of covering our mouths when we yawn. Otherwise, it used to be said, the devil would fly straight inside the tempting hole.

Once inside the person, the demon would begin to take over and gradually drive his host insane. In some cases the victim might be forced to take on a bizarre animal shape, another aspect of the werewolf legend.

However, belief in 'possession' of this kind is by no means confined to legend. Today there are many exorcists operating both within the church and outside it.

It is thought possible to expel a devil from a person if a specially trained holy man or priest intervenes. The religious ceremony he performs is known as exorcism. A clergyman in ceremonial vestments holds his hands reverently above the head of the possessed man or woman and begins to pray. He makes the sign of the cross and reads from the Gospel, eventually directing the demon to leave the body of its victim and 'return to the place from whence it came.' The shrieks, moans and bodily contortions which follow, all classic symptoms of insanity, indicate the struggle taking place between the forces of good and evil.

Although many victims who have been possessed by demons claim that they were cured by exorcism, it can

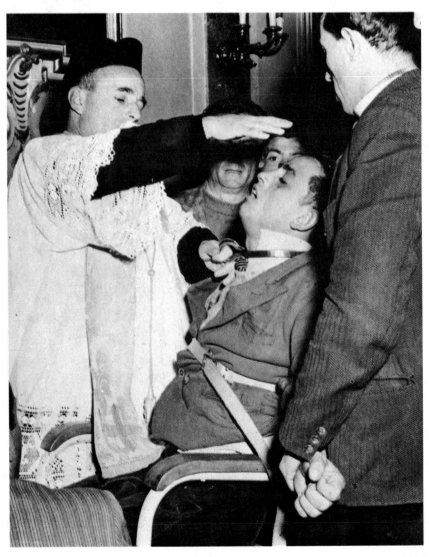

Below: **The priest, Don Alessi, holds a 'penitent's ring' around the neck of a writhing victim of possession by evil spirits. All the while, the priest prays to exorcize the demons within the young man.**

sometimes have a dangerous side. In Yorkshire, England, in 1975, a man who had been diabolically possessed went mad and killed his wife following the ordeal of exorcism.

One of the best known exorcists of today is the Reverend Christopher Neil-Smith. He claims to have driven evil spirits from many hundreds of people over the years. However, he prefers to use the word 'deliverance' rather than 'exorcism' to describe what he is doing since he claims that his procedure delivers the sufferers from the powers of evil. In his book he talks about Jesus Christ as the 'Great Exorcist', since Christ could drive out demons by laying his hands on the afflicted person and commanding the evil forces to leave.

Nowadays, psychiatrists are occasionally called upon to treat patients who are convinced that evil spirits have possessed them. Sometimes the patients respond to skilled medical treatment and are cured. However, as Peter Underwood, the well-known authority on the supernatural, makes clear in his *Dictionary of the Occult and Supernatural*, a religious exorcism can produce equally impressive results. This is due, he suggests, to the effect this highly dramatic ceremony has upon the imagination of the person who is possessed.

It would probably be safe to say that no material proof of demons is known to exist. It is only when we examine the behaviour of people who claim to be possessed that we can get anywhere in our understanding of what demons

may be. They might best be described as the un-named and unknown forces that prey on our subconscious mind, and thus their reality is a psychological one. Although we may no longer think of them as being grotesque little creatures of the Devil, they nevertheless continue to torment us. The demons we fear and suffer today are just as real as they have always been.

Witches

A series of heart-rending screams rang out from the witches' prison, or Hexenhaus, in Bamberg, Germany. The year was 1629, and Frau Anna Hausen was undergoing interrogation by the local Inquisition which suspected her of involvement in the black arts. Finally, having been tortured until she confessed her guilt, Frau Hausen was beheaded and burned. She might be considered fortunate, for witches were more commonly burned alive.

Over a period of 300 years, from the 1400s to the 1700s, about 100,000 men and women were executed for practising witchcraft in Germany alone. Throughout Europe, it has been estimated that 200,000 all told were put to death for this crime.

The last official execution of a witch in England took place in 1684. But eight years later in Salem, Massachusetts, there was a purge of witches during which 19 men and

Above: **This exorcism was performed in dramatic cliff-top surroundings, a setting that gives the entire ritual a somewhat overblown and theatrical flavour.**

Right: **The typical witch of folklore was an old hag given to flying through the night sky on a broomstick.**

women were executed. Some time after this famous American witch trial there was an official expression of regret by the authorities for the injustice of the sentences.

Why was witch-hunting considered necessary at the time? The answer lies in the old belief that it was possible for human beings to sell their soul to the Devil in return for wealth and power. This transaction was known as the Satanic Pact, and the document was supposed to have been signed in human blood. In return, the Devil compelled witches to turn against their fellow human beings and to destroy their health, life and property with black magic spells. Witches were supposed to use their magic like a kind of secret energy. It was generated by uttering incantations and spells. Power was then asserted over an enemy by taking possession of a piece of his property, perhaps a glove, or by modelling his image in clay.

Another important contributing factor to witch beliefs of the past was ignorance about the diseases which prevailed at that time. A mysterious death from an unknown ailment could arouse fears that the victim had been killed by a witch's curse. Any man or woman who had previously quarrelled with the dead person might then come under suspicion of having bewitched him.

Fear of witchcraft has gradually declined as our knowledge of medicine and psychology has advanced. Today the witch is usually thought of as a folk figure, an ancient crone with a pointed hat, a weather-beaten face and a black cat as a companion that flies with her on her broomstick.

However, there is one feature of witchcraft that is still a common superstitious belief—fear of the 'evil eye'. In Latin counries, especially Italy, Spain, Portugal and in South America, certain men and women are believed today to have the power to kill or harm their enemies by means of a single, dreadful look. An elaborate series of defences is needed to protect oneself from the terrible effects of the evil eye.

Also, a kind of witchcraft still survives in some counries in the form of voodoo (meaning a spirit, god, or sacred object). Voodoo's deepest roots are in Africa, but this kind of sorcery is

Above: **During the 16th and 17th centuries, the persecution of witches became a mania in Europe and all kinds of gruesome instruments were devised for their torture. In Germany, witch hunts led to the death of thousands of innocent people.**

113

practised among some Negroes of the West Indies and southern United States. One typical voodoo superstition claims that graveyard dust scattered on an enemy's doorstep will cause the person to waste away until he or she dies. Lucky charms, such as horseshoes, are needed to guard against this kind of black magic.

In 1951, it became legal for the first time in Britain to practise witchcraft. This was followed by the establishment of Wicca, a cult of witchcraft with priests and priestesses who worship a horned god. The cult later spread to the United States, particularly California, where it is most active. Wicca holds seasonal festivals at springtime, midsummer and Hallowe'en when the members meet in woodlands and on prehistoric sites to dance and cast spells. Fortunately, these are of the helpful kind since Wicca is opposed to any form of black magic. The followers of Wicca are convinced they are descended from the witches of history,

but there is no evidence to support this belief.

Cases occasionally occur in which modern black magic users violate graves at night to obtain human bones with which to cast spells on their enemies. Black masses, which are perversions of the Catholic mass, are also celebrated secretly in churches as an

act of homage to Satan. This sort of black magic witchcraft has few followers, however, and those who practise it are often mentally disturbed.

There are a number of theories which try to explain the origins of popular belief in witches and witchcraft, but none offers any clear-cut answer. One of the more likely explanations is that the ability to bewitch people corresponds with certain kinds of telepathic powers. Some people seem able to transmit their thoughts and suggestions to others without communicating with them in any other way. This ability may explain, in part, how witches were able to influence other people by sending them telepathic messages.

Another explanation of the powers of witchcraft is that people are very susceptible to things they have great faith in. A strong belief in witches, therefore, could make someone very vulnerable to the powers any witch might claim to possess. There is plenty of evidence that people have fallen ill

Above: **A 16th century account of the trial and execution of three witches at Chelmsford in England described their torture and their supposed crimes in loving detail.**

Left: **A young priestess of the small, but flourishing, modern witch cult of Wicca celebrates the ceremony of worship.**

114

and even died after becoming convinced that an evil spell was placed on them. We do not know quite how this works, but the fact that it does gives credibility to the extraordinary powers attributed to witches, and makes it hard to dismiss witchcraft as ancient and innocuous folklore.

Spirit Investigations

In the year 1937, Harry Price, ghost hunter extraordinary, moved into Borley Rectory in Essex, a place reputed to be the 'most haunted house' in Britain. Supported by a team of experts, he set to work to determine the exact character of the occult phenomena which had attracted first nationwide and then worldwide attention. More than 200 witnesses were interviewed during the course of the investigation.

In the grounds of the old rectory, a phantom nun had been seen occasionally peering through the library windows, while a spectral coach pulled by ghostly horses was claimed to glide along the drive. Even more mysterious was the name 'Marianne' which some invisible hand had inscribed on an interior wall. At various times the following phenomena were also reported at Borley Rectory: a girl in white, a ghastly dismembered hand and a series of headless figures. Eerie wailing sounds were often heard, while bells rang out, crockery crashed and many kinds of 'luminous phenomena' were also observed.

Left: **Among the many ghostly phenomena at Borley Rectory, it was claimed that headless figures, a pale young girl in white and a ghastly dismembered hand had been seen in the building.**

A possible clue to these psychic disturbances was provided by the discovery, in 1943, of the jawbone of a young woman in the rectory cellar. Presumably, she had been murdered. This fragment of her body was buried with proper ritual in a churchyard in an attempt to end the hauntings. For, although these had ceased as far as the rectory itself was concerned when the house burned down in a mysterious fire in 1939, some people claimed that the site of the buildings was still haunted. Many believe it is haunted to this day.

The Borley Rectory case was a landmark not only for the immense public interest that it aroused but also for drawing attention to 'ghost hunting', otherwise known as psychical research. Harry Price was one of the pioneers of this work. He investigated almost every aspect of the supernatural including mediums, magic and poltergeist activity. By the time of his death, in 1948, Price had amassed hundreds of records of occult phenomena, together with a file of over 20,000 letters on the subject. His vast library of books was bequeathed to London University, where it can still be consulted by serious students of the occult.

Left: **Until it burned down in mysterious circumstances in 1939, Borley Rectory in England was reputed to be the most haunted house in the country. Despite being repeatedly studied, no evidence was ever found to explain the strange phenomena that were claimed to occur here.**

The blaze of publicity that surrounded Price's work tended to hide the fact that a psychic researcher is an investigator who proceeds in a scientific manner and who aims to study the evidence of psychic phenomena. Much of the work includes investigating the various reports of hauntings and ghostly apparitions which are brought to his or her notice.

Psychic research has not only been the domain of scientists. Many churchmen have taken to studying the occult in the past. In 1905, Father Jovet, a French priest, investigated the story of a female phantom who materialized 'all aflame as though in a fire of burning oakum'. It was claimed that the apparition even left scorch marks on her husband's nightcap with her fiery fingers when she appeared before him during the night. The hauntings ceased after Father Jovet prayed on her behalf. His success with this case led him to check further and he discovered that ten similar fiery hauntings had been reported between 1696 and 1903.

Serious scientific research into the occult and the psychic dates from 1882 when the British Society for Psychic Research was established. It included a professor of psychics and a professor of philosophy among its notable founders. In 1884, a similar body was

Left: **Harry Price was a renowned 20th century researcher who devoted his life to investigating and cataloguing bizarre psychic phenomena. His activities, though controversial, were some of the most sustained attempts at giving psychic research a sound scientific basis.**

founded in America. Both organizations undertake investigations and research into events which mainstream science cannot explain. The range of study includes inquiry into apparitions of the living and of the dead, clairvoyance, dreams, dowsing, hypnotism and telepathy.

One of the most interesting sides of the work carried out by the British Society is the collecting of case histories of ghosts. The vast majority have proved to be 'crisis apparitions', spectres of people seen at the time of their death by close friends or relatives. One line of thinking is that such ghosts are telepathic messages sent by the dying person in a moment of great stress.

In 1894, the Society published the results of a survey carried out on 17,000 people on the subject of hallucinations. About one person in ten of those interviewed claimed to have had a psychic experience. Most often, this was linked with an especially critical period in their lives.

Later research techniques into spirit hauntings have included tape recorders triggered off by sound, temperature recording equipment to measure the supposed fall in temperature that occurs when a spirit is present and automatic cameras that can take normal as well as infra-red photographs. All of these techniques are used to establish whether spirits have a physical dimension. It is equally possible that they only exist as psychological phenomena.

Although many leading scientists have shown an interest in psychic phenomena, to date no way of conducting reliable scientific experiments has been found. Since World War II, the United States has become the main centre for psychic research. However, experiments here were confined to Extra Sensory Perception for the most part rather than to the problems of life after death.

The full potential of the human mind is a long way from being understood by science. It is conceivable that forms of communication like telepathy really do exist between people. If they do, they might go a long way towards explaining the remarkable and mysterious world of human experience we choose to call the supernatural.

Left: **Father Jovet, a French priest, conducted his own investigations into hauntings that were associated with fire after his experience of a husband who claimed that his wife returned to him as a flaming ghost during the night. To his surprise he discovered a similar pattern of hauntings that dated back more than two centuries.**

Left: **Harry Price established a laboratory where he conducted his examinations of psychic events and attempted to classify their common factors.**